DUBLIN KINGS: BOOKS 1-4

THE COMPLETE SERIES

L.K. SHAW

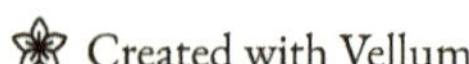 Created with Vellum

CIAN

DUBLIN KINGS, BOOK 1

CHAPTER 1

Nessa

Loneliness isn't about being alone. It's being in a room full of people where every one of them stare. Where they judge. Where they whisper to each other behind raised hands that don't block their hateful words. And Dónal Sheehan takes every opportunity he can to be the center of attention, making sure I'm right by his side. Not because he actually wants me there, but because then he can put on a front of doting Da to his fat, ugly, and motherless daughter. So all those people can applaud his efforts at raising her after his first wife—my mother—and second wife both died. Except it's nothing but a show. A façade. If they only knew what went on behind closed doors.

I'm not sure they'd care.

"Would you like another cup of tea, Miss Sheehan?" The housekeeper asks from the doorway of the library.

"Yes, please."

Deirdre dips her head and leaves me to the book I've been trying to read for the same number of hours that Dónal has been gone. He stopped being Da a long time ago. If I do address him, it's always sir. Even that is more than he deserves. I push my glasses farther up my nose and finger the end of my braid draped over my shoulder, nervous gestures I can't help. Not when I don't have a clue when he'll be back.

It's just one more thing I hate him for.

Books let me escape. It doesn't matter that it's only for a few short hours. Not long enough to forget, but long enough that I can blissfully ignore reality. *My* reality. At least for a little while. Except I can't even do that. Not tonight. Because I have to be ready for his return. A low fire burns, providing an extra bit of light in the dim room. An ember pops, causing a small spark to fly and me to jump. I sit back in my reading chair and stare into the flames. If I were anyone else, maybe I'd lose myself in a daydream. But I stopped daydreaming years ago. It's pointless.

The rattle of metal startles me, and I whip my head in the direction of the door. The heart that dropped into my stomach returns to its place, beating a bit faster than it had a moment before. Deirdre steps into the room carrying a serving tray. She sets it on the side table next to me, picks up the teakettle, and fills my nearly empty cup.

"Thank you, Deirdre."

"Yes, miss." She places it back on the tray and exits the library, no doubt to also prepare for the return of her employer.

From down the hallway, my mother's grandfather clock bongs, calling out the hour.

One.

Two.

Three.

Four.

It's the middle of the night, and I should be sleeping. Only sleep won't come. It never does when Dónal goes out. Because going out means drinking. Gambling. Losing more money. Worse than that, it means adding bruises to the collection he's already given me.

One would think I'd be used to it after all these years. I take a sip of my hot tea, blowing on it to cool it down enough not to burn my mouth, and stare into the fire again. My eyes burn with fatigue, but my mind races and my palms sweat.

Another hour's passing is marked by the sound of the clock. Five a.m. And still I wait. Maybe he finally cheated the wrong person. Maybe I'm free.

In the distance, there's a crash. My eyes slowly close and I curse the stupid part of me that dared to hope.

"Where's that ungrateful daughter of mine?" Dónal bellows, his words slurred from drink. "Nessa. I know you're still awake. Get your fat arse out here and help me."

Setting down the book, I stand and head out of the library to where the bastard waits. I learned the first time he hit me not to stall or ignore him. It's only worse when I do. I step into the entryway where he struggles taking off his jacket. His porcine face with its flappy jowls is red. A mix of alcohol, rage, and exertion, I'm sure. His shirt is missing a couple buttons, and the pasty white flesh of his round belly peeks through the gap.

"Don't just stand there," Dónal snaps.

I take a few quick steps forward, grab the neck of the jacket, and tug it down his flailing arms, which is only making it more difficult.

"If you'd keep still, I could get it." I've just managed to get both of his arms out of the sleeves, so I'm left with the coat dangling from my hands. Which means I can't block the blow.

The back of his hand collides with the side of my face. Stinging pain follows, my head snaps to the right, and my glasses fly off my face. There's a ringing in my ear which muffles whatever Dónal is saying. I cover my hot cheek with my palm and turn toward him. He glares at me with hatred burning in his eyes.

"Hang that up and come to my office." He curls his lip and walks down the hallway.

Deirdre comes rushing around the corner and scoops my glasses up off the floor. "Let me help you, dear."

I shake my head and take them from her, putting them back on. "No, I'll do it." If nothing else, it gives me an extra minute to compose myself.

Once the jacket is put away, I head toward more punishment for imaginary infractions. The minute I step through the door, a painful and vicious grip wraps around my upper arm. Nails dig into the underside of it, and I can't bite back that whimper of pain. The fingers only clamp down harder as Dónal drags me across the room.

"Make me a drink."

He nearly pushes me toward the bar, his steps unsteady, despite the fierce hold he maintains. At last, he releases me. My entire arm flares with pain, and already I can feel the finger-shaped bruises forming on my skin. I pour the exact amount of whiskey he prefers into the glass, and with shaky hands, pass it to him. He tosses it back in a single swallow. Then he paces. I remain standing there, doing my best to make myself invisible. He mumbles and runs his hands through his hair, leaving it to stick up all over.

Dónal's bleary gaze lands on me and he sneers. "You might finally be good for something."

Uncertainty fills me. What does he mean?

He glances at his watch and then out the window. Faint light shines in as dawn approaches. His eyes return to me and scan me from head to toe. There's no disguising the disgust in them. I'm wearing a shapeless flannel nightgown that hits mid-shin and pulls around the waist and hips. My feet are covered by tall wool socks that disappear beneath the hem of my sleepwear. I'm dressed for comfort not fashion. It's not as though anyone is going to see me anyway.

"Any minute, Cian Donnelly will be here."

Dónal hates the Donnellys, and vice versa. Why is one of them coming here? Especially at this hour? I don't ask any questions. A slap or punch is always the answer I'm given when I do.

"You're going to go upstairs and change into something less...

pathetic before he arrives. Something that doesn't make you look like a cow, if such a thing exists."

After twenty-six years, I should be immune to his insults, yet they still have the power to dig in where it hurts the most.

"Why?" It slips out before I can stop it.

An open-handed slap is his response. Even drunk, Dónal has enough strength to make me bleed. Thankfully my glasses stay put, but they're knocked slightly askew. I straighten them and swipe at the small cut in the corner of my mouth.

"Stupid. How many times are you going to make me do this? If you would just listen the first time I tell you something."

Yes, because him hitting me is always my fault. If only I were smarter. Thinner. Prettier. Less of a burden. I quickly bypass him and rush out of the hated office. I make it to the entryway just as Deirdre opens the front door. In steps the man I first dreamed about when I was twelve years old. Back when I still believed in dreams.

Cian Donnelly.

I come to an abrupt halt and swallow. On his heels is one of his brothers, although I'm not familiar enough with either of them to be sure which. Cian's sapphire eyes travel down the length of me, stopping at my feet. I curl my toes inside my socks. He raises his gaze back up to meet mine, pausing at my mouth for a fraction of a second. So fast, I'm sure I imagined it. His expression is blank. Then his gaze shifts over my shoulder, past me, and that changes in an instant.

His lips curl in disdain. "I'm surprised you didn't find some hole to crawl in and hide like the rodent you are, Sheehan."

I pivot a half turn and take a step back. My gaze bounces between the two men. The air is thick with hate and tension that makes me nervous. What's going on?

"You're not welcome here. Take her and go," Dónal bites out. "Consider my debt paid."

Take *who*? What debt? I blink and my mind races. Is he here for me? But why? I glance at his brother behind him, but he's focused on Dónal as well.

Cian's gaze leaves his enemy's and collides with mine again. "Let's go,"

"Go? Go where?" It comes out on a whisper.

He moves to the door and glances over his shoulder. "You belong to me, now."

CHAPTER 2

CIAN

NESSA SHEEHAN IS ALMOST EXACTLY AS I REMEMBER HER. All the way from her plain brown hair and glasses to the plump figure. One that hideous nightgown she's wearing does nothing for. Is this how she really dresses? Christ.

From her expression, it's obvious Sheehan is too much of a coward to tell his daughter what he's done.

"Will someone please explain what's going on?" she rasps out as she plays with the tail end of the braid that grazes the crest of her lush breast. "Did your dear old Da not tell you?"

Nessa shakes her head, her gaze still bouncing between him and me.

"Apparently your virginity is worth about twenty-five-thousand euros." No sense keeping it a secret.

"M—my what?" Her face loses all its color.

Shit, she's not going to faint, is she?

"Your Da lost a game of cards to me. He couldn't cover the bet, so he added you—and your virginity—to the pot to make up the difference." I could do anything I want to her. I stare at Sheehan, who doesn't demonstrate any type of remorse.

Nessa takes in a deep shuddering breath, her chest rising with the effort. I can't help but be drawn to her breasts again. It takes more willpower than I expect to drag my gaze away from them. The color has returned to her face. In fact, it's turned pink and getting darker with each passing second. Behind her glasses, those deep blue eyes shimmer as she stares at her father.

"Do you really hate me that much?" she whispers.

To his credit, Sheehan actually flushes, but he won't meet her gaze and doesn't answer her. Fucking coward.

"If we're done here?" I'm impatient to get back to the manor. Being in this house is only pissing me off.

Nessa sputters out a laugh tinged in bitterness. "Yeah, we're done."

Thank fuck. "Let's go then."

Finn clears his throat. I glance at him with a raised brow. His gaze travels quickly up and down Nessa and he tips his head sideways just slightly. I sigh. "Go change your clothes and grab some of your things."

She hesitates, but finally stiffens her shoulders and stands tall. "I won't be long."

Then she strides out of the entryway like a queen, with her head held high. I follow her with my eyes until she disappears around a corner. Laughter sounds behind me. I turn to Sheehan. My jaw clenches. I want to punch the smarmy grin off his face.

"She's not much to look at, is she? What with that face and fat arse. You got the short end of the deal."

I bite back any words I might say, refusing to take the bait. Instead, I move to stand next to Finn. I'm not good at waiting, unless it involves a game of chance. Especially when it means I have to remain in the presence of a man I want to kill, but can't. Not yet, anyway.

"Deirdre," Sheehan calls out.

The housekeeper who'd let us in and then quickly disappeared steps into the entryway. "Yes, Mr. Sheehan."

"I'm going to bed. Wake me at lunch." He waves a hand in our general direction. "Make sure they're gone the second Nessa gets back."

Without another word, he turns his back on us and heads in the opposite direction his daughter had gone. The man is either confident or stupid. The housekeeper sends a wary glance our way and then conspicuously makes herself absent again, although I'm sure she hasn't gone far.

"Jaysus, he's a right bastard." Finn's tone is dry. "She's better off without him."

I face my brother. He's always had a soft spot for people in trouble. For some reason, he has this need to rescue them. "Sheehan has gotten just a bit too cocky with this cease-fire. He seems to think he can do whatever he wants without consequence. I think it's time we had a family meeting to re-evaluate this little truce."

"While I don't disagree, there might be other things you should be worrying about."

I regard my brother closely. "Like what?"

Finn's eyes widen slightly. "Oh, I don't know. Like maybe the woman that just left here."

"I'm not worried about Nessa Sheehan. Nothing in my plans have changed."

He crosses his arms and stares. I glare right back. Footsteps grow louder until the subject of our brief discussion appears with a large suitcase. Thank god, she's not wearing that ugly flannel gown still. Instead, she has on a pair of dark jeans that accentuate her thick thighs and wide hips, but nips in slightly at the waist.

The green shirt that's tucked in gapes between several buttons, providing, to my surprise, a small glimpse of red satin and lace beneath. I'm suddenly reminded of Christmas. Soon enough, I'll unwrap Nessa. My cock hardens at the thought of discovering what's hidden under those clothes.

Finn steps forward to take the suitcase from her, but she clutches the handle tightly and moves a fraction to the side to partially block it from him.

"I'll get it," she says with a bite.

He holds up his hands and retreats a couple paces. I'm not sure what Nessa's trying to prove, so I close the distance between us, until there's barely an inch between our bodies. A soft fruit fragrance surrounds her. She inhales a sharp breath and stares somewhere in the middle of my chest. I don't move or speak. Just continue looking down at her until finally, she tips her head back to meet my eyes. Behind the glasses, hers appear big and round.

Her tongue darts out to wet her lips. *Fuck*. I grow even harder. Without a word, I reach out and gently pry her clenched fingers off the handle. She trembles beneath my touch. Once she's let loose of it, her arm drops to her side and I pull the piece of luggage around the both of us. Finn takes it from me and the door opens. Light spills in, bringing the cold air with it.

"Get a coat. You're going to need it." I follow my brother, leaving Nessa standing there alone.

I take a deep breath once I'm outside, dragging in the odors of the city. Anything to get rid of her scent. On my way to the vehicle, I meet Finn, who's heading back toward the house. He stops me with a palm across my chest. I glance down at it and then at him. He opens his mouth as though to say something, but merely closes it with a short shake of his head and drops his arm and continues walking away.

I stop at his SUV and glance back. Nessa glides past him, staring straight ahead as she makes her way toward me.

She'd be terrible at cards. Every emotion is on display. They're on her face, in her eyes, and in her posture. I suppose that can be a good thing. At least a person will always know where they stand with her, because she can't hide it. And at this moment, she vibrates with everything she's feeling. Hatred. Fear. There's even a hint of relief under the surface.

Nessa stumbles slightly and my brother reaches out to steady her, but she jerks her arm away from him with a hiss and rights herself, pushing her glasses higher up her nose. I can't help the half-smile that curls my lips. It would seem there's a bit of spirit lurking under that mousy appearance. In a mocking gesture of a gentleman, I open the back door and bow, sweeping my hand for her to enter.

Her eyes narrow and her lips thin. At her side, tiny fists clench tightly. I imagine she'd give anything to punch me. With a small huff, she climbs in and then stares straight ahead, her fingers laced together on her lap and her entire body stiff.

"I have no intention of crawling over you, so I recommend moving to the other side."

Nessa snaps her head in my direction. "Why do you need to sit back here, when there's a perfectly good seat right up in front?"

"Because *you're* not up there. And if I have to choose between sitting next to my brother or beside a beautiful woman, I'll choose the woman over him, every single time."

Twin flames of red rise in her cheeks. "Fine."

She practically flings herself to the passenger side. Behind the movement is rage. I study her another minute. No, not rage. I'm mistaken about the reason behind the change of color in her face. She's embarrassed, but why? I'll have to puzzle out her reaction another time. I'm fucking exhausted. Finn's already behind the wheel, so I settle in behind him and close the door.

I glance at Nessa out of the corner of my eye. She's twisted partially away from me and faces the window. We haven't even made it out of the drive and she reaches up and swipes beneath her glasses. I turn away to offer her a small bit of privacy. I'm not sure what she's mourning, though. She should be happy to be away from that bastard Da of hers.

CHAPTER 3

Nessa

We pull up to a massive wrought iron gate. Cian's brother pauses only briefly at the entrance before it jerks slightly and opens. He drives through the opening and down a narrow lane lined with massive trees that tower over the lawn. The sun peeks through the naked branches, giving the ground a dappled appearance. Like a strobe light, it flashes over my face as we continue forward until the sprawling manor comes into view.

Large windows cover the front of the home, bookending double doors, right in the center. The trees surround the manor on either side, no doubt providing it with shade during the warm months when the leaves are in full bloom. It's probably a stunning view.

Cian's brother comes to a stop behind two other vehicles and gets out. He doesn't wait for us. Instead, he heads straight inside, closing the door behind him. I'd gotten brief glimpses of sympathy from him through the rearview mirror on the drive here. I quickly glanced away each time, not wanting his pity.

"Home sweet home. At least for a little while."

My gaze flicks to Cian. The sun shines in through the back window bathing him in its bright light. His auburn hair burns like the hottest flame. Small freckles that weren't nearly as visible before dot his forehead, cheeks, and the bridge of his nose. His eyes drill in to me with a nearly hypnotizing affect until his words finally penetrate.

"What do you mean for a little while?" This isn't a permanent arrangement? He said I belong to him, even if I hate the fact.

His expression quickly matches the one his brother kept showing me. Pity. I swallow. Have I gotten it wrong?

"It means that once I've finished with you, you'll be returning to your beloved Da. Whenever that might be," Cian says it so casually, as though it is—as though *I am*—of no consequence.

Nausea churns in my belly. *Oh god, please don't throw up.* My fingers clench so tightly my nails dig painfully into the backs of each hand. "I see."

His eyes drop to my lap and I quickly loosen the grip I have and reach for the door handle. Anything to get away. I struggle to draw in a breath as I jump out and the cold hits me. *That's what you get for refusing to wear a coat just because Cian suggested it.* I sharply inhale and my lungs burn from the freezing air. I welcome the pain of it.

A door closes behind me and footsteps crunch, drawing closer. I close my eyes for a second, take another deep breath, ignoring the sting of cold, and pivot toward the approaching man.

"Well, grab my bag, then," I instruct Cian before he can say anything.

I stride past him, keeping my gaze averted, and around the back of the SUV before proceeding toward the front door of the manor. I've hidden my fear and insecurities with fake confidence for long enough that it comes easily. Still doesn't mean it's real, but at least I can maintain the front for a little while. I make it to the long porch and up the few steps to wait. I'm not bold enough to just walk in alone.

"We're not going inside." He approaches with my suitcase.

I fold my arms and try to control my shiver. Not from his baritone, either. It's only because I'm cold. *Yeah, right.* "Where are we going then?"

"Follow me." This time, it's Cian leaving me standing there as he heads along a narrow path lined with large, octagonal shaped stones that lead toward the side of the house.

Having no other choice, I trail behind him as he walks around to the back side of the manor, where the sprawling landscape travels farther out until it blends into the rolling fields. A well-kept guest house sits about halfway down a shallow slope where it levels out. Cian is almost at its front door. Treading carefully down the grass, I reach him.

He turns the handle, pushes it open, then takes a small step back, and similar to when I got in the vehicle, he gestures for me to enter. With only a quick glance in his direction, I move inside. A pleasant floral fragrance, as well as warmth, greets me.

"I'll put this in the bedroom."

I move out of Cian's way as he strides past with my suitcase. Taking a moment, I glance around the living area. A pale blue sectional is situated against the wall to the right of the entrance. There's a small side table at the nearest end and a narrow coffee table in front. Opposite it is a large, flat-screen TV on top of a long, rectangular entertainment table. Stunning artwork decorate the walls. A kitchen lines the back of the open concept space separated from the living space by a four-seat, square table. It's not fancy, but I suppose there are worse places I could have been sent to lose my virginity.

He comes out of the doorway just past the sofa, and I nervously shift a few steps back. As though my reality is hitting me, I struggle to meet his gaze. I have no idea what happens next. Is he going to just fuck me? There's nothing I hate more than uncertainty. I've had far too much of it in my life.

A warm hand palms my cheek and I jump, my eyes instinctively moving to meet his. Those freckles are noticeable again this close. As is the length of his eyelashes. And god, the way he smells. I'm used to the scent of whiskey and stale sweat. Cian Donnelly smells like rain on a spring day with an undercurrent of ginger that reminds me of Deirdre's gingersnap biscuits. I've been trying to ignore it since before we got in the vehicle, but with him standing so close—touching me—it's almost impossible.

"Don't look so terrified, sweet mouse. I promise you'll enjoy everything I do to you."

The arrogance of his statement—along with that stupid pet name—raises my hackles. I bat his hand away and put distance between us, giving him my back. "I'm not scared."

"No? Then why do you tremble beneath my touch."

I whirl on him. "Maybe because I'm furious and tired of men who think they can control my life."

Cian folds his arms and an amused gleam brightens his eyes. "Are you going to be this feisty in bed? I'll have to say it's a bit unexpected."

Seriously? Some mad compulsion propels me toward the door. I open it and glare back at the man who doesn't appear to have any regard for common decency. "I'd like to be alone, now, so I can get some sleep. Leave."

I would never treat Dónal this way, because I'm well aware of the consequences. I suppose I've been hit enough times that once more won't make a difference. But it will give me a better understanding of the kind of man Cian is. Will he do as I say or will I regret my outburst? I prepare for the worst and hold myself rigidly while I wait for the reckoning.

With long, powerful strides he moves toward me. I can't help but take in his broad shoulders or how defined his upper arms muscles are beneath the taut fabric of his tight-fitting long-sleeve shirt. Or how well his jeans fit and the noticeable bulge there's no hiding. I avert my gaze, hating how hot my neck and cheeks get. I'm sure they're bright red to match. There's no keeping secret when I'm embarrassed or self-conscious.

Cian stops beside me and I brace myself.

"I'm not your Da, mouse. I don't need to hit a woman to show her how strong I am." He runs a finger along my jaw from the bottom of my ear to the point of my chin and then traces a line down my throat.

I swallow beneath the tip of it before it continues moving. There's a slight tug, then another. My heart pounds and my pulse races. Another one of those mad compulsions hits and I swivel my head to face him. There's an intense heat in his gaze, but it's not focused where I expect it to be. Instead, his attention is on where that finger drags along the skin that is exposed by the buttons he had undone.

A line of fire burns down my sternum and between my breasts. I draw in a shaky breath which causes them to rise.

"Such a pretty color."

"Wh—what?" The question is a whispered rasp.

Finally, Cian lifts his gaze to mine. "Your bra. I hope you'll wear it for me again soon. If for no other reason than because I know I'll enjoy taking it off you."

A soft breeze wafts over me, and I blink away the dizzy haze. He's no longer standing in front of me. I turn to find him walking up the slight incline toward the manor house. There's so much confidence in his stride. I keep standing there with my hand on my chest, the heart beneath it pounding out a quick beat. Not once does he glance back. He merely disappears inside.

I sag, nearly stumbling back a step. Rousing myself, I manage to close the door and then sink down on the couch. My heartbeat slows and whatever energy I'd been running on wanes. I'm suddenly exhausted again. There's an ache deep inside me that Dónal could be so callous. I shouldn't be surprised, and yet, I am. How could I not be? Not once would I have ever expected him to be so cruel.

Then you're stupidly naïve.

I must be. He hits me. Why should selling me to his enemy come as any big shock?

My eyes close as I lean back into the soft cushions. I'll just sit here for a few minutes to rest. Try to regain some focus. Some clarity. And prepare myself for whatever else might lie in store for me.

CHAPTER 4

Cian

Nora is making breakfast when I step into the kitchen. She glances up at my arrival.

"Good morning, Cian. I didn't expect to see you up and about so early."

I snag a warm croissant from the plate on the counter and break a piece off. "Just getting a guest settled in the cottage."

Her gaze darts out the window and back to me with a wrinkle between her brows. "I didn't realize anyone was visiting. Will I need to prepare meals for them?"

"It was only decided last minute she'd be visiting. And yes to meals, please, although I'll deliver them to her." I take another bite of my favorite flaky pastry. Nora is a master at baking.

Her eyes widen. "Her?"

Considering her relationship with Da, I assume she'll discover my guest's identity soon enough. "Nessa Sheehan."

There are questions brewing in her eyes, but she also knows

when—and when not—to ask them. She's well aware that Sheehan is our family's enemy. Has been for decades. And while Nora is more than just our housekeeper, she's not involved in the more unsavory—criminal—aspects of our family business.

"I see." There's definitely a hint of disapproval in her tone. "I'll make sure Miss Sheehan will have plenty of things to choose from. Please let me know of any allergies or dislikes she might have."

I can't help the grin from forming. Nora mother hens everyone. Even my brothers and me despite the fact we're all adults who have been taking care of ourselves for well over a decade. "Of course. I assume Nessa will be resting for a few hours, but I'm sure she'll be hungry by the time lunch rolls around."

She dips her head. "I'll have something prepared."

"Thank you, Nora." I finish my croissant as I leave and head toward the wing of the house where my brothers and I reside. Except I don't make it past the entryway.

"You're back." Da stands at the entrance of the hallway that leads to his office. "We have a few things to discuss."

He turns and walks away. Sleep is going to have to wait, it would seem. With a sigh, I follow. As soon as I step through the door, he closes it behind me and moves to his desk. "Have a seat."

I drop into the leather chair and lean back to get comfortable.

"Finn tells me you had an interesting night and morning." Leave it to Da to get right to the point and leave it to my brother to be the one who let him in on things.

"As I'm sure you're already well aware, Dónal Sheehan showed up at *Anamacha Caillte* last night. Which should not have happened. A fact I will remind my little brother of as soon as I see him again."

Da reclines in his chair and places his forearms on the armrests. "I think the more pressing matter is what happened later."

Is that a hint of disapproval from him? I expect it from Nora, but not Da.

"I assume you're referring to his daughter." Carrick Donnelly can drag something out forever until a person finally tells him everything he already knows, but wants to hear them say it. "As I already told Finn, don't worry about her."

He sits up and rests his steepled hands on the surface of his desk. "You know there's a war brewing. It's only a matter of time before it strikes."

"I'm well aware."

"And yet you're bringing her right into the middle of it."

This has me leaning forward as well with my elbows on my thighs as I stare at the man I admire most in this world. "Nessa Sheehan has nothing to do with her Da, Liam Campbell, and whatever is about to go down."

"You know she's a pawn," Da says softly.

"Is she, though?" I cock my head. "There didn't appear to be any love lost between her and Dónal. And Campbell hates Sheehan even more than we do. He's also never shown any interest in Nessa."

"That doesn't mean Campbell won't. Especially if he, not only discovers the exchange you and Sheehan made, but also accomplishes what he's been setting out to do."

As the head of our family—and the man who controls all of Dublin—I understand Da's concerns, but it also annoys the fuck out of me that he still questions me at times. I'm the oldest. The one who will be in charge of our organization one day. Far into the future, I hope. I stand and stare down at him. "You worry about Campbell and Sheehan. I'll worry about his daughter."

With that, I walk out of his office and head straight for the wing where my brothers and I live. Finn is nowhere in sight. Which is probably a good thing, because otherwise he and I would be having a chat. One that may or may not involve fists. Aidan, however, is reclined in his favorite chair with a plate overflowing with a giant omelet and potatoes. He glances up at me.

"Why aren't you out back seducing your new little pet?"

Fucking Finn. I throw up my middle finger and keep walking through the common room we all share and down the hallway toward my room. My brother's laughter follows me the entire way until I close my door, cutting it off. Exhaustion hits me. I take a quick shower and then crawl naked into bed to stare up at the ceiling. A vision of Nessa comes to mind.

I want to take her hair out of that braid and run my fingers through it so it spreads out over the pillow she's lying on. I can picture the flush she'd exhibited earlier spreading down her chest. She'd surprised me with that bright red bra. What other surprises are in store for me? I'm looking forward to finding out.

Virgins have never interested me. Yet, there is something about Nessa Sheehan that intrigues me. Even beyond the fact of who her da is. It will make our time together tolerable at least, because no matter how intriguing she might be, nothing in my plan has changed since Sheehan offered her to me.

Fuck her.

Make her beg for my cock.

Then send her home with a cunt full of my come that her father will smell the second she walks through the door.

Remind him who holds the power in this city.

A LOUD BUZZING PENETRATES MY AWARENESS AND I reach out for my phone. I shut off the alarm and roll onto my back, lying there for a minute before crawling out of bed. Memories of the past twelve hours greet me. Today begins the seduction of the sweet mouse out in the cottage. This is also the last morning I plan on waking up alone. At least until I'm done with Nessa. I dress and make my way to the kitchen to get food to take to her. I'm sure she's awake, and no doubt, hungry.

The common room is empty, as is the kitchen, but there's a covered platter on a tray with a note. I grab the juice from the fridge and head out the door and down to the cottage. Not bothering to knock, I let myself in. The shutters have been closed and only a single stream of light shines through the narrow crack between them. I cross the living area and glance into the bedroom. Nessa is asleep in bed, lying on her side, facing me, with the duvet pulled all the way up to her neck and her hands tucked under her cheek. Her braid drapes forward over her shoulder, caught in the bend of her elbow, and her face is bare of her glasses.

I continue on, set the tray on the counter, and then walk back to the bedroom. Soft, quiet snores reach me the closer I get to the bed. To her. I stand there studying her. She appears younger than the twenty-six I understand her to be. Her cheeks are sweetly rounded as is the hip the duvet curves nicely over. I squat down, balancing on the balls of my feet, so I'm eye level with her.

A few strands of hair have escaped their confines and fall across Nessa's jaw to tickle the corner of her mouth. Gently, I brush them back, grazing her temple and the top of her ear. Her eyelids flutter and open. They widen and she lurches backward with a scream that cuts off abruptly. Her hand covers her chest.

"You scared the shit out of me."

I ignore her words. She has on that hideous nightgown from earlier. "You're not wearing that when I'm in bed with you."

She clutches the fabric, glances down at herself and back up at me. "Excuse me?"

I push off my thighs and stand. "Lunch is in the kitchen. Bring that ugly thing you're wearing out with you so I can take it and burn it."

Leaving her sputtering, I walk out of the bedroom. Mumbled curses follow and the door slams shut behind me. I chuckle at the display of temper. At least her Da didn't beat it out of her. While I wait for Nessa, I grab a couple plates and glasses from the cabinet as well as silverware from the drawer and set everything, including the platter, on the small dinette table.

Da had a few upgrades added to the cottage after our enforcer, Roarke, had stayed here while he was assigned to be the bodyguard for my cousin Caitlín. Almost no one was surprised when the two of them fell for each other and became engaged, much to the annoyance of Uncle Cormac. Only because his youngest daughter will perpetually be twelve in his eyes. It probably doesn't help that Roarke is nearly sixteen years older.

Behind me, Nessa comes out of her room. I glance over my shoulder. She changed her clothes, but her hands are empty. This little rebellion of hers is amusing. I turn around and lean against the counter with my arms folded over my chest.

"I think you forgot something."

She comes to an abrupt halt and glares at me. "No, I didn't."

I straighten and close the distance until only inches separate us. She tips her head back and though her expression grows more mulish, there's a tremble she can't hide.

"Is this really something you want to fight me on, Nessa?"

Her eyes flare with awareness. It's the first time I've said her name. Her jaw clenches and her nostrils flare. With a small huff, she pivots and disappears into the bedroom, only to come back out holding a wad of flannel. She steps up to me and slams it against my chest. "Are you happy, now?"

I reach up before she can release it, wrap my hand around her wrist, and then slowly drag my fingers up and over the ridge of her knuckles until I fist the fabric trapping her hand under mine. Nessa jerks from my hold. One side of my mouth lifts in a smirk. "Immensely. Now, I'm sure you're as hungry as I am, so why don't we sit and have a pleasant lunch that Nora provided."

CHAPTER 5

NESSA

I'M SEETHING. WHAT AN INSUFFERABLE ASS. HOW DARE HE mock me, asking if I really wanted to fight him on it. Yes. Yes, I did. I hate that I backed down, because it only made him even more smug. The bastard.

I've lived in fear since I was six-years old, when my much older stepbrother finally had enough of the abuse and ran away. There was no one left for Dónal to take his anger out on but me. He's punished me for far less than any infraction I've committed since I left the house with Cian. I'm coming to suspect I don't have to fear the man who bought me. Or at least, that he'll use violence against me. Not yet, anyway.

What about any other plans he has for you?

My stomach chooses then to growl, reminding me that I haven't eaten since early yesterday evening.

"Stop being stubborn and come eat. Nora will be disappointed if I go back into the house with food left."

A swirling sensation rattles in my chest at another mention of this Nora person. Who is she? His wife? It's not unusual for married men to have a mistress. Surely Cian wouldn't have brought me here right under his wife's nose, let alone have her cooking for me. Would he?

"What's going on in that head of yours, mouse?"

My head snaps up and I narrow my eyes. "As you're well aware, my name is Nessa. Kindly use it."

That infuriating grin of his returns. Great. Why did I let him get to me and have to open my stupid mouth? Annoyed, I shoulder past him and plop down in one of the chairs at the table. Seconds later, Cian joins me, sitting to my right, which is far too close.

"I didn't check to see what Nora made, but I'm sure it will be satisfying." He lifts the lid off the large, round platter and sets it to the side.

My mouth waters at the simple but delicious-looking fare. On small plates, there are two ham sandwiches with brown sauce spilling out from beneath the top slice of bread and the corner of a piece of cheese peeking out. There's also a single large serving bowl that—after the lid is removed—is full of some kind of soup. It smells delicious.

"I doubt she left it out on the counter for too long before I got into the kitchen, but we might have to warm it up a bit." Cian picks up the soup bowl. "Start eating while I reheat this."

If not for the fact that I'm starving, I would do it myself. I don't want anything from him, but my stomach tells me to argue another day, so I pick up my fork and knife and cut off a piece of the sandwich. Flavors burst across my tongue and I moan. I open my eyes and unexpectedly meet Cian's. There's an intensity in the way he stares at me. Slowly, I swallow and lick away the bit of gravy at the corner of my mouth. His gaze drops to it and his nostrils flare. A newfound awareness ripples through me. No man has ever looked at me the way he is. Flustered and a bit self-conscious, I quickly focus back on my plate.

At one of the many parties Dónal liked to throw, I managed to escape and head for the ladies room for a brief respite. On my way there, I passed the cracked open door of the den, and someone inside said my name. Curious, I paused outside the room—making sure to stay out of sight—to eavesdrop.

I learned my lesson about listening in on conversations after that..

The cruel and hateful things they said about me still make acid churn in my stomach. There are times when I'm lying in bed at night that I can hear their awful laughter inside my head. I shudder. The microwave pings and I shake off the ugly thoughts. Cian wraps a towel around the hot soup and sets it back on the table. He goes to the cabinet, grabs a couple of bowls, and places one in front of me before taking his seat again.

I reach for the ladle that accompanied the food to dip myself a serving, but he beats me to it. His fingers brush over mine, and I jerk my arm back as though I've been burned. I drop my hand into my lap and rub my thumb over the spot where we touched. His lips curl as though he knows just how unsettled I am and he dishes out first mine and then his. The entire time we're eating, my skin tingles with the sensation of being watched. I set my spoon down, stopping long before I'm actually satisfied, because my nerves can't take the scrutiny any longer.

"You haven't finished your meal." Cian's voice sends a shiver down my spine.

"I'm not hungry."

"Eat, mouse."

My head snaps up at the demand. "I *said* I'm not hungry."

"And I say you're lying. Besides, you're going to need all the energy you can get. So, I suggest you eat your fill."

I scrunch my eyebrows together. "Energy? For what?"

That smirk settles across his lips again and he stares at me with a knowing look. It takes several seconds before my brain processes. My eyes widen, and my whole body is on the verge of bursting into flames as understanding hits.

"Ahh, now she gets it."

"Why are you doing this?" Not that I've kept up with Cian's personal life, but I'm pretty sure I'm not his type. He doesn't strike me as a man who likes a quiet woman who's more comfortable with books than she is with people. A woman who doesn't have any fashion sense—probably because I don't care about it. And most definitely a woman who doesn't fit the mold of society's shitty view on beauty.

Which means he's just trying to punish Dónal.

I hold back bitter laughter. The man who fathered me couldn't care less what is done to me. As evidenced by the fact he bid me away in a card game.

Cian lays his spoon down as well and leans back in his chair with his fingers threaded over his waist. His steely stare unnerves me, but I make myself hold it. Something I never would have done with Dónal. The silence lengthens. I'm barely able to keep myself from squirming.

"You should finish eating." He picks up his spoon again and does the same.

I blink. That's it? The nonchalance with which he goes back to his meal makes my blood pressure skyrocket. Snatching up my half-full bowl with enough force that some of it sloshes over the side, getting all over my hand and spilling on the floor, I stomp to the trash and dump it in. I smack the glass down hard enough in the sink I'm surprised it doesn't shatter. Then I head back to the bedroom. Or at least, I try to. Instead, as soon as I pivot, I collide with a solid chest. One that smells divine.

"Excuse me, please." It's a tightly controlled command through clenched teeth. Tears of anger and frustration threaten to fall, and I refuse to meet Cian's eyes.

"You want to know why I'm doing this?"

My head jerks up. His pupils are dilated, almost blurring out the blue around them. Words clog my throat.

"I'm doing this because I can. Because it galls your Da to know that he lost. To me. Anyway, you should be thanking me for bringing you here."

I gape at him. "*Thanking* you? I should be *thanking* you for ruining my life with this little power struggle you have going on with Dónal?"

"Yes," Cian bites out. "At least I won't hit you."

Something inside me snaps. I slam my hands against his chest and push as hard as I can. He stumbles back in surprise, but I keep shoving him, again and again, my rage spilling out until we're in the middle of the living area.

"I am not"—shove—"some pawn." Shove. "I'm a human being"—shove—"with feelings."

I push again, but this time Cian braces and holds his ground. He's like an immovable wall that my puny strength can't budge. He captures my face between his palms—knocking my glasses askew—and his lips crash against mine, moving over them roughly. My mouth opens in shock, and he takes advantage of the opportunity. His tongue sweeps in as though he's claiming his territory.

I've been kissed before—once—but not like this. This isn't a kiss. It's a ravaging storm. Battering waves of pleasure crash into me. Through me. It's fire and ice burning me with both heat and cold that coalesce and settle straight in my core. I'm bombarded with sensations. My brain keeps trying to send me a message that my body is ignoring. It only wants Cian to keep kissing me like he'll die if he stops.

But stop he does—just as quickly as he started—leaving me breathless. My chest heaves with the need to bring in the air he took from me. A tiny flicker of pride swells. He's breathing just as hard. There are two small areas of bunched fabric over his chest. My fingers tingle with the memory of fisting it between them, holding tightly onto him. With trembling hands, I reach up and straighten my glasses.

As though breaking some spell cast on him, Cian blinks and shakes his head just slightly. His gaze focuses and I swallow at the intensity that sears into me from his stare. It happens slowly, but a change comes over him. Whereas seconds ago there was an almost stunned glaze in his eyes, a calculating gleam enters them. Something I'm not sure I like.

"Well, well, that was unexpected."

Huh?

"Maybe the mouse isn't such a mouse after all."

CHAPTER 6

Cian

"Well, you're still an ass."

No one is more thankful for the anger in Nessa's eyes than me. Because I'm still reeling from that kiss. What had started out as punishment morphed into something entirely different. She's attractive, but not what most people would call a beauty. Not with her ill-fitting clothes, librarian glasses, and full figure. Except it's her lush curves my fingers itch to touch. To explore.

Remember why she's here. "I've been called worse."

"I'm sure you have." Nessa folds her arms over her chest, doing nothing more than drawing my attention to her tits. As though sensing where my focus lies, she drops her arms back to her sides and a pretty flush colors her cheeks. It takes effort to lift my gaze to her face.

"If you're done with your little tantrum, Nora wanted me to ask what you like—or don't like—to eat, so she can get an idea for meals to prepare."

Nessa's fists clench at her sides. I'm having a little too much fun egging her on.

"Your wife doesn't have to make me anything special."

Why would she think Nora is my wife? And is that a hint of jealousy in there? "Don't worry, she doesn't mind."

"Well I mind. Does she know I didn't choose to be here?"

"Yes, she knows." I bite back a laugh at Nessa's gaping expression.

Then her eyes narrow and she cocks her head. "You're finding something amusing about this aren't you?"

I try to act innocent, but I'm clearly failing at it. "You have no idea."

She fists her hips and glares. "Please, enlighten me then. I can make my own food, you know."

Moving closer, I drag my finger lightly down Nessa's nose. She wrinkles it and smacks my hand away. "Nora isn't my wife, mouse. She's our housekeeper and my father's long-time lover."

That adorable shade of pink colors her cheeks again and her anger deflates like air let out of a balloon. She breathes out a quiet "Oh," and darts her gaze away almost shyly.

"You were jealous." The fact amuses me.

As intended, that gets her back up.

"I was not *jealous*."

I chuckle. "You were."

Verbally sparring with her is a huge turn on. I'd rather Nessa rage at me than hold it back. My gut tells me she isn't given the opportunity to show her true self. Not with that bastard Da of hers. *And you're going to send her right back to him when you're done with her.*

I ignore that little voice.

She closes her eyes and takes in a deep breath. "Look. It doesn't matter who Nora is. The fact remains that she doesn't have to cook for me. I've been doing it myself for long enough."

"Unfortunately, she won't see it that way. If there's one thing she loves it's to make sure people are fed and taken care of. It's how she's wired. So, let her feel useful. She'll drive my Da insane otherwise."

It's a sneaky trick to play on Nessa, but I'll do what I have to. Although I'm not sure why I'm pushing the matter.

"Fine."

"Now, why don't you come back and finish eating?"

She shakes her head. "No, thank you. I'm really not hungry anymore."

I study her and decide to let it go. This time. I'm sure there will be bigger battles than this one I'll need to fight with her. I nod and head back the kitchen to clean up. Behind me, a door closes. I glance over my shoulder to find exactly what I expected. Nessa's shut herself in her room. I hope she doesn't think a piece of hollow wood is going to stop me from coming in. But I'll give her some privacy and time to cool off. I need to take this stuff back to the house anyway.

Putting the remaining soup in the fridge—Nora made enough to feed us for a couple days—I stack the platter back on the tray along with the jug of juice and head up the incline. She's once again in the kitchen when I enter. I set it on the counter. "Everything was delicious, as always."

She shoots me a glare that says she knows I'm trying to stay on her good side. Nora has been part of our lives for over a decade. She's also been more of a mother to my brothers and me than our real one ever was. Because she can never stay mad at us for long, I brush a kiss across her cheek and give her my best smile. She just shakes her head.

"Did Miss Sheehan enjoy the meal?"

"Of course she did. How could she not, when it's no doubt the best one she's ever had?"

Nora laughs. "You're really laying it on thick, aren't you?"

I palm my chest and try to appear innocent. "You know I'd never lie about something like that."

She waves me away, takes the dirty dishes off the tray, and loads them in the dishwasher. Da made sure she had a state-of-the-art kitchen when she proposed becoming our housekeeper. She refused to merely be his lover. Said it made her feel sordid. I still haven't figured out why they've never gotten married. It's not as though Da's never asked. Their love for each other is obvious.

"Is there anything she prefers not to have?"

"Sorry, I forgot to ask. I'll do it when I head back down there."

Finn walks into the kitchen, takes a single glance in my direction, and turns right back around. Oh, no. He and I need to have a discussion. There's no more avoiding me like he's done since we left for Sheehan's to get Nessa. First by making himself absent at the casino and second when he spent the whole drive on some bullshit phone call.

"Thanks again, Nora," I call over my shoulder as I stride out of the room to follow my brother trying to make his escape.

When he enters our common room, I'm right behind him.

"Why are you bothering me?" He heads straight to the bar. "Don't you have a woman to seduce?"

I ignore his reference to Nessa. She wouldn't even be a part of this if Finn had banned her Da from the casino in the first place. "What the fuck were you thinking, letting Sheehan into *Anamacha Caillte?*"

He winces as he pours a hefty portion of whiskey into a glass. "That was an accident."

"How, exactly?" I rest my forearms on the top of the bar and wait for whatever story he's going to make up.

"Ennis had to step away from the door during a small altercation happening just inside. Which meant that, briefly, no one manned the entrance. I checked the security feed. It was just bad luck Sheehan showed up right about that time."

I raise an eyebrow. "Bad luck, or did he plan it, knowing we couldn't kick him out once he got inside without looking weak?"

Finn cocks his head. "I'm not sure Sheehan's smart enough to have thought of that, but maybe I'm not giving him enough credit."

"I hope you at least docked Ennis' pay for leaving his post. We have enough security that someone else could have taken care of it." While the three of us own equal shares of the casino, my youngest brother is essentially the one who runs it. He has the head for numbers and takes care of all the books.

"I spoke to him, and it won't happen again."

"It better not."

"So," Finn draws out. "Why are you up here instead of down in the cottage with your new possession?"

Despite the fact that is essentially what Nessa is, for some reason, I bristle at him calling her that. "Like I told Da, you let me worry about her."

He takes another drink and makes a noncommittal sound. I'm not sure I care for the way he's studying me. There are things I need to do, so with only a final glare, I go to my room. From my closet, I grab a bag and fill it with clothes and toiletries. I'm not going to traipse back and forth from the cottage to the house every time I have to take a shower.

With enough things to last me for at least a few days, I walk back down the hill and let myself in again. At least Nessa left her room. The shutters have all been opened and light spills in through them. A few dust motes float within the beams of pale sunshine. The sound of water reaches me. I carry my bag into the bedroom and set it on the floor just inside the door.

Faint, off-key humming comes from the en-suite bathroom. I cross the room and push open the door. Condensation covers the mirror and hangs thickly in the air. From above the frosted glass of the half wall, steam rises, and behind it is the outline of a naked Nessa. I can just make out her curves and when she raises her arms to her head, the shadow of her breasts rise.

I lean my shoulder against the doorframe, cross one ankle over the other, and wait. Less than two minutes later, she shuts off the water and reaches for the towel that hangs on a bar built into the back wall of the shower. She continues humming the unfamiliar song while she dries off and wraps the bath sheet around her. Nessa steps around the thick opaque barrier, spots me, and grabs tightly onto the cloth wrapped around her. Her shriek is loud enough to make my ears ring. She dives back behind the frosted glass still clutching the towel.

"Oh my god, get out."

"I was rather enjoying the view."

Nessa peeks around the corner, her long, wet hair hanging over her shoulder. "I don't care what you were enjoying. You can't just walk in here while I'm showering."

"Actually, I can. I do own the place after all."

She growls and dips back behind the wall. I remain right where I am, waiting. She has to come out eventually. As though guessing my intent, she blows out a heavy breath and steps around. Her neck and face are bright pink, and she won't meet my eyes. I drink in the sight of her. Droplets of water hang from the tips of the hair that cascades down her chest before dropping off and gliding down porcelain flesh. The edge of the towel skims her knees.

Nessa curls toes that are painted a bright red that reminds me of the bra she wore. Each little discovery shows me a new side of her. I raise my gaze back to her face. She's finally glaring at me. I much prefer the heat and fire she spits than the timidity.

"Are you done staring? I need to get dressed."

One corner of my mouth tips up. "Go ahead. Don't let me stop you."

With a little huff, she marches forward, snaps her glasses off the counter, and puts them on while pushing past me toward the bed where her open suitcase lies with half of its contents spilling out. She rifles through the clothes and then, without removing the towel, steps into a pair of panties and draws them up her legs. I get only the briefest glimpse of the lush globes of her ass before the cloth drops down and covers them again. Next she pulls on a pair of pants. Her modesty is adorable, really, even if pointless. Before tomorrow, Nessa's body won't hold any secrets from me.

A fact she needs to be reminded of.

CHAPTER 7

Nessa

Twin flames of heat burn my face. I haven't been naked, or even partially naked, in front of anyone since my first—and only—year at uni. I don't have to turn around to confirm Cian's watching me. My prickling skin tells me he is. It's not that I'm ashamed of my body. In fact, I quite like it. There are times when I imagine I'm one of those voluptuous Greek goddesses—Aphrodite, perhaps—that men worship.

It doesn't matter that my breasts are large and not quite perky. They're mine. I love the way my butt is shaped. It's almost a perfect heart and looks great in a pair of jeans. Maybe my belly could be a little flatter and my hips a little narrower, but it's not the end of the world that they aren't. Overall, I feel feminine and womanly. The few vague memories I have of my mother were that she was soft and squishy and gave the best hugs. I'd like to think I resemble her, not only in our features—I certainly don't look like Dónal—but in softness. Every hug I got from her felt as though I was surrounded in love.

But the constant scrutiny only reminds me of all the times I'd been forced to parade alongside Dónal and of the people who would examine me like a bug under a microscope. And then the mocking voices I once overheard ring in my ears again. I firm my lips and snatch up the plain and so-not-sexy skin-toned bra out of the pile of clothes. How the hell do I put this stupid thing on without removing the damn towel?

A soft touch glides along the line of my shoulder and I jump.

"I like the red one better." Cian's breath ghosts across my skin. Goosebumps run down my forearms and a small chill skates down the back of my neck from his voice alone. It's the only movement I can make. I almost don't even dare breathe.

He runs his hand gently down my arm until he reaches the fabric gripped in my fist and then plucks the undergarment right out of it. It's tossed back in the mess and then he leans forward, the fabric of his shirt rubbing across my sensitized flesh, and picks up that damning red satin I'd bought on a whim. It had been a bit of self-indulgence I didn't normally partake in.

The bra hangs off his finger by a single strap and dangles in the air, slightly swinging. I snatch it from him and hug it to my chest like a shield. Behind me, Cian chuckles.

"Such a shy mouse."

With a growl, I whirl on him. I hate that mocking nickname, although I hate the fact I take the bait every time he uses it more. "I'm not a woman prone to violence, but you certainly tempt me to change my mind."

All he does is smile, completely unconcerned with my threat. "Since it doesn't look like you've put anything away yet, you won't mind if I take one of the drawers."

He moves toward the door, and I stare after him in confusion until he leans down and picks up the bag from the floor.

"Oh, no, you can turn around and take whatever is in there right back to where you got it."

Completely ignoring me, Cian strides past, plops the duffel on the opposite side of the bed as my suitcase and unzips it. I must be living in some bizarre universe, because I just keep standing there as he empties his clothes and then takes the small amount of toiletries, including a bottle of shampoo, body wash, toothbrush, and razor into the bathroom. Then he sets a bottle of cologne on top of the dresser and dumps a handful of silver, square packets in the night-stand drawer before tossing the empty bag just inside the walk-in closet.

He pauses beside the bed and his gaze tracks down my body and back up. "Why aren't you dressed yet?"

Hysterical laughter explodes out of me. That's it. I've gone barmy. Completely off my rocker. Cian stares at me as though he agrees. I can't stop laughing—wheezing—even as tears spill down my cheeks. I'm finally out from beneath Dónal's thumb, even if it is only temporarily, and yet another man completely disregards me and any of my wishes.

Maybe he senses how close to the edge of a breakdown I am, because he walks to the door. My eyes follow the path he takes.

"Finish putting your clothes on, and I'll show you around the estate," he says over his shoulder and then closes it behind him.

I stare another minute, waiting to discover if this is a trick and Cian's going to walk back in to try and catch me naked. Then I shake off the thought. I can't picture him sneaking a peek. If he wanted to watch me get dressed, he wouldn't have left. I push my glasses up and swipe the wetness from my face, pulling in a shaky breath. In my other hand, I'm still clutching the red satin. With a groan of disgust, I throw it down and in an act of rebellious control, I pick up the beige one again and quickly put it on. A simple pink shirt with a frilled hem goes on over it.

Once I've hung up the towel, I blow dry my hair, quickly braid it, and swipe my lips with a clear gloss. I glance around, but there isn't much else I can do to put Cian off. I'm sure if he has to wait too much longer, he'll come barreling back in here. I slip on my flats, run my hands down my waist to smooth out any wrinkles, and take a deep breath. My hand trembles as I turn the knob and open the door.

He's made himself at home on the couch with an ankle crossed over his knee and his phone in his hands. He finishes typing out whatever message he'd been in the middle of and stands. His gaze rakes over me. Nothing about his expression gives any of this thoughts away. *Why do you even care what he thinks?*

" You're going to need a coat. It's not much warmer than it was this morning."

Too late for that. "This will just have to do, since I don't have one." *Whose fault is that?*

"We'll stop at the manor. I'm sure Nora can find you something."

Despite the fact she isn't Cian's wife, but rather his father's mistress, the way he says her name still makes me...prickly. Which is stupid. Maybe it's because there's so much affection behind it. "I'll be fine."

In two steps, he's right in front of me. I have to tip my head back to keep my eyes on his.

"Are you going to fight me on every little thing?" There's a hint of exasperation in his tone.

I rock my head slightly. "Probably."

To my surprise, Cian's lips curl and he huffs out a breath. "I look forward to our skirmishes and seeing who comes out the winner then."

I've never had a competitive nature, but a part of me relishes the idea of sparring with him. I smile back. "As do I."

His mouth straightens and his gaze drops to mine. Heat burns in his blue eyes, turning them a shade darker. Beneath my bra, my nipples tighten. My tongue darts out to wet my lips and his nostrils flare as though drawing in my scent. The part of me I've buried so far down that craves affection stirs to life. I snuff it out, though. Cian has already said I'm nothing but a pawn in his stupid game with Dónal. Wishing and hoping for a different outcome is only opening myself up to a broken heart. I'll play along, for the moment, but make sure I keep a tight rein on my emotions.

I step around him and make my way to the front door. "Let's get this tour started, why don't we."

"Yes, let's." He moves toward me, and just as my hand closes around the door knob, Cian's fingers wrap around it.

My skin tingles with awareness, but I manage to not yank out from beneath his hold. I don't want him to see how much he affects me. I'm not sure why I try, though, because the flash of amusement across his face indicates he's well aware.

"Allow me," he says as though he's some gentleman when there isn't anything farther from the truth.

The cool air hits me the second he opens the door. I clamp my jaw shut tight to keep down the sound of discomfort and clench my fists to keep from wrapping my arms around myself to try and hold in some of the warmth.

"You might give my cousin Caitlín a run for her money in the stubbornness department." Cian chuckles and closes the door.

He walks away with long strides, and I have to skip a few steps to catch up.

I vaguely recall whispered murmurs at one of Dónal's last house parties about the American cousin who came to visit and fell in love with the Donnelly patriarch's enforcer. "She's from Brooklyn?"

He nods. "Uncle Cormac moved there nearly forty years ago to expand our family's business dealings. They aligned themselves with the Italian syndicate about eleven or twelve years ago when his oldest daughter Brenna married the head of their organization."

I've always found America fascinating. Maybe because I've never been outside of Dublin. "Do you ever visit them?"

"Not often. I think the last time we were there was three or four years ago for a wedding. Caitlín's brother Nathan lives here in

Dublin with his wife and two kids. Or maybe they have three kids now. I don't pay much attention."

"Don't you like children?" Why did I ask that? It's none of my business.

"I don't have any strong feelings one way or the other about them."

I always thought I wanted children, but the older I've gotten, the more undecided I become.

The wind kicks up and I can't control my shivering. We reach the large patio at the back of the manor. "Come on, let's go."

I blink at the command and when my eyes focus, Cian is standing at the door of the manor with it halfway open. It's obvious he's going to get his way, and since I'm freezing, I'll let him. This time.

CHAPTER 8

CIAN

NESSA AND I STEP INTO THE WARMTH OF THE DINING room. I glance in the kitchen, but Nora isn't there. At this time of day, there's only one other place she might be. *You didn't think this through, did you?* I don't want to leave her alone in case Aidan or Finn wander by, but I also don't want her in Da's office. That's the only option, though. Not unless I want to take her into my wing of the house and give her one of my coats.

I don't want her scent invading my space or lingering in my clothes, so down the hall it is. "This way." I jerk my head the direction we're heading and take off that way.

Voices from inside get louder the closer we get. I pause outside the closed door and knock. Nessa comes to a stop behind me.

"Enter." The command is deep and gruff.

I open the door and step inside. Nora is attempting to rise from Da's lap, but he tightens his hold around her waist. Knowing it's pointless to resist, she collapses back against him with a small harrumph. She never flaunts their relationship in front of us. Out of respect for our mother, I overheard her telling him once. As much as I shouldn't speak ill of the dead, our mother doesn't deserve the respect. Kathleen Donnelly had been a terrible mum.

"Sorry to interrupt, but Nessa needs a coat, and I was hoping you might have one she could wear."

Da raises a brow in question, but doesn't say anything. Nora pushes on his chest. He sighs and releases her so she can stand. She dips her head slightly. "Of course. I'm sure I can find something for her."

She shuffles passed us. "If you'd like to follow me, dear, I'll see if perhaps Caitlín left something here the last time she stayed."

Nessa glances in my direction as though seeking my permission, and I give a short nod. She turns and follows Nora out of the room. My gaze doesn't leave their retreating forms until they're no longer visible. Bracing myself, I face Da, who I'm sure is full of questions.

"So that's Sheehan's daughter."

"Yes."

"And you brought her up to the house, so Nora could find her a coat." There's a tone to his words I'm not sure I like.

"It's four degrees outside and I was taking her for a tour around the estate. She's proving as stubborn as Caitlín. What was I supposed to do? Let her freeze?"

Da leans back in his chair. "I see."

"Any word on Sheehan or Campbell?"

He smirks, knowing exactly what I'm doing. "Only rumblings, although one of my sources mentioned a business deal between Campbell and an unknown player. One that signals he's about to make his move against Sheehan."

"I wonder, how long after Campbell takes over is he going to break the cease-fire we have with Sheehan? Dónal isn't going to go down without a fight, either. He does still hold a small amount of clout in this city with a few remaining allies."

Da's mouth tightens. "I fully anticipate Sheehan will attempt to align himself with our organization to try and stop Campbell."

Dónal has always been a weaselly thing. I suspect Da is right. A creaking floor signals someone's approach. I glance toward the door as Nora steps in. Right behind her is Nessa, wearing a dark blue coat she's trying to button over her breasts without success. She growls under her breath and gives up. At least she has a wool scarf draped over her neck, so it's something.

I cast a quick glance Da's way and then Nora's. "Thank you."

She smiles in the all-knowing way she has. I cross the room and place my hand on Nessa's low back to guide her out the door. We can't get out from beneath the scrutiny fast enough. We make it back to the dining room door that leads out back.

"Nora is very kind," she says.

"Yes, she is."

"How long has she...worked for your family?"

My eyes dart to her. "Is that your subtle way of asking how long she and my da have been lovers?"

Nessa stumbles and I reach out to steady her with a chuckle. Her fiery gaze snaps in my direction. "I would never be so rude."

I open the door and beckon her out. "There's nothing wrong with being curious. And to answer your question, Nora has been working for my father for years. In fact, they first had an affair over twenty-five year ago. Right after my youngest brother Finn was born. Nora broke it off, though, and moved to Belfast. They reconnected about ten years ago, I'd say."

She blinks. Nearly everyone in our organization knows their history, so it's not as though I've shared any dark secrets. Da has never hid his relationship with Nora. Or been ashamed of it. Not even when he was married to my mum. Some judge him, but he ignores them. None of those people know what our lives were like back then. When our mum was still alive.

We wander around the estate. I point out Nora's vast vegetable garden along the west side of the manor, the trees that have been standing longer than I've been alive, as well as the small hedgerow maze that sits in the center of a clearing on the east side of the property. It takes far longer than I remember to make it to the center of the maze where a short statue sits.

"This is beautiful." Nessa turns in a slow circle.

"Da had it built for us when we were kids. The three of us as well as Caitlín and Nathan would run around the estate. This was our favorite place to wander."

A fleeting sadness crosses Nessa's face and she releases a heavy sigh. "That sounds lovely."

Yes, I suppose it was. While we fight as any siblings do, I know that Aidan and Finn will always have my back. Same with Caitlín and Nathan. Hell, my brothers and I were the ones who taught her how to shoot, fight, and play cards. It must have been lonely being an only child. *Don't forget who either she or her Da are.* Pushing away any sympathy, I clear my head.

"I'll make you a bet."

Nessa stops. "What kind of bet?"

I jerk my chin up. "If you can make it out of the maze before I catch you, I'll bring you breakfast in bed tomorrow."

"And if I can't?" she says slowly.

"Then my reward is a kiss."

Nessa crosses her arms. "Neither of those sound like a good bet to me. You're familiar with how to get in and out of this place."

I gasp in mock affront. "This is the first time I've been inside these walls in over fifteen years and it was pure luck that got us to this spot. Besides, what woman doesn't want a sexy man bringing her breakfast in bed or a kiss that will have her forgetting her name?"

She snorts. "You have an awfully inflated opinion of yourself."

"And you're avoiding answering." I move closer and walk around her, leaning in to whisper in her ear. "Are you scared you'll lose?"

She turns her head just slightly and our breath mingles. Our eyes meet. She drops her gaze to my mouth and lingers there for a second before lifting it back up to mine. "No, I'm not scared."

In a flash, she pushes me, causing me to stumble and nearly fall on my arse, before taking off into the hedgerow. I laugh. Sly little mouse. It *has* been years since I've been inside the maze, but I've never forgotten the way out. Nessa's footsteps are loud, as is her breathing. There's a flash of blue and pink through the greenery. My prey thinks she can escape me. Down one row, then a right turn, followed by two lefts has me at an intersection where I stand and wait.

Seconds later, she bursts around the corner and comes to a skidding halt with a soft cry. Spinning on her heels, she darts away in the direction she came from. I casually make my way in the other direction. This is the only way out of here. She's going to have to make it past me if she wants to win. I whistle a tune and shove my hands in my pocket, slowly striding down the narrow pass without a care in the world. Another intersection is in front of me and just as I turn right, a soft body collides with mine.

My hands grip Nessa's hips to steady her, and big, blue eyes filled with disbelief peer up at me.

"Gotcha."

CHAPTER 9

Nessa

Breathless, I can only stare up at Cian. It might have been sneaky on my part to shove him back there, but it had been out of desperation. I don't want to feel his lips on mine again. At least not as part of a game. If he's going to kiss me, I want him to do it because he wants to.

I want him to mean it.

Which will never happen.

"Fine, you won. You can let go of me now." I try taking a step back. Anything to get away from the heat of his body seeping into mine and warming me from the inside out.

"Maybe I like holding you." His grip tightens and then shifts, so the tips of his fingers splay across the outside of my butt cheeks, just above the crease of my thighs.

I'm painfully aware of my chest squished against his. The slightest movement generates friction and makes them ache for more. I have to force myself to hold still and avoid the temptation of rubbing myself all over him. Cursing my body for betraying me, I once again try to put some distance between us, but Cian is like a solid statue. Completely immoveable.

"Let's just get this over with then." I quickly lift up on my toes, press my mouth to his, and drop my heels back to the ground. "There. Freely given. Debt paid."

Cian scoffs. "That wasn't a kiss."

"Yes, it was. My lips were on yours. Which is the definition of a kiss. So we're done." I flatten my palms against his rock-hard chest and push.

"I should have expected a Sheehan to cheat. Just like your Da."

Indignation rises up from my belly. "Don't you dare lump me in with Dónal. We're nothing alike."

Cian glares down at me. "Then prove it."

Any other challenge I might back down from, but not this one. Not after being called a cheat. Which is probably his intention. He wants me to prove it? Then I will.

I palm the back of his neck and go up on my tippy-toes again, pressing my mouth to his. I part my lips and tilt my head enough that our noses don't bump. As if I know what I'm doing, I flick my tongue out, gently caressing the seam of his mouth, keeping my touch soft. Coaxing. Teasing.

Just when it's becoming clear that this is one-sided, he wraps an arm around my waist and pulls me into him. At the same time, he deepens the kiss. Our tongues tangle. Breaths mingle. The ginger and spring scent of Cian makes my head spin. The hand still gripping my hip tugs me close enough that the hard line of his cock presses against my lower belly. Right where a swirling ball of heat is centered and spreads outward, warming me from my head to my toes.

He nips my bottom lip and the slight sting is like a bucket of water being dumped over my head. It brings me back to reality. I jerk my head back and struggle out of Cian's far too pleasant hold. Surprisingly, he lets me go. I clear my throat and awkwardly shift my weight while not looking him entirely in the eye.

"There was your kiss. Are you satisfied now?"

"Not even remotely."

My eyes jerk to his face and the intensity of his stare nearly burns me with its heat. I straighten my shoulders. "Well, you're going to have to be."

I swiftly hurry away from Cian and the arousal he evokes in me.

"You're going the wrong way," he calls out with a hint of amusement.

An abrupt turn has me locking gazes with him again. Marching forward, I make to pass him, but he blocks that narrow passageway. "If you'll excuse me, I'd like to get out of here."

He pivots a half-turn and sweeps his arm out. "By all means, go ahead."

There's hardly any room between him and the hedgerow wall. The only way I'm going to get by him is to squeeze through. I twist sideways. The sharp, broken twigs that make up the greenery scratch my back forcing me to take a tiny step forward, which means my still-aching breasts and tight nipples brush across his chest. I keep my head facing straight ahead until finally I make it past. A soft chuckle at my back makes my fists clench. I breathe through the irritation which only brings in more of Cian's scent.

My mind replays the kiss. The glide of his tongue across mine. His flavor. The way he held me. *Don't fall for his kisses. His touches. Be strong.*

Without his help, it takes forever, but I finally make it out of the maze and into the clearing. I don't wait for him. Instead, I make my way directly to the cottage behind the manor.

I close the door, but something stops it. Cian. Damn it. I forgot he brought his clothes here like he plans on staying. *Just ignore him.* Yeah, right. As if it's going to be that easy. I take off the borrowed coat and hang it on a nickel hook that juts out from the wall behind the door. Needing to wash the far too delicious taste of him from my mouth, I grab a glass from the cabinet, fill it with water from the tap, and guzzle it down.

Warmth spreads across my back, and the whisper of a breath ghosts over my neck before I'm caged between Cian's arms as he lays his palms on the edge of the counter. My eyes close and I try to control my breathing.

"Why are you fighting this so hard?" Cian murmurs into my ear and runs his tongue along the shell of it. "We're two adults attracted to each other. You can't deny our chemistry. There's nothing wrong with going where the attraction leads us."

If only it were that simple.

"For my entire life, I've been used by someone more powerful than me. I won't be used by yet one more person." I take in a shuddering breath. "I have no illusions about my value to Dónal's organization. My virginity is the one thing that belongs solely to me, and I won't let anyone take it from me. I don't care what the terms of your bet were. He offered something that isn't his to bargain with."

My heart pounds so hard I could swear I can hear it over the silence that hangs heavy in the air. I swallow and wait for whatever Cian might say or do. One second, he's crowding me and the next he's gone. Still, I remain where I am. Then the door behind me opens and closes.

Slowly, I turn. The room is empty.

I sag back against the counter with a sigh. I'm not sure what Cian's leaving means. Will he be back? Do I want him to?

A single tear spills from the inner corner of my eye and slides down my nose. I reach up and swipe it away. Too many men have been the cause of my tears. First Liam when he ran away all those years ago and left me entirely alone. Then Dónal. Why am I more hurt and surprised that Cian is the cause of these? I sniff and rise up. I'm away from the house I grew to hate. Out from under the thumb of someone I lost respect for long ago. I need to embrace the freedom I've been given. Even if it's only yet another façade.

CHAPTER 10

Cian

I've spent most of the day avoiding Nessa. I even
sent Nora down to the cottage with her evening meal. And because I
didn't want to deal with any questions, I headed into the city to take
care of some business. Nathan and I have been going over the details
of our newest shipment that's supposed to be coming in from our
German suppliers some time in the next couple of days. Despite the
fact he took over as our head of acquisitions more than three years
ago, and is perfectly capable of handling everything, I use it as an
excuse to stay busy. So I didn't keep hearing Nessa's words inside my
head.

"Is there a reason you're still hanging around?" Nathan closes his
desk drawer and locks it. "Not that I don't want you here, but I'm
pretty sure this is the longest amount of time you've spent in my
office in at least a year."

I take another sip of whiskey from the bottle of The Devil's Keep he keeps stocked in the bar. "Which is precisely why I should be here. It's important I know every aspect of our business dealings."

My cousin cocks his head. "Planning on replacing me already?"

"What? No." I don't have the patience or the temperament to deal with the kind of bullshit he does. Not that I'm a hot-head, but Nathan has a way of putting people at ease when he talks to them. He's far more suited to the job than I'd be.

He chuckles. "Just making sure. Which means there's got to be some other reason why you're still here, despite the fact that you have no interest in dealing with contracts and paperwork."

"Like I said, I'm just keeping up-to-date on how things are running."

Nathan leans back in his chair and studies me. "I heard about the card game last night."

I pause taking another drink, the glass barely touching my lips. Slowly, I lower it. No doubt Finn shared the news. My brother seems to have forgotten how to keep his mouth shut. "Yes, and?"

He flips his palms up and lays them flat against his armrests again. "And nothing. I just never pictured you as someone who has any interest in virgins."

"I don't. Except this one is Dónal Sheehan's daughter. She's a means to an end."

He studies me a little too critically. "I've known you my entire life. We may not have grown up together, but I know the kind of man Uncle Carrick is. What kind you, Aidan, and Finn are."

"What's that supposed to mean?" I bristle.

My cousin rises from his chair and circles the desk. He props himself up on the edge of it and crosses his ankles. "This life can be— is—brutal and violent. There's no escaping it. We aren't without our enemies. We've killed our fair share of them. But the one thing we've never done, not since Grand-da's death anyway, is hurt innocent people—especially women."

He strides past, claps me on the shoulder, and disappears out of the office. Nathan has no idea what he's talking about. I'm not hurting Nessa. I could have already forced her if that had been my goal. Dónal is who I'm hurting. Showing him he can't fuck with us. Reminding him who holds the power in this city. The only plan I have for the little mouse back at the estate is pleasure. For both of us.

I throw back the last swallow of whiskey. I'm sure Nessa has had time to cool down. The entire drive home, I plot my next move in the seduction of my little mouse. By the time I'm through, there won't be any taking of her virginity. She'll gladly give it to me.

IT'S DARK BY THE TIME I PARK IN FRONT OF THE MANOR. The gravel on the drive crunch beneath the soles of my shoes. Soft lights glow from several windows at the front, including Nora's room. I walk along the stone pathway that circles to the side before it gives way to grass. The night critters fill the air with chirps and whirs, and a cool breeze blows causing the tree branches to sway and dance. Overhead, the section of the moon not hidden beneath cloud coverage shines brightly, providing a bit of illumination as I head down the sloped lawn to the cottage. Light spills from its windows as well. Which means either Nessa is still awake or she left them on knowing I'd be back.

I don't bother knocking. From the couch, she jerks her head up, her eyes wide behind her glasses and body stiff, but then she relaxes slightly. She's wearing another one of those ugly nightgowns and a blanket is thrown over her lap. In her hands is a book. I'm pretty sure neither Roarke nor Da had left one in here, so she must have brought it with her. I stand there for another few seconds, neither of us looking away from the other.

Finally, I close the door behind me. Nessa clears her throat. "Nora left supper if you're hungry. I didn't"—she pauses and swallows—"know when you'd be back so I didn't keep it warm."

She's either a people-pleaser or she's forgotten about earlier. My guess is the former. I stride through the living area into the kitchen and grab the pitcher of filtered water from the fridge. "That's fine. I ate earlier at the office."

Once I've filled my glass, I move back to the living room and sit on the sofa next to her. Not close enough to intrude on her personal space, but close enough that she can't just ignore me. I swivel a half turn toward her and cross my ankle over my knee, taking a drink. Nessa shifts an inch. It's a subtle movement, as though she's actually giving me more of her attention, but it draws her body back and farther from me.

I tip my chin toward her lap. "What are you reading?"

There's another shift, this one uncomfortable. "Nothing you'd be interested in."

"You might be surprised." I arch a brow.

Nessa closes the book and folds her hands over it. "Fine. It's about a young woman whose long-term boyfriend breaks up with her, instead of proposing marriage like she'd been expecting. She's feeling lost, so she and a friend travel the world. Throughout their travels, they meet and help people from all these different countries and cultures. She begins to discover things about herself she never knew or expected. Then something happens and she has to choose between her old life and her new one."

"Which one does she choose?"

Nessa gives a small shrug. "I don't know yet. I haven't made it that far."

I study her. Her hair has been braided again and the tail drapes over her shoulder. She doesn't appear to be wearing any makeup. Not that I really noticed any before. I lift my gaze to meet hers. "What would you choose, if it were you?"

Behind the glasses, those big eyes of hers blink. "I don't know. I suppose it depends."

"On what?" I'm genuinely curious.

"I guess on whether or not I'd be returning to my old life because it's familiar, and although shitty, there's comfort in the safety and security of the known. Sometimes, the uncertainty of your future is far more terrifying than the familiarity of your past."

Carefully, I palm the side of her neck, gently running my thumb along her cheek. She doesn't pull away. "That's what makes new things all that more exciting. The way your pulse races and your heart pounds. There's a bit of exhilaration in not knowing what the outcome might be. How do you know that this new life won't be better? Isn't it worth a bit of risk to find out? The reward could be so worth it."

Nessa blows out a harsh breath. "Says the person who hasn't lived their whole life faced with uncertainty, only to discover it's far worse on the other side of it."

"I don't confess to knowing what your life with Sheehan was like, but nothing says you have to go back to stay there. You're a grown woman. Get out there and live."

She draws her head back, turning it to force my arm to drop, and then returns her sharp glare to me. "How do you propose that? I have no money of my own. No skills to speak of. I've basically been kept locked away under the guise of a loving Da who can't live without his precious daughter. I don't have any real friends, although not for lack of trying. All I can hope for is that either one of these days Dónal's luck will run out and I'll finally be free, or I find a man I want to marry and who wants to marry me. Although, considering the company Dónal keeps, the chances of that happening are pretty low." Nessa stands up. "Now, if you'll excuse me, I've suddenly developed a headache and am going to bed."

She moves toward the bedroom, walking around the outside of the coffee table to keep far enough away that I can't reach for her without getting up. The door closes with a soft *snick*. I glance over my shoulder toward it and smile to myself. Every little wall she puts up only makes me that more determined to tear it down. I set the glass on the floor near my feet and pull my phone from my pocket. After typing out a quick text message, I pick it back up, take it to the kitchen and sit on the sofa again. I'll give Nessa a bit of time to get settled before I head in there. Allow her the illusion of control.

CHAPTER 11

Nessa

I've been lying awake for hours. How could I not, after discovering Cian in bed with me some time before dawn? Although shouldn't I have expected it after he placed his clothes in the drawer and personal items in the bathroom? My bladder had pulled me out of a deep sleep, and still groggy, I slipped from beneath the blankets and went to the bathroom. When I walked back into the bedroom, I'd stopped short at the large human-shaped form lying there. I'd stood for the longest time debating. Do I just go back to bed and pretend he's not there or go out to the living room and sleep on the couch? Neither prospect sounded appealing.

Stiffening my shoulders, I went back to my side of the bed and laid under the covers staying as close to the edge of it as I could without falling out and onto the floor. I'd kept my eyes closed and prayed for sleep to come, but it didn't. I lie frozen, waiting for every shift of his body. I'd still been awake when he got up, showered, dressed—my eyes had remained firmly shut—and left. That had been at least an hour ago.

I roll onto my back and stare at the ceiling. My arms lie folded over my chest with the fingers threaded. I loosen them and smooth down the fabric of the duvet nervously even though I'm alone. I've never slept in the same bed as anyone before. For Cian to be the first has me feeling all sorts of ways. The conversation from last night comes back to me. As well as the one before he'd left earlier yesterday. I wish I knew what to make of him. I mean, he shows up at my house at dawn, claiming I belong to him. Then we spend the rest of the day in this weird dance that alternates between making me furious and falling under some spell he's putting on me.

I'm not fooled by his kisses and the way he touches me. As though I'm someone he cares about. Every interaction we've had has been calculated to get a reaction from me. I'm not stupid. I've learned how to judge people's sincerity, dealing with Dónal and all his hangers-on.

And yet, despite knowing I'm being played, I can't control my own emotions. Everyone in the world I live in is playing a game. One that earns them power, money, and control. It's one I want no part of and yet I've been forced to become a player.

Perhaps Cian is right. Maybe I need to start playing by my own rules for my own benefit. Take back the control Dónal has exerted over me. That I've *let him* exert.

Except where do I start? I'm stuck out here in the countryside with no one to call. Even though I got the sense that Cian's brother didn't approve of him bringing me here, I doubt he's going to go against his brother by taking me home.

Not that I want to go back there anyway.

For the briefest second, I consider trying to figure out how to reach Liam, although I've only seen him twice in the last twenty years. Once was over ten years ago, and the other nearly ten years before that on the day he'd had enough and ran away. While he was never cruel to me, he hates Dónal. I don't suspect he has any more charitable thoughts toward me, even if, for a few short years—until his mother died—he was my step-brother. We're practically strangers.

Lying here feeling sorry for myself isn't getting me anywhere. I throw back the duvet, grab clean clothes, and hop in the shower. The blast of water revives me. Once I'm dressed and my hair is dried and braided, I grab the coat Nora loaned me yesterday and head up to the manor house. It's a bit of a bold move, but I'm not going to let fear stop me. I'm not going to sit inside that cottage, alone, and wait for things to happen, or remain hidden like some dirty secret.

Except my boldness only takes me so far. I stop outside one of the French doors and knock. Hopefully someone is nearby and will hear me. Otherwise, I suppose my only other option is to walk around to the front and ring the bell like an uninvited guest. Thankfully, Nora appears through the glass and opens up the right side.

"Miss Sheehan, is everything all right?"

"Oh, yes. I just thought I would see if there was anything I could do to help you. It's a bit boring out there all by myself."

She steps back, opening the door wider. "Please, come in."

The house smells divine. A mix of fruit and something sweet.

"I'm just baking some treats for Carrick's grandsons. Nathan and Lucia are stopping by tomorrow with the boys." There's affection in her tone when she speaks of them. "You're welcome to come and keep me company."

I follow Nora out of the dining room and into the kitchen where the scent of chocolate and shortbread fills the air. She gestures to one of the stools pushed under the counter. "Take a seat if you'd like. Have you eaten breakfast yet, dear?"

"I'm not really hungry, but thank you."

"You're welcome to a biscuit or two once they've cooled."

In the distance, a door opens and closes.

"Yoo-hoo, I'm here. Where is everyone?" a feminine voice calls out and footsteps grow closer.

Nora makes an excited noise, brushes her hands off on a towel, and rushes to meet the new arrival. A stunning red-head comes around the corner and the older woman wraps her in a hug. "Caitlín, love, what are you doing here?"

They separate and the younger woman leans around her and locks eyes with me. "I'm here to introduce myself to Nessa, who I assume is you?"

Caitlín? Where do I know that name? It takes a second. *Oh, yeah.* She appears friendly, but there's a gleam in her blue gaze that makes me wary. I slowly stand and swipe my palms on my thighs. "Hi, yes, I'm Nessa. You must be Cian's cousin."

Her smile widens. "Whatever he's told you about me is probably true."

Nora threads her arm through Caitlín's and drags her farther into the room. "Come and have a seat. Tell me all about your trip to Brooklyn."

"Actually, would you mind if Nessa and I chatted for a bit first?"

The older woman's gaze bounces between us and then settles back on Cian's cousin. As though some silent exchange occurs between them, Nora nods. "Of course. You two ladies go and get acquainted."

"Thanks, Nora." Caitlín kisses her cheek and then steals a biscuit from a cooling rack on the counter and breaks half of it off in her mouth with a moan of delight. "You've outdone yourself as always."

The housekeeper shoos her off, but a pink flush rises in her cheeks. Caitlín turns to me. "The sun is finally out and burning some of the chill out of the air. Up for a walk?"

There's a weight in my gut that says I'm being ambushed, but I'm not sure I have a choice. "Sure."

"Great. We'll go out the front." She snags one more biscuit and then marches out of the kitchen.

At a much slower pace, I follow her. It's my first glimpse of the inside of Cian's home. To say I'm a bit surprised is an understatement. It's warm and inviting in here with family pictures hanging on the walls. There are fresh flower arrangements on mantels and side tables. The color scheme is a mix of blues, greens, oranges, and reds.

Yes, there are signs of wealth, but they're not quite so ostentatious as Dónal tries to make our home.

"I hear you're going to be staying for a while," Caitlín says over her shoulder as she reaches the double doors in the entryway.

I almost laugh. "So I've been told." *Or at least until Cian gets tired of you. Isn't that what he said?*

"At least the guest house is cozy. Did Cian tell you that I lived out there for a little bit? Okay, so maybe not actually *lived* there, but it was still a nice place to stay."

We walk down the narrow lane that makes up the drive. Even though the sun peeks through the branches, it's still shady enough to be a bit cool. I tug the coat a little tighter around me even if I can't close it all the way. Caitlín glances over at me and her eyes widen, as though just realizing what I'm wearing. "That's where I left that thing. I wondered. It's a good color on you."

Her comment hadn't been laced with any snarky undertones, but I'm a bit uncomfortable with the fact it had been loaned to me without her knowledge.

"Thanks." I smile weakly.

"Tell me about yourself. I'm still getting to know other women around my age since I spend most of my time with either my fiancé or my sister-in-law. It's a lot harder making new friends as an adult, which is kind of weird."

I stop short. The uneasy sensation grows in my belly. "I'm sorry, I'm not trying to be rude, but why are you doing this?"

Caitlín pauses and faces me with a questioning look. I brace myself for her reaction.

"Doing what?"

I wave my hand, gesturing between the two of us. "This. Being here. Introducing yourself to me."

The little crease between her eyebrows deepens. "Cian sent me a text message last night. He told me you were visiting for a while and thought it might be nice if you and I got to know each other. I'll admit it seemed a bit out of left field, but like I said, I'm always up for making friends my age."

That's it? She's here because Cian asked her to come? Why? "Did he tell you why I'm visiting?"

She cocks her head. "Now that you mention it, no."

I can't help it. This time I do laugh, mostly because it's so sad and pathetic. "My Da lost my virginity to Cian in a game of cards two nights ago. Apparently, I belong to him now. Or so he says."

Good god. Why did I just blurt it all out like that?

If I expect Caitlín to be scandalized, I'd be dead wrong. Instead, her face twists in anger. "What the actual fuck?"

CHAPTER 12

CIAN

MAYBE ASKING CAITLÍN TO COME INTRODUCE HERSELF TO
Nessa hadn't been the smartest decision I've ever made. I'm taking
the chance that Nessa won't tell her why she's really staying at the
cottage.

Not that I'm scared of my cousin, but I don't want to listen to
her bitch me out. Caitlín has strong opinions on how women should
be treated and has no hesitation about sharing them whether a
person wants to hear them or not. It's a calculated risk. If nothing
else, she'll be even more inclined to take Nessa under her wing. Then
again, I could also go home and my little mouse will be missing.

A thwacking pain pierces the middle of my forehead. I reach up
to rub where Aidan flicked me with his finger and glare at him as he
leans back in his seat next to me. "What the fuck was that for?

"Because your mind is elsewhere and you need to pay attention."

I glance around Finn's office. It's just Aidan, him, and me. "You guys are going over the books and numbers. Pretty sure you don't need me for that."

Aidan shoots me an annoyed glare. "We were done discussing casino business at least five minutes ago. Finn's said your name three times and you haven't heard him once. Is it your little virgin that's got you distracted? Although, I suppose she's not one anymore."

He and Finn share an amused glance. I'm suddenly reticent about sharing anything regarding Nessa with them. "Don't worry about her."

Finn's expression flattens. "You keep telling us that, and I can't help but wonder why."

I glare at him. "Because it's none of your business."

"I beg to differ," Aidan rumbles. "You've got the daughter of our family's enemy stashed out in the guest house while her Da is teetering on the edge of ruin. In the meantime, that psychopath step-brother of hers, Campbell, is doing everything in his power to destroy not only Sheehan, but us. All so he can control Dublin. The fact that your plaything could come in handy in winning an upcoming war is exactly our business."

An unwelcome haze of anger distorts my vision. "We're not using Nessa as some type of bargaining chip."

"Why not? She's a Sheehan." Aidan leans forward in his chair. "Neither Dónal nor Campbell would hesitate to use anyone against us. We have the upper hand here."

"We're not using her." I push myself out of the chair to loom over my brother. "End of story. I'm done here."

I jerk open the door to leave.

"Make sure you're not thinking with your cock, Cian," Aidan calls out and I slam the door behind me.

Caitlín's car is gone by the time I park in front of the house. Is my mouse still here, or has she tried to escape me? I head into the house first to grab something to eat. I missed breakfast and spent the last few hours at the casino. I step into the kitchen to take a few things out of the fridge. I turn and come to an abrupt halt. Da stands in the open entryway, his features tight.

"What's happened?" I set everything down and brace myself against the edge of the counter.

"Liam Campbell initiated his take-over less than an hour ago. Strolled right into Sheehan's home, presented him with the deed, and announced he was in charge of the organization now."

"Fuck. We knew it was coming, but I didn't expect it so soon." I lean into my hands balancing me and then push myself upright. "What are we going to do about it?"

"We wait a few hours and then call for sit-down with him. Try to gauge where he's at and get a lead on what his plans are. He's smart. And dangerous. Far more dangerous than Sheehan. Campbell's predecessor let drink control him. He talked a bigger game than he could back up. If for no other reason than to continue living under his own delusion that his organization was just as powerful as ours." Da rubs the back of his neck. "It was my mistake in letting him continue. We all know I could have taken out the entire thing and everyone in it. But so long as he didn't interfere in our business deal-ings, I let things lie."

"How could you have known that Campbell would gain the support of Sheehan's men? At least this quickly. He's only been making noticeable allies for, what, a few years? He's an outsider. Not even blood. It doesn't matter that Campbell is Sheehan's stepson. Loyalty shouldn't be bought."

Da shakes his head. "Yet in this case, it has been. Young Liam has gained himself some powerful backers. He's played the long game well. And now, he's finally won."

"We need to let Aidan and Finn know."

"I called them. They're on their way home. I also put the word out to the heads of the families that we will be having a meeting in two days to discuss this latest development. Campbell wants it all.

Money definitely. But more importantly, he wants to rule Dublin. He's not going to abide by the truce. He's going to come for us, and he's going to come hard." Da's gaze intensifies. "We'll need to be ready for a war."

Christ. I run my hand through my hair. For more than half my life we have had a cease-fire between our two organizations. We'd all gotten tired of our men—our families—dying. Campbell's takeover changes everything.

My gaze shifts to the cottage halfway down the hill. No doubt he's also discovered that Nessa is mine. He's never shown any interest in her. Hell, his entire focus has always appeared to be bringing Sheehan down. Except what if that changes?

My mind goes back to Aidan's suggestion. Use Nessa as some type of bargaining chip. A part of me wants to instantly dismiss it, but I hesitate. It might come down to that.

"Be careful, son."

I blink away my thoughts and nod. Da walks out of the room, no doubt to go to his office for a drink and a smoke. He only brings out his tobacco pipe when he's got a lot on his mind. Nora isn't a fan and playfully scolds him, but that's the extent of it. She knows not to try and make him stop. I quickly put together a sandwich and eat it on the way down to the cottage. It's more important than ever to make sure Nessa is still here. I should have gone down to check as soon as I got here. I walk in and actually exhale the breath I'd been holding. She's sitting on the couch with the same book from last night in her hands. Her head lifts without the surprise it had at my entrance the previous evening.

"I honestly wasn't sure if you'd still be here." The confession is pulled from me before I can stop it.

Nessa lightly shrugs. "I wasn't either. But the sad fact is, at the moment, I have nowhere else to go. Even though Caitlín offered me the spare room at her and her fiancé's place."

Closing the door behind me, I stride forward and sit at the other end of the couch, leaning forward with my forearms resting on my knees. "You didn't take her up on it?"

"And be the third wheel?" she laughs, but there's a tinge of self-deprecation to it. "No, thanks."

I tilt my head to peer over my shoulder. "I'm not sure I would have blamed you if you had."

There's a slight pink hue to Nessa's cheeks. Otherwise, she remains still. Her breasts rise and fall with each breath she takes. I turn to face forward again. "Campbell forcibly took over your Da's organization earlier today."

She sucks in a sharp breath. "Liam?"

A bright flare of anger erupts at his name coming from her lips. "Walked right into the house with his men."

"Was...was anyone hurt?" Her voice trembles.

I sit upright. "Not that I'm aware."

Nessa visibly relaxes, but her white-knuckled grip on her book doesn't ease. She swallows. "He actually did it."

"You knew that was his plan?" It comes out sharply.

She shakes her head. "Not really. Dónal has grown paranoid over the last two or three years. Always mumbling something about revenge. He started drinking more around the same time so I didn't put much stock into it. There were a few late-night meetings where I caught bits and pieces of conversation on occasion. Liam's name was mentioned a couple times. I thought Dónal was over-reacting. Now I see that he wasn't."

I relax slightly. "How much contact have you had with Campbell?"

Nessa jerks her head my direction. "What's that supposed to mean?"

I shift and twist so we're more face-to-face. "It's just a question, Nessa."

"That wasn't *just* anything. There was a tone in your voice. Like you're accusing me of something."

"I'm not accusing you of anything." Am I?

"For your information," she huffs. "I haven't talked to or seen Liam in ten years."

My jaw clenches at the name again. "You two weren't close then, I take it." I make sure to keep my tone measured and neutral.

Nessa doesn't answer at first. She studies me while I try to maintain a blank mask. Finally she sinks back into the cushion behind her and loosens her grip on the book. "Never. Not even after he and his mum moved in when she and Dónal married. I was still quite young, but I remember being so excited to have a big brother. Except Liam was always a bit distant. Thinking back, it almost feels like he was intentionally trying not to get attached. Considering how Dónal treated him, I guess I'm not surprised."

"Did your Da hit him, too, or just you?" I can't help asking. Maybe I just want confirmation that he laid hands on her.

"He didn't always hit me."

That doesn't really answer my question. "When did he start?"

Nessa averts her eyes. "After Liam left."

I clench my jaw. Campbell is ten years older than her. If he left as a teen, she had only been a little girl. "How old were you?"

"Does it matter?"

Does it? For some reason, yes, it does.

"Maybe not, but tell me anyway," I coax, softer than I thought possible.

"I was six when he escaped."

CHAPTER 13

Nessa

I'm not even sure why I'm telling Cian all this. Maybe so he can have an idea what my life was like. What Liam's was like.

I can't fault Liam for taking over the organization. Truly. If I were a man, I might have even done the same. But despite the fact I haven't talked to Liam in a decade, it doesn't mean I haven't heard things. Whispers of how cold and uncaring he's become. How brutal. My heart aches a bit for him. I'd sensed his loneliness all those years ago. It matched my own.

"What do you mean 'escaped'?"

I glance at Cian. "If you lived with a man who mentally, physically, and emotionally abused you for four years, would you not consider getting away an escape?"

His face twists with anger. "Not if it meant leaving a little girl behind."

It's nice that he has the luxury of believing that. Especially since he has a family who loves him. Living in our world is hard.

If Liam could have a moment of happiness being out from under Dónal's thumb, then I envy him. He's had twenty years of freedom. I can't even imagine what that's like. And I doubt anything I say is going to change Cian's mind. I'm not sure what it means with Liam in charge, although I'm going to bet we'll all find out soon enough. Tired of the conversation, I change topics.

"So Caitlín wasn't at all what I expected."

He snorts softly. "I'm sure."

"I should probably warn you...I think you're on the list of people she's quite unhappy with."

That brings a laugh. "I assumed so, if she offered to let you stay with her and Roarke. I take it the reason behind your visit came up?"

"It might have been mentioned." I place my book on the end table and swivel, bringing my leg up onto the couch and tuck it beneath me. "Aside from that, we had a lovely visit. Thank you for having her stop by."

"You're welcome. Caitlín needs to be kept busy, or she causes trouble. I figured having her stop by for a few hours was one way to do that. I'm sure Roarke will thank me later."

That makes me chuckle. From everything she told me about her fiancé, I got the impression he liked the kind of trouble she caused. Even that reminder has my cheeks heating.

"Are you blushing?"

I startle and grow flustered. "Wha—? No. Why would I be?"

Cian smirks. "You are. What were you thinking just now?"

"Nothing." I shake my head and jump up from the couch.

He snags my hand and tugs me straight down onto his lap.

"Hey. Let me up." I wiggle and squirm, trying to get up, but he tightens his hold. Then I freeze, because his hardness grows beneath me.

"Thought that might settle you down." Cian smirks.

It galls me to admit I like being this close to him. To be able to admire the freckles sprinkled across his face. I'm not sure he'd appreciate the fact, though. For some reason, they make him more human. More fallible. They remind me of the Cian I met before his face lost its boyishness and he matured into the man he is today. Still, I remain rigid in his grasp.

"I'm not a child, you know. I'm too old and too big to sit on anyone's lap."

He shifts beneath me and I settle deeper against him. The tingle I get each time he's touched or kissed me starts up again. I have to make myself not rub my thighs together to ease the ache that throbs between them.

"A woman is always welcome on a man's lap, no matter how old or grown she's gotten."

That annoying flush rises in my chest and neck again. I'm glad my shirt covers most of it. "We'll have to agree to disagree, I guess."

"I guess so. Now, are you going to answer me?" Cian asks with a raised brow.

What was the question? My brain's gone stupid from the near proximity of him. A fact that annoys me greatly. I've never gone stupid over a man before. Why does he have to be the first? Oh, yeah, the question. "There's nothing to answer, because I wasn't blushing."

"You were. We were talking about Caitlín and Roarke and suddenly your cheeks turned red." He tips his head. "What did she say to you?"

"My god, you're like a dog with a bone that doesn't let go, aren't you?" It's beyond irritating.

"If it's something I want, then, yes." He says it without an ounce of shame, too.

Quick, think of something. "Fine. She just gushed about their relationship. How they met. How Roarke proposed. Their visit to Brooklyn to meet her parents and the rest of the family. That was all. It was sweet."

Cian narrows his gaze. "That is not blush-worthy conversation."

"Maybe not to you it's not."

"Wow, that's really sad." His face falls with sympathy.

I smack his chest and quickly draw my hand back. "I'm sorry."

He makes a sound. "For what? That little tap? I'm sure I deserved to be slapped harder than that. If not now, then for some infraction in the near future."

"No." I shake my head. "There's never an excuse to put hands on someone. Not even in jest. I'm also sorry I pushed you yesterday. I shouldn't have done that."

Cian's hand cups the side of my face and turns it toward him. His eyes hold mine, more serious than they've been. "You don't have to apologize. I did deserve it. Both times. I'll probably continue to deserve it."

I open my mouth to argue, but he presses his thumb over my lips. "No arguing."

The breath leaves me and I sag. He gently continues gliding across my mouth with the slightly roughened fingertip. My tongue darts out before I can stop it and catches on it. Cian's eyes darken with heat and the hardness beneath me gets even harder. Slowly, he leans forward and kisses me. It's soft. Gentle. The way I kissed him, although he's far less tentative than I'd been. He doesn't deepen the kiss, which only frustrates me.

I curl my arm around his neck and thread my fingers through his hair. It's finer than it appears. I flick my tongue out again, wanting more of a taste of him, until finally Cian answers my call. He swoops in, deepening our connection and taking my breath with him. Swirling sensations dance inside me. I lay my other palm against his cheek. The coarse bristles of the hair along his jaw tickle my skin. He's hot beneath my touch, warming my hand all the way up to my elbow.

Cian's ginger scent surrounds us and makes my mouth water. I'll never eat a gingersnap again without thinking of him. When he kisses me like this, it's easy to forget why I'm here. While I'm in his arms I could almost fool myself into thinking I'm safe from the outside world. That he'll protect me from anyone who wishes me harm.

Except I'm not and he won't.

Because he's the one who poses the biggest threat. If only the two parts inside me could both see that, instead of just my brain. *Stop thinking, Nessa. Just feel and enjoy what Cian's doing even though it's a lie.*

The kiss goes on until far too soon, he draws back. A smile curls his lips. "I guess that's one way to stop you from arguing."

I match my smile to his. "I guess so."

His phone rings. He shifts his weight, tightening his hold on me, and raises a hip to drag it from his pocket. "Give me a minute."

Curious, I wait while he answers.

"Yeah?"

There's a short pause. The faint voice of the person on the other end filters through, but I can't make out what they're saying.

"I'll be up in a minute."

Cian ends the call and tosses the phone on the cushion I'd recently vacated. His arms around me tighten. "As much as I'm enjoying our current seating arrangement, I need to go back up to the house for a meeting. I'm not sure how long it will be."

I point to where I set my book. "I'll be fine."

He follows my finger. "Did your character choose her old life or the new one?"

He remembers that? "Neither, yet, but I get the sense it's coming soon."

Cian dips his chin. "Let me know what she decides."

He taps my thigh, and robotically I climb off him, still a bit stunned that he actually remembered our conversation about a random book I'm reading. Once I'm standing, he does the same. He leans in, gives me a quick kiss, grabs his phone, and then he's closing the door behind him. I bring my fingers to my mouth holding onto the touch of his lips to mine. Why does Cian have to go and do things like that? It makes it hard to keep a tight rein on my emotions when he's so damn...nice.

I flop back on the sofa and pick up my book, but after two pages, I set it down because I can't focus on the words. I keep feeling the kiss and being irritated at myself because I want more. God, I'm in so much trouble.

CHAPTER 14

Cian

I glance impatiently at my watch and then toward the windows where the first signs of dusk are visible. It's been hours since I left Nessa with a hint of arousal in her eyes. In that time, I've had to sit through a family meeting to discuss Campbell's takeover—and our strategy plan—along with waiting to hear back on whether he agreed to meet us or not. The soft din of conversation, along with the occasional clink of glassware, fills the air of the small restaurant in the middle of the tourist area where we sit until Campbell shows up.

I'd half expected him to tell Da to fuck off when he arranged the sit-down, but instead he agreed to it. If I had to take a guess, it's because he doesn't want us to think he's nervous about a face-to-face meeting. I also suspect it's his way of getting a quick read on us and our thoughts on this new leadership change. It's what I would do. Hell, it's what we *are* doing. The bell over the door rings, and in steps a mountain of a man with a jagged scar across his face and a black suit that strains at the seams over his shoulders. He moves a fraction of an inch to his left and two paces behind him is Liam Campbell.

Cold eyes stare out from a rough-hewn face. He's only about five years older than me, but he's got an edge that ages him. His suit is tailored, and from this distance, I don't spot a single wrinkle. It's the vibe he gives off that people take note of, though. As the two men stride toward us, the patrons at each table they pass all glance up and stare, tracking their every move. When they reach our table, Campbell sits across from Da while his bodyguard takes the seat opposite me. We glare at each other with barely contained contempt.

"How's Nessa, by the way?"

I turn my gaze to Campbell's and my jaw clenches despite my best effort to remain unaffected by his presence as well as his question. He wears a smirk that raises my guard. It's as though he's hoping for some sort of reaction. I can sense Da's eyes on me. I smile tightly back. "I'm surprised you give a damn."

"I don't, actually. Call me curious."

"That isn't why we're here, Campbell," Da speaks up.

The bastard's gaze leaves mine and slowly drifts across the table. I turn back to his muscle, whose eyebrow quirks as though he's also amused by my reaction.

"Ah, yes. A man who wants to skip any pleasantries and get straight down to business." Campbell's words drip with sarcasm.

Da leans forward and rests his forearms on the table. "I understand you have taken over your Da's organization."

"Dónal Sheehan is *not* my Da."

Finally a crack in his veneer. Apparently mentioning a familial bond with Sheehan triggers Campbell's rage. Interesting. Although, considering what Nessa told me about his relationship with the older man, it doesn't surprise me.

Da smirks, clearly interpreting Campbell's reaction the same way I did. "My mistake. Your *step*-Da, then. That's awfully ambitious of you. I hope that means we can continue to remain on...friendly terms."

"I assume by 'friendly' you mean you expect me to be as weak as Sheehan." Campbell casually leans back against his chair. He's certainly nothing like his step-Da.

Da opens his mouth, but closes it as someone passes our table. Once they're out of earshot, his attention returns to Campbell. "I'm not sure you have any idea the kind of power I hold in this city. Just because you managed to acquire enough to take over Sheehan's organization doesn't mean shit. Like you said, he's weak. Had I wanted him to be, your *Da* would long be dead by now. I merely chose to let him run his business as he saw fit, so long as he didn't interfere with mine."

Campbell's expression shifts and it's clear he doesn't take kindly to the veiled threat. "Maybe that's where you went wrong. You were too soft-hearted. Make no mistake, I'm nothing like Dónal Sheehan. I cower from, and answer to, no one."

Da continues staring quietly, his gaze assessing. He slowly sits back, and a small half-smile appears. "I can see that. You certainly have a lot of ambition. I admire that in a man."

Even I almost wince at the condescending tone. Campbell's mouth flattens into a thin line and his right arm twitches as though he wants nothing more than to reach for whatever weapon I'm sure is on his person. Another button pushed. Da chuckles lightly and my lips twitch. The man across from me goes rigid.

"Did you call this meeting for any other reason than to try and intimidate me?"

"I have no need to resort to intimidation. This was merely a friendly chat to get to know each other a bit better. As one powerful businessman to another." Da flips both his palms up, flaring his fingers in a patronizing gesture.

"If there's nothing else then?" Without waiting for a response, Campbell stands, as does his guard. "Enjoy the rest of your evening, gentlemen."

With complete disregard for whether we had anything more to say or not, he walks away from the table toward the exit. The hulking muscle follows on his heels. Some of the tension drains from me and I relax into the chair. "That was certainly enlightening."

"It's pretty clear that Campbell is far more dangerous than Sheehan is or will ever be." Da stares in the direction where our newest enemy disappeared. "He's got something planned, I can tell. I just don't know what yet. Let's move up the meeting of the families to later tonight. We'll meet at the casino. Reach out to our associates that have their ear to the inner workings of Campbell's new organization and see if any information has started trickling down their ranks."

I nod. "I'll take care of it."

Da faces me. "You do realize it wasn't strictly curiosity that had him asking about your...guest. He was testing you."

"I know." It had been too calculated for that. I don't like the fact, either. Nessa needs to stay far off his radar. She might not think he's a danger to her, but Liam Campbell isn't a man to be trifled with. "She's safe enough out at the cottage."

"How long do you plan on keeping her there? Because that isn't the type of man who is going to give up his new position any time soon. That's a long time to hold onto a woman you're only fucking because she's Sheehan's daughter and because it's a way to lord power over him. Especially considering he just lost control of his entire organization." Da cocks an eyebrow.

He's absolutely right. There's no telling how long this impending war could go on. At least until Campbell is dead or he has all four of us killed. Unless he catches us all together, the odds are stacked in our favor. On the off chance he happens to succeed, he'd then have Uncle Cormac, Uncle Conor, and the rest of the family to answer to. *I'll take my chances.*

"I plan on keeping her until I'm through with her. Whenever that happens to be. Could be next week. Or it could be a month from now. For the moment, she's proving entertaining."

"You're walking a fine line, Cian," Da warns. "Be careful you don't fall onto the wrong side of it."

He rises from his seat, buttons his jacket, and heads for the door. Roarke gets up from the table by the far wall where he'd stationed himself to keep watch over things in case they went south. He and Da step outside, and their departing figures disappear from sight. I remain seated for another minute, replaying his words. Why am I so determined to keep Nessa at the cottage? *Because I haven't had a taste of her yet.* And I want to.

Not just because she's Sheehan's daughter either, although that certainly plays a large role. It's also because she fascinates me. I've witnessed enough facets of her to keep me intrigued. Something not many women can do. I'm itching to discover all the lines and curves Nessa keeps hidden beneath that atrocious wardrobe of hers. I can't get the image of that red satin and lace out of my head. It's a total contradiction to those frumpy, flannel nightdresses.

I want to dress her in a sheer flowing gown that hugs her waist and flares out over her hips. One that offers the barest tease of her nipples. One so thin I'm able to make out a hint of her sex. Does Nessa keep herself bare? Or maybe the smallest bit of hair? I want to draw out every bit of wetness she produces and then drink it down.

Fuck, I've got it bad.

I adjust my aching cock behind my zipper and then I make my way out the door and to my car. Before the night is over I plan on going through her entire wardrobe, removing anything plaid or flannel, and setting it on fire. Then it's time to get my first—but certainly not last—taste of Nessa Sheehan's body.

CHAPTER 15

Nessa

Cian's been gone for hours, and all I've managed to do is eat a late lunch, try to read three different books without any luck, and wander around the property. At least the weather has been decent. I explored the maze again and memorized the way out. I'm not going to get caught in any more bets with him that I might actually lose. I've been back to sitting on the sofa after giving up trying to watch TV. Nothing even remotely interesting had been playing.

If I were at home, at least I'd have Deirdre for company. It's far too awkward going up to the main house and talking to Nora, especially after Caitlín's visit this morning. Lord knows I don't want to bump into Cian's brothers, or his father. The intense way he'd studied me for the brief time I'd been in his company still lingers. I'd tried hard not to stare, but it had been impossible to ignore the striking resemblance between father and son. Even seated, Carrick Donnelly left an impression. It's understandable how he's the most powerful man in Dublin.

And then there's Liam.

An uneasy sensation inside me says something bad is coming. I hate it, because I don't want anyone getting hurt. This is why I always say women should be in charge.

The doorknob rattles and I snatch my book up so I can at least pretend I'm actually reading. Cian steps in carrying a take-away bag and bottle of wine in one hand, and a single, short-stemmed white lily in the other.

I quickly jump to my feet. "Can I carry something?"

"I've got it, but you can have this." He presents the flower out in a dramatic fashion.

My hand trembles slightly as I take it from him. No one has ever given me flowers before. Not even for my birthday. "Thank you. It's beautiful."

"Don't tell the neighbors at the end of the lane that I nicked it from one of the bushes along their fence line." Cian winks and goes into the kitchen.

Still carrying the gorgeous bloom, I follow him and stand at the imaginary threshold separating the two rooms. He sets everything on the counter and takes the square, paperboard containers out of the bag. He glances over his shoulder and tips his chin up. "I don't know much about gardening, but you might want to put that in some water."

Jolted out of the shocked trance that has me frozen in place, I rush around the kitchen to search for anything that would work as a vase. To my surprise, there's actually one in the cabinet to the left of the sink. I fill it with water and drop the stem in. Unable to resist, I finger the satiny soft petals, taking care not to pluck too hard. My lips curl into a silly grin.

"Do you want to eat out of the container or would you prefer plates?"

I jerk guiltily and spin toward Cian.

His back is to me and he's getting a couple of wine glasses from a cabinet. "It's nothing fancy. Just pasta from this little Italian restaurant nestled on a side street near St. Patrick's my cousin Nathan—Caitlín's brother—introduced me to. I ordered three different entrees, so hopefully you'll find something you like."

"Um, containers are fine. No sense in dirtying dishes when the food is pretty much already in a bowl."

Cian chuckles and pops the cork on the bottle making me jump. "Feel free to check which is which. There's mushroom risotto, pasta carbonara, and chicken Alfredo."

"They all sound delicious. Do you have a preference?" I've never been good at making decisions.

He pivots with a glass of red wine in each hand. "Truth be told, I'll eat just about anything. Whatever you don't want I'll be good with."

I play a mental decision-making game, bouncing between all three choices until I land on the one in the middle. "This one, I guess."

"Good choice." He raises both arms slightly and brings them down. "Let's eat."

Once I pick up the container and grab two forks from a drawer, I sit in the seat where Cian places my glass. He grabs his meal choice and takes the seat next to me. It's almost beginning to feel like a date. *Remember this is only a game.*

"Thank you again for the beautiful flower and for bringing food."

"You're welcome." He takes a sip of wine. "I hope you weren't too bored while I was gone."

I shake my head, lying. "Not at all. I told you I had my book to keep me entertained."

Cian's lips quirk. "It must have been hard to read with the book upside down."

The bite I just took goes down the wrong pipe making me cough and choke. My eyes water and I grab my glass. After a couple swallows, I manage to get myself under control. "Excuse me?"

"When I walked in, you were holding the book wrong side up. I imagine it makes it challenging to actually get any reading done." He leans back in his chair almost daring me to deny it.

My cheeks heat and I fold my arms trying to look stern, but probably failing miserably. "You know, it's rude of you to point that out."

Cian bursts out laughing. "I've never claimed to be otherwise. So, since you weren't reading, what *were* you doing?"

I'm about to burst into flames. He's always managing to unarm me. Maybe it's my turn. "Fine. If you must know, I was impatiently waiting for you to get back so maybe you would kiss me again."

All hints of amusement are erased from Cian's face. I hold eye contact with him, and the flare of heat along with his dilated pupils make me want to squirm in my seat. I'm not sure being bold suits me. He leans over into my personal space, palms the back of my neck, and brings me closer to him until only a whisper separates us. His wine-scented breath ghosts across my skin.

"There's no maybe about it," he murmurs against my lips before claiming them in a passion-filled kiss.

Cian tastes earthy with a hint of fruit. Blackberries, perhaps. I'm swept away by sensations. Electricity sparks everywhere he touches me. It's heady and overwhelming, yet, at the same time, not enough. My tongue meets his as he swoops in and they tangle together. Beneath my hand—the one that, to my surprise, grips him—his muscled forearm ripples, the single vein that runs down it bulging. Who knew men's forearms were so sexy? Or maybe only Cian's are.

Far too soon, he draws back and rests his forehead against mine. His breathing is harsh in the stillness surrounding us. My heart gallops a mile a minute.

"You tempt my control. I hope you know that, mouse." His low, gruff tone rumbles through me. A shiver dances down my spine.

"I suppose it's only fair, since you tempt mine."

Cian chuckles lightly. "Yes, I suppose it is."

As though moving through mud, he slowly releases me and sits back in his chair. I move away as well and pick up my wine glass before drinking down half of it.

Where's a fan when a girl needs it? Every part of my body tingles and aches, begging for more. That single kiss wasn't nearly enough. Just because I don't have any practical sexual experience doesn't mean I haven't dreamed about it. Yearned for it. I've given myself orgasms before, but there's always been something missing.

For the rest of the meal, we chat about banal topics. I cast discreet glances beneath my lashes at Cian, getting caught more than once. All my nerves buzz with awareness. It's hard to concentrate on even simple conversation. When I can't eat another single bite, I drop my fork in the container with the remaining risotto and push it away from the edge of the table.

"That was delicious." I lean back, my hunger sated.

"I'm glad you enjoyed it." Cian rises and gathers up things.

I quickly stand and grab stuff as well. "Let me help."

Together we clear the table and put away the food neither of us had eaten. Cian holds up the wine bottle. "Another?"

Already my cheeks are hot and probably bright pink—it always happens the rare times I drink—but my single glass has relaxed me enough to not worry so much about whatever Cian has planned next. I offer him my glass. "Yes, please."

Once both our glasses are full, sudden shyness hits. *Now what?* As though hearing my unasked question, he places that solid, warm, and almost comforting hand across my lower back and leads me out to the living area and the sofa. He turns off one of the lights, leaving only a soft glow from the kitchen. I fiddle with the stem of my wine glass, tapping my nails in a rapid staccato beat. The flutter in my belly picks up its pace while Cian turns on the TV and scrolls to one of those channels that displays a crackling fireplace and plays romantic instrumental music.

He sits far too close to me, his thigh pressing against mine with his arm slung along the back cushion behind me. "Do I make you nervous?"

"What? No, of course not." I laugh, but it comes out as more a panicked giggle so I take a deep inhale. "What I mean is that I'm not so much *nervous* as I am uncertain. And I've already told you my feelings on that."

A soft caress glides along my neck. "Yes, I recall. But you might also remember my response to those feelings. That the excitement of discovering new things outweighs the fear of the unknown."

I take a sip of my wine, trying to control the trembling in my hand. Wasn't it only a few minutes ago that I wasn't worried about what would happen next? Where did that feeling go? The reality is, I *am* nervous.

Because once I give in to Cian's seduction, there's no going back.

CHAPTER 16

Cian

I shouldn't have offered Nessa another glass of wine. Her cheeks are flushed, and despite her obvious nervousness, she's a bit too relaxed for my taste.

I want her coherent and in full control of her faculties. I'm not above seduction as a means to an end, but even I draw the line at force. There are too many women in my life who would cut off my balls, Caitlín being at the front of the line. Roarke would probably hold me down if he thought it would make her happy. Besides, I'm nothing like Grand-da.

Nessa's skin is soft beneath my fingertip. Along the side of her neck, her heartbeat is faintly visible. I brush against the stem of her glasses. I'd only gotten a brief glimpse of her without them when I caught her showering yesterday. They don't hide the blue eyes that are almost too big for her face. Or the thickness of her lashes. I'm actually glad she doesn't wear any cosmetics. Her natural appearance is far too pleasing without it.

"Tell me what you enjoy doing? Besides reading, of course." I'm not one for small talk, but if it eases the nervousness she denies feeling, then I'll do it.

"I don't really do anything else." Nessa raises a shoulder almost in a self-conscious way. "Although I suppose I enjoy musicals, even though I've only ever watched them on TV and not in a theatre. So it's probably not quite the same."

That can't be it. "Nothing else interests you?"

I can't tell if the redness of her cheeks is still from the wine or if it's there for another reason.

"There are a lot of things that *interest* me. I've just never had a chance to try any of them. Dónal thought they were all a waste of my time and his money."

Fucking Sheehan. I unclench my fist. "Why do you call him by his first name and not Da?"

"Because he doesn't deserve the title," she bites out. Finally some fire from her. "A Da is someone who loves you. Cares for you. Protects you. Dónal is none of those things."

What can I say to that? Finn was right. Sheehan is a right bastard. "If you *could* try anything, what would it be?"

Nessa sits quietly and continues playing the stem of her still full glass. I don't press her. Instead, I wait and give her time to think. My patience is rewarded.

"I think I would love traveling." She huffs out a small laugh. "Do you know I've never even left Dublin? Not even for the one semester of uni I was able to attend before I was made to come home. Wielding a lot of money will get people to do anything you want them to, including kicking your daughter out of school."

Christ. Every new thing I learn has me wanting to kill Sheehan that much more. *Soon.* Once he's dead, Nessa can go back to her life and live it any way she wants. I'll make sure of it. "If you could pick one place to go first, where would it be?"

"Promise you won't laugh?" She says cautiously.

"You have my word."

"I've always wanted to visit America."

Not quite what I'd expected, but I see the appeal. I've only been to Brooklyn and Manhattan and it was like another world. I shouldn't care, but I want that for Nessa, too. As soon as Sheehan is out of her life, I hope she does all the things she's dreamed of doing. "I don't doubt, one of these days, you'll get there."

She throws me a disbelieving glance. "That will never happen. Not as long Dónal is alive."

"Then I guess I'll have to fix that."

Nessa goes still. Is she even breathing? She swallows. Her knuckles go white around her wine glass. "Does it make me a terrible person if I say that I hope you do?"

I take it from her hand before she breaks it and set both hers and mine on the coffee table. Then I face her again and cradle her jaw in my palm. A sheen in her eyes reflects the light coming from the other room. "No, it doesn't make you a terrible person. If there's anyone in this world who has a place reserved in hell, especially for him, it's Sheehan. I plan on helping him get there."

Nessa jerks her head shakily, takes a deep breath, and slowly releases it. "God, I've thought about his death so many times. And the guilt always crept in. What kind of daughter wishes her father dead?"

"The kind who's been beaten down for far too long and only wants to be happy."

"I'm not sure I even know how to be happy. Maybe once I did, but it's been so long, I've forgotten what it even feels like." She reaches up and lays her hand over mine. "Will you show me? Even if it's not real. Maybe for a little while I can pretend."

Christ, she's killing me. I must hesitate too long, because Nessa leans forward and brushes her lips across mine. Once. Twice. Unable to resist the desperation behind it, I deepen the kiss. She opens for me and I sweep my tongue inside, lapping up the taste of her. There's no shyness in how she meets me stroke for stroke and sinks against my chest, pressing herself into me. I should put a halt to this. At least until the wine wears off. A better man would, but then again, I've never claimed to be one. This is where we've been heading from the start.

Nessa knows it as well as I do.

I slowly pull away and come to my feet. Nessa raises her eyes to mine, a plea shining behind her glasses. I reach my hand out and she places hers within my palm, letting me help her stand. Without loosening my hold, I lead her into the bedroom and switch on the lamp near the door. A light brightens the room enough to cast soft shadows along the floor and in each corner. We stop short of the bed and I pull her to me.

Carefully, I lift her glasses off her nose and place them on the nightstand. Then, at last, I take the band off the end of her braid and toss it away before unraveling the plaited hair. I comb my fingers through Nessa's thick, silken strands until it falls in soft waves over her shoulders. Without her glasses on, her big, blue eyes are truly visible. Between her wine-reddened cheeks, long flowing hair, and bright, wide stare, Christ, she's absolutely beautiful. Even more so, because she doesn't realize it.

"I've been wanting to see you with your hair down since you first got here. I keep imagining it splayed out on the pillow." I meet her gaze and brush it off her forehead with a fingertip. "It's gorgeous. I'm not sure why you don't wear it down."

She dips her head. "I guess because it's easier not to. And since I rarely left the house, I never really saw any point in doing anything more than that with it."

With a finger under her chin, I tip it up. "While you're here, I want you to wear it down for me. Please."

Nessa blinks a few times and then gives a slight nod. She parts her mouth, closes it, and then visibly straightens. "Can I touch you?"

"Mouse, you can do anything you want with me."

If I expected caution or hesitancy on her part, I'd have been dead wrong. She places her hands on my chest and glides them up and over my shoulders and down my arms, pausing to trace a vein along my forearm. My cock hardens at the innocent touch. Nessa continues tracing a path back up my arm and then walks around me, dragging those fingertips along my shoulder blades until she's circled back in front of me.

"My turn." I take several steps around her and sweep her hair over one shoulder, exposing the long line of her neck.

Whether intentional or instinctively, she tilts her head a fraction, but it's enough invitation for me. I brush my lips just behind her ear and then kiss down the the exposed slope until I reach the neckline of her shirt. Then I move toward her spine and up her nape to bury my nose in her hair and breathe in the fruit fragrance of her shampoo. A small shiver rushes over her and to my satisfaction, Nessa lets out a quiet moan.

"I love the way you taste." I press an open-mouthed kiss along her flesh and flick my tongue out to draw in more of her flavor. At the same time, I tug the fabric down, exposing her upper shoulder.

I drag my lips across her porcelain skin. My gaze is drawn to the beige strap that digs slightly into her. I can't help but smile at Nessa's small act of rebellion. I slide my finger over the strap. "This doesn't look red."

"That's because it isn't."

I chuckle and step back around to face her. A pretty pink flush climbs up her check and neck. "What a pity. I rather liked that one. It suits you far better than this bland thing."

She glares. "Well, I happen to like *this* one."

"No you don't."

Nessa crosses her arms and juts out a hip. "*Yes* I do."

"This is what you're choosing to fight me on?" I chuckle. "Especially when we both know you're lying. You just don't want to admit that the real reason you're wearing that boring old thing is for spite."

"Fine," she huffs. "Yes, I'm only wearing it because you so badly want me to wear the red one."

"See, that wasn't so hard to admit, was it?"

She unfolds her arms and places her hands on my chest. "Are we going to argue about my bra all night? Because I'm pretty sure there are better things we could be doing."

God, I love her spirit and sass. No matter that's she's lived under Sheehan's thumb for so long, he wasn't able to snuff out her fire. "You mean things like this?"

Without giving her a chance to respond, I wrap my hand around her waist and claim her lips in a savage kiss. Tinder sparks and flares to life in a storm of heat and burning desire. Kissing Nessa is like that burst of flavor that hits just right when you bite into a juicy piece of fruit. It only makes me hunger for more. Virgins have never appealed to me because of all the effort it takes, but the woman in my arms is worth all of it.

Everything about her is soft and warm. For a man who's surrounded by hardness, it's a welcome sensation. I want more of it. I grab the hem of Nessa's shirt and tug it upward. I break our kiss only long enough to drag it over her head and toss it to the floor and then my lips are back on hers. Still holding tightly to her, I walk her backwards until we reach the bed. I'm not sure I've ever been on my knees for a woman before, but I slowly lower myself until I'm staring up at her.

I drag my gaze from her face, down past her breasts that rise and fall with each breath she takes, until I reach her rounded belly. Jagged, silver-white lines run vertically along the curve of it. I kiss the tip of one and another. Then my hands go to the button of her jeans. I lift my eyes to meet Nessa's again with a silent question in them. A voice inside my head keeps telling me to move faster, but I quiet it. I plan on savoring this woman.

"Tell me who you belong to." The command is harsh in the stillness around us.

"You."

CHAPTER 17

NESSA

IS IT POSSIBLE FOR A PERSON TO COMBUST INTO FLAMES? If so, I'm seconds away from it. My whole body is burning up from head to toe. The way Cian stares up at me makes me feel like the most beautiful woman in the world. This must be how Aphrodite felt with men falling to their knees at her feet. It's an addictive sensation I could certainly get used to. As though my answer unlocked something, he undoes my jeans and slides them down and over my hips, continuing the whole length of my leg until he reaches my ankles. Using his shoulder for balance, I lift one foot and then the other. He tosses my pants to land somewhere near my discarded shirt.

He leans into me again and breathes in. A soft caress glides across my lower pelvis directly above the place that is throbbing so hard, it wouldn't surprise me if Cian can feel it. Nerve endings I didn't even know existed tingle as he continues rubbing his face against me.

Needing something to ground me, I thread my fingers through his hair, holding him to me. I ache deep inside in a way that only he'll be able to satisfy.

Except how do I ask for it? The words are lodged in my throat.

As though he hears my unspoken plea, Cian rises to his feet and wraps me in his arms again. Gently, he guides me down onto the bed. A shiver courses down my spine from the cool fabric against my back. I don't remain cold for long, because he covers me with his warmth. The fabric of his clothes are rough against my skin. Who could have imagined being that sensitive to the slightest touch?

My nipples are hard, and there's a throbbing pulse between my thighs. I almost regret not wearing the red satin. Then any thoughts of what I'm wearing dissolve like smoke when Cian pushes one side of my bra up and his mouth closes over my breast and he sucks on the hardened tip. I shudder at the pleasure and arch up into him. His teeth graze my flesh and then he switches to the other side giving it equal attention.

The air is cold from the wetness left behind and my nipple is so hard it nearly hurts. Yet somehow that slight sting of pain only makes the pleasure he's giving me that much greater. As if not wanting to keep all his attention in one place, Cian kisses down my belly, dragging his tongue along and lapping at my flesh. He teases along the waistband of my panties and lifts his gaze to mine as he presses several kisses from one side of my body to the other. The fire in his eyes sears through me.

Without looking away, he hooks his fingers under the thin cotton and drags it down my hips, along the entire length of my legs, and drops the scrap of fabric over the side of the bed. How must I appear with my bra pushed up to my neck and nothing on my lower body leaving my breasts and everything below them completely bare and exposed and open to his gaze?

The faint ugly whispers that still ring in my ears at times tell me to cover myself. To hide my body from view. But another voice right behind them starts as a low murmur and then grows louder that says all those people can go to hell. *That sounds like me.*

"You're beautiful."

That definitely wasn't my voice. I blink and lock eyes with Cian who stares down at me with something like awe in his expression. Maybe he's only saying that because I'm finally naked in his bed and he's getting what he set out to from the beginning, but I'm choosing to believe he's not. I went in to tonight with my eyes wide open. Tomorrow, I might have regrets, but tonight, I won't let them interfere in my chance to grab a tiny bit of pleasure and enjoyment in life.

If anyone deserves it, it's me.

"And you have far too many clothes on."

Cian grins. "We can't have that, now, can we?"

He stands at the edge of the bed and drags his shirt up and over his head making his hair stick up on end. A few auburn curls dust his chest and form a narrow arrow that bisects carved abs and disappears beneath the waistband of his low-hanging jeans. Various scars pepper his skin. Two diagonal lines at either side of his hips point inward as though directing wandering eyes to the sweet spot right in the center where the already impressive bulge has only gotten bigger. I swallow, a bit intimidated and only the slightest bit worried. How much will it hurt? God, am I really going to do this?

Cian leans over me and palms my jaw. "Hey, look at me."

I lift my gaze from where it had gotten stuck below his belt to meet his.

"It's going to be okay. I promise," he vows.

Letting out a shuddering exhale, I nod. He mimics the gesture. Then, as though wanting to lessen my anxiety, he quickly finishes disrobing and before I can get more than a brief view, he's back in the bed and pulls the blankets to our waists.

"We should probably get rid of this, don't you think? Make ourselves a little more comfortable." He gently rolls me toward him and reaches behind me to unhook my bra.

I help Cian tug down the straps and then it joins the rest of our clothes on the floor. Finally, we're both completely naked. It's weird, lying intimately like this with someone. I've imagined making love with a man before, but it had always been this fuzzy concept of how it went. I'd expected my first time to be filled with sweet words of love and gentle kisses. Soft touches and loving gazes. Reality is so different. Instead, it's uncertainty. A bit of awkwardness. A lot of anxiety.

A caress whispers across my cheek. I blink and focus on Cian's face above me. His eyes are intent and serious. "I'm not sure you're supposed to be thinking this hard."

I almost smile. "I'm afraid it can't be helped. It's what I do. Overthink. It's a blessing and a curse at times."

"There are worse things to be blessed and cursed with, I suppose."

"Like what?"

Cian brushes the tip of his finger down the side of my face. "I don't know. Maybe like lying in bed with a stunningly beautiful woman with glorious breasts and lush curves you're aching to touch and explore but you feel like an overeager teenager who can't control his raging cock."

It takes my brain a second to catch up, but then laughter explodes from me and Cian's lips curl into a huge grin. My laughter turns to a giggle and then a few chuckles. "Yes, I can see how that might be a worse problem to have. What a horrible woman to do such a thing to you."

His expression shifts and turns serious again. "That's the thing. She's actually pretty incredible."

All of my amusement fades away, and I swallow. *This is what you asked for isn't it? To pretend you know how to be happy.* Afraid of the heavy silence that descends between us, I lift up and kiss Cian. Anything to distract myself from doing that overthinking thing I'm so good at.

Thankfully, he takes over. The kiss is full of fire and passion. His tongue sweeps into my mouth and lashes against mine. I clutch tightly to him running my hands over the muscles that he could have used against me if he wanted to, but that instead provide me a sense of safety and security. I continue to explore the dips of valleys of his arms before trailing my fingers down the ridges and valleys along his back. The strength and power he holds in them ramps up my desire.

Cian's hands gently caress me as well, learning my body like I'm learning his. He searches for and finds all the places that make me gasp and makes wetness spill from between my thighs. Maybe I'm supposed to be embarrassed by how wet he makes me, but I don't care. He boldly palms my breast, kneading it and plucking the sensitive hardened tip. He discovers the ticklish place right below my ribs, and I giggle into his mouth.

He also finds a place behind my knee that makes me moan with pleasure.

Cian kisses his way down my body again until he reaches my center. I stare at him, my body vibrating with nerves and anticipation, waiting for whatever comes next. Far too slowly, he lowers his head and licks. My fingers curl into fists, clenching the sheet tightly. I pant with desire and throw my head back almost unable to bear the overwhelm pressing down on me. It's too much and yet not enough.

Cian settles even deeper between my spread thighs and pushes his face harder into my core. He thrusts his tongue into the entrance of my body. I cry out . His growl sends a rumbling vibration through me. I shake with it. When he replaces his tongue with a finger, slowly thrusting it inside, I stiffen. He murmurs words of reassurance.

"Relax, Mouse. Let me in."

I close my eyes and focus on just that as I take slow, calming breaths. My body adjusts to the feel of Cian, and then he drags his finger in and out. Slowly. Gently. His mouth and tongue go back to doing what they were. Tasting me. Teasing me. There's a sting. Did he add another finger? He latches onto my throbbing clit, and whatever worries I have vanish as sensation takes over.

The pressure mounts. A tension builds and grows. It tightens until the only thing it can do is snap. Cian bites down on my clit and it does. The pleasure goes off like a cannon.

It travels up my body and releases on a scream. My whole body shudders and soars. Sound ceases to exist. There's an echo of silence and then a whoosh and it returns. There's our harsh breaths rushing through my ears. Whispers of praise and encouragement. In the background there's the drag of wood against wood, and then foil ripping.

So many new and unexpected emotions well up inside me.

My eyes fly open and meet Cian's. Our gazes stay locked together as he positions his hardness at my center. There's pressure and stretching. I whimper when it shifts to pain. He stops all movement while my body adjusts. Then he kisses me softly. Gently. The way I always imagined my first time would be. He whispers loving words against my lips and for a moment I imagine they're real.

Cian shifts again and the stinging grows and swells. He reaches between us and rubs my clit, bringing back the toe-curling pleasure from before. Our kiss becomes more urgent. Just...more. He pulls away slightly and I breathe him in.

"I'm sorry," he mumbles against my lips, and then he thrusts upward hard and the sting becomes a sharp pinch.

A pained cry spills from my lips, and Cian swallows it down. He holds himself still, and his jaw clenches with the effort it takes him. Sweat beads on his forehead. We lay connected to each other while my heart beats hard and loud. *Move.* It's a tiny whisper that grows with need. I shift my hips and above me he groans. Cian rests his forehead against mine.

"Give me a second," he whispers and sucks in a breath.

A second passes. And another. Then he moves, rocking his pelvis, grinding against me, and deepening the penetration. I push my hips upward needing more of something I can't name. Whatever it is, I can almost reach out and touch it. He pulls out and thrusts back in building speed and momentum until the only thing that can happen is a booming crash.

Cian increases the friction against my clit, varying the way he rubs and circles it. A spark is lit and the ember pops, a brilliant light that explodes in a rainbow.

Another orgasm rips through me. I scream and buck my hips. There's a deep pressure inside me as he roars out his own release. Scalding heat burns me and then the warmth settles soothing away some of the pain. Tears threaten to spill. Not because I hurt, but because I feel too much. Being with Cian had been more than even my imagination could have made up.

He lowers himself gently onto me. His weight is like a heated blanket.

Neither of us move until our breathing returns to normal. He raises himself up and stares down at me. "I didn't hurt you too much, did I?"

I shake my head and bite my lower lip, unable to come up with the words to describe what's going on inside my head. Because this was more than only pretending to be happy. Cian studies me and I have to fight to keep from crying. Thankfully, whatever he sees satisfies him.

"I'll be right back. I need to take care of things." He rolls off me and I'm unsure what he means by things until I drop my gaze to his...cock.

It's covered by a condom that's slick with wetness and tinged red. Oh god, protection hadn't even crossed my mind. I'm grateful to Cian for thinking of it. He disappears into the bathroom. A shiver wracks my body and I bring the blankets up to cover myself. A minute or two later, he comes back and lays down beside me. The night isn't over, which means I can still pretend to be happy. Not waiting to ask permission or waiting for him to deny me, I scoot as close to him as I can and lay my head on his shoulder and my arm over his chest. Cian stiffens, just slightly, but enough to be noticeable. I remain still, waiting for him to push me away or tell me to go back to my side of the bed. But he doesn't say anything. Instead, he slowly slides his arm under me and pulls me a little closer. Neither of us break the silence that falls. What is he thinking? Too scared to ask, I close my eyes and let myself drift off to sleep and hope that when I wake up, I'll go back to being the me before he...fucked me. The one who didn't believe that dreams could come true.

CHAPTER 18

CIAN

NESSA LIES CURLED ON HER SIDE WITH HER HANDS tucked beneath her cheek and her long-lashed eyes closed. She makes soft snuffling sounds, but doesn't awaken. Tonight was unexpected. Wasn't it only yesterday that she'd been so determined to hold onto her virginity? What made her change her mind?

The only thing that's changed since then is Campbell's takeover and Caitlín's visit.

Despite her inexperience, she'd been so responsive. She'd been a wholly active participant in her downfall. I'd drank down every cry that spilled from her lips. There hadn't been an inch of her body I'd left untouched. And still, my desire for her is all-consuming. I haven't been anywhere near satisfied.

From somewhere on the floor, my phone buzzes. Careful not to disturb her, I slip out of the bed and rifle through the pile of discarded clothes until I find it. I grab it and head out to the other room, closing the door behind me.

"Donnelly."

"Where the fuck are you?" Aidan growls.

Christ. "I'll be there in twenty."

"Hurry up." He ends the call.

I step back into the bedroom. Nessa is still sleeping. As quietly as I can, I quickly dress and brush a kiss across her forehead. She doesn't stir.

The drive through the countryside is quiet and I'm only one of a few cars out due to the late hour. The lights of Dublin are bright as I make my way through the city center and then into the more residential area until I park in one of our designated spots on the street beside the casino.

The neon sign displaying *Anamacha Caillte* glows like a beacon on the darkened street lighting the way toward our den of iniquity. Millions of dollars are exchanged within these walls, most of it landing in our pockets. We run a clean and fair establishment, but at the end of the night, it's the house that always comes away with the majority. Ennis mans the front door. He dips his head at my approach and pulls the handle to open it.

"Mr. Donnelly."

Not enough days have passed that I've forgotten his mistake. "I hope you don't plan on letting any more of our enemies through."

He shifts his weight back and forth and he lowers his gaze as his shoulders drop a fraction. "No, sir. I apologize. I swear it won't happen again."

"It better not. I won't be as forgiving as my brother." I stride past him without another word.

The gaming floor is packed and at first glance, it appears as though there's not an empty seat at any of the tables in sight. The hum of conversation fills the air. Absent are the sounds of bells and *cha-ching*s of slot machines. Caitlín has pushed more than once for us to add them, but I keep vetoing the idea, because to me, they don't represent money or class. All I picture are grans sitting in front of the machines and feeding them their one-eurocent coins. That's not what I envisioned for this place when she convinced us to buy the derelict property from its previous owner.

I zig-zag around tables as I head to the elevator and make my way to the top floor where Finn's office, as well as the security center, is located. Not bothering to knock, I walk in. Heads turn at my arrival. The room is filled with not only my brothers and Da, but from a quick count, the heads of the clans that comprise our entire syndicate.

"Glad you could join us." Da quirks his eyebrow, whether in annoyance or amusement. "Close the door and have a seat."

Aidan glares disapprovingly when I sit in the open chair next to him. I'm not sure what crawled up his ass, but I don't care for this new attitude he's giving me. I'm still a little pissed about how he spoke of Nessa earlier.

"Now that everyone is finally here, we need to discuss a few new developments," Da announces.

We all exchange glances. Has something else happened in the short number of hours since our meeting with Campbell?

"As you all should know by now, Liam Campbell has taken over Dónal Sheehan's organization. Cian and I met with him earlier this evening. This is a man whose power far outweighs that of his step-Da. He's smart and calculating, as evidenced by the connections he's made and loyalty he's gained in a relatively short time." Da's gazes travels over the room, pausing slowly on each person. "Although nothing was said directly, it was made pretty clear that Campbell has no intention of honoring the agreement between our two organizations. Which means we all need to be watchful and prepared for anything."

"Have there been any reports from our inside associates regarding Campbell's next step?" Finn asks.

Da shakes his head. "Nothing yet that we didn't already know, although they did mention there were vague references to tomorrow. They couldn't get any more details than that."

"So essentially, we're blind," I note.

"One new thing's come into play, although I'm not quite sure how to use the information." To my surprise, Da hesitates. It's only for a split-second, quick enough that I might be the only who caught it, but it definitely occurred. "Yesterday morning, Liam Campbell kidnapped a young woman, Imogen Walsh, off the street and took her to his estate. With the unexpected help of his cousin, she managed to escape this evening, while Cian and I were having our sit-down with him."

"How did you find that out, and what does that have to do with us?" Aidan asks the same question I have.

There's that pause again before Da answers. What the hell is going on?

"Because she showed up at the manor shortly before I returned from the meeting with Campbell requesting protection." The announcement is met with stunned silence.

"So, Campbell is trafficking women now?" I ask in disgust. Flesh traders are scum.

"Not to my knowledge," Da corrects. "According to Imogen, she was taken because he professed to be fascinated with her and liked the challenge. In his words, he wanted her, and he always gets what he wants."

What a fucking sociopath.

"Why did she come to you and not the Gardaí?"

"Because during the duration of her captivity, she learned who Campbell is, as well as who we are. She decided to take her chances with us, rather than him. For the moment, she is at the estate."

"Our estate?" Finn gapes.

Da pins him with a hard glare. "Is that a problem?"

My youngest brother shows his palms. "No, no problem."

"Maybe we can use her," Aidan suggests. "Especially if Campbell wants her bad enough."

I snap my head in his direction. "What the fuck is wrong with you? She's not some pawn either."

"No one is using anybody," Da barks loud enough that our attention quickly shifts to him. He's standing behind the desk leaning into his fists on its surface. His features are harsh as his gaze burns into us. "Until we figure out exactly what Campbell's plans are, Imogen *and* Nessa both remain exactly where they are. Are we understood?"

Mumbled replies of assent ripple through the room, Aidan's offered begrudgingly.

"Now that we've got that settled, I want everyone to keep their eyes and ears open. Stay alert, but continue with business as usual," Da warns. "Tomorrow is the arrival of our next shipment of goods from our supplier in Germany. Cian and Nathan are in charge of that. Report back when you've accounted for it all."

I nod. When nothing else is said, we all disperse. I'm anxious to get back to the cottage and Nessa. I'm halfway across the casino floor when someone calls out my name. I glance back, and Aidan sidesteps one of the floor girls. Annoyed at the delay, and him in general, I ignore him and keep walking.

"Damn it, Cian, wait up."

I grind to a halt and slowly turn. "What's your problem?"

He stops a few feet from me and sighs. "Look, I'm sorry for being such a dick."

"Fine. Is that it, then?" I'm not in a particularly forgiving mood.

Aidan studies me. "You've got a thing for Sheehan's daughter, don't you?"

My jaw clenches. "First, her name is Nessa. Second, I don't have a *thing* for her. I enjoy fucking her and she's turned out to be quite entertaining. That's the extent of it."

I don't need to be told how embarrassed and disappointed she'd be if she knew I spoke of her like that. *Why do you care? She's all part of the game.*

"How long are you going to keep lying to yourself?" His look is one of sympathy, and then he walks away.

I shake off his words. He has no idea what he's talking about.

CHAPTER 19

Nessa

I'm surrounded by warmth and the scent of ginger. Did I only dream last night? The ache between my thighs tells me I didn't. I slowly open my eyes. Cian is lying on his side, facing me, with his eyes closed and his chest rising and falling evenly. Afraid he'll wake up, I hold perfectly still and study him. Faint morning light shines through the crack in the shutter and hits his face. He appears younger—maybe even a little softer—in his sleep with his auburn hair curling over his forehead. The freckles that dot his nose and cheeks give him a more vulnerable appearance. Or maybe more earthly as opposed to the god-like presence he radiates when he's fully awake.

I wait for the embarrassment to hit, but it doesn't come. Neither do the regrets. For the first time in my life, I actually did something for myself. Something *I* wanted. No one, not even Dónal, can take that away from me. And I want to do it again. And again.

Don't forget there's a time limit on this...relationship? Affair?

What do I even call this? Maybe arrangement is a better term.

I can't forget to keep my emotions in check. The last thing I need is to be sent home with a broken heart and pining for something— for *someone*—that can never be. I just need to enjoy whatever time I have with Cian so I have the memories to keep me company later.

The temptation is too great for me to resist. Trying not to disturb him, I reach out and brush one of the curls that fall forward. It's soft to the touch. He shifts his head, his cheek rubbing along the pillow and then his eyelashes flutter and lift. A small grin appears.

"Good morning." His voice is sleep-filled.

"I'm sorry. I didn't mean to wake you."

"If it means seeing a beautiful creature beside me, then by all means, feel free."

Heat warms my cheeks. Cian makes me feel beautiful. He reaches out and runs a finger down the side of my face. Like always, tiny sparks run along its path, lighting me up from the inside. "I must not have debauched you enough if you're still blushing. I guess that means the next time I need to try a little harder."

I laugh. "Maybe so."

He raises an eyebrow. "Do I hear a challenge?"

"I'm not sure I'm ready for your next level of debauchery quite yet."

Cian chuckles this time. "I *definitely* heard a challenge there."

He playfully tackles me and rolls us so I'm on my back and he's on top. The weight of him is a heavy but comforting presence. Beneath him, I feel protected. Safe. Although he is the danger.

"What are you thinking about so hard that has that look on your face?" He pushes a few stray strands of hair back and tucks them behind my ear.

I blink and focus on him above me. There's such tenderness in his expression it makes me ache a little. "Nothing really. Just that if I was going to give my virginity to anyone...I'm glad it was you."

Maybe I'm mistaken, but I could swear there's a flash of guilt in his eyes. Before I can puzzle it out, Cian lowers his head and kisses me. I wrap my arms around him and fall into it.

Bring on the debauchery.

I OPEN MY EYES AND THE PLACE BESIDE ME IS EMPTY. THE indentation in the pillow from Cian's head is absent as well. Based on the brightness of the sun, I suspect it's close to mid-day. My stomach growls. I stretch and move, luxuriating in the sheets against my naked skin. Until last night, I've never slept in the nude before. It's rather freeing. My entire body aches, but in a really good way. I toss back the blankets and open the closet for clean clothes. First thing first, I need a shower. Sex is...messy.

After I've washed myself from head to toe, I dress and dry my hair, making sure to keep it down the way Cian asked. I pause and stare in the mirror. Do I look different today than I did yesterday? Not that I expect to walk out the door and people are going to know I'm no longer a virgin. But I study myself trying to decide if *I* notice anything. Maybe I'm standing taller. Holding my head up a little higher. There's definitely a new awareness in my eyes. Almost as though the secrets of the universe have opened up to me.

I cup my breasts. It's not the same as when Cian had done it. And when he'd taken them in his mouth...I melt with the memory of it. I place my hands over my belly, spreading my fingers and running my palms out to either side of my waist. I'd had to blink back tears when he kissed the stretch marks. Everything about last night—and this morning—was perfect.

But the reality of my situation is slowly sinking in. No matter how hard I fight it, all those new and exciting emotions twelve-year-old me experienced are rushing back in and I have a feeling they're not going to stop. Which means I either have to leave or brace myself for when Cian breaks my heart. Because he will. There's too much hate between his family and Dónal for him to forget who my father is. I'm going to need to make a decision soon, before it's too late for me.

Spinning away from the mirror, I head back into the bedroom. What to do today? My stomach growls again. Fine, food next. I heat up a bowl of soup that is still in the refrigerator from the other day and take it out to the living room to eat while I read. Once I'm settled, I open my book to the bookmarked page and a handwritten note is in its place.

Cian's handwriting is as bold as the man himself. Thick, harsh lines make up each word he wrote. There's no romantic greeting. It's simply addressed to "Mouse" and that he had an appointment and would be back later in the evening. There's no "I'll be thinking of you." Just his name. As far as love letters go, it's more than lacking.

Except the part of me that has been starved for affection my whole life holds it against my chest, soaking up every bit of it. It's the first time a man has ever written to me.

A knock at the door makes me jump. I stick the note back inside the front cover and go to the door. It's definitely not Cian, since he always walks right in. I crack it open with a bit of caution. Caitlín is on the other side.

"Oh, good you're dressed. I love your hair by the way. It's so pretty." She pushes past me into the room and spins around. "Get your shoes on. We're going into the city."

"We are?" I blink. "And thank you."

"Yep. You've been stuck out here for three days with no one but Cian to keep you company. How boring. Unless of course you've met Imogen?"

"Imogen?"

"I guess not, then. She's staying up at the manor visiting Uncle Carrick. And since you haven't, I'm here to pull you from your misery." She claps and her smile is almost maniacal.

There's only a brief hesitation and then I nod. "All right, let's go."

"Excellent."

I hurry back into the bedroom, slip on my flats, grab my small purse, and then head out into the living room again. "I'm ready."

She eyeballs me, but doesn't say anything for so long, I get twitchy. I glance down at myself. Did I miss a button or something? Nothing is noticeably askew. I raise my head. "Is something wrong?"

"There's something different about you today. You're not so timid and self-conscious."

Thanks? "That's a good thing, right?"

Caitlín waves her hands in front of her. "Shit, I'm sorry, I didn't mean anything bad by it or to hurt your feelings. I tend to say the first thing that pops in my head without thinking and with zero filter. It's a curse at times. It's a very good thing. It means I don't have to kick Cian's ass now."

I sputter. "No, you don't need to kick his ass. We've come to a mutual agreement." Sort of.

"A mutual agreement, huh?" Caitlín waggles her eyebrows up and down and my cheeks heat even as I laugh.

Is this what it's like to have a girlfriend? "Something like that."

"You can tell me about it on the way." She loops her arm through mine and drags me out the door. "And I want all the juicy details."

Surely she doesn't mean...? We make it up the incline and into her car. It's a gorgeous blue-sky day with the sun shining and warming the inside. Caitlín pulls out onto the road and glances over at me.

"Okay, spill it."

My mind goes blank and I panic. What am I supposed to say? "I'm not sure what you want to know."

"For starters, based on what I'm seeing"—she gestures up and down with her finger in my direction—"I assume your...debt was paid to Cian last night."

Oh god, can she really tell I'm not a virgin any more?

"Stop freaking out, okay. I don't want *those kind* of details—gag —just confirmation."

I'm not sure that's any better. "Um, yes?"

Caitlín narrows her eyes. "It was consensual, right?"

I frantically nod. "Absolutely. Yes, totally consensual."

"Good, because I would have castrated him if it hadn't been," she almost growls. "Cousin or not."

The image makes me wince. Would she have really? I glance over at her. Yes, I do believe she would have. It's kind of...sweet, actually.

"He brought me a flower," I admit.

"Only one?" She shakes her head. "Cheap ass. What kind?"

"A white lily. It was perfect, actually. As was the dinner and wine that came with it."

Caitlín whistles. "At least he made some effort. I'm not a flowers kind of girl, but I suppose I can see the appeal."

Until last night I had no idea what kind of girl I was, but it would appear flowers might be my thing. "If it had been a real first date, I'd say it was nearly perfect."

"You still haven't elaborated on this mutual agreement thing," she points out. "Because when I was last here, there was bitter resistance coming from you. What changed?"

I drop my head back against the seat, inhale deeply, and then turn it to stare at Caitlín. "You can't tell Cian."

She darts a glance my direction and then focuses on the road again. "My lips are sealed."

"It was my former stepbrother, Liam."

Her eyes bulge and she coughs. "As in Liam Campbell? The man who is about to start a war ?"

I wince. When she puts it that way. And he's obviously made a reputation for himself. "I know it sounds awful and crazy and terrible. It got me thinking about him and Dónal and my life. Or rather the one I didn't have, but always wanted to."

Caitlín glances my way again, but she doesn't say anything, so I continue to explain what even I still don't fully understand.

"I've had twenty years to envy Liam and the courage it took him to run away from the abuse he suffered at Dónal's hand. And look at him now. According to Cian, he walked right into the house where that very abuse took place and gave Dónal a pretty big fuck you." I almost wish I could have been there to see it. "And while I'm sorry it pits him against your family, I admire him for it. It also made me think. Why couldn't I be that courageous? I've let Dónal control every aspect of my life. Where has it gotten me? Absolutely nowhere, except to leave me as nothing more than a woman whose only apparent value is her virginity. I'm worth far more than that. And I don't want to live that way any more. Cian wanted to seduce me, so I let him. Because it was *my* choice to allow myself to have that one thing. It put me in control."

"What happens next?" Caitlín asks.

"I keep making choices for myself. I'll enjoy my time with Cian, and then, when it's over, I'll go back to my life and live it without anyone ever telling me what I can or can't do again." If Cian does what he says he'll do, I'll never have to worry about Dónal trying to control me again anyway.

CHAPTER 20

Cian

"Earth to Cian."

I blink at the voice and shake myself. "Sorry, I'm distracted."

Nathan chuckles. "Obviously. Need to talk about it?"

"No, I'm good."

My cousin twists his lips and nods slowly. "If you say so."

We've been sitting here waiting for the shipment from Germany to arrive, but it's late, and I'm getting antsy.

I just keep picturing Nessa still asleep in bed when I left. I can't recall ever being this conflicted about something. She's nothing like I expected when I took Sheehan's bet.

The only thought I had that night was showing him up. Making him appear weak in front of everyone. Mission accomplished. Anyone standing within the vicinity of that table heard the desperation in his tone when he offered up Nessa's virginity. I'd reveled in it. Still do.

But it's become complicated. After last night and this morning, it feels like it's more about her than her Da. She's smart. Funny. Brave. Beautiful. I didn't fuck her because of Sheehan. It was because I wanted to. I can admit to myself that when she returns to her home —to her old life—I'll miss our conversations. I'll miss verbally sparring with her. Being out from under her Da's thumb has made her bloom like a flower. It looks good on her. But both of us are still who we are. She's still Sheehan's daughter and I'm still one of his bitter enemies.

Nathan smacks my arm. "There's our cargo. Let's go."

We exit the vehicle and head toward the dock where the large ship is being unloaded by several dock workers. Nathan approaches one of them.

"Paul, my friend, how's Niamh and the kids doing?" He shakes hands with the man.

"They're doing good, Mr. Donnelly. Very good." Paul swipes his other palm down his thigh. There's a tremble in his voice and he struggles to meet Nathan's eyes.

He and I exchange a glance. What's that all about?

"Is everything okay?" My cousin asks. "You seem a little nervous."

"There, um, is just a wee bit of a problem with the shipment you're expecting."

I straighten. "What kind of problem?"

Paul coughs. "The shipping manifest is missing. The new owner won't allow any of the crates to be offloaded without the proper paperwork. So, until it's located, they have to remain on the ship. If the manifest can't be found, then everything will return to its port of origin."

"What new owner? How are we only now hearing about this?" Nathan bites out.

The dock worker shrugs and flips through the paperwork he's holding. "Apparently it was a buyout in the last day or two. Looks like the order was signed by a Liam Campbell."

"Fuck." I jerk and run my hand through my hair. Then I turn back to Nathan and we exchange a look.

Is this Campbell's plan to start? To cut off our supply of weapons? This shipment alone cost us over ten million euros. Yes, there are other shipping companies, but none have the reach, resources, or manpower. Our suppliers are going to be a lot more cautious if they have to deal with someone they've never worked with before. Nathan faces Paul. "Perhaps we can work out a deal?"

The other man shakes nervously. "I'm sorry, sir, but I have to think of my family's safety."

Christ. "Let's go."

My cousin and I walk back to the car in silence. Once we're inside I punch the dashboard. "That motherfucker."

"I'll make some phone calls. See if I can put some feelers out for any new contacts."

I shake my head. "Don't bother. It's not going to make a difference."

Nathan drives away from the docks and heads back to the casino where he picked me up. I call Da to have him and Aidan meet us there. The tall brick building comes into a view. It's unassuming appearance is a far cry from the goings on inside. He parks in a family spot and we enter through the unmanned front door. The place won't open for a few more hours, so it's quiet and empty. Only a few lights along each wall are lit, leaving everything mostly in shadows. We step into the elevator, and I press the button for the top floor. Anger burns hot inside me. I want to locate Campbell and put a bullet in his brain. End things.

I barge into Finn's office, slamming open the door, and come to an abrupt halt at the weapon pointed in my direction. The woman bent over his desk taking his cock screams.

"Jaysus, Cian, don't you know how to knock?" Finn sets the gun on his desk beside her, withdraws from her cunt, and yanks his pants up.

She, in the meantime, pushes down her dress to cover herself and rushes out of the office without sparing Nathan or me a glance. I glare at my brother who sits in his chair and locks the weapon away in his desk drawer.

"Isn't she one of the floor girls? Don't you know any better than to fuck an employee?"

"Not that it's any of your business, but Aoife doesn't work here any more. Hasn't for several months."

Still, shit's messy.

"Since you've ruined a perfectly good fuck, why are you here?" Finn snaps.

"We need a family meeting. Campbell just made his first move."

My brother jerks to attention. "I'll call Da and Aidan."

"They're already on the way. As are the clan heads." I cross the room to the bar and glance at Nathan. "Want a drink?"

He takes a seat in one of the many leather chairs with a nod. "Yeah."

I pour us both a glass of The Devil's Keep and take the seat next to him, passing him the whiskey. Ten minutes later, Da and Aidan walk through the door. The family leaders quickly trickle in after and the last arrival closes the door behind him.

"What's going on?" Da asks once everyone has taken their seat.

After I lay everything out, he leans back in his chair and sits quietly. I can't read his expression. Finally, he sits forward and rests his chin on steepled fingers. "Campbell has two cousins, Declan and Aran. Finn, I want you, Nathan, and several of our soldiers to pay them both a visit. Give them a message to pass on to Campbell. One that won't be misinterpreted. In the meantime, I'm going to stop by his office for a chat."

"Do you think that's a good idea?" Not that I don't trust Da to take care of himself. It's Campbell I don't trust.

"I'm in possession of something he wants, and I'm going to make sure he's aware of it if he isn't already."

"I'm going back to the docks tonight for some recon. If they won't give us our shipment, then we'll have to take it." I won't sit back and wait for Campbell's next move.

The buzzing intercom on Finn's desk interrupts the conversation. He answers the call. "Donnelly."

His gaze pans the room, pausing on Da. "Send him up."

Who would be coming to *Anamacha Caillte* this early in the day?

Finn hangs up the phone and returns his gaze back to Da. "Dónal Sheehan is on his way."

What the fuck is that rat doing here?

He must truly be desperate if he's coming to the casino.

The knock on the door echoes in the quiet. I quickly stand and move across the room. I want to be the the first to witness him begging. After only a brief pause, I open the door. Sheehan's eyes widen, but quickly return to normal. He stands there with his hair sticking up on end and an unbuttoned wrinkled suit coat. His tie is askew and two buttons are missing from the equally wrinkled white dress shirt. His face is even redder than usual, and he smells like he bathed in a barrel of whiskey.

"Aren't you going to let me in?" he sneers with complete disregard for a man in his position.

I stare in disgust before finally moving back and opening the door wider for him to enter. He pauses just inside. His sallow complexion whitens with the presence of a room full of his enemies. Did he expect only Finn to be here? Sheehan quickly composes himself. He straightens his jacket—as much as he can—and buttons it. As if that will impress anyone. I close the door a lot harder than I normally would and he flinches. I smile in petty satisfaction. It's time someone shows him what it's like to know fear.

"Carrick," he greets my father with a friendly nod, his expression far too jovial for a man who I suspect is about to ask for our help.

"Sheehan."

The other man loses his grin at the sharp formality. What did he expect? I stride past, ramming my shoulder into him as I do. He stumbles. I take my seat again and glare while we all wait for what we suspect is coming.

"I understand you boys ran into a little trouble at the docks earlier."

It doesn't surprise me Sheehan heard about it. My guess is Campbell spread the news to every business associate in Dublin.

Da sits back in his seat and crosses his ankle of a knee as though he doesn't have a care. "Nothing we can't handle."

The other man waves his hand as though to appease us against any unintentionally implied insult. "Of course you can. I wouldn't expect anything different."

"What do you want, Sheehan?"

He turns his affected charm on me. "I thought I might offer my assistance putting that whelp Campbell back in his place."

"We don't need your help." I make the decision before Da can. He may get angry with me in private, but he'll back me in front of everyone.

Sheehan tries to plead his case. "Carr—"

"You heard my son," he cuts him off. "We have no need for your...assistance. Now, if you'll excuse us, we're in the middle of a *family* meeting."

The other man's entire face turns bright red. He straightens his sleeves and tugs down the hem of his jacket trying to maintain whatever dignity he might have left. "Yes, of course."

Da nods at Brenn, who's closest to the door. He stands and opens it for Sheehan's departure. Our enemy casts one final glance around the room and then scuttles out of the office.

"Brenn, why don't you follow our guest and make sure he arrives safely at the front door?"

"Yes, Mr. Donnelly."

Our man exits and closes the door behind him. Da stands and moves to the front of the room. He stares out over the rest of us, his gaze pausing on me. "Back to business."

CHAPTER 21

Nessa

I'VE NEVER LAUGHED SO HARD IN MY ENTIRE LIFE. I SWIPE
at the tears spilling down my face and try to catch my breath. The
stories Caitlín has told me have me in stitches. I'm almost glad she
isn't my sister. She's ruthless. From the sounds of it, the only person
immune to her antics is her brother-in-law's cousin, Pierce. He
sounds absolutely terrifying. It takes another minute, but I finally get
myself under control.

"Thank you for inviting me to hang out with you today." I
chuckle lightly again before taking another bite of the delicious salted
chocolate torte we stopped in to try.

We've been sitting at this lovely cafe for nearly an hour, enjoying
some wine and dessert. It's one of the best afternoons I've ever had.

"You're welcome. We'll have to make a plan for Lucia to join us
next time. Give her enough notice so she can have Nathan watch the
boys. Oooh, we need to go out dancing one night." Caitlín jumps up
and down in her seat. "Roarke and I have fond memories of one of

those nights. Well, he might disagree slightly with that assessment, but *I* have fond memories."

"I've never been to a dance club before." It's a sad admission.

She gapes and then composes herself. "We definitely need to change that. I'll call Lucia and we'll make a plan for the Friday after next. How's that?"

While I'm out from under Dónal's rule, I'm determined to experience every small thing most people take for granted. "I'm in."

"Excellent."

I press my lips together. This is probably a stupid question, but... "What should I wear? I didn't anticipate going to a club when I packed my things. The nicest outfit I brought with me is probably what I have on."

Caitlín leans to the side and eyeballs me around the table. I've got on my favorite dark wash jeans that make my butt look incredible and a deep purple silky shirt that shows off the tiniest hint of cleavage. She sits back up, and from her expression, this isn't going to do. "While you look adorable for a day out with a girlfriend—that's me, by the way—you need something that is going to drive the men at the club wild. You have a bangin' figure you need to be showing off."

Bangin? That must be an American phrase, because I'm not sure anyone of my acquaintance has ever used the word before. I like it. Especially if it's used to describe me. "I've never really been that into fashion. I wear what I like, not necessarily what's the most flattering."

Caitlín shoves the rest of her torte in her mouth and covers it with hand, but goes right on speaking. "Not to worry, my friend, because I can help you." She swallows. "I love shopping, and you and I are going to pick out the sexiest outfit that will showcase you in the best way possible."

My belly flutters with excitement.

"What the hell are you doing here?"

A lead weight drops in my gut smashing every butterfly flittering around in there. I glance up. Dónal is barreling toward us, his drink-reddened face twisted in a mask of rage. Words get clogged in my throat. He grabs my upper arm and digs his nails in. I whimper in pain.

"Get your fucking hands off her," Caitlín snaps, already rising from her chair.

"Don't, please," I manage to rasp out. Dónal will hurt her too. I struggle in his grip, but he's too strong.

She ignores me completely and steps into his personal space, getting right up in his face. "I said take your hands off her."

He sneers. "You don't know who you're dealing with. Nessa is my daughter to do with as I please."

"I know exactly who you are. A piece of shit bully who doesn't deserve a daughter as amazing as Nessa. I'm only going to tell you one more time." Caitlín leans in closer. "Get your goddamn hands off her."

To my surprise, Dónal does exactly that. In fact, he whimpers, and his face contorts in pain. Confused, my gaze moves from their faces down and I nearly gasp. Digging into his gut is a knife. On the other end of it is Caitlín. A bit of blood seeps through his white shirt. He steps back and the blade disappears somewhere on her person.

"I'll be sure to let my cousin Cian know that a woman nearly made you shit yourself." She wags her hand at him. "Now go fuck off somewhere else."

Dónal shoots us both a hate-filled glare and hesitates while he decides how far to push. Then he's gone as quickly as he appeared.

I sit in numb silence. Caitlín stares after him another second and then grabs her purse before tossing down a bunch of bills. She gently places her hand on my arm and I jump. "We should probably get going before someone calls the Gardaí."

I nod, still in shock over the whole encounter, and stand. She grabs my hand and leads me out of the tiny restaurant while the patrons whisper to each other and stare at us. We step out into the bright sunshine which finally jolts me out of the haze. Horrified, I meet her eyes. "I'm so sorry."

She pauses with her phone in her hand and her eyebrows wrinkle. "Why are you sorry? You didn't do anything."

I flap my arm toward the restaurant. "For that. For Dónal."

Caitlín hugs me and then draws back. "Don't you dare be sorry for that son of a bitch. Back there was all on him. He needed someone to put him in his place, and I was happy to do it."

Turning away from her, I shake my head. "But you shouldn't have had to. I just...froze. All this talk about doing what I want. Making my own decisions. It's nothing but talk. The first time I see Dónal and I couldn't do anything but let him hurt me again."

"Hey, look at me." Caitlín lays her hand on my arm.

Reluctantly, I lift my head and meet her gaze.

"You've spent your entire life being abused. That kind of conditioning isn't going to go away overnight. Or even in three days. But it *will* go away, because you're strong. I promise." She gently squeezes me. "Okay?"

I nod jerkily, but I'm still not convinced. "Okay."

She types out a message and puts her phone away. "Roarke is on his way. He's calling Cian, who will probably reach us first, considering he's at the casino. It's only about ten minutes away. In the meantime, let's go get lost in Stephen's Green. No sense in standing here in case the cops show up."

We head down the block. My whole body is on full alert. I scan the entire length of the street waiting for Dónal to jump out at us. I won't relax until Cian gets here. Caitlín and I check traffic and dart to the opposite side and take one of the paths that leads into the tree-covered garden park. It's too cold for many people to wander through, but it's not entirely empty. We pass several couples walking and a cyclist whizzes by us.

"This is my favorite place to visit in the city. It reminds me so much of Central Park back home, except on a much smaller scale," Caitlín fills the uneasy silence.

Grateful for the diversion, I glance over. "Is it really as big as it looks?"

She chuckles. "Bigger. You could easily get lost inside. I have more than once, in fact. But there are worse places to got lost, I suppose. There's this huge concrete fountain surrounded by this wide, circular brick terrace where street performers like to put on shows for the crowd. I love hanging out around there to watch some of them, especially the small dance troupes. There's this group of five or six guys that are my favorite. They know how to work the crowd, let me tell you."

I try to imagine the scene she paints, but it's almost more than I can fathom. The pictures I've seen of Manhattan are mind-blowing. All those buildings packed tightly together. They all look so tall. And all the people. *I bet it's incredible.*

We continue our circuitous route until Caitlín stops. "Looks like your man has arrived."

I glance in the direction she tips her head. Cian plows forward, his pace quick and his expression surprisingly unreadable. At least until he gets close. His eyes tell me everything. My heart skips, but my stomach sinks.

I care about him.

I do. Far more than I should. Far more than I swore I would. I take a few steps forward to meet him. He cradles my face between both palms and stares intently at me. "Are you all right?"

My arms go up and I lay my hands over his wrists, squeezing gently. "I'm fine. Caitlín was a total badass."

Cian's gaze darts in his cousin's direction before locking back on me. "I'm going to kill him."

The fierce declaration shouldn't make happiness soar like a weightless balloon floating in the sky. But it does. Surprisingly, there's no swarm of guilt. Dónal has crossed the wrong people one time too many. Whatever his fate is, he brought it on himself.

"I think I've had enough excitement for one day. Can you take me home, please?" *Since when did I start thinking of the cottage as home?*

"Let's go." Cian tucks me against his side and we walk toward Caitlín.

She falls in line with us, soon joined by a silver fox with a scar along his face. She tips her head up for a kiss. So this is her fiancé and infamous enforcer for Carrick Donnelly. The four of us stride out of the park and then go our separate ways. Caitlín and Roarke get into a vehicle and Cian opens the passenger door of his for me. Once I'm in, he closes it and gets behind the wheel.

It isn't until we hit the straight-away that he reaches for my hand. It trembles beneath him. Today had been going so well. I'm furious at Dónal for ruining it.

"Are you sure you're okay?" Cian's thumb glides along my skin.

I nod. "I'm fine, thanks to Caitlín. My god, she actually pulled a knife on him. Even stabbed him hard enough to make him bleed." I'm still a little in shock by the fact.

He blows out a breath. "Sounds like something she'd do. I swear since getting engaged to Roarke she's even more bloodthirsty than before."

I can't even imagine. I'll admit to being a bit envious of her bravado. She isn't someone whose bad side I'd want to be on.

"If you want, I can teach you how to fight. Or at least to defend yourself."

Is that something I want? I'm not scrappy and fearless like Caitlín. I'm not sure I could ever be like her. I'm just a woman who loves sitting in a library with her books. "Can I let you know?"

"Of course. The offer is open-ended."

"Thank you."

We make it back to the estate and a sense of home washes over me. This is the first place I've truly felt like my life is going to be fine. It hadn't started out that way. But in the short time I've been here, it's as though I've changed. Or rather, I *had* changed.

Dónal managed to smother the new me down in a single encounter. Cian gets out of the car and comes to my side to help me out. He threads his fingers through mine as we make our way to the cottage.

Once inside, he leads me to the sofa. Before I can sit, he's already there and pulling me onto his lap. I snuggle close, absorbing his warmth, and lay my head on his shoulder. I sense a difference in him even from only this morning, but I can't quite name it. Instead, I keep still, breathing in his scent and letting a sense of peace settle inside me. I'm going to enjoy it for as long as I can, so that when it's time to leave, I'll have the memory of my time with Cian. Of the time, where, briefly, I almost started to believe in daydreams again.

CHAPTER 22

CIAN

NESSA CURLS UP ON MY LAP AS IF SHE BELONGS THERE. I'M
still trying to control the rage that fires through my veins.

I'd left in the middle of the meeting still in progress, Da calling
my name as I ran down the stairs, too impatient to wait for the elevator. It had taken far too long to arrive at Stephen's Green. Rationally,
I knew Nessa was safe. But the irrational part of me—the part I'm
still fighting—wants to keep her locked in the cottage and never let
her leave again.

I shouldn't feel this way about her. As though I'll never get
enough.

Almost desperately, I try to remind myself that she's only here
because it's another way to rub our power in Sheehan's face. To make
sure he remembers in the future not to fuck with us. Except it's all so
petty. Nessa's words from that first day come back to me. She's not a
pawn to be used in some game between her Da and me. Once
Sheehan is dead—which will be soon—I'll let her go.

In the meantime, I'll continue to enjoy her body. To enjoy *her*.

"I'm glad you and Caitlín are getting along."

Nessa nods, rubbing her cheek along my shirt. "Me too. I had fun today. Well, until Dónal ruined it."

"Soon you won't have to worry about him ever again. I promise."

"I keep waiting for the guilt, except it never comes. I'm not sure what that says about me."

"It doesn't say anything about you other than that you've had enough. Bad things happen to everyone. Some just deserve it more than others." No one deserves it more than Sheehan. There's no room for guilt when it comes to justice. Karma. Vengeance. Whatever a person chooses to call it.

"I suppose you're right."

"Hey."

Nessa raises her head.

"I know I'm right."

She huffs and smiles a little then lays her head back down on me. "There's that ego again."

"You like my ego."

"Maybe."

The quiet that settles between us is comfortable. It's a bit unsettling *how* comfortable. Needing to break it up a bit, I tap her thigh. "Come on."

Nessa sits up. "Where are we going?"

"*I* am going to run you a hot bath and then *you* are going to relax with your book. I'm still waiting for you to tell me what she chooses." I help her to stand and then I'm on my feet and leading her into the bathroom. "Strip."

Without waiting for her, I turn on the hot water and stop the tub. I vaguely recall there being some bath crystals or one of those small balls that dissolves in the water in one of the drawers. After a quick search, I find it and add it to the steaming water. I glance over my shoulder, suspecting Nessa will be standing there fully clothed, but once again, she's done the unexpected. Her clothes lay in a pile on the floor and she's in the process of braiding her hair.

For a second, I take her in. From the slope of her breasts to her rounded belly to the dimples along the back and side of her thighs. My gaze is drawn to those adorable red-painted toes. Everything about her is soft and sweet. I lift my eyes and find her watching me with a flush over her cheeks.

"You're staring." Nessa plays with the end of her braid in a way I'm coming to recognize as her being nervous.

"Am I?"

She narrows her eyes. "You know you are."

"My apologies." I cover my heart and her lips twitch. Probably because I'm not at all sorry.

Nessa points behind me. "I think that's probably full enough."

Bubbles rise over the rim of the tub. I shut off the water, check the temperature, and face her again. "Climb in and I'll bring you your book. Stay here as long as you like and call me when you're ready to get out."

She pins up her braid and lets me help her into the bath. She sinks down and releases a long sigh. "This feels so good."

"That's what I like to hear. Be back in a second." I grab her book from the end table in the living room and return to her. "Did you find my note?"

Nessa reaches for it. "I did. Are you going to forever call me that silly nickname?"

I pause passing her the book for a fraction of a second at the word 'forever'. Like this thing between us is more than just temporary. I recover quickly and hand it over while I attempt to appear amused at the question.

"What, you don't like it?"

She cocks her head. "I don't know. It's kind of growing on me."

All amusement leaves me. "I'm going to make a couple phone calls and order us something to eat. Any requests?"

"I'm good with whatever you want." Nessa shakes her head.

"All right. Yell if you need anything...Mouse." I turn for the door.

"Cian," Nessa say quietly.

I pause and glance back.

"Thank you. For being there today."

"You're welcome." I can't leave fast enough. What the fuck is wrong with me?

With a glance at the door, I grab my phone and head out to the living room. There are five missed calls as well as several text messages. I call Da first, already dreading the conversation.

"Did you take care of whatever business you had that was more important than our meeting?" he draws out with sarcasm.

"Yes." He doesn't need to know any more than that.

"I'm going to assume it had something to do with your guest. Nora said Caitlín stopped by and the two of them left together."

"Look, I'm sorry I left the meeting without an explanation."

Da sighs. "What's going on between the two of you, Cian?"

"No disrespect, sir, but it doesn't really concern you."

"It does when it interferes with our business and costs us millions of euros," he snaps. "Liam Campbell needs to be dealt with. As does Dónal Sheehan. His daughter is proving a distraction, and distractions get us killed."

I run my hands through my hair and collapse back into the couch. Fuck. He's right, though. I have been distracted by Nessa. This agreement between us is merely her paying her Da's debt. I've taken her virginity, so this should be the end of it. I'm making it into something more than it is. "It won't happen again."

"It better not. Now, when do you plan on doing recon at the docks?"

"Tonight. After midnight sometime."

"Report back what you find. Points of entry. Number of guards. Shift changes. We need to know how much firepower and how many men we're going to need, as well as the fastest way to get in and get out without drawing more attention than we need to."

"Yes, sir."

"And Cian? Keep your head in the game and stop thinking with your cock."

I move my phone away and glance at the screen. He's gone. I sit and stare at nothing. The splash of water shakes me out of my haze. I search for restaurant numbers and place an order, but the weight of Da's disappointment is heavy, and I'm not all that hungry. Tomorrow is Sheehan's last day on this earth. Then I can send Nessa on her way and she doesn't have to worry about her Da again.

"Cian, I'm done," she calls out.

I blow out a breath and head back into the bathroom. Tendrils of hair stick to her forehead and her cheeks are red, whether from the heat or shyness I can't tell. "I think I'm turning into a prune."

Forcing a smile, I chuckle softly. "We can't have that."

I help Nessa out of the bath. Bubbles cascade down her naked flesh, playing peek-a-boo with her nipples and her cunt. While the water slowly drains, I turn on the shower. "Rinse."

She steps under the rainstorm and is soon free of any suds. I grab a towel. "Let me."

If this is going to be our last night together, then I'm going to make every minute one she—*I*—will remember. Carefully, I dry every inch of Nessa's body, paying special attention to her breasts and between her thighs. The musky scent of her arousal overpowers the floral scent the bubbles left behind. I need to taste her. Everywhere. Tossing the towel to the floor I drag her to me and my lips crash against hers. There's no subtlety to my want. I'm going to fuck Nessa hard—claim every inch of her— so she'll never forget tonight.

No matter who beds her in the future, I want her to remember who had her first.

CHAPTER 23

Any sort of relaxed state I'd been in disappears as Cian kisses me. This one is different than any other. There's a thread of desperation beneath it. I try to analyze it, but I'm swept up in an ocean of pleasure. It swirls around me, inside me, filling me up so full I'd be afraid of drowning if I weren't in his arms. Instead, I let the sensation wash over me, basking in its depths.

A cool burst of air dashes across my back. I shiver, and my nipples tighten. Cian lifts his head, and the blue eyes I've come to love darken to near pitch black. Before tonight, I never would have guessed the amount of power I have over him. I could bring him to his knees. Except I don't want that. I want nothing more than to savor this moment.

"You're beautiful. I hope you know that."

My heart swells. "You make me feel beautiful."

Before I can guess his intent, Cian sweeps me up in his arms and carries me out to the bedroom. He gently lays me on the bed and slowly begins to undress. Any cold I'd felt has burned away under the heat of his gaze. I can't resist taking him in. The last time, I hadn't been able to fully appreciate his nakedness. I absorb everything. Commit it to memory. My fingers itch to trace the lines defining each one of the muscles surrounding his shoulders. I want to feel them shift and move beneath my touch with the strength he possesses.

"You're staring," he repeats my words back to me.

A smile curls my lips. "Am I?"

Cian barks out a laugh. "You are. But don't let me stop you."

I won't. Instead, I drink him in. My eyes drift across the light smattering of hair that covers his chest then down to the narrow strip that runs from just below his belly button to his swollen cock. My cheeks heat merely thinking the word.

"Are those dirty thoughts running through that mind of yours? Should I feel objectified?" He smirks.

I nod slowly. "Most definitely."

"Good." Cian places one knee on the bed and then prowls toward me, his gaze hot and intense.

He positions himself between my legs, spreading them wide and opening me up for him. His hands go on either side of my head, caging me in like I'm prey he's about to devour. He leans down and his lips are on mine and his tongue swoops in. Every kiss is like the first. The flutters rise in my belly. There's that hint of excitement. Of danger. Of the feeling that one kiss will never be enough.

Cian drags his mouth away, but only to move it along my jaw. The soft bristles of hair along his jaw abrade my skin in the most delicious way, sending a shiver of delight through me. Unable to resist touching him, I run my hands over the rounded arches of his shoulders and down his arms. They flex beneath my touch. I find the vein that runs its length and drag my finger along the line of it. I'm not sure I'll ever get enough of touching him.

At least until our time together is over.

I push away any thoughts of the future and focus on every sensation bombarding me. The tightness in my breasts. The throbbing in my lower belly. The heat of Cian's body covering mine, warming me in spite of my nakedness. He burns hotter than any fire ever could.

"Where did you go just now?" The words are rasped in my ear as he nuzzles the shell.

"Nowhere. I'm right here with you."

He lifts his head and stares down at me. I hold his gaze letting him read the need in my eyes. Whatever he sees must satisfy him, because he kisses me again and then moves down my body. Wet heat engulfs my breast. His tongue laves my nipple before he draws it fully into his mouth, capturing it tightly and sucking. The pleasure runs through my whole body, and my toes curl. Never had I imagined how sensitive I am. Or maybe Cian just knows how to pull it from me.

He pays homage to the other one, and I thread my fingers through his hair. I love touching him. Grounding myself in him. As though I'm reassuring myself that he's real. That *this* is real. His breath whispers along my belly as he presses gentle kisses to it. He lifts his gaze to mine as his lips keep moving downward. I can't tear my eyes from Cian's as he gently lifts my leg and lays it over his shoulder. My muscles tense with the need to close my thighs and hide myself from his front row seat to...everything.

Then any thoughts disintegrate, as overwhelming pleasure takes over. Cian devours me. Every swipe of his tongue draws more wetness from me. He opens me up and explores every inch of my flesh inside and out.

Tidal waves of emotion crash into me.

No one has made me feel as cared for as he does. No one whose attention has been more focused on my needs—on my enjoyment—than his.

I'm not sure how I'm going to make it through each day without him.

Stop thinking about it.

Except it still lingers there, in the background, rushing forward at the worst times, like when I should be enjoying this moment. Cian latches onto my clit and there's a stretch as he thrusts his fingers inside me. I gasp and my back arches.

"That's the reaction I was looking for," he murmurs against my sensitive flesh. "Should I be offended that your mind doesn't seem to be on what I'm doing? Maybe I need to try a little harder."

He bites down on the nerve-bundle, and I let out a keening wail before sucking in deep breaths. "If you try any harder, you might kill me."

Cian chuckles and draws his fingers out partway before pushing them back in deeper and hitting something inside me that makes my whole body tremble. "We wouldn't want that. Now, get out of your head and just *feel*. Enjoy being fucked, and stop thinking so hard."

As though my mind needed to be given permission, I let every thought that continues to sneak past my barriers get locked away. I curl my fingers in his hair and nod, encouraging him to continue. That's the only signal he needed. Fingers and tongue go back to playing. Wetness pours out of me, soaking my inner thighs and dripping down to my ass. Cian licks every bit of it up. His tongue flicks out and I stiffen slightly.

"Relax, I'm not going to do more than this." He licks my asshole again, and I try not to clench. "At least for the moment."

I'm not sure I like the devious chuckle that accompanies that—no, in fact, I definitely don't—but I do my best to listen and force my body to relax. The second it does, he returns to his scandalous pleasuring of my backside. Everything centered between my legs tingles with awareness, as though every sensation is amplified. It's a little terrifying that I can feel all of them at once.

It's too much.

Unable to take it any longer, explosions rock through me.

My skin buzzes and tingles in a way it never has before. Almost like electricity runs through it, sending sparks along my nerve endings, making my hair stand on end.

As quickly as it hit, I come down. My chest rises and falls as I drag in breaths. I open my eyes to meet Cian's. A similar fire burns in his. He crawls up my body and kisses me, thrusting his tongue inside my mouth. I taste myself on him.

There's a slow stretching as he pushes his cock inside me. Panic hits. I push at his shoulder. "Condom."

He curses, and his weight lifts off me. There's the sound of the drawer opening, a package tearing, and then a brief groan before he's settling over me. "Sorry. I didn't mean to forget."

I nod jerkily. He kisses me again, probably trying to bring the mood back that I ruined with my frantic single-word command. I'd caught the glimpse—of not irritation but maybe regret—when I mentioned protection. Not that I'm worried about any diseases. I trust Cian to be safe. But there had been a blip of a thought of pregnancy. I'm not ready for a baby, especially since I'd be raising it alone.

Thankfully, Cian knows exactly how to touch me, and in only minutes, I'm writhing beneath him, begging to be filled. He's made me insatiable. He pulls his fingers from me again and replaces them with his cock. The slow stretch is agonizing.

"More." I lift my hips to pull him in deeper, but he's determined to torture me and draws back. Far enough that only the tip remains inside.

"Patience is a virtue, Mouse."

I growl in frustration, but he only laughs.

"I hate you," I rasp with mock heat.

"No, you don't. You l—"—Cian's mouth snaps shut, and there's a brief pause before he finishes quietly—"like me."

That pause echos loudly though, making it ring in my ears. Then he thrusts hard and impales his entire length, as though he's trying to distract me. It's working, too, because Cian moves, and nothing else matters except the release that is building.

The tension tightens even more, begging to be released. I mewl in frustration when it's just out of reach.

"Do you need to come, little mouse?" he rocks hard into me, hitting the spot deep inside and making stars and colors swirl behind my eyes.

"Yes, please." I'm panting and dig my heels into his lower back urging him for more.

"Who does your pleasure belong to?" Cian rasps into my ear, his hand going between us to finger my clit.

"You." I barely get the word out.

"Who does this cunt belong to?" He pinches the nub at the same time he thrusts and that's all it takes.

"You." It explodes out of me on a scream.

Two pumps later and Cian roars out his climax, the tendons in his neck bulging as he throws his head back. Our sweat-slicked bodies glide over each other as he lowers himself onto me and buries his nose in my neck. I unlock my ankles and they fall from his waist. He settles deeper in the cradle of my thighs, still inside me. I run my fingers up and down his back. This is the kind of intimacy I never imagined. The quiet time after release, when our bodies are still connected and our hearts almost beat as one.

I'll miss this.

Slowly, Cian rolls off and covers me with the blanket while he goes into the bathroom to dispose of the condom. He comes back with a wet cloth, and even though there's no blood this time, he washes me. He disappears into the bathroom again, but seconds later, climbs in beside me and tugs me against him. I like that he wants to cuddle.

I snuggle closer, breathing in both his ginger scent and the musky odor of sex. I'd say something, but I don't want to disturb this moment between us. Tonight had been perfect, even if I sense something different with Cian I can't put my finger on.

I close my eyes and absorb everything I'm feeling. We'll have to get up in a couple hours to eat supper, but until then, I want to lie here in this bubble we've created and ignore the outside world. Because something inside is telling me we won't be able to for much longer.

CHAPTER 24

CIAN

THIS IS THE SECOND TIME WE'VE MADE LOVE TODAY.
Earlier, we'd taken a short nap, and then my rumbling stomach had
pulled us from bed to eat. Nessa and I sat on the sofa afterwards and
watched some movie whose plot I wouldn't be able to recall if asked.
Instead, I'd spent the entire time thinking. About everything. Dónal,
Campbell, but mostly about the two of us and what I'm going to do
about it. When we'd finally gone to bed, I still hadn't come up with
any answers.

I lie on my side facing Nessa and brush her damp hair off her
forehead. The length of it lays tangled around her shoulders and all
over the pillow. She smiles softly and opens her eyes. I love seeing her
like this.

"You've gotten into the habit of staring." She shifts and nestles
deeper into the bed.

"What's wrong with that? I enjoy the view."

Even in the dim light, the flush of her cheeks is visible. "I don't know that I'll ever get used to someone—you—studying me so intently, I guess. It feels a little weird."

"Then everyone is missing out on the beauty in front of them."

Her expression evens out to one more serious. "You're the first person to ever think so."

"Maybe because they've never seen you the way I have."

That gets a chuckle from her. "You mean naked in bed?"

My smile is devious. Mostly to hide the burning jealousy at the thought of anybody but me seeing her like this. "Exactly."

She shakes her head. "I've always been a joke to people. It used to bother me at first. When I was younger, I'd cry myself to sleep at night wondering why they all laughed at me. But the older I got, the more I realized that they were mean and spiteful people who hated anyone who wasn't like them. And no matter what I did, I would never be good enough. They were going to continue to talk about me. To whisper about me behind my back. All that said more about them than me. So, I stopped caring what anyone thought."

Fuck all those people. "I've never thought of you as a joke."

She lifts her eyes to meet mine. "I know. I remember this one time when I was twelve, Dónal had taken me to the theatre. In the middle of the show, I excused myself to the bathroom. I was just coming back and didn't realize my dress had gotten caught in my underwear so I was baring half my butt. The son of one of Dónal's cronies saw and started teasing me. He even went so far as to smack my butt cheek, then laughed when he said it jiggled."

My blood boils. Who the fuck does that to a twelve year-old girl? It makes me want to find the bastard and ram a knife through his hand. Teach him not to fucking touch things he has no business touching.

"Anyway." Nessa shifts and pulls the blanket up higher. "That's when this young man steps between us and punched him and told him if he ever so much as looked at me again, he was dead."

A vague thread of memory surfaces and I stare harder at her.

"That was you?" Christ. I remember the incident, but I'd had no idea that was Nessa. I'd been seventeen or eighteen at the time.

She nods, dropping her gaze from mine. "I saw you after the show ended and asked Dónal who you were. He'd been livid and cursed the whole way home about you and your family. When we got inside, he beat me and told me to never mention you again."

I palm her cheek. "I'm sorry he did that to you."

Nessa shuffles closer and buries her head against my chest with a yawn. "I never forgot what you did that night. You were my hero."

She doesn't say anything else, and when I glance down, her eyes are closed and her breathing even. I continue lying there with her in my arms unable to sleep. All I do is replay her words over and over again.

I'm no one's hero.

Hours later, I'm still awake and for the second night in a row, I have to leave Nessa sleeping while I take care of family business. Just once, I would have liked to hold her in my arms for an entire night. I creep out of bed, quickly dress, and then I'm heading into town toward the docks. The city is quiet. No tourists roam the streets and all the businesses have closed until morning. It's oddly my favorite time to absorb all the wonders Dublin has to offer without people clogging the walkways.

I park my car, grab the gun from beneath my seat, and stuff it in the waist of my jeans at my back. I walk the rest of the way. No need to signal my presence. I stop a short distance away and take in the area. The entrance to the container terminal is blocked by a levered gate that wasn't closed when Nathan and I were here earlier. The guard house is empty. A placard on a brick pillar displays the hours of operation. With the right vehicle, it's easily bypassed. I scan for security cameras, but if the place is equipped with them, they're well hidden.

Another few minutes pass with nothing but silence so I duck under the gate and sneak along the fence line, staying within the shadows until I reach a small outbuilding near the docked ship. Stacks of large, metal cargo containers line up around the loading area. A crane is parked nearby, its lever reaching to the sky, while the chain and hook dangle toward the ground like a string swaying slightly. Port workers enter and exit the ship at random, and only one or two at a time.

Voices reach me, and I cast a glance around the corner of the outbuilding. Two security guards, deep in conversation, pass by, not paying attention to their surroundings. I stand there—hidden—a while longer. It takes the security guards another fifteen minutes before they make a second round in front of the cargo ship containing our goods.

Once all is quiet again, I keep moving farther along the fence to observe the other ships docked nearby. Every so often, a port worker will exit or enter the ship. I do another sweep of the area for cameras and still come up empty. Overall, security is lax.

My cousin, Paddy, employs a hacker. I bet they'll be able to find out what type of cameras, if any, there are and probably bypass them if necessary. I'll reach out later today. By my guess, I've been here for nearly an hour and gathered as much intel as I'm going to. Slowly, I take the same path back toward the gated entrance, pausing when the two guards wander by again. I just make it out of the gate, walking back to my car, when my phone vibrates in my pocket. I stop next to the vehicle before I answer. It better be important.

"Donnelly."

There's no response.

"Hello?"

A stick snaps nearby. I spin in that direction, reaching for the gun at the small of my back. There's a loud pop and a searing pain stabs through my chest. I stumble back a step. My eyesight darkens, and I collapse to the ground. My phone drops from my hand and hits the cement with a crack.

Fuck.

I've been shot enough times to know what a bullet feels like. Footsteps approach. I clutch my wound, warmth spreading beneath my hand.

I blink away the dark spots that fill my vision, but there's too many of them. They multiply until there's only a shadow hovering over me. I can't make out more than that. I groan as the pain engulfs me. My eyes slowly begin to close and I fight against it. The agony vibrating through my chest is too much.

Darkness consumes me.

"Liam Campbell sends his regards," the voice whispers and then fades away.

CHAPTER 25

Apparently Cian is going to make a habit of disappearing before I wake. Based on the faint light filtering through the crack in the shutters, it's barely past dawn. I'm trying—and failing—to withhold my disappointment as I lie there, staring at the ceiling. What am I going to do? The longer I stay here, the harder it's going to be to not fall deeper under his spell. I'm coming to discover I'm not one of those women who can separate their emotions from sex.

I can't just enjoy what Cian does to me, compartmentalize it in some vault inside my head, and then go about my life as though it was nothing more than scratching an itch.

All I do is replay every kiss, every touch, every sweet word he murmured in my ear, trying to read a deeper meaning into it. As though he feels what I do. As though I'm special and not merely payment for a debt owed.

God, I'm so screwed. There had been a brief moment last night where it felt like he was back to playing the role of seducer, similar to those first couple days. When it was all a game.

"You're overanalyzing it. It was your imagination." *Do you really believe that?*

Ignoring the taunting voice, I crawl out of bed, shower, and dress. Since there's no telling when Cian will get back, I'm going to finish my book. It became pretty obvious what choice the protagonist is going to make, but I want confirmation. Because I'm not sure I agree with her. I curl up on the couch and don't even make it two pages before there's a knock at the door. I'm not sure I'm up for another outing with Caitlín so soon. A second knock sounds.

"Coming. Give a girl a minute." I climb to my feet and turn the knob to open it. "I don't think I can handle—"

Dónal shoves the door open, and I stumble back with a cry. "You little bitch. Turning against your own Da."

A stinging slap to my face knocks my head sideways, and my glasses go flying. I moan at the pain that reverberates through the whole right side of my head. He grabs my hair and yanks it back. I scream. Spittle sprays all over me. "After everything I've done for you, and this is how you repay me? By aligning yourself with those fucking Donnellys?"

I claw at the hand gripping my hair. He's ripping it from my scalp. "Stop, please."

Dónal shakes me harder. Blistering pain surrounds me. I grow nauseated from it. "I'm going to teach you a lesson. Remind you who's in control. You dare tell me what to do?"

I'm thrown face-first into the sofa, and twist onto my back. My arms go up to block the blow, but it's too late. Another ear-rattling punch collides with the side of my head. Nails dig into my arm. I'm yanked to my feet. I scream again. How did he get past anyone at the house? Where's Cian?

"Let's go." Dónal drags me out the door and up the hill.

I scratch and hit everywhere I can reach. Another punch lands and my head pounds so hard I nearly pass out from the pain. I stumble, but he yanks me upright, squeezing my arm so tight my fingers go numb. Agony radiates throughout my entire body. A car door opens, he shoves me into the backseat, and then climbs in beside me.

Blindly, I lunge for the door. My fingers curl around the handle and Dónal snatches a fistful of my hair again, yanking me back. Using his hold, he slams my head into the window. A ripping sensation spreads along my temple. Warm wetness glides down the side of my face and the explosion of every nerve ending rioting is more than I can take, and my vision goes dark.

I SLOWLY OPEN MY EYES, BLINK AT THE SUN SHINING IN through the window, and then wince, as my body sends pain signals to my brain. My entire face throbs like my heartbeat is located inside it, pounding away. I reach up and touch the side of my head and flinch. Memories return.

I can make out the shape of the furniture that fills the unfamiliar room, but the fine details are impossible to make out. Where am I? Does Cian know I'm missing? What is Dónal going to do with me? He's been in a rage before, but never like this.

Carefully, I sit up in the bed and make my way across the room. Outside the window is a narrow, residential street lined with trees, and a few cars parked along the curb. There aren't any people walking down the sidewalk. I try opening the window, but it won't budge. A quick glance around the room confirms there's nothing I can use to break it. I'm not sure what good it would do anyway. I'm on the second floor, and even if I tried to jump, I can't imagine I won't break...something.

A lock clicks. I whirl around as the door opens, and Dónal strides in.

"You're awake," he says with a small slur.

His hair is a riotous mess and his cheeks are far too ruddy for just drink. Did he sleep in his clothes? A dark red splotch covers the bottom section of his shirt. Is that the blood from Caitlín's knife? She must have cut him deeper than it appeared. I stare at him, expecting the same fear, the same sense of uncertainty, but both are gone.

In their place is hatred.

A sense of calm fills me as I take in this man who has tormented me for twenty years. I'm not afraid of him anymore. Any power he had over me is gone. "Cian is going to kill you."

Dónal's face twists in rage and he makes a move toward me.

"I wouldn't do that if I were you." I don't raise my voice nor does it tremble. The warning is clear. He must hear it, because he stops, a bit unsteady on his feet. "By taking me, you've guaranteed your death. And you know what? I'm glad."

He sneers. "You've always thought you were better than everyone. Smarter. Well, you're not too smart now. Cian Donnelly is dead."

My stomach lurches and I sway. Tears threaten, but I refuse to let him see me cry. "No. You're wrong."

Dónal laughs. "I'm the one who put out the order to shoot him, and I watched it happen. Your precious *Cian* is dead. I almost wish he weren't, so I could see his face when he realized he'd lost. To me."

I blink and then laugh until I wheeze. "You stupid, stupid man. If you'd done nothing more than take me away from the Donnelly estate, then maybe that would have been the end of it. But if Cian is truly...dead"—my heart aches just speaking the word—"then Carrick Donnelly and his sons will hunt you to the ends of the earth to make you pay."

His expression shifts to self-satisfaction. "Except they think Liam Campbell killed him. They're going to get rid of that little whelp for me. Then I'll be back in control."

"And what about me?"

Dónal's brow crinkles. "What about you? You'll return home with me and everything will be like it was before."

My fists clench and I take a step forward closing the distance between us. "I will *never* go back with you. I will kill you myself before I let that happen."

He rocks back at the vehemence I spit out, but recovers. "I'll give you a few days to see things my way."

Without another word, he disappears out the door. The lock snaps back into place.

Cian can't be dead. He can't be. I'd know it if he was, right? I stumble to the bed and collapse onto it just as the sob rises in my throat. Grabbing the pillow, I hold it against my face and cry until the pillowcase is soaked with my tears and my throat is hoarse.

Once I've spilled every tear I'm going to, I pull myself together. I wipe my nose and then start to plan. Because I refuse to believe Cian is dead. He and the rest of the Donnellys are going to come for Dónal. And when they do, I'll be ready.

CHAPTER 26

Why does everything fucking hurt?

"Stop moving or you're going to tear your stitches. Again."

I open eyes far too heavy for just sleep, and the blurry figure looming over me slowly comes into focus. Aidan stands there, disheveled, his hair sticking up everywhere and a wrinkled shirt, which isn't like him. He always makes sure he's put together.

Then the rest of my surroundings become clear. I glance at all the machines I'm hooked up to and then down at myself. A large white bandage is wrapped around my chest and shoulder, and an IV is stuck in the back of my hand.

What the hell?

"Do you remember what happened?"

I lift my gaze to meet Aidan's expressionless face. *Think.* "I went to the shipping docks to scout things out. Then I walked back to my car. I remember my phone vibrating, and I answered it."

I close my eyes.

"Anything else?" he asks.

I replay everything. The guards walking by. The dock workers moving in and out. The quiet as I walked back to my car.

Wait.

"Someone was waiting in the trees near my car. I answered my phone, but no one was there. Something cracked close by—a stick—and I turned. Then I heard the gunshot. I remember hitting the ground and then a figure standing over me. He said Liam Campbell sent his regards."

My gaze darts to Aidan. "How long have I been here? Where's Nessa?"

I try to lift myself up, but my brother lays his hand on my uninjured shoulder and holds me down. "Relax. You're going to undo all the hard work the doctors did. It's a couple hours past dawn. Bullet went in through the fleshy part directly beneath your collarbone and came out the other side. Nothing vital was hit, but they still needed to close up the wound and stop the bleeding. You'll be fine in a few days."

He's avoiding eye contact. "Aidan. Where's Nessa?"

Finally he meets my gaze. "I don't know. Da called Nora and asked her to go down to the cottage to let Nessa know what happened, and she was gone. Her glasses were on the floor, and one of the cushions had been knocked off the sofa."

Campbell's a fucking dead man. I grab the IV to rip it out, but the movement sends stabbing pain through me and my vision darkens. I collapse back onto the bed, breathing hard. Aidan curses. "You're not going to do Nessa any good if you bleed to death. Finn and Nathan are doing what they can to gather intel. We'll find her, Cian."

Sweat beads across my forehead. I've never felt so helpless before. "Campbell's time on this earth is limited. I am going to destroy him, along with anyone or anything he cares about."

"You're going to have to heal first. Let us take care of things for a change. You don't have to do everything all on your own."

The door opens and Da walks in. His haggard appearance makes him appear as if he's aged overnight. He kisses my forehead like he used to when I was a kid. "I thought we lost you."

"It's going to take more than a single bullet to take me out."

"You lost a lot of blood." His eyes appear haunted.

"I'm here, Da. I'll be back on my feet before you know it." I have to be. Nessa needs me. "Any news from Finn or Nathan?"

He shakes his head. "Nothing yet, but word is making its way through our organization. We've called an official halt to the cease-fire and declared war against Campbell. Our soldiers are gathering all our weapons and we're planning a full on assault on Campbell's estate as well as any other properties he owns. Wherever he's hiding, it won't last long. Whereever Nessa is, we'll find her too."

"When are you making your move?"

"Tonight," Aidan answers.

Da glares at me. "I see what you're thinking, son."

"I'm coming with, whether you like it or not. If anyone is going to take down Campbell, it's going to be me."

He shakes his head and Aidan sits in the chair pushed against the wall under the window. "You've always been far too stubborn for your own good."

The door flings open again and Caitlín rushes inside, Roarke right behind her. Christ, is the whole family going to show up? Fatigue is beginning to creep in. The pain in my shoulder is lessening a bit as well. Probably from the pain meds being pumped into my system. My cousin squeezes my hand and glares down at me.

"I had to come and confirm for myself that you were okay. Now, you better hurry up and get better so you can go and get your woman back," Caitlín growls fiercely.

"That's the plan." I'm glad Nessa has my cousin to count as a friend.

"Good. And I hope you bury that fucker Campbell." Hatred burns from her eyes. Roarke places his hands on her shoulder and they step away from me.

"He's as good as dead." I stifle a yawn.

"All right everyone, Cian needs to rest. Especially if he plans on joining us, against our better judgment." Da ushers everyone toward the door. He pauses with it partially open and glances back at me. "I didn't realize what she meant to you. I'm sorry for what I said yesterday."

Before I can dispute him, he walks out and the door closes behind him. Too tired to examine my feelings for Nessa, I close my eyes and let sleep come. I have to be ready for tonight.

~

I'VE SLEPT OFF AND ON ALL DAY. THE NURSE UPPED MY pain meds earlier. Just enough to numb me for a while. At least until Campbell is dead. The faded sunlight shines through the bottom half of the window. Soon it will be completely gone as dusk hits. The door opens and the doctor walks in.

"It's going on record that you're leaving against medical advice. A nurse will be in to have you sign the paperwork and remove your IV. Then you'll be free to go."

I nod and he leaves the room. Time passes far too slowly while I wait for the nurse. There's a short knock and then Da walks in carrying a small bag.

"Any news on Campbell?"

"He's denying he had anything to do with it. Said if he wanted to kill you, you would have seen him coming. He wouldn't have hidden in the bushes like some coward."

The nurse enters and the conversation stops while she works. I sign the form and then she turns a valve on the tubing before taking the needle out of my hand. "Your clothes are in a bag in the cabinet, but they're ruined."

"I brought him some." Da lifts his arm.

The nurse nods. "Pain medication can be picked up at the hospital pharmacy."

"Thank you."

She leaves without another word. I wait another minute to make sure she isn't going to return before I resume our conversation. "Do you believe Campbell?"

"I don't know him well enough to say yes or no. However, we do have to consider the possibility that he is telling the truth. Which means someone is trying to make it appear as though he's behind it."

I nod. "The only person who would gain anything from us taking Campbell out is Sheehan."

"That's a pretty strong incentive," Da says. "Especially after we declined his invitation to join forces."

"There was an altercation yesterday with him and Nessa. She and Caitlín were at a cafe together and he made a scene. Tried dragging her out, but Caitlín managed to...persuade him otherwise."

Despite the seriousness of the situation, he chuckles. "I can only image how she accomplished that."

"She drew blood, I was told."

"Christ, I bet he didn't take kindly to being bested by not only a woman, but a Donnelly at that." Da rubs his hand down his face. "It's certainly enough for him to want to see one of us, especially you, taken down."

I sit there a moment in indecision. Do we take the risk that Campbell is telling the truth and put a temporary halt on the assault while we try to find Nessa? Or do we move in and destroy everything he owns while she remains missing? For the first time in my life I'm considering putting someone—putting Nessa—before the organization. Before family.

"What do you think we should do?" I meet Da's eyes.

He studies me and I make myself stay still during the scrutiny. "Before we rush into things, let's have a family meeting. Discuss our options. In the meantime, I'll see if anyone has seen Sheehan. Perhaps if we let him know we've changed our minds about the alliance, we might get some answers."

Da tosses the bag on the end of the bed, and I pull everything out and get dressed. I bite back the wince putting on my shirt. By the time I'm finished, I'm breathing hard, and sweat pops along my forehead. I slowly stand up, taking measured breaths, and face Da. "I'm ready."

"I'd try to talk you out of this, but I know it won't do me any good."

He's right. All I've thought about during my waking hours is Nessa. Whether Campbell has her or Sheehan does, I plan on finding her before the day is over. Then killing whoever it is that dared take her. And if they've hurt her, I'll make them suffer before I put them out of their misery. Roarke has learned a few new...techniques for delivering pain from Pierce de Luca when he and Caitlín were back in Brooklyn. Campbell's already proven that he'll kidnap a woman to get what he wants. Who's to say he won't hurt another if it means weakening us any further?

I only hope I get to her before it's too late.

NESSA

I STARE OUT THE LOCKED WINDOW AGAIN—STILL—AND wait for...something. Anything. The sun has crested the sky and despite the deceiving hint of warmth it gives off, a cold chill still seeps in through glass. My feet are half-frozen, but I'm tired of doing nothing but sitting on the bed with them tucked under the blankets to try and keep them warm. I'm going to have to use the bathroom again soon, and my stomach is growling with hunger.

Movement outside draws my eyes. An elderly man walks a tiny dog down the sidewalk, and they're heading this direction. If I can get his attention, maybe he'll call for help. I glance over my shoulder, afraid someone is going to come in. I'm also afraid someone will hear if I pound on the window. As the man draws near, I wave my hands over my head. He doesn't even glance toward the house. I refuse to stop. Back and forth I scissor them, desperation evident in my movement.

"Here. Look up here."

He's crossing the drive. In a minute, he's going to be completely past the house and all my efforts will have been wasted. Not caring if someone inside the house hears me, I pound on the glass and press my face to it to yell. "Help. Please help me."

The dog's ears perk up and the man pauses. My heart skips. *Please, look up.*

Behind me, the lock clicks.

I scream for my entire worth. The man on the sidewalk pauses and glances at the house. He lifts his gaze at the same time a raspy voice speaks in my ear.

"Unless you want to be the reason that poor old man and his little dog meet with an unfortunate accident, I recommend you just smile and wave."

The sharp end of something jabs into my back. My gaze jerks from the window to Dónal's man, standing far too close to me. The scent of his cologne is overpowering and gives me a headache. There's an edge to his eyes that make me uncomfortable. I glance back outside. The elderly man is staring up at us. Fionn presses the gun harder into my back. With a forced smile, I lift my hand and quickly put it back down. He glares at me, and then he and his dog keep walking.

Tears blur my eyes, but I blink them away. I try to spin away from Fionn, but he catches me around the arm and drags me against him. I squirm, but that only makes him laugh. His rotten breath assaults me.

"If you're not careful, I might have to punish you." He thrusts his pelvis and my stomach lurches. "Hell, maybe I'll just do it for fun."

I bite my tongue, not taking the bait. I can't show him fear. "If you so much as touch me, Cian will kill you. He might, just for fun, anyway." I throw his words back at him.

Fionn studies me another minute and I stare right back. Finally, he lets me go. "Don't try that again. The next time, you won't get a warning. It'll be a bullet to the brain of whatever poor soul it is. Now, I'll be back in a minute with food."

He backs away slowly without taking his eyes off me. His grin is creepy enough to send chills cascading down my spine. At the door, he salutes me with the weapon. I blow out a shaky breath and nearly collapse to the floor. My body needs to sit, but if he's coming back, I want to be as far away from the bed as possible. I brace myself against the windowsill instead and concentrate on slowing down my racing heart.

It isn't long before footsteps approach and the lock clicks again. Fionn steps inside, carrying a tray with a covered dish and glass of water on it. It smells like shepherd's pie. He sets the tray on the bed and moves to leave.

"I need to use the bathroom." I hate asking him, but I don't have any other choice.

"Let's go."

He leads me down the hall to the door at the end. I close it, quickly take care of my needs, and wash my hands. He's waiting for me when I finish. The hairs on the back of my neck prickle as he walks behind me to my room. I can't get there soon enough. Finally we make it back and with only a single lingering glance, Fionn locks me in again. I don't trust him or the way he looks at me. I lift my gaze to the ceiling.

"Please, Cian, hurry."

SEVERAL RAISED VOICES COME FROM DOWNSTAIRS. THIS IS the first time I've been aware of anyone's presence in the house besides Fionn. It's been quiet since he brought me lunch and not once has Dónal been back since he left early this morning. *What is happening?*

The front door slams. I rush to the window and peer out. One of Dónal's men storms out to his car and speeds away, but not before glancing up. It's too dark to tell, but it's almost as though our eyes meet. Why did he leave in such a hurry?

More raucous noise filters in through the door. I fold my arms and rub my hands up and down them trying to get warm, but the cold isn't only from the temperature inside the house. It's also coming from inside *me*. Like a warning.

I pace the length of the room, my gaze darting to the door often. The noise remains at a steady level with the occasional burst of laughter. Only Dónal would be careless enough to have some sort of celebration of his alleged success in getting the Donnellys to do his dirty work for him. Are they all killing each other at this exact moment?

For almost my whole life we've lived with a truce between my family and Cian's. Is it all going to be destroyed by stupid men who can't be satisfied with what they have?

My head jerks toward the door. Are those footsteps? It's hard to tell with all the other noise. There it is again. Yes, they're definitely footsteps. A shadow forms beneath the door, and then comes that damning snick of the lock. A pit of ice forms in my belly.

Fionn steps in, and my blood turns cold at the expression on his face. "Everyone downstairs is enjoying themselves. I thought you and I could have a good time up here." He prowls forward.

"Get out." I vibrate with anger and fear.

Fionn snarls. "Always was an uppity bitch, weren't you? No matter how many times I tried to catch your attention, you always acted like you were too good for me."

I shake my head and back farther away, trying to keep distance between us. What is he talking about? Fionn's never indicated he was interested in me. Not once.

"You always looked right through me."

I hold up my hand. "I'm sorry if I ever made you feel slighted. It was never my intention."

He keeps stalking forward, the evil grin on his face growing wider with each step. "Well you won't be able to ignore me tonight."

I move, trying to put the bed between us, but I'm not fast

enough. Fionn lunges and grabs me around the waist, yanking me hard against him. He buries his face in my neck and palms my breast in a rough grip. I claw at the hands holding me. "Stop it. Let go of me."

My fingernails rake across the back of his arm, drawing blood. He howls.

"You stupid bitch." He pushes me facedown on the bed and locks my wrists in a tight grip behind my back.

I writhe and kick, trying to break his hold, but I don't have the leverage. I scream, and Fionn shoves a pillow over my head. I suck in as many deep breaths as I can. He reaches beneath me for the fastening on my pants. Either some unknown strength fills me or he's distracted, because his grip loosens. I jerk my arms free and swing the right one back as hard as I can, twisting my body at the same time. My fist connects with the side of Fionn's head. He bellows out a curse and stumbles. I don't wait for him to recover. Instead, I scramble upright and race for the door. My fingers wrap around the knob. A weight crashes into me.

He grabs my hair and yanks my head back. I cry out in pain.

"You stupid cunt. Just for that I'm not going to go easy on you. I'm going to fuck every hole and make you scream."

A loud pop comes from downstairs. Was that a gunshot? Whatever it was, Fionn freezes. Several more pops come in rapid succession. Still keeping hold of me, he backs us away from the door and pulls a gun from behind his back. He places it against my temple, and I go rigid. Pounding footsteps draw closer.

Fionn moves the gun from my head and fires at the door. "I'll kill her if you try to come in here."

"There's no place for you to go. If you hurt her, you're a dead man. Let Nessa go, and we'll let you walk out of here."

My knees nearly give out with relief and tears spring in my eyes. My heart hadn't been wrong.

"Cian," I scream.

Fionn's entire body trembles. "I swear I'll kill her."

"Listen to me. You don't want to do that. I swear, if you let her go, you can walk away. No one has to die."

Behind me, he's breathing hard, the sour odor of his breath making me sick. I keep my mouth shut, afraid I'll make it worse.

"O—kay," his voice wobbles. "You swear you'll let me out of here?"

"I will. Just let Nessa go."

Another beat of silence, and then he straightens as though he's made his decision. "We're coming out. I have my gun against her head. If anyone tries anything, the bitch is dead."

Keeping his hand wrapped around my waist and the weapon at my temple, Fionn walks us toward the door. "Open it."

With shaking hands, I reach for the knob. Tears spill down my cheeks. Cian is standing in front of me. His face is ashen, making his freckles stand out against the paleness of his skin, and his curls form a wild cloud around the top of his head. But he's alive.

"You swore," Fionn reminds him.

Cian nods shallowly, but doesn't take his eyes off me.

Then I'm free and in Cian's arms. A single gunshot rings out. I scream. In Cian's outstretched arm is a gun, and Fionn crumples to the ground, his eyes wide, and a bullet hole that seeps blood between them.

Oh, god.

I fling myself away from Cian and vomit all over the floor. He holds my hair back and murmurs words I can't make out as I dry heave, having lost the little bit of what had been in my stomach. Once there's nothing left, he hands me a cloth. I wipe my mouth with it.

"Come on, Mouse, let's go home." Cian wraps an arm around me, but he stumbles and falls.

I cry out and drop to my knees, calling his name. He's still breathing, but it's shallow.

"Fuck, I knew he shouldn't have left the hospital," someone says.

Hands gently clasp my shoulder. "Nessa, I'm Finn, Cian's brother. He's going to be okay. But we need to go."

I lift my head. It's the same brother as when he took me from Dónal's house. Somehow I manage a nod and he helps me to my feet. We back up a few steps, several men pick up Cian, and carefully carry him out of the house while his brother and I follow. My mind and body are numb. I'm moving on auto-pilot. Finn puts me in the back-seat of the same SUV I'd been in before. All I can do is stare straight ahead. He gets behind the wheel and drives, leaving that nightmare behind us.

CHAPTER 28

CIAN

CHRIST. IF I NEVER WAKE UP IN A HOSPITAL AGAIN, IT'LL be too soon. I glance over and once again find Aidan. Only this time, he's asleep and snoring, sitting upright in the chair. It doesn't look at all comfortable. Vague memories of last night—or however long it's been—filter in. Finding Nessa and killing that fucker who dared threaten her life. I'm not ready to jump out of this bed to find her, but only because I trust my family to have taken care of her while I was...incapacitated. The door opens and Da walks in.

"You're awake. How are you feeling?" he whispers, trying not to disturb Aidan.

"Like I was shot." I huff out a small breath. "Is Nessa okay?"

He grabs the chair from beside my brother, moves it next to my bed, and takes a seat. "Caitlín is with her, the last I heard. Finn called her."

"I appreciate it. And Sheehan?" My fury is still at a slow boil.

"Roarke has him secured. They've been having a one-sided conversation with our enforcer doing all the...talking."

I can imagine. It's not enough though. "You told him to keep him there until I can join the discussion?"

Da nods. "Of course."

Good. Because if anyone is going to end Dónal Sheehan's life, it's going to be me. I made a vow to Nessa. "Any word on who our anonymous caller is?"

"Nothing."

We'd been in the middle of our family meeting to decide on our plan of attack when Da got a phone call. The person said they worked for Dónal, but didn't agree with what he did to Nessa. The caller gave the address where Nessa was being kept. It had been a calculated risk to believe him, but it had paid off.

From his chair, Aidan shifts and groans. He sits upright and runs his hands up and down his face. "You're not dead yet, I see."

"It's going to take more than one bullet to put me in the grave."

"Let's hope the next time someone shoots you they don't use two bullets then."

I grin. "You sound as though you'd miss me."

"Like an itchy nut sac."

"If the two of you are finished." Da sighs. "We do have other important things that need to be dealt with. Liam Campbell continues to be a problem, as does the fact we still don't have our shipment."

"You met with him the other day, didn't you? Is that woman—what was her name, Imogen—still at the estate?"

Da nods. "I did, and she is."

"And?" Aidan pipes up.

"And that's all I'm going to say on the matter."

My brother and I share a glance. Da isn't normally this evasive. Who exactly is this woman and what connection does she have to Campbell? There's no sense in pushing. It's obvious we're not going to get anything else from him.

"When she's rested, can one of you or Finn bring Nessa by? I need to see her." And speak with her.

Aidan stands and heads to the door. "I will. In the meantime, *you* should rest."

"If you keep saying things like that, I'm going to start thinking you really do care about me."

"Arsehole," my brother calls over his shoulder as he walks out of the room.

Da rises as well and pushes my hair off my forehead before leaning down to kiss it. "I love you, Cian."

"Love you too, Da."

He follows Aidan and closes the door behind him. I shut my eyes and try not to think about the conversation ahead with Nessa.

I SLOWLY OPEN MY EYES AND ORIENT MYSELF. I'M STILL IN the same hospital bed. Except there's a new scent in the room. One I'll smell even after she's gone. I turn my head, and Nessa sits in the chair Aidan vacated earlier, reading a book. Her slightly crooked glasses are perched on her nose, and the hair I love so much lays in soft waves around her shoulders.

My jaw clenches at the bruises marking her beautiful face. The ones I plan on making Dónal Sheehan pay for. Slowly. Painfully.

My fingers curl into a fist.

As though sensing the movement, Nessa lifts her head. Her eyes widen, she slams the book shut, and rushes over, collapsing into the chair pushed up near the bed. "Oh my god, Cian." She clutches my fingers, careful of the IV. "You had me so worried."

"I'm sorry I wasn't there to keep you safe."

She jerks back a fraction. "What? No. You saved me. If it weren't for you, Fionn would have..." Nessa's voice cracks.

That fucker died too easily.

"Do you know where Dónal is? Caitlín either wouldn't, or couldn't, tell me."

I don't want to lie to her, but I'm also not sure how she'll feel about her Da being tortured for his betrayal. "He's being detained someplace where he won't hurt you again."

Nessa's eyes meet mine. "I'm going to assume 'detained' is code for something else."

I don't answer for a minute. "Yes."

"I see." She nods, but just barely.

"He tried to have me killed. Then he beat and kidnapped you." It's as though I'm trying to justify my actions to her. Something I've never done, or cared about doing, before. Why this time? Because it's Nessa?

Her fingers tighten their grip on mine and her gaze shifts to where our hands connect. "I've had a lot of time to think about my life the last week. We all make choices. Some good. Some bad. And whatever decisions we make, we have to live with them. I know the kind of person Dónal is. I've witnessed it over the last twenty-six years. I also know the kind of person I am. The choices he made have consequences. As do mine. Which is why I'm going to have to live with knowing that I'm a daughter who believes her father deserves whatever consequences he receives, no matter what they are."

"Nessa." I wait until she lifts her head. "If there is anyone who deserves to be free to live her life as she chooses, without fear, it's you. I can make that happen for you, so I'm going to. There's nothing for you to feel guilty about or be sorry for or afraid of."

She laughs softly, the light in her eyes shining a little dimmer than normal. "One day, I might believe you."

"You will. I promise. I'm letting you go. Any debt Dónal owed me has been paid."

Nessa's brow wrinkles and she leans back, her fingers loosening their hold on mine and returning to her lap. "What do you mean?"

"I mean that you're no longer indebted to me. You can do whatever you please. Travel to America or any other place. Attend the theatre. Anything you want. I've put away some money—"

"I don't want your money." She jumps to her feet and her fists clench at her side. "Is that what our time together means to you? That you can *pay* me as though I'm some...?"

"Ness—"

She slashes her hand through the air. "No." The force of the word reverberates around us. She takes in a deep measured breath. "I won't take your money, Cian."

There isn't anything I can say that will make this better, so I say nothing at all. Nessa walks back to the chair and picks up her book. A familiar book. She clutches it tightly to her chest and stares at me for a moment longer. I return it, refusing to look away, so I can continue absorbing everything about her and committing it to memory. Her jaw clenches, and I wait for her to say something, but instead, she moves across the room and pauses at the door.

Then she turns around. "She and I chose the same thing."

I'm not sure what she means. My confusion must be evident, because Nessa lifts her book slightly. "She chose to let go of her old life and embrace the new one. The new...*love* she finds. I'm just glad she didn't end up with a broken heart. Like me."

And then she's gone.

CHAPTER 29

WHY DID NO ONE EVER TELL ME THAT WHEN A HEART breaks, the person actually feels it?

It's a stabbing pain in the center of my chest that takes my breath away. I lean against the wall outside Cian's hospital room. *How did no one hear it shatter?*

Just like with everything else in my life, I'll endure the pain of this, too. It's not as though I don't have decades of practice.

I stride down the hallway without a destination in mind. I'm supposed to call either Cian's brother or Caitlín for a ride to the estate, but I can't go back there. Not anymore. I wander through the hospital until I find myself out in front. The day shouldn't be as beautiful as it is. The sun should be hidden behind dark clouds and misty rain should be falling.

Who knew you were so melodramatic?

"Hello, Nessa."

My head snaps up and my heartbeat quickens at the sight of a man leaning against the front of a town car with his ankles crossed and his hands in his pockets. "Liam. What are you doing here? How did you know where to find me?"

He smiles, but it doesn't quite reach his eyes. I study him again. For whatever reason, I don't sense any ill intent from him, although I'm not sure I should trust my own judgment. It's obviously severely lacking. He cocks his head. "Trying to figure me out, are you? Others have tried and failed. I'm not sure you'll have any more luck than they did."

"Are you that complicated?"

"You have no idea."

I close the distance until only a meter separates us. Liam stares down at me, his face a bit harder, with more craggy edges than there were the last time I saw him.

"I missed you, you know. When you left." I laugh a little awkwardly. "I even cried when Dónal told me."

The muscles along his jaw flex and something flickers in his eyes. "Sorry you wasted your tears."

"They weren't a waste. You were my brother, even if you never let me be your sister. I loved you. I understood why you ran. Goodness did I envy you."

Liam jerks, but I almost missed it, the movement was so slight. "Like I said, wasted."

It's clear he won't believe anything different. "You still haven't told me what you're doing here."

"I came to see you, of course."

My head cocks. "Which goes back to my second question. How you knew where I was. Unless you're following me. Or maybe not me, but Cian, rather." Just saying his name hurts.

He palms his chest. "You make it sound as though I have nefarious plans."

"Nefarious, huh?" Despite his condescension, I'm not scared.

"I like to use big words sometimes. It makes me look smart."

I burst out laughing. "Yes, I can see how that would do it. What about this one? Prevaricating."

Liam smiles, and this time, there's a spark of amusement in his eyes. "I'm here because I thought perhaps I could give you a ride back to the Donnelly estate."

"That won't be necessary, but I appreciate the offer."

"It's no trouble. I mean, I'm already here, after all." That gleam of hardness is back.

"I'm not going back there." I'm proud of myself for getting it out without breaking down.

"Oh?" Liam quirks an eyebrow.

"I understand you took ownership of Dónal's house."

"I did, but I have no intention of living there. Sheehan is lucky I didn't burn the thing to the ground," he grinds out, his hatred evident.

"While I have no desire to go back there either, I don't really have a choice." I sigh. "I don't suppose you'd be willing to let me stay there? At least until I can find somewhere else to live."

"What happened with Donnelly? As I understand, there had been some sort of debt."

I snort, but my cheeks heat. *Some sort of debt.* Yes, something like that. "My virginity to cover a card game. Well, that's been paid, and I've been released from any obligations."

"I see."

"Yes, well. So, then, the house?"

Liam unfolds his massive frame and towers over me. "It's currently not in any condition to be lived in. I'll admit to having all of its contents removed and sold."

My heart drops, but I try not to let it show. "Everything?"

He hesitates, almost not even long enough to be noticeable. "Everything."

It all hits me at once. Being kidnapped. Beaten. Nearly raped. Waiting to hear if Cian will live or die and him turning around and breaking my heart. And then this. All my belongings...gone. My books. My *mother's* things. It's all just...gone. I have *nothing*.

A sob rips from my throat and my knees give out. Strong arms catch me before I hit the ground and cradle me against a hard chest. That only makes me cry harder, because it's not Cian's.

I hold my book even tighter and bury my face in Liam's neck, tears still pouring out. He carries me somewhere, and then we're in the backseat of the town car, driving away. I don't even care where he's taking me. All I can do is cry. I must doze, because we come to a stop, and when I open my eyes we're in front of a massive two-story house that spreads out across the property.

A throat clears, and I jerk upright. Oh god, I'm on Liam's lap and his suit jacket is soaked. "I'm so sorry."

He studies me. "You're not the first woman I've made cry, and I'm certain you won't be the last."

"Where are we?" I almost try and climb off, but with my luck I'll end up sprawled on the floor, so I remain still, even though this is so awkward.

I duck my head and peer out the window.

"We're at my estate."

I open my mouth to protest, but Liam holds up his hand. "You can stay for the night and make a list of things you'll need for your house to get you started. I'll make sure they're delivered tomorrow, and then you can return there."

"Why are you doing this?"

"I have my reasons."

It's obvious he has no intention of sharing them with me, either. I lean in and kiss his cheek. "Whatever they are, thank you."

Liam clears his throat. "You should probably get out now."

"Oh, yes, sorry." I scramble off of him and nearly tumble to the floor, but he steadies me with a hand. I mumble another thanks just as someone opens the door. I jump out and keep my gaze averted while he exits the vehicle with far more grace.

Liam straightens his suit coat and then heads into the house. Not having any other choice, I follow. The entryway is tiled in a black-and-white square pattern and the U-shaped staircase leads to the second floor. The fireplace against one wall is unlit. I stare at everything as he leads me into a large, sunken living space and gasp at the waterfall running down the wall into a small pool in the floor. He's certainly done well for himself.

"I'll show you to your room."

I close my mouth to stop gaping. He moves down a short hallway off the back of the living area. I peek in the open doorway of the first room we pass. It's a large bathroom with double vanity and walk-in shower. He pauses outside the next door and gestures for me to enter.

It's a beautiful room with a large bed covered in a cream duvet. At the foot of it is a narrow taupe settee. I walk around and take the rest of the furnishings in. A small and simple wooden desk is pushed against a wall with a cream chair tucked beneath it. Another cream accent chair is parked in front of a massive bow window that is nearly as tall as the ceiling, with a view of a well-trimmed hedgerow, its opening guarded on either side by tall stone plinths and a stone gargoyle perched on each one. I glance over my shoulder at Liam.

"Your home is lovely."

"Thank you." He bows his head. "Make yourself comfortable. I have some business to attend to, but if you're hungry or thirsty, help yourself to anything in the kitchen. It's behind the staircase off the entryway past the dining room. And if you need me for any reason, I'll be in my office in the hallway on the other side of the living area."

"I still don't know your reasons for helping me, but...thank you."

Liam's gaze holds mine for a second and then he turns and walks out. I stand in the middle of the room another minute and then sit on the edge of the bed, setting my book beside me. I caress the cover, and tears well in my eyes, but I sniff them back. I've done enough crying today. Liam said my tears were wasted on him, but I don't believe any tears are truly wasted. They can be cleansing. Healing.

I can't imagine what Cian would say if he knew I was with Liam. Although maybe that's Liam's goal. Maybe he has every intention of telling Cian I'm here. To taunt him. Lord it over him. This isn't the seventeen-year-old boy I remember, nor the serious, intent man I observed from afar when I was sixteen. Liam is so much harder. Angrier.

I'm going to trust that he isn't going to harm me. That he's going to do exactly what he says. Take care of having items delivered to Dónal's old house and let me return there tomorrow. Perhaps it makes me foolish, but like I told Cian, we all make decisions and then have to live with whatever rewards or consequences come with them.

I believe Liam is telling me the truth. His reasons might not be altruistic, but they're his.

I pick up my book and settle into the chair by the window. I've already finished it, but I'll reread it as though, this time, Mia won't make the same choice we both did.

CHAPTER 30

Cian

There's a short knock and Finn walks into my hospital room. He pauses and glances around. "Where's Nessa?"

I turn my head and stare up at the ceiling. "She left a couple of hours ago."

He comes and stands next to the bed as the door closes behind him. "What do you mean, 'she left'?"

My eyes close. I'm not in the mood to explain.

"Cian, what do you mean she left? She was supposed to call Caitlín or me to come get her. Except I haven't heard from her all day. I thought she was still here with you."

"Where's my phone?"

He rifles through my belongings packed away in a bag stored in the closet and drags it out. I snatch it out of his hand. No missed calls or texts. Did I ever give Nessa my number? I hit the speed dial for my cousin.

"I'm in the middle of something, so this better be important," she answers, panting like she's out of breath.

"What are you—? Never mind, I don't want to know. Did you pick up Nessa from the hospital?" Is that a thread of panic?

"Roarke, stop," Caitlín murmurs in the background. "Is she not there with you?"

Fuck. "No. I thought she was going to call you or Finn to come pick her up."

Loud rustling comes from her end. "Are you sure she didn't call Finn?"

"He's here with me and hasn't heard from her."

"Son of a bitch," she snaps. "Okay, no freaking out yet. Have you called Aidan or Uncle Carrick? Maybe one of them picked her up."

"I'm calling them now." Someone better have heard from Nessa.

I will raze this city to find her.

Before I can call Aidan, my phone rings, and an unknown number appears on the screen. "Donnelly."

"Have you misplaced something?"

A wave of red-hot rage burns through my veins. "Campbell, I swear to Christ if you hurt her, I will rip apart anyone you ever cared about. You'll be begging for death before I'm through with you."

"My, my, so blood-thirsty." The bastard chuckles and then it fades away. "It's a good thing I don't care about anyone then, isn't it?"

"What do you want, Liam?"

"I didn't realize we were on a first-name basis."

"What. Do. You. Want?" I don't have the time or energy for his fucking mind-games. All I care about is that Nessa is all right.

"Why do you assume I want anything? I'm not the one who lost something." He *tsks*. "You know, you really should take better care with your possessions. There are a lot of unsavory people in this world."

"I will bury you and piss on your grave."

"Stop being so dramatic. Nessa is fine and will remain so. In fact, she's comfortably settled in her room for the evening. I'm not sure what you did to her"—he pauses, and I clench my fist around the phone so hard I might actually break it—"but my suit is still drying from the tears she cried against my shoulder. Then again, isn't that what dear brothers are for? To comfort their sister when some bastard breaks her heart."

"If you so much as touch her—"

"Cian—I can call you Cian, right—since we appear to be on a first-name basis after all? There is only one woman I want to touch at the moment. And from my understanding, she is currently under your protection."

So that's what this is all about? This Imogen woman? "Fine, you want her? She's yours. Just let Nessa go."

Campbell laughs. "And they say I'm a cold-hearted bastard. Trading one woman for another? That's awfully callous of you. I mean, I could do anything I wanted to with Imogen. Or Nessa for that matter. She *has* grown quite lovely over the years."

"Name the time and place," I grind out.

"Tomorrow. Two o'clock. I'll call you twenty minutes ahead of time with the meeting place. The only two people who better be there are you and Imogen. I'd hate for anyone to get hurt if you try to double-cross me," he pauses. "I'll be sure to tell Nessa you said hello, by the way."

"Campbell?"

Silence.

"Campbell?" I throw the fucking phone across the room. "God damn it."

"What the hell is going on, Cian?"

"He has Nessa. Says she's fine, but he wants to make a trade." I blow out a fatigued sigh.

Finn's brow creases. "For what?"

"Imogen."

My brother gapes. "And you agreed? What the feck is wrong with you? Da will never allow it."

"There isn't any other way."

"There has to be." He runs his hand through his hair. "We just need to figure out what it is."

I feel like an invalid in this damn place. I've got to get out of here. If I'm going to lie in a bed all day, I'll do it in my own. My pain's under control. "I'm coming home. We can try to come up with another plan when we get there."

"Jaysus, you nearly died twice. Are you really going to try for a third?" Finn stares, his eyes narrowed.

"If it means making sure Nessa is safe, then I'll do whatever I have to. Even if it kills me."

AFTER IGNORING ANOTHER BITCH OUT SESSION BY THE doctor, and a stop by the hospital pharmacy, Finn and I are on our way back to the estate. Roarke and Nathan are meeting us there. The iron gate opens and we drive down the lane to the house. Several extra cars, include our enforcer's Vanquish, are parked out front. I reach across my body with my good arm and open the car door. Da greets us on the porch with resignation written all over his face. Still, he carefully hugs me at the top of the two steps.

"I'm glad you're home."

"It's good to be here."

He backs up and gestures for Finn and me to go ahead. "Everyone's in my office."

The three of us stride down the hallway towards the room at the end of it. The familiar scent of pipe tobacco grows stronger the closer we get. Apparently Da's been smoking again. Once inside, the smell of his favorite stout joins it. Nathan and Roarke are seated in the white, blue, and red striped wingback chairs that match the Donnelly Coat of Arms positioned on either side of the French doors. Aidan leans against the bar with a drink in his hand, half of its contents already gone.

Finn takes one of the other wingback chairs near the bookcase and I sit in the leather one in front of Da's desk. Da circles to the other side, but remains standing. "Cian, since you called this family meeting, you can tell us what it's all about."

"Liam Campbell called me a few hours ago."

"What did our new business associate want?" Da raises a brow.

I can sense Finn's stare boring into me, full of disapproval. "He has Nessa. According to him, she's unharmed and will continue to be."

"That bastard," Aidan spits out and unfolds his frame, setting his glass behind him. "When do we attack?"

My gaze turns back to Da. "We don't."

Dead silence follows my announcement. I don't take my eyes off Da.

"He wants something, doesn't he?" I suspect he knows what.

I nod. "He wants Imogen."

Da finally sits. "You know that's not going to happen, Cian."

"Unless we come up with another plan, it's already done. Tomorrow at two. No one else can be there or he hurts Nessa."

Da radiates disappointment. I don't blame him.

"Then we better come up with something."

"You don't need to," a feminine voice comes from behind me.

I spin in my chair and glance toward the door. A short young woman, around Nessa and Caitlín's age, with teal and purple streaks in her black hair stands there. She meets my stare straight on, and guilt pierces me.

"Imogen," Da says in a low tone and her gaze leaves mine and meets his. Something passes between them.

"Liam won't hurt me," she says.

Da shakes his head. "You don't know that."

"Yes, I do." She nods firmly. She believes it. Or perhaps she's only telling herself that. "He wants me because he sees me as a challenge. The fact I was able to leave right out from under his nose only made it worse. So if it means helping the woman Cian loves, then I'll go with him."

I open my mouth to deny it, but...I can't. The only reason I'd risk so much is because I love Nessa. I collapse back into the chair.

Imogen chuckles. "Didn't have that figured out yet, did you?" Her smiles fades slightly. "She's a lucky woman."

Da circles the desk and stops in front of Imogen. "You don't have to do this. We'll come up with something else."

"Don't worry about me. It'll be fine. Truly. I'm not afraid of Liam." She reaches out and squeezes his hands. "Thank you. After this is all over and I go home, maybe I'll see you again."

The tension in the room is thick.

Imogen glances around and laughs again. "Don't all stare at me like I'm about to die, for fuck's sake. Nothing that drastic is going to happen. Liam's just pissed I left. In the short time I was with him, I learned he's not a man who likes to give up any type of control. Once he gets the challenge out of his system, I'll go back to my life. Besides, I have no intention of making *his* life easy. By the time I'm finished with Liam, he'll be begging me to leave."

From the devious expression on Imogen's face, she might actually be telling the truth.

CHAPTER 31

Nessa

I take a final glance around the room. The bed's been remade, and the t-shirt and boxers Liam loaned me to sleep in lie folded neatly at the foot of it. I grab my book and small bag off the desk and head out to the living area. As promised, he arranged for the few pieces of furniture I ordered to be delivered today. They should arrive shortly after he takes me to the house.

Liam's on the leather sofa speaking to someone on his phone, and I only catch the tail end of the conversation before he ends the call. I step farther into the room, and he glances up. "You ready, then?"

Am I? Not at all, but I'll go all the same. I smile and nod. "Ready. Thank you again for letting me stay, and for lunch."

"Of course."

I'm finally free.

Dónal is dead or soon will be. This is my chance to live the life I always thought I wanted. Like Cian said, to do all the things I never got to do. Except why is that suddenly so terrifying? I keep my hands folded over my book in my lap so they don't shake as we leave Liam's estate.

"I need to make a quick stop first, if that's all right?"

"Of course." I almost breathe out a sigh of relief that our arrival will be postponed even if it's only for a short time.

The driver travels through the city and finally comes to a stop in front of a church. I duck my head and glance out the window gazing up at the spire that reaches toward the sky. Why's Liam stopping here? He turns to me. "I'll just be a few minutes."

I nod and he exits the vehicle. He adjusts his suit coat and strides up to the doors of the cathedral. I expect him to enter, but he doesn't. He simply turns around and stands there like he's waiting for something. I glance up and down the sidewalk and the breath leaves me. Coming around the corner is Cian and beside him is a woman. A beautiful woman.

My gaze darts to Liam. He's staring at them as well, his expression unreadable.

Unable to just sit here any longer, I climb out. My eyes meet Cian's, but I glance away. I'm standing next to Liam when the other couple comes to a stop in front of us.

"Together again, minx," Liam greets the woman, his intense stare locked on her.

My gaze bounces between him and her.

"Go fuck yourself, Liam."

I blink at the calm way she says it and the fact he does nothing more than smile.

"How do you two know each other?" And what does that have to do with Cian being here?

"Imogen is an old friend, aren't you?"

The woman barks out a rough laugh, but it is filled with disdain. "Why, Liam, are you actually afraid to tell Nessa the truth?" She turns to face me. "I'm your brother's prisoner."

Nothing about this makes sense. I turn to him. "Prisoner? What is she talking about?"

Liam doesn't say anything. Not a single muscle in his face moves.

"You got what you wanted, Campbell. We're leaving, but this isn't the end of things." Cian steps closer and gently pulls me to him. I blindly stumble forward.

The woman, Imogen, swaps places with me, but keeps her distance from Liam. Finally the confusion clears. With it comes white-hot fury. I move before Cian can stop me—before I can stop myself—and slap Liam across the face. "I *trusted* you."

He doesn't even flinch, and the red hand-print glows on his cheek. "That was your mistake. I told you you'd wasted tears on me."

I shake with rage. Cian yet again tugs me to him. Liam takes the few steps toward Imogen and wraps his hand around her upper arm. She jerks out of his grip and leaves him behind as she marches over to the waiting town car and gets into the backseat. With barely a glance our way, Liam follows, and as soon as he slides in beside her, the driver closes the door, climbs behind the wheel, and pulls away from the curb.

"Nessa."

Dragging my gaze from where the town car disappeared, I lift my gaze to Cian's. "Why would you do that to her?"

He flinches slightly at the accusation. "For what it's worth, she volunteered. But I was prepared to do what I needed to if it meant you were safe. I can't—won't—apologize for that."

I jab my arm behind me. "You didn't have to do that. Liam was taking me back to Dónal's house. Since he had it gutted, there was nothing left, so I ordered a bed and a few other things. They're being delivered today. You gave that poor woman to him for *nothing*."

Cian cradles my jaw. God, I've missed his touch so much. I'm too weak to move away.

"Do you really believe he didn't have this planned when you went with him?"

Do I? Liam said he had his reasons. But was *this* truly what they were? No matter how hard I try, and even after everything that just happened, I still don't want to believe it. I don't want to believe that I've now had my heart broken by the only two men I've ever loved. Regardless of his feelings, Liam has always been my brother and I loved him. "Take me to Dónal's house. Please."

Cian jerks back like I betrayed him somehow. "Why?"

"Because I have to see for myself." I need some kind of proof that my trust hadn't been misplaced. Because there had been an emotion in Liam's eyes when I slapped him—something that will take a while to forgive myself for. It had been regret. I'm sure I wasn't supposed to see it, though.

Cian nods and reaches for my hand. He threads his fingers through mine, and I let him. Because I can only deal with one thing at a time, and right now, that thing is Liam. We walk to his car.

Neither of us speak as he winds his way through the city. I stare out the window, but everything we pass is a blur. Finally Cian slows. I blink and focus on my childhood home in front of us. I stare at it. Study it.

Does it look any different than it did a week ago?

So much has changed since then. *I've* changed so much since then. It stands to reason that the house would too. Except...it doesn't.

It still stands there with an aura of sadness. Of bleakness. Almost none of the memories inside that house are good ones. There are a few, though. Mostly of when my mother was still alive, but sometimes I question if even those are real.

There is one difference, though.

The large delivery truck that several men are unloading.

I walk up to the front door. Behind me, a car door shuts. I step through the entrance and breathe in the familiar smells.

It's completely empty, just like Liam said. At least the entryway is. I doubt the rest of the house is any different. Cian comes up behind me.

Bong.

Bong.

Bong.

I follow the sound, passing empty room after empty room, until I come to a stop just inside my mother's sitting area where her favorite grandfather clock still stands. For some reason, Dónal never got rid of it after my mother died. I'd like to think it was because she loved it so much that he couldn't part with it.

I guess I'll never know.

"Liam told me he'd gotten rid of everything." I run my hand down the wood as the pendulum behind the glass swings back and forth and turn to Cian. "Of all the things to lie about, why this? It was my mother's favorite thing. Mine too. He didn't even know her."

He studies the clock, eyes scanning it, and then they're on me. "I don't know."

A throat clears from the doorway. I peek around Cian. A man in a delivery uniform stands there with a clipboard in his hands. "Sorry to interrupt. Are you Nessa Sheehan?"

"Yes."

He lifts his arm and drops it. "I need your signature."

"Of course." I cross the room and sign where he indicates.

The man dips his chin and walks away. Footsteps echo through the emptiness and then the house is quiet aside from the faint sound of the clock counting the seconds behind us. Only Cian and I are left. We need to talk, but I can't. Not after today. I'm wrung out. The hardwood floor creaks behind me and I turn. Cian stands far too close to me.

"I'm not ready to talk to you right now." I look him in the eyes.

There's a flash of pain in them and his mouth thins. "I shouldn't ask, but I'm going to anyway. When do you think you'll be ready?"

"I don't know. You hurt me. Just let me go, as though things between us hadn't changed. It wasn't all some grand seduction on your part and you know it. Then you gave an innocent woman to your enemy, because you thought it meant that I would be safe. I don't care that you say she volunteered. I was there, Cian." My voices rises slightly and I clear my throat. "Regardless of what she said, she didn't want to go with him. I saw it in her eyes. It was obvious she felt like she didn't have a choice though. And no woman, no matter who she is, should be given to a man against her will. After what Dónal did to me, I thought you, of all people, would understand that."

He knows what his touch does to me, so, of course, he'll use it to his advantage. Cian cradles my face between his palms. "I'm sorry I hurt you. More sorry than I've ever been in my life. I've never apologized in my life. Not to anyone. But I'm apologizing to you, Nessa. I thought I was doing the right thing by sending you away. You'd already been taken from me once. I didn't think I could survive a second time."

Cian's eyes scan my face. "Campbell is ruthless and will do anything to get what he wants. You saw that today. I was willing to risk your hate if it meant that he left you alone. The only way I could think to make him do that was to send you away. If he thought you didn't mean anything to me, then he wouldn't be able to use you as leverage against us. Against me. And no matter how much you might despise what I did, Campbell isn't above using people. Even women. I love you too much to let that happen."

Tears well and I step into Cian's arms, laying my cheek on his chest. He holds me close and I breathe in my favorite scent of ginger. I hug him tight, afraid to let go.

Except I do.

My arms drop, and I step away from him. "I love you, too, but I need some time. Alone."

His jaw muscles ripple and he swallows. "I'll give you all the time you need, Nessa. I'm not going anywhere. Ever. So, when you're ready, whenever that might be, I'll be here."

Cian walks through the house, and because I'm not quite ready to say goodbye despite telling him to go, I follow him all the way to the front door. He pauses and glances over his shoulder. "I love you."

All I can do is nod and raise my hand in a small wave, because a giant lump sits in my throat. One corner of his mouth turns up and then he's gone.

CHAPTER 32

Cian

I DRIVE DOWN THE NARROW LANE BISECTED BY A LINE OF grass and weeds that need tending. A large copse of trees provide a barricade. No nosy neighbors to bother a person. It's quiet out here in the countryside. The path continues winding through the near-forest, until a small, run-down building appears out of thin air. The rotted wooden structure almost leans in the direction the wind blows. No doubt someone could push it over with only a gentle nudge of their finger.

Parked beside the building is a gorgeous Vanquish. One Caitlín still has to beg or bargain to drive. I come to a stop behind it. Outside, I pause and breathe in the scent of sheep and cows. Twigs and dead leaves crunch beneath my feet until I reach an almost new door at the backside of the dilapidated ruin of a house. Or what is meant to appear that way to anyone who approaches. I enter a dimly lit room with no windows. I take the hallway that branches off to the right. Muted screams filter down the length of it.

I pause outside another door and knock four times. Only seconds pass and it opens. The scent of burnt flesh and blood assaults me. Roarke moves to the side and lets me pass. Dónal Sheehan lies naked except for his pants on a granite slab marked with dark stains around his bound and bloodied body. His mouth is gagged. I don't blame Roarke; I wouldn't want to listen to him, either.

"How's that new device working out?" I tip my chin toward the small box centered on a table next to Sheehan. It's one of the many new toys Pierce de Luca recommended for this room.

Roarke lifts a brow. "He's not dead yet, is he?"

Sheehan slowly turns his head my direction. His eyes are glassy with pain, and he whimpers. Probably because he knows why I'm here. I stroll forward and stop at the edge of the mounted slab. He stares up at me, and tears mixed with blood spill down his temples.

I bend close to his ear. I don't want him to miss anything. "How does it feel to be at the mercy of someone who abuses you day in and day out? To feel fear, never knowing when the next strike might come?"

Sheehan screams behind the cloth and his body writhes beneath the ropes. I straighten.

Roarke is slowly driving an ice pick through our prisoner's shoulder. Nearly the entire length of it disappears before he drags it back out, flips on the machine, and sets a wand to the wound. It sizzles and smokes. The stench of burning flesh fills the room. Faint cries still spill from Sheehan's mouth as sweat pours off his face, mixing with the bloodied tears. Once Roarke is satisfied, he turns the machine off.

I circle the table, keeping my eyes on Sheehan. "This is an ingenious device our enforcer learned about from my cousin's Italian relative in Brooklyn. He says he can torture a man for days, weeks even, without killing him. They just burn over and over again. Apparently they all beg for death before it actually comes."

I pick up the corded wand Roarke had set down, examine it, and return it to its place before glancing at Sheehan. "Did you know the

Italians all get a crown tattooed on the left side of their chest when they initiate into the organization? It's to signify their loyalty. When someone bearing that crest betrays them, they use one of those machines to burn the tattoo off the body before they bury it. It's quite a handy tool, if you ask me."

Sheehan mumbles behind the gag. I pull it from his mouth. "Please, just kill me."

"I'm not sure you've suffered enough to make up for the twenty years of abuse you dealt Nessa. Your own daughter. A daughter one of your piece of shit associates nearly raped. For what? Did it make you feel powerful? Significant?" I sneer. "Look at you now. Lying in your own shite. Desperate. Alone. Begging your enemy to end the pain you deserve. Not so powerful now, are you?"

Tears spill from his eyes. "Please, I'm sorry." he begs.

"You're sorry?"

Sheehan nods as a sob rumbles up his throat. "Yes, please tell Nessa to forgive me."

I punch him in the face. There's a sharp crack, his head snaps to the side, and he cries out. "I'm not telling Nessa to do fuck all. Because you know what? She doesn't forgive you. Never will. In fact, she was glad to know that soon you'll be dead. How does it feel knowing that your daughter—your own flesh and blood—doesn't even care if you die? You get to go to your grave knowing that the kindest, smartest, most loving person to exist in this world, not only hates you, but also fell in love with your greatest enemy."

Wanting this to just be over with, I snap up the ice pick and ram it straight through Sheehan's heart. His eyes widen and lock on mine and his mouth parts on a soundless scream. We stare at each other until the glaze of death moves in and his head lolls to the side.

"Didn't know you had it in you."

I lift my gaze to Roarke's. "Have what?"

"Mercy."

"That wasn't mercy. That was ending a man who wasn't worth any more of my time. He knew who had all the power in the end.

Besides, I didn't do it for him." I glance down at the dead body. "I did it for Nessa."

"How is she? Caitlín planned on calling her today to check in. Invite her out for dinner maybe, since I told her I'd be late getting home."

It's been nearly twenty-four hours since I left her at her former home. Everyone has been avoiding me since. Even Nora.

"Hurt. Angry. Told me she needed time." I slept in our bed out at the cottage, because it smells like her.

Roarke lays a hand on my shoulder. Something he never would have done before Caitlín. She's softened some of his rougher edges. "She loves you. It'll work out."

I hope he's right. "Thanks. You good here, or do you need me for anything?"

"I'm good. The pigs will do most of the work."

Not bothering to spare a final glance at the body, I exit the house and then I'm driving back down the narrow lane on my way home. I head straight out to the cottage when I arrive. Once I pour myself a drink, I sit on the couch and pull my phone from my pocket. I take a sip, savoring the oaky flavor. There's no better whiskey in Ireland than this one. Even our cousins in Brooklyn drink it. We have to ship bottles to them every few months.

I lean forward, set the glass on the coffee table, and rest my fore-arms on my knees to stare at the phone I'm holding. *Fuck it.* I unlock the screen, hit contacts, and tap on her name. Then I type out a short text message.

Mouse. I hope it's okay that Caitlín gave me your number. I thought you should know that I fulfilled my promise. It's done.

Set it down.

Except I can't. I keep staring, waiting for those three dots to appear. My heartbeat counts out the seconds. At seventy-three, they pop up. I sit up. They disappear. Then they're there again.

Nessa: Thank you.

I wait for more, but after another minute, no other messages come through. I lean back against the sofa with a sigh and toss my phone onto the cushion next to me. My phone pings. I snatch it up and swipe the notification.

Nessa: I miss you. I just wanted to tell you that. Goodnight.

"I miss you too."

Christ. I grab the glass of whiskey and down the rest of it in a single swallow, then take the glass to the kitchen. On the counter is one of her books. It's not the same one she'd been reading. The one she finished. I open this one to the page that's bookmarked, lean against the counter, and start reading from where it appears Nessa left off.

My phone pings again. Taking the book with me back into the living area, I pick it up. It's just a text from Aidan. I type out a short response and take a seat to go back to reading, but I open it to the beginning.

Page after page, I flip.

This is actually good. I'm not sure I've picked up a book since university. I do all of my reading online and that's mostly things related to business. I can't remember reading something for pleasure. My stomach rumbles and I groan. Reluctantly, I set the book down and grab a quick bite to eat. I also jump in the shower, but as soon as I have on a pair of boxers I sit back on the couch and keep reading.

The sun is just peeking through the windows I never shuttered last night by the time I finish. Hell, if this is the kind of novel Nessa reads, no wonder she loves books so much. I pick up my phone, check the time, hesitate, but then type out another text message.

C: I read the book you left on the kitchen counter last night. And this morning. Stayed up all night actually.

Not expecting an answer this early, I set it down and go into the kitchen to grab some breakfast. I warm several of the croissants Nora had made a couple days ago and poach three eggs. Once it's all done, I take my plate and sit on the sofa. I turn on the news while I'm eating.

Ping.

Muting the TV, I grab my phone.

Nessa: I hope that means you liked it <smiley face>

C: I'll admit to being a little surprised by the fact, but yes, I did. It was actually quite good.

N: You better not spoil it for me then. I haven't finished reading it.

I smile.

C: I wouldn't dare face your wrath by spoiling it.

My fingers hover over the screen without hitting send. And then I type again.

C: I'd be happy to bring it by later today if you want. Then, when you've finished reading, we can discuss it.

Before I erase the last part, I hit send. I don't want to push Nessa too fast, too soon, but I miss her. I miss holding her at night. I miss just talking to her.

Those three dots appear.

N: I'd like that.

Relief floods me.

C: How about one? I can bring us lunch. Pick something up from the Italian place. Mushroom risotto?

N: That would be lovely.

C: I'll see you then.

N: I'll see you then.

Those four words give me hope.

CHAPTER 33

NESSA

It's probably not the best idea to have CIAN come over, but I've had some time alone to process everything. Caitlín provided some details at dinner last night that had previously been left out. Why hadn't he told me? *Maybe you should have trusted him.*

I stand in front of the mirror and fluff my hair then smooth it down. I'm still in awe over the fact he stayed up an entire night just to read a book I'd started reading.

I glance over at my bed and what lies on it. When someone rang the bell yesterday, I'd been surprised. Had Cian come by? Instead, it was a young man somewhere in his teens, holding a package.

"Can I help you?"

"Delivery for Nessa Sheehan." He hands me the small item wrapped in plain brown paper.

"Who's it from?"

"Don't know, miss, was just told to deliver it." The young man nods and hops down the three steps before heading down the street.

I close the door and walk back to my room. Sitting on the edge of the bed, I carefully tear the paper off. Inside is my book. The one I'd accidentally left in the backseat of Liam's car after the whole debacle outside the church yesterday. I smooth my hand over the front cover and open it. A folded piece of paper falls out and floats to the floor. I pick it up and unfold it.

For what it's worth...I missed you, too, when I left.

~L~

Liam was right the other day. He is far more complicated than I could have imagined. I hope one day I'll be able to forgive him and maybe we can have some sort of relationship. Given the current situation between him and Cian's family, it's probably only wishful thinking on my part.

The front bell rings. I take one more quick glance in the mirror and then head for the door. I'd been glad to hear from our former housekeeper Deirdre yesterday. Thankfully she found another job quickly after Liam took ownership of the house. She told me she had only stayed working for Dónal because of me. Before we ended the call, we both promised to keep in touch with the other.

I pause as soon as I reach the entryway and take a deep breath. On the other side of the frosted glass stands a large shadow. Giddy excitement swirls around in my belly.

I've missed Cian. We have a lot of things we need to work through, but the only way we can do that is by talking. Neither of us are perfect, but I love him. Flaws and all.

I open the door. The sun shines down on him, brightening his auburn curls. In one of his hands is a take-away bag, in the other is a single, long-stemmed red rose, and tucked under his arm is a book.

"Hi," I breathe out.

That slow smile curls his lips. "Hi."

Neither of us say another for a minute. We just stare at each other. Then I blink. "Please, come in."

I step back and Cian strides past, his familiar and missed scent wafting around me. He turns and holds out the flower. "For you."

"Thank you." Taking it from him, I breathe in the sweet, floral fragrance.

It's a stark difference from the white lily he'd given me before. I'd looked up what it signified and almost laughed when I read 'purity'. Especially considering that had been the first night we'd had sex. Still, I'd been sad when its petals shriveled and fell to the counter.

"And also for you. Spoiler-free, of course." Cian chuckles and holds out the book.

My laugh matches his as I take it from him. "It better be."

"It's a beautiful day. If you have a place, we can sit and eat outside? I had them pack utensils just in case." Cian slightly lifts the bag.

"There isn't any furniture out there, but I've taken a meal or two on the terrace steps before. Otherwise, we can sit on the sofa." Thankfully I'd had one delivered yesterday.

"Steps are fine with me."

"Good. Let me go put this in some water and get us something to drink from the fridge. Then we can head out there. I'll be right back."

The sun hasn't risen high enough to clear the roof entirely, so a section of the terrace is still covered in shade, including the steps. But the breeze is warm enough to keep the chill out. I take a seat and Cian settles near me, placing the bag between us next to the bottled water I set down like a buffer, and then he pulls out the first container.

"Mushroom risotto for the lady." He passes it, along with a set of utensils, to me.

"Thank you, sir." When I take it from him, our hands brush, and a warm tingle travels up my arm. My eyes jerk to his. Judging from the expression on his face, he felt it too. Then again, it's always like that when Cian touches me.

"You're welcome." His voice is low and husky.

To distract myself, I open the container and take a bite. The long, uncomfortable silence slowly shifts as the familiarity of a pleasant meal together settles between us. I take a drink of water and swallow my food.

"How's your shoulder feeling? It seems to be better." There, that's a neutral enough topic, right?

"It still stings if I move it the wrong way, but it's fine. Nothing that time won't heal. Although I'll have another scar to add to the collection."

"I'm glad you're okay."

I understand violence is a part of Cian's world. I don't like it, but I understand. He's a member of a crime organization led by his father. They deal in dangerous things with dangerous men. Caitlín had told me about the time Roarke and his elderly neighbor lady had almost been killed by the Moroccans, not that long ago. Dónal had been more interested in drinking and gambling, trying to impress associates, than he had been in some of the more unsavory business aspects of our family's organization.

We finish our meal just as the sun creeps over the top of the house and shines directly down on us. I lean back on my hands and lift my face to the sky with my eyes closed and absorb the warmth. We don't get as many days of sunshine as I wish we did, so I make sure to fully enjoy the ones where we do.

"Roarke told me Caitlín was going to invite you out for dinner last night."

I sit up and glance over at him. "She did, and we had a nice time. I got to meet your cousin's wife Lucia as well. She's a lovely woman."

"No wild nights at a dance club, I hope? I heard rumors of one night the two of them were together and got a bit too drunk. Caitlín can corrupt the most innocent."

I laugh. "No clubs. At least not last night. Although, we do have plans to go soon."

Cian groans. "I'm not sure my cousin is the best of influences. Before you know it, she'll be teaching you how to cheat at cards and throw a punch."

Neither of those sound like terrible ideas. I have a lot of experiencing new things to do. I doubt I'll ever have any use for either of those things, but they're not the worst skills to have in my tool box, I suppose. "I guess we'll have to see. One thing we did do, though, was talk."

Neutral conversation time is over. Might as well get everything out.

"Oh?" Cian raises his brows.

"Why didn't you just tell me you had a plan to rescue her, instead of letting me believe the worst?"

He leans forward, rests his forearms on his knees, and stares straight ahead. "Because I had hoped you would trust me."

I lay my hand on his arm. "I'm sorry I didn't."

He slowly nods. "I understand why you didn't though. I'm not sure I've really ever given you any reason to."

We sit together in silence. "Do you know when you're going to go get Imogen back from Liam?"

"Tomorrow night."

Worry runs through me. Not only for Cian, but for Liam. I don't want either of them to get hurt. Imogen either. "You'll be careful?"

He turns his head toward me. "I swear."

"What happens next?"

He pivots his whole body in my direction. "With what?"

"With us."

Cian reaches out and takes my hands. "Whatever you want to happen. I love you, Nessa, but I know how much I hurt you, so I'm trying to honor your wishes and give you the time and space you asked for. I'm not always going to get everything right. I'll probably do things you don't agree with, but I promise to at least do my best."

I want it all, but I want to take things slow, too. We've done everything backwards. "Do you know I've never been out on a date? I mean a real one where the guy picks you up for a special night he has planned. I think I'd really like that."

Cian stares at me with a burning intensity. "Nessa Sheehan, will you go out on a date with me tomorrow night?"

I nod slowly. "I'd love to."

EPILOGUE

Four months later

MY NOSE IS PRACTICALLY PRESSED against the plane window as I stare out and take in all the giant buildings packed tightly together and surrounded on two sides by water. There, in the middle, is Stephens Green times fifty. My eyes widen at how big Central Park—how big *the city*—is. Aerial photos on the internet don't even come close to capturing the magnitude of New York City. I drag my eyes from the scenery and turn to Cian.

"This is where your family lives?"

He chuckles. "It's something else, isn't it?"

I go back to staring out the window. "It's magnificent."

All those millions of people walking around down there, living their lives, probably not even paying attention to the wonder around them. Of course New York isn't perfect. Caitlín prepared me, but I'm choosing to focus on the positives. I don't take my eyes off the skyline until the plane lands and we taxi to our gate.

Cian had booked our flight to make sure that we arrived when it was daylight, so we could sleep through the night and hopefully avoid jet lag. Plus, he wanted me to experience the city from the sky both during the day and at night when it's all lit up. I'm so wired with excitement, I'll probably be awake until tomorrow.

We make it to the bottom of the escalator when a familiar voice calls out my name. I glance around and there's Caitlín, waving her hands like a mad woman, with Roarke at her side. She rushes forward the second I step onto level ground and throws her arms around me.

"I'm so happy you guys made it. How was the flight? What did you think of your first view of the city?" She releases me and then grabs my hand to drag me away.

I laugh at the rapid-fire questions as Cian and Roarke fall into line behind us. "The flight was fine. Our layover was so long in Boston that we actually left the airport and wandered around the city for several hours. We stopped at this restaurant, and I got to try a lobster roll and Boston cream pie. I wanted to bring another slice with me onto the plane, but I wasn't sure if I was allowed."

"Wait until you try New York pizza and our bagels. There's this amazing bakery not far from my parents' brownstone, where they make the best garlic bagel I've ever tasted." She brings her fingertips to her lips and kisses them. "We'll have to walk down there one morning before you leave."

"I can't wait to try it all."

We make it to baggage claim and wait for our luggage. The four of us chat about the upcoming wedding. Cian and I were the only ones who came, but once Caitlín and Roarke get back from their honeymoon, they're going to have another small ceremony at home so the rest of Cian's family can attend. Once we have all our suitcases, we walk to the parking garage.

It's slow going from the airport to Caitlín's family home. There is so much traffic. More than once I have to close my eyes and pray a car changing lanes doesn't hit us. And so many horns honking. I'm not even driving, and my nerves are on edge. Unable to deal with the anxiety it's causing I put my back to the window and face Cian who's been chatting with Roarke and Caitlín.

"Thank you for letting us stay at your home, by the way."

She glances over her shoulder. "Are you kidding? Mother and Da wouldn't let you stay anywhere else. They're so excited to meet you. I've told them all about how wonderful you are, especially for putting up with this one here."

I snort. "Well, we really do appreciate it."

Finally, we take an exit off the massively busy motorway and enter a residential area with far less vehicle traffic. Staggered between homes are small businesses. Mobile stores. Restaurants. Boutiques with expensive-looking clothes displayed in the window. Some windows are even covered with bars. As we make our way through the streets, the homes become bigger and much more well-kept until at last, we come to a stop in front of a three-story brick building that sits back a bit off the street and sandwiched between two shorter ones. Trees and cars line the curb.

"This is it," Caitlín says.

The four of us exit the car. She loops her arm around mine while Roarke and Cian get all of our suitcases out of the boot. The front door of the house opens and a woman who is obviously Caitlín's mother steps out onto the patio with a huge smile. Then I'm tugged forward and up the narrow path toward her.

"Mother, this is Nessa. Nessa, my mother."

"It's lovely to meet you, Mrs. Donnelly."

To my surprise, she pulls me in for a hug. "Please, call me Moira. I'm so happy to meet you. Caitlín has told me all about you. My daughter Brenna loves books, so we have a library full of them. You're welcome to borrow as many as you'd like while you're here."

"Thank you so much."

She releases her hold on me and glances over my shoulder. "Cian, it's always great to see you."

He embraces her as well. "Same with you, Aunt Moira."

"Cormac and the boys are all at a meeting, but he'll be here for lunch. Come in and let's get you both settled."

Caitlín's mother leads us inside. The entryway walls and the hallway leading away from it are covered with family photos and the scent of fresh flowers greets me. To the left is an actual elevator. Moira presses the button and within seconds, the door slides open.

"You guys get settled. I'm sure you must be tired. We'll be around if you want to get together and chat," Caitlín says.

"Thank you."

Cian and I load our luggage inside, and Moira taps the button numbered two. "I've put you in Jack's old room since it's the biggest and has its own bathroom. The library is up on the third floor and you're welcome in there any time. We're having a family lunch out in the garden at one if you'd like to join us, but don't feel obligated if you're not feeling up to it. It won't be anything fancy. We tend to be pretty casual around here. In the middle of the floor is the door to the stairwell. If you're feeling like a bit of exercise, you're welcome to use it."

I'm experiencing a bit of overwhelm at the moment so all I can do is say, "thank you."

My gaze darts to Cian's and he winks at me. The elevator comes to a smooth halt and the door slides open. We all get out and Moira comes to a stop in front of door partway down the wide hallway. "Here you are. There are plenty of towels in the closet inside the bathroom as well as any toiletry item you might possibly need, but if there's something missing, don't hesitate to ask."

Once again she wraps her arms around me. "We're all really glad you're here."

I hug her back just as tightly, overcome with emotion. It's been so long since I've had a motherly hug. It makes me miss mine more than ever. "Me too."

Moira steps away and walks back into the elevator with a small wave before the two panels slide closed and she disappears from sight.

"It's a lot, isn't it?" Cian chuckles lightly and brings two of our bags farther into the room. "You get used to it after a while. Aunt Moira is like another mum to all of us."

"She is so kind." I get both our carry-ons and set them on the bed.

"Uncle Cormac's a bit gruffer and quieter, but he's a good man. You'll like him as well."

I've gotten to know little things here and there about Cian's cousins over the last few months. Between him and Caitlín I've been told so many stories about the entire Donnelly clan and their significant others; Jack and Rory, Paddy and Anya, and Brenna and Emilio whom she calls Jacob. Growing up an only child after Liam had left, I was always envious of people with lots of siblings.

"I'm sure I will."

"Other than being bombarded with affection, how are you feeling? I know it's been a long trip."

"I'm still pretty giddy over the fact that I'm really here. In *America*." I throw my arms out to the side and tip my face to the ceiling.

Cian laughs and then he grabs me around the waist, lifts me, and spins us around in a circle. I squeak and throw my arms around his neck. He sets me on my feet and kisses me until I'm breathless. I stare up at him and my heart is so full I'm afraid it might explode sometimes.

"I love you."

"I love you, too." He brushes my hair off my forehead in a sweet gesture that never gets old. "If you're not too tired then, why don't I show you around Aunt Moira's famed garden."

My eyes widen. "Famed, is it?"

Cian nods. "You'll see."

He threads his fingers through mine and leads me outside. I gasp. A stone path is bordered on either side by a mass of flowers in every color imaginable. We travel the direction the stones lead and are greeted with rows and bushes over-flowing with blooms.

"Told you. Wait until you see it at night, though. Aunt Moira has all these strings of lights she calls fairy lights that give this place a magical glow. It's incredible really. She's been adding plants and flowers and growing this place since Brenna married Emilio, so going on eleven years, maybe. It started out as only a small, simple garden until it became this."

My goodness. We continue strolling through the stunning foliage, but I stop to smell several different blooms. There's a large open space of lawn on the left-hand side of the house where a tall white tent is erected. Beneath the cover are white folding chairs. This is where Caitlín and Roarke will be married in three days.

From my understanding, the reception will be held here too, with more tables set out in the grass and a small dance floor will get laid under the tent for dancing later. I'm excited to be part of the ceremony. When Caitlín asked me to be one of her bridesmaids, I bawled with happiness. After all these years, I belong to a family.

Cian and I keep walking around the large garden. We're at the far back, out of sight of the house and near a giant trellis woven through with a rose bush in full bloom, when his hand drops from mine. I stop and turn back with a question. My whole body goes weak and tears well in my eyes. Cian is down on one knee. He reaches into his pocket and brings out a small velvet box that he slowly opens.

"I wasn't sure when I was going to do this, because I didn't know when an opportunity would present itself. And I know it's technically supposed to be Caitlín's week and all attention should be on her, which I'll never understand, but this just felt like the perfect time and the perfect place. I love you, Nessa. I love the fierce woman that you are. I love your warm and kind heart. I love your laugh. Your smile. I love that you make me want to become a better man for you. I love that you're my best friend who I can talk to about anything. The nights we sit together and spend the whole evening just talking and being with each other are my favorite time of the day. You're the woman I want to spend the rest of my life with. Mouse, will you marry me?"

I drop my hands covering my mouth and nod, the tears spilling down my cheeks. "Yes, I'll marry you."

Cian rises to his feet and takes the gorgeous sapphire and

diamond ring from the box. I hold out a shaking hand. He wraps his warm one around mine and slides the band down my third finger. The heaviness and weight of it is something I'll have to get used to. I throw my arms around him and kiss him with everything that I am.

When Cian showed up in the early morning hours of that day not so long ago claiming that I belonged to him, I never would have believed that he was was right. He owns my heart, body, and soul, just as I own his. Our life won't always be easy, not with the families we have, but together, we can get through anything. And there's no one I'd rather have by my side.

Thank you for reading **CIAN**. I hope you enjoyed it. I'd greatly appreciate a review on the platform of your choice. Reviews are so important!

Can't wait to find out what happens with Liam and Imogen? Get your copy of LIAM!

Doms of Club Eden
Submission
Desire
Redemption
Protect
Betrayal
Mistletoe
Absolution
Merry Eden

To Love and Protect
In Too Deep
Striking Distance
Atonement
Bullet Proof
For Always
Point Blank
Saving Evie

Brooklyn Kings
The Devil I Don't Know
The Enemy in My Bed
The Beast I Can't Tame
Irish Devil
Irish Rogue
Irish Charmer
Irish Rebel

Dublin Kings
Cian
Liam
Aidan
Finn

Other Books
Love Notes: A Dark Romance
SEALs in Love
Say Yes
Black Light: Possession

LIAM

DUBLIN KINGS, BOOK 2

CHAPTER 1

Imogen

If Stalkers Anonymous were a real organization, I'd be standing at the front of the room staring out over the assembly as they reply to my confession with, "Hi, Imogen."

Although maybe stalker is too strong a word. I like to consider myself more of an observer. A student, really, of life. Or, more specifically, of other people's lives. Just because they have no idea I'm watching them is beside the point. I lean back in my gaming chair and pluck at the torn leather of the arm rest. I should probably upgrade to something less tattered, but this one has the perfect imprint of my ass and it's comfortable. It's a pain breaking in a new one.

My gaze drifts to the giant computer monitor on my desk. One of many that fill my small inner sanctum I keep cut off from the outside world. On the screen are four video feeds separated into quadrants. Each square displays different angles of two different locations. And four different people I might have developed an unhealthy obsession with. I've tried breaking myself of it, but it doesn't last more than two or three days before I'm logging back in and stalk—observing—them again.

"Jesus, Imogen, you really need to get a life." I shake my head and force myself to turn off the feed.

My stomach growls, reminding me I haven't eaten since—I tap my phone screen to check the time—late last night. Since a significant number of my clients are American, my work hours are fucked. I grab my messenger bag, shove my laptop in it, snatch up my keys, and head for the door. Once I secure the lock and engage the security system, I gallop down the stairs at the end of the hall and slam open the exit.

Dawn hangs over the city, the sky a palette of pinks, purples, and blues. I breathe in the scent of fresh-baked scones and the citrus fragrance of my favorite tea from the bakery two storefronts down. The footpath is empty and only a delivery van is parked on the street. The brisk air sends a cold shiver across the back of my neck and down my spine. I should have snagged my scarf off the hook before I left.

Picking up my pace, I hurry toward the bakery and tug on the door handle. Warmth and delicious smells bombard me.

"Morning, Imogen," James calls out.

"Morning."

"The usual?"

I get to my regular table and plop down onto the seat. "You know it."

While he's making my tea and warming my scone, I bring out my laptop and set the bag on the chair next to me. I open the computer, unlock it with my fingerprint, and log in to check any messages left in my encrypted inbox. There's one from a client in Dubai. This young and reckless prince I've done a couple things for needs video wiped of him at a club with a woman who's not his wife. There's another from a spoiled heiress who wants a virus planted in her cheating boyfriend's computer. All boring stuff that, while the pay is decent, takes less than two minutes of my time. I'm in a rut and have been for a few months.

Ever since Mum died, and I discovered she's been lying to me for twenty-seven years.

"Order's ready, Imogen."

After closing my computer, I grab my breakfast with a "thanks" and return to my seat. For a moment, I savor my tea, the warmth of the cup heating my palms wrapped around it. I slather the jam and clotted cream onto my scone and take a few bites before brushing the crumbs from my shirt and hands, and opening my laptop back up.

The bakery door opens, bringing with it a gust of cold air that quickly dissipates as the door closes again, locking in the warmth, but I don't bother looking up. My focus is on my screen. I quickly take care of the two tasks waiting for me and have another bite of scone. With that done, I need to search for something else that will occupy my time. A few keystrokes later, I'm scouring the dark web for jobs.

A chair scrapes the floor, far too close, and finally, I glance up and blink. Then stare. Well, more like glare.

"Can I help you?" It comes out a bit snippy, but how else should I react to finding some bloke—albeit a fucking gorgeous one—sitting in the chair directly across from me, when there are ten other tables where he could have sat?

"Perhaps." That single word is a deep rumble that makes my lady parts suddenly pay attention. His full lips—the kind that would make any woman envious—curl up almost cruelly and then quickly flatten. There's a hardness in his bright blue eyes that sears into me.

I've never quite gotten rid of the toxic trait of being attracted to men who radiate danger. This man is screaming it. But I also hate men who play games—no matter how breathtaking they are—and there's a little voice whispering inside me that says he's most definitely playing one. I'm just not sure what the rules are. Considering I've been awake for almost twenty-four hours, I don't have the time or energy to find out, either.

"Well, get on with it. I'm kind of busy here."

His gaze drops to my laptop, no doubt judging my "F*ck the Patriarchy" and death metal stickers. He raises his eyes to meet mine again. "Yes, I see that."

I keep my mouth shut and continue staring, my fingers tapping an impatient beat on the table top. That cruel smirk comes to those lips again, and my belly flutters. He takes a drink from the cup in front of him, sets it back on the table, and stands. He buttons his perfectly tailored, pin-striped suit jacket, while his gaze never leaves mine. I try not to squirm under the intensity of those sapphire eyes.

"Enjoy your scone." He turns and strides toward the exit, his steps confident and measured. The broad shoulders that fill out his jacket perfectly block some of the light coming through the glass as he stops in front of it. His hand is on the door, and he pivots to glance back at me. "I'll see you again soon, Imogen."

It takes far too long for his words to register. By the time they do and I make it to my feet and across the length of the bakery, he's gone. I head to the counter.

"Hey, have you ever seen that guy before?" I ask James. "The one that just left."

"Yeah, over the last couple months he's been in a few times in the mornings. Usually comes in right after you do."

Creepy, much?

"Do you know his name?" It will make searching for him that much easier.

James shakes his head. "Sorry. I've tried making conversation once or twice, but he's the strong, silent type. I gave up."

I blow out a harsh breath. "Thanks, anyway."

Hadn't I just said I'm in a rut?

I have some digging to do. I pull up the security feed from the camera mounted outside the window of my workroom and start going through it.

There you are.

My mystery man gets out of the backseat of a fancy black town car. I zoom in and get a good view of the registration. The feed still plays after I've memorized the number. I reverse it to try and capture anything else, but there's nothing. The windows are tinted so dark I can't even tell who the driver is. Having gotten what I needed, though, I run some more code while I wait. I finish off my scone and grimace at the tea gone cold.

Finally, there's a soft beep and I key in the plate number and run the search. Within seconds, I get a hit.

Fuck me.

I open a new tab and run another search just to be sure. This one gives me the same result, just as fast. I stare at the man in the photo, whose angry gaze stares right back at me. It's no less effective than in person. As though he can see straight into my soul.

Liam Campbell. Aged thirty-seven. Stepson of Dónal Sheehan—not only the head of the second-most powerful family in Dublin, but also the bitter enemy of Carrick Donnelly, head of the Irish mafia.

Fuck me twice.

CHAPTER 2

LIAM

MY COCK IS STILL SEMI-HARD FROM MY ENCOUNTER WITH Imogen. The way she glared at me and her obvious irritation shouldn't arouse me, but it does. It's a refreshing change from the women who would suck me off just for a fraction of my attention. They all bore me. Every single one of them, with their tear-streaked faces and my come still drying on their lips as they realize I have no intention of giving them anything except that. They aren't worth more of my time than a quick fuck or suck before I send them away.

The driver comes to a stop in front of my office building and opens the door for me to step out. I button my suit jacket and tug down my sleeves. The cold Dublin air dances across the back of my neck, but I ignore the chill, glance around briefly, before climbing the three steps and entering through the front. It's too early for my assistant to be in, so the waiting area is empty and dark.

I cross the polished hardwood floor and head toward my office. Everything around me is kept clean and shiny. I make sure of it. I like to surround myself with luxury and only the best of things. I want business associates to envy what I have. The door to my office is cracked and the overhead light turned on. I pause before pushing it open the rest of the way.

"Don't you have your own bed to sleep in?" I put away the gun I'd drawn and glare at my cousin.

Declan doesn't move from his sprawled position on the chaise except to open one eye and then close it again. "But then I wouldn't see your smiling face. Besides, I'd been hoping to catch a glimpse of Ashlynn."

Normally, I'd let him attempt to seduce any of my assistants he wanted, but she's the first one I've had that I can at least tolerate and who hasn't quit within a week. "Leave her alone or I *will* actually shoot you."

He heaves a sigh and finally sits up. It's not an empty threat and he knows it. "Didn't you just go stalk your little obsession? You should be in a much better mood than you are."

"You're lucky you're my cousin." I round my desk and take a seat. The scent of new leather swirls around me. "Was there something you needed besides wanting to annoy me?"

Declan wipes away his amusement. He leans forward, resting his elbows on his knees and clasps his hands in front of them. "I wasn't sure if you had heard yet that your dear old stepda went to *Anamacha Caillte* last night."

"Of course he did." I shake my head in disgust but also in annoyance that I hadn't been informed. "How much did he lose this time?"

My cousin shifts in his seat. "All of it."

"Fucking bastard."

"There's more." Declan clears his throat. "He couldn't meet the bet with cash, so he wagered Nessa's virginity to make up the difference. His opponent took the deal and won."

"Who was it?"

He doesn't answer.

"Declan." It's a warning.

"Cian Donnelly."

My jaw clenches so hard, it's a wonder my teeth don't break. A better man would care that his much younger step-sister had just been used to pay a debt, but that's not what pisses me off. It's the fact that Dónal Sheehan lost more of *my* money to the Donnellys. Whatever pittance my worthless stepda has left is also my money. Just as soon as I take care of him. He has no idea how many of his men have turned their backs on him. Lost respect for him. Their loyalties have switched to someone who has what it takes to gain control of Dublin. Who doesn't give a fuck about truces.

That someone is me.

I've bided my time. Made more and more money, garnered high-powered business associates, and earned the respect—or perhaps, fear —of those who will soon belong to the most powerful organization in the city. The Donnellys have ruled for too long. It's time fresh blood reigns. I don't intend on that being Dónal Sheehan, Carrick Donnelly, or any of his sons either.

"Do you think he'll marry her?"

"Donnelly?" I huff out a breath. "Not a chance. He has no interest in aligning their families. They hate Sheehan nearly as much as I do. My guess is he'll fuck her a few times and then send her back to her loving Da disgraced. Virginity is a high commodity when it comes to alliances. Although I'll never understand why a man would want to deal with an unskilled lover who'll probably flinch and cry every time he tries to touch them."

Declan nods. "I assume then that this news doesn't change your plans in any way?"

"Why would it?"

"Sorry, I forgot who I was talking to. The man who doesn't care about anyone. Not even an innocent young woman—his *sister*— who's done nothing to him." My cousin sits up and leans back into the couch.

I stare at him, bored with this conversation already. "Nessa

Sheehan is not my sister, a fact of which you are well aware. You're also aware that your continued attempts at being my conscience are pointless. Because you're right. I don't care about anyone."

Declan scoffs. "Not even me."

"Not even you."

He stands and studies me. I merely return his stare, not flinching under the disgust he can't control in his expression. With a small shake of his head, he turns and heads for my office door. He pauses just as he reaches it and glances back at me.

"You know, I used to look up to you when we were growing up. Both Aran and I did." Declan laughs harshly. "Not anymore though. I'm not sure when you changed, but this new you? I don't even know who you are. Best of luck with your little coup. I hope it brings you some measure of happiness. Although I'm not sure you even know what that emotion feels like."

Declan walks out the door, not even bothering to close it behind him. I continue sitting there while his footsteps fade the farther away he gets until, finally, they—and he—are gone. His contempt stings a little. If I did care about anyone, it would be him and his brother. The three of us had been close once. But that time has passed, and the only person I care about is myself.

I unlock the top right desk drawer, open it, pick up the manila envelope lying on top, and set it in front of me. For a second, it remains unopened.

I've memorized its contents. Still, I reach inside and flip through each of the photographs.

The subject of them is far more vibrant in person than in this flat, two-dimensional rendering. The purple and teal streaks that add color to her shoulder-length black hair. Those bright blue eyes that sparked annoyance at my intrusion of her personal space this morning and made my cock hard. Still makes it hard. I can't wait to sink deep inside her cunt. And I will, too. No doubt her eyes will spit more than just irritation. I'm actually looking forward to it.

Setting the pictures down, I glance at the paper with minimal details on it. Imogen Walsh. Twenty-seven years old. Mother: Maire Walsh (deceased). Da: Unknown. An address is also listed. Graduated at the top of her class from University College Dublin with a degree in computer science. Other than that, I haven't been able to find anything else out about her. Declan isn't far off, calling her an obsession. From the first moment I laid eyes on her, she'd unknowingly drawn me in. I've wanted her ever since. And I always get what I want.

CHAPTER 3

Imogen

The ear-splitting alarm jolts me awake. I grab my phone from the nightstand and shut it off. Not ready to get up yet, I roll onto my back with my eyes closed. Dreams of Liam Campbell plagued my sleep. Some were terrifying. The majority of them, however, elicited a far different reaction. A throbbing heat low in my belly returns as I recall the vivid images of sweat-slicked bodies writhing together. *Don't forget who he is.*

He isn't classically beautiful. In fact, there's a harshness to his features that some might find unattractive. His skin isn't smooth and unblemished. It appears rough and rugged beneath the close-cut beard. Still, he is a striking figure with his full lips, piercing blue eyes, thick brows, and overly-long hair that sticks up just the slightest bit in front. Don't get me started on the way he filled out his jacket. I may not have the best fashion sense, but I can pick out an expensive suit anywhere. Which makes sense considering who he is.

What did he mean he'd see me again soon? More importantly,

how did he know my name? I still can't figure that out. My second phone rings. The completely secure one I use for business. Liam will have to wait.

"Maddox." The built-in digitizer disguises my voice.

"It's Donnelly. Got a job for you."

I sit upright on high alert. For nearly ten years I've been doing various jobs for Padraig Donnelly. He's one of my highest paying clients and always hires me for things that utilize some of my best skills. It's crazy I didn't connect his relationship to Carrick Donnelly until five or six years ago. Then again, Padraig does live in Brooklyn.

"What do you need?" I rush across my bedroom and grab my laptop from where I dumped my bag when I got home from the bakery before I crashed.

My fingers fly across my keyboard as he gives me the details of the job. Adrenaline pumps through my veins and wipes away any sleep that still remains. Finally a task worth doing. Not just for the money either. "Give me a couple hours, and I'll have something for you."

"Payment is already on its way to your account."

I end the call and get to work. Of all the jobs I've done for him, this is certainly one of the easiest, but still hard enough to let me flex my skills.

Everyone in Dublin is aware of who the Donnellys are. Mostly because they run the largest crime syndicate in the city. They have the Gardaí in their pocket, so the authorities look the other way. They also run the most successful—and exclusive—casino in Dublin. Generally speaking, gambling is illegal. But they've gotten around the law through a couple loopholes.

My laptop pings, and I sit forward to analyze the data on my screen. I enter more code and let it run. Hopefully, it doesn't take too long. There's nothing I can do until my program finishes, so I hop in the shower, throw on a thermal shirt and my favorite pair of black jeans. The hardwood floor is cold under my feet, so I grab an old pair of wool socks Mum bought me for Christmas one year and sit on the edge of my bed to put them on.

Tears come to my eyes as I stroke the slightly scratchy material. Grief is weird. I'm still angry at her for keeping secrets from me, but I miss her so much. She'd been all I had, my best friend. Swiping away the tears, I put the socks on and head back into the bathroom to comb through my hair. I stare at myself in the mirror, picking apart my features. Annoyed that I still look like myself, I go out to the kitchenette and boil some water for tea. Just as the timer goes off on my electric kettle, my computer pings.

I pour myself a cup, grab a couple biscuits off the counter, and head over to my small table and computer. Taking a seat, I start typing, and within seconds, I've got bank accounts loaded onto the screen. I scan the transactions, trying to locate the ones of interest. I run a search, but nothing comes up. Still, I keep searching.

Fifteen minutes later, I've got nothing. I key in a couple more queries. It takes me far longer than it should, but finally, I get a hit.

"Gotcha."

Grabbing my work phone, I call Padraig back.

"Your friend has an offshore account with a long list of transfers from a bank in Poland. Each deposit is for the same amount and arrives in regular intervals. I'm still waiting on confirmation of the owner of the Polish account, but the money is definitely being transferred in."

"Thanks," he says. "Let me know when you have an identity."

Another ping comes from my laptop. "Looks like it's all coming from a corporation called Grupa Polska."

Not very imaginative of them.

"Got it, thanks."

"I'll let you know if anything else comes up." I end the call and set the phone on the table beside my cup of tea that has, no doubt, gone cold. Damn it.

I snatch up one of the biscuits and shove it in my mouth while I reheat my drink. Once it's hot again, I waste no time drinking it down, savoring the slight citrus flavor. There are only two things I splurge on: tech and tea. Probably because they're the two things I can't live without.

After I finish off another cup and the second biscuit, I throw my hoodie on over my thermal, shove my laptop back in my bag as well as my cell phones, and walk out the door. Once the security alarm is set, I head downstairs. I spend more time out of my flat than I do in it. Probably because I want that space to be my sanctuary away from work. That call from Padraig was unusual. It's still barely dawn in the States. I've normally made it to my workroom before any calls come in.

The cold wind hits me the second I step outside. I pull my hood up and tuck my hands inside my sleeves and front pocket as I make my way down the walkway toward the internet cafe where I start my day before spending the rest of it at my main base. Mum was always disappointed that I don't have some fancy corporate job, but instead choose to do freelance work. The pay is less, sure, but I more than make up for it with off-the-books jobs I'm hired for by people who aren't always stand-up citizens. I'm choosy about who I work for, though, even if half of them are criminals. I do my research before accepting a job from just anyone. The nice thing is, most of my new clients come my way through a referral from an existing one. Being my own boss is a definite perk. Granted, the hours suck, but it's something I can live with.

I cut through the narrow passageway between two buildings. The scent of cooked meat wafts around me as well as rubbish as I pass a few bins. It's usually pretty empty this time of day and it's the quickest route to the cafe. I hop over a puddle of water gathered beneath a rainspout. The wind is still blistering cold and blowing straight into me. I keep my head tucked down to try and ward some of it off. I'm so focused on the ground, I miss the massive barrier in front of me and collide with it.

"Shit, sorry." I tip my head up and freeze.

A suit-clad man with a large, mottled scar across one whole side of his face stands there. Trying to bluff my way past, I apologize again and force my feet to move and walk around him, but he sidesteps and blocks my path. "Mr. Campbell would like you to come with us."

Walking the streets alone at crazy hours of the night, I've learned not to act intimidated, so I stand as tall as I can, which isn't much considering I barely come up to his chest. "You can tell Mr. Campbell to go fuck himself. I'm not going anywhere with you."

Is this what he meant this morning by 'seeing me again'? That he was going to send one of his goons after me? The question is why?

"I don't want to hurt you." He takes a step forward—closer— and I turn to run.

Except I don't make it far. I slam into another brick wall.

I open my mouth to scream, but a hand claps over it, muffling the sound, and an arm wraps around my waist, lifting me off my feet. I'm held against a hard chest. I kick and flail, reaching back to try and punch the guy holding me. His hand is so big, not only is my mouth covered, but so is my nose. I can't breathe. Still, I try everything to get away until my strength flags and my vision turns black.

CHAPTER 4

LIAM

My phone buzzes, and I check the message.

Finally, they're back. I make my way to the front door and open it for the new arrivals. First Craig steps past, carrying a black messenger bag, his expression blank. Next is Darragh. Slung over his shoulder is a body. I'm guessing she gave them some trouble.

Why am I not surprised?

"I'm going to assume she's merely drugged and not dead?" I ask drily.

"Yes, sir."

"Place her in the bedroom attached to mine and lock the door on your way out." He walks away. "And Darragh, I'd take care with her if I were you."

He nods and disappears down the hallway. I hold my hand out to Craig who passes the bag to me. "Anything of interest?"

He follows me to the kitchen. "Just a laptop, keys, and a couple phones."

Why does my lovely guest need two phones? I reach inside for the laptop first, set it on the counter, and open it. Without a fingerprint, this is as far as I'm getting, it would appear. I shut the top and bring out the cell phones. Both are locked with facial recognition. Clearly someone has trust issues. Something we have in common. Darragh returns as I place the items back in the bag.

"Is my guest settled?"

"Yes, sir. She was just starting to come around."

"I take it she didn't come quietly?" Which should be obvious considering the condition he brought her in, but I want to know what to expect when she wakes. Fear or rage? I'd prefer the latter rather than dealing with tears.

Craig coughs and Darragh glances away before meeting my eyes again. "I believe her exact words were 'you can tell Mr. Campbell to go fuck himself'."

The silence hangs for a beat and then I throw my head back and laugh. My two men share a glance. I'm not one for laughing. They probably didn't think I even knew how. It does sound a bit rusty. But at least my question has been answered. I should expect one pissed off woman when she finally awakens. And based on the banging and yelling that reaches me, that would be now.

"That will be all." I dismiss the two men, who leave with a brief nod.

Taking my time, I wander out of the kitchen and through the rest of the house toward the pounding punctuated frequently by swear words I've never heard before. I enter my bedroom, unlock the connecting door, and lean against the open doorway.

Imogen stands at the other door, slamming her fist against and then kicking the locked barrier. Her chest heaves and obscenities spew from her mouth.

"You fecking cock-knobber, open this goddamn door before I shove my foot straight up your arsehole."

I barely hold back my chuckle, although my lips do curve.

Standing upright, I stride across the room and stop right behind her. "That's quite the gutter-mouth you have."

Imogen whirls with a screech and throws a punch at my face. I catch her fist easily and dodge the knee headed straight for my cock so it hits my thigh. Using my hold, I spin her around and push her against the door, covering her body with mine. She bucks against me, cursing over her shoulder, her words garbled from her cheek pressed to the wood, but clear enough to make out.

"Let go of me, you cretin. I swear to god, I'm going to murder you."

I grind my rock-hard cock against her ass. "Don't threaten me with a good time, minx."

Imogen freezes. I lean closer and breathe in her scent. Her jaw clenches. I can only imagine the amount of control she's using to not curse me out again. This is going to be a lot more fun than I expected.

"As much as I'm enjoying our current position, I'm sure you'd prefer we continue this conversation face-to-face. Are you going to behave if I let you go?"

She nods. With great reluctance, I loosen my hold on her and take a couple steps back. Imogen spins and glares up at me. "You're a dick."

"You've just been taken captive by two strange men and delivered to another stranger's home. Although it sounds as though you knew who I was when Darragh and Craig...detained you. I could do any number of depraved things to you. Yet, you're not showing any fear."

Imogen tugs her sweatshirt down and shoves her way past. I turn and track her lush ass as she moves farther into the room. She rounds on me. "*Detained me*? Is that what they're calling kidnapping these days? Besides, why should I be afraid? It's not like you're going to chop me up into little pieces and dump them in the Liffey."

"This is true." I pause. "I'd probably choose the Bay."

For a second, there's a flash of fear in her eyes, but she clears it and continues glaring with her arms crossed. The bulky clothing doesn't hide her tits. "Why am I here?"

Normally, I don't care for a mouthy woman, but on Imogen, it's such a fucking turn on. I want more of her fire. "You're here because I want you to be."

She gapes. "Are you fucking serious? You just grab any woman off the street because you *want to*?"

I lean back against the door and cross my ankles. "I didn't grab any woman. I specifically grabbed you. And I always get what I want."

Imogen swivels her head back and forth and throws her arms up in the air. "You're a fucking lunatic. That's not how things work." She strides forward until we're toe-to-toe. Her head tips back as she stares up at me. "Move. I'm leaving."

"I'm afraid that isn't going to happen. Not until I'm done with you, anyway. Then you'll be free to leave. Until then, you'll remain here as my guest."

She fists her palms and screeches. "God you are infuriating. Fine, if you're going to hold me captive, then at least give me my bag. Your lackeys *did* bring it, didn't they?"

I nod. "Your things are safe and sound. However, you will need to earn the privilege of having them returned."

Imogen snarls. "I'm not fucking you just to get my shit back."

"Oh, don't worry, you'll fuck me because you want to and not for any other reason."

She makes a sound of disgust. "You really are a nutter, aren't you? There's not a chance in hell I'm going to want to fuck you. You're holding me captive, in case you have forgotten."

I move forward and for each one step I take, Imogen takes two backward until she collides with the corner post of the bed. She goes rigid but holds her ground. I stop when my chest brushes hers. Blue eyes are filled with hatred, but a lesser man wouldn't notice the flicker of a deeper emotion behind it or the catch of her breath. I palm the back of her neck and thread my fingers through her hair before slowly lowering my head to brush my lips across hers. A tease really. Merely a prelude of what's to come.

I'll give her credit. She tries not to react, but beneath my thumb, her pulse races. I flick my tongue out and at first she resists, but I continue my gentle coaxing until she opens sweetly for me. Beautifully. Oh, yes, I'm going to enjoy seducing, and taming, this fiery minx. I deepen the kiss and Imogen meets my tongue stroke for stroke. She tastes of shortbread with a hint of citrus. It might be my new favorite flavor. I draw back after taking one final lap of her sweetness. She slowly opens her bright blue eyes that have gone dark with arousal.

"I could fuck you right now. Couldn't I?" I can't help but goad.

Her emotions change in the blink of an eye and the arousal is replaced with fury. Her body vibrates with it. God, she is glorious in her rage.

"Get. Out."

I dip my head in a mocking gesture, a smirk shifting across my lips, and go back through the open doorway to my room. I close the door behind me and turn the lock. For a minute, I stand there, straining to capture any noise coming from the other side, but it's completely quiet. No sobs. No angry tantrum. Only the silence.

I'm tempted to pull my cock out and stroke it to release, but I have more self-control than that. Instead, I head for my office, where I finalize plans for my takeover.

CHAPTER 5

IMOGEN

THE LONGER I'M LOCKED IN THIS ROOM, THE MORE PISSED I get. A feat I didn't believe possible. There isn't a clock in here, but based on the fact that it's dusk outside, I'm guessing I've been in here for at least four hours. Thank god I have a bathroom. Someone also kindly left a bottle of water. *How nice of them.* That doesn't change the fact that I haven't eaten more than my scone since this morning and a couple biscuits and I'm fucking starving. Which is only making me hangry.

I slam my fists into the mattress and growl. My feet had gotten tired standing and pacing. So even though I'm bored out of my goddamn mind, I've been sitting at the head of the bed with my knees pulled to my chest ever since—stewing. Alternating between glaring at both locked doors and plotting how to get out of this damn place. And when I do, Liam Campbell is going to regret taking me. Already, I've figured out what organizations I plan on donating all his money to when I hack into his bank accounts and drain them dry.

I've already cried twice. Not because I'm scared—although I am certainly that—but because I'm furious. Aside from Mum's funeral, the only time I ever cry is when I'm rage-filled. And being kidnapped off the street, held captive in a dangerous man's home, belongings withheld, and not given proper sustenance is enough to make any girl rage-y. I'm also pissed at not only Liam, but myself for that kiss. And how much I liked it.

A lock clicks. I freeze.

The door opens and he strides through. Gone is the expensive suit jacket and tie. Instead, the top few buttons of his white dress shirt are undone, and his sleeves are rolled up exposing his forearms. The right one is decorated in colorful tattoos that climb upward and disappear beneath his shirt. How far up do they go? *You're pissed off, remember?*

Who cares?

"If you behave yourself you can come out to the dining room for dinner."

I grit my teeth. "Do you treat all your prisoners like a child who's been sent to their room or am I the lucky one?"

That smirk I want to punch off his face returns briefly. "Is that how I've been treating you, then? Like a child? Because that's certainly not how I see you. I'm more than happy to demonstrate again if you need reminding."

There's a small flutter in my belly that votes yes for that, but I only give him a patronizing smile and climb off the bed. I hate giving in to his little game, but my stomach is the one in charge at the moment and vetoing every decision except the one that ends with being fed. I move across the room and sweep past him without a word. I brace for him to grab me or stop me in some way, but when nothing happens, I continue walking. His footsteps follow me.

The hallway is brightly lit by recessed lighting in the ceiling. The full length of the wall to my left is made entirely of glass. I pass a single door on my right. The passageway opens to a large, contemporary sunken living area with a massive fireplace and sleek black furniture. The warmth is comforting. I nearly gasp at the water cascading down another wall.

"Welcome to my home." Liam strides past me, since I've stopped in the middle of the room to admire the indoor waterfall.

I don't want to find anything appealing about my prison. Forcing my gaze away, I follow him as we cross the entryway with a white-and-black marble floor and spiral staircase leading to the second level and into the next room. Finally the delicious scent of food hits me. The dining room table is set for two people. One at the head of it and the second at the seat to the right. A covered baking dish is set between them.

"Come. Sit." Liam gestures toward the table.

For a brief second, I'm tempted to move the place setting to the opposite end, but I don't want to jeopardize my chances of eating. I'll pick the battles worth fighting. Once I'm seated, he does the same. "Please, help yourself. It's my famous shepherd's pie."

I shoot him a quick glance. *His shepherd's pie?*

Liam's eyes widen innocently. "What, you don't believe I can cook?"

"I hadn't given it any thought, actually." Without waiting for him, I dig into the generous helping I dipped out onto my plate. Oh my god. It's delicious. Refusing to give him the satisfaction of seeing how much I'm enjoying it, I keep my expression as blank and as bored as I can.

"Is the food not to your liking?" There's almost a mocking tone to his question, as though he knows quite well it is.

"It tastes like shepherd's pie." I manage a shrug trying for nonchalance. "Considering I haven't eaten since your creepy stalker visit to the bakery this morning, I'm sure anything would taste good at this point."

His face darkens. "That was over twelve hours ago. Why haven't you eaten since then?"

"Oh, I don't know, let me see. Your goons kidnapped me off the street on my way to get food, and I've been stuck in a locked room for fucking hours. Why do you think?" My words drip with disdain. Not that I expect Liam Campbell to feel an ounce of guilt, but whatever scrap of decency he *might* have in him, well...I hope he chokes on it.

To my surprise, he doesn't have a rebuttal. Instead, his expression clears and he dishes out his own helping. The rest of the meal is eaten in silence. Which is fine by me. I'm not sure I could speak civilly anyway. For the moment, I'll play nice—or as nice as I can make myself play—and when he gets bored, I'll go home.

Despite my head start and my hunger, Liam is finished before I am. He sets his silverware on his plate and pushes it away from him. He rests his clasped hands on the edge of the table. "Did the clothes in the closet fit?"

I'd inspected the entirety of the bedroom and bathroom I'd been given after he had left earlier. A ridiculous amount of women's clothes—none to my taste—were hung in the closet. If they were there for me, then my captor doesn't know shit about me.

"Don't know. Didn't try them on," I mumble through a mouth full of food.

Liam's jaw clenches and he inhales deeply through his nose like he's trying to breathe in patience. "May I ask why not?"

"Sure." I set down my own set of utensils and swallow that last bite. "For two reasons. One, there was nothing in there that I even remotely liked. And two, I'm not wearing clothes you provide like I'm some little doll you can dress up."

"I see."

Unable to sit here any longer like we're a normal couple having a nice quiet dinner at home together, I toss my napkin onto my empty plate and rise from the chair.

"Where do you think you're going?"

"Back to my prison cell," I call over my shoulder, already walking away.

A chair scrapes across the floor behind me, but I don't stop. Liam grabs my arm and I turn on him with a hiss. "Get your hands off me."

"You seem to think you're the one in charge here. Maybe you need to be reminded that I'm the one in control."

I jerk my arm, but his grip doesn't loosen. "So, what? Are you going to rape me now?"

He sneers. "I think we already established that I don't have to resort to rape."

"Go fuck yourself."

"The only person I'm going to be fucking is you." He yanks me against him, wraps his hand around the back of my neck, and slams his mouth down on mine in a blistering kiss full of fire and rage.

It's a battle of wills, both of us trying to prove a point, and neither of us wanting to concede. Except I can feel myself giving in to the pleasure. The desire. I whimper, almost pleading for more. Liam's beard scrapes my skin in the most delicious way, abrading it harshly and sending a spark of pleasure-pain dancing through me. I bite him—hard—but he only deepens the kiss. The warm, briny flavor of his blood glides across my tongue. It's the taste of it that brings me to my senses. I rip myself from his arms.

We stand there, panting, and glare at each other. Shame creeps up my neck, heating my flesh. Liam's tongue flicks out and laps up the bit of blood spread across his bottom lip. That tiny movement makes my pussy throb, as I imagine him licking me instead. Sliding through my wetness, drinking it down. Feasting on me like I'm his favorite dessert. A shiver runs over me and a knowing glint flashes in his eyes.

"Go ahead and run away like a scared little girl," Liam goads me. "We both know, though, that when you go to sleep tonight you'll be dreaming of me fucking you hard and fast. And when I'm lying in bed stroking myself, I'll be thinking of you."

My face flames, both from rage and embarrassment, and without another word, I spin and rush out of the room while his mocking laughter chases me the whole way.

CHAPTER 6

LIAM

IGNORING THE SPUTTERING HOUSEKEEPER, I STRIDE through the front door of Dónal Sheehan's sprawling manor house as though I own the place. Which I will, as soon as this meeting is over. Behind me are Darragh and Craig. Our footsteps beat a rhythmic staccato on the hardwood floor. God, I hate this fucking house. Always have. It's cold and emotionless. For someone like me, it should be perfect then. Instead, it only serves as a reminder of its owner—former owner anyway. If my dear stepda is lucky, I might not burn it to the ground.

The door to his office is partially closed. Without even pausing, I push it open the rest of the way and keep walking in. Sheehan sits behind his desk with his gaze focused on a stack of papers in front of him. He jerks his head up at the intrusion, taking in the two men who follow and flank me on both sides. His eyes narrow, and his lips curl in a familiar sneer that fans the flames of my hatred.

"Always the uncouth mongrel, aren't we, Liam? Barging into a man's home like he's the king of the place. Couldn't even come alone, like a real man. Worried I might teach you some of the same lessons I did when you were a little brat?"

His insults roll right off me. I merely offer a faint smile, because there'd been a slight waver of apprehension—of fear—behind them. So slight, I'm not sure if anyone else took note of it. I stride closer, unbutton my suit jacket, and take a seat across from him. In a lazy gesture, I sit back and cross my ankle over my knee. Sheehan bristles at my lack of reaction and the disrespect.

"I'm going to give you two choices." I stare straight into his eyes. "You can vacate the premises with your pride barely intact or when my men drag your corpse out of it."

Red climbs up his porcine face, giving his cheeks a ruddy appearance. His eyes flash with rage. "You dare come into my house and threaten me? I don't think you know who you're dealing with. You're a dead man."

Sheehan jerks open a side drawer, but before he can bring out the gun he keeps stored in it, there are two weapons trained on him. His eyes widen, and he slowly brings his hands up to rest on the desk surface.

"You see, Dónal." I rise from my chair and casually button my jacket. "While you've been losing your fortune, I've been amassing mine."

His wary gaze follows me as I slowly circle behind him.

"While you've been losing the respect of your men, I've been gaining it." I place my hands on his shoulders. He goes rigid. I squeeze the tiniest bit before I clap the right one, and Sheehan flinches. I continue my small trek until I'm in front of my recently vacated chair. Instead of sitting, I turn, place my palms on the desk top, and loom over him. "I now own the deed to this house. It, as well as the entirety of what's inside, belongs to me."

His complexion goes white. "That's not possible. I didn't sign it over to you."

I straighten and reach into my inner jacket pocket, pull out a rolled up sheet of paper, and toss it on his desk. "Didn't you?"

Sheehan unfurls the damning evidence with trembling fingers. His eyes scan the document and he swallows hard, his jowls shaking with the effort. It drops from his lax hold, but his gaze remains locked on it.

"The original is in my possession for safekeeping."

Finally, he raises his head. "When? How?"

"You should be careful who you trust when they hand you a stack of papers to sign and you don't bother reading them." I pluck the document up and pocket it again. "Now...get the fuck out."

We stare at each other a moment longer, until, at last, Sheehan breaks contact and slowly stands. His shirt is rumpled and gapes open at the bottom. With as much dignity as he has left, I suppose, he buttons his jacket and rounds the desk with his gaze locked straight ahead. He passes me and continues through the narrow space between Darragh and Craig, neither of whom have holstered their weapon.

Sheehan makes it to the door and pauses. He turns and finally meets my eyes. "You have no idea what you've just set in motion. If you think that by taking over my organization you'll also be able to take control of Dublin from the Donnellys, you don't know Carrick or his sons very well. They will kill each and every one of you before they'll let that happen."

I sneer. "Let them try."

He stands there for another second, his hate-filled gaze drifting over the three of us, and then walks out. I jerk my chin, and Craig follows him to ensure he doesn't *accidentally* lose his way or take anything that no longer belongs to him.

The stench of stale sweat makes my stomach turn. I can picture all the times I stood in here and was disciplined by the bastard who just left. He tried to break me. Almost did. But I refused to let him win. He would have enjoyed it too much. Satisfaction washes over me at the recent play of events. It couldn't have gone better. Unless, of course, Sheehan had given me an excuse to kill him. I glance up to find Darragh studying me.

"Now what?" he asks.

"We let word get out. I expect it will reach Donnelly by the end of the day. No doubt he'll want to set up a meeting ."

He glances around. "And the house?"

"It can stand, but sell everything in here. I want it gutted. When the eldest Donnelly son gets tired of fucking Nessa and discards her, she'll at least have somewhere to go. Don't let it be said that I'm entirely heartless." Which reminds me of my completely fuckable house guest. "Now that that's taken care of, update me on getting into Ms. Walsh's flat."

"It's completely secure. Not even our best guys could figure out the code to get in."

Imogen is turning out to be quite the conundrum. Why does she have two different cell phones and a locked-tight laptop, as well as a high-tech security system? What's so important it needs that much protection? I glance at my watch. Perhaps when I get back, we can play nice and maybe she'll answer some of my questions. Unable to stand being in this house any longer, I exit the office just as Craig returns.

"Has the trash taken himself out?"

He nods. "Yes, sir."

"Excellent. You and Darragh are in charge of arranging for this place to be stripped of everything." I continue out the front door to the waiting town car, get in the backseat, and, once the driver's behind the wheel, tap the cracked-open window divider between us. "Home."

As soon as he pulls away, I reach into the bar and pour myself a glass of whiskey. Then I sit back and toast to the new Dublin King.

CHAPTER 7

Imogen

If Liam doesn't kill me, the boredom will. Once again, I've been locked in this stupid room with absolutely nothing to do. At least I've been fed. For someone who kidnaps a woman because he wanted to, my captor has been notedly absent, aside from that disastrous dinner last night. *Don't forget the kiss, though.*

I groan. As if I could. I'd love to scrub my brain of it forever, but the memory won't go away. Nor his taunting words after. Had he actually thought of me when he masturbated? Because the bastard had been right. I had dreamed of him. Dirty, filthy dreams. I woke up needy with my pussy throbbing so bad, I ended up taking care of it myself.

Liam doesn't strike me as a man who can't get any woman he wants. Especially without resorting to kidnapping her off the street. So what exactly does he want with me? I find it hard to believe it's just a fuck. Does he know who I am, and this is just some giant mind-fuck? No, he can't know. I only do because Mum told me as she lay dying. I used every one of my computer skills, and, other than her confession, I couldn't find a single piece of evidence—nothing—that backed up her claim. Had she been mistaken? Confused? *Lied*?

Since it's not possible for Liam to know my secret, there has to be some other reason I'm here. Never one to shy away from conflict, the only thing to do is ask. This time, though, I won't settle for a simple "because I want you here". Bored, I climb off the bed and pace the room. I glance up at the ceiling. *Are you happy now, Mum? I'm exercising.*

I've made close to ten passes when the lock on the door clicks. The main one, not the other that connects to his bedroom. I stop in the middle of the room and wait. It opens, and Liam stands there wearing another perfectly fitted suit that accentuates his muscular form. I push away the attraction I'm not supposed to feel.

He leans a shoulder against the door frame and takes me in. My temperature rises from that single glance. "Have you been keeping yourself busy while I've been away?"

"Oh, yes." I wave my hand around in a flippant gesture. "I've managed to take two naps and walked at least three miles back and forth across the floor of this well-appointed prison cell, thank you, very much."

His lips flatten. "Perhaps, instead of a prison cell, you might think of this as your...home away from home. A vacation, if you will."

I laugh without humor. "If this were a vacation, I'd be sitting on the beach in the Maldives, under a large umbrella, drinking a stiff cocktail brought to me by a stunningly gorgeous Italian named Raffaele."

Liam cocks his head. "I don't really picture you as a beach go-er. I see you more on a yacht, cruising around the Mediterranean, lying on the deck completely naked, soaking up the sun, while I bring you a large glass of red wine and rub lotion on your back. And front."

The picture he paints appears unwillingly in my head. I can almost feel the sun heating my skin—I'll ignore the fact that I burn like a lobster—and a dark shadow forming over me. Of shading my eyes as I peer up at him. Him—Liam—kneeling at my side and the rough, but tender touch of his hands as they rub all over my body. A shiver rushes over me.

I shake my head and blink, pushing away the image and swallowing a moan. His smirking face says he knows exactly what had been going through my mind. Doing my best to ignore the tingles that still ripple over my skin, I cross my arms and glare.

"I assume you're here for something?"

Liam steps fully out of the doorway and into the room. "I propose a truce."

"A truce," I parrot. "And what exactly happens during this *truce*?"

"You remain civil, and perhaps I'll let you out of this room."

I bite my tongue to keep my sarcasm—my *civility*—in check. Only, it doesn't work. "I assume you mean compliant. Fawning. Grateful that you would bestow such generosity on me."

Liam's fists clench at his side and a tight smile flattens his lips. *Way to go Imogen.* "Fine," I huff. "I shall attempt to remain civil."

He loosens his fingers and cocks his head. "Why do I not believe you?"

I toss up my hands. "Hey, I said I'd attempt it. That's the best you're going to get out of me."

Liam scans my face, perhaps gauging my sincerity. I didn't lie. I said I'll do my best, and I will. But it's also on him to not be a dick.

"You may have free run of the house. If I'm away, one of my men will remain here to...make sure you stay out of trouble."

Keep your mouth shut, Imogen. Keep it shut. "And my bag with my belongings?"

"Will remain in my possession. Speaking of, I attempted to have someone retrieve a few items for you. To ensure your comfort during your stay, but they were unable to gain access to your flat." He places both hands behind his back and studies me with an intensity that almost makes me fidget. "I find it curious why you would need such a robust security system."

I stiffen at the fact he tried breaking into my place as well as his probing question. But if I've learned anything in my short time here, it's that Liam will do what he needs to, to get what he wants. Better to give him something, at least. "I have an expensive computer in there that I use for work. I don't want someone breaking in and stealing it. It carries sensitive information."

While technically true, all the information I have on that computer is highly encrypted. It would take an extremely talented hacker to break my code. So, not impossible, but also unlikely. I'm one of the best for a reason.

"What sort of work do you do?"

"I'm a freelance contractor." Amongst other things Liam doesn't need to know about. "Which is why I need my laptop. I have bills to pay, you know?"

He drops his hands to his side. "While you're my guest, I'll take care of anything that comes due."

"Wow," I draw out the word. "Does that make me your whore then?"

Liam actually growls. Before I blink, he's got me pinned me to the wall with his hand around my neck, tightening his fingers enough to provide a warning, but not hurting me. Yet. He leans forward, his face close to mine.

"Why do you have to keep pushing?" he grinds out, his breath hot against my cheek.

My chest heaves as I try to breathe and not panic. For the first time since his men took me, I'm truly afraid. *You can never leave well enough alone, can you?*

"I've shown you far more patience than anyone else who would dare speak to me the way you have, because it amuses me. But my amusement has its limits." Liam's fingers tighten a fraction more, and I whimper. "I could have fucked you raw without giving a shit about whether you liked it or not. All I've asked of you is some polite discourse. This is the only warning you are going to get. Do not test my patience again, Imogen. I promise, your stay here won't be nearly as pleasant as it has been."

As quickly as he grabbed me, his hold loosens and he steps back. I don't move, only stare in fear as my body trembles. He tugs down the sleeves of his dress shirt and straightens his tie.

"Now that we have that unpleasantness out of the way, perhaps you would prefer a change of scenery. I brought back lunch from my favorite restaurant and thought you might like to join me."

All day I've been wallowing in my boredom, but despite the freedom currently being offered, I'm not sure I want it any longer. I'd almost rather stay safe behind the locked door.

"Okay." It's the only response I can make. Warily, I lift myself away from the wall.

Liam heads for the door and stops when he reaches it, turning to stare back at me with a questioning glance. Forcing my feet to move, I cross the room, pass him, and continue walking, trying to ignore the feel of his eyes following me all the way down the hall.

CHAPTER 8

Liam

I want to punch something. There aren't many things in my life I regret. In fact, only two stand out. As Imogen walks rigidly down the hall, I could add one more to the list. I'm pissed at her, but more at myself for letting my temper snap. It shows a lack of control. And I'm nothing if not in control.

I'm not a kind man. In fact, I've never claimed to be. But the terror in her eyes shifted something inside me.

I refuse to apologize, though.

We reach the dining room where our food waits. I stop at the seat where Imogen sat last night and pull it out for her. Cautiously, she moves closer, pauses with a quick glance in my direction, and sits while I push the chair in behind her. I follow suit.

"I hope you enjoy fish and chips." I reach into the brown bag for the two boxes inside. "No one makes them quite like Braden McCarthy does. No matter how many times I've asked, though, he won't tell me his secret recipe."

Imogen hesitates before opening the large white box I set in front of her. Gone is the smart mouth who spits fire at me with every turn. In its place is a shadow hiding her flame. *Goddamn it*. It's my fault. Guilt is a useless emotion and makes me defensive. "I never took you for a coward."

Her head snaps up and—there it is—that familiar flash of anger lights up her eyes. "I'm merely being civil. Providing you polite discourse like you requested."

I have to withhold my smile. Thank fuck she found her spirit again. "Considering, until this moment, you haven't said a single word since we came out here, there isn't much discourse happening, now is there?"

Imogen sighs and sags back against her chair. "What is it you want from me? You could have any woman you wanted without having to kidnap one. Why, out of all of Dublin, did you take me? To my knowledge, we've never met before. It's not as though we run in the same social circles."

"Do you know who I am?"

Her face crinkles like she's confused. "Of course."

"I don't just mean my name. Do you know *who* I am?"

She pauses as though considering. "I know you're the stepson of Dónal Sheehan and part of an extremely powerful family that may or may not abide by any man's law."

I chuckle at Imogen's description. "Correct. Mostly, anyway. I'm not just part of that powerful organization. As of a few short hours ago, I'm now the head of it. And to answer your previous questions... yes, I can have any woman I want, although that wasn't really a question. However, it's tiresome dealing with sycophants. Women who want the money and power that comes with being with me. I needed a challenge."

Imogen's mouth drops. "You're telling me that I'm here because you're *bored*?"

"If you'd like to call it that. I'd like to think of it more as a game of strategy. One where I seduce you while you try—and fail—to deny me. In the end, perhaps, we both win."

"Jesus, you really are barmy, aren't you?" She shakes her head. "That still doesn't answer why me out of the whole city?"

"Because you intrigue me, Imogen Walsh. Also, are you sure we've never met before?" I lean forward, fingers threaded, and rest my forearms on the table.

She harrumphs. "I'm pretty sure I would have remembered running into one of the biggest criminals in Dublin. No offense."

I merely smile and sit back in the chair. "None taken. To refresh your memory, it was several months ago. I was coming out of a restaurant after a business meeting. Your head was down and you were staring at your phone, not paying attention. You ran straight into me. Most people would have apologized. Not you, though. If I recall correctly, you looked me up and down with distaste, called me an extremely colorful, and vulgar, name, and kept walking, while sending me the middle finger over your shoulder."

Imogen's cheeks flush.

"Anyone else would have been...shown the error of their ways, but surprisingly, I was amused. I sent one of my men to follow you. Since then, I've learned a few things about you."

She stiffens. "Like what?"

"Sadly, only the basics. Useless things, really. Which has me curious. Why can't I find more out about you? You have no digital footprint to speak of. You have one of the most complex security systems at your home. You also have two separate cell phones, which in and of itself isn't unusual, but combined with other things, has me questioning why."

"I told you—"

"Yes, yes, you have sensitive data involving your 'work' on your home computer." I pin Imogen with a stare. "Except you're not being quite truthful with me. You see, in my line of work, it's important to be able to spot when someone's lying. There are tells. Over the years, I've become quite adept at identifying them."

She shifts in her chair. "That sounds like a neat trick."

"It does, doesn't it? So, why don't you tell me what you're really hiding."

Imogen sits quietly for minutes. I can almost see her mind spinning. The stories she's making up. I patiently wait for what she's going to say next. "Fine. I'm a hacker."

I blink. Of all the things she could have confessed, that wasn't in the top five. Probably not even the top ten. I also believe her. It makes sense, really. "A hacker."

"What? You think I'm lying?"

"Actually, no, I don't. I'm just a little surprised. Something that doesn't happen often. Are you any good?"

Imogen straightens and tips her chin up a bit. "One of the best, as a matter of fact."

A smile splits my face. "Now *that* doesn't surprise me."

Just then, her stomach growls. Of course, our lunch has long grown cold. I pick the box up I'd set in front of her and place it back in the bag. "It would appear you'll have to sample McCarthy's fish and chips another time. They're shit warmed up. Come into the kitchen and I'll make us something."

"You really do know how to cook?"

I raise an eyebrow. "Follow me and find out."

Grabbing the bag, I stand and head to the other room. Soft footsteps follow. I toss the food in the trash and open the refrigerator to grab the few things I'll need. Imogen stands on the other side of the L-shaped counter. I set everything down and crook my finger at her. She narrows her eyes, but rounds it to stand barely within arm's reach. Without giving her time to object, I wrap my hands around her waist and plunk her on the countertop next to where I'm working.

"Seriously?" She makes to jump down.

I side-step in front of her, separating her legs as I do and move between them. Imogen's eyes widen and she sucks in a breath. The sweet scent of her cunt rises up and I breathe it in. Let her deny her attraction. Her mouth says one thing, but her body says another. I'm not above taking advantage of that. I lean in until our chests brush and our lips are so close I could flick out my tongue and taste her. Neither of us move, both of us waiting for what the other will do. Imogen remains frozen. Which means I'm the one who takes charge. It's the way I like it anyway.

"Sit here and be good." And just because, I nip her bottom lip.

I return to the food I'd set out. From the corner of my eye, Imogen's tongue darts out and runs across the spot I marked with my teeth. Fuck if that tiny movement doesn't make me hard. While I work on preparing our lunch, she kicks her legs slightly and hums a little.

"How did you learn to cook, anyway? You don't strike me as the type."

"Why's that?" I glance over at her. "Because I'm ridiculously wealthy and spoiled?"

"Pretty much. Also, that's some ego you have."

I finish cubing the chicken and toss it in the skillet with the rest of the ingredients I'd been letting simmer in oil. "When I was a kid, I spent a lot of time at O'Doyle's. The owner, Seamus, brought me back to the kitchen and put me to work. He showed me how to make nearly everything on the menu. To my surprise, it was something I enjoyed. Everything else I've learned how to make has been self-taught. It relaxes me."

Imogen makes a small choking sound. "If that's the case, you probably shouldn't ever leave the kitchen. You could do with a bit more relaxing."

"I'll take your suggestion into consideration." I chuckle. "What about you? What relaxes you? I know a few things that work wonders I'd be happy to add to your list."

"I bet you do," she mumbles under her breath, but I can still make it out. "Being at my computer relaxes me, actually."

I shoot a glance in her direction. "Your computer?"

"Yes. I love the challenge of trying to break past firewalls. The harder it is, the more fun I have. It makes me think, and then, when I finally hack into a system, I fully enjoy the feeling of success it brings me."

The scent of garlic and ginger wafts around us. "What I'm hearing you say, then, is that being a criminal makes you relax."

Imogen shrugs nonchalantly. "We all have our vices, I guess. Besides, I don't *do* anything once I'm in. No nasty viruses or stealing information. Not usually, anyway."

I can't hold back my laughter. "The words of a criminal mastermind."

Her neck turns red, but she doesn't deny it. I take the skillet off the stove and nudge her to lean over so I can grab a couple plates out of the cabinet above her head. She studies me while I serve us both. I turn with my hands full, and Imogen glances down.

"Damn, I'll have to say I'm impressed. I hope it tastes as good as it looks." She finally hops off the counter and heads back into the dining room.

I trail behind her, set both plates down, and then have a seat. Imogen doesn't hesitate. She's already taken her fist bite. I wait for her verdict, although there's no question on what she'll say. She glares at me.

"Yes, it's good. I know you're over there waiting to gloat."

"Gloating is beneath me."

Her lips quirk, but she doesn't have any comeback. We finish our meal and after wiping my mouth, I place my napkin on my empty plate.

"I have some work to get done in my office. You're free to roam around inside while I do it." I rise and stare down at her. "Don't make me regret extending you the privilege."

I'm not sure how well Imogen plans on listening to me.

I almost hope she doesn't.

CHAPTER 9

Imogen

"*'Don't make me regret extending you the privilege',*" I mimic the mocking words in a snarky tone. One minute, Liam is bordering on being a decent person, and the next, he's a giant asshole. Or a dangerous criminal. I'm still a little shaky from the incident in my room. *Don't think about it.*

I'm tempted to find out if there's any type of security system engaged, shut it down, and waltz out the front door, but I won't give him the satisfaction. I also don't want to test his temper.

I guess I should go exploring then. Partly to get a layout of the place, but mostly because my curiosity is piqued. I'd be lying to myself if I didn't admit that I'm considering Liam's little proposal. Not that it's much of one. But being stuck in this house—in that room—has made me feel extremely out of control. Something I'm not fond of. This has all been about him dictating things. Take me off the street. Seduce me until I give in. Because he's *bored*, regardless of how he wants to see it. Maybe I shouldn't make it such a challenge, then. I'm the one who says we're doing this. Because the sooner he gets whatever boredom out of his system, then the sooner I can go home. *If he doesn't kill you first.*

Am I terrified of him? Absolutely.

I've also learned over the last ten years not to let men intimidate me, whether in real life or behind their keyboards. There's only one other hacker who knows I'm a woman. Maybe I have some sort of signal that only another female hacker can recognize, because she's one too. An American in California. We've passed each other jobs when we're busy. I don't know her real name, and I haven't tried to find out. I only hope that over the last few years, she's extended me the same courtesy.

Since Liam left our plates on the table and he did the cooking, I guess it's only fair that I clean up. I have no idea if he has a house-keeper or not. As hard as it had been to picture him knowing how to cook, it's even harder for me to imagine he also cleans. Once the kitchen is tidied and the dishes washed, I stroll around the house.

In the entryway there's a fireplace, as well as the staircase leading to the next level. The floor is polished to such a shine, my reflection is almost visible. The scent of fresh flowers on the mantle remind me of my walks through Stephens Green when I'm taking the long way around from my flat to the building where my work room is located. There's a gorgeous chandelier hanging from the ceiling with lights that sparkle like diamonds.

Figuring I'll start upstairs and work my way down, I climb the stairs, my fingertips gliding along the railing, which doesn't have a speck of dust on it. I step into the first room down the right hallway and gasp. "Oh, wow."

It's a gorgeous sitting room with wall-to-wall windows that over-looks Dublin Bay. There's an inset fireplace surrounded by white and gold marble and bookended by a pillar on each side. Two plush and cozy sofas face each other, and a matching accent chair forms the bottom of the u-shape they make.

I can picture myself up here in the evenings with a roaring fire while I peck away at my computer and drink my favorite tea. The image shifts, and Liam steps into the room and gently plucks the laptop from my hands. He sets both it and my teacup on the side table before returning to where I sit. I stare up at him, marveling at how the firelight flickers across his face, casting him in shadows that should make him appear frightful. Instead, it only makes him appear that much more dangerous. Alluring. Like he's hiding secrets he wants me to discover.

With a hand curled around the back of my neck and his lips against mine, he guides me until I'm lying down, covering me with his body. A skillful hand palms my breast, kneading the sensitive flesh, before traveling down my stomach and lightly tickling me, eliciting a soft giggle. Liam smiles against my lips. A genuine one, too. Not any of the fake or condescending ones he's given me in the past. His warmth heats me inside and out. I suck in a breath. His roaming hand slips beneath the waist of my pants and he palms my wet, throbbing center teasing my slit with his fingers.

Somewhere, a floor creaks, and the image disappears in a flash of smoke. Son of a bitch. It's clearly been too long since I've been laid. Especially if I'm having waking wet dreams about Liam. Then again, that only cements my decision to let him seduce me. Be the one in control of the game he wants to play, and then get the fuck out of here. I hope.

I finish my tour of the upstairs with two more bedrooms, each with an en-suite, and a small office that isn't nearly as warm and inviting as the sitting room. Back down the stairs, on the opposite side of the entryway as the main areas of the house, is a long hallway. I follow it, admiring the view of the backyard. It's stunning. What truly has me in awe are the hedgerows that encase the sprawling lawn bisected by a narrow canal of water. The soles of my feet tingle, just imagining how the lush grass would feel beneath them. On either side of where the hedgerow splits to form the opening are two towering stone plinths topped with massive gargoyle statues. It has such a gothic vibe. I love it.

At the end of the hallway, I open the door to a large conservatory. Lush plants and vines rise up providing a canopy over everything. Flowers in every color of the rainbow are either planted in the soil or in pots that line up along either side of the winding stone pathway. I wander through, slowly turning while I walk, making sure I don't miss a single thing. I travel the whole loop until I finally make my way back to the main door.

I come to an abrupt halt. Liam stands at the entrance. He's removed his jacket and is only in his white dress shirt and slacks. His hands are in his pockets, and my gaze automatically moves to where the fabric is pulled taut across his impressive package. I lift my eyes to meet his, expecting a cocky grin, but instead there's a burning intensity that raises the already humid temperature of the room a few more degrees.

Liam doesn't move an inch, but somehow I find myself in front of him. It's like an invisible tether between us pulled me to him. I'm standing so close I can smell his citrus cologne, along with a clean, manly scent that's all him. I wet my lips and his gaze is drawn to them. His pupils flare black, almost erasing the bright blue surrounding them. *Fuck it. Might as well start.* I slowly begin to unbutton his shirt. My eyes stay on his, waiting for him to put a stop to it, but he remains still. Rigid like a statue, but giving off a pleasant warmth.

With each button I undo, more of his body is exposed until I tug the tail out of his pants and push the fabric open. A small patch of hair covers the upper part of his chest, narrowing to a thin line of fur that bisects his stomach and disappears below his waistband. Growing more confident, I push the shirt over his shoulders and down his arms until it's completely off. When I hesitate, unsure what to do with it, Liam takes it from me and tosses it away.

Unable to resist, I place my hands on his chest. His heartbeat is strong beneath my palm. The heat of his skin nearly burns me. I trace the lines of his muscles across his chest and up over his shoulder. Continuing to touch him, I slowly circle around, dragging my fingertips along the swells and valleys of his muscled back that shift with each brush of my finger over them until I reach his right side. The tattoo I'd been curious about begins at the top of his shoulder and travels the whole length of his arm. It wraps all the way around it as well, leaving only a few empty spaces where his own skin tone peeks through. The colors are as vibrant as the flowers that surround us. I take my time, paying close attention as I trace the lines that make up each design.

His head is turned toward me and I glance up. "What do these all mean?"

"Different things." Liam's voice is a low growl that rumbles through me. "Reminders, mostly."

"The Chinese dragon?" It's a stunning red and teal creation that decorates his entire bicep and runs down to his forearm, its body twisting and curling along the way.

"It signifies strength and luck."

I glance up again at the huskiness in his tone. His jaw is clenched and his body has gone completely rigid. For a second, I'm worried I've made him angry again. "Is this okay?"

"Is what okay?" Another vibration stutters through my chest.

"Me touching you."

Liam huffs out a ragged laugh. "Imogen, leannán, you haven't touched nearly enough of me yet."

Ignoring the 'lover' endearment, but encouraged by his words, I complete my pass around him until we're face-to-face again. I palm the back of his neck and rise up on tiptoes to press my mouth to his. My breasts push into his chest, making my nipples hard. Beneath my fingers, his hair is soft. Beneath my lips, his are dry. I flick my tongue out to wet them. Making me work for my pleasure, he doesn't open for me. Not to be deterred, I continue the kiss, putting my all into it, until, finally, Liam's lips part, and he lets me in.

We kiss long and hard until I draw away. Without breaking eye contact, I unbutton his pants, drag the zipper down, and slowly lower myself to my knees. Not surprising, he's bare beneath them.

Gently, I free his cock. He continues watching me with hooded eyes. I lean forward and swirl my tongue around the head of it. The musky scent of him fills my nose. I curl my fingers around the thick base and lap up the tiny bit of pre-come leaking from the slit before taking his length into my mouth.

My hand and lips work together to make Liam lose control. I slide down his fat shaft, my spit making it easier to swallow more of him. What started out as me wanting to prove a point has morphed into something more. I want to do this for him. Coaxing pleasure from this dangerous and violent man, who I shouldn't be attracted to for so many reasons, makes me wet. I want to reach inside my jeans and finger myself at the same time my mouth sucks him dry so we reach our release together.

Hell, it might not even take that much for me to orgasm. My pussy is dripping and my clit throbs. I rotate my hips to generate friction, not once slowing down tasting Liam. I shift my hand down to roll his sac and take him so far down my throat my nose brushes against the well-groomed hair surrounding his cock. I swallow, and he inches just a bit farther forward. His fingers spear my hair and hold me there. I can't breathe. My eyes water and saliva drips from the corners of my mouth. Fuck, I'm almost there.

I once again raise my eyes to his face. His expression is tight, as though he's fighting for—and losing—control. Just as I'm about to reach my limit, Liam stiffens and come explodes from him. His release triggers mine, and I shudder while I drink him down as fast as I can, until finally, he loosens his hold on me. I jerk my head back, gasping. A string of spit still connects us.

He yanks me to my feet and slams his mouth down on mine, thrusting his tongue inside and sweeping up the come that coats the surface of it. A tiny ripple rushes through me again, as a smaller, but no less powerful, orgasm hits. He draws back and stares down at me with eyes gone black.

"You liked sucking my cock. You came just from that, didn't you?" Liam steps back and tucks his softened length into his pants.

I can only nod, still too breathless to form words.

"Good girl."

To my surprise, I preen a little at the compliment. Praise kink? Who knew?

"Unfortunately, we'll have to continue this later. I have to leave for a business meeting. But Imogen?" He pauses. "When I get back, that cunt is mine."

LIAM

Fuck, she'd been perfect. I can't recall any woman whose mouth is as good as hers. If I'd had more time, I would have fucked her right there on the dirt floor. I make a quick stop in my office and grab my jacket from where it hangs on a hook behind the door. Once I put it on, I make sure it's buttoned, the sleeves are straight, and I'm satisfied there aren't any creases. Then I head for the front door.

Imogen steps into the entryway just as I do. Her cheeks are flushed and her hair is still a tangled mess from my grip. She's fucking beautiful. "A couple of my men are stationed outside. You're welcome to use the indoor pool just past the conservatory, although, I'd also recommend exploring it a bit more. There are a few hidden treasures I don't believe you've uncovered yet."

"Will I be fending for myself for dinner then?" she pouts.

I've apparently spoiled the little minx. "I'm afraid so. I'm not sure how long this is going to take. One never does when they're meeting with the man they're going to destroy."

Imogen cocks her head, her brows furrowed. "That sounds ominous. I thought you already took over your stepfather's organization. I assume that's what you meant when you'd said you were now the head of it."

"And now I plan on taking over the whole city."

She freezes. "What do you mean?"

I study her more closely. Her hands tremble at her sides. I close the distance between us until I'm towering over her. Imogen tips her head back and I lean down until our breaths mingle.

"Carrick Donnelly has ruled Dublin for far too long. It's time for a regime change," I murmur against her lips before slanting my mouth over hers and gliding my tongue inside to taste her own flavor mixed with mine.

I thread my fingers through her hair to deepen the kiss, clenching my fist and tugging slightly. She sucks in a breath. My cock hardens again—like it always does when she's near—even though I just spent myself. This meeting better be fast so I can get back and fuck her pretty pink cunt.

Christ.

One blowjob and I'm addicted to her. That gives me pause. I draw back slightly, tugging her bottom lip with my teeth before releasing it.

Imogen opens her eyes and stares up at me with arousal burning in their depths. She blinks and her vision clears leaving another emotion. She's trying to hide it, though. It's fear. I've witness it enough times to recognize it in an instant. What is my little minx afraid of?

"Be good while I'm gone." I head out the front door where the driver waits beside the town car, along with Darragh.

Two of my other men, including Craig, have already been instructed that Imogen is to remain inside the house while I'm away. Darragh and I climb into the backseat, and the door closes. Neither of us speak. My mind should be on this meeting with Donnelly, instead, it's on the woman I just left. She'd still been off-balance from her orgasm when she'd come into the entryway. Then something changed. I can't put my finger on what though.

We drive through the city until we reach the meeting place where, inside, Carrick Donnelly waits. Word had spread far more quickly than I'd expected and just before I'd gone in search of Imogen, I'd received a phone call that he wanted to meet within the hour. Briefly, I'd considered telling him that I was unavailable, but then decided the sooner he understands how things are going to work with me being the one in charge, the better. I certainly don't want him getting the idea that I'm intimidated.

Darragh steps out of the vehicle first and I follow. We're in one of the most populated area of the city, overrun with all the tourists who come to experience Dublin. It's smart of him to set up the meeting here. Too many witnesses. We enter through the red wooden door of the establishment and make our way toward the table in the back where Donnelly and his eldest son, Cian, already sit.

It's more than obvious the two men are related, despite the near black hair Carrick has and the son's reddish-brown. In fact, all three of Donnelly's sons bear the same features. The bright blue eyes, the pronounced nose that widens slightly at the base, and the shape of their face. Something tickles the back of my mind, but I can't put my finger on it.

I take a seat across from the elder Donnelly, while Darragh sits across from the younger. The two men glare at each other with barely contained contempt. To the other patrons, this probably appears to be a simple business meeting, when it's anything but. I glance at Cian.

"How's Nessa, by the way?" I can't help but inquire. Not that I particularly care. I'm merely hoping for some type of reaction.

His jaw clenches and he smiles tightly. "I'm surprised you give a damn."

"I don't, actually. Call me curious."

"That isn't why we're here, Campbell," the elder Donnelly speaks for the first time.

My gaze slowly drifts to meet his. He's far more relaxed than his son. There's a hardness in his eyes that clearly says he is a man to be feared. Too bad for him, I'm not one who scares easily.

"Ah, yes. A man who wants to skip any pleasantries and get straight down to business."

Carrick leans forward and rests his forearms on the table. "I understand you have taken over your Da's organization."

"Dónal Sheehan is not my Da." I regret snapping out the words the instant they leave my lips.

Donnelly's smirk says he knows he pushed the right button. "My mistake. Your *stepda*, then. That's awfully ambitious of you. I hope that means we can continue to remain on...friendly terms."

"I assume by 'friendly terms', you mean you expect me to be as weak as Sheehan." I casually lean back against my chair, unconcerned with the implied threat beneath his words.

He opens his mouth, but closes it as someone passes our table. Once they're out of earshot, his attention returns to me. "I mean, I'm not sure you have any idea the kind of power I hold in this city. Just because you managed to acquire enough to take over Sheehan's organization doesn't mean shit. Like you said, he's weak. Had I wanted him to be, your Da would long be dead by now. I merely chose to let him run his business as he saw fit, so long as he didn't interfere with mine."

I bristle at the insult. "Maybe that's where you went wrong. You were too soft-hearted. Make no mistake, I'm nothing like Dónal Sheehan. I cower from, and answer to, no one."

Donnelly stares silently, his gaze assessing. He slowly sits back and a small half-smile appears. "I can see that. You certainly have a lot of ambition. I admire that in a man."

His condescending tone grates on my nerves. It takes all of my self-control not to kill him and his son right here. He must sense how close to the end of my patience I am, because he chuckles lightly.

"Did you call this meeting for any other reason than to try and intimidate me?" I've reached my tolerance limit for sitting here any longer. Imogen's hot, needy cunt waits to be filled with my cock back at the house. That's worth far more of my time than this meeting that's grown tiresome.

"I have no need to resort to intimidation. This was merely a friendly chat to get to know each other a bit better. As one powerful business man to another." That patronizing—mocking—smirk returns.

"If there's nothing else then?" Without waiting for a response, I stand. Darragh does as well. "Enjoy the rest of your evening, gentlemen."

Trusting my guard to watch my back, I walk away from the table and the two men who will soon topple from their castle, and out to the waiting vehicle. I climb into the backseat with Darragh right behind me.

"Do you think they understand what's coming?" he asks once we're on the road toward my estate.

The silence hangs for a moment. "They have no idea."

CHAPTER 11

IMOGEN

I'VE TORN APART THIS ENTIRE HOUSE SEARCHING FOR MY
bag, but wherever Liam put it, it's well-hidden. The first place I
checked was his office. All the bookshelves, the desk drawers, and
even behind the paintings on the wall, hoping one of them concealed
a safe. No matter where I've looked, I continue coming up empty.
His departing words haunt me. What did he mean by a regime
change? Is he planning on killing Carrick Donnelly?

"God damn it, where would he have put it?"

"Put what?" a disembodied male voice comes from behind me.

I scream and whirl around, ready to throw a punch. A tall, dark-
haired stranger stands in the entryway of the living room. He's casually dressed in jeans and a polo. Far different from the suit-clad men
I've spied wandering around outside.

"Who are you?" I eyeball him warily.

He steps farther into the room, but when I move back he stop and holds up his hands. "Sorry. I'm not going to hurt you. I'm Declan, Liam's cousin. I stopped by to see if he was here."

"He left a couple hours ago." I relax slightly at his identity, but still remain watchful. Despite the less hardened look of him, it doesn't mean he's not as dangerous.

"Figures. You don't, by chance, happen to know where he is, do you?"

"A business meeting is all I know." Does this guy really think Liam would tell me?

Declan studies me long enough to make me uncomfortable. Then a new tension radiates off him and his features harden to finally bring out the resemblance to his cousin. "You must be Imogen. Christ."

"Excuse me?" I'm almost offended by his obvious irritation.

"I can't believe him." He shakes his head and it's apparent he's not talking to me. Finally he turns his gaze my way again. "Please tell me you're here by choice."

My heart skips a beat at his wary optimism, as though he really wants me to say yes. Will he help me if I tell him I'm not? Or is this a trick?

"Fuck. You're not, are you?" Declan runs a hand through his hair and paces. "First Sheehan, and now this. Goddamn it, Liam."

That flicker of hope flares and I step toward him. "Will you help me get out of here?" *Please don't let me be putting my trust into the wrong person.*

He hesitates, and his expression already tells me he's going to say no.

"Please." I can't remember the last time I've begged for something, but I'm begging him.

"Fuck. Liam is going to kill me."

Hope flares again. "Thank you."

"You better have somewhere you can go that's safe. Because he knows where you live, and I have no doubt he'll come for you." There's a heavy tone of warning in Declan's words. "If for nothing else than for the fact that Liam doesn't like to lose. And you disappearing from right under his nose is really going to piss him off."

For a second, that bright flame dies, until an idea comes to me. It's probably the dumbest thing I've ever done in my life, but it's most likely going to be the only thing that keeps me safe. *If he believes you*. I glance at Liam's cousin and nod.

"Yes, I have somewhere to go, but you're going to have to take me there."

Declan drops his head back between his shoulders and blows out a heavy sigh. He better make a decision before it's too late. "Fine, let's go."

I wish I didn't have to leave my shit here, but there's nothing I can do about it. We head for the door, but he stops before opening it and turns to me. "I'll distract Craig. Give me two minutes and then you can come out. Go straight to the silver Mercedes, get in the backseat, and lie down."

With that, he steps outside while I count the time. My belly dips and twists with nerves. I'm wracked with fear that any second Liam is going to walk through the door. I almost want to tell Declan to forget it. Leave me here and I'll continue to play Liam's game. What I'm about to do may totally backfire. Then I'm completely fucked. I send a short pray up to my mum and ask for strength.

I take a deep breath and crack open the door. No one is standing at the entrance, so I risk a peek around the corner. Craig's back is to me and he and Declan seem to be in some sort of argument. I take a quick glance in the other direction, but the coast is clear. *Go. Now, Imogen*. I run the short distance between the house and the only silver car, carefully open the back door, crawl inside, and as quietly as possible, close it behind me.

Lying on my side with my head behind the passenger's seat and my knees bent, I try to slow my racing heart. The front door opens and I jump.

"It's just me." Declan starts the vehicle and within seconds drives away.

Still frozen with fear, I stay lying down. Maybe five minutes pass before he gives me the all clear. "You should be fine sitting up if you want. We're far enough away."

Slowly, I push myself upright and glance out the window behind me before facing forward. Declan's eyes meet mine in the rear view mirror. "Where are we headed, then?"

I twist my lips with indecision. Can I really do this? *You have to.* It's really my only option. "Carrick Donnelly's estate."

His head whips to the side, as does the car.

"Fuck." He quickly corrects, his fists gripping the steering wheel tightly. Once the risk of crashing has passed, Declan glances carefully back at me. "Are you shitting me right now?"

"No. You said to go someplace where I'm safe. That's where I want to go."

"Christ." His eyes return to the road, but he continues mumbling to himself. I'm pretty sure I catch a Liam in there somewhere.

Finally, the car slows, and I open my eyes. Declan comes to a stop at a massive iron gate. He swivels in his seat to face me. "This is as far as I can go. The Donnellys aren't going to allow a Campbell, especially Liam's cousin, to approach any closer. Nor do I want to. I'm afraid you're on your own from here."

I swallow a few times and take in a shaky breath. "I understand. Thank you for helping me."

He stares a moment longer and looks like he wants to say something, but he just jerks his chin up. "You should probably get going."

I nod shallowly and step out of the car. Declan slowly backs away from the gate and then out onto the road. He casts one more glance in my direction, tips his head, and drives away. Christ. Turning, I walk over to the security box and press the button. A few seconds pass and then the speaker crackles.

"State your business." Static sounds behind the voice.

I clear my throat. "My name is Imogen Walsh. I need to speak with Mr. Donnelly. It's important. Please."

There's no reply for so long, I'm worried that whoever is on the other end is going to just ignore me and I'll be well and truly fucked. Then, there's a click from the gate and it opens. Not waiting another minute, I walk through the narrow opening. The gate stops once I'm past and closes behind me. I glance at it for a minute before continuing my trek down the narrow lane that leads to the manor house I can just make out through the break in the trees.

It grows larger the closer I get until finally it looms over me. The trees form a canopy over the entire front lawn as well as most of the house. Windows make up almost the entirety of the front of the manor aside from a set of double doors in the middle that open just as I reach the porch.

A lovely older woman with strands of gray threaded through her reddish hair answers my knock. Her face has lost some of its color. "Ca—can I help you?"

"Yes, I'm really sorry to bother you, but I need to speak with Mr. Donnelly. Any of them, I guess, but preferably, um, Carrick."

She continues staring at me with a weird expression, but finally, she blinks, and it clears. The smile she gives me appears forced, but she steps aside and gestures for me to come in. "Mr. Donnelly should be home any minute. Would you like to wait in the library?"

I wring my hands and try not to gawk at my surroundings. "If you don't think he'll mind."

"This way, please."

She leads me to the left of the entryway and into a gorgeous library full of books lining nearly every shelf. The scent of old paper and must fill the space. It's absolutely stunning.

"I'll let him know you're here when he arrives."

I turn toward her and smile. "Thank you."

The woman dips her head and walks away. I wander around the room, taking everything in. My fingers drag along some of the spines and I pause every once in a while to read some of the titles. A throat clears behind me. I spin around with a gasp and immediately choke and cough. Carrick Donnelly stands in the doorway. He doesn't even have to introduce himself. I'd recognize him anywhere.

"Nora said a young woman was here to see me, although for the life of me, I can't figure out why." His voice is a bit raspy. It must be from the pipe he smokes.

Somehow, with him in the flesh, right in front of me, everything I'd planned on saying disappears from my head. I can only stare. My chest hurts, and I'm breathing heavy.

Carrick cocks his head. "Why don't you come to my office and sit. I'll have Nora bring you something to drink."

I manage a nod and make myself move. He heads back toward the entryway, bypasses it, and walks down a hallway until we reach the room at the end. Everything about it is familiar and yet, not. He sits at the chair behind his desk and gestures for me to take the one on the opposite side of it. Slowly, I sink down.

The same woman—Nora—enters carrying a small tray with a glass of water on it. She hands it to me. It shakes slightly in her grip as I take it from her. "Thank you."

Once again she bobs her head and then she's out the door—closing it behind her—leaving me alone with Carrick. I take a large drink to wet my dry mouth. He continues observing me.

"Feeling a bit better?" he asks once I've emptied the entire glass.

Not really, but I'm here. "Yes, thank you."

He leans forward with his forearms on the desk top surface. "Now then, would you care to explain who you are and why you're here?"

I take a deep breath. "My name is Imogen Walsh, and yesterday Liam Campbell kidnapped me."

Carrick, who until this moment had been relaxed, goes rigid, and his whole demeanor changes. His lips tighten and his cheeks turn ruddy. On the desk, his fists clench. "Go on."

"His cousin helped me escape."

Carrick sits back in his chair again. "That still doesn't explain why you're here."

"I'm here because I hope you'll protect me from him."

"Not to be cruel, but why should I care what Campbell does, so long as it has no bearing on me or my organization?"

It's not said unkindly, but Carrick's question still hurts. I push down the pain, take another deep breath, and stare him straight in the eye. If I didn't let Liam intimidate me, I certainly won't let the man in front of me either, no matter who he might be. "Because Maire Walsh was my mum. And on the day she died, she told me that you were my da."

CHAPTER 12

Liam

The rage from my meeting with Carrick and Cian Donnelly fades the closer we get to my estate. Instead, it's replaced with anticipation. Lust. I pull up the vision of Imogen on her knees —swallowing my cock—with desire and a hint of contempt warring in her eyes. For herself or me is the question. Perhaps a little of both.

It had been more than obvious she's trying to manipulate me. Except I've been mastering the art of manipulation far longer than she has. I'll continue to let her believe she's playing me, because I'm amused by the fact she thinks she can.

The driver comes to a stop in the middle of the wide lane in front of the house. Darragh exits the town car and I step out behind him. The moon is a pale, speckled orb sitting low in the fading light of day. The setting sun rivals it for control of the sky, but soon, its counterpart will declare victory. At least until the morning.

Craig rounds the corner, his body tense and alert. He relaxes slightly as his gaze lands on us.

I stride toward the front entrance—Darragh on my heels—where he meets me. "Any issues with our guest?"

"No, sir. But Declan was here about an hour ago to speak with you."

"I assume you told him I was unavailable."

Craig dips his head. "I did. Still, he entered the premises. Said he'd leave you a note."

I stiffen. "How long was he inside?"

"Less than ten minutes. He came back out, we had a brief discussion, and then he left."

Without another word, I walk into the house. The moment I cross the threshold, I sense a difference. The air is still. Quiet. Heavy. I stride out of the entryway, through the living area, down the hall, and open Imogen's bedroom door. It's empty. The bed hasn't been made and a towel lies crumpled on the floor.

I search the rest of the house, although it's pointless. It's obvious she's not here. Still, maybe I'm wrong. Perhaps she's in the conservatory or taking a swim. I walk down the hall, around the winding path in the humid air taking in the fragrance of all the flowers that are blooming, but unable to appreciate them. Nothing. There's not a single ripple in the pool water, either. I backtrack and take the stairs two at a time. The sitting room is warm from the sun shining through the windows, but she's not here either. Not that I expected her to be.

"Goddamn it."

My vision turns red. Cousin or not, Declan is going to regret this. I keep my steps slow and unhurried as I make my way downstairs, out the front door, and behind the wheel of the Porsche I drive only on rare occasions. My fingers squeeze the steering wheel as I push my emotions down to maintain control of them.

The minutes tick by far too slowly until I finally arrive at the house Declan and Aron share, the moon hanging fully in the sky at last. A few faint lights shine through the cracks in the shutters along the front. I don't bother knocking. Not when there's a spare key poorly hidden under a rock lying in a dried up flower box that sits on one of the window ledges.

I stride into the vacant living area. The TV is on, but the volume is down. Clinking glass comes from the kitchen. My footsteps are quiet on the hardwood floor until I'm halfway to the next room and a board creaks. Light spills down the short hallway and I step across the imaginary threshold.

Declan's back is to me. He sets down the bottle of whiskey he just poured from, takes a small sip, and places the half-full glass on the counter. His palms flatten on the granite surface and he releases a puff of air.

"I figured you'd show up sooner or later." My cousin picks up the drink, and at last, turns to face me, not showing the least bit of surprise—or guilt—at my presence. "Can I get you one?"

"Where is she?" A thread of warning lies beneath the question, although if he hears it, he ignores it.

"Some place she seems to think is safe from you."

I clench my fists. At least he's not trying to deny anything. "I won't ask you again, Declan."

One side of his mouth curls up. "Hmm. Looks like there *is* something that threatens the iron-clad control you work so hard to hold on to. Nice to see you are human."

He moves forward and then right past me, without a single care for what I might do to him. Or as though he assumes I won't do anything at all, actually. I follow him back out into the front room. He sits on the couch and raises his glass, pointing a finger at the open chair. "If you're not going to have a drink, at least take a seat. I'm sure it's been a trying day."

The hint of sarcasm and Declan's blasé attitude is only pissing me off more. Even as kids he always knew how to push my buttons. Since it's clear he's going to keep fucking around, I sit with my entire body rigid and unmoving.

He takes another sip of whiskey. "Do you remember the time you, Aran, and I skipped school and spent the whole day at

Kilmainham Gaol? Then we freaked out because we thought someone had kidnapped Aran and just knew our mums were going to murder us. I swear I can still hear mine yelling at me sometimes."

Christ, that had been a lifetime ago. Before Dónal. Before...everything. Despite the adventure we had that day, I hadn't really been happy. Fuck, had I ever been? Maybe Declan is right and I don't know what it actually means. "And your point? Because you seem to think bringing up our past will make me forget you betrayed me today."

Declan laughs, but it's filled with bitterness. "*Betrayed* you? Liam, you were the one who tossed Aran and me aside a long time ago, so don't think for one second that I give a fuck about owing you any kind of loyalty. We both know we're beyond that by now."

There's a slight twinge deep in my chest that makes me want to rub it, but I ignore it and keep still. Because he's not wrong. The three of us aren't who we used to be. Most likely never will be. Too much time has passed. Too many hurts caused. All by me.

"Is this payback then? I hurt your feelings, so you try to get back at me?"

Declan shakes his head. "Jesus. Not everything is about *you*, Liam. No matter what you seem to think, you don't always get what you want. We're not kids anymore. Imogen is a person, not some toy I stole away from you because you were mean to me. You *kidnapped* her for Christ's sake. Do you even comprehend what that means?"

"All these feeble attempts at trying to be my conscience bore me and if you continue, you won't like the consequences." I rise from the chair and Declan's gaze follows my every move. "I'm going to break my own rule and ask you one more time. Where is she?"

He takes another drink of his whiskey and rests his glass on the arm of the sofa. His eyes stare into mine. "You can fuck right off, Liam. Now, get out of my house, because I'm not telling you shit."

Driving his point home even more, he picks up the remote, turns the volume up on the TV, and his attention shifts to the screen, effectively shutting me out. Since I won't be getting any answers without force—and maybe not even then—I stride across the living room and out the front door. The wind has picked up and fallen leaves dance and float down the walkway with the force of it.

Not ready to return to my empty house, I tug my collar more closely around my neck, shove my hands in my pockets, and walk down the quiet street. A dog barks in the distance, but otherwise, there aren't any other sounds besides an occasional car that drives by. I breathe in the fresh air. Ten or fifteen minutes pass before I head back to my car and to my estate.

There's no sign of Craig or Darragh when I return. Once the front door is alarmed—something I should have done when I left Imogen alone earlier, instead of trusting that my guards would deter anyone—I head straight for my bedroom and open the door to the large walk-in closet I'd had specially designed after I purchased the estate. Reaching around the doorframe, I press a button. On the right side wall, a narrow opening appears. I push my clothes out of the way and pull back the small section that protects the hidden safe behind it. I key in the security numbers, press my thumb to the fingerprint scanner, and the beep sounds.

I open the door and bring out Imogen's laptop. With it in hand, I secure the safe again and make my way to my office. Once there, I set the computer on my desk and take a seat. Slowly, I open the lid. Aside from the instruction to place my finger on the scanner the screen is black. My reflection stares back at me. I slam the lid shut with a curse.

"You're not going to get away from me that easily, Imogen. You're mine."

CHAPTER 13

Imogen

Emotions shift across Carrick's face. Shock. Disbelief. Confusion. Until, finally, one settles into place. Pity. "I'm sorry, but I don't know anyone by that name."

A weight drops in my stomach. *Don't get sick. Don't get sick.* "But, you have to have. She told me. My mother wouldn't lie to me." Would she?

"Perhaps she was mistaken. Or confused. You said she was dying. Maybe she didn't want you to feel like you were alone. I'm sorry for your loss, but I did not know your mother."

Tears threaten to spill. I clench my fists and dig my nails into my palms trying to distract myself with the pain. Better it be there than the stabbing sensation in my chest. Carrick isn't saying anything that I haven't already told myself. Maybe she was confused. Giving me something—even if it wasn't real—to keep my mind on instead of her dying. A puzzle to try and solve, even if she knew it was impossible.

I take in a shuddering breath, the act proving more difficult than it should. It's as though someone is standing on me, crushing me.

Why can't I breathe?

My eyes close. Someone is talking, but it's like I'm underwater. Sounds are muffled. Something tightens around my arms. I force my eyes open. My vision is blurred. Hazy. Slowly an image comes into focus.

Carrick kneels in front of me, his mouth moving and brows dipping with concern. He brushes a thumb across my cheek, wiping away the tears spilling down it. Finally, his voice reaches me.

"It's going to be okay, Imogen. Just breathe. That's it. In and out."

"I'm sorry." I study his features, still trying to see myself in them despite his denial of parentage.

His smile is soft and kind. "Don't be. I'm sure the past couple days have been difficult. Why don't I let Nora show you to a room? You can stay for a little while, if you'd like. At least until you feel a bit better. There's no rush. We have plenty of space, so stay as long as you need to."

I'm not sure I can. Not after this.

Carrick must sense my unease, because he cups the side of my head, the weight of his palm heavy against my ear. It's such a paternal gesture, tears threaten again. "It'll be okay."

I nod shakily, and he rises to his feet.

"Let's go find Nora and get you settled."

We leave his office and make our way through the house. I do my best not to stare at everything, but it's difficult not to. The entire manor reeks of wealth. It's not gaudy or pretentious, but certainly evident. Between the furnishings, the artwork that decorates the walls, and the architecture, it's clear that a wealthy family lives here. There isn't a speck of dust or dirt on a single surface.

Vases full of flowers are littered throughout, their fragrances filling the air and providing a homey feel. Family pictures, mostly of when the boys were younger, dot the walls of the living area. The scent of cooking meat reaches me. We must be approaching the kitchen. Seconds later, we step through the doorway.

The same woman who answered the door and took me to the library to wait moves around the room, an apron tied around her waist. As though sensing our presence, she turns. Her eyes dart from me to Carrick and her expression shifts slightly. I can't read it though. Then her lips barely curl up.

"Carrick." She dips her head formally. "Miss."

He steps close to her, touches her hand with the familiarity of someone he's intimate with, and speaks in a low voice. Low enough I can't catch what he says. Carrick turns to me and I jerk my gaze away.

"I have a bit of business to attend to, but Nora will show you to your room. You're welcome to join us in the dining room for dinner in about an hour."

Not quite sure I'm ready for that kind of sit down, I simply say, "thank you."

Carrick glances at Nora one last time and then strides out of the room, leaving me alone with her. I shift uncomfortably under her scrutiny. Finally, she shakes off whatever has a hold of her. She clears her throat. "If you'd like to follow me, then, I'll take you to your room."

I follow her back toward the entryway and then up the staircase to the second floor. Nora turns down a hallway to the left, pauses at the second door, and reaches in to turn on a light. She gestures for me to enter. A beautiful four-poster bed sits in the middle, the white and lavender duvet smooth and neatly tucked under the sides of the mattress. Four fluffy pillows are arranged at the head of it.

"The en-suite bathroom is just there." She points to the open door on the far wall. "It should be stocked with any toiletries you might need, as well as towels. If something is missing, please let me know. There are also some clothing items in the closet that should fit. I understand you don't have anything with you, so feel free to borrow whatever you need."

This is all so much to take in. Whatever I'd been expecting when

I asked Liam's cousin to bring me here, this certainly isn't it. I finally pull my attention from the room and place it on Nora. I'm overwhelmed with emotion again. Something I don't particularly care for. I clear my throat and shove it all down. "Thank you. I appreciate what you've done."

Her expression is almost pained, but she bobs her head again like she'd done for Carrick. "I need to get back to making dinner. If you'll excuse me."

Without waiting for a response, she turns and disappears down the hallway. I quietly shut the door and sag against it. My eyes close and I drag in a deep breath. Once I'm a bit more grounded, I open them and take in the rest of the room. The dusk sky is visible through the windows as is the giant moon that is climbing higher and higher. A large dresser sits against the far wall, while a different door than the one that leads to bathroom is opposite it.

I walk over and open it. A few shirts, a pair of jeans, and black yoga pants hang inside. Considering my rather eclectic taste in clothing, I'm surprised to find that I don't hate everything in here. Not like all the shit Liam had supposedly chosen for me. Turning from the closet, I head for the bathroom. The light is overly bright, and I blink a few times at it.

Fatigue hits me. I search for, and find a towel under the sink. Feminine scented hair products and body wash sit on a shelf inside the shower. I run the water and shed the clothes I've been wearing since I left my flat yesterday morning. The warmth hits me as soon as I step under the spray. I hug myself tight and let the thudding pressure hit my back. Slowly, some of the tension in my shoulders eases.

Christ, what am I going to do? A small part of me had hoped Mum told me the truth. Discovering this is one more lie on top of all the rest only makes the anger I'd tried to get rid of return. I could almost hate her. Tipping my head back, I let the water wash away my tears. Tomorrow I'll figure out what to do next. Where to go. I could call Teagan, but I'm not bringing her into this mess. It's better if she's not involved in any way. It was stupid of me to come here though.

I should have just stayed at Liam's. I mean, there are worse things than some dangerous criminal wanting nothing more than to fuck me, I suppose. Would it have been so bad? Let him get me out of his system and then go home, none the worse for wear? I might not trust him for shit, but I believe him when he said he'd let me go. Fuck. I'm too tired to think straight.

Hurrying to finish my shower, I shut off the water and grab the towel from where I'd hung it nearby. I wrap it around me and go back to the closet and pull on a plain green t-shirt and the yoga pants, foregoing my dirty bra and underwear. Once my hair's towel-dried and combed, I turn off all the lights and crawl under the duvet. For a brief second, I contemplate actually going down to dinner, but discard the idea. I'm not sure an uncomfortable meal is how I want to spend the evening. My stomach grumbles, protesting the decision, but I ignore it. It won't be the first meal I've missed.

I stare up at the ceiling and the shadows that dance across it. A hollow sensation settles in my chest. One I haven't felt since that first month after Mum died. I rub at the ache, wishing for it to go away, but it continues to grow and burn. Things will look different tomorrow, after I've had some sleep and cleared my head.

I hope.

CHAPTER 14

The sun has barely risen when the town car heads toward the docks. A shipment arrives today and I have specific instructions for this one. I put out several discreet calls last night wanting answers about Imogen, but so far there's been nothing. It's as though she's disappeared off the face of the earth. She didn't return to her flat and that idiot who works at the bakery she favors was useless. No one of her acquaintance has seen or heard from her. Wherever she is, she's well hidden. I have no intention of giving up though. If she thinks I'll just forget about her the longer she's away, she's sadly mistaken.

The driver scans his keycard at the security box and the metal gate guarding the entrance opens with a grating sound. He pulls through and comes to a stop next to a small out building. Dock workers tread back and forth along the wide loading area, up and down ramps leading onto the massive cargo ships, and supervise cranes lifting and stacking containers in the surrounding area. The smell of fish and sea water lingers strongly in the air as I stride through the herd of workers, intent on my destination.

The freighter I'm searching for looms ahead of me. I blink against the sun creeping over the top of it. The din of conversation grows louder the closer I get as men disembark. I approach a gentleman with a clipboard.

"I'm looking for Paul Hanlon."

The man turns. "That'd be me."

From my inner jacket pocket, I pull out some paperwork and hand it to him. "My name is Liam Campbell and I'm the new owner of Emerald Shipping. I understand there is a special shipment of crates inside the cargo hold for the Donnelly family."

Hanlon glances from the papers I'd produced to the freighter and then back to me with a hard swallow. I smirk at his nervousness. The Donnellys must be paying him an awful lot of money to turn a blind eye to the illegal cargo packed within legitimate items.

"There's no point denying what we both know. Is there?"

"No"—he squeaks and clears his throat—"no, sir."

"Good." Makes things easier. "Now then, Paul, this is what's going to happen. You're going to make the shipping manifest disappear. When our mutual friends come to collect their products, you're going to let them know there's been an unfortunate turn of events and their cargo is unable to be offloaded until the manifest is found. Which it won't be. Without the proper forms, sadly, all shipments are going to have to return to their port of origin. Are we understanding each other? By the way, you're quite the lucky man, what with that beautiful wife of yours. Niamh, isn't it? Your children are adorable as well."

Hanlon pales. "I understand, sir."

My smile is fake as I clap him on the shoulder. "Glad to hear it. Oh, and be sure to let them know that the edict came from me, would you?"

With a single nod, I walk back to the waiting town car. Once settled in the backseat, I pour a drink from the bar. "Take me to my office."

From the other side of the dividing window, the driver nods. "Yes, Mr. Campbell."

I savor the oak flavor of the whiskey as it burns a path down my throat and settles into a warm puddle in my stomach. That couldn't have gone any better. The first stage of my takeover is in full operation. Soon it'll be time to initiate the second stage. I can hardly wait.

A short time later, we arrive in front of the brown brick building that houses the office space I purchased about six months ago. The white door doesn't show an ounce of dirt and the windows reflect the sun that is slowly rising, nearly blinding me with its brightness. I step through the entrance and the slight scent of wood polisher greets me beneath the fragrance of flowers my assistant Ashlynn insists on displaying around the waiting area.

"Good morning, Mr. Campbell," she greets me from behind her desk as she sets a large mug of steaming coffee on the raised platform attached to the side of it. She learned the first day that I despise tea. "Here is the list of voice messages. I've also added several appointments to your calendar."

I grab the mug and disappear into my office with only a brief nod. Ashlynn has also learned that I don't care for conversation beyond giving her instructions. Most of our interactions happen through email. As long as she does her job efficiently and effectively, then there's nothing else I care about. I overhead Declan telling her once she must be desperate for a job to put up with me. She deflected the conversation. It's the only reason I didn't fire her. That, and she's the first assistant I've been able to tolerate since I opened my business. Perhaps she is desperate.

Once I've flipped through the messages and scanned the calendar, I pick up the phone and call Darragh.

"Yes, sir."

"Any news?" Not that I expect there to be. He would have called me immediately if there had been.

"Nothing yet. I'm waiting to hear from one of my contacts. Hopefully later today."

"Keep me posted."

"Of course," Darragh says.

I disconnect the call, turn on my computer, and open my email. Except I can't concentrate. Where would Declan have taken Imogen? Fuck. Forcing myself to focus, I get to work. Distractions mean a lack of control. Several hours pass before my intercom buzzes.

"What?"

"There's a Carrick Donnelly here to see you, sir," Ashlynn's tinny voice blares through the speaker.

A smirk pulls at my lips. This is a surprise. I never expected him to personally pay me a visit. "Send him in."

"Yes, sir."

I sit back in my chair and thread my fingers over my waist and wait. The door to my office opens. Ashlynn steps in and then to the side. Directly on her heels is my adversary. Donnelly strides in, his movements fluid. His lean body is relaxed. He certainly has presence and power even at his age. There's a cunning gleam in his gaze as he takes in his surroundings. My assistant closes the door. The snick of the latch echoes in the otherwise silent air.

"Campbell," the older man greets me as he crosses the remaining distance of the room.

Donnelly takes a seat without my invitation to do so. A bold but unsurprising move. It's not as though there's any respect between the two of us. I remain reclined.

"To what do I owe the pleasure?" Might as well get this conversation started. My curiosity is piqued.

"I understand you're the proud new owner of a shipping company. Congratulations. Quite the business deal you made there." Donnelly nods his head, the movement only slightly mocking.

"Yes, it's been a lucrative decision. I might actually acquire a few more. One can never have too many business ventures, can they?"

Donnelly crosses an ankle over his knee and mimics my pose. "I agree. Although, as one businessman to another, I would caution you about putting too much stock into one industry. It's better to diversify. Spread your assets into other ventures that can make you a profit."

I tip my head as though giving thought to his suggestion. "You're right. I actually have my eye on this casino."

He stiffens and then smiles thinly. "Best of luck with that." Donnelly's words ooze with insincerity and sarcasm.

"I don't believe in luck."

"You're Irish. Luck is part of our heritage."

My brows raise. "You really believe that shite?"

Donnelly merely stares at me.

I'm tired of these word games. "What do you want?"

"Ah, we're done with the pleasantries, I see." He uncrosses his legs and sits forward. "I just stopped by to ask how your cousins are doing? Declan and Aran, right? Have you heard from them today?"

I grit my teeth. "Is that what we're playing at, now?"

He stands, forcing me to tip my head back to maintain eye contact. "Have a good day, Liam."

My fingers ache. I've gripped my knuckles hard enough to stop the blood flow. Donnelly glances down, and I have to force myself to unclench them. He lets out a short chuckle and heads for the door where he pauses and glances over his shoulder. "By the way, I met this nice young woman—Imogen—yesterday. I believe the two of you are acquainted. It's been lovely having her visit my estate. She's certainly enjoying her stay much better than the last place she'd been."

He walks out the door and closes it behind him. I continue sitting there long after he's gone and then I stand, pick up the large crystal paperweight that's merely for show, and throw it against the wall where it shatters. Moments later, the door flies open.

"Sir, are you okay?" Ashlynn asks.

"Get out," I roar, slamming my fists down on the desk top.

She pales and quickly leaves without a word. I snatch up my

phone and dial Declan. Straight to voicemail. Same with Aran. My third call is answered.

"Take Craig and two more men over to my cousins' house. Let me know what you find." I end the call and only barely refrain from hurling it across the room as well.

I stand over my desk breathing hard. *Get control of yourself.* Slowly, the rage slows in my veins, setting into a low-burning flame instead of an explosion of fire. If Donnelly doesn't kill Declan, I'll do it myself. What the fuck was he thinking taking Imogen to their estate? More importantly, why would she go there? I recall that trace of fear she'd tried hiding when she learned where I was heading after our encounter in the conservatory. Is she connected to them in some way? No, Donnelly said he'd just met her. He didn't know her until she showed up there. But why?

What secrets does that computer of hers contain? One of her phones has rung a few times, but whenever I've answered, the person on the other end disconnects the call. Imogen said she's a hacker. I'm guessing that one is for clients. Hearing a man's voice has probably deterred them from responding. I pick up my own phone again and dial another number.

"Hello?" a man answers.

"Do you have any hacker contacts? One who might be able to bypass security on another hacker's computer? One reputed to be one of the best?"

"I know a guy."

"Call him. I have a laptop I need access to. Now." I finally return to my seat.

"Yes, sir. Give me about thirty minutes."

"You have fifteen." I disconnect the call.

CHAPTER 15

Imogen

My eyes fly open and my heart pounds. I place my hand on my chest. What woke me? The knock on the door makes me jump. I drop my arm back down onto the mattress with an exhale.

"Just a minute," I call out.

Throwing back the blanket, I pad to the door and open it. Nora stands on the other side holding a serving tray with a stainless steel covered dish and a glass of juice. "I'm sorry if I woke you, but I thought you might be hungry since you missed dinner last night."

Is that a hint of disappointment in her tone?

"It's fine, thank you." I step to the side and wave her in. "It smells delicious."

She crosses the room and sets the tray at the end of the bed before turning to me. Her hands are clasped in front of her and she rubs her thumbs against the other. "I understand you need some-where safe to go."

I blink, not expecting her to bring it up and also not sure why she appears so nervous. "Basically."

Nora nods. "I have some extra money and friends in Belfast you can stay with for a while. At least until Mr. Campbell loses interest."

In a weird way, Liam getting bored with wanting me stings a little. God, I'm so fucked in the head. I study the older woman. She's pretty, with streaks of gray through her reddish hair. A few wrinkles flare from the corner of her eyes and she has quite a few laugh lines. Like someone who smiles often. Except she's not smiling at the moment. There's a tightness around her lips, in fact.

"Why would you want to help me?"

"I understand a little what you're going through. Not being kidnapped, of course, but the need to get someplace safe. To protect yourself. And the people you love most."

What does that mean? I pull my brows together. "And you want to help me, because of that?"

Nora wrings her hands tighter. "Yes."

Am I really willing to leave Dublin? Even for a little while? This is my home. I've never lived anywhere else. Everything I've ever known is here. *Jesus, Imogen, it's not like you're moving to the other side of the world. It's just Belfast. And it's only temporary.* "Can I think about it?"

"Of course. Anyway, I'll leave you to your breakfast." She strides past me and out the door.

I stand there a minute longer wrapping my head around Nora's proposal and then sit on the bed to check out what she brought to eat. Food always makes me think better.

"Oh, god." I nearly moan at the full Irish breakfast in front of me.

When's the last time I had a real meal like this? I certainly don't cook for myself. Pre-packaged tapas I throw in the oven doesn't count. I stuff myself, eating every bite and drinking all the juice, until my gut aches, but in a good way. Nora certainly knows her way around the kitchen. I'd consider staying here for her cooking alone. I chuckle to myself, but it quickly dies away. With a full stomach and a solid seven hours of sleep I haven't had in years, I have a decision to make.

I've never quit or run away from anything in my life. Do I really want to start today? It feels cowardly to take the easy way out. Still torn with indecision, I pick up the tray and venture downstairs. The only areas of the house I've seen have been Carrick's office, as well as the room I've deduced over the last few months as the sort of man-cave his three sons share. I have caught the occasional glimpse of the their bedrooms when they've taken their laptops in there, but I make sure to turn off the feed on my end when that happens. I *do* have limits on how much privacy I'll invade.

All is quiet. I'm not sure if it's because of the hour, and everyone besides Nora is still asleep, or if no one is home. Despite how often I observed them from my computer room, there had never been any noticeable pattern of the Donnelly men's routine. I envy that. My daily life is predictable. I chuckle. There hasn't been any predictability about the last few days.

I've gotten brief glimpses of how they all live in the time I've been watching them. I'd like to think I've learned a few things about them as well.

Like how Aidan always drinks his whiskey without ice. Or how Finn is screwing one of the casino's former floor girls. And, the eldest, Cian? Well, he gives off a confident vibe when he's with his brothers, but on the rare occasion I've caught a glimpse of him alone, he lets his guard down. I'm surprised he hasn't rubbed a raw spot between his brows for as often as he runs his finger back and forth across it.

Then, of course, there's Carrick. The way he always smokes his pipe when he's stressed. Or that he puts three ice cubes in his stout. No more. No less. I also learned how much he adores Nora, and she him. For months, I've imagined all of them as my family. A father to offer advice and guidance when I need it and three older brothers to talk and laugh with, but who are also over-protective and annoying at times. A part of me mourns something I never had.

Someone should really tell the four of them how easy it is to bypass security on their computers and hack into their cameras.

Nora is in the kitchen cleaning up from breakfast when I enter. She rushes over and takes the tray from me. "You didn't have to bring that down. I would have come to get it."

"I think I just needed to get out of the room for a bit. Stretch my legs." I glance out the window.

There's a cute little cottage-style guesthouse in the back near the bottom of the sloped yard. Outside of the few rooms I've been privy to through my computer screen, I haven't gotten a glimpse of any of the property surrounding the manor.

"Would it be okay if I went outside for a little?" I'm not usually a fresh-air kind of girl, but without my computer, I'm bored. I'd been locked inside Liam's house long enough that in the few short days since, I've come to appreciate being able to move about freely.

"You're welcome to go wherever, although we do have a guest staying in the cottage at the moment," Nora mentions.

I shake my head. "I won't bother them. Thank you for breakfast, by the way. It was delicious."

Her cheeks flush. "I'm glad you enjoyed it."

Nora returns to her task and I make my way to the front door and onto the circle drive. Breathing in the cool late morning air, I set about exploring.

I close the book with a soft thud. My entire morning had been spent wandering the Donnelly estate. It's much bigger than it appears from my walk down the narrow lane yesterday after Liam's cousin dropped me off. I discovered a hedgerow, a garden, and even a small hideaway built into one of the trees a good distance from the manor. Inside it, there had been a few toy soldiers.

Clearly something a child had left behind. I try to picture any of Carrick's sons playing, but I can't. Do children of the head of the mafia have a normal childhood like those of us that don't belong to Dublin's most powerful criminal organization?

Despite having the most sleep I've had in a while, fatigue has settled in. No one will mind if I take a short nap. It's not as though there's been anyone keen on keeping me company in the short time I've been here. I put the book back on the shelf where I found it and head out of the library. Just as I cross the threshold into the entryway, the front door opens. I brace myself for whoever is going to step through.

A young woman near my age comes to an abrupt halt. "Oh."

Based on my research of the Donnellys, this is Carrick's niece. *Catriona? Kathleen? No that was his wife's name.*

Her forehead crinkles. "You're not Nessa."

"Hmm, no, I'm not."

She stares at me then widens her eyes slightly and cocks her head in expectation. Right, yes.

"Sorry, yeah, I'm Imogen."

"Are you Aidan or Finn's lover?"

I nearly choke on the spit I swallow. It takes a few seconds to get my cough under control enough that I can talk. I clear my throat a final time. "Definitely neither. I'm just visiting for a few days."

She doesn't appear satisfied with my answer, but what else is there to say? I thought your uncle was my Da and I showed up here unannounced only to be told I was wrong?

"Caitlín-love, what are you doing here?"

I cast Nora a look of gratitude and silent thank you for saving me as she joins us. The older woman rushes forward and hugs Carrick's niece.

"I just wanted to pop in and say hi before I commandeered Nessa and headed into town."

"I'm so glad you did." Nora's gaze darts to mine. "I see you've met Imogen. She's the daughter of a friend from Belfast come to visit me."

Caitlín's shoulders drop and relax when she turns my way again. I smile almost lamely and give a little wave. "Nice to meet you."

"You as well."

I thumb over my shoulder. "I'm just on my way to take a wee nap, if that's okay?"

Nora gestures me off. "Of course, dear. Dinner will be ready around seven."

"Thank you." I dart a glance at Caitlín and then nearly run up the stairs, closing the door of the bedroom quickly, but quietly.

Well, that was awkward. I'm grateful for Nora's explanation—albeit untruthful one—about who I am. Makes things easier for sure. Especially if I take her up on her offer to go to Belfast. Something I haven't ruled out yet. Too keyed up after that uncomfortable meeting downstairs, there's no way I'm going to be able to sleep. Which leaves me stuck up here. Alone. I'm no better off than I'd been at Liam's.

A bit of melancholy washes over me. As does loneliness. My chest aches. God, how I miss my mum. I miss the sound of her voice. Her laugh. Even her chiding me about not having a "real job". I'd give anything to be able to talk to her one more time. There's nothing for me in Dublin anymore. Although Teagan has been my closest friend since uni, she travels so much with her job, I only see her when she manages to come home for a few days every couple months. Once I get a new computer and burner phone, I can work from anywhere. Including Belfast.

Decision made, I make myself lie down and try to get some rest. I'll talk to Nora tomorrow and let her know I accept her offer of help. Maybe a change of scenery will do me good. A chance to explore a new place that doesn't have so many memories tied to it.

CHAPTER 16

Liam

Everything on the screen in front of me only leads to more questions than answers. Allen's hacker contact finally got into Imogen's computer. Despite it taking him most of the day to do so, I haven't left my office. Instead, I remained here while he sat at my desk and worked where I could keep an eye on him. Allen might trust him, but I didn't. Which meant the laptop hadn't left my sight.

"I've only ever seen this level of security twice before. Whoever's system this is...they're good. Probably one of the best there is." The awe in his tone had been unmistakeable.

Imogen hadn't exaggerated her abilities. Considering the things she has on her laptop, it's no wonder the security was so tight and nearly impossible to break. I click another video, this one also without sound. It's almost identical to the twenty-some I've already gone through. They date back months. Based on the minimal intel I've collected on Imogen Walsh, they appear to start around the time her Mum died.

Why has she been watching the Donnellys? The video playing is of Carrick and his housekeeper in his office. I study the two of them. Not because I give a shit that the family patriarch is fucking his employee, but because I'm focused on trying to decipher what they're saying. It became clear at the beginning the woman isn't happy about the pipe he's smoking. She says something to him, he gives her a look, and she just shakes her head.

There have been videos in a common living space the younger three Donnellys appear to share, as well as ones from inside Finn Donnelly's office at their casino. But the ones I've found the most fascinating—mostly because of the sheer volume of them—are the ones in Carrick Donnelly's office. His inner sanctum. If only the fucking things had audio.

My gaze is drawn back to the image playing. I fast forward until Carrick waves someone in and the housekeeper disappears. Fuck. Who is he talking to? Since the feed is coming from his computer, he's the only one on the screen. I jam my finger down on the mouse and the video pauses.

Today has turned to shit. It started perfectly with my visit to the docks. I'd experienced a perverse sense of satisfaction for having won this round. I'm not opposed to taking things by violent means, but the fact that I'm slowly strangling the Donnellys financially first gives me great pleasure. But then to find out Imogen is at their estate? The people I hate nearly as much as that bastard Sheehan? It feels exceptionally like betrayal. I still haven't heard anything about Declan or Aran either. No matter how things stand between us, they're family. And no one touches my family.

The doorbell rings. I glance at the clock. It's just before midnight. The only people who would show up at my house at this hour unannounced are either Darragh or Craig. It better be one of them and it better be important. I grab my gun from the drawer, stride through the house to the front door, and check the security camera. Darragh stands on the other side. I let him in. His gaze darts to the gun in my hand and back up to meet mine.

"We found Declan and Aran," he says, his voice rough.

"And?"

"They're alive, but in bad shape." Anger colors his tone. He and Aran are friends. "They came with a message."

"From Carrick Donnelly, I take it?"

He nods.

"The old man clearly doesn't have the stones to do what it takes to send a real message to not fuck with him. If he did, he would have killed them both. It's what I would have done."

Darragh jerks slightly as though my words surprise him. Have I ever given any indication, in all the time he's worked for me, that there's nothing I won't do to rule Dublin? "Is there anything else?"

"No, sir. I just thought you might want to hear about them in person." He turns to the door at the clear dismissal.

I set the security alarm again and go back to my office. It's obvious I'm not going to get any answers tonight. Especially not about Imogen. I close down the computer and head to my bedroom. The door to the room she'd occupied stands wide open. Turning on the light, I pause within the doorway. It's exactly as it had been last night and this morning when I stood here. The bed is still unmade and the towel still lies crumpled on the floor. Besides that, her smell lingers as well. Not just the scent of the shampoo she used, but the underlying essence that is purely Imogen. My fists clench the doorframe, and I force my fingers to loosen and to exit the room and step into my own.

Each item of clothing I remove gets tossed into the basket for the housekeeper to wash. Naked, I climb into bed. Tomorrow, I plan. Not another night will pass that Imogen isn't under my roof. I swear it.

❧

IT'S TAKEN ALL DAY, BUT BY EVENING, NEARLY everything has come into alignment. The timing has to be perfect, though, for it to work. I'm confident it shouldn't be a problem. Darragh and Craig should be here any minute. I put away Imogen's computer again, grab my two weapons locked into the shoulder holster, and shrug into it. I pick up two extra magazines and pocket them. On my way out of my office, I flip off the light. A bright illumination guides my way out to the living area.

The sound of the water flowing down the wall eases some of my tension, but not all of it. I'm too keyed up to fully relax. My phone chimes, signaling the two men's arrival. I open the front door before they can knock. They stride through the entrance and immediately there's a sense something is wrong.

"I just got word from someone I know that works at the hospital that Cian Donnelly was shot some time late last night," Darragh says without preamble. "He's still alive."

I go rigid. "One of us?"

He shakes his head. "No, sir. They're all denying it."

"Do you believe them?" I care less that Donnelly's been shot than I do about my men being disloyal and not following orders.

"Yes, sir. Your men know better. They understand the consequences if they disregard what you've told them."

Without a word, I walk back to my office. Darragh and Craig follow. I remove my weapons, set them on my desk, and cross the room to the bar to pour a glass of whiskey. Once I empty it, I refill it and return to my desk, taking a sip as I go. I gesture toward the bottle. "Help yourself."

Darragh shakes his head and sits in one of the chairs, but Craig gets himself a glass.

After a few sips, I lean back. "You said he was shot near the docks. Where?"

"From what my contact has been able to gather from snippets of conversation, it was a few blocks away. Next to his car, which was parked near a copse of trees. No one knows if he was heading to the docks or coming back from them. The civilian who found him was returning home from somewhere and spotted the body on the ground. Called nine-nine-nine." Darragh glances away and shifts in his seat.

I stare at him. He's uneasy. "There's something you're leaving out. What is it?"

"There are rumblings about retaliation."

"Against who?" I ask even though I suspect the answer.

"You. With Donnelly being shot near the docks where you now control the majority, the blame is falling on you. Especially after the incident with the cargo yesterday. With Carrick thinking you're responsible for what happened, he's done with the word games and innuendos. He's out for blood."

I need to disabuse him of the idea that I put out the order. There's only one person who would benefit from casting the blame on me. I glance over at him. "Find out where Sheehan is. Now."

After they're gone, I pick up my phone. "Get me Carrick Donnelly's phone number."

I tap my finger on the desktop while I wait. Less than five minutes later, I get a call. Once I've written down the number, I dial it.

"Donnelly."

"I understand there's a nasty rumor going around that I find I need to dispel."

He growls. "You're a dead man, Campbell."

"That may be, but it won't be for something I had no part of," I reply. "A little birdie told me a story. You should be aware that were I to take out one of your family members, it wouldn't be from some hidden locale like some coward. Whoever winds up on the other end of my weapon will see me coming."

There's a pause on the other end.

"You have the greater motive," Donnelly says.

"Are you sure about that?"

"Where's Nessa?" he counters, surprising me.

"What do you mean? Don't tell me that your son has lost his little prize?"

The older man makes a noise. "You really are a cold bastard aren't you?"

"So I've been told," I reply blandly.

There's another moment of quiet.

"Just know that if you're lying—about anything—you'll regret it. We'll be coming for you."

"I look forward to it."

CHAPTER 17

IMOGEN

THE LAST TWO DAYS HAVE BEEN CHAOS. EVER SINCE
Dónal Sheehan shot Cian and kidnapped his girlfriend Nessa. Thank
god they were able to rescue her last night. I haven't felt right bothering Nora about leaving. Not when she's been busy trying to keep
Carrick from losing his shit. His son could have died, for Christ's
sake.

Members of their organization have been coming and going at all
hours. I've passed Aidan and Finn more than once as they've headed
down the hall to their Da's office for family meetings I may or may
not have eavesdropped on. They stare at me each time, but neither
have spoken. Which is fine, because what do I even say? Has Carrick
told them who I am or why I'm here?

I head into the kitchen to grab a snack and pause just inside the
doorway. The man I've believed to be my father these last few
months stands against the counter. To my surprise, he's alone. Ever
since he got the news about his son, Nora hasn't been far from his

side. I quietly study him. Dark circles under his eyes make the rest of his face appear paler. I could almost swear that a few more lines mar his forehead. His shoulders sag as though weighted down. It's like he's aged ten years in only a couple days.

Not wanting to intrude on his solitude any longer, I turn to leave. The floor creaks beneath my feet. Carrick's head jerks up and his body goes rigid. He relaxes slightly when our eyes meet.

"Imogen."

"Mr. Donnelly."

A soft smile makes its way to his lips. "No need to be so formal."

I thread my fingers together, for once hesitant to speak. What if I say the wrong thing? "I'm sorry to hear about Cian, but I'm glad he's going to be okay."

For a second, rage flashes in his eyes, but it clears. "Thank you."

A wave of envy hits me. It's obvious Carrick loves his son very much. "Cian is really lucky, you know. Aidan and Finn, too. Not all fathers care as much as you do."

I can't help but wish things were different. That I really was his daughter. Would he love me as much as he does his sons? He crosses the room and stops in front of me. He slowly reaches up and gently tugs on a small section of my hair, running his fingers down the length of it. His eyes are tired, but kind. "I've always thought of my niece Caitlín as a daughter. She's more like me than she is my brother. I know you and I don't know each other, but something tells me, given the chance, you'd end up like one as well."

"Thank you...Carrick."

A throat clears. I jump away like I've done something wrong, and my gaze bounces between Carrick and his middle son.

"Cian and Finn should be here any minute." Aidan glances in my direction before returning to his father. "Campbell called him at the hospital, but he wouldn't say any more. Just that when he got here, we all needed to meet."

Why would Liam call Cian? And why would he be leaving the

hospital so soon? I turn to Carrick whose jaw is tight with tension. "I'll leave you men to your meeting."

I glance once more at Aidan before walking away. Instead of heading up to my room, I go to the library. Before long, low voices reach me and then they fade. I wait several more minutes and then quietly make my way down the hall, careful to avoid the spot that creaks, until I'm standing outside Carrick's office. The door hasn't been shut completely, so I nudge it just a fraction.

"Cian, since you called this family meeting, you can tell us what it's all about." That's Carrick.

"Liam Campbell called me a few hours ago."

"What did our new business associate want?"

There's a heavy and tense pause. "He has Nessa. According to him, she's unharmed and will continue to be."

How is that possible? She was with Cian at the hospital.

"That bastard. When do we attack?"

Damn it. Who said that?

"We don't." Cian again? It isn't his Da.

This time the pause is longer. I hold my breath. What's going on in there?

"He wants something, doesn't he?" Carrick's question is almost inaudible.

"He wants Imogen."

I barely contain my gasp. Then my whole body heats with rage. *That son of a bitch.*

"You know that's not going to happen, Cian."

"Unless we come up with another plan, it's already done. Tomorrow at two. No one else can be there or he hurts Nessa."

"Then we better come up with something," Carrick replies.

Without hesitation, I push the door fully open and scan the room. My gaze lands directly on Cian. "You don't need to."

He stares back and obvious guilt flashes in his eyes, but his lips firm like he has no intention of taking back his words or changing his mind.

"Imogen," Carrick says in a low tone, and my gaze leaves Cian's and meets his.

We stare at each other a moment, maybe both of us wishing for the same thing.

"Liam won't hurt me."

Carrick shakes his head. "You don't know that."

"Yes, I do." At least I did before I escaped. I'm not so sure any more. "He wants me because he sees me as a challenge. The fact I was able to leave right out from under his nose only made it worse. So if it means helping the woman Cian loves, then I'll go with him."

Cian opens his mouth as if to deny it, but then closes it and collapses back into his chair.

I chuckle at his realization. "Didn't have that figured out yet, did you?" *What would it be like for someone to love me that much*? "She's a lucky woman."

Carrick circles the desk and stops in front of me. "You don't have to do this. We'll come up with something else."

"Don't worry about me. It'll be fine. Truly. I'm not afraid of Liam." Unsure if I should, I squeeze his hands trying to convey every emotion with that touch. "Thank you. After this is all over and I go home, maybe I'll see you again."

He nods and slowly releases me. The tension in the room is thick.

I glance around and laugh again. "Don't all stare at me like I'm about to die, for fuck's sake. Nothing that drastic is going to happen. Liam's just pissed I left. In the short time I was with him, I learned he's not a man who likes to give up any type of control. Once he gets the challenge out of his system, I'll go back to my life. Besides, I have no intention of making *his* life easy. By the time I'm finished with Liam, he'll be begging me to leave."

My words ease some of the heaviness. I even manage to get a snort and guffaw out of a couple people.

"I think we're all forgetting something."

We all turn to the man who spoke. Carrick's enforcer, and his niece's fiancé, stands. He's an intimidating man, with a scar down the side of his face and ice-blue eyes that track the room, pausing at every person in here. It travels back and meets his boss'. "Just because Imogen is returning to Campbell's estate doesn't mean she has to remain there. He's made it clear that he'll win by any means necessary. Instead of waiting for him to make his next move, why don't we make ours? If he wants a war, then let's give him one."

Our gazes shift from him to Carrick. Before he can say anything, I do. "I can't let you do that. There's no way I'd be able to live with myself if people were killed because of me."

"This game that Campbell is playing? It's been leading to this point from the beginning," Carrick says. "He wants to control Dublin. The only way that will ever happen is if all of us are dead. And I won't go down without a fight. People are going to die sooner or later, Imogen. That's how our organization works."

I swallow, because he's probably right. What do I really know about the mafia anyway? I'm just a computer geek who sits in a small room and thinks she's cool by playing with code and hacking into other people's systems. Judging from the expression on the faces of the men in here, nothing I say is going to change their minds. This is the kind of life they lead. I suppose, in the end, violence and death are inevitable.

"I understand."

Carrick nods and turns to his men, effectively ignoring me as the plotting and strategizing begin. No one consults me on anything, so I leave. I run into Nora at the end of the hall. "Looks like I won't be needing to go to Belfast after all."

Her gaze jerks over my shoulder and back. "What happened?"

"I'm going back to Liam's tomorrow."

Her face pales. "What? No, you can't."

"He has Nessa. The only way he said he'd let her go is with a trade."

Nora's features harden and she storms forward. I stop her before she can take more than two steps. "It's fine. They're working on a plan to come get me. I won't be there long."

At least I hope not. I don't say that, though.

"He's going to get himself killed," she nearly whispers, her voice filled with worry.

A compulsion makes me reach out and squeeze her hand. This is the most I've touched anyone since Mum died. She jerks her head in my direction. There's fear in her eyes. "We both have to trust him. All of them. Okay?"

Slowly, she nods. "You're right."

I release my hold on her. "If it's okay, I think I'm going to go upstairs and take a shower before I go to bed."

"Of course."

With one final glance down the hall, I take the stairs two at a time and then close myself in my room. Come two o'clock tomorrow, I'll be back with Liam. I'm not looking forward to it.

CHAPTER 18

Liam

The ceiling creaks and I glance up. When Nessa had stepped out of the hospital yesterday alone, I hadn't been able to pass up the perfect opportunity. She's nothing like I remember. Of course, she was a child when I escaped that hell-hole Dónal called home. In only the short time she's been here, it's clear she has none of her Da in her. She's far too sweet and innocent for having grown up under his control. If I were anyone else, I might feel guilty for what I'm doing.

Although, that uncomfortable knot in the center of my chest tightens a fraction again at recalling yesterday when she'd told me she had missed me and cried when I left all those years ago. Maybe, in another life, things could have been different. My phone rings bringing me back to the present.

"Campbell."

"Declan and Aran are out of the hospital and home," Darragh tells me.

"Good to know."

"Do you really think the Donnellys are going to just let you have her?"

"Of course not. Which is why once Imogen has been returned to me, we're going to take a small trip away from Dublin, and you're going to have Declan and Aran moved to the safe house," I announce. "Also, make sure the cottage in Killarney is ready for our arrival in the next four hours."

"I'll make the call to the housekeeper and let her know to expect you."

"I want the closet stocked with clothes. Black jeans. Hoodies. Long-sleeve thermals." I almost smile, picturing her saying that none of it is anything she would wear just to spite me. Vicious minx.

"Yes, sir."

I end the call and toss the phone on the couch next to me. I've bided my time over the last few years, garnering business acquaintances and money, in anticipation of my taking over Dónal's organization. Not once have I lost my patience. I've played the long game. But the knowledge that in less than an hour, Imogen will be back in my sights makes my skin itch with impatience.

Needing to burn off some restless energy, I head for the bar and pour myself a whiskey. The amber liquid gives off an oaky fragrance that eases some of my tension. I sip it down, savoring the flavor. Above me, the ceiling creaks again. I glance at my watch. Footsteps come from the second floor. Tossing back the rest of my drink I pick my phone up off the couch and dial a number.

"Donnelly." There's a hard bite to the name.

"Meet me in front of John's Lane Church. Be there in twenty minutes. Don't forget to come alone when you bring the package." I disconnect the call without waiting for a response.

Movement out of the corner of my eyes makes me glance up. Nessa stands there holding the same book she'd had with her yesterday. I rise. "You ready, then?"

Her smile wavers, but she nods. "Ready. Thank you again for letting me stay, and for lunch."

"Of course."

I walk her out to where the town car and driver wait with the door open to the back. She gets in first and I follow. The driver makes his way out of the drive. I glance over at Nessa. Her face is bruised and battered. Rumor has it the Donnellys have Sheehan locked up some where. While I'm a bit disappointed that I'm not the one to put the bastard in the ground, I suppose it's only fitting that the eldest Donnelly son be the one to do it. Especially since Dónal put hands on his daughter. I have no doubts her Da won't see the light of day much longer.

"I need to make a quick stop first, if that's all right?"

"Yes, that's fine."

The driver travels through the city and finally comes to a stop in front of a church. I dart another glance in Nessa's direction. She thinks I'm taking her to her childhood home. Will she forgive me?

Where did that come from?

She ducks down and stares out the window, glancing upward to where the spires shoot upward.

"I'll just be a few minutes," I tell her and exit the town car.

I button and straighten my suit coat before striding up to the doors of the cathedral where I stand and patiently wait for the arrivals. My wait isn't long. With her back straight as an arrow and her head held high, Imogen turns the corner. My attention only flickers to the man beside her, because it's all on her. The way the sun brings out the slight undertone of red in her black hair. How her eyes meet mine and then harden. God, she's going to burn me alive with the heat spewing from them.

A car door shuts, and then Nessa stands next to me. A few short minutes later, Imogen is right in front of me.

"Together again, minx."

"Go fuck yourself, Liam."

Because it will add flames to her fire, I smile.

"How do you two know each other?" Nessa asks with some hesitation.

"Imogen is an old friend, aren't you?"

She barks out a rough laugh, but it is filled with disdain. "Why, Liam, are you actually afraid to tell Nessa the truth?" She turns to face her. "I'm your brother's prisoner."

I should have known she wouldn't come quietly. Maybe this will prove to Nessa the kind of man I really am and that perhaps she shouldn't be so trusting in the future.

"You got what you wanted, Campbell. We're leaving, but this isn't the end of things." Donnelly steps towards Nessa and gently pulls her to him.

She stumbles slightly forward with a dazed expression. And then Imogen stands in her place beside me, although she keeps distance between us. She can have her space for the moment, because after this, we're going to get nice and cozy. I spare a brief glance at the other couple. Nessa's eyes widen in understanding and flash with fury. Before I can guess her intent, she strikes, slapping me across the face hard enough that the pain radiates through my head and down my neck. I've had worse so I don't even flinch. My cheek burns like fire, though, no doubt with the shape of her hand-print brightening it in color.

"I *trusted* you," she snaps.

"That was your mistake. I told you you'd wasted tears on me."

Her whole body vibrates with rage. Donnelly finally pulls her to him again. With my sole purpose accomplished, I shrink the distance between Imogen and myself and wrap my hand around her upper arm. Or try to. She jerks out of my grip and storms over to the waiting town car and gets into the backseat. Holding back my amusement, I follow and get in beside her.

She stares straight ahead. Her lips are pressed tightly together and hostile energy wafts off her. Imogen is more pissed than the day Darragh and Craig brought her to my estate. My cock twitches. I plan on funneling all that anger into passion when I fuck her. The explosion will be magnificent. Already I can feel her nails scoring my back as I pound into her. I'll keep her on the edge of orgasm as a form of punishment until she's begging me to let her come. It's the least I should do to her. It will be glorious torture for both of us.

Because it will gall her to have a conversation, I push. "Did you really think I wouldn't find you?"

Imogen ignores me. Her fists tighten in her lap. I stay alert in case she tries to throw a punch. When she remains rigid and unmoving, I continue. "Fascinating videos you have on your computer, by the way. Although the obsession you appear to have for the Donnelly family could be construed as stalker behavior. And you're the one judging me?"

"How did you get past my security?" She gapes and pivots in my direction, my taunt finally prompting a reaction.

"You may be smart, but nothing is completely unbreakable when you have the right incentive and the time."

"You had no right to go through my personal property," she snaps.

I relax back into the seat unconcerned by her outburst, but remain prepared for violence. "You left. I only assumed you were abandoning your things as well."

"You hid them. If I would have found my stuff, I would have taken it with me."

"My mistake."

Imogen growls. "I hate you."

Finally, I give her my full attention. "That may be, but it still doesn't mean you don't want to fuck me."

Her lips part, and I take full advantage by grabbing her behind the neck and slamming my mouth against hers. Our tongues fight for control. Our teeth gnash together. A pinch of pain follows and then the copper flavor adds to hers. We can't seem to stop drawing blood. It only makes the rage hotter. She keeps battling against me. Not to stop the kiss, but to show me she'll be the one to win this. My cock is harder than it's ever been. Soon.

Imogen jerks her head back, and I loosen my grip on her. Both of us are breathing hard. She swipes the back of her hand across her mouth as though that will wash away the taste of me. I flick my tongue out and lap up both our flavors as well as the blood still smeared across my lips. Not putting it past her to murder me in my sleep, I bite back the words "I'm right.". Besides, she doesn't need them. That kiss proves it.

If she needs further proof, having her naked beneath me tonight should cement it. Imogen will be begging for my cock before the night is over.

CHAPTER 19

Imogen

I may hate Liam, but I hate myself more. Because that disastrous kiss only confirms the affect he has on me. I glance at the passing scenery and my forehead creases. *I don't remember any of this from the other day.* We've also been driving for much longer than it took Declan to get to Carrick's estate.

"Where are we going?" They're the first words I've spoken since he made his point. "This doesn't look like the way to your estate."

"That's because it's not."

My head snaps in his direction. No, we have to go there. Carrick is coming to get me. "What do you mean?"

Liam glances over at me. "It's pretty self-explanatory."

I take a deep breath and ask for patience. "If not to your estate, then where are you taking me?"

"Are you worried your friends won't be coming for you now? Do they know you've been spying on them for months?" he continues. "Which leads me to an even more important questions of *why* are you spying on them?"

Fuck. I want to wipe the smirk off his face.

"Since you asked, I thought it would be nice if you and I had a change of scenery. Dublin is so boring this time of year, don't you think?"

"No, I don't, actually."

"A pity. You really need to get out more then, Imogen," Liam says, almost scolding me. "Experience new places."

"I'm perfectly content right where I am. I happen to *like* Dublin." Just not your estate, arsehole.

"Well, I'm sure where we're going will have plenty of things to offer you as well." He tips his head to the side. "Then again, since this *is* a romantic getaway, we probably won't be leaving the house—or bedroom—much."

I snap my mouth shut, because it's obvious I'm not going to get any answers and Liam is pissing me off even more. I'll sit back, wait until we arrive at our destination, and figure out where to go from there. Considering the degree of hatred he has for the Donnellys, I'm almost surprised he isn't more angry. Or maybe he is and I'll reap the consequences of my actions soon enough.

WE'VE LONG LEFT DUBLIN BEHIND AND THE CITY STREETS have turned into green, rolling hills dotted with sheep. We pass an occasional farmhouse and barn. Liam has periodically checked his phone, while I've stared out the window as the stunning landscape flies by. I picked up the book from beside me on the seat—Nessa must have left it—and tried to read, but it wasn't for me.

Mum and I would take trips to county Cork every once in a while, but for the most part, we were city lasses. I like being able to walk out of my flat and go to my favorite coffee shop or restaurant. It's the convenience of everything that does it for me.

I'm not opposed to the countryside, I guess, but it's certainly not the first place I'd choose to go. I close my eyes and try picturing the white sands and blue-green water of the Maldives. Instead, the vision shifts and I'm on the deck of a yacht that slowly dips and rises with the waves as it floats in the middle of a giant body of crystal-clear water. The scent of salt and coconut is in the air and the heat of the sun warms me. A gentle finger runs down my arm along with a deep voice that whispers in my ear almost teasing me with what's to come.

I jerk my eyes open and force the vision away. No fucking way am I fantasizing about that again. The bastard has been in my head far too much. My gaze darts around as the town car finally slows. We've been driving for hours. On my side of the road is still a vast field of green hills. I duck my head to glance out Liam's side. The driver turns into a lane guarded by a wrought iron gate similar to the Donnellys. It slowly opens and we head through. That's where the similarities end.

While both of their estates are massive and sprawling with the house taking up a huge portion of the landscape, the small cottage that sits in front of me is minuscule in comparison. It's quaint actually. Adorable, even. And not a place I can picture Liam owning. I consider myself a good judge of character and based on everything about his home, he enjoys showing off his wealth. He wants people to admire, but more, to envy what he has.

This cottage is old. It's been kept up, but the signs of age are there from the stained stone walls to the thatched roof. The driver comes to a stop next to another black vehicle. In a move that surprises me, Liam reaches across my body for the book, and, with it tucked under his arm, exits without waiting for his door to be opened. He holds out his hand for me as though he's some sort of gentleman. Slapping it out of my way, I climb out on my own. I can't think when he touches me, so I plan on avoiding it as long as possible. Behind me, he chuckles.

I'm glad I amuse him.

I let him lead me into the cottage. A boot room where a coat hangs from one of the hooks in the wall leads into a cozy kitchen with a mammoth stove and wood plank table. The scent of cinnamon lingers in the air. I continue following him into an open space with a staircase on one side and a set of double doors on the other. Through a doorway in the third wall, I get a peek of a sofa. A familiar scarred man steps into view. He briefly glances at me before his attention shifts to his boss.

"Everything is ready that you asked for, sir," the man says. "The housekeeper also made sure the kitchen is fully stocked."

Liam turns to me. "Stay here."

He and his lackey walk into the living area and leave me standing in the entryway. I spin in place, taking in my surroundings. It's a nice house. I really like the stone floor and the simple artwork on the walls. This reminds me of a home, not just something to showcase a person's wealth. This is where a family could live.

Since I'm not a dog to be commanded, I move closer and stand out of sight near the doorway. I dare a quick peek around the corner. Liam is at a small desk scrawling something on a piece of paper. He tucks it inside the book and passes it to the other man. I duck back out of sight.

"Have this wrapped and delivered to her. Anonymously. Also make sure to keep an eye on our mutual friends and update me on any movement. Continue forward with all the other arrangements we discussed."

For a moment I almost forgot where I am and who I'm with until Liam's instructions ground me. I step into the room, not caring if they see me. "Carrick isn't going to let this go."

Both men turn.

"*Carrick* is it?" Liam's eyebrow raises. "Only with them a few days and already calling the old man by his first name. Does his lover know how close you two have gotten?"

"Don't be gross." I make a face. "Carrick was—is—a friend. Something I'm sure you know nothing about."

"I know what friends are. I just don't need them," he scoffs. "They only let you down. You should remember that."

I stare at him. He's serious. "You know, I actually feel sorry for you. Somebody must have really fucked you over."

"Nobody *fucked me over* as you so eloquently put it. Now, I'm bored with this conversation." He turns to the other man who glances away and shifts his weight like he's uncomfortable with having to listen to us. "Call me when you get back to Dublin."

His lackey nods. "Yes, sir."

The man steps around us and several seconds later a door opens and closes. Liam's focus is back on me. "Why don't I show you to our room?"

"I'm not sleeping with you." I fold my arms.

He strides forward, closing the distance between us. I force myself not to take a step back, even when the fabric of his suit jacket brushes against my shirt. I tip my chin up a fraction and stare him down. Almost daring him to contradict me. The lines shooting out from the corner of his eyes are clearly visible. As are his long lashes and the flecks of brown in his blue irises. I try not to breathe in his masculine scent, but it's useless. It assaults me anyway and sends unwanted signals of arousal down south.

I expect Liam to repeat the kiss from the town car. Being as discreet as possible, I press my thighs together to ease the throbbing. He smirks like he knows exactly what I'm doing and leans down. His lips caress my cheek, then my jaw before he nibbles his way up toward my ear, pushing my hair out of the way, and then down my neck. It takes every ounce of control I possess not to tip my head to give him better access. A chill skates across the back of it and I shiver. His chuckle vibrates through me causing another involuntary quiver. Liam's tongue flicks out and he tastes his way back toward my mouth.

With a gentler than any kiss I've ever had, Liam's mouth moves over mine. His tongue sweeps carefully inside. There's no taking. Only giving. There's a message of intimacy—of tender emotion—in the way he touches me. I fall into him, unable to resist the intoxicating pull. The fabric of his jacket glides beneath my hands as I raise my arms and loop them around his neck. His hair isn't coarse like I expected it to be. Instead, it's like silk.

Liam's hand cradles my jaw while the other circles my waist. His chest is hard beneath my breasts and I want to rub them over it and increase the friction against them, but I hold back because I don't want to break the spell I'm under. Except he slowly pulls away. I feel myself leaning into him, trying to bring him back. My eyes flutter open and meet his. There's a flicker of something in their sapphire depths and then it's like a door shuts, closing it off from view. He blinks and the familiar devilish gleam enters.

"That was almost too easy." A full-blown grin appears. "I don't think much sleeping will be happening anyway, do you, Imogen?"

Liam gives me his back and heads up the stairs. He makes it all the way to the top before I have myself under control. I steel my emotions, the fragile ones that are supposed to be buried, but that the damning kiss brought to the surface instead. I won't give him the satisfaction of raging at him. It's what he wants. A reaction. Turning on my heel, I follow.

CHAPTER 20

Liam

That did not go as planned. Soft footsteps follow me up the stairs, and seconds later, Imogen comes into view. Her cheeks are flushed, I'm sure from anger, but I'm conceited enough to believe it's also from arousal. She can profess her hatred all she wants, but that doesn't stop her from wanting me. A weakness I will use to my advantage.

Except I didn't like that kiss either. Rather, I liked it too much. It might be the first time I've ever experienced a certain kind of intimacy with a woman.

What started out as a way to drive my point home, turned into something...sweet. The way Imogen's fingers curled in my hair. The way she leaned into me. For a second, I savored the simplicity of it and enjoyed the kiss for what it was. There had been no ulterior motives. No captor and captive.

It had just been Liam and Imogen. The Liam I could have been in a different life.

I push that shit away. It's weakness talking. I have one life and this is it. There's no room for tenderness or *sweetness*. There's only room for ruthlessness and control.

I stop in front of the bedroom and wait for Imogen to reach me. Once she comes abreast, I walk inside and turn on the light. The bed sits in the center of one wall, its duvet already folded down as though beckoning us to climb beneath it.

"There are clothes in the wardrobe for you. Perhaps these will be more to your taste," I can't help but say drily.

She glares at me before she crosses the room and flips through the items hanging in the wardrobe. Finally, she turns. Her expression is blank. "They're fine."

My lips twitch. It must have hurt to admit that much. "High praise."

Imogen doesn't wait for the rest of the tour. She marches into the adjoining bathroom and closes the door. Since there is only a second bedroom and bathroom up here, there's not much else for her to see other than the grounds. Considering the late hour, I'll assume she's getting hungry. Leaving her to sulk, or whatever it is she's doing in there, I head downstairs to the kitchen.

Darragh hadn't exaggerated when he said the housekeeper stocked the kitchen. I pause for a moment and take in everything in the fridge before grabbing what I need for a stew. It's one of the first things Seamus O'Doyle taught me how to make. It had filled my belly during those early cold winters when I'd been near starving and freezing my arse off living on the streets. If not for him, I'd most likely be dead. Cancer took the poor bastard too soon.

The broth is simmering, the meat added, and I'm just tossing in the vegetables when Imogen walks in. She glances around, squares her shoulders, and moves to one of the cupboards. To my surprise, she brings down a couple bowls and glasses and sets the table. We both perform our tasks in silence until there's nothing left to do but let the stew simmer for thirty or forty minutes.

"There's still enough light outside. Why don't I show you around the property?" I offer.

She pauses as though she's going to refuse. "Fine."

I set the lid on the pot, wipe my hands on a towel, and head out of the kitchen into the boot room. Plucking the coat off the hook, I hand it to her. "Wouldn't want you to catch a cold."

"If only I could be so lucky," she snarks, but puts it on.

The thing swallows her whole. I like her wearing my clothes far too much. Pushing away the sensation, I lead the way out the door to the empty drive. The cottage sits at the top of a hill surrounded by trees. We walk down the narrow gravel lane bisected by short grass and cut weeds toward the road. To the left is a line of almost bare bushes a couple feet taller than me. Near the bottom a doorway shaped opening is formed.

I glance over at Imogen whose cheeks have turned rosy again from the bite of the wind. Her black, purple, and teal hair flutters around her head and she tucks it behind her ears. Her gaze wanders. I study her and somehow am at a loss for words.

"What made you buy a modest cottage all the way out here? Wherever *here* is?" she asks, finally breaking the silence.

"Trying to get me to tell you our location are you?"

She glares at me. "I'm merely making polite discourse. Isn't that what you asked for a few days ago?"

I throw my head back in laughter. Imogen stares at me like she has no idea who I am. I rein in my amusement with a final chuckle. "I think we've gone beyond *polite discourse* don't you think?"

"No, I don't."

"Still trying to deny this thing between us, I see."

She stops in her path and folds her arms. "Fine. Am I attracted to you? Of course. There's no sense denying it anymore. But whatever you think *this* is?" She waves a finger back and forth between us. "It's just an illusion of civility as you say. You want to seduce me? Go ahead. You want to punish me for going to Carrick for protection *from you*? Go ahead. But let's not make me being here into anything more than that. Do whatever it is you're going to do so I can go home and get on with my life."

Before I can utter a single word, Imogen walks back up the hill and into the cottage.

Fuck.

~

DINNER IS UNCOMFORTABLE. I'M HONESTLY SURPRISED Imogen didn't refuse to eat it with me. Although, from the first day she arrived at my home, I discovered she'll never turn down food if she's hungry. Not even to spite me. I consider being a twat and goading her into conversation, but for some reason, I don't want to argue with her. Not tonight anyway. *What the fuck is wrong with you?* I block out the inner voice and finish up my meal.

From that first meeting, Imogen presented a challenge. She still does. Even more than I imagined. I need a new strategy, because this one clearly isn't working. She pushes away her bowl. "If you'll excuse me, I believe I'm going to lie down. It's been a shit day."

She gets up and scurries away from the table. Probably thinks I'll chase after her and try to bend her to my will, but I let her go. This time anyway. Because the only thing I think about when she's near is all the ways I plan on fucking her. I have every intention of having her, but forcing her to acknowledge the attraction between us has made her all the more determined to fight it. Fight me. Which means, I need to change tactics. It means I can't seduce her. I have to woo her. Court her. The only problem is, I'm not sure I have it in me.

I clean up the kitchen and then go to the living area to call Darragh.

"Hello."

"Are Declan and Aran secured?"

"Yes, sir. Although they didn't come quietly."

I snort. Of course they didn't. That would have been expecting too much.

"Also, Aran wants to talk to you."

"I'll ring him tomorrow. In the meantime, watch the estate, but don't engage," I instruct Darragh. "Let me know when they strike and be ready to make the call. It'll be soon. Keep an eye on my other properties as well, including the docks. I wouldn't put it past Donnelly to hit everything."

"You got it, boss."

I end the call, toss my phone on the sofa, and go to the bar to make myself a drink. There hasn't been a single footstep since Imogen went upstairs. I'm not worried about her going anywhere. We're out in the countryside with no close neighbors. It's one of the reasons I purchased this property. The other being that it once belonged to my grand-da and the only person who ever loved me. Before my Da sold it right out from under him.

Bastard.

May he rot in hell.

I take a deep breath in and swear I can still smell the ale he used to drink even though the old man's been dead for thirty years. I miss him.

Tossing back the rest of the whiskey, I shake off the fucking pity party. Christ, is that what being in this house is going to do to me? If that's the case, I never should have brought Imogen here. Pity is for the weak. I haven't spent the last two decades working toward who I am today only to be brought down by memories and some woman. No matter how much I want to fuck her.

I smack the glass down on the bar top with almost enough force to break it and pivot out of the room and up the stairs. The light in the main bedroom is on. I step inside and Imogen lies with her back to the door on the farthest side of the bed with the duvet tucked under her arm. She doesn't turn when I enter. A quick glance confirms her eyes are closed. Not that I care either way.

I undress.

A sharp inhale comes from behind. Naked, I pull out my clothes for tomorrow and hang the clean suit on the handle. Then I turn to face her.

Imogen's eyes are open and locked on me. My cock specifically. I let her look her fill before padding over to shut off the light and then to what is apparently my side of the bed. I lie down and her body stiffens. Since I've already decided on a different tactic, I remain unmoving while I lie on my back and stare at the ceiling. Eventually, she relaxes, but stays where she is. It takes far too long for her breathing to slow and even out.

It's going to be a long night.

CHAPTER 21

I snuggle against the warmth next to me and the firm, yet soft, pillow under my cheek. Then freeze. Mentally preparing myself, I open my eyes. Fuck me. I'm half sprawled over Liam. My head is on his bicep, an arm is flung over his chest, and one of my legs is threaded between his. And because it can only get worse, he's staring down at me. There's no delicate way to extract myself, so I stay where I am. It's not like I can hide the fact that I'm plastered against him. Maybe if I act like it's no big deal—it's a damn huge deal —he won't say anything.

"Are you aware that you snore?" he asks, clearly trying to torment me.

I glare up at him. "Snoring happens when you sleep. And since I'm *asleep*, then, no, I am not aware of it."

"Haven't any of your previous lovers mentioned it?" He says it like he's one of many even though we haven't even fucked. *Yet*, a little voice whispers.

I try to move away, but Liam's hold on me tightens. With a sigh, I stop. "No, no one has ever mentioned it before. They're probably too *polite* to do so."

He snorts. "Are you saying I'm not polite?"

"You're the farthest thing from it."

His gasp is more than fake. "I should be offended. If it weren't true, that is."

The way he says it, in such a self-deprecating way, actually makes me smile. At least Liam is honest about the kind of person he is and makes no apologies for it. I could almost appreciate the fact if I also didn't hate him. *Now who's the one lying?* Fine, so maybe hate is too strong of a word. It doesn't mean I like him, though.

Him getting undressed last night shouldn't have been as sexy as it was. It's not like I haven't seen a man get naked before. But with Liam, there is something different. Probably because his body is pure perfection. He's muscular without being bulky. The tattoos that cover the canvas of his skin are hot. Don't get me started on his cock. He's maybe slightly longer than average, but whatever he might possibly lack in length—which isn't much—he makes up for in girth. I've always been partial to a fat cock. It's a shame that beautiful cock is attached to such a giant *dick*. I snort at my own joke.

"Care to share what's so funny?"

"You wouldn't get my humor."

He raises an eyebrow. "Try me."

"I'd rather not."

Liam launches his assault. He tickles my side and a squeal erupts from me. I roll to my back to get away, laughter spilling from my lips, but he looms over me with a devious grin. "Tell me."

I wiggle and squirm, but he's relentless. Finally, out of breath, I cave. "Okay, okay."

He stops, but doesn't move off me. I stare up at him. His eyes are bright with his own laughter. The smile slowly leaves my face. I can't look away from him. The fun, light-hearted atmosphere shifts into acute awareness of his nakedness lying on top of me. Heat pools in my belly. My legs part enough that Liam settles into the cradle of them. Only the thin layer of fabric of my yoga pants separate us. The area right above my clit pulses. He brushes away a stray strand of hair stuck at the corner of my mouth. My tongue darts out to wet my suddenly dry lips and his gaze drops to them. Desire darkens the blue of his eyes to nearly black. Then...he's gone.

I blink away my confusion and push myself up on my elbows. Liam's already rolled out of bed and heading to the bathroom. He glances over his shoulder. "I'm going to take a quick shower. Why don't you go down to the kitchen and get out the eggs and whatever else you want inside your omelet? I'll be there soon."

The bathroom door closes. Stunned, I don't move for several minutes. Not until the water turns on. What the fuck just happened? I throw the duvet off me and sit up. My feet dangle over the edge. I glance over at the bathroom, but the door remains closed. Shaking off the weirdness, I hop down and put my socks from yesterday back on. I'll search the wardrobe later for a clean pair.

I make my way down to the kitchen and grab everything he asked for from the fridge. I'd start breakfast, except I have no idea how to make an omelet. Instead, I pour myself a glass of orange juice and sit at the table. I dart my eyes up to the ceiling. An idea hits. I run back up the stairs, careful not to make any noise, and pause outside the bedroom. The shower is still running. I peek around the door. Empty.

With careful steps, I walk across the room and search. There's nothing in either drawer of the table on Liam's side of the bed. I rifle through suit jackets and pant pockets in the wardrobe. Shit, where did he put his phone? I swivel my head toward the bathroom and curse. He stands in the doorway in all his wet, naked glory with arms crossed over his chest. I try not to stare at his cock. Again.

"Looking for something?" he asks drily.

I clear my throat and straighten. "Yes, as a matter of fact."

"Oh?" He's not stupid, so no sense acting like he is.

"I was trying to find your phone."

Liam's eyes widen a fraction. Good, I've shocked him with my honest reply.

"What? You thought I was going to lie?"

He unfolds his frame. "Yes, actually."

I lift a shoulder. "No point. We both know what I was doing."

"You didn't think I'd make it that easy, did you?"

My cheeks heat, because I really did. He chuckles, shakes his head, and walks back into the bathroom. Although this time he leaves the door open. I blow out a ragged breath and go downstairs again. I haven't given up. Just postponed my search. Since I didn't get to explore any of the grounds except the lane up to the house, I open the set of double doors in the entryway.

A beautifully landscaped courtyard greets me. Despite the chilled weather, beds of blooming flowers dot the space between sections of green grass and narrow stone pathways. I step out onto the patio. Shit, it's cold. Sucking it up since my shoes are upstairs, I walk around admiring the well-tended area. Liam must have a thing for gardening as well as cooking. Another piece of the puzzle I can't seem to fit together with the rest of them.

I stay to the path in case the grass is wet. Nothing grosser than walking around in wet socks. The stones wind through the beds, twisting and turning until they lead me back to the house. I'll wait until I have shoes on before I take on the rest of the property. The scent of bacon greets me as soon as I step inside. I guess Liam wasn't worried about me running off anywhere. Not that there's any place for me to go. The last town we'd passed yesterday certainly isn't within walking distance nor were there any houses close by that I can recall.

Closing the door, I head for the kitchen, the scent of food reminding me how hungry I am. With still damp hair, Liam stands at the stove. The sizzle of grease is loud in the quiet. He glances over his shoulder and then goes back to his task without saying anything. Is he leaving it up to me to make conversation? Because if that's the case, he's going to have a long wait. I sit at a computer all day. Alone. My social interactions are extremely limited.

The only people I talk to are the clients, James, and Teagan, my best friend from Uni. None, except hers, are social calls. The only thing James and I ever talk about is the weather and while T and I text weekly, she only calls me when she's back in Dublin between jobs. There isn't much I can do to help cook since that's non-existent in my wheelhouse. Instead, I do like I had last night and set the table, refilling my half-empty glass of juice I'd left sitting here when I rushed upstairs. At least I can't fuck that up. Once that's done, I take a seat to observe him.

When the silence stretches to an uncomfortable length, I can't take it any longer. "The flowers outside are pretty. I never took you for someone who gardened."

"There are a lot of things you don't know about me." Liam plates the last of the bacon and slides both omelets from two separate pans onto two more plates. He somehow manages to bring all three of them to the table at once and then sits in the chair next to me.

"Why don't you tell me one thing, then." It's almost a dare.

He leans back and there's a calculating gleam in his gaze. "What will you give me in return?"

Why do I even care if he shares anything personal with me?

Because he's a puzzle to solve, Imogen.

Oh yeah.

I mimic Liam's pose. "What do you want, and we can negotiate from there?"

The familiar smirk appears. God only knows what he's going to ask me. I'm regretting bringing the whole conversation up.

"I want you to enjoy yourself while you're here. Think of this as a vacation."

What? I blink and wait for him to say something else. Or ask me a question. Like why I went to Carrick's. Or why I had all those videos. But a vacation? Enjoy myself? There has to be a catch. I cock my head and narrow my eyes. "Why do I feel like this is a trick?"

Liam shows me his palms. "It's not my fault you have a suspicious nature. No trick."

The quiet lingers again while I weigh if I trust him or not. He doesn't try and persuade me. Just sits there with one eyebrow raised like he's calling my dare.

"Fine."

He dips his head slightly. "Fine."

I open my mouth and he raises a finger. *I knew it.* "I'll tell you one thing. Any more than that will require another trade."

I'll have to take it. "Deal. Now, stop procrastinating and spill. It better be something good, too."

"My middle name is Noah."

"Seriously?" My jaw slackens. "That's it? I could have found that out myself without even breaking a sweat."

"You know what you have to do if you want more."

"That was a dick move," I huff.

Liam stands with his plate and takes it to the sink. "Hurry up and finish eating. We're going out."

Going out where?

CHAPTER 22

Liam

I'm not sure why I'm taking Imogen into Kenmare. Or anywhere, in fact. We should be up in bed while I fuck her every which way until we're both sweaty and exhausted. Then do it again.

Except we're not.

There's still no word from Darragh. Everything's been quiet. No raid on the estate, my office, or the docks. It's obviously a tactic to keep me guessing or make me show my hand. As if that will happen. I have far too much patience for that. I can wait the Donnellys out. Dónal is still missing as well. If rumors are true and they do have him, I doubt his body will ever be found.

The floor creaks several times and then Imogen walks into the living area where I've been waiting. She's pulled her hair up and she's wearing a different outfit than the one she had on earlier. Which means she got it from the wardrobe. I scan her from head to toe and meet her eyes again with a knowing glance, but I don't mention what she's wearing.

I stride toward her and stop less than an arm's length away. Her head tips back slightly and I want nothing more than to pull her to me for a taste, but it's not part of my strategy. "The driver should be here in a few minutes."

"You still haven't told me where we're going."

"I know." With that, I walk around her and head to the boot room.

Imogen growls low in her throat, but follows me. Who knew it was this fun to antagonize someone just for the hell of it? I love that she gives as good as she gets. Yet again I hand her my coat. Already it smells of her.

"I don't need that. I'll just go up and get a hoodie." She starts to turn but I move to block her path.

"Wear it."

She huffs but puts it on. Unable to resist the temptation any longer, I cup Imogen's jaw. She stops moving, maybe even breathing. I wait until her eyes meet mine before I slowly lower my lips to hers. It was just yesterday that we kissed, but it feels like a lifetime ago. I draw back and stare down. Her eyes flutter open. That same sensation hits me in the gut. I can't name it, but I'm most certain I don't like it.

I release her and turn for the door to open it. "After you."

Confusion, then annoyance, flickers across her face as she sweeps past me out to where the driver waits. She climbs into the backseat and I can't help but admire her ass. I get in as well. Moments later we're out on the road.

"Have you ever driven around the Ring of Kerry?" I glance over at Imogen.

She shakes her head. "Not unless it's near Cork."

"Is that the only place you've been besides Dublin, then?"

"Aye. My mum and I would go every once in a while on a weekend getaway. Before she got sick, anyway," she says softly with a tone of sorrow.

"How did she die?" It hadn't been in any of the research I'd done on her.

"Cancer."

"Mine, too," I admit before I can pull the confession back.

"I'm sorry. You were still a kid, weren't you?" She doesn't wait for an answer. "That must have sucked. At least I had twenty-seven years with her. Not that it hurts any less, but I think it would have been harder if I'd been young."

Would Imogen be surprised to know that I hadn't been all that sad? No, probably not. But why mourn someone who hated me? A warm hand lays over mine and I jerk my head to the side. Sympathy lines her face. I slide out from under her touch and hurt flares in her eyes. She clutches her fists together in her lap and for a second, I want to apologize.

Except I don't apologize to anyone. Ever. Not anymore.

"What did you and your mum like to do in Cork?"

Imogen narrows her gaze. "What's with the sudden interest?"

"You're the one who wants to stick to polite discourse." I throw the words back at her.

She snorts. "Since when do you let anyone else get what they want? You've been pretty clear that the only thing that matters is what *you* want."

"Perhaps you've helped me see the error of my ways."

This time Imogen laughs outright. "I doubt it. You don't strike me as the type of man who ever thinks he's wrong."

I lay my hand over my chest. "You wound me."

She studies me with a suddenly serious expression, her gaze traveling over me. Every spot it lands is like a physical touch. She lifts her gaze to mine and cants her head like she's trying to figure something out. I stare steadily back. Waiting. Except Imogen turns and faces forward without a word.

"Since when have you kept your opinions to yourself?" I snark.

She sighs and pivots a half-turn in my direction. Probably because she knows by now I won't let it go.

"Fine, but remember I tried to keep my mouth shut, so if you're going to be pissed at someone it better not be me," she warns.

There's a short pause. I wait her out, because my curiosity is more than piqued.

"I was just wondering if there *was* anything that truly did wound you? Not like I actually think you'd tell me if there was. Because let's be real. You're an arsehole. I just wondered what made you this way, is all. You couldn't have always been like this." She raises a shoulder. "Then again, maybe you were."

Imogen's mouth snaps shut, and she visibly braces herself, but she maintains eye contact. Her words hang in the air. Lingering. Taunting. I like the fact she's unafraid of me. There's nothing worse than a terrified and crying woman.

"You're right."

She blinks and jerks slightly, clearly shocked I'd admit it.

"I am an arsehole." I nod for emphasis.

For a second, I could swear disappointment flashes behind her eyes. What did she expect? That I'd tell her some sad tale about how horrible my life has been?

"So? Cork?" I nudge, redirecting the conversation to its original question.

At first, Imogen doesn't answer. There's a mulish tilt to her chin. "Mum loved all the castles," she finally says begrudgingly with a small smile. "Her favorite was Blarney, of course. Every time we went there, we always kissed the Blarney Stone."

I can just picture her trekking up all the stairs to the top and lying backwards to press her lips to the piece of stone said to bring the person the gift of eloquence and persuasiveness. Considering her sharp tongue, it appears to have worked.

"I'll take you to go see a castle tomorrow. It's not Blarney Castle, but I think you'll enjoy it just the same. The view of the surrounding mountains is quite the spectacle. Today, however, you'll have to be satisfied with the rolling hills and water." I point out the windscreen.

Imogen ducks her head and takes in the view. Her eyes widen.

Colorful buildings line the street on either side, and the cathedral tower rises up to the sky on the horizon. Grand-da would bring me here during the summer, and we'd rent a fishing boat and head out onto the bay. I'd forgotten about that.

"Where are we? It's so pretty," she gushes and turns to me.

"Welcome to Kenmare."

The driver makes his way through the town and into the car park while Imogen's head swivels side to side as she takes in everything. Across from us is an old cathedral and a short stone wall lines the footpath on that side of the street. A few people stroll past.

I exit the vehicle and hold out my hand. There's a brief hesitation, but she takes it. I help her out and when she tries to release me, I tighten my hold. Her lips thin, but she relents. Hand-in-hand we walk along the footpath toward town center. The weather is cool this early, but the sky is a bright cerulean and clear and soon the sun will climb high overhead and bring warmth with it.

"You're pretty familiar with this place," Imogen notes leaving an unasked question hanging in the air.

I glance down at her. What will it hurt for her to know? "My grand-da and I used to come here quite often when I was young."

"You two were close, then?"

There's a short pause. "For a while."

She makes a small sound, but closes her mouth on it. Maybe she can sense my reticence to talk about him. Whatever it is, Imogen doesn't ask another question. "That must have been nice to have that kind of relationship with him. I never knew mine."

"Your mum never spoke of them?" I'm relieved to change the subject.

She shakes her head. "Only to say they disowned her. After that one time, she never spoke of them—or any other family—again."

"You're a computer expert. You can't tell me you weren't ever curious? Didn't you ever use your skills to track them down?"

"By the time I reached an age where I could try and track them down, I'd gotten it in my head that if they really wanted to know me, they would have. If they cut my mum out of their life, then I doubted they were interested in me. And judging by the lack of phone calls or birthday cards, I was right." Imogen tips her head to the side. "So it's always been just Mum and me. Or it was. Now, it's just me."

It's just me as well. A fact that's never bothered me. I suppose I should consider Declan and Aran. They *are* the only family I have left, even if we've been estranged for years and they'd rather not admit we're related. Imogen and I stop at an intersection and once traffic has passed, we cross. Considering the hour and that it's the middle of the week, I'm surprised by the number of people out and about. Then again, it's been years since I've visited. Maybe it was always like this and I just don't remember.

"What was your favorite place coming here?" Imogen asks.

I glance over and find myself smiling a little. "You'll see."

CHAPTER 23

Imogen

My breath catches. This might be the first genuine smile Liam's given me. There's always been a hint of sarcasm behind all the previous ones. Yes, he's laughed a few times, but it also felt like each one held a hint of mockery. But this? The hardness in his features softens just a fraction and he looks younger. The same thing happened when he mentioned his grand-da. Not a lot, but enough. Christ, if he smiles at me like this all the time, I'll probably fall straight into his bed.

He's even more beautiful than before. Fuck.

"What's got that look on your face?" Liam asks.

I shake off the wandering thought. "Nothing. I just got distracted for a second."

His side-eye says he doesn't believe me, but he doesn't push the issue. We make a turn down a lane between a row of buildings. A short distance ahead of us, at the end, is a stone wall about chest high. To the left is a blue storefront with a hanging placard displaying the name of the bookstore. I picture all the books in Carrick's library. It also reminds me of the book in Liam's car and the note he'd slipped inside the cover before passing it off to his goon. What had he written on it? If I thought he'd tell me, I'd ask.

We reach the end of the road and a dirt path veers off into a wooded area. I dart a glance in Liam's direction, but keep walking. The sound of water reaches me. He guides me along the wall and I peek over it. A narrow river flows down a shallow ravine guarded on either side by trees. We round a bend and I let out a soft, "Ohhh."

A beautiful, old stone bridge with patches of moss growing on it arches over the water. A steel barricade blocks this end of the entrance to it to prevent pedestrians from crossing. Liam and I come to a stop not far from it.

"This is Cromwell's Bridge, one of Kenmare's more popular tourist attractions," he explains. "There's a ton of history connected to it. The Brits claim it's named after their commander Cromwell who tried to squash the Irish uprising, but others say it was built by monks in the seventh century as a way for them to reach a nearby holy well. No one knows the real story for sure though. It's all just a bunch of speculation."

I follow the walking path—Liam's hand still entwined with mine—to get a closer look. The trees are too overgrown to determine what this place might have looked like when the bridge was functional, so it's hard to tell what's on the other side of them. Still, there's a sense of history and wonder that comes from the structure alone. It's one of the reasons Mum loved visiting all the castles around Cork. She'd always been fascinated with their background and historical significance. Maybe some of her interest rubbed off on me.

"It's beautiful. Thank you for showing me."

"Oh, we're not done yet," Liam teases. "Come on."

We backtrack the same way we came. I toss a glance over my shoulder for one final look before he and I round the corner to the street and lose sight of the wooded area behind us. We walk out to the main road and turn. More colorful buildings in yellow, blue, and pink line the streets. The footpath becomes a bit busier as we pass shops, bakeries, and other restaurants. Elderly men tip their hats and several groups of women stare, their eyes glued to the man at my side. I edge a little closer to him like I have some sort of claim. For Liam's part, he doesn't pay them any attention.

As we walk, the sun creeps higher in the sky and burns off some of the chill. Soon, it will be too warm for his coat, but until then I'll keep wearing it. It smells like him. The citrus fragrance of the cologne he wears—that reminds me of my favorite tea—along with the slight musky scent that is all Liam. I can't reconcile the man from before I escaped to Carrick's with the one whose hand hasn't released mine since we stepped out of the town car. *You know he's playing a game.* I do, but he keeps changing the rules. Until I figure out what they are, I have to keep playing, too.

Soon, the buildings thin out just a bit and we come to a roundabout.

"Are you sure you know where you're going?" I can't help but ask. We've been walking for ten minutes.

"What? You don't trust me?"

"Not even a little bit."

Liam squeezes my hand. "You're probably right not to."

I clearly need the reminder. He glances both directions and we cross the street. A drive way on the left is marked on either side with two curved stone walls facing each other. An iron placard on both of them reads "Park Hotel Kenmare."

"Are you sure we should be walking down this way? It looks like private property." Trees line the perimeter forming a canopy over the lane.

"I'm positive. This is the main entrance to our next destination."

"You're taking me to a hotel?"

"Worried you won't be able to resist me any longer?" Liam smirks.

I glare at him. "Don't get your hopes up."

His knowing expression tells me he's perfectly aware he's wearing me down. It's not as though I haven't admitted to the attraction between us. Even to myself. Hell, I practically sucked him dry before he left for his meeting with Carrick that night. As though he, too, recalls exactly what happened in the conservatory, his eyes heat with desire that sends a shiver coursing through me. The musky flavor of his come lingered on my tongue for hours after that. I can almost still taste him.

Then he blinks and whatever awareness that had hovered between us is gone. "Don't worry, you'll like where we're headed."

Is this his new tactic? Drive me insane with desire and then leave me hanging? Because, if so, it might actually be working.

The bastard.

Having no other choice, I keep quiet and let him lead me to where ever it is he's taking me. We pass the hotel and keep walking even as the road curves and then abruptly ends. Except there's still a path that leads straight into a massive copse of trees.

"Is this where you chop me up into little pieces and dispose of the body?" I can't help but joke.

"I'm saving that for the Bay, remember?"

"Ah, yes, now I recall something to that effect."

The path widens and then turns into a descending staircase, with wide pieces of carved wood serving as the steps. We follow it down to another path. With the trees blocking out the sun, the chill has returned. I snuggle deeper into Liam's coat. We continue along the nature-formed walkway until we veer to the right where it suddenly straightens into a long stretch. My eyes widen and my mouth drops. I tug my hand loose and he releases me. My feet keep moving me forward as I slowly pivot with my head tipped back and my eyes scanning everything.

Inward leaning trees with purple flowers curve and form an archway down the entire length of the path creating the illusion of a circular tunnel, almost as though it leads to a fairy dimension. Scattered across the ground as far as visible into the imagined tunnel are the same purple petals that grace the trees. The only whisper of sound is the quiet breeze fluttering the remaining flowers and leaves high above us.

"What is this place?" It's a hushed whisper. I don't want to disturb the magic that surrounds me.

"The entirety of it is Reenagross Woodland Park, but this particular section is the Lover's Walk in the Rhododendron Forest. They say at night you can see the sparkle of the fairy dust from the fae that live within the hollows of the trunks and knolls in the ground." Liam's voice is equally quiet.

A mystical sensation skims across my skin and raises the hair along my arms. I could almost believe he's right. There is something special—almost otherworldly—about this place. I come to a stop, close my eyes, and spread out my arms, breathing in the floral fragrance. For a second, it's as though I've been transported to another dimension.

I let it continue washing over me and then slowly open my eyes. Liam stands several yards away. *Too* far away. I'm not sure if this has been his plan all along, but, if it is, I have to give him credit. It fucking worked. Isn't this what I decided on that day in the conservatory anyway. Go ahead and let him get me out of his system and be done with all of this? Why does that have to change? *Is that really why you're doing this*? I close the distance between us. In a single move, I rise up on my toes, palm the back of his neck, and claim his mouth with mine. I slip my tongue between his lips, and he groans as his hands grip my ass.

Liam pulls me against him, and I grind my pelvis against his hard cock. The friction is a sweet pleasure-pain that won't be satisfied until he's buried deep inside me. Maybe not even then. I'm royally fucked. Considering he's trying to rule all of Dublin, I guess it's only appropriate. The kiss goes on as though nothing outside this magical realm exists. I drink from his lips like I'm parched. The sweetness all around us makes Liam taste better. Like a fruit-flavored cocktail. My thirst may never be quenched.

A branch snaps and a stifled cough breaks us apart. He glances over my head and glares with marked annoyance at whoever inter-rupted us. I'm sure my expression mirrors his. I want to gnash my teeth and growl at the interloper. I'm guided a few steps sideways toward the edge of the path. Two people pass by, but my gaze is locked on Liam's. We stare at each other long after we're alone again. As an Irishwoman, I hold to a lot of superstitions. One of them being that the fae are real. This magical place only proves it. And maybe the words whispered in my ear are merely my brain rationalizing my actions, but I can't help believe that they're coming from the fairies who live in the forest.

Mind made up, I seal my fate. "I'm ready to go back to the cottage now."

CHAPTER 24

LIAM

WHO KNEW THE EFFECT THIS PLACE WOULD HAVE ON Imogen? On me? I brought her here because the few times I'd come with my grand-da I'd been captivated by the magic of the forest. It could have been that I was only a kid, but the feeling stayed with me longer after he'd been gone. I wanted her to experience the magic of it too. Judging by the expression on her face, she does.

In no time we're in the town car and on our way back to the cottage. The air around us is charged with desire. Imogen casts several glances my way, each one lasting a little longer as her gaze travels over me and her eyes darken with arousal. My cock strains against my zipper, begging for release.

I could have her suck me off again, or I could slip my hand inside those leggings of hers and bring her to completion. Except I have no intention of letting the driver get so much as a glimpse of Imogen's pleasure. It's only for me to witness.

After far too much time, we finally pass through the gate at the base of the hill and then we stop outside the cottage. I step out of the back and give her my hand. Each time I do, her hesitation to take it lessens. We walk through the boot room and the kitchen before I can't make it any farther. I pull her into my arms and claim her mouth. She clings to me and falls into the kiss. I palm her ass and hike her up, forcing her legs to wrap around my waist. Imogen gasps against my lips and holds tight as I walk us up the stairs and into the bedroom.

My grip loosens and she slowly slides down my body until her feet touch the floor and only then do I drag my mouth from hers. Imogen's eyes are glazed with arousal and she holds my arms like she needs to steady herself. I cup her jaw and rub my thumb across her bottom lip until she tips her chin up.

"I have no intention of stopping until I've wrung every orgasm out of you and you're screaming my name."

Imogen's gaze narrows. "Maybe you'll be the one screaming *my* name."

Always with the smart mouth. "We shall see. Now strip."

I expect her to have some sharp rebuttal, but she surprises me by stepping away and yanking her shirt up and over her head. It dangles from her outstretched palm before she tilts her hand and it drops to the floor. Her bra comes off next. She's absolutely exquisite. My fingers itch to trace the subtle line of her waist before it flares out to her hip. Her breasts are small, but stand firm and proud with their bright red tips.

Imogen glides forward, and with the same drawn-out, teasing way as she'd done back in the conservatory at the estate, she unbuttons my shirt, exposing more of my chest with each one until the last of them is released and she pushes the fabric over my shoulders and down my arms. With a careless toss, it falls somewhere near hers.

"I think you forgot something." I glance down at her leggings.

"No, I didn't. I'm leaving the rest of the honors to you. But first..." Her fingers dance across my skin, lingering along the tattoos that run down my arm and the furrows and valleys of my stomach.

Her eyes darken with arousal as she touches each new spot. My cock aches with the need to be buried in her cunt, but I plan on savoring this first time. First of many.

Imogen continues her exploration until her fingertips trace my jaw. She scrapes her nails through the stubble that covers it. My fists clench with the need to reach out and touch her, but I breathe in patience for a moment longer while she makes a lazy circle around me. Without taking her eyes off me, she walks backward until she reaches the bed and then crooks her finger at me.

I cross the distance in only a few steps and crash my mouth against hers. Heated passion rises as I lower her, neither of us breaking the kiss. My tongue teases hers with only a flick, drawing her out. Imogen surrenders to me and meets each of my parries with one of her own. The cool sheets quickly heat beneath her.

My fingers skate across her skin and I reach for her small, firm breast. She's satin to the touch and as fragile as the petals of the flowers in my conservatory. She should be handled with care, but she's strong enough to take everything I give her. I knead the mound and pluck at the turgid point. Imogen arches into my touch.

"More," she pleads.

I pinch the diamond-hard nipple harder and a shudder runs through her. I lower my head, take the rigid peak in my mouth, and lash it with my tongue, suckling the hardened tip before catching it between my teeth. Her chest rises on a quick inhalation at the bite of pain, but I soothe the sting with gentle kisses. I give her other breast the same sweet torture, and she lets out a breathy sigh. My nostrils flare at the smell of her perfume like a beast scenting its mate. I've waited long enough to finally sink into the wet heat of her cunt. I come to my knees.

"Lift up," I command, tugging at her leggings.

Imogen raises her ass and I pull them over her hips and down the length of her legs. I discard them somewhere over the side of the bed. Her breathing grows shallower, her chest rising and falling with the effort. I separate her knees so she's fully displayed to me. My cock jerks at the exposed flesh.

"I wish you could see yourself right now. How wet and pink your cunt is waiting for me to devour it and lap up every drop." My mouth waters in anticipation of Imogen's flavor.

Will she be sweet? Musky? Without taking my eyes off her, I rise from the bed, quickly remove my pants, and step out of them. Her eyes home in on my cock. Like the predator I am, I prowl forward and wedge my shoulders between her legs, spreading them farther until she's wide open for me. I slide my hand under one hip and loop her knee over me. Her bare pussy glistens with wetness, and her clit swells.

I nibble her inner thighs, and her breaths come in short gasps the closer I move to her center. For a single beat I consider prolonging Imogen's agony, and mine, but I can't do it. I'm going to make her come over and over again until her only thought is me. I dip my head and lap up her juice. Every movement of my tongue is meant to push her to heights she's never reached.

I worship her cunt, feasting on it as though nothing has tasted sweeter. Her fingers thread through my hair, and the sting from her clutching me hard only makes me hungrier.

"Fuck, yes," Imogen whimpers. "I need more."

I spear her with my tongue and lift my gaze. She's stunning. Her whole body is flushed as she writhes and moans beneath me. Her heel digs into my back and she pushes herself harder against my face, the tension building in her muscles. I slide one finger, then two, deep inside at the same time I bite down on her clit. Imogen's entire body jerks. Her back arches and her fingers clench into tight fists yanking at the strands of my hair she holds within them. My scalp stings, but I don't stop.

A third finger joins the first two, and I suck her clit hard, grazing it again with my teeth. Another powerful orgasm rocks her body and her head thrashes from side to side. A thin layer of sweat coats our skin making it so slick her leg slides off my shoulder, which only gives

Imogen more leverage to push upward. Begging for more of what only I can give her. Her cunt pulses around the digits, milking them like she'll soon be milking my cock.

Her ragged breathing slows as I kiss my way back up her body and bury my nose in the crook of her neck to breathe in the scent of Imogen and sex.

"Is that all you got?" she mumbles into my ear.

I push myself up. Her eyes are glassy and her lips are puckered and pouty. God, this woman. "I don't think I've wrung every orgasm out of you yet, which means I'm far from done."

Imogen's vision clears and she arches a brow. "Then get to it."

My mouth curls at the challenge. "Don't forget you asked for it."

I climb higher up the bed and reach into the bedside table. Between my fingers is a foil pouch that I quickly tear open and slide the condom down my length while she watches with hooded lids. I settle between her thighs again, holding myself up on my elbows and slowly inch inside her cunt.

Imogen gasps at the sensation, while I groan deep in my chest at the tightness surrounding me. It's incredible. I bite my cheek to distract myself from the sensation, and blood coats my tongue. Once I've gained control, I thrust, gaining momentum with each push and pull. I slam my mouth down on hers, feeding her the copper-flavored fluid, and my tongue mimics the movement of my cock. A growl rumbles out of me every time she clenches down. I'm not sure how long I'll last.

I slide my hand between us and play with her clit, rocking my pelvis faster, going deeper. Imogen pushes her hips up to meet me with each forward thrust of my cock.

"Do you have any idea how good you feel? How much you turn me on," I mumble against her lips. "I could fuck you all night and into tomorrow. And the day after. Your cunt was made to be filled by me."

"Yes." The muscles in her body tighten as though she's seconds away from release already.

Increasing the pressure on her clit, my movements quicken and my balls draw up. I'm about to explode like a fucking teenager, but she needs to come again first. With only a small bit of friction, Imogen's cunt contracts, and the orgasm rushes through her. She throws her head back and screams my name as my cock erupts.

Her body trembles and I half collapse on top of her, keeping my full weight off with my elbows. Our breathing is harsh in the empty room. I rise up a little and push damp strands of hair off her sweat-beaded forehead and brush a kiss across lips that curl up in satisfaction.

"I think you killed me," she whispers harshly, throwing her forearm over her eyes. "But what a way to go."

A chuckle is pulled from me as I roll to my side. "That was only a sample of what I have planned for you."

I lie there for a minute to catch my breath. I turn my head and glance over at her. She's still smiling. I could get used to it. Leaning over, I kiss her quickly, and then rise to discard the condom before I crawl back in beside her. She scoots close and cuddles into my side. I've never been one for snuggling after sex, but I find myself slipping my arm beneath her head and bringing her closer.

Imogen murmurs a small happy sound and I kiss her forehead. "Rest so you're ready for round two."

She wraps herself tighter around me with a giggle and her entire body relaxes. I bring my hand under my head and stare at the ceiling, reliving the most intense orgasm I've ever had. I'm not sure if I'll ever get enough of her. A fact that worries me more than I care to admit.

CHAPTER 25

Imogen

I SHIFT AND THEN WINCE AT THE TENDERNESS BETWEEN my legs. After a two-day fuck-a-thon my lady parts are cursing me out. But it is so worth it. Other than breaking to grab a quick bite to eat or use the bathroom, Liam and I haven't left this bed since we got back from Kenmare and the fairy forest. I slowly swivel my head in his direction. He's on his side, facing me. The shadow of hair on the bottom half of his face has thickened. My skin burns with the abrasions he's left, especially between my thighs. Lord, I've never been with a man who likes to eat pussy as much as Liam. Not that I'm complaining.

Along with genuine smiles, apparently multiple orgasms also give him a more youthful appearance. The fine lines that radiate from his eyes have smoothed out. There's also a lot less tension around his mouth, like he's not trying so hard to maintain his resting bastard face. I reach up to stroke my fingers across his rough skin of his cheek but let my arm fall.

I don't want to wake him. I'm not sure I'm ready to look him in the eyes.

I've never had any trouble disassociating sex from emotion. Hell, men do it all the time. I'm one of the few women of my acquaintance who can. Sometimes, I just need an itch scratched. It's fun, and the men I've slept with have been perfectly content to provide their services and then be on their way. Liam is supposed to be nothing more than a scratcher. Damn it, he *is* just a scratcher.

Then why do you want to get to know more about him?

I steel myself. I don't. There's no need for me to. He's selfish. Dangerous. Heartless. Cold. Except he wasn't any of those things these past couple days. Liam saw to my needs more than any man ever has before. Yes, he benefitted from it, but still, he always made sure I orgasmed at least twice before he came. He's been sweet. Taking me to the park and for a walk through the forest was the most magical thing ever. He's been tender. A feat I couldn't have pictured before two days ago. Especially not after I went straight to the Donnellys.

More than that, he's opened up, although that might be a bit generous. But he has actually told me little slivers of things about his life. Like how he, Declan, and Declan's brother Aran used to get into all sorts of trouble. He shared more about his summer trips out here to visit his grand-da. From everything I've managed to gather, all of his stories are from before his mother married Dónal. He hasn't mentioned her, his stepda, or Nessa in any of the stories he's told, and I haven't asked.

It's probably a good thing Carrick's not my father, even if it hurts for me to finally admit it. I'd wanted it to be true so badly. God knows what Liam would do.

The sudden need to escape runs through me. Doing my best not to disturb him, I inch my way out of the bed.

I manage some cold leftovers and then fill up my glass with juice and take it into the living area and turn on the TV. There's nothing on this early, but I keep scrolling through the channels before I pause.

Oh fuck.

Surrounded by a pack of Gardaí is Aidan Donnelly with his hands handcuffed in front of him. They're all walking into some building. Microphones are shoved in his face from various reporters and men with cameras are taking photos. He doesn't flinch, just stares straight ahead. I gasp and my hand covers my mouth, because right on their heels, another group of Gardaí escort a handcuffed Cian. Then Carrick. My eyes remain glued to the TV while I wait for more handcuffed men to be escorted through the mob of people, but once Carrick disappears through the door, the excitement of the crowd dims. What the hell is going on?

"Well, well, it actually worked." Liam chuckles behind me.

I whip around to face him. "What did you do?"

His gaze flicks from the TV to me and he tsks. "I had armed intruders at my home arrested, of course. You do know guns are illegal in Ireland?"

The minute I soften toward him in the slightest, he goes and pulls some shit like this. "That isn't the point. You got what you wanted. I'm here, aren't I?"

Liam scoffs. "Are you really that naive, Imogen? Did you actually think that this was only about you?"

I flinch at the hurtful words. "So you waited until they came for me and had them arrested?"

He folds his arms. "I've worked far too hard to acquire everything I have just to let the Donnellys take it from me."

"And it's still not enough for you." I stand. "I'm just one more thing you've *acquired*, aren't I? God forbid that I didn't ask for this or to be here. I've now just become collateral in this stupid battle you have against Carrick. It doesn't matter that I'm a fucking person and not some toy for you all to fight over."

Liam's eyes burn with growing anger and he steps closer. "I didn't hear you complaining about being here these last two days over the sound of you screaming my name as you orgasmed time after time."

My cheeks heat and not only from embarrassment. My temper is just as fiery as his. Maybe more so. "Fuck you."

He smirks, but it's an ugly twist of his lips. "Oh, I believe we've already done that, don't you?"

God, he's so infuriating. I glance back at the TV, but the news anchors have moved on. I turn to him again. "Why is controlling Dublin so important to you? What are you trying to prove? Isn't it enough that you overpowered your Da and are now the head of his organization?"

"*Dónal Sheehan is not my Da*," Liam roars, spittle flying from his mouth, and in a sweeping motion shoves everything off the side table to crash onto the floor. "It will *never* be enough."

My eyes go wide, and I stumble back a few steps away from the vitriol. He was angry before, but this is something entirely different. His face is flame-red and his chest heaves. His fists clench. I remain frozen in front of the couch, doing nothing more than swallow, afraid to move and set him off even more. The air is thick with tension until he slows his breathing and stretches out his fingers. An apology hovers on my tongue, but I bite it back.

Liam takes one last inhale and meets my gaze. His eyes shutter and lock out the deep emotion that, only seconds ago, had been pouring from them. He turns around and walks away. I collapse onto the couch. A minute later he comes back and I go rigid. Except he's holding a broom and dustpan and cleaning glass from the floor. He picks up the books and the small pieces of the broken wood-carved wolf figurine and places them back on the table. All I do is stare until he disappears again and sounds from the kitchen reach me. The scent of bacon cooking soon follows.

What the fuck did his Da—*stepda*—do to incite that much hatred? Because that response went far beyond any emotion Liam has displayed in the short time I've been with him. All the air around him had been charged with so much rage. If Dónal Sheehan had been standing in this room, I suspect he'd be dead.

Hopefully he's had enough time to cool off. I head to the kitchen, my steps a bit more cautious, and pause at the entryway. Liam stands at the stove and flips the half-made omelet in the skillet he's tending. He takes several pieces of bacon out of another pan and sets it on a nearby plate. I stand there another minute, but he doesn't acknowledge my presence more than the slight stiffening of his shoulders when I first walked in.

Like the last meal we had down here, I grab our place settings from the cupboard and drawers and set the table. I pour each of us a glass of orange juice. By the time I'm finished, he's plated the first omelet and sets it in front of the same chair I sat before.

"Eat before it gets cold," Liam grumbles and returns to the stove.

I take a seat and dig in. My gut tells me it's not the time to push. For once, I heed it. I'm halfway through my meal when he finally comes to the table and takes his first bite. We eat in uncomfortable silence. His outburst reminds me that I'm stuck in a house out in the middle of wherever it is we are with a dangerous criminal. My throat tightens remembering his fingers wrapped around it the last time I pushed him. *Don't forget who he is.*

I push my plate away, my hunger leaving me as the food turns to sawdust on my tongue. Liam cleans his plate and takes it to the sink. My gaze follows him as he exits the kitchen. A door opens and then slams shut. I sit back in my chair, my stomach a swirling mess of nerves. Since I doubt I'm going to be able to eat any more, I dump the remaining omelet in the trash and clean up the kitchen. No sense in having the housekeeper come when I'm perfectly capable of doing a few dishes.

Hours pass and there's still no sign of Liam. Unless I missed it, there hasn't been any sound of a car arriving. Which means he's either still close by or he's been walking...wherever this whole time. I run upstairs and slip into my shoes. Then I open the double doors off the entryway and step out onto the terrace. He's not here. I wander around the lawn, circling the cottage, as if he'll miraculously appear.

A sharp noise draws my attention. My gaze travels and, finally, I spot Liam. The bottom half of a pair of stretched out legs is visible, while the rest of the body they're attached to are hidden behind a massive looming tree. I cross the expanse of grass and move closer. More of the figure appears until he's fully revealed. He sits on a two-person swing that hangs by ropes attached to a thick branch high off the ground.

Liam stares straight ahead, not even acknowledging my arrival. *Go back inside, Imogen.* Except I can't. I take a seat next to him. We sway forward and backward in short jerky motions, stuttered by his planted feet. I look out in the same direction he is, but there's nothing in front of us except a giant green field and rolling hills filled with sheep. I chance a quick glance in his direction. There's a distance in his eyes that tells me it's not the field he's seeing anyway.

"Not once since you took me have I ever thought you'd truly hurt me." My voice is shaky. "Until now."

Nothing. Yet, I plunge ahead.

"If there's any ounce of kindness inside you, I'd like to go home to Dublin. *My* home," I hesitate before continuing. "Please."

He swallows, his Adam's apple bobbing with the action. It's the only part of him that moves. I can't even tell that he's breathing. The swing jerks as he stands, but he doesn't turn around. I stare up at his back, stupid tears stinging my eyes.

"I'll take you back tomorrow," he says softly and walks away.

LIAM

"COME TO MY OFFICE. NOW." THE COMMAND IS BOOMING and rattles through me.

I leave the library and follow him down the hall, keeping my head bowed and my eyes focused on the floor. My body quakes and my back and ribs from yesterday's beating still ache. I'm not keen on having more bruises added to them. Although it's not always something I can avoid, no matter what I do.

He steps inside the room and after I pass through, he closes the door behind him. I glance up and then down just as quickly. My mind races. Who is that seated there? The man behind me circles to the other side of the desk and lowers himself into his chair, the leather creaking under his weight that only grows more substantial with each passing day.

"There he is," my stepda announces.

Is he talking to me?

"Yes, I see that."

No, it's to the stranger in here with us. There's a small hint of *movement and then a shadow creeps along the floor. Black dress shoes polished to such a high shine I can almost make out my reflection move into my field of vision. The man grips my chin between his thumb and finger and tips my head up. Up close, he's familiar. One of my stepda's business associates. He has a friendly face.*

Why is my stomach dipping with unease then?

He scans me from head to toe and then releases his hold on me. I stand stock-still as he places his arms behind his back with one hand gripping the opposite wrist and slowly walks around me.

I don't turn my head and track his path. Instead, I stay frozen, barely breathing. What's going on? Seconds later he completes his trek around me. He stares long enough to make me uncomfortable and shift my weight. When he reaches up to run his fingertip along my jaw, I flinch. A sense of dread creeps under my skin, making it itch. I clench my fists to keep from scratching.

"Well, do we have a deal?" my stepda still seated behind the desk asks.

Nausea churns in my gut. This isn't right. My gaze bounces back and forth between the two men.

I find my voice. "What deal?"

Dónal finally meets my eyes. There's an evil gleam in his. "You're finally going to earn your keep, boy."

Already I'm shaking my head and backing away toward the door. The man near me grabs my arm. That's all it takes and I'm fighting off his hold. I thrash and kick, but he's a grown up twice my size and when he throws me to the ground, I smack my head against the corner of the side table. Pain explodes through my skull and warm liquid tracks down my temple.

I push myself up on all fours with a groan and a hand grabs my hair and yanks me to my feet. Dónal's grip tightens and he pulls my head back, straining my neck, and I whimper. My vision swims as I stare up at two of him.

"I'll give you a choice. Either you play nice with Brendan and give him everything he wants or it will be Nessa taking your place. I

know more than one person who has a special fondness for little girls."

God, he's a monster. Nessa's just a baby. Barely out of nappies. What kind of da would let someone touch his daughter? Especially a three-year old?

"What's it going to be, Liam? Are you going to become good friends with Brendan, or am I going to have to call the nanny to bring Nessa in here?" Dónal jerks my hair harder.

I close my eyes so he can't see my tears. "I'll do what you want. Just leave her alone."

"I thought you'd see things my way." His evil laugh reverberates through the pounding inside my head.

My eyes jerk open, and I suck in a sharp gasp. Beneath me, the sheets are soaked with sweat. Wet hair sticks to my forehead. My chest heaves, and I try to slow my breathing. Something brushes my arm.

"Don't touch me!" I roar and throw a wild punch.

A pained cry fills the air, and I jerk my head to the side. Imogen's hand covers her cheek and her eyes are wide with shock. I scramble to sitting and reach for her, but she scoots away. "Fuck, I'm sorry. I didn't mean..."

"It's alright, I know you didn't." She lowers her arm to display the flaming red mark marring her flesh.

I run my hands down my face. "Christ."

"Do you..." she pauses. "Do you want to talk about it?"

"Jesus, no," I snap at her. "There's nothing to talk about."

Imogen drops her gaze and stares at her hands clasped in her lap where the duvet pools around her waist.

"Look,"—I clear my throat—"I'm...sorry. I didn't mean to do that. I just don't want to talk about it."

"I understand. If you change your mind," she says softly. "I'm a really good listener."

I've spent the last twenty years trying to forget what happened to me. There's no way in hell I am going to intentionally bring that shit up. God, how long has it been since my last nightmare? Months? A year? It pisses me off that Dónal still manages to have me in a chokehold.

Pale light creeps in through the window. It's barely past dawn. Except there's no way I'm going back to sleep after this. I climb out of the bed and into the shower. No amount of scrubbing will ever wash away the memories. I've tried.

I keep picturing Imogen's red cheek. It's one of the reasons I don't let women sleep in my bed. I may be a ruthless bastard, but I don't abuse women physically. It's why I regret that second day she was at my estate. I hadn't hurt her, but the fear that flickered in her eyes as my hand tightened around her throat reminded me of that scared boy I used to be living with Dónal. But that was nothing to fear she expressed yesterday. Even I'd been shocked at the rage that spewed from me. I hadn't liked what I'd seen.

After turning off the water, I dry myself and walk back into the bedroom to grab some clothes. Imogen is gone. I dress and head downstairs to find her at the stove attempting to cook. She's pulled her hair up into a messy knot on top of her head. Long tendrils of teal and purple skim the back of her neck and shoulders. She's also got on a pair of black lounging pants with a skull spanning her entire ass and a white tank. She glances over her shoulder at my arrival.

"I thought I'd try to make us breakfast, but I'm not sure it's going so well. You should probably give me a hand so I don't poison both of us." She chuckles and gives a self-deprecating shrug.

I find myself smiling. Something I've done more of in the last three days with Imogen than I have in years. I'm not sure what it is about her. I cross the kitchen and gently hip bump her out of the way, reaching for the spatula in her hand.

"Give me that before you destroy perfectly good eggs. Do you know how much these things cost these days?"

She snorts, but passes it off to me. "As if you can't afford it, you cheap bastard."

I focus on the eggs in the skillet, turn down the heat, and grab a few more things from the fridge. "You can help by setting the table. At least I know you can handle that."

Imogen gasps in mock affront and I laugh. "How rude, even if true."

Soon, breakfast is done and we're sitting down to eat. I glance over at her. "When you're done, I'll call my driver."

She swallows. "Thank you."

I nod shallowly. I'm nowhere near tired of her yet, but being here, in this cottage, is reminding me of too many things. My grand-da and who I used to be...before. I'll never be that person again. Too many things have passed. I finish eating first and take my plate to the sink. Imogen joins me shortly and together we clean up the kitchen. After the last dish is done and put away, I turn to her.

"Feel free to take any of the clothes in the closet."

"What? You don't think you'll need them for the next woman you decide to kidnap because you're bored?"

"I doubt they would be to her taste," I deadpan. "Besides, I'd hate to be accused of trying to dress her up like a doll. If that doll were a death metal loving goth chick who hates the patriarchy."

Imogen barks out a huge laugh. "What are you trying to say?"

I hold my palms up in a display of pure innocence and lower them with a small smile. "Go on. Pack whatever you'd like. I'll call my driver. He should be here in about fifteen minutes."

We stare at each other for several beats before she finally turns and leaves the room. The floor creaks a few times before everything goes quiet. I lean on the countertop and drop my chin to my chest with a heavy sigh.

CHAPTER 27

Imogen

The drive back to Dublin is quiet. But it's a
different kind of quiet than when we left. There's this weirdness in
the atmosphere around us, but I can't name it. I also don't want to
disturb what feels like an uneasy peace between us. Which means I
keep my mouth shut, even though everything inside me wants to
break the silence.

We come to a stop in front of my building. The driver gets out,
and I wait for Liam to do so as well, but he remains where he is. Am I
supposed to get out on my side or does he expect me to climb over
him? It's not like him to not burst out of the vehicle before the driver
can open the door.

Anxiety rolls around in my belly. I've only ever been this uncertain when I first started my hacker business, unsure I could find any
clients or jobs worth taking.

Forget this.

I'm not turning into some namby-pamby who needs a man to

make all her decisions for her. Tired of waiting, I reach for the door handle on my side, but Liam grips my arm and stays me. I turn toward him. His eyes bore into mine, but he doesn't speak. Just stares. Why do I feel like he's memorizing my face?

Why does it feel like I'm memorizing his?

At last, he releases me. He opens his door and steps out before pivoting and offering me his hand just like he did when we went to Kenmare. He helps me out but, unlike Kenmare, as soon as I'm on my feet he lets me go. I swallow and swipe my palm down my thigh. The driver rounds the back of the car carrying a small bag. I take it from him, and he makes himself scarce.

"I guess this is goodbye," I tell Liam.

"Yes."

I clear my throat. "Thanks for showing me the fairy forest. It was beautiful and I'll never forget it." *Or you.*

He dips his head. "You're welcome."

My gaze darts around, not settling on anything, especially him. I should be celebrating the fact that I'm finally back in Dublin. Finally home.

"Right, then." I rock on my heels and my bag sways.

Liam doesn't respond. Done with the awkwardness, I step around him with a short nod, but I've barely moved when he palms the back of my neck and kisses the hell out of me. With my free hand, I grip the lapel of his suit jacket and tug him closer. We stand there in the middle of the footpath in the middle of the day just kissing as pedestrians pass by. It's the whistle that draws us apart. I stare up at him, breathing heavy. Then before I can blink, Liam climbs into the backseat, closes the door, and the town car drives away.

I stand there until it disappears out of view. Christ.

Shaking myself out of whatever the hell that was, I let myself into my flat. There's a vacant smell to the place. The dirty teacup still sits next to my electric kettle and the bag of biscuits is unsealed. They're probably stale. Not bothering to taste one, I throw the whole package in the trash.

My desk is bare. Damn it. Liam still has my laptop and phones.

I dump the bag of clothes I'd brought back with me, lock and arm the door, and jog down the stairs. This time, I take the long way around to my secret work room. I keep glancing around, but there doesn't appear to be anything unusual. No strangers trying to discreetly follow me. Do I really believe that Liam is finished with me? That he didn't agree to bring me home only to put a tail on me? He sure acted like whatever was between us was over.

My favorite citrus scent reaches me. I'm tempted to stop at the bakery and get a cup, but I keep walking. Glancing around once more, I punch in the lock code for the door and jog up the stairs. Nothing on my floor appears to be disturbed. The door to my space remains closed, and the red light indicates the alarm is still on. I'll check the log to make sure no one has bypassed the security. Not that anyone should be able to, but one never knows the connections Liam has.

I head inside—locking the door behind me—and fire up my main desktop. Once I've gone through the video feed from the hidden camera as well as the log—satisfied that no one's been in here —I open my encrypted email. Shit. I've got fifteen unread messages. I click on the one from Padraig. This is only the second time he's ever emailed. All our interactions have been over phone, but I gave him my address once in case of an emergency and he couldn't reach me any other way.

A quick reply later confirms I'm still alive along with an apology for ghosting him with a family emergency. I scan the rest of the messages. There is nothing there that can't wait another day. Next, I'm bringing up the video feed. Not that I expect there to be anything considering Carrick, Cian, and Aidan were all arrested. I'm not sure how the judicial system works for a family like the Donnellys, but I doubt they'll be in jail long. I assume Carrick pays a lot of money to expensive attorneys—and maybe judges—to stay out of prison.

Just as I predicted, the feed coming from Carrick's computer is dark. Same with Aidan and Cian. I manage to get a hit from Finn's though. He's sitting behind his desk at *Anamacha Caillte* going through the books. There are dark circles under his eyes like he hasn't been sleeping and his hair is uncombed and a mess like he's been running his hands through it. Poor guy.

I need to let him know that I'm okay.

I rifle through my desk drawer for an old burner phone. Once I find it, I plug in the charger, wait until it gets some juice, and then dial the number to the casino. With my eyes still on the screen, I wait until the assistant who answers the phone transfers me. Finn absently picks up his phone.

"Finn Donnelly."

Despite staying at their estate for several days and passing him and his brothers multiple times in the hallways, this is the first time we've spoken. I'm assailed by nerves for some strange reason. "Um, hi, this is Imogen Walsh."

He sits up straight in his chair. "Jesus, Imogen, where are you? Are you okay?"

I bite my nail. "I'm fine. I saw on the news what happened. I'm so sorry. How are your dad and brothers doing?"

"Where are you? I'll come get you." Finn is already on his feet.

"No, no, you don't have to. I'm actually home." God, this is awkward. "Liam just dropped me off."

Through the feed, he sits abruptly. Worry lines crease his forehead. "Did he hurt you?"

I shake my head even though he can't see me. "No, he didn't hurt me."

"Still, why don't I pick you up and take you back to the estate? I know it will make Da feel better knowing you're safe."

Liam won't hurt me.

He'd been horrified that he'd hit me yesterday morning. I don't blame him for it. Whatever nightmare he'd been having must have been truly awful for him to lash out like that. Did it have anything to do with his hatred for Dónal Sheehan? It had to.

"Imogen, are you there?" Finn asks.

"Yeah, sorry." I focus on the conversation at hand. "I am safe. Swear. But I need to know that your family is okay."

He sighs. "They're still in jail, but our lawyers are working on getting them out. Should be tomorrow. I'm going to go visit in a little while. I'll let Da know you're all right."

"Thank you."

"Call if you need anything," Finn says.

"I will." I won't. "Thanks again."

After I disconnect the call, I shoot a quick text to Teagan, turn the phone off, unplug it, and toss it back in the drawer. With a sigh, I collapse back into my chair and pluck at the tattered armrest. I can't take my eyes off the monitor until he closes the lid on his laptop and the feed goes dark. I'm back where I wanted to be. Except it doesn't feel the same as it did before. I've never minded the quiet space and being alone in here with all my computers. They've been the things I love the most. But I'm not sure it's enough anymore.

CHAPTER 28

THE HOUSE RESEMBLES EVERY OTHER HOUSE IN THIS ROW with its red brick exterior and white trim. There's no need for me to knock, because as soon as my foot hits the top step, the door opens. Craig stands on the other side. He dips his head and moves back for me to slip past. I walk through the entryway into the depth of the house. The lock clicks behind me and his footsteps follow.

Cheers and hollers grow louder the closer I get to the living area. On the TV is a football match and sitting on the sofa yelling at the players on the pitch who can't hear them are Aran and Declan. Both of them are battered, with various cuts all over their faces. Declan's arm is in a cast and sling, while a shorts-wearing Aran's upper thigh is wrapped in a bandage and propped on a low table in front of him. A pair of crutches lean against the arm of the sofa.

Two other guards stand at attention near the back of the room. For a moment I stand at the threshold and observe my cousins. How long has it been since the three of us were in a room together? Christ, a decade at least. Maybe two. The three of us were inseparable as kids. Two years younger than me, they were the closest thing I had to brothers.

Aran raises the beer bottle over his head, his gaze not leaving the telly. "How about another?"

"A bullet to the leg, and it suddenly doesn't work?" I toss out.

The two men whip around. Aran's face lights up with amusement, while Declan glares and turns back to the match. Still pissed at me. Aran grabs his crutches and stands with ease. He hops around to the other side and I meet him partway. To my surprise, he transfers a crutch to the other hand and throws an arm around me in a hug. I hold back my flinch at being touched.

"Oy, ya bastard, made it back to Dublin, I see." He claps me on the back not the least bit put off that I don't return the embrace. "Ya done fecking around with the Donnellys yet, or just getting started? Where's your little captive by the way? I hear she's a fiery colleen."

Imogen is off the table for discussion. I take a step back and straighten my jacket. "Of course I'm not done with them."

Clearly not offended by my lack of affection, Aran laughs. "Why did I think you'd answer otherwise? Next time, though, I'd appreciate *not* getting shot."

"It gives you character. Besides, weren't you the one who told me that the women love playing nurse to an injured man? You should be happy about that." I jerk my chin in the direction of his wound.

"I was talking about fake injuries or the flu. Man colds as they call them. I don't want a fecking bullet-hole scar to mar my beauty." He holds an arm out to the side showcasing his body.

As I'm sure is his intent, I can't help but shake my head. Between the twins, Aran has always been the one to not let shit bother him. Declan, on the other hand, holds a grudge for fucking ever. I'm sure we'll both be dead before he talks to me again.

I turn back to my younger cousin. "I'll try better next time."

He blinks and then smacks my chest. "Oy, did you just tell a joke? It sounded like a joke, but then I remembered who I'm talking to.

Are you sure you're Liam or did your pretty captive murder you, peel off your skin to make a mask, and hire someone to play you?"

"You're fucking weird, you know that right?" I'm not sure why I put up with his craziness.

"Thank you. Now, some one does need to get me a drink, so I can sit down and get off this leg. Christ, it's killing me." He transfers his crutch over to the other hand and hops back to the couch where he drops onto the cushion.

One of my men moves and I wave him off. I walk to the bar, grab two beers, pop the tops, and then take them over. He pours back a large swallow while I sit in the chair nearby and sip mine. Declan still hasn't looked at me again. Aran just shrugs. We both know how his brother is.

"Don't think I haven't noticed you've avoided answering my question twice now about...what's her name? Oh, yeah, Imogen, right?"

He knows good and well what her name is. "Because it's none of your business."

"Ah, so it's like that," he says good-humoredly.

Yeah, it's like that. I clear my throat and my gaze darts to my three men trying to remain inconspicuous and back to Aran. "I'm glad to see you two are okay."

There's a rush of air as though everyone sucked it all out of the room. Every single person in here is dead silent. And staring at me. I take another drink of beer.

Aran is the first to recover. "Jaysus, ya really have been invaded by a body snatcher, haven't ya?"

I glare at him and bite my tongue for the first time ever. Suddenly uncomfortable in a way I've never been before, I set my beer down and stand. "I just came to make sure you were both still alive. Feel free to go home whenever you want."

I walk out of the living area and through the front door. Just as I reach the town car my name is called. I turn. Declan stands on the stoop. "Did you let her go?"

It's on the tip of my tongue to tell him to fuck off. Instead, I jerk a brief nod and then get into the backseat. I grab the bottle of whiskey from the bar, not bothering with a glass. It's half gone by the time we arrive at my estate. I stumble out of the vehicle and into the house. It's just as empty as the day I discovered Imogen missing.

I take another swig straight from the bottle and make my way down the hallway toward the bedroom. The bed is still unmade, and the towel still lies crumpled on the floor. I throw back one more swallow and set the bottle on the nightstand. There's a vague thud sound and an oaky scent fills the air overpowering the lingering fragrance Imogen left behind. I collapse into the bed and bring the pillow up to my nose so I can breathe her in.

"Imogen."

My head pounds and cotton fills my mouth. I groan and roll over. Not ready to open my eyes yet, I lie there for a few minutes more, swallowing to try and wet my tongue and wishing for the headache to go away. Vague flashes of memories come to me. Stopping at the safe house to check on Declan and Aran. Whiskey. A lot of whiskey. Imogen's smell. I open my eyes and squint at the bright sunlight flooding the room. A room that isn't mine. I glance around. Christ, why am I in Imogen's bed? Oh, yeah, because that's where my drunken self landed.

The scent of stale whiskey fills the room. I sit up on the side of the bed and cradle my head. On the floor the bottle is on its side, a small amount of liquid still inside. I pick it up, drink what's left, and let out a groan. "Fecking disgusting."

I glance down at myself. I'm still wearing all my clothes. Even my shoes. Stepping through the connecting door between our rooms, I undress and throw everything in the basket. Twenty-five minutes later, I'm showered and wearing a clean pair of jeans and button down. I roll up the sleeves and head for the kitchen to make something to eat that will settle the rolling in my gut.

I'm at the stove and all I can picture is Imogen padding around to get plates out of the cupboard and setting the table. *Get out of my head*. I need to go into the office. Work will keep my mind off her and back where it belongs: on destroying the Donnellys and taking over Dublin. Nothing has changed in that regard. I turn the burner heat down and call Darragh.

"Give me the latest," I say in greeting.

"They're being released, as soon as the paperwork is finished."

"Any news on the next business venture?"

"We made another visit to O'Neill as an extra incentive to sell. He'll be ready to sign over the deed later today," Darragh confirms.

I transfer the phone to my other ear and stir the chicken. "Good. I'll meet you there shortly after four."

"Yes, sir."

The silence lingers another second. *Don't ask.*

Goddamn it.

"And Imogen?"

"She was home for a short time, and then she left. I followed her to the bakery, but she kept walking past. Instead, she entered a door a few storefronts down. She was inside for a couple hours and then left. Stopped at a nearby restaurant, grabbed some takeaway, and then went back to her flat. Hasn't left since as far as I can tell."

"That's all for now. Leave her be."

"Yes, sir."

CHAPTER 29

I SMOOTH DOWN THE FABRIC OF MY DRESS. THE ONE MUM bought for me for my twenty-fifth birthday that I only wear on special occasions. I twist side to side and the black and white skulls knee-length skirt flares out around me. My black combat boots and black cardigan complete the outfit. I run the brush through my hair one more time, take a final glance in the full-length mirror, and then grab my keys off the stand.

Once the alarm's been set on the door, I jog down the stairs and outside. The sun is still shining but hangs low in the dusk-shaded sky nearly hidden behind the neighboring buildings. It's still chilly in the evenings, but warmer weather is slowly coming and staying a little longer each day. People are out and about, and I dodge a few of them as I walk down the footpath. I've been too nervous to eat anything all day, so my stomach clenches on emptiness and grumbles in preparation of food.

Ten minutes later I step through the front door of an Italian restaurant I've never been to before. I've passed it more than once, but for some reason I haven't ever stopped in or ordered takeaway. Probably because I'm more of a greasy fish and chips kinda girl. I glance around the fancy place with wine bottles stuffed in a built-in wall-to-wall wine rack that covers two of the interior walls from floor to ceiling. Every surface shines. I'm almost afraid to touch anything, in case I break it.

I spot the person I'm meeting and head to his table. Blue eyes meet mine and with a smile he stands. It's been just over two weeks since we last spoke.

"Imogen, dear, it's good to see you." Carrick cups the side of my head in that sweet paternal way I could get used to and gestures to the empty chair opposite his. "Please, have a seat. Would you like some wine?"

I've never been much of a wine drinker, but I need something to settle these damn nerves. "That would be great. Something on the sweeter side, please, if they have it."

"Of course." He waves over a waiter and places an order.

Once we're alone again, he picks up his stout. "How have you been?"

"I'm doing okay, thanks. What about you? How's Cian feeling?" I don't want to bring up their arrest directly for fear of igniting Carrick's anger towards Liam. Plus, I've been doing my best not to think about him either. *How's that going?*

"We're fine. Business as usual. Cian is resting, but only because Nessa's forcing him to do so. Although, honestly, I don't think he minds much. In fact, I have a feeling he's taking the invalid role a little too far because he has a pretty nurse taking care of him." He chuckles.

I'd been so worried. "That's good. I'm glad he's okay. That you all are."

"Don't you worry about us Donnellys. We always come out on top."

Carrick's words should put me at ease, but it only makes that uneasy sensation in my gut—that I haven't been able to get rid of since Liam dropped me off at my flat—grow. Nothing's been right since that day. I can't sleep. All I do is toss and turn. I certainly can't concentrate. I've missed out on more than one job, because I haven't responded to emails or returned phone calls. Hell, I even completely overlooked something for Padraig.

A hand covers mine. I jerk my eyes up to meet Carrick's. Concern wrinkles his brow.

"Are you *sure* you're okay?" he asks.

I laugh awkwardly. "Sorry, yes, I'm fine. Really. My mind just wandered for a second."

He doesn't look like he believes me, but he lets it go. Thankfully, the waiter approaches with a bottle of wine and pours me a glass.

"Are you ready to order?" he asks.

Crap. Carrick glances at me. "Give us just another minute."

The waiter dips his head and leaves. I pick up the menu and glance over it without paying attention to anything listed. *Get it together, Imogen.* I blink, make myself focus, and pick something random. I'm not sure it matters what I order. It'll all taste the same. I set the menu down and glance up. Carrick's face has hardened, and his gaze lingers over my shoulder. I turn and my breath catches.

Liam stands in the doorway glancing around as though searching for someone. He turns slightly and our eyes meet. His widen and for several beats of my heart that races they stay locked on mine. Then his gaze shifts just past me and his eyes narrow. It's obvious, even from this distance, the hatred that flares in them. I move my head to block his view—Carrick's as well—and his expression softens a fraction. His lips twitch as though he's fighting a smile.

I'll probably regret it, but I stand. Carrick snags my hand and I stare down at him with what I hope is a reassuring expression. "Just give me a minute. Please?"

He doesn't appear convinced. "If you need anything, I'm here. So is Roarke."

It shouldn't surprise me that his enforcer is somewhere nearby.

He probably doesn't go anywhere without his guard. I nod in appreciation though. It's a nice feeling that someone cares enough about me to make sure I'm safe and protected. Carrick releases his hold on me and I walk toward Liam.

I stop within arm's reach. "Hi."

He's still as beautiful as ever, but he also looks tired. There are dark spots under his eyes like he hasn't gotten a good night's sleep in...two weeks? It doesn't appear as though he's shaved in a few days either.

"Hi," he echoes. "How've you been?"

"Fine. You?" Is this what we've been reduced to? Awkward, banal conversation as though we're just two strangers.

His lips curl on one side. "Fine."

"I'm glad."

Liam raises an eye brow. "Are you, though?"

I glare at him. "Yes."

"I wasn't sure." His gaze travels down me. "You look good in that dress. I didn't think you wore them."

"Just because I didn't wear those ugly pink girly ones you picked out doesn't mean I don't wear them." I huff. He doesn't need to know this is the only one I own.

"How rude of me to think otherwise," he deadpans. "Well, I like this one. Very much."

I preen a bit with the compliment. *Aren't you glad you wore it now?* Yes, maybe. "Thank you."

"Even if I don't like who you're wearing it for."

Of course, Liam has to ruin it by being a dick. The regret kicks in. I turn to walk away, because I'm annoyed he had to turn a nice thing into something shitty, but he grabs my arm. I spin around, a curse already on my lips but his words stop me.

"I'm sorry."

My mouth snaps shut and I stare at him. His jaw clenches and he presses his mouth into a thin line like it's his turn to regret something. I'm also certain if I ask him to repeat it, he'll deny me, so I won't.

"I really am glad to see you," Liam says softly and releases me.

My skin still tingles from his touch. I rub the spot where his hand had been, not because hurt me, but because I want to hold onto it a little while longer. "I better get back to the table." I pause, undecided if I should tell him how I feel, and then do it anyway. "It's nice to see you as well."

I hold his gaze for another second, taking in features I've already memorized, and then head back to Carrick's table. His narrow-eyed gaze is still locked over my shoulder, which I can understand. Nothing between them has changed just because Liam brought me back to Dublin. I hate that I feel stuck in the middle between them. I have no reason to be.

Once I'm seated, Carrick finally turns his attention back to me. "Is that the first time you've seen him since you got back?"

"Yes."

"He hasn't harassed you or had any of his men harass you?"

"No one. I've gone about my business as though he and I had never met," I assure him with a hint of...some emotion in my tone.

If Carrick notices, he doesn't mention it. "I'm just surprised since he shows up five minutes after you. Seems a little too coincidental."

"Isn't his office nearby?" Yes, I did a whole lot more digging in Liam's personal and business life the second I got back. Apparently my stalker tendencies decided to add a new subject, although I've mostly stopped watching Carrick and his family.

"It doesn't make it less conspicuous. My nephew and his wife are frequent patrons here. If Nathan had ever seen Liam Campbell here before, he would have mentioned it."

Could it be a coincidence that Liam showed up tonight of all nights? Is he having me followed? I should probably be more upset about it than I am. Because I *had* missed him. Or at least I'd missed the Liam from the cottage in Killarney. I'd searched the real estate records and discovered its location. From what I could find, his grandfather had owned it for close to forty years until he got behind on taxes. According to the paperwork, Liam's father sold it, forcing his grandfather out. The elderly man died a few years later. Then about three years ago, Liam bought it for far more than it was worth.

"It doesn't matter," I finally say. "We both know Liam does what he wants. If he's going to have me followed, there isn't much I can do about it. So long as that's all it is, then I'm not going to get worked up and cause myself unnecessary anxiety. I have enough of it with the rest of my life."

Carrick doesn't say anything for a minute, but then he sighs and sits back in his chair. "You're as stubborn as Caitlín, do you know that?"

I snort. "Thank you."

"It wasn't a compliment." Still, he chuckles.

"I'm taking it as one anyway." I grin.

At last, the waiter returns and takes our order. Despite the awkward interaction with Liam and the tension that lingered after his arrival, Carrick and I have an enjoyable evening with conversation. So much so that time passes far more quickly than I expect.

"Thank you for a lovely dinner," I tell him. "But mostly, thank you for checking up on me. You certainly didn't have to. I know that I'm not really anyone to you, except a stranger who showed up on your doorstep with a wild accusation. Most people in your position would have sent me on my way or worse."

Carrick reaches across the table for my hand and gives it a small squeeze. "Despite the organization I head, I'm not a bad man. I love my family. I believe in God. I give to charity. I'm also a good judge of character. If I'd seen anything other than a scared young woman desperate for help, I wouldn't have been as charitable."

A slight shudder runs over me at his words. I lucked out, then. But I also understand what he's saying.

"Do you need Roarke to walk you home?"

"No, but thank you. I'm only ten minutes from here. I'm used to walking by myself. Can't start getting scared, now, can I?" I refuse to.

"I suppose not."

I stand, and on impulse, round the table to give Carrick a brief kiss on the cheek. "Thank you, again. For everything."

He pats my arm. "You're welcome."

With a small wave, I exit the restaurant and head for home. I'm two blocks away when the hairs on the back of my neck stand up. I stop in the middle of the footpath and whirl around. "Whoever's following me, you can fuck right off."

A tall shadow emerges from a doorway. My heart races and then a mix of emotions slams into me as it becomes a familiar form. Anger. Annoyance. Relief. I sag at the last one and release a sigh. "You scared the shit out of me."

He comes closer and a streetlight illuminates Liam's face.

CHAPTER 30

Liam

None of my focus had been on the two investors I'd met for dinner. Which is obvious, considering they've declined to sign the paperwork sealing our mutually beneficial business arrangement. I should be more pissed, except I can't stop picturing Imogen sitting at the table with Carrick Donnelly. What the fuck were they doing together?

From where we were seated the two of them weren't in my line of sight. I could only imagine what was happening over there. When Imogen finally walked past my section of the restaurant to leave, I threw down a bunch of bills—enough to cover our server's salary for a week—and excused myself, cutting our meeting short. I hadn't intended to follow her, but here I am stepping out of the shadows like a creep.

"You scared the shit out of me," Imogen growls. "I've already been kidnapped once before. It's not something I'd like to repeat."

I move even closer. "I'm sorry."

She cocks her head. "You know what? I actually believe you."

For someone who never apologizes, I've done my fair share of it tonight. "I don't usually say things I don't mean."

"I suppose that's true. Well, since you're already here and know where I live anyway, you might as well walk with me." She pivots and keeps going in the direction she'd been, clearly expecting me to follow.

Which, of course, I do. I fall in line beside her and glance over at her several times. Imogen's hair cascades down in waves around her shoulders and the neckline of her dress shows the barest hint of cleavage. Not so low as to give away all her secrets, but enough to make a person want to discover them. The skull skirt bounces with her steps on feet covered by—I raise a brow—combat boots. On anyone else, the outfit wouldn't work, but on Imogen, it's perfectly her. I still laugh at the stickers on her laptop.

I'd given a listen to some of the bands she apparently enjoyed. They'd done nothing but make my ears bleed.

"Did you have a nice dinner?" she asks.

"It was fine."

She glances over at me. "Judging by your tone, I'm not sure I believe *that*. Not a fan of Italian food?"

I slip my hands in my pockets. "The meal was palatable."

Imogen whistles. "That's some high praise, right there."

"It would have tasted better if the restaurant did a better job of choosing who they allow in."

"Nope." She shakes her head. "We're not doing that. If you want to walk with me, then we're going to have polite discourse where certain topics are off the table for discussion."

I almost laugh at the fact she thinks that she gets to decide if I walk with her or not or that she dictates our conversation. Except I don't want her to push me away or stop talking so I bite my tongue.

"Did I tell you you look pretty tonight?" I ask instead.

Imogen glances at me out of the corner of her eye and her forehead wrinkles like she's confused by the compliment before she smooths it out. "You said you liked my dress."

"I believe my exact words were 'you look good in that dress'."

"Isn't that the same thing? Not that I'm fishing for compliments," she rushes to reassure me.

"Are you sure you aren't?"

She turns her head toward me, snorts, and then, to my surprise, steps close enough to loop her hand around my elbow and presses herself to my side. I glance down at her, but she just shrugs. "What? I'm getting cold and you're warm. Don't read too much into it."

A grin tugs at my lips. "I wouldn't dream of it."

Arm-in-arm we continue toward her flat while we pass other couples on the way. The silence settles comfortably between us. I'm not sure I've ever walked with a woman like this. A casual stroll through town. I've had women hang on my arm as we make our way through the lobby of a hotel where I'm taking them for a quick fuck. But none for no other reason than because she wanted my warmth.

"You know, you still have my laptop and phones. Are you ever going to return them?"

"I don't know." I've continued watching all the videos she has on there. "At the risk of broaching forbidden topics, are *you* ever going to tell me why you have all those recordings?"

"Nope," Imogen says with a loud *pop*.

"Didn't think so." It also didn't hurt to ask.

She harrumphs. "Have you been back to your grand-da's cottage?"

"I don't think I ever told you it belonged to him."

"I'm a computer genius," she says as if that explains everything. "You didn't really think that I wouldn't do some digging and figure it out?"

"I hadn't given it any thought, actually. And, no I haven't been back." It's too soon. In fact, I'm not sure I'll ever be able to go back and not have it remind me of Imogen and the time we spent there. It might have only been a few days, but things changed during them. "What about you? Have you gone back to work? Hacking, I mean?"

"Here and there." She lifts her shoulder.

What does that mean exactly? We turn a corner onto a familiar street. Two more buildings and we come to a stop in front of hers. She lets go of me, and already I want to call her back. Imogen bites at her bottom lip and won't meet my gaze. She's not usually nervous. "Well, here we are."

I glance up at the darkened windows behind her. "So it would seem."

Another few seconds pass where we both stand there, neither of us saying goodbye or walking away. She straightens and at last looks at me. "Would you like to come up?"

I take a step forward. There's not a chance I'm turning down the offer. Imogen quickly spins and heads inside. I follow her up the stairs. She unlocks and opens the door, disarms her security system, and after flipping on a light switch, walks in, leaving it open. I close it behind me and study the small studio where she lives. The kitchenette is neat and tidy with a single tea cup sitting on the counter next to an electric kettle. The bed is unmade and clothes are tossed everywhere, including hanging over the chair tucked under a desk where I can picture her sitting with her laptop. I assume a partially closed door just past the bed leads to the bathroom.

Imogen takes off her sweater and hangs it in the wardrobe. She scoops up the rest of the clothes strewn around the place and tosses them into the bottom of it and shuts the door. Then she turns to me. "Can I get you some tea or water to drink? I might also have a bottle of beer that's most likely been in the fridge for at least a year. Then again, you probably don't want that."

"No, but thank you."

She stands in the middle of the large open space rocking slowly back and forth on her heels. I cross the room until I can reach out and touch her, something I've been wanting to do since she approached me at the restaurant. I brush her hair back and over her shoulder. She stares up at me with eyes darkening with arousal.

"Why did you invite me up here, Imogen?"

She blows out a puff of air. "Ever direct."

"Since when do *you* hold back?" I counter.

"Since I'm not entirely sure why I invited you." Her pained expression makes it like the admission had been dragged from her.

I close the last remaining inches between us so her breasts brush my chest and trace my thumb across her bottom lip. "Are you sure about that? Because I have a pretty good idea."

"Then why don't you tell me," Imogen whispers, caressing my flesh with her warm breath.

Leaning down, I let my lips ghost along the shell of her ear. She makes a small noise and tilts her head slightly, but it's enough. "You want me to fuck you, don't you?"

"Yes."

That's all she has to say. I claim her mouth and slip my tongue inside. She tastes exactly the same and I drink her down like a man who's parched and in need of sustenance only Imogen can provide. Her fingers thread through my hair and she clings to me. There's almost an underlying desperation in her kiss. In mine as well. Her hips curve gently beneath my palms as I cradle them and hold her tightly against me.

While we reacquaint ourselves with each other's flavor, the kiss is soft and gentle, but soon grows harried and deep. The musky scent of Imogen's arousal perfumes the air. My cock throbs against my zipper, begging for release. I slide one hand down her leg and fist the fabric of her dress, tugging it higher and exposing more of her sweet flesh. Her skin is like satin as I explore. I glide my fingers upward until I encounter the soaking material between her thighs.

"So wet already," I murmur against her lips.

She moans into my mouth and presses herself into my touch. I reward her by slipping under the scrap of fabric and circling her clit with my thumb. Imogen's throaty whimper grows louder. The sounds she makes and the way she rubs against me almost has me spilling my seed, but I focus on her pleasure. Wetness pours from her and drips down my hand. I easily slide two fingers into her cunt and increase the pressure on the sensitive nub, pushing her higher toward release.

With only a few more practiced flicks, Imogen goes rigid and cries out. Her body shudders and her back arches. She squeezes me and I tighten my hold on her hips as her knees weaken and nearly fold. I pull her closer, supporting her as she slowly comes down from her peak. A pretty shade of pink covers her upper chest that heaves with each breath she draws in. Finally, it slows and eyes that had closed with drowsy arousal slowly flutter open until she stares up at me.

A sensual smile curls Imogen's lips. "That was a good start. You better not be done, though."

I chuckle and a tiny voice in the back of my head whispers I may never be done with her. "I think you owe me a few more orgasms. Besides, I have every intention of sinking deep inside this hot, needy cunt before I leave here tonight." I push my fingers in farther eliciting another tremor from her.

"Are you sure? Because you seem to be taking your sweet time," Imogen nearly taunts.

Never one to back down from a challenge, I strip and in seconds I'm standing there naked. Her gaze tracks over me and she whistles in appreciation.

"Now who's taking their time? Unless you want me to rip that dress off you, I suggest you remove it."

She gasps. "You wouldn't dare. It's my only one."

I take a step forward, intent on proving her wrong. She squeaks and quickly shimmers out of the thing until she's left in only a pair of barely-there panties. I reach for her and she pushes them down her legs, still encased in those black boots. She bends, her fingers just touching the laces, but I stop her.

"Leave them on."

The space between Imogen's eyebrows crinkles. "Are you serious?"

I give her my most imperious glare. She just shakes her head with a soft chuckle. "Hey, you won't hear any kink shaming from me. I just didn't realize combat boots were your thing."

Ignoring the taunt, I scoop her up and toss her on the bed. She yelps, and before she can recover, I'm kissing my way down her body. I settle in between her thighs, drawing one leg over my shoulder, and feast on her sweet nectar. The hard rubber sole of that boot digs into skin, marking me. I lash my tongue against Imogen's clit and bite down on it the way she loves, milking another climax from her.

I spear her with three fingers. She cries out my name and tremors vibrate around them, the inner walls of her cunt clenching down as though trying to suck them deeper. A surge of raw power flows through me. I'm the one who makes her come again and again. The one who satisfies her. The one who…

Chasing away the thought, I yank out my fingers, move over her, and in a single move plunge my cock in until I bottom out. Imogen screams and fists the sheets. She wraps her legs around my waist, and I pump my hips, thrusting harder. Deeper. Then one last time before I roar out my own release and spill myself inside her. We're connected in a way that it's like I've become a part of her and she's become a part of me.

My chest tightens with panic, and I try to draw back, but Imogen's squeezing me so hard I can't move. My breathing grows ragged until whispered words penetrate the haze. Her words are nonsensical, but soothing in tone, and she strokes the back of my head in a calming gesture. The tremors that wrack my body slow and the buzzing inside my mind quiets.

Imogen continues her tender ministrations until slowly it all recedes and a sort of stillness settles in its place. We lay together, neither of us moving, until at last, she unhooks her ankles and her legs drop to either side of my hips. The vulnerability I squashed twenty years ago threatens to rear its head. I shudder and move to roll off her. Thankfully, she loosens her hold and I push myself to sitting on the the edge of the bed.

My elbows rest on my thighs and my hands dangle between my legs as my chin bows to my chest. There's the rustling of fabric before the mattress dips and warm touch glides across my back. I stiffen, but don't pull away. Imogen places a kiss on my shoulder and wraps her arms around me, pressing her cheek to my spine. She doesn't say anything. Just embraces me like she cares.

CHAPTER 31

THE FACT LIAM HASN'T RUN AWAY COMES AS A SURPRISE. Which says more than any words could. I hug him even tighter.

"I'm sure you don't want to talk about it—although I'll listen if you do—but will you at least tell me if you're okay? And, you know, be honest." I won't press him for more than that, but I say a silent plea for him to give me...something.

He clears his throat and swallow is audible. "Have you ever just had a moment of overwhelm?"

My heart leaps and then races. I try to calm the thing, to rein in the excitement that he actually answered, because it also aches at the pain in his voice. "I have lots of moments like that."

"How do you handle it?"

"It depends."

"On?" Liam asks.

"On what caused it. For instance, when I'm in new social situations, I get a panicky sensation that swirls around in my belly. I'm not good with people. I'm awkward. A little inept at times. Which means I avoid them as much possible." I give a mock shudder. "But if, for some reason, I can't avoid it, then I find ways to excuse myself, so I can be alone for a minute or two. I might go to the bathroom or even step outside. And the second it's acceptable for me to leave, I do."

Liam makes a small noise. When nothing more is forthcoming, I don't push. Instead, I kiss his shoulder blade and climb out of the bed. I walk to the bathroom and pause in the doorway before glancing back at him. There's an almost uncertain expression on his face. My heart aches as he just stares at the floor. What is he seeing? Finally, he lifts his gaze to mine.

"I could use someone to wash my back if you're up to the task." Without waiting for a response, I disappear inside and turn on the shower.

I quickly divest myself of the boots I'm still wearing, get in, and duck my head under the water. The steady pressure thumps my skin. I sweep my wet hair back and wipe my face. A large, warm body brushes against mine. I open my eyes and stare at Liam. He reaches around me, and then he's squeezing shampoo into his palm.

"Turn," he demands in a rough growl.

Slowly, I pivot and give him my back. Gentle hands massage my scalp and the fruit scent wafts through the steam that floats in the air. I moan in pleasure. Liam certainly knows how to work those fingers of his. He continues pampering me, including rinsing all the suds out, repeating his relaxing massage with the conditioner, and then rinsing it all out. He takes just as much care with washing my body. I'm a noodle by the time he finishes. I'm not sure I've ever been this relaxed.

When we're finished, he helps me out of the shower and dries me off first, then himself. He shocks me again by putting a dry towel over the wet spot in the bed. The sight of it makes my brain fire and my mouth go dry. Shit. *Don't freak out. You're on birth control.* Not that it's perfect, but it's something at least. Still...

"I know it's a little after the fact, but we forgot a condom."

Liam pauses and straightens to glance over at me. "Are you on birth control?"

"Yes." Did his shoulders just relax? "That's also not the only reason I mentioned it."

"I'm good," he says. "Had bloodwork done not that long ago."

I nod vaguely. This is a first for me. I've never fucked anyone without protection. Never had to ask about it. The guys have always taken care of it on their end. Who knew how awkward a conversation this would be? At least for me. Liam doesn't appear bothered by it at all. Then again, I'm not sure anything bothers him. Well maybe nothing except being vulnerable.

He moves in front of me and tips my chin up with a thumb and forefinger. "I'll make sure to wear a condom next time. Now, get in the bed and rest. The night isn't over, and I'm not finished with you."

I'll save my anxiety for later. Instead, I grin up at him. "I'm going to hold you to that."

I lie down and Liam climbs in behind me. His arm wraps around me and he drags me against him so my back is flush with the front of him. His cock nestles in the cleft of my ass and he palms my breast. Beneath him, my nipple hardens. I wiggle backwards, and he pinches the hard tip hard. I gasp at the pain that quickly morphs into pleasure.

"Behave," he growls into my ear.

I snort, but do as he says. Between the hot shower, the massage, and Liam's warm body and masculine scent surrounding me, my eyes grow heavy and I slowly relax against him. One second my thoughts are on what's going to happen tomorrow and the next day and the day after that, and then I'm not having any at all.

A SLOW BUZZ OF AWARENESS HITS ME. I HAVE TO PEE, BUT I'm also comfortable and cozy and I don't want to move. Ugh, I might as well get up. I roll over, expecting to find Liam, but that side of the bed is empty. I push myself up on my elbows. Nothing. I glance over at the bathroom. The door is open and the light's off.

Maybe he went to grab us some breakfast and will be back?

An hour later, it's obvious he didn't and he won't. In the meantime, I stripped the bed, put clean sheets on it, and started a load of laundry. I also did nothing but overthink. What did last night mean? Hell, maybe I'm the only one who is trying to put any meaning to it. Or at least more meaning than just a fuck. I collapse onto my back on the bed with a groan. What the hell is wrong with me?

I'm sitting here obsessing over a man—a criminal—who kidnapped me. And while Carrick isn't my Da, for months he *could have been*. Which makes these stupid feelings for Liam worse. I keep hoping it's just lust. I can deal with being attracted to him. Who wouldn't be? But *feelings*? I'm so screwed. What kind of idiot develops feelings for her kidnapper, a man who is doing his best to destroy the person she believed to be her father? Apparently, this one. My poor Mum is probably questioning my sanity from her grave. Hell, I'm questioning my own sanity.

My phone rings, and I jump. Thank god. I needed something to stop the whole mental spiral I'm about to go down.

"Hello?"

"Imogen Walsh?"

"Yes."

"My name is Arthur Tobin with Hill Solicitors and Company. I've been overseeing your mother's estate. We spoke a couple of months ago."

I have a vague recollection of some solicitor calling me right after Mum died, but most of the first few weeks were a blur. "How can I help you?"

"There is some paperwork I need your signature on and there are some personal effects that your mother wanted you to have. If you're free, could you come to the office, and we'll get this taken care of?"

Personal effects? I cleared out the whole house a month ago. What else is there? "I'm free now."

"Wonderful." He gave me the address to the office and said his assistant would let him know when I arrived.

I put on my boots and slip my hoodie over my head before walking out the door that had been left unalarmed when Liam snuck out. Almost thirty minutes later I walk into solicitor's office and approach the dark-haired woman behind the desk.

"I'm Imogen Walsh."

"If you'll have a seat, I'll let Mr. Tobin know you're here."

The waiting area has four chairs and resembles exactly what I'd picture a solicitor's office to look like. Everything is brown. Dark. There aren't even any flowers or plants to give the place some color. It's plain and boring. An older, gray-haired man wearing glasses rounds the corner and comes toward me.

"Ms. Walsh? I'm Arthur Tobin. If you'd like to follow me."

He circles his desk and gestures toward the chair. "Please, have a seat."

While I try and get comfortable, he settles in and drags closer a folder from one side of the desk, opens it, and pulls out several sheets of paper. "Yes, now then. These are the forms that need your signature. They're just to say that all of your mother's accounts have been settled, and that, as her sole beneficiary, the remaining balance will come to you."

Mr. Tobin pushes them toward me and I scan them. It's all legal jargon I don't understand, but I do my best to read through it. It all appears to be exactly what he's said so I pick up the pen lying on the desk, sign, and hand them back.

"Excellent." He nods and returns the sheets of paper back to their folder. "I'll make sure my assistant gets you a copy of everything before you leave."

"Thanks." I'm not sure what else to say.

"Now, as for the personal effects." The solicitor hands me a single, white C5-sized envelope.

I take it with trembling fingers, glance down, and back up at him. My heart races, and that swirly sensation I always get in my belly when something bad is about to happen starts up. I swallow down the spit that fills my mouth. It takes me two tries to open it, and I manage to give myself a paper cut in the process. I slide out a piece of paper folded in half. A picture falls to the floor. I lean down and pick it up. Then stare at it a few minutes. I turn it over, read the words written on the back again and again, and slowly flip it so I can stare some more, unable to make sense of what's in front of me. My whole body goes numb and the sound of ocean waves crashing against the rocky cliffs fills my ears.

A muffled voice pushes its way past. I blink and jerk my gaze up to meet the solicitor's. Sympathy lines his face. "Are you all right?"

Crazed laughter echoes inside my brain. *Am I all right? Do I look all right?* I don't ask either of those questions. I nod and take in a shuddering breath. "I'm fine."

He doesn't appear to believe me, and rightfully so. I jump to my feet and my fists clenches tightly around the picture in one hand and the envelope and sheet of paper in the other. "Is there anything else?"

"No, that's all of it."

"Okay, I need to go."

He reaches for the folder on his desk. "Let me have Siobhan make copies of these."

I wave him off, because I need to get out here. "Just mail them to me. I have to go."

I'm almost running out of his office and the building. I slam open the front door and make it a few blocks before coming to an abrupt halt. I throw my head back and breathe in the fresh air. It doesn't help. Tears flood my eyes. I stumble a few steps and drop to my ass on the stoop of the nearest building. All I do is sit there for a few minutes, blinking back the wetness threatening to spill down my cheeks.

When I finally have myself under control, I smooth out the crumpled picture and study it longer. Then, I set it down beside me, unfold the sheet of paper, and read the letter written in my mother's handwriting.

Dearest Imogen,
Please forgive me...

CHAPTER 32

I'm distracted. For a third time—or is it the fourth?—I read the documents in front of me, but I don't make it through two paragraphs before my mind drifts again. Always back to Imogen. Fuck. I slam the folder closed and collapse back into my chair.

There's a single knock on the door before it's opened and Aran comes limping in.

"You know, most civilized people wait for someone to answer a knock before they come barging in," I say drily, grateful for the interruption despite my irritation.

"Only when they think the person on the other side will actually let them enter," he lobs back with a grin and makes himself comfortable on the couch.

"Can I get you a drink?"

Aran waves me off. "Not at the moment."

For nearly a minute we just stare at each other. Finally I raise an eyebrow. It's not like him to stay quiet this long. "Was there something you needed?"

All traces of amusement he usually exhibits are gone. It's one of the subtle ways I can always tell him apart from Declan. With this serious demeanor, he more closely resembles his twin than ever.

"Are you okay?" Aran asks. "You seem different. And yes, I know I made that whole joke about the body snatcher thing, but I'm being real here. You're not the same Liam from a few weeks ago."

"Of course I am. I'm the exact same cold and ruthless arsehole I've been for years."

"No, you're not. I noticed it, and so has Declan. Ever since you got back from wherever it is you took Imogen. Hell, Liam, you actually showed up at your little safe-house to make sure we were still breathing." He throws his arm out, pointing in a random direction. "Do you even remember the last time the three of us were in the same room together? Let alone having an actual conversation?"

Didn't you ask yourself the same question? I don't have an answer for him, so I keep my mouth shut.

"It's been twenty-one years, in case you were wondering. Your sixteenth birthday."

Has it really been that long?

"Do you remember now?"

I go rigid. Of course I do. It was the beginning of the end of the three of us.

"Dónal caught us drinking and beat the shit out of me."

"Didn't stop you from sneaking out later, though, did it?" A small smile creeps onto Aran's face.

"I wasn't going to let that bastard ruin my birthday." No, that came after.

"You sure didn't." He shakes his head. "Except something did. You met us at Blaine's house. All the kids were having a great time, even you, no matter how hard you tried to hide otherwise. Except one minute you were chuckling at some lame joke I made and the next you cut us out of your life. No explanation. Just...done."

"I know." Destroying our friendship is one of my only regrets in life.

Along with not killing Dónal.

Then there's Imogen.

"For what it's worth, it was never about the two of you."

It had taken every bit of control I possessed not to vomit when Blaine's father came to check on us. It was one of the many faces of my nightmares. Both waking and sleeping. His secret, knowing smile sent cold chills rushing through me, especially when he squeezed my shoulder, lingering a second too long. No one could ever find out what he did to me. It's why I killed him.

"You're never going to tell us why, either, are you?" Aran asks, although from his flat expression he already knows the answer.

"No."

He nods in understanding and carefully stands. "Whatever it was, don't let it continue to eat away at you and destroy your life or other's. You're stronger than that."

I don't reply. He limps to the door and pauses at it. "She's good for you, you know? If there's a smallest chance she could make you happy, you should take it."

The door closes behind him. I sit there a while longer.

"Don't let it eat away at you."

I can't get Aran's words out of my head. Since I was seventeen, everything I've done has been with one goal in mind. Be the most powerful man in Dublin. No matter what I had to do and no matter how long it took. Except my focus keeps getting distracted from it and onto something—someone—else.

I open the folder again and try to read, but, finally, I have to give up. I pick up the phone and call Darragh. "Last night was a no-go. Which means we need to find some new investors. Reach out to any of your contacts and see what you can find."

He hesitates. Something he's never done before.

"What?" I bite out.

"There are whispers that you might not be ready to control

Dublin," he finally admits. "They say you've been distracted. While you've managed to derail the Donnelly's import business, people are worried it's only temporary. Carrick Donnelly still holds far too much power in this city and some aren't sure you have the focus to take what you think is yours."

My fist tighten around the phone and my jaw clenches so hard it aches. "I see. And what do you think?"

Another hesitation is all the answer I need.

"I think your priorities have shifted, Liam." He rarely uses my name and only when he's concerned about something.

At least he didn't say I'm distracted. *Aren't you, though*? "Reach out anyway and let me know."

I disconnect the call. Without investors, I can still purchase the land and build the casino. Like Darragh said, I've already crippled the Donnelly's weapons importing and cost them millions, but it's not enough. I have to bankrupt them. If that doesn't work, then it'll be time to take things to the next level. War. Except I keep balking at taking that step.

I'm not afraid of death. I'm also not afraid to kill. I just don't want Imogen caught in the middle. Goddamn it, what has she done to me? Christ. When did things change? What am I, if I'm not the one with all the power in Dublin? More importantly, what am I going to do about Imogen? I'm not sure anymore if I can have both.

The intercom buzzes and Ashlynn's voice comes through. "Carrick Donnelly is here to see you, sir."

What the hell does he want?

"Send him in." I sit back and wait for his arrival.

Moments later, the door opens and my assistant gestures for him to enter. Like the first time, he strides in with the grace of a predator and takes a seat without my leave. Not in the mood for whatever games he wants to play, I'm blunt. "What do you want?"

"Not even going to bother with fake pleasantries, I see," Donnelly muses.

"There's not really any point, is there? Besides, the sooner you say whatever it is you came here to say, the sooner you can get the fuck out of my office."

The older man smirks. "I hear you lost the support of a couple investors last night."

Apparently word travels fast. I paste a smile on my face and wave a hand. "There are plenty more. I have no concerns."

"You should." There's a warning in his tone I can't ignore.

"Why's that?"

"Because up until now I've enjoyed watching you play at being leader of your organization, so I've let it continue. But the game has gotten boring and I'd hate for anyone to get hurt."

"And by anyone, I assume you mean those three sons of yours?" I arch a brow.

Donnelly's expression hardens. "By anyone, I mean Imogen."

I go rigid and slowly sit up. "Are you threatening her?"

"I'm merely giving you fair warning regarding the stakes in this little power play you think you have going on. What are you willing to lose?" He stands and stares down at me. "Think on it."

Rage has me in a chokehold as he walks to the door. I manage to fight past it, not even considering the consequences of my words. "If you so much as touch her, then you better be prepared. I won't stop until every single one of you are dead."

"Always a pleasure, Liam." He nods, and then he's gone.

CHAPTER 33

THERE'S THE SNICK OF THE FRONT DOOR BEING unlocked, but I ignore it. Same with the annoying beeping sounds as someone disarms the security system. What I can't ignore is the person who grabs the duvet and yanks it off my head where I've been hiding for two days.

"Jaysus, have you not showered since we last talked?" Teagan wrinkles her nose.

"Aren't you supposed to be in London? Or Berlin? Or wherever it was this time?" I grumble, regretting giving her both a key and the security code a few years ago.

"Berlin. And I *was*, but then I get a call from my best friend who sounded like she was one second away from jumping off a cliff—figuratively, I hope. Did you really think I wouldn't come rushing home to check on you? Because there was something in your voice I *really* didn't like," she declares as if that explains everything.

And it does. There is no one who knows me better than Teagan.

I roll to the side, grab the photo and letter off the bedside table, and silently hand them to her. She glances at me and then sits on the edge of the bed while I scoot to the head of it. The first thing she does is stare at the picture, the same way I did. With confusion. She lifts her gaze to mine and then turns the photo over and reads the back. Her eyes widen.

Teagan sets the photo down next to her and unfolds the sheet of paper. Her eyes move side to side as she reads it and then widen. She mouths something that looks a lot like holy shit, which is a gross understatement. Her arm drops like a weight and she sits there not blinking. Finally her gaze meets mine.

"Where did you get this?"

"Mum's solicitor."

Because she's Teagan, she crawls across the bed until she's practically sitting on top of me and laces her fingers through mine, holding my hand tightly between us. "Christ, Genny, I don't know what to say."

I laugh bitterly. "What is there to say? My entire life is nothing but a lie. What if she hadn't gotten sick? Would she still be keeping this from me?"

"Probably." She says it kindly, but leave it to her to give me the unbiased truth. "But she did get sick."

"I hate her for this." I sniffle, tears I swore I'd stop shedding threatening to start up again, and swipe my nose with my free hand.

"I think, given the circumstances, you're allowed."

"What am I going to do, T?" I turn toward her.

Teagan's eyes scan my face. "You have a few choices, I suppose. One, you can ignore the letter and picture and live your life like they never existed. But we both know the likelihood of that happening. Which leaves you with option B. Find out the truth. Do you know who that is in the photo?"

I've stared at it so many times since Mr. Tobin handed it to me that I have it memorized. "I have a pretty good idea."

"Alright, then start there."

I huff out a laugh, but it's forced. "It's not as easy as it sounds."

"Why not?"

So I tell her. Everything. Like the best friend she is, Teagan listens quietly until I'm done. I brace myself for the reaction that's going to come in three...two...one...

"You were fucking kidnapped and you didn't think to tell me before *now?*" She screeches and jumps out of the bed to pace. "Jesus, Genny."

I wince at the disappointment in her tone. But of all the things she could have fixated on, it had to be Liam. "I'm sorry."

She pauses in the middle of the room and pivots my way. "Only you would get kidnapped and then catch feelings for your kidnapper."

A grin tugs at my mouth. I fight it for as long as I can, but Teagan's obvious exasperation tickles me and it's a losing battle. I burst out laughing, because it's ridiculous. "There is something seriously wrong with me."

She comes back to the bed and sits beside me again, still chuckling and shaking her head. "Yes, there is. It's one of the many reasons I love you." She snags my hand. "Since there is way too much to unpack with everything you told me, let's start with this Liam bloke. Do you plan on seeing him again?"

I drop my head backwards and it thumps against the wall. "He left two mornings ago and I haven't heard from or seen him since. I think that speaks for itself."

"And it was two weeks before that since you'd heard from him, and yet it happened." Teagan eyeballs me. "Besides, you haven't left your flat to *be* seen and your phone is either turned off or on silent, because you didn't answer any of my calls or texts in those same two days, hence the reason I showed up. I had to make sure you weren't dead."

I flinch. "Sorry."

She squeezes my hand in forgiveness. "He's probably busy trying to take over the world. Which means you're going to have to make the first move."

"He's not trying to take over the world," I grumble.

"Sorry, he's probably busy trying to take over Dublin." Teagan glares, because she knows I'm avoiding answering.

"Fine," I blow the word out on a breath. "I'll stop by his office tomorrow."

She shakes her head. "Today. After you've showered, though, because good Christ, ya stink."

"Hey, now." I shoulder bump her.

She lets go of my hand, smacks my thigh, and stands. "Go get cleaned up and I'll pick you out something to wear. Then, you're going to introduce me to your kidnapping mobster boyfriend. After that, we'll figure out what to do about your Mum's letter. One thing at a time, all right?"

"But what if it's true?" I push.

Teagan shakes her head. "One thing at a time, right?"

"Right."

AN HOUR LATER, TEAGAN AND I ARE ON OUR WAY TO Liam's office. I've balked more than once, making excuses about why I shouldn't show up unannounced like a weird stalker. Every time, she reminds me that he *kidnapped me*, so us randomly stopping by shouldn't be an issue. And if it is, then he'll just have to get over it. We turn the corner onto his street and my feet keep pivoting so I'm walking in the opposite direction.

Teagan snags my arm. "No you don't. We're already here."

I groan, but let her pull me forward. This is the first time I've actually been this close to Liam's office. We walk up the three steps and through the front door. It's exactly what I'd expect from him. Everything from the high-polished floor to the decor screams wealth and power. The soles of our shoes squelch as we cross to where a pretty woman sits behind a desk.

"Can I help you?" she asks with a polite smile.

My mouth opens, but nothing comes out. I can only gape like a fish. Teagan elbows me and I cough, clearing out the rocks that had been blocking my throat. "We're—*I'm*—here to see Liam."

"I'm sorry, but Mr. Campbell isn't taking any visitors at the moment."

Sagging with relief, I wag my hand out. "Oh, okay, that's fine, no problem, thank you." Then I try walking away.

Teagan grabs me with a glare and turns back to the assistant with a saccharine smile. "Mr. Campbell would be extremely upset if you didn't let him know that Imogen Walsh was here to see him."

The other woman's gaze bounces between us. I give her a pained expression, while my best friend stares her down with an imperious glare that almost puts Liam's to shame.

"Just one moment, please." She picks up the phone and presses a button. "Mr. Campbell, there is an Imogen Walsh and...associate here to see you."

There's a brief pause before she nods. "Yes, sir."

She stands and rounds the desk. "If you'd follow me, please."

Teagan, the traitor, pushes me in the assistant's direction. "You go ahead. I'll wait out here for you."

Sending her a look of betrayal over my shoulder I follow the woman until she knocks on a door and opens it, stepping aside to allow me to enter. I swallow and step past her. My gaze lands on Liam, who's sitting behind his desk, and I can't tear it away. The door closes behind me, and still I can't move.

"Imogen," he breaks the silence.

"Liam." My greeting is far more formal than his.

A quick grin crosses his face, but he smooths it out and gestures for me to have a seat. I cross the room, sit, and fidget. What the hell's wrong with me? Where'd the take-no-bullshit Imogen go? Straightening, in my chair I narrow my eyes.

"You left without a goodbye the other day, you know?"

He blinks. Almost like he's surprised I'm calling him out. "Is that why you're here then? To chastise me?"

I snort. "You make it sound like you're a naughty schoolboy and I'm your teacher about to punish you."

"I think I prefer the picture of you being the naughty schoolgirl I bend over my desk, toss up your plaid skirt, and spank your ass red." Liam's blue eyes glow with heat.

My center throbs, and I press my thighs together. "I might be able to arrange something. I'd have to borrow my friend's skirt, though."

He barks out a laugh. I love the sound of it, because it doesn't happen nearly enough. I also love how it softens the harsher features of his face making him appear not as cold.

"I look forward to it," he say with a low growl that perks up my lady parts more.

Shifting in my seat to alleviate some of the ache, I clear my throat. "Do you want to grab some lunch?" I blurt out.

Liam's eyebrows raise. My tongue almost bleeds from being bitten to hold back the invitation retraction. My heart thumps in my ears as I wait for an answer.

"Like a date?" he finally asks with no small amount of...something in his tone I can't identify. Disbelief? Mockery? Anticipation? Coming from him, it could be any of the above.

"If you want to call it that." *Hello, don't forget Teagan.* "Um, actually, no, not a date. At least not this time." Oh, no, it's much worse. It includes my best friend, which is essentially like introducing him to my family. My sister.

"So there will be a next time?"

"That's up to you. But this time, my friend is actually waiting out in your lobby." I thumb over my shoulder. Might as well get all the awkwardness out of the way.

"I see." He steeples his fingers. "Well, then, we should probably get going on this non-date then."

With that, he stands and buttons his suit jacket. I clamber to my feet as well. Liam rounds the desk and heads for the door. He glances back at me and I shuffle over to him. He palms my jaw and rubs his thumb across my cheek. "For what it's worth, I was going to stop by your flat later today."

"Oh yeah? Why's that?" I expect him to say something about returning to my bed.

"Because for some reason, I can't stay away even though I should."

I stare up at him. "Why should you?"

"I'll only end up hurting you. I'm not a good person, Imogen."

I rise up on my tiptoes and kiss him softly. "Why don't you let me worry about that?"

Because it's already too late. I care about Liam far too much. He's shown me the kind of person he is from the beginning, and yet, I'm still falling for him. God, I'm so screwed, especially when the truth comes out. But that's a worry for another day. First, let me get through introducing him to Teagan. By the time she's done grilling him, he may never want to see me again anyway.

CHAPTER 34

Liam

Once again, Imogen's arm is looped through mine as we walk down the footpath a few blocks from the restaurant where we went to lunch. It's another surprisingly sunny day, but the clouds in the distance are moving closer.

"Thank you for putting up with Teagan's interrogation. You were far more patient than I expected you to be." She glances up and squeezes my arm.

I only tolerated it because Imogen obviously cares for her deeply, and I didn't want to hurt her. A fact I'm still adjusting to.

"How long have you two been friends?" A month ago I wouldn't have cared enough to ask.

"You mean you hadn't already learned that when you stalked me?" she mock gasps.

"Apparently my stalker skills don't compete with yours."

"No one's does, so don't feel bad," she says pertly.

"And you said my ego was big." I huff. "So...Teagan?"

"Right. We met at university our first year. Ended up having quite a few classes together and randomly sat next to each other. We hit it off and have been best friends ever since." Imogen leans into me. "This is the first time I've seen her since Mum's funeral. She works cyber security for this huge corporation and is always traveling to their international offices."

"Cyber security, huh? So basically she keeps people like you out of their computers?"

She grins up at me. "Exactly."

"Have you ever...?"

"Only when she asks me to so she can test their system's safeguards. I would *never* betray her trust like that."

I blink at her firm tone and let that revelation sink in for a minute. Do people like Imogen really exist? What would it be like to have someone that loyal to me? Who wouldn't dream of stabbing me in the back? I don't surround myself with the kind of people who wouldn't take advantage of someone else. Not even if that person was an alleged friend. *I* wouldn't. Will I only end up corrupting Imogen's goodness if whatever this thing between us continues?

"What are you thinking right now?" she asks.

We turn and walk through the arched entrance of the Dublin Castle garden. God, I haven't been here since I was a kid. She nudges me with a gentle elbow, and I glance down. A lie forms in my throat, but I swallow it down.

"I was thinking that you're far too good for me."

She studies me for a moment, her eyes scanning my face.

"What if we're both far too good for the other?" Imogen's gaze wanders across one length of the garden to the other. The flowers are starting to bloom and the grass is, as always, a beautiful shade of green. She continues. "I'm just as much a criminal as you are. I've altered financial statements to make people appear guilty of taking bribes. I've planted viruses that have wiped out entire systems. Those are just tiny examples. But I've done more. All because the right people paid me. I'm not sure that makes me the most moral person. So I don't judge others by their worst mistakes."

I stop and draw her to me with my hands around her waist. She loops hers over my shoulder, clasping them behind my neck. "Like I said, you're too good for me."

She lifts up on her toes and kisses me. "Did I ever tell you that I kind of have a thing for dangerous men?"

That makes me laugh. "No, actually, you didn't. How dangerous?"

"Enough to have some woman kidnapped off the street and brought to his house because he's *bored*."

"Not just some woman." I pull her closer. "A specific woman. And I wasn't bored."

Imogen grins. "If you say so."

I kiss her once more, wrap her hand around my elbow again, and start walking. "Would you like to go back to the cottage with me this weekend?"

There's a short silence.

"I'm not sure I can. There's something I have to take care of first. I'm also not sure how long Teagan is going to be in town. I'd like to spend some time with her before she leaves again. Maybe another weekend?"

"Yeah, maybe." I try to hide my disappointment. "Well, I should probably get back to the office."

"I didn't mean to keep you from work."

I stop and palm Imogen's cheek. "You're not keeping me. Any time you want to go to lunch or just stop by, I'd love to see you."

A slow smile tugs at her lips. "You may regret that open invitation."

"Doubtful."

We make it to the door of my office building right as the sky opens up and it pours. She laughs as we run the last bit of distance, both of us getting soaked, and dash inside. Imogen shakes off the water like a dog. "Man, I love the rain."

Droplets cling to her eyelashes and her hair is stuck to her head. But her cheeks are rosy and she radiates happiness.

If there's a smallest chance she could make you happy, you should take it. Aran's voice whispers inside my head.

If anyone could make me happy, it's Imogen. But can I make *her* happy?

"Would you like me to call my driver to take you home?"

"No thanks. I'm already wet. Besides, I'm one of those weirdos who loves walking in the rain. It's one of my favorite smells."

"If you're sure. Here." I get out my wallet and a business card and hand it to her. "My mobile number."

Imogen studies it and looks up with a cheeky grin. "Saves me the trouble of having to search the 'net for it."

"Thought I'd make it easy on you."

"As if it would be hard." She scoffs. "All right, I'll let you get back to work. Thank you again for lunch."

"The pleasure was all mine."

She waves as she walks backward and then swivels on her feet. There's a brief pause and in a swift move Imogen runs back to me, throws her arms around my neck, and kisses me like it's the last time. I respond by deepening it. *Something's different.* I can't figure out. Before I can try, she almost pushes me away and runs out the door. What the fuck was that?

I call Darragh. "I need you to keep an eye on Imogen for a few days. Don't approach or engage her."

"Yes, sir."

Not remotely satisfied, I toss the phone on my desk and get back to work. Except I can't get either of the visits I've had in the last two days out of my head. First, Aran and then Carrick and what sounded like a threat to Imogen. It gives me one more reason to destroy him. Which means I need to get my focus back. No more distractions. Find a couple new investors and build the casino to rival theirs.

Next, I call Craig. "Reach out to your man and tell him to put the plan in motion."

It's time to ruin them from the inside next. No one wants to lose their money at the tables when the house cheats to get it.

THE TOWN CAR COMES TO A STOP IN THE DRIVE. BEHIND the house, the setting sun sparkles across the Bay. It's one of the reasons I bought the place. It reminds me of the time spent fishing in Kenmare with my grand-da. It's the first time I've acknowledged the fact.

He wouldn't be proud of the man I've become. The things I've done. I'm sorry for that. Not for doing them, but that I'd be a disappointment.

I loosen my tie, tugging at it until it's completely undone and hangs around my neck. The suit jacket comes next. I toss it over the arm of the couch and head for the kitchen. Ever since Imogen left, I've been waiting for her to call me. Only she hasn't. Aside from the other night and lunch today, have I given her any reason to?

Christ. *Why don't you call her?* Because that would mean there's something between us. Something...more. I've never needed anyone.

I put my attention on making dinner. Has it always been this quiet in here? So empty? It feels more so since Imogen left. She may have hated me, but there had been more life in this house when she'd been here. It was nice.

Nice? It was more than that. For the first time in probably ever, I'd been content.

What's the deal with her and Carrick, though?

Why she was watching them is still a mystery. One I don't suspect she's going to clear up for me. She told me they were *friends*. How can this thing between us work if she's friends with my greatest enemy? Imogen would never betray her friend. I suspect that means she wouldn't betray any friend.

What if I have to choose between her and my mission to destroy the Donnellys? A few days ago it would be an easy decision. I'm not sure it is any more.

CHAPTER 35

Imogen

Teagan comes to a stop right before the narrow lane and swivels to face me. "Are you sure you don't want me to come in there with you?"

"No. This is something I need to do on my own." I take a deep breath.

She nods. "Okay, but I'm waiting here for you."

I reach across and hug her. "I love you."

"Love you, too."

A push of the button releases my seat belt and in seconds I'm standing at the security box pressing the intercom button.

"State your business," the staticky voice intones.

"This is Imogen Walsh. I was here visiting Mr. Donnelly a few weeks ago. Could I come in, please?"

The same extended silence from the last time passes until finally the iron gate groans and slowly opens. I walk the familiar lane, the leaves of the trees starting to fill in the all the empty spots that were present before. The swirling sensation in my gut gets faster and faster the closer I get to the manor, until I have to stop and swallow several times before I can continue. My footsteps get heavier with each step, but finally, I make it to the house.

The door opens and Nora stands there with a welcoming smile despite the fact I'm showing up unannounced. Again. "Imogen, dear, what a surprise. Is everything all right?"

"Not really."

She gestures me forward. "Please, come in."

The weight of my feet grows and both the letter and photo burn a hole in my bag as I climb the three stairs and walk into the house. It's exactly as it was the last time I was here. There's the scent of flowers and behind it a hint of some dessert that must be in the oven or just came out. Not a speck of dirt touches a single surface.

"I'm afraid Carrick isn't here at the moment. And the boys are all out as well. They'll be disappointed to have missed you," she says.

I'd intentionally come when no one was home. I swallow. "I'm not here to see any of them."

Nora freezes, but it's so fast I'm not sure if my eyes are playing tricks on me. Her gaze quickly darts away before returning and she clasps her hands together in front of her like she's nervous. "Oh? Who are you here to see then?"

"You. But I think you already know that, don't you?"

A flash of something like pain appears on her face. "Why don't we go to the library?"

I follow her down the hall and through the double doors. During the short time I stayed here, I visited this room a few times. It's warm and cozy and I love the smell. Every time I step inside, I'm transported back to my childhood when I would spend hours at the library with Mum. These days, all my reading is done electronically, but nothing beats the scent of old paperbacks. Except I can't enjoy the smell this time.

Nora pivots in my direction. I study her and how tense she is. My hand shakes as I reach into my bag and pull out the photo. It's wrinkled and creased from being clenched in my fist so many times. Her gaze darts to it. I raise my arm, holding it out in front, and she pales. As if it might bite her, she slowly takes it from me and stares down at it.

A tear slides down her cheek as she caresses it with her fingertip. My stomach hurts and my chest tightens as if someone is squeezing it. Choking it. I can barely draw in a breath.

"Is that you?" I whisper.

Nora raises her head. More tears stream down her face. "I forgot all about this picture."

That doesn't answer my question. "Is. That. You?" I repeat, louder.

She straightens her shoulders and wipes away the wetness. "Yes."

That single syllable slams into me with more force than if she'd punched me. A sharp pain stabs me in the belly. But right behind it is a stronger emotion. I snatch the picture from her hand and yank the letter out next, shoving it at her. Just as carefully, she takes it and reads what I've memorized word for word.

"Is what she said true?" I grit out between clenched teeth.

"Imogen," she pleads, reaching for me.

"Is it true?" I scream, lunging away from her.

Nora's whole body deflates. "Yes."

Tears of anger and pain fill my eyes. "Who was she to you?"

"My sister." With the truth finally revealed, she no longer hesitates.

Lies. It has all been nothing but lies. "You knew, didn't you? When I came here for help the day after Liam kidnapped me. You knew I was your daughter."

"Yes."

"Nora? What's going on?"

We both whip around at the deep voice behind us. Carrick stands in the doorway, his eyes filled with confusion.

"Did you know?" I snap at him.

His gaze darts to Nora who's suddenly aged right in front of us before meeting mine again. "No."

At least that's one less betrayal. Something nags at me. What is it? My chin drops slightly and my eyes sweep side to side. *Think, Imogen.* Oh, god. Is it possible? I lift my head. "Who's my Da?"

The pleading look for forgiveness she sends Carrick says everything. The utter devastation on his face is one I won't soon forget. It has to mirror mine, because with that confirmation, everything I could have had is...gone.

The pain and anger leave. In its place is only numbness. *I'll grieve later.* "I deserve to know why. We both do."

Sorrow radiates off Nora as she wraps her arms around herself and walks over to the window. She stares out, silent, before breathing deeply. "Because she was going to kill you."

"Who was?" Carrick's voice booms, startling me.

She turns to us, but her eyes are locked on him. "Kathleen."

His wife?

"Jesus Christ," he rasps out and runs his hand down his face.

"I got pregnant shortly after Finn was born, but didn't tell anyone. I couldn't. Somehow, though, Kathleen found out. She showed up at my house and said if I didn't get rid of it, she'd find someone who would." Nora's voice cracks. "So I ran."

Carrick curses again. What kind of person would do that? I have to know the rest, though. "Where did you go?"

"Belfast. To Maire."

I flinch at my mother's name. "You said she was your sister. If that's true then why are there no records of that? When Mum died, she told me Carrick was my father..."—I jerk my gaze to him. His bounces between her and me like he's not sure he believes this is happening. Like he doesn't know if he should be angry, betrayed, sad, or hopeful. All the emotions bombarding me. I start again. "When she said he was my father, I searched every database out there, looking for evidence. I researched anyone connected to him, including you. If you really are her sister, then why couldn't I find any proof?"

"Because you and I are the same. My mother had an affair with my father while he was married. The only difference is that my father knew about me. I was never acknowledged and my mother never told anyone except me."

Carrick walks to the bar and pours himself a drink. I turn back to Nora. "So how did my mum find out?"

"When I was fifteen, I confronted my father. Of course, he denied it. Maire overheard us and forced him to tell her the truth. She was the perfect daughter. One he'd do anything for," she sneers. "She refused to forgive him and we grew close after that. We still didn't tell people we were sisters, but only because Maire didn't want to hurt her mother."

"So you get pregnant and hide in Belfast. That doesn't explain why my entire life has been a lie."

Nora hugs herself again. "Because Kathleen found me. Or at least the men she hired did. I'd been walking home from the pub where I worked when I was attacked. They said they were going to beat the bastard out of me. One of them kicked me in the stomach. I was bleeding so much, there's no way you had survived. I was wrong." She chuckles softly and smiles. "When you cried for the first time, it was the most beautiful sound I'd ever heard. I knew then that you were a fighter. Which meant I had to fight as well to make sure you were safe."

Tears spill down my cheeks. Carrick crosses the room and pulls Nora to him. He murmurs in her ear, his expression hurt-filled, but also full of love and forgiveness. The pain returns. With it, anger. They have each other, yet I'm here. Alone. My mum is dead and I have no one.

"What happened then?" I snap. "You just gave me away?"

She lets go of him and takes several quick steps closer, but I back up. She stops. "I loved you more than anything and I was trying to protect you the only way I knew how. Which was making Kathleen believe that she'd succeeded."

"Carrick's wife has been dead for over fifteen years. You could have told the truth then," I accuse.

"How could I do that to any of you? By then, you were Maire's daughter in every sense of the word. I'd long ago accepted that fact. What good would it have done? It would have been selfish of me. Everyone I loved would be hurt and there was a chance you would end up hating us both."

"Too bad for you, all of that came to pass anyway."

Nora palms her chest like I stabbed her, but I ignore any pain I caused her. I can only focus on my own. My heart races and there's buzzing inside my head. I pace a few steps, growing more restless with each one. My hands tremble. I squeeze them into fists to try and stop it. "I have to go."

I swing around toward the door and rush forward.

"Imogen, wait," Carrick pleads.

Ignoring him, I move faster until I'm running out the door and down the lane toward the road. The iron gate looms in front of me, blurred by the tears that won't stop. I grab the bars and shake them as hard as I can and scream. "Open this right now."

I keep shaking and screaming until finally, it groans and a crack appears. I bounce up and down, flapping my arms with impatience until there's an opening wide enough for me to slip through. Teagan's already there. I jump in beside her and she drives away. The only sound are my sobs. She doesn't say anything, but she reaches out and grabs my hand. I clutch it tight like it's only only life line.

We've almost made it back to the city before my tears dry up. She parks close to my building and walks with me up to my flat. As soon as she disarms the security system I go straight to my bed and curl up in it. A minute later, Teagan sits beside me and lifts my head onto her lap. We sit together in the semi-dark as she strokes my hair and I grieve for everything that was and could have been.

CHAPTER 36

Liam

I KNOCK ON IMOGEN'S DOOR AND WAIT. SEVERAL MINUTES pass with no answer, so I knock again. According to Darragh, neither she nor Teagan have left since they got back from the Donnelly estate yesterday. I want answers and I'm not leaving here until I get them. I knock again. And a third time. A few seconds come and go and still nothing. I raise my hand to knock a fourth time, but before my knuckles can connect, the door is jerked open.

"What the fuck do you—?" Teagan's mouth snaps shut. "Liam."

"I need to talk to Imogen," I say without preamble.

She shifts and closes the door a bit, blocking the narrowed opening with her body. "I'm sorry, but she's not feeling well. I'll let her know you came by though."

She attempts to close the door the rest of the way, but I stiff arm it. "I'm not leaving until I talk to her."

Teagan bristles and stands straighter. "I appreciate the fact you're some powerful mobster who thinks he can command everyone around him, but I've already told you she doesn't want to see anyone right now. You should respect that."

Other than Imogen, no one has ever told me no before. It's a novel experience. The old me would push past her without caring, but I hesitate.

"It's okay, T, let him in." Imogen's voice is fatigued.

Teagan glances over her shoulder. Whatever she sees makes her sigh and step back, bringing the door with her. Imogen sits in her bed with the blanket pooled around her waist. Her hair isn't combed and her eyes are bloodshot and red like she's been crying. There are bruises under them as well.

Her friend walks across the room where the two of them speak softly to each other. Imogen shakes her head and the other woman's shoulders drop. They hug and Teagan walks by me and out the door, closing it behind her. I turn back to Imogen, who still hasn't gotten out of the bed. Is she really sick? No, there's more going on here.

I grab the chair from her desk, drag it over to her, and take a seat. "What's wrong?" I'm not going to bring up her visit to the Donnellys. Yet.

Imogen wrings her hands. I hate how deflated she appears.

Reaching out, I take one hand in mine. "Talk to me."

"Has there ever been anything you wanted, but didn't realize how badly you wanted it until you discovered you could never have it?"

"No. I always get what I want, remember?" I say it in a way I hope will bring a smile to her face.

I'm rewarded with a small one, but it quickly disappears. "If only we were all so lucky."

Every part of me wants to demand she tell me what the fuck is wrong, but I clench my teeth and draw on the infinite patience I've cultivated over the last twenty years. I continue holding her hand, rubbing my thumb up and down hers in a soothing gesture. Tears shimmer in her eyes, but she blinks them back and sniffs.

"Might as well get this over with." She shrugs but the movement is so sluggish like she's been weighted down I want to tell her I changed my mind. She continues before I can. "Teagan and I went to the Donnelly estate yesterday."

"Oh?"

Imogen glances up at me. Her eyes track my face. I keep my expression blank. Except I must not succeed, because she turns away. "You already knew, didn't you? It's why you're here."

"Hey." I squeeze her hand making her look at me again. "Yes, I knew, but it's not the only reason I'm here."

She doesn't ask what that other reason is, and I don't tell her.

"You know my mum died several months ago. The other day, I got a call from her solicitor asking me to come by." She draws her hand out from under mine and reaches over to her bed side table. "He gave me this."

I take the envelope she holds out in front of her and glance up.

"Go ahead." Imogen dips her head. "Open it."

Slowly, I lift the flap and pull out the contents. I glance at the photo of two women and then unfold the sheet of paper.

> *Dearest Imogen,*
> *Please forgive me and know that I love you with all my heart.*

"Are you sure you want me reading this?" Isn't it personal?

"Yes."

I go back to the letter.

> *By now I am gone, but I wanted you to know that you were the best thing to ever happen to me. No one could have asked for a more perfect daughter than you. You're smart. Kind. Loving. Beautiful inside and out. I have*

few regrets in my life, but the biggest one is that we've kept the truth from you. Please know that it was not done out of malice, but rather, out of love. My god, when the doctors put you in my arms, I knew I'd do everything in my power to make sure you were safe and protected. But mostly, that you were loved. And you were. You ARE. So, so much. Not only by me, but also by the woman who gave birth to you.

My eyes jerk up to meet Imogen's tear-filled ones. What the fuck?

I understand if you're confused, hurt, and angry right now. All I can do is hope you will one day forgive me. Forgive both of us.
With all my love,
Mum

Setting down the letter, I pick up the photo again. On the left is a black-haired woman. On the right, an auburn-haired one who lovingly cradles her large, pregnant belly. A breeze must be blowing because both women's hair almost appears to be moving. The sun shines high above them and they're standing on a bridge overlooking a body of water that shimmers. Their smiles are bright and happy, and they each have an arm around the other's waist. I bring the picture closer and stare at the redhead. She's somehow familiar, but not. I flip it over. The handwriting on the back matches the letter.

Maire, Nora, and baby Imogen (May, 1996)

I study the women again. My eyes widen. Jaysus. Is that who I think it is? I lift my head. Imogen's bottom lip quivers.

"Maire wasn't your mother." It's not a question, but she shakes her head anyway. "And this other woman, Nora? Is that...?"

She slowly nods and new tears spring to her eyes before sliding down her cheeks. I drop my arm to the bed, loosening my hold on the photograph, and rise to my feet. Imogen's gaze follows me. Nora Martin is her mother. I freeze for a second and grab the picture again. 1996. Based on how far along in her pregnancy she is, she probably gave birth only a few months later. So if Nora is her mother, then that would mean...

"Fuck."

She chuckles but it's the most pitiful sound. "Figured it all out didn't you?"

I turn and glance down at her. It's been right there in front of me this entire time. The color of her eyes. Her hair. The nose. The shape of her face. Every single aspect of her face is a Donnelly. *How could you not see it*? I run my hands through my hair and tuck my chin. Goddamn it. That's why she has all those videos of them on her computer. Her mother must have told her Carrick was her father.

"You had Declan take you to his estate because he's your Da, didn't you?" The question is flat. Emotionless.

"Yes."

At least she didn't lie.

"Are you working for him?"

She startles at the question and that little crease between her eyebrows appear like it does whenever she doesn't understand something. "Am I what?"

"You know, spying on me to get information to pass off to him? Or maybe you were supposed to seduce me. Make me have feelings for you. Make me fall in lo..."—I cut off abruptly.—"Are you working for him?"

Imogen stiffens, throws back the blankets, and jumps to her feet. Her chest heaves and I'm reminded of her rage that first day at my estate. At least the tears have dried up. "Is that really what you think of me? That I would whore myself out for someone?"

I flinch at the word.

"Fuck you, Liam," she spits. "I just found out I've been lied to my entire life. I've done nothing but sit in this bed since yesterday agonizing over the fact that the man I care about—might even be falling in love with—is going to hate me because of who my father is. Not everyone is out to get you, you know? Or has ulterior motives. If that's what you really think of me, then you and I were never going to work anyway. I'm glad I found out now."

"What else am I supposed to think? You ran to him for help. He tried getting you back after the trade for Nessa. How about when you and he were having dinner together on the same night I show up at the restaurant and then you invited me back to your place? Aren't you the one who came by my office when you hadn't heard from me in two days?" I throw my hands up.

She laughs bitterly. "You both are so paranoid, you know that? Carrick said the same thing about you. That you only came to the same restaurant because we were there. As for inviting you to my place, *you* followed *me*. I had no intention of going to your office. I'd already told Teagan it was obvious you weren't interested, but she harassed me into going anyway. Look what good that did? Just because you'd use and manipulate someone doesn't mean everyone would. It doesn't mean *I* would, and the fact you think that of me tells me everything I need to know."

Imogen pushes past me and opens the door. She won't even look at me. "I'd like you to leave now."

For another minute, I stand there and try to reconcile everything I learned. Except I can't. Not while it's this fresh. Yes, I'd vaguely considered what I'd do if I had to choose between her and everything I've worked for, but never in my wildest imagination did I really believe I'd have to make the choice. It should have been easy.

I cross the room until I stop directly in front of her. She still won't meet my eyes. "You and I aren't finished, Imogen."

At last, her gaze settles on me. "I guess this is the one time you *don't* get what you want."

She's wrong. I have to come to terms with things first, but I'll be back.

CHAPTER 37

Imogen

Teagan throws her arms around me and we hug each other hard. "I wish I didn't have to leave."

"I wish you didn't either, but you have a job to go back to." I draw away, but clasp her hands and take in a deep breath. "And I have a life to figure out."

She huffs and shakes her head. "Why is it you're the one who gets to have all the fun?"

I snort. "Oh yes, because finding out my true parentage after twenty-seven years and falling for my Da's enemy is every girl's dream."

"When you put it that way..." Teagan drawls.

One more quick hug later and I shoo her toward the door. "Go before I cry. You know I how much I hate doing it. Plus you don't want to miss your flight."

She grabs her messenger bag and dips her head under the strap so it lies across her body. "I'll call you when I get to Berlin. In the meantime, get some rest and eat all your veggies."

Tears burn my eyes, but I sniff them back. "I love you."

"Back at ya, babe." She waves and walks out the door, closing it behind her.

She's been an amazing distraction since Liam left the other day, but with her leaving, I'll be alone with my thoughts.

I've neglected clients for so long, my reputation is slightly tarnished. Word moves quickly in the hacker world of who people should stay away from. I'm sure I've lost more than one client over the last few weeks. I grab my bag and keys and head out the door.

My new laptop should be here in a couple days. In the meantime, I have to work from my secret office near the bakery. I stroll down the streets, head up, intent on my destination. I round the corner a block from my destination and nearly collide with someone. "Shit, sor...Liam."

His massive frame blocks my path. Instead of his usual suit, he's wearing a pair of jeans that fit far too well and a cream Henley that outlines his broad shoulders and chest to perfection. In one hand, he's carrying a white paper bag and in the other, a paper cup with a tea bag string dangling down the side.

"Imogen." His deep growl rumbles through me settling low in my belly.

"What are you doing?"

"I was on my way to your place with a snack from the bakery you frequent." He hands me the cup and the citrus fragrance wafts up.

Unable to help myself, I inhale the scent, savoring it. "You brought me tea."

"Your favorite, I believe. As well as this."

Clasping the cup between my forearm and chest, I open the bag and glance up. "A scone?"

"With jam and cream."

Liam was bringing me breakfast? Wait. "How did you even know what I like?"

"Because I pay attention to the women I stalk," he says it like it should be obvious and reaches into the black messenger bag slung over his shoulder. *My* messenger bag. "By the way, you have god awful taste in music."

I blink at the laptop in his hand. A familiar one with death metal stickers and one that says "F*ck the Patriarchy". He slides it back in the bag. "Your phones are in here, too."

Is this the equivalent of a break up? Him giving me all my stuff back? *Isn't that what you wanted?* I've run out of hands to reach for it, though. He must notice my dilemma, because he adjusts the bag's weight over his hip. "I'll carry it for you."

"Thanks."

"Were you heading somewhere specific?"

"My office." I'm not sure why I'm telling Liam. I've kept the place hidden for two years. No one, not even Teagan, knows where it is.

He arches a brow. "I didn't realize you had an office. I thought you did freelance work from home?"

"Not much I can do without a laptop." I sip my tea and head down the footpath. "Come on."

He steps in line beside me so we're walking side-by-side. My face tingles like I'm being watched, but I keep my eyes forward until we reach the entrance to the building. I hand him the paper bag without a word and unlock the door. We climb the stairs to the top floor and walk down the hallway until coming to a stop outside my office. I disarm the security system and step inside. Liam follows and whistles.

His head swivels as he takes in the small room filled with computer components, a giant server taking up the entire length of the wall, and several monitors and towers. I set my tea on the desk and close the door, engaging the alarm again.

"This is where you work?"

"Some of the time. Depends on what I'm working on. The server is completely secure so I do most of the"—I cough—"more illegal things on it."

Liam glances over at me with amusement. "I didn't realize there were levels of illegal."

I stick my tongue out. "You know what I mean."

He chuckles and strolls around the room observing everything. He pauses, darts a look over his shoulder, and I nod before he picks up various things, studies them, and puts them back in their place. The room isn't that large, so his circuitous route is a quick one. He stops short of me.

"Impressive," he says.

"Thanks." I hesitate. "You're the only person who's ever been in here."

Liam closes the distance and cradles my jaw. "Thank you for trusting me."

I lean into his palm, unable to help myself. *You're broken up, remember*? Although were we going out in the first place? I step back with a soft sigh. "What are you—*we*—doing, Liam?"

He doesn't say anything for a minute.

"I'm trusting you." He unloops the strap from over his head, sets my bag on the chair, and props his butt on the corner of the desk. "I was thirteen when my mum married Dónal. He needed a mother for Nessa, so it wasn't a love match. I spent the next year in what I thought was hell. It wasn't close to it. By the time I turned fourteen, my mum had been dead a little over six months. Dónal beat me every single day of them."

Liam's fists clutch the edge of the desk and his gaze is focused straight ahead, although I'm not sure he's seeing anything except the past. "I was small for my age. Thin and weak. I was also a teenage boy who ate everything in sight. Dónal always complained about the amount of money he had to spend on food. Until one day, he came up with a way for me to pay him back. Told me if I didn't, then Nessa would. She was just a baby for fuck's sake."

He pauses and takes in a deep breath. That same swirly sensation I got in my belly when Mr. Tobin handed me that envelope returns. The one that signals something bad.

Really, really bad.

Tears well, but I try not to shed them in case Liam mistakes them for pity.

"For three years I 'earned my keep' with several of his business associates who paid him a lot of money. That's when I discovered what hell truly was. But everything changed when I was seventeen." His voice changes. Hardens. "I'd grown tall and strong. Far stronger than any of those cunts. Stronger than Dónal. And one night I proved it. Sent him to the hospital. It was the first time I realized what having control over someone meant. Then I ran and tracked down each one of those pieces of shite and put them all in the ground. I swore then and there that no matter what I had to do and no matter how long it took, I'd destroy Sheehan. I vowed to become the most powerful man in Dublin. I would never be weak or at the mercy of anyone again."

Finally, Liam turn his head my way. The intensity of his gaze sears me to the soul. "Then I met you."

I walk forward, slowly narrowing the distance between, not stopping until he separates his legs and I step within the V of them. He straightens and I wrap my arms around his waist and lay my head on his chest. His heart beats strong in my ear.

"You've made me question everything I've worked toward for twenty years. What it means to be strong and powerful. What it means to be loyal. To be worthy of someone's trust." Liam gently takes my head in his hands and lifts it so we're eye-to-eye. "Of their love. I don't know if what we have—what we *could* have—will last forever. But I want to find out."

The tears I'd be trying to hold back fall and I give him a watery smile. "Maybe you do always get what you want."

CHAPTER 38

IMOGEN SNUGGLES DEEPER INTO MY SIDE AND HER FINGERS dance across my chest. "You know what we have to do, right? Both of us."

I glance down at her, but her attention is on whatever invisible design she's drawing on my skin. "Is that your devious plan then? To fuck my brains out so you can then persuade me to do your bidding?"

She lifts her head. "Is it working?"

"Ask me after I lose myself in your cunt again." I bend to kiss her and she meets me halfway, but before I can deepen it, Imogen nips my bottom lip.

"Don't you dare distract me," she scolds, but soothes the non-existent pain with a flick of her tongue. "I'm being serious."

"I know. That's why I'm trying to distract you."

"We can't stay in bed and ignore them forever," Imogen wrong-fully points out.

"I'm pretty sure we can do anything we want. Remember? Which means if we want to lie here and do nothing but fuck for days on end, we can. If we want to order takeaway, we can. And if we want to avoid uncomfortable family reunions—for both of us—then we can."

She sighs. "Just because we can, doesn't mean we should. Because no matter how uncomfortable we are, the fact remains that Carrick and Nora are my parents, Cian, Aidan, and Finn are my brothers, and Nessa is your sister." Imogen places a finger over my open mouth. "She *is* your sister. I'm not saying you ever have to be friends with with my...family, but you don't have to be enemies either. Besides, I would really like to get to know Nessa. I always wanted a sister."

Fuck. When she puts it that way, how am I supposed to refuse her?

"Fine."

Imogen leans up, kisses me, and then pushes off my chest and jumps out of bed. "Good, because we have to be at Carrick's in an hour."

"What?" I roar.

"If I told you beforehand you'd find some way to avoid going. Now you can't."

"The fuck I can't."

She comes back and crawls on all fours toward me, her tits grabbing my attention. I lose some of my anger. For only a second. I snap my gaze up to hers. Imogen's eyes are pleading. "I'm sorry I didn't tell you. It was wrong of me to sneak it in out of nowhere. Please come with me."

"You're going whether I come or not, aren't you?" I resign myself to the fact.

"Yes, because no matter how much I don't think I'm ready, I need to go." She sits back on her heels and reaches for my hand. "I would feel better if you went with me. At least with you there, I'll be a little more comfortable."

I've trained myself to gauge lies and people's sincerity. Like Imogen once said, it's a neat trick to have. Yes, she might have ambushed me, but she really is nervous about going and isn't just trying to manipulate me. "I'm only doing this for you."

"I know, so thank you."

We finally get out of the bed. Is it just me, or are we both taking far longer to get ready than normal? Finally, though, we're both dressed. Imogen is beautiful with her hair down in waves. She had it colored again the other day, and the purple and teal ends are vibrant against the black of the rest of it. I step behind her and wrap my hands around her waist to stop her from nervously smoothing down the fabric any longer. My chin rests on top of her head and she leans into me, staring at me through the mirror in front of us.

"You are stunning."

Imogen glows at the compliment. "I just want to look nice. I don't feel comfortable in a dress and, well, you've seen my closet."

I turn her to face me and cradle her jaw. "If they can't accept the death-metal loving goth girl vibe you have going on, then they're not the kind of people you should have in your life. Besides, they should be the ones trying to impress you."

As I'd hoped, she laughs. "You're right. I'm being ridiculous."

"Let's do this so we can get it over with." The fact I'm stepping onto my enemy's property tells me how much I'd do for Imogen.

We head outside where the town car waits. The entire drive from my estate to the Donnellys she clutches my hand and quietly stares out the window. At last we pull up to an iron gate. The driver announces us through the intercom and a few moments later the gate groans and opens. Trees line both sides of the path forming an archway over it that stretches into the distance. I grow tenser the closer we get to the manor. This feels like a trap.

The town car comes to a rolling stop in front of the massive home. Sunlight bounces off the window panes across the entire front nearly blinding me. Clinging vines thread the empty spaces and climb upward toward the roof. A set of double doors opens and

Carrick Donnelly steps out. I scan the premises, searching for anyone lurking, but it all appears quiet.

"It's going to be fine." Imogen squeezes my hand.

I should be the one reassuring her. "Of course it will be. I'll kill them if they upset you."

She leans across and gives me a quick kiss. "I shouldn't find that incredibly sexy."

My lips curl. "But you do."

Imogen's eyes search mine. I let her find whatever it is she's looking for because she relaxes a fraction. "I'm ready."

I dip my head and exit first before giving her my hand. She grips it hard and, with grace and poise, steps out. Together we approach the house where Donnelly waits. He stares at her with a hopeful gleam in eyes so similar to hers. I *almost* feel bad for the bastard. He's just found his daughter after twenty-seven years.

"Imogen," he greets her warmly, ignoring me entirely. "Thank you for coming."

"Carrick." Her voice is soft. Hesitant. Completely unlike her. I hate it.

He glances briefly my direction and his features harden. "Campbell."

For Imogen. Be civil. Polite discourse. I almost smirk. "Donnelly."

Several awkward seconds pass as none of us say anything else. There's tangible hostility and thick tension radiating around us. Finally, Carrick breaks it. "Why don't you both come in?"

I can tell the invitation pains him, but only because he has to include me. It's more than obvious he couldn't be happier that Imogen is here. As we walk through the house, I take it all in, but also remain aware of the woman beside me. I glance down at her, and give her hand a light squeeze. She steps closer and relaxes against me. There's the scent of something baking and signs a family lives here. Like the pictures on the walls with the Donnellys as children. The wealth is understated, but clear.

Instead of going into a study or library or even Donnelly's office, he takes us out the back door and onto a large patio. Nora sits with her hands clenched on the table top, but she quickly rises and a tentative smile appears. "Imogen, I'm so glad you came."

Imogen bobs her head in greeting. "Nora."

The older woman circles the table, but there's caution in her movements. She comes forward and her gaze lands on me. She offers me the same politeness. "You must be Liam. It's lovely to meet you."

I study her. There's a desperation lurking in the depths of her eyes. I'm not sure if either of them realize it, but despite Imogen's strongest features coming from Donnelly, the resemblance between mother and daughter is present as well. "A pleasure."

Nora takes a few quick steps backward and sweeps out her hand. "Please, why don't we all have a seat. I've got a tart cooling in the kitchen that should be ready soon. In the meantime, how about we get to know each other."

Jaysus, this is painful, but I lead Imogen, who's been far too quiet, over to the table where the four of us sit. This time, Carrick is the one who fills the silence. "We didn't want to overwhelm you, so Aidan and Finn are out of the house today. But they would really like to be here next time."

That leaves...

"Sorry we're late."

Imogen and I twist around. Walking up the incline from the small guest house that sits at the bottom of it are Cian and Nessa. The two of them hold hands like they're a united front and the symbol isn't lost on me. Loathing radiates from the eldest Donnelly son and his eyes spew hatred at me, but I don't give a shit. I'm not here for him.

My gaze takes in the woman at his side. Whatever anger she'd had against me the last time she saw me is gone. The same hopeful gleam is in her eyes that had been in Carrick Donnelly's when he looked at Imogen. They stop close to the table where we sit.

"Hi, Liam," Nessa greets me.

"Nessa."

She turns to Imogen. "It's nice to see you again as well."

"Same here." Finally, there's strength in her voice.

Cian and Nessa share a glance and something unspoken passes between them before she turns to me. "I was hoping you and I could take a little walk around the property. To talk."

I don't want to leave Imogen with these people, but she lays her hand on my arm.

"Go. I'll be all right."

Not giving a shit what they think, I palm the back of her neck and bring her to me for a kiss. I end it and press my forehead to hers. "You're too good for them as well."

"Polite discourse, don't forget," she murmurs with amusement.

Standing, I nod at Nessa to lead the way. Tension marks every line in Cian's body, but he doesn't follow, so it's only her and me. We walk down the sloped incline until it levels out, but still well within sight of the four people sitting at the table. I doubt her lover wants her anywhere he can't see her.

"You seem happy," Nessa breaks the silence. I'm thankful for it, because for once, I'm at a complete loss for words.

Am I happy? Declan once claimed I didn't know what it meant. My eyes are drawn to Imogen and a sort of peace settles inside me. Is that happiness? If so, then I suppose I am. "She's the best thing to happen to me."

"I'm glad. You deserve good things in your life."

I glance at her in shock. "You didn't think that a few weeks ago."

Nessa winces. "I'm sorry for striking you. I never should have done that."

There's no need for her to apologize, because I deserved it, but it's obviously important to her. "Apology accepted."

The tension leaves her. "Thank you. And thank you for returning my book. I got your note."

I clear my throat. I don't do apologies, but I owe her that at least. "I'm sorry I couldn't take you with me. I wanted to."

She shakes her head. "Dónal never would have let you live if you had."

Does she not know what I did to him? No, probably not. There's no way he would have told her. "It wasn't because I was scared of your Da that I didn't. I had no money and no place to live. The streets were no place for a little girl to grow up. I barely survived. There's no way I could have protected you. Although, from what I understand you weren't much safer with Dónal. I am sorry for that."

Nessa loops her hand around my arm like Imogen does, but she doesn't lean any closer. That simple touch though eases some of the tightness inside me.

"I understand. Besides, look at us now. We have partners who love us, and Dónal got what was coming to him. I think things worked out."

I'll take that as confirmation that the eldest Donnelly took care of business. "Yes, I suppose they did."

We continue our stroll around the lawn, but the longer we're away from Imogen, the more agitated I get. Nessa must sense it, because she leads us in that direction.

"I know things aren't going to be easy, but I really hope that you and I can get to know each other," she says. "I've always wanted an older brother. A sister would be nice, too."

Christ. These women have far too great a hold over us—on me— because I glance down at her. "I'd like that as well."

Her entire face lights up and we crest the hill where everyone waits for us.

CHAPTER 39

The uncomfortable silence stretches as Liam and Nessa walk away. Cian joins us at the table.

"It's good to see you again, Imogen." He inclines his head and takes a seat next to Carrick.

"You look like you've healed up well. I'm glad." And I am.

The table is round and the way we're all sitting feels as though the three of them are on my opposing side. Like it's them against me. I don't particularly care for it.

"Christ, this is awkward." Cian sums it up perfectly when the silence grows to an even more uncomfortable length I hadn't thought possible.

For some reason, having someone else put into words what's in my head snaps me out of this timid, uncertain fog I'm in. That is not who I am. I'm a death-metal-loving, patriarch-hating goth chick, and if they don't like it, then it's on them.

"Extremely," I agree. "So let's just start talking so we can move forward."

Nora, Carrick, and Cian all shift in their seats, but none take the lead. Guess it's on me.

"I'm Imogen Shannon Walsh. I graduated from University College of Dublin with a major in computer science. My favorite tea is Fortnum's Ginger and Sicilian Lemon. I'm an independent consultant by trade as well as a computer hacker who, by some random act of weird coincidence, counts your nephew Padraig as one of my clients." I take a quick breath before finishing. "Also, you all have shite security on your computers."

A beat of silence continues and then Carrick laughs and laughs. Nora and Cian share glances and their lips twitch. Mine soon follow until we're all chuckling, and the tension at the table eases.

"So you're the infamous Maddox?" Carrick muses. "Paddy speaks highly of you. You must be good at what you do considering how long he's been using your services."

"I'm one of the best." It's said with a certain amount of pride. "I think my first job for Padraig was about nine years ago."

"I think only Aunt Moira calls him Padraig when he's annoyed her." Cian smirks. "He's our—your—cousin. I'm sure you can call him Paddy now."

A nervous tread of tension works its way back in at the mention of my new-found blood relation. I clear my throat. "I'm sure that will come as quite a shock to him."

Everyone smiles and relaxes again. Nora reaches out, but stops before she actually touches my hand. I glance up at her soft features.

"My middle name is Shannon," she says, her eyes misty. "I didn't know Maire gave it to you as well."

I nod. "It's pretty. I like it."

She nods shallowly and her lips quiver, but she manages to smile.

"What's this about our shite security?" Carrick asks.

Nora and I turn from each other and I focus on my...Da. "I

might have hacked into your computers after Mum told me who you were. I wanted to see you for myself."

"And you've been watching us ever since?" he asks in a bland tone.

"Yes." I'm not going to hide anything.

"I hope you didn't see anything that would scar any of us for life," Cian adds.

I bark out a laugh and shake my head. "Definitely not. I always cut the feed if there was any hint of...goings on."

"Good to know. I hope that also means you'll add the proper security we need so no one else can observe us without our knowledge."

"I'd be happy to." I glance at Carrick who's still sitting there, his face void of any emotion. Shit. "I never told anyone anything I saw or did anything else other than peek every once in a while. I swear."

Finally his lack of expression eases. "I'm sorry, Imogen. I didn't mean to scare you. I'm just more concerned by the fact that there's a weakness in our security. Any hacker could have been spying on us and we would have never known."

"Like I said, I can put up some safeguards if you'd like," I offer again.

"We can work out the arrangements later."

Cian's eyes narrow and his gaze snaps over my shoulder. I glance behind me. Liam and Nessa are back. She lets loose of his arm and makes her way to Cian who snags her around the waist and pulls her into his lap. Liam drags a chair closer, until it nearly touches mine, and takes a seat. He reaches out and threads our fingers together. I'll admit to loving the bit of public affection.

I glance over at Nora. She sits quietly with her shoulders curled just the tiniest bit forward. She appears so defeated. I haven't been too kind to her. While I'm still angry, at some point I need to forgive her, which means I should be making an effort. That's why we're here. Leaning over, I whisper into Liam's ear. He stares at me for a second before sighing. "I'll behave."

After a quick kiss on his cheek, I turn back to her. "Nora, can I help you in the kitchen?"

She startles slightly, but quickly recovers. "Yes, that would be lovely, dear, thank you."

We both get up, and I spear Carrick and Cian with a sharp glare telling them without words they better play nice. I follow Nora into the house. The delicious fruit smell fills the air and my stomach grumbles. We step into the kitchen, and my eyes are drawn to the dessert on the counter. It looks as good as it smells.

"If you'd like to get the plates from that cabinet"—she points at one near the end of the counter—"I'll cut into this."

While she gets a knife from the drawer, I pull the plates out and set them next to where she works. "If this is anything like all the rest of the food I ate while I was here, it'll be to die for."

Nora smiles over her shoulder at me. "I'm glad you enjoyed everything."

"Where did you learn how to cook? I can't boil water."

"My Mum," she says in a loving tone. "She worked for a wealthy family preparing their meals. There were a few times she took me with her and I'd watch. Sometimes I'd get to help."

"It sounds like you two were close." I lean against the counter.

"We were. Like you and your Mum."

My heart aches at the mention of my mother. "Liam is actually a really good cook. He's tried teaching me a few recipes, but I'm a terrible student." I pause for a breath. "Maybe you could show me. Something simple, I mean."

Tears fill Nora's eyes. "I'd like that."

She finishes cutting and plating the tart and rinses off the knife. I pick up a couple plates, but her hand on my arm stops me. I glance over.

"Maire will always be your mother," she says softly. "I don't ever want you to think I'd try and replace her. You have every right to hate me and never forgive me. That is something I will have to live with the rest of my life. I hope you do though, and that, maybe, one day, you and I can be, if nothing else, friends."

I swallow down the lump in my throat. "Friends would be nice."

Nora smiles and nods. We each pick up three plates and take them out to the patio. Thankfully, no blood has been spilled, although Nessa appears to be monopolizing the conversation while the men all glare at each other. Once everyone has a piece of dessert, I sit down next to Liam again and glance around at everyone at the table. Things won't be easy, but then again, often the best things aren't.

THE SECOND WE WALK THROUGH THE DOOR OF LIAM'S house, he jerks his tie off with a groan. "I'm never doing that again."

I bite my lip to hold back my giggle at his aggrieved tone. "Thank you for doing it today."

He glances back at me and narrows his eyes. I try to appear innocent, but I'm not sure I succeed. We walk into his bedroom, where he changes into a plain tee and pair of jeans. This man is nearly a god in a suit, but put him in casual clothes and he's reached perfection status. It grounds him. I close the distance between us and lay my hands on his chest.

"Do you have any idea how hot you are when you're not in that power suit of yours?"

Liam palms my ass. "You don't like my suits?"

"Oh, I most definitely like them, but I like it more when you let yourself relax. You hold yourself differently when you're in jeans and a regular shirt. Like you don't have be the scary, intimidating businessman the world sees, but instead get to be the Liam I see when he lets his guard down."

"And you think that's hot?" he lifts a brow like he doesn't believe me.

"Extremely hot." I rise up and brush a kiss over his lips. "I know I've already said, but thank you for coming with me today. I know it couldn't have been easy for you being at Carrick's house."

"I shouldn't admit this, but I find it difficult to say no to you."

I'm sure the admission cost him a lot. "I promise I won't abuse the privilege."

Liam tugs me closer until nothing separates us. "I know you won't. It's the only reason I told you."

"Thank you also for not killing anyone while I was inside with Nora."

He bends and nibbles at my jaw, kissing his way along its length to that one spot that drives me wild. I bend my neck to give him better access.

"That's a lot of thank yous." He nips my earlobe. "Maybe you should show me *how* thankful you really are instead of just telling me."

I shiver, arousal coursing through me. "I should, huh?"

"Most definitely."

Liam walks me backward until my knees hit the bed. He lowers me to it and covers my mouth with his. The kiss grows heated and quickly our clothes come off. After some maneuvering, he has a condom on and then he's surging forward, entering me in one powerful thrust. He fills me perfectly. As always, he makes sure I've come at least twice before he finally roars out his release. I cry out his name and clutch him tightly to me while our harsh breaths fill the air. Slowly, they return to normal and he rolls to the side bringing me with him.

I lay my head on his chest, content in a way I've never been before. After twenty-seven years, I have more than just my Mum. I have a Da. Brothers. I have Nora, and while she'll never replace my mother, it doesn't mean we can't be close. I've also gained a sister. I lift my chin and meet Liam's gaze. Most importantly, I have him.

Thank you for reading **LIAM**. I hope you enjoyed it. I'd greatly appreciate a review on the platform of your choice. Reviews are so important!

Are you ready for more Dublin Kings?

Be sure to get your copy of AIDAN!

Other Books
Love Notes: A Dark Romance
SEALs in Love
Say Yes
Black Light: Possession
The Bratva's Enforcer (co-written with Rachel Everly)

AIDAN

DUBLIN KINGS, BOOK 3

CHAPTER 1

AIDAN

THE WORLD IS FULL OF LIARS.

Some of them tell the harmless white lie. The black lie for personal gain. Or the red lie because they want to hurt the other person or get even for some transgression against them. Me? I've told them all.

"Don't you dare touch that." Sorcha doesn't pause filling up the pint glass with the nearly-black ruby red stout as she threatens Aisling.

The young girl flashes me a wide-eyed, guilty glance as she slowly lowers the arm that had been reaching for the basket of fish and chips sitting on the counter behind her much older sister. My whiskey glass hides my grin. Inside O'Connell's pub, fishermen slowly trickle in after a long day out on the water, all of them wanting a cold drink and a hot meal.

Sorcha tips the glass and expertly leaves less than an inch of foam at the top, before spinning to grab the basket and round the other side of the bar. She sets down both in front of a white-haired, white-bearded man and then moves to a nearby table to take their order.

"She was crying the other night."

I drag my gaze from the lush curves showcased by the jeans she wears and turn to the tiny black-haired girl who moved to stand next to me. "I'm sure things have been hard for all of you."

What else do I say to a six-year old whose Da's been dead less than a month?

"She lied though and said she wasn't." Aisling pouts.

I guess even Sorcha can count herself amongst the liars of the world. "She probably just didn't want to upset you."

"Lies are bad. Da said so."

I'm barely able to stifle my snort. Her Da was one of the biggest liars of them all. "Sometimes people tell white lies so they don't hurt someone's feelings or make them sad."

Aisling shakes her head, her dark curls bouncing around her shoulders. "Da said even white lies are bad. We're always supposed to tell the truth no matter what."

"Well, then, you should probably listen to him." Look at me giving out sage advice.

Except her bottom lip trembles and her bright blue eyes, exactly like her sister's, shimmer with tears. "I can't listen to him no more, cause he died."

Christ. I shoot a desperate glance Sorcha's way. She catches it and her gaze drops to Aisling. With a quick word to the men sitting at the table, she rushes over and crouches in front of her sister, palming the little girl's cheek. "What's wrong?"

"Aidan told me to listen to what Da says, but he's dead and I miss him and I'm sad and I don't want him to be dead," she sobs.

"Oh, my sweet little nightmare." Sorcha pulls Aisling into her arms and holds her tightly. She glances up at me with a sheen in her own eyes, but continues hugging her sister until finally the girl stops crying. Sorcha draws back and swipes away the tears still clinging to Aisling's lashes. "I miss him, too. But just because he's gone doesn't mean we can't still talk to him or hear his voice."

The girl runs her sleeve across her snotty nose and takes in a shuddering breath. "I didn't mean to cry."

"You can cry any time you want."

"Then why do you keep telling us you're not crying when you are?" Aisling presses.

Sorcha winces and stands, although most people would have probably missed it. "You're right. I'm sorry. I won't do that anymore."

"Promise?"

There's a brief hesitation before she answers. "Promise."

Lie.

But I understand why she said it. "Why don't you go upstairs and make sure the twins aren't getting into trouble?" Sorcha tells Aisling. "I'll send dinner up soon and be there to tuck you in later."

"Okay. Will you read me a story then, too?"

"Yes. Pick out a good one."

The little girl throws her arms around her sister again, then just as quickly releases her, and runs toward the kitchen and the stairs that lead to their flat above the pub. She turns and waves. "Bye, Aidan."

I return the gesture, but she's already dashed around the corner. Then I face Sorcha. Her gaze lingers where Aisling disappeared before she shifts it to me. *Where did the dark circles under her eyes come from? Or the rigid way she stands like she's bracing for something?* They weren't there earlier tonight, were they?

"You'd tell me if things weren't okay, right?" I have to ask, then cock my head. "And don't lie to me either."

"Of course I'd tell you." Sorcha doesn't even blink.

A fucking lie.

"Oy, can I get a drink?" A rough voice calls out behind her.

She jumps, fists the apron she wears, and spins away from me to hurry over to the impatient man. I throw back the rest of my whiskey and set the glass on the smooth wooden bar. While Sorcha takes and fills each order that comes through, I study her. She smiles at each patron, but the longer she does, the harder it appears for her to maintain it.

Do I offer her money to help her get by for a while? *You know she'll refuse.* Probably, but I should still offer it. Then again, how can a guy who allegedly works as an underpaid security guard for a Dublin-based business afford to loan or gift her that kind of cash? It would lead to a lot of questions I don't plan on answering.

The hours drag by as slowly the patrons leave until there's no one left but Sorcha and me. She locks the door, turns off the front lights casting darkness over the entrance, and walks back behind the bar. Her steps are slow like she can barely pick up her feet.

"I wish you would have let me help you." I also should keep my mouth shut, but I hate seeing her like this.

She wipes down the bar and shakes her head. "You're a guest, not an employee. Besides, it's easier if I do it. I have a system."

Some system. Sorcha has one cook, who could barely keep up with the orders, which left her to serve as both waitress and barkeep. With her Da gone, why hasn't she hired extra help? "Can't you teach your system to someone so you're not left doing it all yourself?"

"I don't have time to teach anyone." Sorcha sighs and puts a bunch of dirty glasses in the sink. "Can we please not argue about this? You're only here for a couple days, and I've barely gotten to talk to you at all. I feel bad that you came to visit and I have to work the whole time."

Getting up from my seat, I circle around to stand next to her. "Don't feel bad. I'm the one who showed up without calling first." With everything that has gone down with Liam Campbell and the whole family, I needed to get away for a bit. "Now, move over. I'll wash."

Sorcha opens her mouth, no doubt to argue, but I shush her.

"Don't make me pick you up and carry you over to the stool. Sit down. I'm perfectly capable of washing a few glasses."

I hold out my hand for the towel draped over her shoulder. With an annoyed growl, she slides it off, smacks it into my palm, then walks around to the other side and hops up into the bar stool I recently vacated. "How's your cousin? Caitlín, isn't it? Did she get engaged yet?"

"She did. Maybe a month or so ago." I dip the glass into the hot as shit sudsy water, rinse it off, and set it on the mat beside the sink. "It's a short engagement, too, from what I hear. They're getting married in a couple months at Caitlín's parents' house in Brooklyn."

"Wow, that is fast." Sorcha leans her elbow on the bar and props her head on her fist. "Then again, when you know you've met the right person, why wait?"

I glance up at her. "I had no idea you were a romantic."

She lifts one shoulder. "I wouldn't say I'm romantic. More pragmatic. If you love someone and want to spend the rest of your life with them, then do it without all the long, drawn-out fuss."

"What if it doesn't work out?"

"Then it doesn't work out," she says it so matter-of-factly. "Why stress about what-ifs and hypotheticals?"

I stare at Sorcha. No, definitely not romantic. Which makes me glad. When we first became friends, I'd worried she hint at wanting something more between us, but she never has. It's been nice not having to worry about hurting her feelings when things didn't work out between us. Our friendship is the longest relationship I've ever been in.

"Man, I hope the poor bastard who falls in love with you knows you won't be too broken-hearted if you two ever break up." I snort.

A weird expression crosses her face, but then she glares. "I didn't say I wouldn't be broken-hearted. I just said I'm not going to bother worrying about something that may or may not happen."

I finish the last of the glasses and dry my hands on the towel. "What else needs to be done?" Sorcha opens her mouth, but I interrupt. "Just tell me, so we can get it done instead of arguing about who's doing it."

"It's rude to assume you know what I'm going to say before I say it."

"So you weren't going to tell me you have a system for this, too?" I arch an eyebrow.

"Smug doesn't look good on you."

I bark out a laugh and spread my arms out. "Are you kidding? Everything looks good on me."

"Let's get going. I don't want your head to get so big it explodes and I'm left cleaning up the mess." Sorcha grins and hops off the stool.

Together we wipe down all the tables and stack the chairs on top of them. I sweep and mop while she does a quick inventory and double checks that the kitchen has been put to rights. At least the one employee she has is competent. She wipes her brow and sags against the bar. I stand next to her and lean back.

"Thank you for your help." Sorcha shoulder bumps me.

"You're welcome."

Pounding footsteps filter through the ceiling and we both glance up. She tilts her head and glances over me. "I better go and make sure they're not destroying anything up there."

"Breakfast tomorrow?"

"Same place as usual. I'll see you at nine." Sorcha turns and hugs me. "I'm really glad you're here, Aidan."

I hold her for a minute, the faint scent of her coconut shampoo reaching my nose. She lets go and walks toward the door. I'm right behind her as she opens it, and I step out into the late evening air that brings with it the briny scent of fish and ocean water.

"Get some rest."

"I will." She gives me a small wave and then slowly closes and locks the door.

I stand there until the interior goes dark, and then I make my way down the street toward the small bed and breakfast where I'm staying. The tiny fishing village of Burtonport on the northwest coast is a far cry from Dublin. The people here keep to themselves. It's the one place where I can disappear for a while when I need to get away from everyone. And *everything*.

No one here knows who I am. Or the family I belong to.

Not even Sorcha.

CHAPTER 2

Aidan couldn't have come at a worse time. No matter how much I might want him here. I climb the stairs up to my family's flat, alternating between wanting to cry and wanting to curse my Da the entire way. Except I can't cry, because every time I do I'm not sure I'll ever be able to stop.

I reach the landing and the sound of the TV and arguing filters through the wood barrier. Taking a deep breath, I open the door. Kellen is sitting on the floor leaning against the sofa, while Carson sits on it and stomps his feet a couple times. They're playing a video game and trash talking each other or whoever's on the other end of their headsets. I step around to stand in their line of sight and both of them jerk their heads in my direction.

"Did you finish your homework?" I interrupt their game. I love my brothers, but I hate being their parent.

"Yes." They nod and reply in sync then turn their attention back to the TV.

It's a bald-face lie, but I'm too tired to call them out on it. Instead, I head to Aisling's room. Her twinkle lights are lit and projecting shining stars onto the ceiling giving her room the appearance of an enchanted forest with the murals I drew on both it and the walls. I quietly walk over to the bed. She's lying on her back, sleeping, and hugging the book she picked out for me to read to her.

I'd planned on being upstairs a little earlier, but tonight had been busy and even with Aidan's help, it had taken longer to clean up than it usually did. Gently, I take the book from Aisling's arms and bring the blanket up to her chin. She stirs and blows out a heavy sigh, but her eyes remain closed. I ghost a kiss over her forehead and go back out to the living area.

The twins have turned off their game in anticipation of me telling them it's time to go to bed. They know they have school in the morning.

"Aisling said Aidan's here," Kellen says.

I nod. "He came in about an hour before the dinner crowd started trickling through the door. I'm sure he would have liked it if you'd come down to say hello."

"We'll see him tomorrow," Carson adds. "We figured you'd want to spend some alone time with him tonight. Or at least as alone as you can with a pub full of people."

My cheeks heat, which is ridiculous. The boys don't have any idea about the stupid feelings I have for my best friend. We've been friends for five years, which isn't long in the grand scheme of things. Especially since we only see each other when he comes to visit every four to six months or whenever he can get time off from work. But he's been my closest and dearest friend during that time. Over the years, for various reasons, I've drifted apart from everyone else. Which is why I refuse to ruin our friendship by doing something as monumentally dumb as telling Aidan how I feel.

"You didn't have to do that on my account, but thank you. Now, it's time to go to bed, please." I shoo them off. "And I'll be checking your homework tomorrow."

They wince and scuttle off to their room. Once they're gone I grab a beer from the fridge and bring it back to the living room where I collapse on the sofa. I toe off my shoes, stretch my legs out in front of me, and almost sigh with relief. My feet ache and throb. What I wouldn't give for a nice foot massage. After I've washed the stink off first, though. My back hurts along with them.

I take a sip of my beer and drop my head to the cushion behind me. Tears threaten, but I squeeze my eyes shut as hard as I can to push them back. Twenty-eight years old and I'm not only a parent to a pair of twelve-year olds and a six-year old, but the owner of a pub I'm probably going to lose. This place had been everything to my Da. Except he's dead.

I didn't just acquire kids and the pub. I also acquired debt I'll never be able to repay. What was Da thinking? How am I supposed to keep this place running when I can't afford to pay anyone to help me? How am I going to buy supplies with the ever rising costs? What am I going to do?

~

"SHOULD WE WAKE HER?" A STAGE WHISPER FILTERS through my awareness.

I drag my eyes open, blinking slowly with the effort, and a figure appears. Three figures to be exact. My brain finally catches up with my vision. Kellen, Carson, and Aisling stand over me. Sunlight filters through the windows, and I squint against its brightness. I shade my face. "What time is it?"

"Half seven," Carson answers.

"Shit." I jump up. The kids need to get to school, and I need to get ready to meet Aidan. "Boys, go get your bags packed."

I rush into the kitchen to make them breakfast, but they stop me.

"We already did," Kellen says. "We ate breakfast, too."

They did? Sure enough, dirty bowls are in the sink and the box of cereal is still sitting on the counter. Along with the milk. With a sigh, I put both of them back where they belong.

"You spilled your drink, but we cleaned it." That's Carson.

I turn back. What drink? Fuzzy memories of last night come back of me checking on Aisling, the boys going to bed, and then me sitting on the couch. With a beer. Shit, I can't believe I fell asleep. Actually, yes, I can. The late nights of staring at the accounting books and trying to come up with a solution clearly caught up with me.

"Thank you for doing that."

Aisling comes to stand in front of me with her lips down-turned. "You didn't read to me like you promised."

I kneel down to her level. Her hair has been brushed, and from the bright pink skirt with white polka-dots and white shirt with purple horizontal stripes, it's obvious she picked her own outfit.

"I'm sorry. You were sleeping so sweetly, I didn't want to wake you up."

"But you promised," she says, her voice plaintive.

A burst of anger at the unfairness of everything bubbles up inside me, but I bite it back. It's not Aisling's fault. She's just a little girl who lost her Da. *You lost him, too.* I hush the ugly voice.

"I'm sorry." I brush back a curl dipping down onto her forehead. "Next time I'll read you two stories."

Seemingly satisfied, she nods, but I'm not sure she believes me.

I stand. "Alright, let's get you off to school."

Once I've made sure everyone's bags are actually packed, we head down the stairs, through the darkened pub, and out onto the street. The sound of gulls fills the air, along with the familiar and comfortable scent of the ocean. Aisling holds my hand while the twins bicker with each other several yards ahead.

Out on the water, fishing boats move away from the shore and toward the silhouette of several islands in the distance. There's a pang of longing in my chest to be somewhere else. This is my home, and I love it. But I never expected to spend my whole life here.

"Are you going to come get me after school?"

I glance down at Aisling. "I have to be at the pub. The boys will walk home with you." I make a mental note to remind them.

"Okay."

I hate the defeat in her tone, but there's nothing I can do. Someone has to take care of the business and the only one around to do it is me. Thankfully the school is only a short walk from the pub and after our goodbyes and the three of them disappear inside, I rush back to the flat. I take a quick shower, throw on my clothes, and pull my hair up into a ponytail. A smidge of vanity has me dabbing on some pink lip gloss and a bit of mascara. There's not much I can do for the dark circles.

By the time I make it out the door, I have fifteen minutes to reach my destination. Which, in a village as small as Burtonport, is plenty of time. I wave at the few villagers I pass on my way to the small cafe. Aidan's waiting outside at one of the picnic tables. It's the perfect weather to be sitting out here, actually. The sky is clear, although it's a bit gray in the distance, but for the time being, it's lovely.

When he spots me, he smiles and stands. I can't help but appreciate the way his shirt pulls across his chest and upper arms. Or how his waist narrows and how snug his jeans fit. I suppose to some, Aidan might be intimidating with all the tattoos that decorate his upper body, covering the entirety of both arms and the back of each hand and all ten fingers. Especially the one that crawls up the front of his neck and wraps around both sides. But to me, they're just a part of him.

"Good morning." He pulls me in for a giant hug. It's how he always greets me.

I squeeze him back, breathing in the woodsy scent that clings to him, and absorb the warmth of his body. "Morning."

Aidan draws back and his eyes track down me. I can't hold back a small shiver. *Please, don't let him notice.* "You look nice."

I relax. "Thanks, so do you."

We take a seat and a minute later, Fiona comes out. "Morning, Sorcha. Aidan. The usual?"

"Yes, please."

Aidan nods. Every once in a while, I'm tempted to surprise her by ordering something different, but not today. I need today to be like any other visit from him. Where my Da isn't gone, I don't have to parent three children, and I don't have to worry about losing everything.

CHAPTER 3

AIDAN

SORCHA'S BEEN TRYING TO HIDE IT SINCE I GOT HERE, BUT something is going on that she won't tell me. Nothing short of force will make her, either. She's that stubborn. And I don't want to spend our last day together fighting. Although, *together* is being generous. Since I got here the day before yesterday, we've had a grand total of eight hours where it's been just the two of us. I'm not complaining— I did show up unannounced. I just don't like the fact that she's working so hard without anyone to help. Tonight, she's going to have to deal with a disruption to her "system".

The pub is mostly empty, with only a couple elderly gentlemen occupying one of the tables, but a few of the fishing boats have already docked. The married men go home, but a large segment of the single ones come into O'Connell's. In a village this small, their options are limited if they don't want to cook for themselves. But what crowd *is* drawn here, is more than enough to keep Sorcha running around.

Aisling sits at the bar, her dangling legs kicking back and forth, with some paper and markers while she picks at the food in the take-away container next to her. She doesn't have the artistic talent of her older sister, but maybe she'll grow into hers as she gets older and has more practice and instruction.

"Are you going to help Sorcha?"

I turn my attention to the twins seated across from me. Carson, the younger by five minutes, has a mouth full of the shepherd's pie I brought from The Wagon Wheel Cafe. It might be tacky to bring another restaurant's food into the pub, but I didn't want to put any extra strain on the cook by ordering for the five of us. Kellen stares at me expectantly, but also with a trace of pleading.

"Is she in trouble?" Perhaps I'll get some answers from them.

The twins share a glance and Kellen turns back to me. "I heard her on the phone the other day talking to someone. She didn't know I was listening. It was something about borrowing money and the pub."

Borrowing money? And what does the pub have to do with anything?

"Do you remember anything else?"

Kellen shakes his head. "Nothing other than she was crying afterward."

Fuck. "Thanks for letting me know. I'll do what I can to help."

The boys and I finish eating before Sorcha sends them upstairs to do their homework.

"No video games until it's done or you'll lose your privileges," she warns. "Don't think I'll forget to check, either."

The two trudge into the kitchen with a wave over their shoulder. I clean up our mess and take a seat at the bar next to Aisling. More men enter. Not willing to go another night sitting here while she does all the work, I vacate the stool and come around the opposite side of the bar. She glances over at me from where she's filling a pint glass from the tap.

"What are you doing?"

"I'm helping. And don't feed me that bullshit line about a system." I glare at her. "I'm perfectly capable of delivering plates of food or filling a pint of beer."

"You're not supposed to curse," Aisling pipes up before Sorcha can argue with me.

I pull a euro coin out of my pocket and toss it on the bar top. "Penance."

She snatches it up and deposits it in her bag hanging from the back of her stool. "You can curse again, if you want."

Her sister groans and then shifts her glare back to me again. I stare back, daring her to contradict me. Finally, Sorcha throws up her hands with a sigh. "Fine."

The rest of the night goes far smoother than either of us expected after a rough start. More than once we ran into each other and I spilled beer on the floor, but somehow we developed a rhythm that worked for both of us. Finally, the last customer leaves and she locks up. Together, we clean up and I'm back behind the bar washing glasses while Sorcha sits in a stool on the other side.

"Thank you for your help tonight. I'm sorry if I was cranky earlier."

"You don't have to be sorry. But, if you want to make it up to me, then how about telling me what's going on." I'm not above manipulation to get what I want.

"There's noth—"

"How long have we been friends?" I interrupt her.

"What does that have to do with anything?"

"How long?" I press.

Sorcha sighs. "Five years."

"And in those five years, have I ever asked you to do something for me?" I finish the last glass and dry my hands off.

Her entire body sags and she rests her forearms on the bar top. "No."

I mimic her pose and wait until she meets my eyes. "I'm asking now."

The silence lengthens between us until finally Sorcha nods. "The pub isn't doing well. Da was behind on payments when he died. By a lot. Except he told me he was able to get a loan. Yet, there's no record of it. I've been getting phone calls from vendors that haven't been paid in several months. If I can't pay them, they're going to freeze our account and I won't be able to order inventory."

She takes in a deep breath and blows it out. "I called the bank to try and get a loan, but they denied me. If I can't pay the bills, I'm going to lose not only the pub, but our home."

"Christ." I run a hand down my face. *Didn't you suspect something like this?* I did, but having it confirmed makes it real. "What can I do to help?"

I would never let Sorcha lose the pub or her home, even if I have to send her a large, anonymous financial gift. She reaches across the width of the bar and clasps my hand. "Thank you for offering, but there really isn't anything you can do. I'll figure things out."

"You don't have to do this all alone."

She huffs. "I'm not taking your money, Aidan."

I bristle in offense. "Why not?"

"What happens when that runs out? Because it will. Then I'll be right back where I am now." Sorcha throws up her hands. "I'll just have to figure something else out. Reduce the menu, maybe. Limit what's on it so I don't need to order supplies for something we're not going to make. I can also not supply a larger range of liquors or beers. I'll work more hours."

"Jesus, you're already working twelve hour days."

"Then I'll work fifteen," she snaps back, finally losing her defeated expression, and sits upright. "I'm done talking about this. I'm not taking your money. End of discussion."

There's no point arguing anymore. Not with the mulish tilt to her chin. All it will do is drive a wedge between us. I'll let it go for the moment, but this isn't over. I'll figure out something. Maybe pay a visit to the bank and *persuade* them to reconsider giving Sorcha the loan.

"You're a pain in my ass. You know that, right?"

"Yeah, well, you're a pain in mine, so we're even." She glares at me then taps her phone screen. "I better get upstairs and make sure the boys did their homework. Plus, I promised Aisling I'd read to her. You'll say bye before you leave in the morning?"

"Of course." I round the bar as Sorcha jumps down off the stool. I wrap my arms around her and she hugs me back. "Don't be stubborn. If you can't figure things out, call me. Swear?"

She nods against my chest. "I swear."

Tastes like a lie. Would she take my money if she knew who I really was and that I can afford to buy out the loan on the pub? Knowing her, probably not. When I get back to Dublin, I'll make some phone calls. Sorcha draws back, rises up on her toes, and kisses my cheek. "Thank you for being my friend."

I kiss her forehead and hug her a little bit tighter. "Don't forget you swore."

She nods.

"I'll stop by in the morning and say my goodbyes to everyone."

We walk to the door and she opens it for me. I make my way down the footpath and glance over my shoulder. Sorcha still stands in the doorway, her face in the shadows. She waves and I return the gesture. Then she steps inside, and, a minute later, the whole pub goes dark. Faint light shines from the windows of the second floor. I blow out a breath and head for the bed and breakfast, already regretting having to leave tomorrow. But I can only be gone so long before Da or Cian starts asking questions. Plus, there is some unresolved family drama that needs to be faced.

CHAPTER 4

"KELLEN. CARSON. CAN ONE OF YOU GO LET AIDAN IN, please? He's at the door. And make sure you lock it behind you," I call out from the bathroom where I'm trying to finish getting ready.

Footsteps pound, vibrating the floor, and then there's more pounding as one of the boys runs down the stairs. I turn out the light and head into the living area. Aisling is finally finishing her breakfast. I kiss the crown of her head. "Go get your shoes on and grab your school bag."

She jumps up from the table and runs to her room, nearly crashing into Carson, who strolls in from the hallway with his bag slung over his shoulder. Two sets of footsteps plod up the stairs and seconds later Kellen appears in the open doorway. Right behind him is Aidan, who shouldn't look this good at just past seven in the morning. Another form-fitting shirt accentuates his broad chest, and the color of it only makes his blue eyes that much brighter. The sun shining in through the window hits his auburn hair, making it glow like fire. My belly flutters as though there's a swarm of bees inside it. Stupid bees need to settle the fuck down.

"Morning." Did that sound normal? I hope it sounded normal.

Aidan cocks his head slightly and his forehead crinkles, but then his face clears. "Good morning."

I glance at Kellen. "Get your things for school, please, and make sure Aisling has hers. We need to be going."

He dashes down the hallway.

"Let me clean this up quick." I wash Aisling's bowl and wipe down the table. By the time I'm finished, Kellen and she appear. "Everyone ready?"

Heads bob, and the five of us trek downstairs and out the front door. With Aidan leaving today, it shouldn't be this pretty out. Aisling grabs Aidan's hand and then mine, so she's walking between us.

"I'm sad you have to leave," she tells him, glancing up.

You and me, both.

Aidan winks. "I'll be back again, before you know it."

"Are you going to come for my birthday?"

"Hmmm, I don't know. When is it again?"

Aisling giggles, because he knows perfectly well when it is. Every year since she turned three, he's sent her a present. Same with the twins since they turned eight.

"It's September seventh," she draws out all three words with a sassy head shake punctuating each one.

"That's right. How could I forget?" Aidan swings her arm gently. "I'm not sure, but I'll see what I can do."

She'll see him before her birthday, since mine is before hers. Except, we may be out of a home by then. While Aisling chatters to him, I try to quell the panic that is creeping in. Didn't I just tell Aidan the other night there's no sense in worrying about things that may or may not happen? I need to take my own words to heart.

Finally, we reach the school. He squats down to give Aisling a hug and he shakes both Kellen and Carson's hands since they've decided they're too old for hugs. The three of them say goodbye and hurry into the building. Then it's my turn. I hold on to Aidan a few seconds longer than I normally would. Or maybe he's the one not letting go.

"Don't forget you swore," he whispers in my ear.

I manage to nod. Far too soon, I step back. Tears burn my eyes and my nose is getting stuffy. "You better get going if you want to beat all the traffic."

He huffs out an amused breath. There is no traffic until he gets closer to Dublin. "I'll text you later tonight."

I raise my hand in farewell as Aidan turns toward the bed and breakfast and his car.

The walk back to the pub is depressing, because I'm alone. I'm on the verge of bursting into tears, but that will only make things worse. I'm glad he left, even if I'm going to miss him terribly, because I don't want him to see me like this. It will only make him that more determined to try and help.

I'd been so tempted to accept his offer last night, but turning it down was the only thing I could do. Like I'd said, what happens when whatever he loans me dries up? I'll be in the same sinking boat. The small amount he'd be able give me would only be a bandaid over a gaping wound. A drop in the bucket. I love him for it, but it also wouldn't make enough of a difference. He might as well save his money.

Which still leaves me with trying to figure out what the hell I'm going to do. *Don't think about it right now.*

The heavy weight of unwanted familial burdens nearly crushes me as I force myself out of our second floor flat and down the stairs. Another day filled with the guilt of bitter resentment awaits me when I reach the bottom. Even if I wanted to get away from the one place I never pictured myself stuck in, I can't. Da saw to that.

I step into our family's pub and the familiar yeast smell surrounds me. It's a scent I've been around since I was Aisling's age, maybe a couple years younger. I sat at this same bar, on the same stool, with my feet dangling while Da stood behind the counter pouring beer and shooting the shit. The villagers loved him. Visitors, too. Da never met a stranger.

Not once have I ever aspired to follow in his footsteps and run this place. I had other hopes and dreams, but I'd been forced to put them aside when Mum died five years ago. With Da's death a month ago, there isn't anything holding me here. I should sell it. Or try to. Except it's impossible. The pub isn't just our livelihood, it's also our home.

It had meant everything to Da. He'd go on and on about how it was his children's legacy. Kellen's, Carson's, Aisling's, and mine.

I don't want it. I never have. But with his death, I'm trapped. With a sigh of resignation, I drag all the chairs down off the tables. Once that's done, I prep the lemons and limes, make sure we have enough napkins, and double check the kitchen inventory one more time, even though our cook Glen always takes care of it. Everything is as ready as it's going to be for the dinner crowd to roll in so I run upstairs and grab some lunch.

By the time I'm finished, there's a little over an hour until I have to open. I go back downstairs and do one more walk-through, because I have anxiety like that. The kids should be here any minute, so I'm not startled by the pounding on the door. I open it with a welcome home smile that sharply drops at the sight of two men—strangers—standing there. The hairs on the back of my neck rise.

"I'm sorry, but we aren't open for another hour."

"I know. We won't be long." The larger of the two grabs my arm, yanks me inside, and pushes me up against the wall, crowding me with his body. The second man closes and locks the door behind him.

My heart pounds and wild panic screams inside my head. The bitter taste of fear spreads across my tongue. Oh, god, the kids will be home any second.

"What do you want?" My voice trembles. The sooner they tell me, the sooner they'll leave. I hope.

"We're just here for a friendly visit and to offer our condolences on the death of your poor Da." Creepy dude's breath is rancid and when he runs a fingertip down the side of my face, I jerk my head to the side. His laugh sends a chill running down my spine. "We're also here to collect this month's payment."

Payment? What payment? "I don't know what you're talking about."

He tsks. "Did Keir forget to tell you? Now that's a real shame." His smile is twisted and ugly. "Maybe we'll have to take what's due from somewhere else."

He thrusts his pelvis forward, and bile rises to my throat at the hardness pressing against me. The other man chuckles.

"Stop," I whimper and try to disappear into the wall behind me.

The devil's hand whips up with lightning speed and grabs a fistful of my hair, yanking my head to the side. I cry out in pain. He leans in close and sniffs the entire length of my neck, dragging his tongue with it. I flinch away, but he's holding me so tight I don't move far.

"Dónal Sheehan was lenient with your Da's payment plan. However, there's been a regime change, and the loan has been transferred to its new owner. He doesn't grant favors to his enemy's old friends. Which means, it's time to pay up."

"I don't know who Dónal Sheehan is or what loan you're talking about," I grind out between clenched teeth. "But I'll have your money tomorrow. Please, just leave."

I'll promise anything to get them to go away before the children get home. Another knock hits the door. This one softer. Both men's gaze shoot toward the sound.

"Sorcha, we're home," Kellen's loud voice filters through the wood.

I whimper. "Please, don't hurt them. I'll have the money tomorrow. I swear."

Tense seconds pass. Another knock and a louder call. "Sorcha. Let us in."

At last, evil eyes releases me and steps back. He glares and puts a finger right in my face. "We'll be back tomorrow. If you're lying, I won't be so nice. To you or the little mongrels."

I suck in a breath and nod frantically, trying not to cry. "I'll have it."

"Sorcha!" Kellen yells this time.

Quickly, I push past the man and open the door with a shaky smile. "Sorry, I didn't hear you. We were in the kitchen." How I managed to speak normally I'll never know.

"Who's we? Is Aidan still here?" The two boys sweep past. Kellen comes to an abrupt halt and Carson crashes into his back.

"Hey, why'd you stop?" Aisling whines.

The twins' eyes widen and dart between the two men and me. I give them a weak smile and wave them in so they're out of the doorway, then quickly swap places.

"I was just giving these gentlemen a tour. They're friend's of Da's visiting from Dublin and opening their own pub. They wanted to see how he ran ours." It's scary how easily the lie slips past my lips. "They were actually on their way out."

The two dangerous men flash evil smiles and stride forward. The shorter man walks past first, but the big bad pauses and stares down at me with a terrifying smirk. "I'm looking forward to doing business with you again tomorrow."

My mouth tightens, and the second he's across the threshold, I slam the door shut and sag against it, my chest heaving.

"Sorcha?" There's a tremor in Aisling's voice

Eyes I didn't realize I'd closed pop open. Kellen, Carson, and Aisling stare at me with equal amounts of fear on their faces. I come away from the door trying my best to forget about the men and what just happened and stride toward them. "How was school today?"

"Fi—fine," Kellen answers.

"Good. Are you guys hungry? I have some stew upstairs if you want to heat it up for dinner." I guide them to the stairs and they all march up with me right on their heels.

The four of us go inside without speaking, but I can tell there are questions on the twins' lips. Thankfully, neither ask any of them. As with every other day, while I heat up their dinner, they tell me about their day, although the conversation is much more subdued than usual. Like the three of them can all tell something is going on and that it's bad. It was the same way the first couple of weeks after Da died.

"I need to get back downstairs, but make sure you clean up the dishes when you're done. Come down and say good night before you go to bed, and don't forget to make sure your homework is done before video games," I warn the boys.

"Sorcha?" Carson, the more sensitive of the two of them, speaks up.

"We'll talk later, okay?" I press a kiss to both of their foreheads—something they allow for the first time in months—and then Aisling's, who's been unusually quiet. "You can stay up a little later tonight since you don't have school tomorrow."

They nod. With a final glance over my shoulder I walk out the door and down the stairs, my legs trembling with each step, it's a wonder I don't tumble down them. For the rest of the night, nausea churns in my gut, and every time someone walks in, I flinch. By the end of the night, my nerves are frayed and my whole body shakes. I nearly slam the door shut behind the last customer, locking it as quickly as I can.

On numb legs, I make my way back behind the bar and call the only person I can.

"Aidan, I need your help. Please," I beg before bursting into tears.

CHAPTER 5

AIDAN

I DON'T GIVE A SHIT HOW LATE IT IS.

I pound on the front door of a pretentious house owned by a ruthless prick. It might be minutes later, or seconds, but it's finally jerked open. In its place is a hulking shadow and, my guess? A .45mm. I don't even blink. It's not the first gun I've had shoved in my face.

"Give me one reason why I shouldn't pull this trigger," the bastard growls.

"Liam, put that thing away," Imogen calls out seconds before her shadowy figure appears behind him.

"Yeah, *Liam*, put it away."

Seconds pass before he lowers the weapon. "What the fuck do you want?"

Imogen continues standing close enough to touch Campbell, and there's tension in her shoulders, but she doesn't say anything else.

"You and I need to have a discussion."

"Make an appointment." He tries slamming the door, but my foot blocks it from shutting.

I smirk. "My appointment time is now."

There's been an unsteady truce between Campbell and our family since Imogen entered the picture almost two months ago. He's still being a cunt and controlling the shipping docks, which has made importing contraband—weapons—more than difficult. He's also moved forward with purchasing a building to open his own casino in order to compete with ours. Then again, that deal had already been in motion before he fell in love with my half-sister. Beyond that, while he hasn't done anything more to try and take Da and the rest of us down, he also hasn't done anything to help us, either. Essentially, we're in a holding pattern that all rests on Imogen's—and his stepsister Nessa's—shoulders.

"Fucking Donnellys," Campbell curses under his breath. "You have five minutes and then I *will* shoot you."

Imogen throws her head back with a groan and stares at the ceiling for a second before dropping her chin and glaring at her lover. He turns on several lights and walks away, brushing his hand against hers as he passes her. No doubt my time has already started, so I trail behind. Apparently she trusts him enough not to follow through with his threat, because she doesn't come with us.

Campbell walks into a room, turns on the light, and takes a seat behind a behemoth desk, setting the gun on its surface but pointed in my direction. He doesn't offer me a chair, but I sit in one anyway.

"Four minutes left. You better start talking."

I lean forward. "Call your men and tell them to leave Sorcha O'Connell the fuck alone."

There's not a single flash of recognition on his face at the name. I'm also sure he's counting the seconds until my time is up.

"Dónal Sheehan loaned money to a man named Keir O'Connell." I pause. "Two...loan collectors visited his daughter earlier today.

She doesn't know anything about it and doesn't have the funds to pay it back."

"Three minutes. I'm also bored already."

Arsehole. "Since you took over Sheehan's organization, I assume *you* are now the new loan holder they mentioned. You need to wipe the debt clean."

Campbell snorts. "I don't *need* to do a fucking thing."

I grit my teeth, because pushing will only make him push back that much harder. "I'll pay the loan."

That has him straightening in his chair and a calculating gleam enters his eyes. "I'm afraid I can't let you do that."

My body goes rigid. "You're such a bastard. Why not?"

"Yes, I am, and because I don't want to. Two minutes."

I stand up and lean into my palms on the desk until I'm in his face. "Call your men off or they're both going to get a bullet in the back of their head. As will every man you send until they're all dead or you start a war. I doubt Imogen will be too happy with you if your force her father and brothers to retaliate."

A dangerous spark flares to life in his eyes. "I highly recommend you back the fuck up."

My gaze drops to where his palm curls around the grip and his index finger lies alongside the trigger. I grin. "What? You gonna shoot me?"

"Yes."

I blink.

Campbell doesn't.

Jaysus, he's serious. I laugh, but I straighten. "You really are a psychopath."

"Test me again and find out," he snarls. "I may have promised Imogen I won't kill any of you, but I never swore not to make you bleed. Your time is up. Now, get the fuck out of my house."

"I *highly recommend* you call off your men. Imogen will be displeased if she finds out they're threatening the woman I'm going to marry." With that pronouncement—*where in Christ had that come from?*—I turn and walk out of the room, trusting he won't shoot me in the back.

Imogen stands at the end of the hall with her arms crossed, biting her lip. Since discovering she's Cian's, Finn's, and my half-sister, we haven't spoken much. It's been awkward to say the least, especially since I've purposely been avoiding her. It's a lot to take in. She walks with me to the front door.

"Is she really your fiancée?" Imogen asks when we reach it.

"Yes." No. Maybe. Fuck.

She glances over my shoulder and meets my eyes again. "I'll have him call them before we go back to sleep."

I nod. "Thanks."

Imogen smiles slightly. "Of course. I'd like to meet her one of these days."

"I'll see what I can arrange."

Footsteps approach, but I don't turn.

"Goodnight, Aidan." She opens the door.

"Night."

Despite the late hour, there's no way I'm going to get any sleep. Plus, after promising Sorcha I'd take care of things, I told her I'd call. Once I'm on the road, I voice activate her number. She answers on the first ring. "Aidan?"

"Everything's going to be fine. You don't have to worry about those guys—or any others—again."

She sobs. "Thank you. But *how*?"

"Do you trust me?"

"Of course." Sorcha doesn't hesitate.

"Then trust that I handled it." She may trust me, but I don't trust Campbell. Even with Imogen's reassurance. "I'm on my way there."

"What? No, you shouldn't be driving this late. I don't want anything to happen to you."

There are barely any cars on the road as I make my way out of

Dublin. "There's no way I'll be able to sleep tonight anyway. Plus, I want to make sure you're okay."

Sorcha hesitates, but then sighs. "Please be safe." She may not admit it, but there's relief in her tone.

"I'll call you when I get close." It's an almost four-hour drive. "Don't wait up, though. Try and get some sleep."

She chuckles, but there's no humor in it. "I'll try, but I doubt it will happen."

"I'll see you soon."

"Bye. And Aidan?" she pauses. "Thank you."

I disconnect the call and focus on the road. It's going to be a long fucking night.

Three and a half hours later, I find a car park a block from the pub and call Sorcha.

"Hello?"

"I should be at your door in two minutes." The village is dark and quiet, but it won't be for long. Fishermen will be rising and heading out on their boats within the hour.

"I'll let you in." She disconnects the call and I pocket my phone.

The door of the pub is already opening before I reach it, like she ran down. Sorcha steps out in her pajamas and then she's sobbing in my arms. I hold her until she's all cried out, stroking her hair and whispering reassurances the entire time. She takes in a shuddering breath, draws back, and swipes at both eyes.

"Will you come upstairs?" she whispers.

"Whatever you need."

We head inside and once she's turned the lock, we climb the stairs. It's dimly lit and I can't help my eyes being drawn to her ass. *Knock that shit off. This is Sorcha.* Still, I'm a guy in his prime who appreciates a beautiful woman, even if she happens to be one of my best friends.

Once inside, I toe off my shoes and leave them at the door. A lamp near the sofa is on and despite the dimness of the room, it's not hard to miss the dark circles under her eyes or the tightness around them and her lips. I sit on the couch and tug Sorcha down beside me. She curls her legs underneath her and snuggles against my side, resting her head on my shoulder.

"Thank you for coming."

I wrap my arm tighter around her and kiss the crown of her head. "You're welcome. Now, close your eyes and get some sleep. We'll talk in the morning."

She nods and tucks her hands under her cheek. Eventually, her breath evens out and she relaxes completely into me. Trust is hard to come by in my world. The fact that Sorcha does so without question is something I've never taken for granted. Which is why I suspect tomorrow's going to be a shit show and that afterward, when everything comes out, she may never trust me again.

CHAPTER 6

Sorcha

I'm resting on a hard surface. This is definitely not my bed. I open my eyes. Blink. Why am I lying on the sofa? My gaze drops to the legs under my head. I sit upright and crack my skull on something. I wince.

"Motherfucker," a male voice roars.

I rub the spot where it hurts. Aidan cradles his face in his palms.

"Oh my god, I'm so sorry." I reach for him, but he gently nudges my hand out of the way with an elbow. "Are you okay?"

He stands up, tips his head back, and pinches his nose. "I'm fine."

I jump up and stare while he paces. There doesn't appear to be any blood, but I rush into the kitchen for a towel just in case. When I hurry into the living room again, he's already lowered his arm. No blood, but his eyes are watering. Everything about last night also comes rushing back to me. I wring the towel nervously.

The sun is barely up, which means we might have gotten three hours of sleep. I glance toward the hallway. The kids will probably be awake soon regardless of the fact it's Saturday. We've always been a family of early risers. I don't want to have this conversation when it might get interrupted.

"I'll make us some breakfast."

Aidan follows me into the kitchen. "We should talk."

I shake my head. "Later. When little spouts with big ears aren't around. They'll probably be out here soon."

He nods. "Can I help?"

The offer surprises me. I've never pictured him as someone who knew how to cook. "If you don't mind getting milk, butter, and an egg out of the fridge, please."

While Aidan does that, I get the rest of the ingredients out of the cabinet and preheat the oven. I don't make scones every Saturday, but today feels like a special treat day after the mess of yesterday.

"I could use a cup of tea, if you don't mind," I tell him. "There's also coffee if you want."

"Sure thing." He nods and gets to work filling the electric kettle. He's been here enough times to know where the teabags and coffee are kept.

I measure everything out, drop spoonfuls of the mixture onto my baking sheet, and just as I put it in the oven, Kellen walks in. He pauses at seeing Aidan standing there.

His gazes darts between the two of us and comes to rest on me. "Is he here because of those guys from yesterday?"

My younger brother has always been too smart for his age. I'm not sure if it's because of the large age difference between us that he's almost like the oldest child or something else. Whatever it is, there's a maturity present in him this morning that I'm not sure was there before. Nearly thirteen is still too young to be worried about or dealing with what's going on.

"Aidan just missed us so much, he couldn't stay away." I laugh, trying to make a joke. *You didn't think his presence here all the way through did you?*

Of course, Kellen side eyes me, clearly not believing my obvious lie.

"I came back because I have a proposition for your sister," Aidan speaks up.

My gaze darts in his direction. *A proposition?*

"What kind of proposition?" Kellen echoes my silent question.

"Something she and I need to discuss first."

My brother cocks his head, but he doesn't press the issue. A few minutes later, Carson stumbles in rubbing the sleep out of his eyes. He drops his arm and also stops at the sight of Aidan.

"Will one of you set the table and the other go wake up your sister, please?" I ask before more questions pop up.

The boys exchange glances—and their own unspoken language —and then Carson turns around and heads down the hallway he just came from. In the meantime, Kellen gets dishes and glasses from the cabinet, silverware from the drawer, and places them on the table in front of each chair.

I fill up the kids' glasses with orange juice and take the cup of tea Aidan passes to me. A few sips temporarily satisfy me and then I grab the jam and cream from the fridge and place them on the table as well. My timer goes off and I bring the sheet from the oven. Carson and Aisling stroll in, the latter's hair a tangled mess.

"Everyone sit. We'll be back in a second." I take my sister's hand and guide her to the bathroom.

Aidan's voice carries in behind us as he talks to the boys.

"I thought Aidan went home," Aisling says as I run the comb through her hair, taking care not to tug each knot.One in particular gives me some trouble and she winces.

"Sorry, little nightmare. He did, but he missed us so much he came back for another day or two."

At six, she hasn't learned quite yet to detect lies and takes what I say at face value. "I missed him, too."

"All done." I tap her on the shoulder and set the comb on the counter. "Let's go get some breakfast."

We walk into the kitchen and Aisling gives Aidan a hug before taking her seat. I put the scones in a basket and set it in the middle of the table before sitting as well. "Dig in."

~

AFTER THE KITCHEN HAS ALL BEEN CLEANED UP, THE FIVE of us head out for a walk along the old Railway Walk trail. It's overcast, but the temperature is pleasant.

"Aidan and I need to talk so why don't the three of you go ahead. We'll be right behind you." I send them off so we can have at least a small amount of privacy.

Aisling opens her mouth to protest, but Kellen takes her hand. "Come on, nightmare."

She pouts, but goes with them, leaving me alone with Aidan. When they're out of earshot, I turn my head toward him. "This is about the only alone time we're going to have for this conversation. And I'm curious what this proposition is that you said you have for me."

There's a wariness on his face, like he'd rather not have this discussion, which makes me nervous. A weight settles over me. Maybe I should just accept that he took care of things and leave it at that.

"What do you know about a man named Dónal Sheehan?" he asks.

I suppose there's no turning back after this. "Like I told you last night, nothing. The first time I've ever heard his name mentioned was when those men said it yesterday."

Aidan nods like he expected my answer. "Up until a couple months ago, Sheehan was head of the second most powerful family in Dublin. He was involved in things that weren't completely legal."

How did Da get tangled up with someone like that? "You said 'was'."

"He's dead."

"Oh," I breathe out the word. "That still doesn't explain how Da knew him."

"That I don't know. But what I do know is that Liam Campbell overthrew the organization. If your Da borrowed money from Sheehan like those men claim, then Campbell is the one who took ownership of the loan."

"How do you know these people?"

Aidan doesn't say anything. I glance over at him and there's a pained expression on his face. I stop in the middle of the trail and touch his arm to stay him. "What's wrong?"

He straightens and finally meets my eyes. "Do you know who the Donnellys are?"

My forehead wrinkles. "I know they're rumored to be Irish mafia and the most powerful family in Dublin—maybe all of Ireland—but that's the extent of it. I don't really keep up with the news and you know everyone around here just gossips about the locals."

Aidan glances to where Kellen, Carson, and Aisling are still walking and back to me. He runs his hand through his hair, something he only does when he's nervous.

I lay my hand on his arm again. His muscles are tense beneath my palm. "What is it? You know you can tell me anything."

"I want you to know I'm sorry."

"Sorry? For what? Aidan, you're scaring me." My heart's pounding.

"My name isn't Aidan Broderick."

I draw back in confusion. "I don't understand."

"Broderick was my mother's maiden name. It's the name I use when I travel and don't want people to know who I am. Anonymity is something I don't often get, so I take advantage of it when I can. I've loved the freedom I've had being around you. I was worried that if you knew who I was, it would change things between us."

Every word coming out of his mouth buzzes around my head, but none of them make sense. "I need a minute, please."

I start walking while I try to process. Aidan's footsteps echo mine.

"Sorcha."

"I said I need a minute," I snap at him, maybe for the first time ever.

My pace increases, and I'm suddenly desperate to get away. Kellen glances over his shoulder. He snags Carson's arm, who then stops Aisling. Seconds later, I reach them. "We're going home."

We turn back in the direction we came, and I usher the three of them past Aidan. The boys' gaze bounces between me and the man who trails us, keeping his distance.

"Why are we running?" Aisling whines.

Are we? I'm not, but she is trying to keep up with us. I scoop her up and set her on my hip despite the fact she's almost too big for me to do so. Still, I can't slow. Kellen and Carson keep up with me until finally, we reach the pub. I'm sweating and my back aches from the extra weight.

"Sorcha, will you stop and talk to me?"

I fumble with the lock on the door with a trembling hand. "I think it's best if you don't come in right now."

Finally, I manage to get it open and push the three of them inside. I'm right on their heels and shut the door in Aidan's lying face. After the stress over the last few weeks of not knowing how I'm going to keep things going and the fear those men caused me yesterday, this new revelation is more than I can handle at the moment.

"Boys, can you please take your sister upstairs? I'll be up shortly. I need to be by myself for a little bit, okay?" I hope they won't ask me any questions.

As though sensing how on the edge I am, Kellen takes hold of Aisling's hand. "Come on little nightmare. Let's go watch a movie. I'll even let you pick."

With only a quick glance back, he guides her toward the kitchen with his brother following.

"Can we watch the scary one with the weird people?" Her voice trails away as they disappear into the kitchen.

I cross the length of the pub and pour myself a gin and tonic, not caring that it's barely nine in the morning. I finish it in less than two minutes and start on a second before I finally collapse into one of the chairs. Aidan's words rattle around inside my brain again. If his last name isn't Broderick then what is it? The only other names he mentioned were Dónal Sheehan, Liam Campbell, and the Donnellys. Sweet jesus, is he a Donnelly? What does that mean? Is he a cousin or something? Surely, he can't be one of *the* Donnellys.

Grabbing my phone from my pocket, I do a quick search. There isn't a lot of information on them. Then again, if they are the mafia, I doubt they want the attention. I search news articles, images, videos, until finally I find a clip from the main news in Dublin. About a month ago, three members of the Donnelly family were arrested for allegedly attempting to break into a Liam Campbell's home. Each one of them were armed. The video shows three handcuffed men being escorted by several members of the Gardaí into a building.

In the lead is a familiar auburn-haired, tattooed, and pierced Aidan.

CHAPTER 7

AIDAN

THAT DID NOT GO AS PLANNED. I DON'T BLAME SORCHA for being pissed, but I'm a little disappointed she shut me out completely before giving me a chance to explain myself. *What is there to explain? You've been lying to her for five years.*

I walk back to my car, grab my bag, and head to the bed and breakfast I'd checked out of only yesterday to secure another room. I'm not sure how long I'll be in town. I should probably touch base with someone at home as well. I pull my phone from my pocket and call Cian. He might be the only one besides Da up this early and the longer I avoid talking to Da the better.

"Why are you calling me at this hour?" he grumbles and then whispers something unintelligible, most likely to Nessa.

"Stop bitching. It's not that early."

"It is when you're in bed with a beautiful woman. Since you've already ruined the mood, what do you want?"

"I'm just letting you know I'm going to be out of town for a few more days."

"I didn't realize you were gone."

Of course he didn't. "Well, I am. I'll be back either tomorrow or Monday in case Da asks."

"Why are you calling me instead of him, then?" Cian complains. "Unless you don't want him questioning where you are."

I pause for a second. "It's complicated."

"Which means there's a woman involved."

"There is no woman." Jesus. I shouldn't have said anything.

Cian barks out a laugh. "You're a shite liar, you know that, right?"

I'm almost offended. I happen to be an excellent liar. I've been doing it for years. "Look, I'm just letting you know I'll be back in a couple days."

"Thanks for ruining a perfectly good morning by calling for something I don't care about. Tell this non-existent woman I said you're an arsehole." He ends the call.

Fuck. I shouldn't have bothered. Cian is always waiting for a chance to bust my balls, so I suspect I'll be getting a call from Da soon. The bed and breakfast comes into view. Once I'm checked back in and settled in my room, I lie down. I'm going to need all my energy to convince Sorcha of my proposition. One I hadn't been able to broach since she kicked me out of the pub. It doesn't bode well for her accepting my offer, either. I'll have to do what I can to convince her then.

IT'S A DICK MOVE, SHOWING UP WHEN SHE HAS customers, but regardless of her being pissed, she's still by herself and needs my help. Even if she won't ask for it. I walk through the door behind a couple regulars. They take a seat at one of the few empty tables and I head behind the bar. Sorcha glances up, scowls, and ignores me. This might be the first time I've witnessed her truly angry. She's kind of adorable.

She skips right past me with the pint of beer and delivers it to a table. I glance down and find a ticket for another order. Grabbing a glass, I set it under the tap and start filling it. She returns, pauses, and sighs in resignation. Like we'd done two nights ago, we form a rhythm and work together seamlessly, although Sorcha only speaks to me when she has to. I'll take it. After the last customer leaves, we go through the closing ritual until the pub has been cleaned and ready for tomorrow.

Taking my chances, I come to stand next to her. "Will you hear me out now?"

She's silent for a few seconds. "Let me check on the kids and I'll be back down."

I sit at one of the booths and wait, drumming my fingers on the tabletop. Nearly ten minutes later, Sorcha walks in from the kitchen and slides onto the seat across from me.

"Alright, talk," she demands, not wasting time. "And let's start by telling me your name."

Fair request. "My name is Aidan Donnelly. My father is Carrick Donnelly and I have two brothers and a recently discovered half-sister." I take a breath. "Nothing else I've told you about myself has been a lie."

Sorcha raises both eyebrows. "So you're really a security guard, then?"

If I could blush, I'd be doing it. "Technically, that's not a lie. Sometimes I guard things."

"Like what?"

I'm toeing an extremely thin here. "I don't want to lie to you, but I also can't share family business."

To my surprise Sorcha appears to accept my answer. "Why do you hide your identity? I'd think you would want people to know who you are. I'm sure they're afraid of your family's name. You could certainly use that to your advantage."

"That's not always a good thing. Plus, we have enemies. Sometimes, it's just easier."

"It's been five years. Once you knew you could trust me, why continue to keep the secret?" There's hurt in her voice.

"Because I didn't know how you'd react. Like you said, it's been five years. Was I just supposed to blurt it out? How well do you think that would have gone over?" I don't let her answer. "Probably about as well as it's going now."

"That wasn't for you to decide. How do you expect me to believe anything that comes out of your mouth now?" Sorcha sags in her seat.

Neither of us say anything for a minute, because I don't have an answer for her.

"I really am sorry I lied." Apologizing and trying to figure out how to make it up to her are the only things I can do.

"You can be sorry all you want, but it doesn't change the fact you did it."

I sigh. "You're right, I did."

Silence settles between us again. It's tense and uncomfortable. Something we've never been with each other. Not even when our friendship first began. We've always somehow fit together with no awkwardness.

"You said those guys won't bother me again and to trust you. Let's say I'm sorely lacking in the trust department at the moment. So, how do I know they're gone for good? Or that someone else won't show up trying to collect money that Da owed them?" Sorcha challenges me, which I can both appreciate, but also hate that I've made her feel like this.

"I told you how Liam Campbell took over Dónal Sheehan's organization." She nods. "Liam also happens to be Imogen's...whatever he is. Either way, they're together. I reminded him how unhappy she'd be if he and I were forced to go up against each other if he didn't call his men off."

"And what happens if they aren't together anymore?" she prods.

"Am I going to be back in the same position because you no longer have something to hold over his head?"

Things are going to go to shite more than they already are. I can tell. I rub the back of my neck.

"What aren't you telling me, Aidan?"

"I've taken on the debt your Da owed Sheehan, and it will be paid by the end of the day tomorrow. You and the kids will be under the protection of my entire family."

"Does your family even know about me?"

"Not at the moment. But they will. Especially once we're married."

"I'm sorry, when we're what?"

"I told Liam you were my fiancée. He's a ruthless prick and unless I gave him a good reason to back off, he won't. He'd find some way to get around the threat of Imogen being pissed. That's just how he is. He's already making me prove we're engaged. There's always a price that has to be paid."

Sorcha jerks back. "So I'm the one who has to pay this price by marrying you? I'm the one who's getting punished for my Da's actions?"

Ouch. "I'm sorry you see marrying me as a punishment."

She throws her hands up. "How else would you see it? What happens if you fall in love with someone else? Or I do? What do I tell the boys and Aisling? I didn't ask for any of this."

Before I can reply, she jumps up and goes to the bar. I don't follow her while she pours a shot and tosses it back. Then another. Finally, I move across the room.

"What are you doing?"

Sorcha glares. "I'm getting pissed. What does it look like I'm doing?"

She throws back a third shot.

I reach across, pluck the shot glass out of her hands, and set it on top of the bar. "That's not going to help or change things and you know it."

"Maybe I'll go to sleep and when I wake up, this will have been nothing but a dream. A nightmare, actually."

"You know, if you keep on, I'll start thinking you don't like me or something." I walk around to her side of the bar, smiling and trying to infuse humor into the situation.

Sorcha blinks those big blue eyes of hers and then they soften. "I know this isn't entirely your fault, and I shouldn't take it all out on you. But Da isn't here and you are so you're the one who gets the brunt of my anger. Not that it's entirely undeserved considering you've been lying to me for *five fucking years.*"

I wince. "I'm sorry."

She growls. "Stop saying you're sorry."

"Fine. Why don't you go upstairs and get some rest then?" With a hand to her lower back, I guide her to the kitchen. "We'll talk again tomorrow when you've had a chance to sleep on everything." And sober up.

"I'm still mad at you," Sorcha slurs the tiniest bit and pokes the middle of my chest.

I clasp her hand and kiss her fingertip. "I know you are."

She climbs the stairs with me right behind her in case she stumbles, but she makes it safely to the top. At the landing she turns and hugs me. I'm going to take that as a sign that she'll forgive me after she sobers up and has time to think.

"Night." I draw back and kiss her forehead.

Sorcha scrunches her nose. "Still mad."

I chuckle. "Go to sleep."

She opens the door and then closes it in my face without a goodbye. I head downstairs and come to a stop at the exit. Shite. I don't have a key to the pub, which means I can't leave. Otherwise, it'll be unlocked the whole night. I guess it's a good thing I slept late today. It's going to be another long fucking night.

CHAPTER 8

SORCHA

MY HEAD IS POUNDING. I LIE STILL HOPING THE PAIN WILL ease, but the throbbing at the base of my skull remains. My mouth is dry as the desert, too. What the hell? I hope I'm not getting sick. I can't afford it. With a groan, I slowly sit up in bed and rest my forehead between my palms. The thud-thud inside only gets worse. My stomach roils, and I swallow back the nausea. Bits and pieces of last night and yesterday return. Oh, yeah. Not sick. Hungover.

I can't believe Aidan has been lying to me all this time. If we're going to remain friends—my heart pinches at the possibility of *not* staying friends—I'm going to have to come to terms with the fact he belongs to the freaking mafia. As much as it should, that isn't what bothers me the most.

The one person I never imagined lying to me is Aidan. How long would he have continued doing so if those bastards hadn't shown up yesterday? *Forever, probably.* That's what hurts more than anything. It's the fact he didn't trust me enough to tell me the truth.

And marriage? What the hell was he thinking telling his... brother-in-law, or whatever he is, that I'm his fiancée? *Would it really be so bad being Aidan's wife?* Yes, since I could easily fall in love with him. Hell, I'm already halfway there. And then what? Spend the rest of my life loving a husband who doesn't love me back? Because *that* sounds like a lot of fun.

Would he still cover the debt even if we're not married? How much did Da borrow from this Sheehan bloke, anyway? If I decline Aidan's non-proposal and ask him to loan the money to me, will I be able to pay it back? The way he described Liam Campbell, I doubt he'd give me any kind of extension. Which means, either way, I'm screwed. In this moment, I hate Da.

Slowly, I crawl out of bed, trying to keep the nausea at bay, down a couple pain relievers, and take a shower. It's barely light outside, which means it's still early and the kids are sleeping. Once I'm done getting dressed, I head into the kitchen and make some tea. While the kettle heats up, I eat a leftover scone, hoping it will settle my stomach. With my cup in hand, I make my way downstairs. I grew up in the pub, and although I never pictured myself running it, especially alone, being inside it soothes me in ways. The familiarity and the reminder of better times, I suspect.

I walk out of the kitchen, turn on one of the lights, and come to an abrupt halt. Lying on his back across four chairs pushed together to form a line is Aidan. His arms are folded over his naked chest and his feet hang over the edge of the last chair. Beneath his head is, only what I can assume, his crumpled shirt. I take a moment to study him. Nearly every chiseled inch of him from just under his pecs, up his chest and neck, across his shoulders, and down both arms all the way to his fingertips is covered in black ink. I asked him once what all the designs and shapes signified and he told me he just liked the way they looked. He also has a couple small facial tattoos, including a tiny four-leaf clover at the corner of his left eye, and a silver hoop through the left side of his nose too.

His hypnotic and bright blue eyes are hidden by closed lids

whose entirely too long lashes make me envious. Same with his full lips. My fingers itch to sketch him exactly the way he is. Relaxed yet still holding on to the slight edge of danger he possesses while awake. My gaze travels the length of him again and then up to his face. This time, he's staring back.

"What are you doing in here?" The words tumble out.

He unfolds his arms and pushes himself to sitting with a groan. "Christ, those are some uncomfortable chairs."

"Aidan?"

He looks over at me. "I got locked inside."

I glance at the door. Oh shit. I stumbled upstairs last night, not even thinking about the fact the door was locked and that he'd have no way of getting out. Well, he could have left, but that would have meant the pub would be unlocked the entire night.

"I'm so sorry. Why didn't you come and get me? I would have let you out or you could have slept on the couch. It would have been far more comfortable than those chairs."

"You were pissed. It's a fitting punishment, being forced to sleep on hard chairs for a night, I suppose." He stands and slips his shirt over his head, hiding the stunning canvas of his body.

Again, my fingers twitch with the desire to put his likeness to paper. "I guess you're right." There's still a twinge of guilt.

"You're up early," he says while he puts the chairs back where they belong and I slide into the nearest booth. "How are you feeling?"

"Like I took three shots of whiskey in less than a minute and barely slept, which five years ago, wouldn't have even stunned me. But I haven't drank more than a a beer here and there in those five years, so it sort of hit me."

He sits across from me and lays his forearms on the table.

I take slow sips of my tea. Thankfully my stomach has settled a little and my head isn't throbbing as bad as it had been. We sit for a few more minutes in silence. I rub my thumb up and down the outside of my cup. "How much did Da borrow?"

"I told you I've taken care of it."

"Tell me," I demand.

Aidan sighs. He knows how stubborn I am when I want something. "Over ten thousand."

I blink back tears and swallow. The nausea returns full force. "I see."

That amount is probably nothing to him. Merely a drop in the bucket. Pocket change. The thought alone is enough to make me sick.

"You don't have to worry about it anymore," Aidan assures me yet again.

"Not worrying about it apparently means marriage. It won't work, though. Your life is in Dublin. Mine is here." I palm my tea cup and squeeze.

"Except Campbell says he doesn't believe we're getting married if you're here and I'm not. Which means he won't clear your debt." His jaw clenches. "Besides, you and I both know running your Da's pub is never what you've wanted to do. Aisling is only six. That's another twelve years of being here until she leaves for uni. Do you really want to be forty and still living in Burtonport working at a pub you don't even want? You live upstairs for fuck's sake. There's no getting away from here."

Aidan's words hurt. Then again, the truth often does.

"So what? I'm just supposed to give this whole place up, marry you, and move the kids to Dublin—uprooting them from everything they know—because your psycho brother-in-law won't believe this farce you've created if we don't? What happens then, Aidan? Do we just go about our daily lives while you do whatever it is that you do in the mafia and I, what? Stay home and keep house?" I lash out.

He reaches out and grabs my hand. "You can do whatever you want to do. You could even go back to art school. Get the degree you wanted. Open the art gallery you always dreamed about."

Tears gather in my eyes and spill down my cheeks. I'd given up that dream when my mum died, because Da needed me here.

"Besides, I know you, remember? You'd be terrible at keeping house." Aidan grins.

I sputter out a watery laugh and swipe my face with my free hand. The offer is more than tempting. "That still doesn't answer the question of what if you fall in love with someone, or I do? I don't want to do that to either of us."

He squeezes my hand. "There are no guarantees with anything in life. But I can promise you this. No matter what happens in the future, I will always take care of you. That will never change regardless of anything else. Besides, weren't you the one who told me not so long ago that you're pragmatic and you aren't going to worry about something that may or may not happen?"

I pout at him. "You know it's quite rude to throw my own words back in my face."

He loses his smile and his expression turns serious. "This is the only way to protect you, Sorcha."

I've never responded well when being backed in a corner, but this time I'm not really sure there are any other options. I can't afford to pay Da's debt and I don't fancy a return visit from those men. I shudder at the memory of the devil's tongue on my skin. If his boss is anything like him, then he's terrifying. How in god's name is Aidan's sister with someone like that?

"Let me talk to the kids. They have a right to know what's going on before I make any decisions." How do I explain something like this to them? Kellen is smart enough to figure out there's more to what's going on and he'll tell Carson. There are no secrets that I'm aware of between them. That just leaves Aisling. She'll be the easiest. She loves Aidan.

He squeezes my hand. "Everything is going to be fine."

I force myself to smile and keep my eyes on his. If only he wasn't such a gifted liar.

CHAPTER 9

Aidan

Why does it feel like I'm lying to Sorcha? There's an itch under my skin that won't go away. She draws her hand out from under mine and stands.

"Come upstairs and I'll make breakfast. The boys will probably be awake in a little while."

I follow her up to the flat and into the kitchen. "What can I do to help?"

She waves me off. "Just have a seat and tell me about this family of yours. I should probably know more about them if there's a chance I'll be marrying into it."

While Sorcha moves around the room and takes things from the fridge and cabinets, I talk. "What do you want to know?"

She glances over her shoulder at me with a small glare. "They're *your* family. What are the important things you think I should be aware of?"

If she's going to be my wife, I guess I should start with the basics.

"Carrick is my Da. He's the head of our organization and is both respected and feared. He loves his family and isn't afraid to show us he cares about us. He's hard, but fair. Nora is his long-time lover who lives at our home. They started an affair while he was married to my mother, Kathleen, which resulted in my half-sister, Imogen. We only recently found out about her, though. She'd been raised by someone else who she always believed was her mother."

"Lord, that sounds complicated," Sorcha remarks.

"It's been a lot for us to deal with. Especially with her and Campbell being a thing and the fact that until they got together, he was doing his damnedest to destroy our entire family and take over Dublin."

She whistles. "I'm guessing that didn't go over well?"

I chuckle. "There will probably always be animosity between him and us, but as long as he keeps his business to himself and we keep to ours, we'll manage to remain civil. For Imogen and Nessa's sake."

"Who's Nessa?"

"She's Campbell's stepsister, and if Cian has anything to say about it, she'll be my brother's fiancée soon as well."

Sorcha turns, leans against the counter, and stares at me. "Let me get this straight. Your brother is soon to be engaged to your, for lack of a better word, adversary's stepsister, and this same adversary also happens to be romantically involved with your half-sister?"

I nod slowly. "That's pretty much it."

She bursts out laughing. "I bet that makes family reunions awkward."

"You have no idea. Although, we've all only been in a one room together twice and it became clear very quickly that it won't become a regular occurrence. Too much bad blood."

"I can imagine." Sorcha goes back to preparing breakfast. "So, Cian is the oldest. He checks in on the various legitimate businesses we own and makes sure they're all running smoothly. Finn runs and manages our casino. Takes care of the accounts and supervises all the employees."

"And what do you do?" she asks.

What *do* I do? Cian oversees our general operations and Finn is the one with the knack for numbers and business. Me? I'm the one with the artistic talent. What would Sorcha say if she knew that I create counterfeit artwork and then we sell it to unsuspecting victims for a fuck lot of money?

"Aidan?"

I shake myself out it and glance up at Sorcha. "Yeah, sorry. I'm security."

"Security like a bodyguard or something?"

"Basically, yes. On occasion, I'll work the floor of the casino and make sure tempers remain in check and that players behave themselves while in our establishment. If they have grievances with each other, they have to take it elsewhere."

She makes some small noise. "And your cousin Caitlín lives here with her fiancé, who also works for your Da?"

"Yes. Her brother Nathan and his wife and kids live here as well. Lucia works at the National Museum of Ireland. Not sure exactly what her title is, but from what I understand, she pretty much runs it."

Sorcha puts the pan in the oven and comes to sit near me at the table. "The National Museum? That's incredible. It's one of the most prestigious museums, aside from the British Museum."

"I'll take your word for it." I huff out a short laugh. "Now you know all the immediate family."

"I'm already overwhelmed and I've never met any of them." Sorcha clenches her fingers together.

"We're all normal people," I try to reassure her.

She snorts. "Normal people don't run the Irish mafia."

"Almost normal, then."

Approaching footsteps draw our attention to the living area where Carson walks in. He glances over at us and waves. "Hey."

I nod in greeting. Sorcha gets up and sends him over to the table while she gets juice out of the fridge and fills a glass for him. Minutes later, Kellen and Aisling trod in and she pours their drinks as well. The three of them are seated and chatting amongst themselves. I glance over at her as she cleans up. She's always taking care of everyone. Who takes care of her?

Sorcha finishes up and finally takes her seat. "Breakfast should be ready soon. But while you're all here, I—*we*—wanted to talk to you about something."

Their gazes bounce between us and the three of them are unusually quiet. Probably remembering the tension from yesterday and the way I'd left. Sorcha's eyes dart in my direction before focusing on her siblings again. She hesitates then opens her mouth and closes it, like she's unsure where to start. She takes a deep inhale.

"Aidan asked me to marry him," she blurts out. "We wanted to tell you first and see how you feel about it."

Kellen and Carson are quiet, but Aisling wiggles in her seat.

"Does that mean Aidan will be my brother?"

Sorcha glances at me. "Yes, I guess it does."

The little girl jumps down from her chair and runs around the table to throw herself in my arms. "Woohoo! I get another brother."

I squeeze her back. "And I get another sister."

Aisling steps back. "You have a sister?"

"Her name is Imogen." I nod. "I also have two brothers, Cian and Finn. So you'll really be getting three more brothers and another sister."

She turns to Sorcha. "Did you hear that? I've got more brothers and a sister."

"I heard. That's exciting." Sorcha smiles at her, but her eyes hold worry as her gaze flickers to her brothers. "What about you two? How do you feel?"

Kellen speaks up first. "Does this mean you won't have to borrow money for the pub now?"

His sister startles. "Where did you hear that?"

"I overheard you talking on the phone last week."

Sorcha's face flushes.

"Yes, it means she won't have to borrow any money," I speak up. "I told you I'd do what I could to help."

Sorcha sputters. "You two talked about this already?" Her pitch rises with each word.

"The boys were worried about you."

Her mouth snaps shut, but I can tell she's upset about it still.

I turn back to the kids. "Before you make up your minds, you should know that if your sister marries me, we would all need to live in Dublin. The pub will still be here for when you get older if you want to come back. I'll take care of it. But until then, you'd have to leave here."

Quiet settles over the entire room until Sorcha finds her voice. "Nothing has to be decided today. I just wanted to let you know that he asked. We can talk about it later tonight if you want. Give yourselves time to think on it."

She heads over to the oven to check on whatever she'd put in there. It must be done, because she brings it out and sets it on the counter. I glance over at the three kids.

"It'll be okay," I mouth to them with what I hope is an encouraging smile.

Sorcha opens the fridge and brings the jam and cream to the table. Then she carries a basket over and sets it down as well. She glances at me. "Hope you don't mind scones again."

"I don't mind."

While we eat, the atmosphere is thick with tension. Aisling's chatter fills the silence, but the boys pick at their food and keep their eyes downcast. This morning is entirely different than yesterday. What if Kellen and Carson are opposed to not only the marriage, but moving? Sorcha's not going to do anything that will make her siblings unhappy. They've had enough unhappiness in their lives. They all have.

I need to find a way to make them happy.

CHAPTER 10

SORCHA

BREAKFAST HAD BEEN AWKWARD. THE BOYS WERE subdued and while Aisling kept up most of the conversation, even she grew quiet. I'm the oldest—the pseudo-parent. I should have been reassuring them that marriage to Aidan is going to be great. That they'll love living in Dublin. There is so much to do there. More friends their age. But my fears and worries are just as big as theirs if for different reasons.

I finish cleaning up the kitchen. The twins and Aisling excused themselves as soon as they were done eating. I join Aidan at the table with my tea.

"What other questions do you have for me?" Aidan asks. "I'll try to answer them as honestly as I can."

I'm still smothered in overwhelm that my brain is struggling to process. "I need to weigh all my options. Let's say I turn down your offer of marriage, and you loan me the money,"—I hold up my hand when Aidan attempts to speak—"and I do mean *loan*, what would happen?"

He sighs. "I don't know. Campbell knows you don't have the money on hand, and he already refused to let me pay it directly. Which means he'll assume I gave it to you. He will probably charge interest you can't pay and despite my telling him I'll kill anyone he sends to try and collect, it will eventually start a war between our families."

I swallow at the image. "Can't your sister talk him into taking the money?"

"Maybe, but that has other potential consequences. It will only cause a further rift between everyone. Liam will accuse us of using Imogen to manipulate him," he explains. "Then, if she doesn't talk him into it, then it pulls at the tentative relationship my Da is building with her."

It's damned if I do and damned if I don't.

"I know it's no consolation, but I'm sorry that you, Imogen, and Nessa are caught in the middle of this battle between Campbell and my family. It's not fair to any of you."

Him saying it actually makes me feel better. Because it *isn't* fair that us three women appear to be the only thing stopping a bitter war. Also hearing Aidan casually mention killing people had been jarring. And more than a little terrifying. Is this really what my life has come to?

"So we get married. Why can't we stay here and you stay in Dublin? You can come visit anytime." Nothing would have to change except I'd be Aidan's wife.

"I can't protect you if you're here and I'm not," he says and there's a hint of impatience in his tone that's easy to identify.

"Why do we need protecting if you pay off Da's debt?" It should be over and done with by then.

"Because we don't know that Sheehan was the only person your Da borrowed money from. What if there's another debt somewhere and more guys show up to collect?"

I hate that with every argument, he presents a counter. Everything he's saying makes sense.

"What happens after we get married, then?"

He shrugs. "I'll take care of Campbell. Then I'll hire a family to run the pub for you. Make sure nothing happens to it. You and the kids come to Dublin with me. Bring whatever personal items you want. I'll need to speak to Da, but there's no reason why, for now, you all can't live at our estate."

Aidan makes it sound so easy. Only he's not the one being uprooted from the only home he's ever known. Kellen, Carson, and Aisling have grown up here. Not just in Burtonport, but in this flat itself. Since the day they were all born. He and I are asking them to leave it all behind. Not to mention, what happens between Aidan and me once we're married? I assume we'll be intimate. He's not going to be celibate the rest of his life and there's no way he'd cheat. That's just not the kind of person he is. Except I'm too scared to ask for an answer I'm not ready to hear the answer to. Call me a coward.

"I'm not trying to appear ungrateful for everything you're doing for me. Truly. It's just a huge decision." I reach over and lay my hand on his arm. "Will you be upset if I ask you to let the kids and I have some time alone to talk about this as a family?"

"Of course not. I'll head to the bed and breakfast. Maybe we can all have dinner together, though?"

I nod.

"I'll call you later." Aidan stands and bends to kiss my forehead. Then he walks to the door.

I follow because I have to lock up behind him. Once he's gone, I sag against the wall with a huge sigh. My life was never supposed to be like this. Except it is. I head back upstairs. The living room is still empty, so I go to the boys' room. They're playing their video games like usual. To my surprise, though, they also recently cleaned. Their clothes have all been put away and all the dirty dishes are gone. Their beds are made, and I don't trip over their shoes or schoolbags they usually dump right inside the door.

When was the last time this place had been tidied? Far too long ago. I hope it lasts.

They pause their game and I sit on the bottom bunk where Kellen sleeps. They pivot from their positions on the floor and face me.

"I want to talk to you about more grown up things before I talk to Aisling."

While I have no intention of sharing everything, there are certain things the boys deserve to know.

"Is this about the money?" Kellen asks again.

I'd put him off once before, but I can't any longer. "Yes. Before Da died he borrowed money from someone to help with the pub. Except now I can't pay back the loan."

"What does it mean that you can't pay it back?" Carson asks.

"And who were those men?" Kellen adds.

I try for a half-truth. "Those men worked for the man Da borrowed money from. They came to look at the pub because if I couldn't pay the loan, then their boss would have been the new owner."

The twins share a concerned glance.

"Will Aidan really keep it for us?" Kellen asks.

"Yes, but the only way to do that is by marrying him. He is going to pay off Da's debt and make sure no one else will be able to own the pub but our family."

"What is Dublin like?" Carson's question is almost hesitant.

I pause as I scramble for how to describe it. "Do you remember going to Belfast?"

They both nod.

"It's a bit bigger than that. But there's tons of stuff to do and see. You'd go to a bigger school so you'd have a chance to make a lot of new friends. There's a really pretty park there called St. Stephens Green. It has a walking path surrounded by lot of trees and flowering bushes. There's a pond and two fountains. I think you'd really like it." I've only ever been there once, but it had been a memorable experience.

"Where would we live?" This is also from Carson.

I clasp my fingers together between my knees. "Aidan said for now, we'd live with his family."

"What's his family like?" Kellen asks.

"I don't know. I've never met them. But they can't be too bad, right? You guys like Aidan, and I bet his family is just as nice as he is." I hope.

The boys grow quiet again. Kellen glances up a few seconds later. "Can we take our stuff?"

I slide off the bed to sit on the floor by them and take his hand. "Of course you can. Anything you want. Aidan said they have lots of room."

He didn't actually, but if he's rich enough to pay ten thousand euros without blinking, he has to live in a massive house. He did call it an estate after all.

"How about this? Why don't you two talk it over for the day. Aidan wants to take us out for dinner. We can let him know our decision then." I make sure to say 'we' because their opinion and decision is just as important as mine.

"You know Aisling will want to go," Kellen points out. "She's excited to get more brothers who do her bidding."

That makes me laugh. "She does have a way of getting you two to do exactly what she wants, doesn't she?"

They both smile which eases some of the pressure inside my chest."I'll leave you to talk."

I head to Aisling's room next. She's sitting at her desk drawing. I stand beside her and stare down over her shoulder. "Oh, that's pretty. I love the colors you're working with."

She glances up. "Yellow, pink, and purple are my favorite."

"Mine, too."

She goes back to drawing the flower she's working on and I sit on her bed staring at the mural on her walls and ceiling. It had taken me over a month to complete it. And that had been doing a little bit every day. It's a piece I'm most proud of. When I'd set out to start on it, I didn't realize how difficult it would be. Sketching on paper is a far cry from almost life-size on perpendicular surfaces and making sure everything was to scale and didn't get distorted. Then there had been choosing the right paint. The end result had been perfect, though. And we'd be leaving it.

Some other family would be sleeping here if we do leave. I have to make Aidan promise they won't change anything about this room. It has to be kept exactly the way it is. My heart aches at the thought of my hard work and Aisling's adoration being destroyed.

"Socha, why are you crying?" Worry colors her tone.

I sniff back the tears and swipe my face. Aisling stands in front of me, her eyes big and wide and scared. I pull her onto my lap although she's almost too big for this too. God, she'd been so little as a baby. Every time I'd held her, I worried I'd hurt her somehow. What can I even tell her?

"I'm just feeling a little sad that you're getting so grown up. Before I know it, you're going to be going off to uni and I'm going to miss you."

"Then I won't go. I'll stay with you and Aidan forever and ever," she says firmly.

Apparently even she thinks it's a given that Aidan and I will be together.

"Will you be okay with him and me getting married and all of us moving to Dublin?" Does she actually understand what that means?

"Is Dublin very far away?"

I shake my head. "Not too far. A few hours."

"Can we come back here to visit?" she asks.

"Of course. We can make a whole weekend of it if we decide we want to come back for a bit."

She quirks her lips and sits quietly for a rule. "Okay. we can go."

"I think you're going to like Dublin. Plus, like Aidan said, you'll get more brothers and another sister. That's exciting, isn't it?"

"Uh huh." She nods rapidly.

I guess it's all settled then. All there's left to do is tell Aidan.

CHAPTER 11

The familiar scent of baking hits me as soon as I open the door. Nora is always making something or another, whether it's for Da or Nathan and Lucia's boys.

She spoils them every time they come over, which isn't often enough for her or Da. He may only be their great-uncle, but they're treated like grandchildren by both him and Nora. Hell, they've got the boys calling them grand-da and mhamó. Learning they're going to be grandparents to three more kids might be enough to ease them into the idea that I'm getting married.

I stride down the hallway to Da's office. The door's open and I peek in. He sits behind his desk with his head bent over some paper-work. A pint of beer sits nearby and the faint scent of pipe tobacco lingers in the air. Although Cian supervises most things, Da still makes sure he also knows what's going on. I knock and he raises his head.

"Finally decide to grace us with your presence, I see." He arches an eyebrow and leans back in his chair. "You've been gone longer than usual."

Despite the fact I'm thirty, he still manages to make me feel like a teenager waiting on punishment for getting into another fight at school. Not that Da truly punished us unless we rightly deserved it.

"I had to take care of some things."

He waves me in. "Sit, so we can discuss this important thing you have to tell me after being absent for six days."

Not once in five years has he ever asked me where I disappear to. I take a seat and mimic his pose. Might as well just throw it all out there.

"I'm getting married."

Da sits forward and rests his elbows on the desk top, tapping his lips with steepled fingers. "I hadn't realized you were seeing anyone."

"It's complicated."

"Is she pregnant?"

My head rattles. "What? No."

"Is she the daughter of another enemy I'm not aware of?" he asks with a bit of irony in his tone.

I bark out a short laugh. "No. Sorcha and I have been friends—and only friends—for five years. She, her three young siblings, and, up until a month ago when he died, her Da live in a small village on the northwest coast. We met in Belfast where she was going to uni."

"Not that I need to know who all your friends are, but why is it that I've never heard of her before today?"

I have to resist the urge to look away like I'm guilty of something. "Because until three days ago, she had no idea who I was. Or rather what my last name is. She didn't know the family I belong to."

Da slowly leans back, his gaze penetrating. "I see. Why is that?"

"I lied to her when we met."

"That's not what I asked."

I straighten. "Sometimes it's nice being just Aidan without every-thing that comes with being a Donnelly. The circumstances around

Sorcha's and my meeting were difficult for her. It felt easier. Safer if she didn't know who I was."

Da's quiet for several minutes that stretch into what feels like hours. "I assume, if she's marrying you, she's now aware of who you are?"

"Yes."

"If you've been lying to this woman for five years, I'll also assume something prompted you to tell her who you really are." It's not a question.

"I haven't figured out how, yet—although it may not matter at this point since they're both dead—but her Da knew Dónal Sheehan. Well enough to borrow over ten-thousand euros to help keep Keir's pub afloat. With Sheehan's death, the debt was transferred to its new owner who sent two men to collect payment from Sorcha. A debt she knew nothing about."

Da's face hardens and his lips thin. "Campbell."

I dip my head. "She called me after they left, completely terrified. I confronted him that night. He was a prick like usual. Refused to accept my offer to pay it. So I did the only thing I could think of to protect Sorcha."

"You told him she was your fiancée," he surmises.

"In front of Imogen."

At last, a spark of amusement lights up his eyes. "I'll bet that didn't go well after you left."

"I transferred the money to him the day before yesterday. As long as Sorcha and I follow through with the marriage, the debt will remain wiped clean. Otherwise, he'll take payment out of my flesh." No matter how much I'd wanted to, I hadn't gloated after it was all said and done.

"Have you set a date for this wedding?"

"Not yet, although Campbell forced my hand and said if Sorcha and I were actually engaged, then it must mean she would be moving to Dublin soon. Plus, I wanted to tell you first. I do need to go back to Burtonport and help Sorcha finalize some things with the pub. I told her I would hire people to continue operating it if she wanted. She's having a hard time letting go though. It's been in her family her entire life. She wants it to stay that way for the boys and Aisling after they're grown. In case any of them decide to take it over." I lean forward and rest my forearms on my knees.

"What about living arrangements?" Da asks.

"That's another thing I wanted to talk to you about. For now, I was hoping to get them settled here at the manor. The boys can take two rooms upstairs and Aisling can take Cian's old room so she's close to her sister. I think it'll be nice for them to get to know the family. Plus, having other people here can help take the burden off Sorcha. It's been hard for her since her Da died. She's running the pub and parenting three kids alone."

Da nods slowly. "I think that's a good idea. You'll need to talk to your brothers. Let them know."

"I also need to introduce Sorcha to Lucia and see how to enroll the kids in school. Plus, Aisling is around Enzo's age."

"You said there are two boys as well?"

"Kellen and Carson are twelve."

A smile comes to his face. "It'll be nice to have grandchildren around. Nora will be delighted."

"Thank you, Da." Having his support means a lot. "I'll sleep here tonight, but I need to head back to Burtonport tomorrow."

He stands and circles the desk. I rise as well and he palms both sides of my head. "You're my son and I always want the best for you."

He kisses my forehead and releases me. "Let's go speak with Nora. We'll need to make sure all the rooms are ready. Then you can call your brothers."

We walk out of his office and into the kitchen where the scent of something sweet grows stronger. Nora is taking biscuits off a sheet and placing them on a wire rack. She glances over her shoulder at our entrance. Delight flashes across her face.

"Aidan, it's so good to see you."

Da crosses the room and wraps his arms around her, pressing a kiss against her cheek. "We have some good news to share."

She sets the cooking sheet down and wipes her hand on a towel she tosses on the counter. "I love good news."

I need to resign myself to the fact I'll probably have to tell the story at least three more times. If I'd planned better, I'd have gathered everyone together and told them all at once. Too late. Quickly, I summarize what I told Da, but leaving out everything having to do with Sheehan, Campbell, and the pub. It's easier that way, although I'll probably tell Cian and Finn.

Nora rushes over and hugs me. "Oh, Aidan, I'm so happy for you and can't wait to meet this Sorcha and the children. Will you all be staying here?"

I almost chuckle at the thread of hope in the question. "For the moment. Until they get settled at least. Later we may decide to buy a house in the city since the kids are still in school."

"It'll be so nice to have little ones around the house," she nearly gushes.

"I'm sure they'll love having a mhamó who makes them biscuits."

Da comes up behind her, tugs her against his chest, and lays his hands over her waist. "Nora, love, I'm going to call the Fitzpatrick boys to clear out Cian's old room as well as two of the rooms upstairs. Would you mind supervising and making sure things get stored in the extra rooms?"

She pats his arm. "Of course."

Ever since Imogen has come into our lives, Da's been much more affectionate and Nora's let him. We've told her for over a decade that it doesn't bother us—she's been more of a mum to us than ours ever was—but she's held firm in her belief to keep what happens between her and Da behind closed doors. I'm glad she's eased up. Da's never been happier. We keep speculating if they'll ever get married.

"Thank you, Nora." I glance at Da. "I'm going to my room to call Cian and Finn and give them the news."

I leave the two of them and make my way down the corridor and into the common area I've shared with my brothers since we built this wing onto the house. The boys will love it in here, between the theatre system and all the gaming equipment we have. Finn's the only one who still uses any of it. I take the hallway that offshoots toward my room and close the door behind me.

This has been my room for most of the last decade. I've never brought a woman here. To my knowledge neither has Cian or Finn brought one to theirs. It's been our sacred space. And come next week, I'll be sharing it with Sorcha.

CHAPTER 12

SORCHA

I STAND IN THE MIDDLE OF THE EMPTY PUB WITH MY ARMS wrapped around my waist and try not to cry. The past week has been a rollercoaster of emotion. Enough to make me sick to my stomach. The nausea has been almost a constant presence. The twins and Aisling have somehow started treating this like some grand adventure. This will be only the second time they've ever left Burtonport.

Footsteps come from behind and then Aidan's warm body is pressed against mine. I lean into him and he holds me without saying anything. He just hugs me tight while I grieve. We remain there for a few minutes before I take a deep breath and turn forcing him to release me.

"The last of the stuff has been loaded in the lorry. They'll make sure it gets to the manor and taken inside. You just tell them where you want it," Aidan says.

This is really happening. It's time I accept it and figure out how to move forward from here. "Thank you for taking care of all this. I'm not sure I would have been able to do it."

"Yes, you would have, because you don't quit. But now you have someone to help so you don't have to do things alone anymore."

Tears threaten again, because this last month trying to keep everything together has been exhausting. I move close again and circle my arms around him, laying my head on his chest. "Thank you."

"Are we leaving soon?" Aisling's voice pipes up from nearby.

Aidan and I separate and my sister joins us. I kneel down. "In a few minutes. As soon as we grab our bags and get them in Aidan's car."

She grabs my hand and tugs me toward the kitchen. "Mine's ready."

I can't help but chuckle at her enthusiasm and glance behind me. Aidan's smiling as well. The three of us climb the stairs and enter the flat. Sure enough, sitting in the living room is her small, pink Hello Kitty suitcase.

The twins walk in, each carrying their own duffel. I guess I'm the only one left.

"Let me get my bag, and we should be ready to go," I say forcing excitement into my tone.

I leave the four of them and head to my bedroom. For several seconds, I stand there, staring at the four walls where I've lived nearly my whole life. We moved in here long before the twins were born when it had just been Da, Mum, and me. Every day after school, I'd rush upstairs so I could finish my homework and then I'd hurry back downstairs and visit with the fishermen who came in. More than half of them still show up. It hadn't just been about the pub for me. It had been about the people.

With a deep inhale, I grip the handle of my suitcase, take one final glance around the room, and walk out, closing the door quietly behind me.

THE DRIVE TO DUBLIN HAS BEEN FILLED WITH CHATTER and more than one argument, but a buzz of excitement comes from the three passengers in the backseat. As we make our way through the city, the chatter increases drowning out the song playing on the radio. I glance back and they're all pointing at different things.

The scenery changes as we continue out of Dublin and into the countryside. Aidan had said their estate was about twenty minutes outside the city center. The rolling green hills on either side of the road remind me of the area around Burtonport and a wave of homesickness washes over me. A warm hand covers mine and squeezes gently. I glance over at Aidan.

"It's beautiful out here." It truly is. Shouldn't I be happier?

"The back of the estate looks out over a field of hills. Once in a while I'll sit on the patio and watch the sunset on the horizon. The view is stunning."

"I look forward to seeing it."

"Are we there yet?" Aisling calls out for only the twenty-third time.

Aidan and I both laugh and he glances over his shoulder for a brief second. "We should be there in less than five minutes."

That must satisfy her, because she sits back in her seat and goes back to drawing. I'd made sure to keep out her small lap desk and a few art supplies before we left so she'd be somewhat entertained during the drive. Having a picture to sketch is about the only time she'll sit still.

As promised, five minutes later, Aidan turns onto a narrow lane guarded by a massive iron gate that opens automatically at his approach. We drive down the lane lined with trees on either side that provide us shade. Dappled bursts of sunlight filter through the branches giving the ground a polka-dot appearance. As we slowly move forward I keep my eyes trained ahead waiting for the first glimpse of our—my—new home.

The road curves softly and then...there it is. I'm awestruck. The kids must be as well, because a chorus of wow and whoa come from them. It's magnificent with its Georgian architecture and creeping vines that climb and weave in between the narrow spaces separating the wall of windows. The panes are so clean and shiny they reflect the entirety of the front lawn and the archway of trees surrounding it. If I didn't believe Aidan about who he really is, I would after laying eyes on this house. It screams wealth.

Several cars—expensive ones, including Aidan's—are parked in the circle drive. He borrowed his brother's SUV because he thought we would be more comfortable in the larger vehicle. We come to a stop and he shuts it off. Before I can exit, he reaches for my hand and rubs his thumb across my skin.

"Everything is going to be okay. I promise."

I nod shakily. He mimics it and then we're both getting out. Aidan opens the back door on his side and the boys jump down. I help Aisling out. Holding her hand, we circle around to meet them and then the five of us walk toward the house. Before we make it to the steps the double doors part and, despite the dark hair threaded with silver, an older version of Aidan appears. His blue eyes glow with warmth, but every inch of him radiates power. It's in the way he holds himself. This is a man who wouldn't hesitate to destroy any person who crosses him.

Aidan's hand goes to my lower back and I draw strength from him. The most feared and powerful man in Dublin is going to be my father-in-law. I can't be—won't be—timid. Keeping hold of Aisling's hand, we walk side-by-side until we reach Aidan's Da. He smiles down at us and once again, Aidan's resemblance to him is visible.

"Welcome, you must be Sorcha," he greets me with a hug that takes me by surprise. "It's so nice to meet you."

For a second, I'm taken back to before Da died and he'd wrap his thick arms around me, smelling like yeast and hops. I'd felt loved. Mr. Donnelly releases me and his gaze shifts to Aisling and the twins.

"I'm happy to meet you all as well. Forgive me for not being able to tell which of you is Kellen and which is Carson," he says with a wink.

I already warned both of them not to play any tricks on Aidan's Da regarding their identity. As the natural leader of the two, Kellen steps forward with his hand outstretched. "I'm Kellen, sir."

The older man gives him a firm, but gentle handshake and turns to Carson to shake his hand as well. "Which means you must be Carson. A pleasure."

At last Mr. Donnelly turns back to Aisling and for a second time shock keeps me immobile when he lowers himself to one knee. "That means you must be Aisling. I understand you're quite the artist like your sister."

Never one to shy away from strangers, she releases my hand and shoves hers out in front of her like the boys did. "Yes, sir, I love to draw."

Chuckling, Aidan's Da shakes it. "Well, there just so happens to be a new sketchpad and box of pencils with your name on them inside. Perhaps we should go in and see?"

Without loosening her grip on his hand, she turns to me. "Can we, Sorcha?"

"Of course, and be sure to tell Mr. Donnelly thank you."

Aidan's Da rises, his hand still held firmly in Aisling's. " Call me Carrick. All of you. You're family now."

With that pronouncement, he leads us inside. Aidan leans close. "See? Nothing to worry about."

I shoulder bump him, because we've only been here for five minutes. There's plenty of time for things to go wrong. While Aisling leads the conversation in front of us, I slow until the boys come up beside me.

"So? What do you think?" I ask.

"This house is huge," Carson stage-whispers, his gaze darting around.

Yes, it is. It's a bit overwhelming in fact, which is why I keep my attention on them instead of what's around me. I'll have Aidan give me a tour when I'm a bit more settled. I glance at Kellen.

"What about you?"

He actually hesitates before finally speaking. "Do you think he'll like us?"

I open my mouth, but Aidan beats me to it. "I know for a fact he already likes you."

"How do you know that?" Kellen asks in an unsure tone.

"Because *I* like you, and my Da knows I have excellent taste in friends. Besides, he doesn't let everyone call him Carrick. Like he said, you're family now and to us, that means everything."

CHAPTER 13

A LITTLE BRIBERY NEVER HURT ANYONE. IT'S A SMART strategy. Win the kids over and Sorcha will soon follow. Especially once she sees there's nothing to worry about. With Da in the lead and still holding onto Aisling's hand, we head straight for the kitchen. Of course, Nora is more than ready for us.

She turns at our arrival and wipes her hands on her apron. "Welcome."

"Nora, this is Sorcha, Kellen, Carson, and Aisling." I point at each of them as I say their name. "Nora is the best cook and baker in Dublin."

She smirks, because we always give her over-the-top compliments when we want something, but her cheeks still turn pink.

"It's lovely to meet you," Sorcha says.

"You as well. Aidan has told me so much about the four of you." Like Da, she gives Sorcha a hug and then faces the kids with a bright smile. "I hope you like biscuits."

They all nod.

"Wonderful. When you get settled, come back and visit me and I'll make sure you get some."

"Thank you so much," Sorcha tells Nora.

"Why don't I show you to your rooms?" Da says. "Then Aidan can bring your bags in."

He and Aisling leave first. I glance behind us and the boys still trail. It probably wouldn't have been as quiet and with far less anxiety permeating the air if it was just the five of us, but it's best to get the nerves out of the way first with the introduction to Da. Get all the uncomfortableness behind us. I'd told Sorcha that my family knew why we were engaged. Maybe I shouldn't have. She's been nothing but worried since. Except I'd also promised not to lie to her again.

Like I said, bribery doesn't hurt anything. Which is why Finn is sitting in the common area playing a video game. Ply them all with what they love most. The boys' eyes are trained on the giant screen. Already they're salivating. After a quick introduction, we head for Aisling's new room. On her bed are the drawing supplies Da teased.

She breaks away from him and rushes over to pick up each item. "Sorcha, look."

"I see." She crosses the room to admire everything.

"Why don't I take the boys up to their rooms while you and Aisling explore in here? We'll be right back." She may not realize it, but I can sense her emotions and her overwhelm. There are tells.

Sorcha glances up, relief filling her eyes. "We'll be here."

Da walks with us. As we pass through the common area again, he glances at the twins. "Aidan tells me you two love video games."

"Yes, sir," they answer in unison.

"You'll have to show me which is your favorite one of these days."

Kellen and Carson stare in awe. As though they're not quite sure what to make of him. Did Keir never play with them? The one thing about Da is that he has never been too busy for us and always took an interest in the things we enjoyed growing up. Granted, it helped that all the hobbies we enjoyed included fighting, gaming, and shooting.

We reach the second floor and stop at Kellen's room first. His gaze bounces between Da and me and his brother.

"Wait, we get our own room?" It's as though he can't believe it.

Da chuckles and squeezes his shoulder. "If that's what you'd like. Of course, if you'd rather, we can rearrange things so you can both stay in the same room. I'll leave it up to you. Either way is perfectly fine with us. But while you're here, you are each welcome to your own room."

Kellen and Carson exchange a look and then turn to Da, nodding their head rapidly.

"That's settled, then. And this is Carson's room." He gestures to the neighboring door and Carson breaks away from his brother to check out where he'll be living. "If neither are to your liking, we have a couple more you can choose from that might suit better."

I'm glad I can give them this. The home they shared with Sorcha was a wonderful place, but there are so many more opportunities for them here.

"Alright, you can enjoy your rooms once we bring your stuff in. We don't want to leave Sorcha or Aisling unattended. Who knows what kind of trouble those two might get into while we're gone," I joke and the boys smile.

Their bodies are less tense and they're far more animated as we head back down to Finn's and my wing. Although, I suppose it's more my wing than Finn's considering Sorcha and Aisling moved into it. Not that my brother spends much time at home anyway. Just enough to catch a few hours of sleep before he goes into the casino. A lot of times, he doesn't even come home, but rather sleeps in the penthouse on the top floor we keep when one of us needs a place to crash.

Da stops us. "I'll leave you to finish your tour. I hope you'll join us for dinner this evening."

"Thanks, Da."

"Thank you...Carrick," Kellen says, with Carson echoing him.

Da pivots and takes the hallway toward his office, while the twins and I walk through the common area where Finn remains. Sorcha and Aisling are still in the young girl's room, where Aisling is pointing out where she's going to put all her stuff. They glance up at our arrival.

"How did you like your room?" Sorcha asks the boys.

"Holy shit, we get our own," Kellen blurts out and then cringes.

I bite back my laugh. Sorcha gives him "the look". "That's wonderful, but next time, how about we leave off the expletive?"

"Sorry."

She waves him off. I step forward. "I don't think Finn would mind if you wanted to join his game. And maybe Aisling can take some of her new art supplies into the kitchen and keep Nora company while Sorcha and I get your things from the vehicle?"

Kellen and Carson are already nodding. Sorcha runs her hand over Aisling's head. "What do you think, little nightmare? I bet if you asked nicely, Nora will give you a biscuit. No more than one, though. I don't want you to ruin your dinner."

"I liked her. She was nice," the little girl declares. "I like Carrick, too."

As expected, she is the easiest to win over. "I'm glad to hear that."

While I get the twins settled in with Finn, who immediately starts speaking gamer with them, and Aisling all set up at the small table in the kitchen, Sorcha and I head outside.

"Was Da as scary as you thought he'd be?" I tease her when we reach the SUV.

She fakes an exaggerated laugh. "Very funny. Besides, you know it's not necessarily your Da that makes me nervous and uncertain. It's this whole marriage thing. And losing the pub. And taking the kids away from their home. It's all of it."

I let go of the suitcase handle and face her. "You're not losing the pub. It will still be there whenever you want to go back to visit. It's an easy weekend trip. You're just not having to be the one to run it. And so far, the kids are taking the move in stride. You know they're resilient."

Sorcha wraps her arms around her waist. "I know. I just can't help but feel like I'm ruining both our lives. Maybe I could have figured something else out or another way to pay down Da's debt. It's like I just gave up and took the easy way out. That's not who I am."

In two steps, I close the distance between us and palm her cheeks. "The easy way out? Are you kidding? You're going to be marrying into the Donnelly family. Nothing about us is easy. We are all stubborn, loud, opinionated, and possess a fiery temper when provoked. While we haven't had too much trouble in the last few months—aside from Campbell—we're not without our enemies. I'm not trying to scare you, because you'll be well-protected, but there is a small level of risk being one of us. So, while you're safe, it's not always easy."

Sorcha's eyes track over my face until she finally nods. "I don't mean to appear ungrateful for your help. Although if we're comparing stubbornness, then I think I'll fit right in with your family."

I snort and pull her in for a hug. Something I've done hundreds of times over the last five years. Except, I'm not sure if it's the fact we're standing in our driveway or the knowledge that tonight, we'll be sharing a bed, but this hug feels different. From the crush of Sorcha's breasts against my chest to the fragrance of her shampoo, there's so much...more. I cough and release her.

"All right, let's get these bags inside and get everyone situated. Da invited us to join him and Nora for dinner tonight if you're up for it."

"That would be nice. I think we'll all appreciate a home-cooked meal. Especially one I don't have to cook." She chuckles.

"If there's one thing that Nora lives for, it is to feed everyone. She's a fantastic cook and an even better baker. Apparently she's attempting to teach Imogen a few recipes." I mock-shudder and sling the boys' bags over my shoulder and grab Sorcha's suitcase. "All I can say is I'm glad Campbell is her guinea pig and not us. From what

Nora says, the lessons aren't going well. But my sister is as stubborn as the rest of us and determined to learn how to make one meal before she calls it quits."

"I'd love to meet her." She brings out Aisling's luggage, and I close the door.

"I'll ask her to stop by. Same with Caitlín. I also spoke to Lucia. She said to give her a call if you need help with getting the kids enrolled in school. Her oldest son is around Aisling's age."

"You've thought of everything haven't you?" Sorcha walks beside me toward the house.

"Probably not *everything*. Just whatever I can to make life easier for you. I know between losing your Da and now this, things have been hard. Aren't friends supposed to be there for you when times are tough? To help you get through them?" I pause at the door and glance at her expectantly.

She huffs out a short laugh. "I think you've gone above and beyond a regular friendship."

"What can I say? I'm an overachiever."

"And so humble," Sorcha deadpans.

I wink and open the door for her. It's like I told her. Everything is going to be fine.

CHAPTER 14

ALL DAY I'VE BEEN TRYING NOT TO HAVE A PANIC ATTACK. Aidan's brother Finn, his Da—*I have to remember to call him Carrick*—and Nora have been wonderful. They're far more down-to-earth than I expected them to be. Carrick, especially, considering who he is. I appreciate how Finn has befriended the boys.

"I think that's everything." Aidan surveys Carson's room and the boxes that the men he hired finished delivering a short time ago. "Go ahead and start unpacking and putting things wherever you want them."

Kellen's already doing the same in his room. The boys are over the moon that they have their own. It's the first time ever. Although, I suspect tonight, and maybe a few more nights after, they'll both wind up together in one room or the other. At least until they get used to having their own space.

Aidan's hand goes to my lower back as we head down the hallway and then the stairs. He's always been affectionate, but today it's like he's taking every opportunity he can to touch me. Little brushes across my arm here. Soft caresses of my fingers there. Every time he puts his hand on my back the heat that sears through me grows hotter. It's enough to drive me insane. Has he always touched me this much?

"Breathe," he whispers in my ear, his hot breath tickling the shell.

"I'm breathing."

"You're ten seconds from a freak out."

I gasp. "Excuse me, it's at least five minutes away."

Aidan laughs. "Whether it's ten seconds or five minutes, it's too soon. Talk to me. What's freaking you out?"

How do I tell him that I had no idea he planned on us sleeping in the same room? Kellen, Carson, and Aisling were all given their own and yet, each time, my only thought was "where's mine?". Maybe I'm jumping to conclusions.

"I'm not freaking out," I insist. "I'm just thinking."

"About?"

I hesitate. "Our sleeping arrangements. Everyone has gotten their own room except me."

Aidan stops in the middle of the hallway and his gaze meets mine. He studies me for a second. "We're getting married. Where else would you sleep but with me?"

My pulse races at the thought of lying in the same bed as him night after night. Of him leaning over to kiss me. A kiss that quickly flares into more. Already I can picture growing even more attached and then my heart breaking.

"But it's not real." I try one more desperate attempt. The lie is bitter on my tongue.

"It's real to me."

I swear my heart stops beating altogether. "What do you mean?"

He steps closer and threads his fingers between mine. "I'll admit that when I blurted out to Campbell you were my fiancée, it was strictly to fuck with him. But I've gotten used to the idea of us being married. You're going to be my wife. Whether it's tomorrow, next month, or next year."

Aidan scans my face. "We might not be starting out with the ideal marriage, but that doesn't mean it's not real."

Except he's not the one who has to worry about his heart. "Why can't we just stay engaged forever?"

There's a flash of emotion in his eyes. "Would it really be that bad being married to me?"

"Yes." I jerk from Aidan's grip and turn away. Hands clasp behind my neck, I face him again with a heavy sigh. "No. I don't know."

"I see." He takes a step away from me. "I'll move into one of the rooms upstairs, then, so you can still be near Aisling."

"Aidan, no." I reach out, but he dodges me. Dread swirls in my stomach.

"It's fine. I understand. You don't have to worry about anything." He walks away.

With that sick sensation growing, I follow him through the large living area he told me he and his brother share. Finn is gone and Aisling must still be in her room organizing all her drawing supplies. He continues into his bedroom and opens the closet. The one he re-organized just so I'd have room to put my clothes in there as well.

I hate this. He's never walked away from me in the middle of a conversation before. Already the engagement is ruining things between us. What's the marriage going to do to it? *Why are you fighting this so hard?* Didn't I just tell myself that this is happening and I'd need to figure out how to make it work?

Besides, what woman in their right mind would turn Aidan down? He's funny. God, is he funny. No one makes me laugh like he does. He's sweet and kind to the kids. There's no one more reliable and trustworthy than him—minor lying about his identity aside. Him being rich doesn't hurt. And the man is gorgeous.

But, he's also stubborn and often inflexible when he puts his mind to something. There might additionally be the small fact that he's a criminal and is part of a whole family of criminals.

He take a bunch of jeans out—still on the hanger—and lays them on the bed. He adds shirts to the pile.

"Aidan, will you please stop?"

He completely ignores me as he sets a stack of boxer briefs on the bed. Then he turns toward the bathroom and my anger blows. I grab the first thing I can reach and throw it at his back. The soft wad of— oh god—underwear hits him between the shoulder blades and drops to the floor. But he stops and slowly turns around. He tips his head down—his gaze flicking to the black fabric lying there—lifts it, and arches an eyebrow.

"Did you just throw a pair of underwear at me?"

I fist my hips. "Yes, because you were being a dick."

"Me? I'm pretty sure there is only one dick"—he pauses, darts a quick glance down, and then glares at me—"okay, *two* dicks in this room, and one of them can't talk."

There's a stunned silence that lingers for several beats until I burst out laughing. "Oh my god, you did not just say that?"

Finally, Aidan smiles. The ickiness inside me dissipates. But then I get serious.

"You're right. I was being a dick. I'm sorry. And I'm sorry for throwing something at you." I extend the olive branch and make the first move this time. Closing the distance, I hug him. "Please don't move out of here."

At first he remains tense, but then he puts his arms around me and sighs. "You know I have a hard time saying no to you, even when I should."

"I know. Ignore me, okay? I'm just being weird." I breathe in the scent of detergent and Aidan's cologne. "I don't want to fight with you."

"I don't want to fight with you, either. But I also don't want you to be miserable."

I lean my head back to stare up at him. "I'm not miserable. Not at all."

Before my brain can send a warning signal, I come up on tiptoes and press my lips to his. It's a mad compulsion. One I'm going to regret in a minute. But for this brief second, I ignore the screaming voice yelling that I just made a huge mistake. Aidan's hold tightens on me and he moves to deepen the kiss, but it's like a tether yanks him, because in a heartbeat he's nearly pushing me away from him.

"I'm sorry," I rush to say. "I shouldn't have done that."

He shakes his head. "No, I'm the one who's sorry. I think I'm giving you mixed signals."

There's a visceral thud in my chest. "Mixed signals?"

"I'm making such a huge deal about you not wanting to share a room since we're getting married, but I also don't want to ruin our friendship with messy emotions."

"Messy emotions?" I can barely get the words out. "You just said this marriage is real to you. Which means I need to start thinking of it as real, too, and the last I checked real meant kissing and being intimate. Real means I assume you hadn't planned on living a celibate life, and I know you well enough to know that you wouldn't cheat on me."

Aidan's cheeks turn a deep red and he won't meet my eyes. I swallow down my uncertainty.

"You wouldn't"—I have to take a breath before I can even continue—"you wouldn't cheat on me. Would you?"

"No," he says a little too quickly. "I just...I guess I didn't think that far ahead either. Thought maybe we could get married without worrying about more than that."

I'm so busy processing his words that it takes a second before I respond. "By 'more than that' I'm going to assume you mean that I won't do something so completely and utterly stupid as fall in love with you? We get married and have sex, but don't let those messy emotions get in the way. So it's real to you as long as I don't catch feelings. Got it."

This time, it's me who walks away. Only Aidan doesn't follow. Which is a good thing, because I'll say something I'll regret. I should go check on Aisling, but I need to be by myself for a little bit. Alone time has been virtually non-existent for me since Da died. Even before then I spent most of every day of the last five years helping him with both the pub and the kids. He'd been so lost after Mum was gone. When was the last time I did something that was solely for me?

I make my way through the house and out the front door. Maybe some fresh air will do me good. I explore the estate, starting with the back. I take a seat at the round table and stare out over the landscape. Aidan had been right about the view. I bet the sunset *is* spectacular. There's an adorable cottage more than halfway down the slope along a level section. Maybe I could stay there?

A door opens behind me. I brace myself and turn in my seat. Except it's not Aidan. Instead, Carrick steps out. "Mind if I join you?"

What, am I going to tell him no? "Please do."

He closes the distance and sits perpendicular to me, but turns toward to the sprawling lawn to stare out at it as well. "Everyone settled?"

"They're getting there. Thank you for giving the boys their own room. You didn't need to do that."

"What's the sense of having this large of a house if everyone doesn't get to have their own space?"

I suppose that's true.

Carrick finally faces me. "My son's lucky to have you."

Excuse me?

"He's different around you. More focused. Centered."

"What do you mean?" I lean forward and rest my forearms on the table. He has me curious.

"Cian is the oldest. He's the one who will take over our organization when I'm gone. It's what he was born to do. He knows what his place is and he's preparing for it. Finn has always had a knack for business and numbers. It's why I put him in charge of the casino. He's the only person I trust with my money. With our family's money." He pauses briefly. "Then there's Aidan. Despite his creative talent, he somehow manages to coast along, rudderless, without any specific direction. He's brilliant, but he doesn't have the patience for things like managing the books or looking after any of our other businesses or being in charge of it all. There's always been this restless energy surrounding him. Like there's something he's missing out on in life, but can't find it."

It's fascinating how Carrick sees his son, because that's nothing like what he's shown me.

"I can tell I've surprised you," he notes.

"Yes, because I've never seen Aidan anything but calm and focused."

He stands. "I find that interesting."

Before I can respond, he walks toward the house, but he pauses at the door. "It doesn't matter what proof Campbell asked for regarding your engagement. Aidan would have figured out another way to pay off the debt and protect you and your family's pub that didn't force you into marrying him."

He goes inside.

What does he mean by that? Is he saying that I can call off the engagement? Or is he saying there's another reason Aidan is going through with the wedding?

CHAPTER 15

Aidan

Thank god this day is almost over. Of course, there's still the question of Sorcha and the shit show from earlier. I'm forcing the confrontation by not moving to another room and waiting in here for her to show up. She ignored me during dinner and instead focused all her attention on the kids and how they liked their rooms and how they spent their day. Of course, they were all more than happy to dominate the conversation. Kellen and Carson disappeared upstairs right afterward and Sorcha has been in Aisling's room getting her settled.

It was nice to see Da and Nora so happy. He's never come out and said it, but Cian, Finn, and I are all aware of how much he would love for us to give him grandchildren. Imagine me being the first. I doubt any of them expected that to happen.

Other than at dinner, I haven't seen her since our argument. Maybe it's cowardice, but I gave her her space. *Because you know what an ass you were.* Jesus, how could I have been so stupid to think she wouldn't have been hurt by my words? My only excuse is fear.

There's a soft knock on the door. I open it to find her standing there.

"Can I come in?"

I step back to let her pass. The coconut scent of her shampoo follows. I've been smelling it off and on all day. Or maybe that's just wishful thinking. She stops in the middle of the room and pivots to face me.

"We need to talk," she states point blank.

"I know. Have a seat." I gesture to the overstuffed chair at the desk.

Sorcha sinks down into it and swipes her hands down her thighs. She's looking everywhere but at me. "I'll go first before I lose my nerve."

I sit on the corner of the bed facing her. "I'm listening."

"I'm not sorry I kissed you. If this marriage is going to be real, then it's going to be real," she states firmly. "But you need to know that there are going to be messy emotions."

I wince, because I deserve that.

"Maybe you can separate sex from emotions, but I don't know that I can. Especially with you." Sorcha finally meets my eyes. "There's a chance I could fall in love with you. No, there's a good chance I *will* fall in love with you. You're my best friend. You're the first person I want to talk to when something happens, good or bad. I've never wanted to screw that up, so, in my head, I've reminded myself that you're unavailable. Forever. That what we have is better than nothing and I refused to give that up.

"I'm also selfish enough to not share you with another woman, so be warned. If we're doing this, you have to swear on everything you hold dear you won't cheat on me. Ever," Sorcha's voice hardens. "There are no such thing as mixed signals. You're either in this for real or you're not."

Can I live with that? With the possibility that no matter what I do, I'm probably going to break her heart. "I'm not saying this to hurt you, but you need to know that I can't promise I'll fall in love with you."

She swallows and nods. "I understand that. But, I also want you to do something for me."

"What's that?"

"Don't completely rule out the possibility."

My brow creases. "The possibility for what?"

"Of falling in love with me."

Her words are a gut punch and instantly have me distancing myself emotionally. Love was never supposed to factor into this. It's a marriage of convenience. A way for me to protect Sorcha. Nothing more. Loving someone gives them power over you. Makes you weak. Bitter. Hateful. All the things my mother was. And I refuse to become like her.

"Can I have the night to think about it?"

I can tell she's disappointed, but she tries to hide it. "I'm probably asking for a lot and springing it all on you, so I guess it's only fair I give you time to decide."

"Do you want me to sleep somewhere else tonight?"

Sorcha gnaws at the inside of her bottom lip like she always does when she has to make a hard decision. I've always thought it was adorable, but this time it's more meaningful. I'm holding my breath while she decides. She shakes her head.

"No. I'm sure we can both make it through a night in the same bed unscathed." I could swear there's a hint of sarcasm in her tone, but I don't point it out.

"Do you want to watch a movie until we're ready to go to sleep?" It's always been our thing when I've crashed at her flat. We watch a scary movie she picks out and then she spends the entirety of it shielding her eyes against my chest.

"I think I'm just going to go to bed, if that's okay? It's been a long and exhausting day."

"Understandable." I concede. "If you want to use the bathroom first to get ready, I'm going to go take care of a couple things for Da."

"Thanks." Sorcha gets up and I stand as well.

Because I can't help myself, I close the distance between us and tug her into my arms. She stiffens for a second, but then relaxes fully against me. The minutes tick by with neither of us releasing the other, until finally she breaks away and closes herself in the bathroom.

There's nothing I need to do for Da. It had merely been an excuse to get away and try to make things less awkward between us. Even if we survive this marriage with our friendship intact, I'm not sure it will ever be the same. For some reason, I'm finding it hard to breathe. I walk out of the room and head anywhere but here.

Of course, I wind up outside Da's office. The door is slightly ajar and the light's on. "It's kind of late for you to be working isn't it? You should be enjoying your evening with Nora."

He glances up and waves me in. "I'm almost finished here and then we were going to read together before bed."

"You reading anything good?" I sit in the chair opposite him.

"Dry, boring stuff about the growth of agriculture in Ireland that you would have zero interest in." He smirks.

"You're right. I'm falling asleep just thinking about it."

"So tell me why you're sitting in here with me instead of with your fiancée? Not that I don't appreciate the company, but Sorcha's much prettier to look at than I am," Da jokes.

"I think I fucked up."

He leans back. "How so?"

"I thought I was doing the right thing. Protecting Sorcha. Saying she was my fiancée seemed like a simple solution. Then Campbell called my bluff. Now, she's moved in here and we're actually getting married. I didn't plan on it being more than on paper. A front to placate Liam's demand. But nothing about this is simple."

"Loving someone never is."

My heart skips a beat and panic rises in my chest. "Sorcha and I are just friends. I don't love her. Not like that."

Da stares quietly at me, his gaze assessing. Then he closes the folder he'd been reading from, stands, and rounds his desk to stand in front of me. "Of all you boys, you have always been my most stubborn. If you didn't want to do something, you wouldn't do it. No matter how much you're threatened or coaxed. Nothing could ever make you do something you didn't already want to do."

He clasps me on the shoulder and walks out of his office. I sit there for several more minutes replaying his words. No, he's wrong. I've never had any plans to marry. I'm not like Cian who, until Nessa, would have married if for nothing more than to produce a few heirs. Or Finn, who has admitted he wants to find a nice woman to settle down with at some point. But only once he's done fucking his way through every former floor girl who used to work at the casino.

Marriage has never been for me. Love, *especially*, has never been for me. I've seen what love does to a person, and I want nothing to do with it. Yes, I care about Sorcha, and if I could love anyone, it would be her.

I make my way back to my bedroom. She's already in bed, lying on her back and staring up at the ceiling. She glances over at me. At least she's not pretending to be asleep.

"Did you get done whatever you needed to do?"

"I did."

"Good."

We stare at each other for several awkward seconds, neither of us breaking the silence. Finally, I head for the bathroom. I brush my teeth and strip down to my boxer briefs. Maybe I should have grabbed a pair of lounging pants from my dresser, but it's too late for that. Besides, Sorcha and I are getting married. We're going to have to get used to seeing each other without clothes.

Instantly, images of her naked filter through my head. Not for the first time, either. She's a beautiful woman with the perfect amount of curves. I've imagined Sorcha naked more than once, especially during the early days of our friendship before I decided it wasn't worth fucking up by sleeping with her. Soon though, we'll be married and she'll be in my bed every single night. Available. Gorgeous. And my wife.

I meet my reflection in the mirror. *You're really going to do this, aren't you?* Her request plays in my head again.

"Don't completely rule out the possibility of falling in love with me."

Before I left Da's office, I'd already decided I'm in this for real. I'm just not sure I can do the only thing she asked me to do for her.

CHAPTER 16

SORCHA

I'M NOT SURE I GOT MORE THAN A FEW HOURS OF sporadic sleep the entire night. More than once I found myself plastered to Aidan's side, but quickly moved away each time, praying he stayed asleep. I woke up a short time ago, only to discover he'd already left. I've been lying here alone since. *You're feeling sorry for yourself.* Maybe I am. The stress of the last month hasn't made it any easier.

There's a soft knock on the door.

"Sorcha, can I come in?" Aisling's voice filters through it.

"Of course," I call out.

She opens it tentatively and peeks around before coming in and crawling into the bed with me. She hasn't done this since the week Da died. I tug her close to me and she lays her head on my chest. I stroke my fingers through her hair.

"Did you sleep okay?"

Aisling shakes her head slowly. "I miss Da. Do you think he knows where we are?"

There's a twinge inside my chest. I kiss her the top of her head. "Of course he does. Remember, he's always in our hearts, so wherever we go, he goes with us."

She tips her chin up and meets my eyes. "You promise?"

"Promise."

Apparently satisfied, she rests back on my chest and is quiet for several minutes. "I miss my fairy forest and twinkle lights, too."

"I know you do. I'm sorry for that."

"Do you think you can draw me another one in my new room?"

Considering our stay here may only be temporary, I'm not sure it's a good idea. "Let me talk to Aidan and I'll see what I can do."

She doesn't say anything, but she does sniffle. Tears burn my own eyes. Crying doesn't do any good, so I force them back.

"Hey." I tap her shoulder and wait until she tilts her head back to look at me. "Why don't we get up and go exploring? I found this really neat hedgerow maze yesterday with a cool sculpture in the center. We can take our drawing supplies down there and do some sketching. What do you think?"

"Okay." There's a little more enthusiasm in her tone.

She moves away from me just as the door opens and Aidan walks in carrying a tray. He pauses at the sight of Aisling. Will he mind she's in his room?

"Everything all right?" His gaze bounces between the both of us.

"Can Sorcha paint me another fairy forest?" she blurts out making me groan.

"A fairy forest?" He arches an eyebrow.

I sigh. "In her room back home, I painted the walls and ceiling with trees and flowering bushes with little fairies hidden in the branches and behind blooms. Then at night, I turned on a light that would project glowing stars and other small shapes onto all the surfaces."

"That sounds pretty," Aidan says to Aisling. "I don't see why you can't have another one in your new room if Sorcha doesn't mind doing it."

She jumps off the bed and rushes over to throw her arms around his legs. "Thank you, thank you, thank you. I'm going to go tell Kellen and Carson."

Without looking back, she runs out of the room. I guess that means we won't be going exploring together. Aidan chuckles.

"To be so easily satisfied." He crosses the room with a bemused smile. "Here, I brought you breakfast."

Surprised, I slowly sit up. The blankets pool around my waist. His gaze flicks in the direction of my chest when he sets the tray over my lap, but darts away. Only that brief heated glance has my nipples aching. I refuse to check if they're hard. If Aidan can ignore it, so can I.

Finally, I remember my manners. "Thank you. That was sweet."

"I can be sweet sometimes." He almost pouts.

A small smile pulls at my lips. "Yes, you can."

He sits on the edge of the bed with one knee angled toward me and faces in my direction. I squirm a little under the scrutiny.

"Eat." He gestures with his chin.

"You didn't bring anything for yourself?"

"I ate earlier."

Never one to shy away from food, I lift the lid off the plate. There's a croissant that smells delicious, along with jam, peanut butter, and a bowl filled with fruit. I pick up my fork and stab a chunk of melon. Sweet juicy flavor bursts over my tongue. "Mmm, this is so good."

I glance at Aidan and his eyes are locked on my mouth. My chewing slows and I swallow with a big gulp. Heat swirls around my belly and the ache in my nipples grows. Almost subconsciously, I flick my tongue out to gather some of the flavor left on my lips. His pupils dilate and his nostrils flare before he lifts his gaze to meet mine. There's a fluttery sensation inside my chest.

"Okay," he says in a husky growl.

"Okay, what?" It's almost a whisper of sound.

"I'm in this for real."

The fluttering gets faster as does my heartbeat. Isn't this what I wanted? "Are you sure?"

"Not really."

The flutters come to an abrupt halt. Ouch. "At least you're honest."

Aidan reaches for my hand and threads his fingers through mine, the slight callouses lightly abrading my skin. "I promised I wouldn't lie to you again."

He's right. I want the truth, even if it isn't always pleasant. "Thank you."

"Why don't you eat and when you're done, we'll head into town. I'll show you some of the businesses we own and I'll take you to the casino. Introduce you to Finn."

Since we're really doing this, I should probably meet the rest of Aidan's family. "Will the kids be okay here?"

"Of course. Nora will keep them entertained. She'll have them calling her mhamó before the day is over, mark my words."

Aisling never knew any of her grandparents and Kellen and Carson only knew our maternal grand-da. He died right before she was born. All the rest of our grandparents were gone by the time I was fifteen. I would love for the three of them to think of Nora and Carrick as their grandparents. Every kid deserves a grand-da and mhamó who spoils them.

"I'll let you finish eating and when you're ready come find me. I'll either be out in the common room or in Da's office." Aidan stands and leans across the distance between us to brush his lips across mine. He draws back, his eyes track my face, and then he walks out of the room.

I lift my fingers to my mouth and press them to my lips trying to trap in his touch. God, I'm in so much trouble.

∼

I RUN THE COMB THROUGH MY HAIR ONE LAST TIME AND then go in search of Aidan. He's sitting in the common room with the boys who are already at the video games. I'll let them enjoy their final days of pseudo-vacation, but by Monday, they're going to be back in school. I'll make some phone calls when we return from our trip into Dublin.

Aidan stands and kisses my cheek. "You look good."

My cheeks heat. When he said he was all in, I guess he wasn't kidding."Thank you."

"You ready then?"

I nod.

"Where are you going?" Kellen asks, barely taking his eyes off the television and the game displayed on it.

"Aidan and I are going to town." It's on the tip of my tongue to invite them, but I bite it, for once being a little selfish and wanting time alone with...my fiancé. That sounds so weird.

"Have fun." He turns his full attention back to the video game.

That was easy enough.

"We'll be back later," Aidan tells them and they both wave distractedly.

He and I exchange smiles and leave them to their entertainment. Nora and Aisling are nowhere to be found. My guess is they're in the kitchen. The weather is mild. Sunlight peeks through the swaying branches of the trees overhead. Aidan and I get buckled in and then we're on our way.

"I sat out back for a little while yesterday. You're right about the view. It's so pretty out here and reminds me of the area surrounding Burtonport."

"Wait until it rains and then clears out. We usually end up with a rainbow that crosses the entire horizon over the field. If the weather holds tonight, we can watch the sunset," Aidan says.

When was the last time I had the time to sit around and watch the sun set? At least before Da died. It almost feels wrong to not be busy doing...something. Of course, ever since Aidan planted the idea of opening an art studio in my head, I haven't been able to let it go. Except there's so much that goes into one, not the least of which is a lot of money. Of which I have none. I'd had to drop out of my master's program when my Mum died, so I could always go back and finish that.

Needing a distraction, I pivot in my seat toward Aidan. "Tell me about this casino of yours."

"We bought it from its previous owner several years ago. Caitlín continuously reminds us that she deserves all the credit for the idea. Her Italian brother-in-law's organization runs a highly successful one in Brooklyn, which is what made her suggest it."

I hold up my hand. "Wait. Her 'Italian brother-in-law's organization'? Like your father's organization?"

Aidan grins like a madman. "Emilio Jacob Ricci is head of the Italian syndicate and the most powerful man in all of Brooklyn. I'm pretty sure Nathan told me he even has the mayor of the city in his pocket."

My eyes widen. Good god, they're all criminals. I rub my hand across my forehead. What have I gotten us into? "Continue. Casino. Crime organizations."

His crazy smile turns into a smirk at my unintentional alliteration. "There's not much more to tell. It was a derelict building that we bought, gutted, and turned into the most lucrative operation in Dublin. It's obscenely exclusive. Our clientele are extremely wealthy and pay for the privilege of being a member. Finn's in charge of the day-to-day operations."

I've never been to a casino before. There's never been a reason to go. Plus, all of them require a person to be a member. I'll admit to being curious what it's like. "What's it called?"

"*Anamacha Caillte.*"

I gape. "You called your casino 'Lost Souls'?"

"All credit for that goes to Cian. He found the irony of it amusing."

"Your entire family sounds quite interesting." That's about the kindest word I can use.

Aidan barks out a laugh. "We're all a bit crazy."

"I mean, you said it."

"Don't worry, you'll get used to us after a while."

Oddly, I find that reassuring. They all sound a bit colorful. I admit to being a little excited to meet everyone. Especially Caitlín and Imogen. *I hope they like me.* I somehow never manage to keep girl friends for long. I'm not sure what that says about me.

The streets turn more residential and narrow with traffic going only one way, until Aidan parks at a curb in front of a metal sign labeled "Donnelly family only". There are perks to being the owners, I suppose. We exit the vehicle and approach a brick multi-story building. A narrow section juts out and large letters stacked on top of each other spell out the name of the casino.

Aidan grabs the door handle, pauses, and glances over at me. He waggles his eyebrows. "You ready for the corruption to begin?"

I snort. "Bring it on."

CHAPTER 17

AIDAN

DIM LIGHTS ILLUMINATE THE INTERIOR OF THE CASINO, but it's mostly covered in shadows. There's a marked difference between the place during the day when it's completely silent and when the doors open and the buzz of bets being placed fills the air.

Sorcha glances around, those eyes of hers soaking everything in. She turns to me once she's given the place a careful inspection. Her expression is blank and it's obvious she's unimpressed. "This is it? Why did I expect it to be gaudy and ostentatious? It looks like a boring business office with a bunch of empty felt-covered tables."

I roar with laughter. "Be careful, you might hurt Caitlín's feelings if she heard you say that. We loosely designed it based on Emilio's casino, but far less grand. It's also intentionally made to look like a boardroom. It makes the players feel more like they're making lucrative business deals instead of gambling away their hard-earned cash."

We make our way across the gaming floor, weaving between Blackjack tables and Texas Hold 'em tables, toward the elevator. I'm sure security has already spotted us. Unless he's occupied, they've already notified Finn we're here.

"I suspect it looks a bit different with all the lights on and people occupying the seats at the tables," Sorcha concedes.

"I'll bring you back one night and you can judge for yourself. I'll even teach you how to play if you want."

Her eyes widen at that. "Really?"

"Who knows, you might even win a hand or two with beginner's luck." I press the elevator button.

The bell dings and the door slides open. I sweep my hand out and she steps in first. I'm right behind her and then we're moving. A few seconds later, we reach the top floor. I place my hand on her lower back and escort her down the hall to where Finn's office is located. Past experience has taught me to knock. I have no desire for Sorcha to witness my brother's bare ass pumping if he's fucking his latest woman inside.

"Come in," the muffled reply comes through the wood.

I open the door and walk in. Finn sits behind the desk with papers strewn across it. I have no idea how he handles the chaos of it all, but it's his system and it works for him. He glances up and his gaze homes in on the woman at my side.

"I don't feel like we got a proper introduction yesterday." He quickly stands and rounds the desk to give her a hug. "Welcome to the family, Sorcha."

"Thank you so much."

When Finn's embrace lasts a little too long I growl. "All right, hands off."

Far too slowly, he releases her, but he clasps her hand, kisses her knuckles, and winks before stepping back. "My brother is one lucky man."

Sorcha's cheeks turn bright pink and she smiles sweetly. I want to punch Finn in the face. *I know what you're trying to do.* He only smirks.

"Yes, he is," she says with a bit of sass.

"Shouldn't you be getting back to work?" I give him a pointed glare.

"Why would I want to do that when there's a beautiful woman nearby?" He glances over at Sorcha again. "Has he given you the grand tour of the place?"

She shakes her head. "Not yet. Unless of course you count walking from the front door to the elevator a tour. I'll admit, it was kind of boring."

Finn palms his chest and staggers back a few steps. "You wound me. I'll have you know that this is only the second most boring casino in Dublin. Liam Campbell's is the first."

Sorcha giggles and I stare at her dumbstruck. She actually *giggled*. Is she really falling for his schmoozy charm? Is that the kind of guy she likes? Does she want me to be more like that? *Why are you even worried about this anyway?* It's not as though I want her to fall in love with me. I don't want to hurt her if—when— I can't love her back. Then why do I have the urge to put a bullet in Finn?

A gentle hand rests against my chest and I blink back the image of my bullet-riddled brother. Sorcha stands in front of me, her body nearly pressed against mine. "Are you okay? You have this weird look on your face."

I glance over her head at my brother who cocks his head at me and then my focus is back on who it should be. My *fiancée*. "I'm fine. Just lost in thought for a second."

"They didn't look like they were nice thoughts. For a second I wondered if you were about to murder someone."

Behind her, Finn coughs.

"No murdering." *At least not today.* "We should get going though."

"I'll give you the grand tour the next time you stop by," my brother promises.

Sorcha turns toward him. "That would be lovely, thank you."

If anyone is going to show her around, it's going to be me. Finn is well aware of this, but apparently he's in the mood to fuck with me. I glare at him and promise retribution. He's not even fazed. As though sensing the underlying tension, her gaze bounces between him and me. She steps closer and puts an arm around my waist. "I'm ready to go if you are."

Shooting Finn a triumphant glare, we walk out of his office and to the elevator. It opens and we both step in. No sooner does the door close than a feral possessiveness washes over me. I push Sorcha against the wall and my lips crash down on hers. Her mouth opens on a gasp, and I sweep my tongue inside, tasting her surprise. I cradle the back of her head with one hand to protect it from the hard surface behind her and my other is free to roam. Instead, I keep it resting on the curve of her hip.

My fingers itch to explore every inch of her, but my brain is sending warning signals that this is Sorcha. My body isn't getting the message as I deepen the kiss. Her hands clutch the fabric of my shirt. I can't tell if she's pulling me closer or trying to push me away. The elevator comes to a jerky halt and we both stumble. I break the kiss, but tighten my hold on her to keep her from falling.

The door opens, but it's as though we're both frozen. Our harsh breathing echoes in the small space, bouncing off the metal walls as the door closes again. Her eyes meet mine and they've darkened with desire, her pupils shot full. I open my mouth, but Sorcha expression shifts fiercely.

"Don't you dare say you're sorry," she growls.

My teeth snap shut. *I wasn't going to, was I?* Probably. Except I'm not sorry. "I have no intention of apologizing."

She blinks. "Oh. Okay, good. Because I'm not sorry either."

"Good."

Another two seconds go by before I manage to hit the button that opens the door. It glides apart and with her spine straight, Sorcha steps out. I follow right on her heels, my cock aching with an unsatisfied need. The taste of her still lingers on my tongue and I can still feel the softness of her body beneath my fingertips. My gaze drops to her ass as she walks in front of me. I'm so fucked.

THE DRIVE HOME IS QUIET. I'D PLANNED ON SHOWING Sorcha a few more of the businesses we operate, but after that kiss I need some time alone to process it. My reaction had been completely unexpected. This is Sorcha. Of course I'm attracted to her, but that went far beyond attraction. That was jealousy. Possessiveness. I've never wanted to maim or dismember either of my brothers over a woman before. But I'd been seconds away from snapping when Finn flirted with her.

I pull through the iron gate and make my way down the lane to park behind Da's vehicle. Sorcha and I walk through the front door of the manor.

"I'm going to go get some work done. You okay by yourself for a little while?" I do my best to keep my tone level.

She glances at me with an unreadable expression. "I'm sure I can find something with which to entertain myself."

"See you at lunch?"

"Yeah."

I nod and head to the library. As soon as I walk in, I close the doors and go straight to the bar to pour myself a drink. I throw it back in a single swallow then lean into my palms on the edge of the wooden surface. *It was just a kiss.* How many times will I have to tell myself that before I start to believe it?

I push off the bar, pour myself another drink, and head for the back corner of the library where I set up a desk for the times I want a little bit of privacy.

Pulling my keyring from my pocket, I find the one I want and insert it into the keyhole of the top desk drawer. Lying undisturbed inside is a leather-bound journal and several charcoal pencils. I grab one and the notebook and close the drawer. While I sip my whiskey, I focus on the project in front of me. It normally takes me a while to start something new, but not this time. My hand flies across the page, lines forming shapes, shapes forming a subject.

I lose myself in the drawing. My fingers ache, but I keep at it like demons are nipping at my heels. They won't stop until I finish what I started. Shadows get shaded in with varying shades of gray giving the image texture and depth. Giving it—*her*—life. After the last line is drawn, I set down the pencil and lean back to admire the work. Jesus, it's perfect. Not because I drew it, but because it's her. There's arousal in her eyes. Her hair lies in tousled waves around her shoulders. Plump lips shine with moisture. Lips whose flavor I can still taste. Sorcha looks exactly how she did after that kiss.

The one that's not supposed to mean anything.

CHAPTER 18

SORCHA

THE LIVING AREA AIDAN SHARES WITH FINN IS QUIET AND empty. Aisling is helping Nora with lunch in the kitchen and I'm not sure where the boys have taken themselves off to after they announced they were heading outside. It's been just me since Aidan and I returned from Dublin and he ran off to hide. The kiss in the elevator spooked him. Or maybe not so much the kiss itself, but his reaction to it. I've known him long enough to tell he'd been unnerved. A tiny flicker of hope, maybe, for this to work between us still hums in my veins.

I sink into the chair with a sigh. After multiple phone calls and more than two hours, I finally have the twins and Aisling enrolled in their schools. Come Monday, they'll be back to classes. Which will leave my days entirely free. The prospect is terrifying. I'm not used to idleness. Already my skin is getting itchy.

In the distance, someone knocks on a door. Seconds pass and feminine voices drift into the room. I sit up. Should I go out and greet whoever it is? No, that's a bit presumptuous of me. It could be anyone. Footsteps approach and then an auburn-haired woman maybe a few years younger than me and a glasses-wearing brunette around my age step into the room. I nearly jump up from the chair and smooth my palms down my thighs.

"Damn, Aidan has good taste," the former says as her gaze scans me from head to toe. I flush under her scrutiny. "No wonder he's kept you all to himself."

"I'm sorry?"

The brunette rolls her eyes and steps forward with an outstretched hand. "You'll have to excuse Caitlín. The filter from her brain to her mouth is broke. Hi, I'm Nessa, Cian's girlfriend. And this, as you might have guessed, is Aidan's cousin."

Still processing Caitlín's comment, I shake Nessa's hand. "I'm Sorcha."

"Oh, we know," she says kindly. "Word has been traveling through the family for a few days. It's nice to meet you."

"You as well."

"Welcome to the family." Caitlín forgoes the handshake completely and gives me a giant hug. "Once we heard what Aidan had done, we couldn't wait to meet you. I'm glad he could give two middle fingers to Liam. That twat needs to be brought down a peg or two. I don't know how Imogen puts up with his ass."

The brunette—Nessa—winces. "He's trying."

Caitlín side-eyes her. "Yeah, trying to be a major prick."

Yikes. Not wanting the conversation to escalate into an argument, I clear my throat. "Thank you for stopping by. I've been wanting to meet you both. Aidan has told me a lot about you."

"That makes one of us." Caitlín pouts. "He hasn't been forthcoming with information about you other than you're getting married so he could pay off your Da's debt and that you have three much younger siblings. Which is why we're here. We wanted to invite you out to lunch so we could get to know you."

Oh. "That's very nice of you, thank you."

"She's not being entirely altruistic. Caitlín is nosy and likes to be in everyone's business," Nessa says with a laugh.

Aidan's cousin shrugs, completely unapologetic. "Sue me. Anyway, lunch?"

I hesitate. Aidan and I were already gone this morning. Should I really leave again when the boys and Aisling are still settling in? I don't want them to think that because we're not in Burtonport anymore, I'm just going to push them off onto someone else.

"I'd love to, thank you. Let me just check on the kids and make sure they're okay with me leaving. I feel guilty for not being here. Just in case they need me. Other than Aidan, they don't know anyone else very well yet."

"I don't have any of my own, but my sister Brenna has a shit ton of them, and I can tell you that as long as someone feeds them they're fine," Caitlín says.

That makes me laugh. "I suppose you're right, but it will soothe my anxiety just to make sure. Maybe I need it more than they do."

"Understandable," Nessa agrees.

The three of us head out of the room in search of Kellen, Carson, and Aisling. On our way to the kitchen, a set of double doors open and Aidan steps out. The library, if I remember correctly. He comes to an abrupt halt and his gaze bounces between us before landing and sticking on me.

The heat in his eyes burns through me. This is the same way he looked at me in the elevator. My core pulses and arousal makes my skin tingle. One of the women clears her throat. I dart a quick glance their way and back to Aidan. "Caitlín and Nessa came by to invite me to lunch. I was just looking for everyone to let them know."

Is that disappointment in his eyes? "That was nice of them. I won't keep you then."

I turn to the women. "Would you mind giving us a minute?"

"Of course." Nessa tugs Caitlín's arm and guides her away.

"Damn it, why do we always miss the good stuff?" Aidan's cousin's voice trails off.

I think I'm going to like her. Clearing the smile from my lips, I face him again. "I don't have to go with them today if you had plans for us."

He shakes his head. "No, you should go. Enjoy some grownup time."

I lay my hand on his chest. His heart beats firmly beneath my palm. "I enjoy my grownup time with you."

Aidan covers it with his. "You know what I mean. It'll be nice for you to get to know each other and have other women to talk to. I know it's been lonely for you without that."

It really has. "You're being sweet again. You know that, right?"

He cradles my jaw and his thumb caresses the ridge of my cheek bone. "Don't tell anyone. I have a reputation to maintain."

"I won't," I say softly.

"Good." Aidan leans down and kisses me. It doesn't last nearly long enough before he rests his forehead against mine. "I'll let the boys and Aisling know you'll be back later this afternoon. How's that?"

The pull to stay here wars with the need to enjoy a little bit of freedom. "Are you sure? What if they need me for something?"

"We'll be fine. If it gets desperate, I'll call you. Go and have fun."

I rise up and manage to bring my lips to his for another brief kiss. Everything in me wants to linger, but I make myself draw back. "Thank you. We shouldn't be gone long."

Aidan squeezes my hand gently and releases me. "Call me if Caitlín gets you guys into any trouble."

"It's just lunch." I chuckle.

"You don't know my cousin. She's like a magnet for trouble. Ask her about the time she drew a knife on Nessa's Da."

My mouth falls open. "You're kidding?"

He's the one to laugh this time. "Not at all. Granted the bastard deserved it. May he rot in hell."

"You know, I'm not sure if I should admire her or be completely terrified."

"Both," Aidan replies. "All right, go. Enjoy."

I wave goodbye and go find Caitlín and Nessa who are waiting at the door. His cousin whistles and opens it. "Holy shit woman, he's got it bad for you."

"What? No. We're just friends," I insist as I follow her and Nessa out to another expensive-looking vehicle. It's a sleek silver sports car that shines. I'm almost afraid to touch it.

"Friends who happen to be getting married," Caitlín points out.

I somehow keep forgetting that. "Fine, I'll admit there's a certain amount of attraction on both sides. At least I'm pretty sure it's on both sides."

"Oh, it's definitely on both sides. When Aidan stepped out of the library, Nessa and I no longer existed," Caitlín says while Nessa nods in agreement.

My cheeks heat. His cousin gets behind the wheel and Nessa takes the backseat.

"Your first ride in this thing should definitely be up front," she says.

Once I'm in, Caitlín takes off. She glances over at me. "I won't even tell you what I had to negotiate to get the car today. Sometimes I think Roarke loves her more than he loves me."

"You know that's not true." Nessa laughs.

"Fine, maybe it isn't. I still had some hard negotiations to make to be able to drive her."

Nessa leans forward and touches my arm. "Don't ask her what she negotiated. It'll be something sexual. Caitlín likes to see how much she can shock people."

Aidan's cousin jerks her head sideways and glares before returning her attention to the road. "Thanks for calling me out."

"You're welcome."

Caitlín glances over at me. "Since Nessa ruined all my fun, tell us about yourself."

It's clear the two of them have a close friendship, which is nice, but also intimidating. "There isn't a lot to tell, I'm afraid. My life is pretty boring."

"How did you meet Aidan? He said you've been friends since you were at university," Nessa says.

Old memories surface, and I shudder. I hate talking about the past, but I'm not sure how to avoid answering without being rude. "My ex-boyfriend was pissed and having trouble understanding what the word no meant. Aidan happened to be nearby and reminded him."

A heavy silence falls until Caitlín curses. "Men are such pieces of shit sometimes. I'm sorry that happened to you, but I'm glad my cousin was there to protect you."

It's as though he's been protecting me ever since. "I am too. He made sure I got home safely and checked on me for a couple days after. That was right around the time my mum died as well. Aidan was there when I got the news. We've been friends ever since. He's always been there for me."

"I know our family has a dangerous reputation—one that's well-deserved—but what people don't know about us is how much we love one another." Caitlín glances in the rearview mirror at Nessa. "There are times we fight, of course, but we are all close with each other. There isn't much we wouldn't do for one of us, even if we were pissed at the person. Except Liam. He can fuck off."

Nessa leans forward again. "In case you haven't figured it out, someone holds a grudge forever."

"Yep," Caitlín ends the word on a pop.

I make a mental note not to get on her bad side. We reach the city and make our way down unfamiliar roads. "I've only been to Dublin a few times in my life. It feels bigger with each visit."

"It's not so bad once you learn your way around. Us girls try to get together once a week for drinks, although Lucia can't always come. Not sure if Aidan's mentioned her or not, but that's my sister-in-law," Caitlín says. "Enzo is in a lot of activities so her calendar is full some times."

"He's the oldest, right? Aidan said he was around Aisling's age."

"Seven going on thirty?" Caitlín jokes.

I laugh. "Something like that."

"The kid's an artistic genius. You should see some of his drawings. He has more talent in a single finger than I do in my entire body."

Caitlín has my attention. "Really? I'd love to see some of his work. I'm an artist and Aisling is a budding one herself."

"You should definitely reach out to her and introduce Enzo and your sister," Nessa suggests. "Especially if they're the same age. They might even be in the same class together. It might make things easier for her if she already had a friend."

"That's actually a great idea. I'll do that, thank you."

So far this outing is going far better than I expected. I'm not sure I've ever felt so welcome. Maybe marrying into Aidan's family won't be so bad after all.

CHAPTER 19

So much for spending the rest of the day with Sorcha. I'm not sure why I'm bitching. I'm glad Caitlín and Nessa are taking her under their wing. Imogen is still balancing getting to know her new family while also being in a relationship with their rival, so we don't see her as often as Da and Nora like. They hope the visits will grow more frequent with time. Still, I need to make it a point to introduce the two women soon.

Sorcha's never said it out loud, but slowly losing her friends from uni really hurt her. She'd been so isolated in Burtonport. The village was full of people over forty or under fifteen. It'll be good for her to have new friends.

I stride through the house in search of the kids. Aisling is in the kitchen standing on a stool next to Nora who's showing her how to make whatever it is they're making.

"Hey, little nightmare. Having fun?" I come up beside her and peek over her shoulder.

"Uh huh. Auntie Nora is showing me how to make the potatoes for shepherd's pie."

I raise my eyebrow at the older woman. *Auntie Nora*, I mouth and she just smiles. Not mhamó yet, but it's close. "That sounds delicious. I can't wait to try it."

Her gaze flits my way. "Where's Sorcha?"

"She went to lunch with my cousin Caitlín and my brother's girlfriend, Nessa, but she'll be back before you know it." I lean against the counter a short distance away. Far enough to stay out from underfoot.

"I wanted to show her what I was making." Aisling pouts.

"You'll have plenty of time to show her another day. Do you know where your brothers are?" I try to distract her.

She lifts a shoulder. "Outside somewhere."

"I'll find them and let them know it's almost lunch time." I head toward the dining room and the door to the back patio.

It's an overcast day, but the temperature is mild. The expansive lawn that stretches out to the rolling fields is empty aside from the guest house that sits on a level area about halfway down. I walk around to the side of the manor where the hedgerow maze sits. When we were kids, my brothers, Caitlín, and I would chase each other through it. On the other side of the house, we used to set up targets while we taught her how to shoot.

"Kellen. Carson," I call out their names while I walk.

Rustling sounds come from the hedgerow. I pause at the entrance and wait. Several minutes and more than one curse later, they appear. I'll leave it up to Sorcha to give them the look for their language.

"It's about time for lunch," I tell them and wave them toward the house.

"This place is so cool," Kellen announces.

"I'm glad you're enjoying it. I'll have to show you the secret passages inside the house that lead out here." I pause. "Although, if you're going to use them to sneak out, make sure you stay out of trouble when you do it. No leaving the property. Stay within the gated walls or it won't be Sorcha you have to worry about."

Both boys swallow and nod sharply and continue walking with me.

"Speaking of Sorcha, it's just the three of us and Aisling for lunch." I open the door into the dining room for them and gesture for them to proceed.

"Why isn't Sorcha eating with us?" Kellen asks.

"She went out to lunch with a couple friends. They'll be back this afternoon."

Kellen nods. "Oh good. She needs more friends. It can't be all that fun for her to just hang out with us all the time, even though we know she loves us."

For a twelve-year-old, he has the maturity of someone much older. I nudge him with my elbow. "You're a good kid, you know that, right? You are too, Carson. Sorcha's lucky to have you both."

They flush but stand a little prouder.

"Why don't you have a seat in here. The food should be coming shortly."

While they sit next to each other at the table that's already set, I go into the kitchen. Nora glances up. "There you are. Cian just arrived. He and your Da asked that you come to his office."

"Thanks. The boys are at the table. Holler at them when you need some help." I turn and head to Da's inner sanctum.

I stop in the doorway. "Nora said you wanted to see me."

My brother's already taken a chair. Da jerks his chin. "Close the door."

I do as he says and sit next to Cian. "What's going on?"

"Word on the street is that Ayman Naji is back in business," my brother announces.

"The Moroccan?"

"One and the same. With Campbell blocking all the imports from our suppliers, Nathan says that Naji has been making deals with the Germans. He's increasing his weapon stores and there's talk of retaliation for our attack a few months ago," Da adds.

"An attack that was provoked when that piece of shite McElroy tried to kill Roarke. An action that wasn't even sanctioned by Naji," I argue.

"He's still threatening revenge since we took out so many of his men. Naji didn't escape completely unscathed. From my understanding, he took a bullet that required more than a month of recuperation," Cian says. "Now that he's back to his full health, he's ready to declare war."

Fuck. "I suppose Campbell is letting his shipments through."

Da's fists clench on his desk. "From the sounds of it. Liam has said he has no quarrel with the Moroccans so he has no reason to deny cargo deliveries for them."

"That bastard. Does Campbell really think Naji isn't going to try and use those same weapons against him if it comes down to it? He can't be that naive?" I scoff.

"I don't think it's naivety. Liam thinks he's untouchable. He's cocky. One of these days, his superiority complex is going to be his downfall. I have no intention of letting Imogen fall with him," Da growls. "Eventually the Moroccans are going to want more than they have and Campbell will be the one standing in their way."

"What's the plan then?" I ask. "Do we have any other way of smuggling weapons into the city?"

Cian shakes his head. "Not Dublin. Our only option is to somehow get them into Belfast. Which isn't so much a problem, although Nathan is running into a couple snags with finding some contacts up there. The challenge is transporting them from Belfast to here. There are too many opportunities for something to go wrong. We don't have enough people in our pockets at the moment."

I run my hand down my face. "Son of a bitch. Completely disregarding the weapons shipments for the moment, what are we going to do about Naji?"

"I'm calling a meeting with the clan leaders tomorrow," Da says.

"We'll strategize then and see how we want to proceed. In the meantime, you boys need to keep your eyes open when you're in town and make sure you're armed."

"Always. Fuck," I curse and move to stand up. "Caitlín and Nessa took Sorcha to the city for lunch."

Da lifts a hand and I settle back down. "Roarke is keeping an eye on them. They'll be fine. He'll call if there's any trouble."

Not that I don't trust our enforcer, but I won't relax until Sorcha walks through the front door.

"Speaking of..." Cian draws out. "I take it this new engagement is the 'it's complicated' thing you were telling me about? And you said it didn't involve a woman."

Leave it to him to bring that up. I give him the finger.

Da clears his throat and stands. "I'll leave you boys to your discussion. Don't argue too long. Nora won't appreciate having her meal grow cold."

He leaves his office and I punch Cian in the arm. He groans. "The fuck? That hurt."

"Don't be a pussy. That's not even near where Sheehan's guy's bullet hit you."

"You're a dick. I can't believe you didn't tell me you were getting married," Cian whines.

"I hadn't planned on getting married until that bastard Liam called my bluff."

"And you've been friends with this woman for five years and not once did she know you were a Donnelly? You ashamed of us?"

I glare at him. "No, I'm not ashamed. Sometimes, it's just easier if people don't know who I am. It lets me go places that I might not otherwise be welcome."

"Since when has being unwelcome stopped you—any of us—from going where ever the fuck you want?" Cian gapes. "Money and power opens pretty much any door."

"Normally, I'd agree. But, at the time, being Sorcha's friend was more important than being a Donnelly."

My brother stares at me for several seconds and then he narrows his eyes. "You're in love with her."

I shake my head. "What? No I'm not. She's my best friend. Nothing more."

Cian stands over me. "Go ahead and keep lying to yourself if it makes you feel better."

Before I can respond, he walks out of the office. I slump back in the seat. He's wrong. I am *not* in love with Sorcha.

CHAPTER 20

I can't remember when I had such a good time. Thankfully, Caitlín has been happy to lead the conversation. She also has a way about her that makes a person feel comfortable. It's not that I'm an introvert or shy. I just tend to let others do all the talking unless I feel like there's something I want to to add to it or if it's a topic I have a lot of knowledge about.

"Are you excited or nervous about the wedding?" I ask Caitlín. "Aidan told me you were getting married in a few months in Brooklyn."

"Both, but I'm even more excited over the fact that my mother loves nothing more than to plan weddings. She's organized nearly all of her childrens'. I think Nathan and Lucia's was the only one she didn't do everything for, and that's only because they got married here in Dublin." She takes the last bite of her dessert.

I'm a bit envious and even more sad. My mother and I had been close. Same with Da. Neither one of them will be here to see me get married. Nessa lays her hand on my arm. "Hey, are you okay?"

I nod and smile a little sadly. "Just thinking about my own parents and how they won't be at my wedding."

"I'm sorry. I feel the same way about my mum not being there if Cian and I ever get married. She died when I was so young, but I still miss her," Nessa says softly.

"I know I'm not a replacement for anyone's mum," Caitlín adds gently. "But I'm happy to help with any wedding planning you want me to help with. Either of you. I don't mind. I'm just letting my own mother do it, because I know how much she loves it."

"Thank you. I really appreciate it. Aidan and I haven't even set a date yet. Or even started talking about it." We only *just decided* it's even real.

"If I've learned anything in my life, it's that men aren't going to make a point to sit down and think about things like that unless you make them. It's not necessarily that they don't care," Caitlín pauses. "No, wait, never mind, they don't."

I'm taking a drink and nearly spew it everywhere. Instead I cough and grab my napkin. Nessa laughs and pats my back.

"I've learned to be cautious about when I drink when she's talking for this very reason," she says.

Unapologetic, Caitlín shrugs. "Even I don't know what's going to come out of my mouth half the time."

I manage to get my coughing under control. "I guess I'll have to be the one to bring it up."

Aidan's cousin chuckles. "Don't make it sound so terrible. Communication is important. How else are you going to know what the other is thinking or feeling if you don't talk about it? It's all part of being in a relationship."

Nessa stares at her like she doesn't recognize her. Caitlín chuckles. "What? I manage to give out decent advice every once in a while."

My gaze bounces between them and Nessa turns to me. "I can't believe I'm going to say this, but...what she said. Talk to Aidan. You two have been friends for this long, it's not as though you don't know how."

I sigh. "You're right. Everything feels different now, but we're still both the same people. Talking is something we've never had trouble doing. We'll figure out this new relationship between us eventually."

We finish our dessert and drinks and the server brings the bill. I get out my pocketbook, but Caitlín waves me off. "It's on me."

"Thank you."

Once she's paid and we leave the table, a tall, scarred man with silver-flecked hair rises from another table and falls in line behind us. I glance over my shoulder at the distance between him and us and lean close to Nessa. Before I can say anything, Caitlín pivots so she's walking backward and blows a kiss at the man. "Thanks for lunch, babe."

She swivels forward and the man shakes his head, but there's a grin on his face. *Ohhh.* That must be her fiancé. My curiosity is raised. Does he always linger nearby when she goes out or is there another reason he's sticking close?

"Who's up for some shopping?" Caitlín asks.

"I should probably get back to the house." The guilt returns about leaving the kids, even though it shouldn't.

"Maybe next time, then."

We reach the vehicle and then we're back on the road.

"Thank you again for inviting me to lunch. I had a really nice time." It's been great getting to know Aidan's family.

"Of course." Nessa glances at me in the backseat. "I, for one, know how intimidating it can be as a newcomer. I've only been around a couple months myself so I know how nice it is to be welcomed. It's great to have friends. Especially ones who understand what it's like being attached to a Donnelly."

"Excuse me," Caitlín gasps. "I'm a Donnelly."

"Exactly my point."

The two of them bicker good-naturedly while I sit back and

enjoy the scenery. It's been a pleasant afternoon. Finally, we drive through the gate guarding the entrance to the estate and down the lane to stop in front of the manor. Nessa lets me out and I wave over my shoulder with a goodbye before entering the house. I head straight for Aidan's wing. He's sitting in one of the chairs with a glass in his hand. He glances up at my arrival.

"You're back. Did you have a nice lunch?" he asks.

I set my purse on a table and sit on the couch closest to him, curling my legs beneath me. "I did. I really liked the both of them."

"Good. I'm glad."

"Were the kids okay?"

"Of course. Aisling helped Nora make lunch and the boys traipsed around outside. They're back out there, although they said they'd be back soon, and Aisling is in the dining room drawing you a picture of her day for when you get home."

"I can't wait to see it." I smile. "What are you doing in here all alone, anyway? I figured you'd have some work to do."

"Just sitting and thinking."

"About what?"

"Things." Aidan takes a sip from his glass.

I study him closer. There's a distance in his eyes. Something...off. "That sounds ominous." I try to joke.

Finally one side of his mouth curls up displaying the dimple that hides in the auburn scruff covering the lower half of his face. "It's not, I promise."

"You know whatever it is, you can talk to me. We're still friends, remember." I reach across the short distance separating us and lay my hand on his. Aidan flips it over and threads his fingers through mine.

"It's just family business stuff that will work itself out eventually."

I've always loved the casual way he touches me. Except after the kiss this morning, I'm far more aware of the texture of his skin than ever before. The way the callouses slightly abrade my flesh. The heat that builds where we're connected and how it travels up my arm. I'm much more aware of the attraction that's been present from the moment we met, but that I've kept tempered for five years because I didn't want to ruin what we had.

Except, after all this time, we have more. Or could. A certain boldness comes over me. I release his hand, unfurl my legs, and stand up. When I settle back down, it's across Aidan's lap. His eyes widen. I try not to blush, but from the heat radiating off my upper chest and cheeks, I'm pretty sure I haven't succeeded.

"You looked like you needed a hug." I shrug with as much nonchalance as I can muster.

Both sides of his lips curl this time and he rests his arm over my thighs. "If this is the kind of hug I get, then I could get used to them."

"I also figured if you can't get away, we can talk."

Aidan arches an eyebrow. "I'm not complaining in any way, but you don't have to become a delectable lap decoration just to talk to me."

My cheeks become even hotter. "What if it's about the wedding?"

His head draws back slightly. "Are you breaking up with me already and you're trying to let me down easy?"

"What? No. I thought that, well, since it's real and all, we should consider setting a date."

Beneath my butt and hips, Aidan's body actually relaxes. *How had I not noticed how tense he'd become?*

"When were you thinking?" he asks.

I wiggle a little, trying to get more comfortable and he goes rigid. All tension that had left him returns and a bulge hardens beneath me. *Don't look down. Don't look down.* I keep my eyes on his. Both of our breathing has sped up. I clear my throat and swallow. "I'm not sure. Caitlín said she's getting married in three months so we should wait until after that. She might think it's rude to do it any sooner."

"There's always a late autumn or early winter option," Aidan suggest, his voice gruffer than usual.

"Hmmm. I *have* always loved autumn. We could do it near the end of September or beginning of October. Wait until after Aisling's birthday."

"Or..." his tone rises a bit at the end like it's a question. "We don't have to wait that long. There's always just eloping. That way there's no long, drawn-out fuss. Caitlín won't mind, I'm sure."

My own words come back to haunt me. "I mean, we're both nothing if not pragmatic."

"Hey." Aidan gently taps my thigh. "If you'd rather wait until autumn and go all out with the big church wedding and reception, we can. The wife of one of the clan leaders owns a shop that makes cakes. Caitlín loves shopping so I bet she'd go dress shopping with you."

Even when I was younger I hadn't pictured—or wanted—a fancy wedding. There was too much fuss involved. Why then am I questioning his suggestion? "No, that sounds like so much trouble. You're right. Why are we waiting? We should just do it and get it over with."

"You don't have to sound too excited," he grumbles.

I nudge his chest with my shoulder. "You know what I mean."

Aidan smirks. "But it's fun giving you a hard time."

I stick my tongue out and his gaze drops to my lips. He stares a second longer before leaning in and brushing a kiss across them. I bring my arm up and loop it over his shoulder while my fingers clasp the back of his neck. His tongue flicks out and coaxes my mouth to part. I open for him and he deepens the kiss. It's not the claiming from the casino, but there's a hint of possession in it.

I'm consumed with need as the kiss goes on. This is Aidan. Soon to be my husband. Something I never would have imagined or even hoped. I caution my heart. Don't read more into this than attraction. It's purely lust. At least we have this between us. Our marriage could be starting out with less than that. His woodsy scent fills my head. It's a comforting smell.

The hardness beneath me grows and with a soft moan, I shift

trying to ease the ache that's building. A warning blares inside my head. Reminding me where we are and that any one of the kids could walk in any second. I stop moving, and Aidan groans against my mouth. The voice of caution speaks louder, and as much as I want to keep going, I slowly break the connection.

"We should probably resume this somewhere more private later," I murmur against his lips.

He rests his forehead on mine. "As much as it pains me—in more ways than one—you're probably right."

Aidan doesn't draw away. Instead we continue breathing in each other's air until the sound of voices reach us and grow louder. With a sigh, I move to stand, but he tightens his grip on my hip.

"Stay."

CHAPTER 21

Aidan

It's not only because my cock is rock hard that I don't want Sorcha to move. I love touching her. Having her close. She surprised the hell out of me when she sat on my lap. I'm not sure I ever want her to leave. Which terrifies me.

Kellen and Carson walk in. Their gazes land on us—widen—and they come to a standstill. They've seen us sitting next to each other on the couch hundreds of times, but never like this. Sorcha stiffens, but remains where she is. Kellen is the first to recover.

"You're back."

"I am. How's your day been? Aidan said you've been outside exploring the property." Her words nearly run together.

The twins move forward. Kellen sits on the couch while Carson takes the floor chair where Finn often sits when he's playing a video game.

"There's a cool hedgerow maze that we got lost in," Carson says with some excitement.

"Yeah, and there's this secret room built into one of the trees out in the woods. Well, it'd be secret if there was a door. But it's really well-hidden. We also found a tree-swing," Kellen adds. "Nora has this huge garden, too, where she grows a bunch of different vegetables."

"Sounds like there are some neat things around here," Sorcha says with an indulgent smile.

Running footsteps approach and Aisling bursts into the room. "You're back," she squeals and runs over.

With a quick glance, Sorcha carefully rises off my lap and Aisling collides with her, wrapping her arms around her sister's legs, a piece of paper clutched in her palm.

"Aidan said you got to spend time with Nora today. Did you have fun?"

Aisling untangles herself and shoves the paper at Sorcha, who takes it gently. "I drew this for you."

"Wow, look at this. You did such a great job," she praises her. "Is that you with Nora in the kitchen?"

Her younger sister nods. "Uh huh. I helped make shepherds pie for lunch. It was delicious, too. Even better than Glen's. But don't tell him I said that."

Sorcha chuckles. "I promise I won't tell him."

"Okay good. I'm going to my room," Aisling says before she walks away and down the hallway leading to it.

"I guess someone didn't miss me too much."

I stand up and hug her from behind. "She missed you. But she also trusts that you were going to be back so she didn't need to worry about you being gone."

Sorcha turns in my arms and loops her arms around my neck, the paper crinkling in her hand. "I suppose you're right. I'm so used to always being available in the pub if she needed me."

"It's good for all of you to have a little freedom from each other. It helps her"—I glance over her shoulder—"and the boys develop a bit of independence."

"You always somehow manage to put things into perspective."

"It's my superpower."

"Oh, I think you have a much greater superpower than that," Sorcha says low enough that there's no way either Kellen or Carson can hear and glances downward before meeting my eyes again. Then she winks.

"You're trying to torture me, aren't you?" I say just as quietly.

"What are you two whispering about over there?" Carson calls out.

We jump away from each other, both of us clearing our throats, while Sorcha swipes her free hand across the top of her thighs and her other clutches the drawing tighter. She turns to face her brother. "Boring grownup stuff. Nothing that would interest you."

He doesn't look like he believes her, but just shrugs and picks up the game controller that had been discarded next to where he's sitting. Kellen's gaze darts between his sister and me and then he gets up from the couch to turn on the television and the gaming system. Seconds later, they're both ignoring us and their attention is on the game.

Sorcha darts a glance my way and her eyes dance with amusement. I thread my fingers through hers and tug her out of the room. "C'mon, let's go for a walk."

"I need to drop this off in my—our—room first." She flashes me the piece of paper. "I'll be right back."

She hurries down the hall and returns a minute later. Taking her hand again, we leave the boys and stroll through the house with no real destination in mind. It's like I'm trying to make up for the far too infrequent times we were able to see each other over the years by keeping her close.

"Have you given any thought to going back to art school or opening that art gallery?" I squeeze Sorcha's fingers.

"Yes and no. I've thought about it, but I'm not sure where to even start. Besides, opening a gallery isn't as simple as you seem to think," she says with not a small amount of sarcasm.

"What does it take?" Whatever it is, I'll make sure she gets it.

Sorcha darts a glance in my direction and widens her eyes, not in surprise, but as though I should already know the answer. "First of all it takes a location. Then I have to reach out to the artists of the type of art I want to showcase and see if they'd be interested in a collaboration. None of whom I actually know where to find. But most importantly, it takes the single thing I don't have."

"And that is?" I raise an eyebrow risking her annoyance with my ignorance.

"Money. A lot of damn money."

I stop her outside the library and wait until she looks at me. "It's a good thing then that I *do* have it."

Sorcha lets go of me and crosses her arms with a glare. "Didn't we have this discussion before. I'm not taking your money, Aidan."

I close the fraction of distance between us until I tower over her. She tips her head back, but the fierce expression doesn't lessen.

"That was before you knew who I was and didn't think I had any," I point out. "We're getting married. My money is your money. And we have *a lot* of it. If you want to open a gallery, then open it. We—*you*—can afford it."

That stubborn tilt in Sorcha's jaw only sharpens. "It doesn't feel right."

I throw up my hands and spin away with a growl before I pivot and crowd her against the wall. Her eyes widen. My chest bumps up against hers and her head is caged in between my forearms. I lean in until my forehead rests against hers. Her lashes flutter before closing. "This is an argument you're not going to win against me. If you really don't want to try and open your own gallery or go back to art school, then that's one thing. But if you're only refusing because of the cost, then you need to get over it. You don't have to do everything yourself anymore. Opportunities you and the kids have never had before are open to you. All you have to do is take them."

Sorcha's takes in a shuddering breath. "You know, it's really not fair of you to use my weakness against me. And I'm an idiot for admitting I have one."

I caress her cheek with my fingertip. Her skin is soft and smooth. I rub the end of my nose against hers and she trembles. "What weakness is that?" I murmur and run my lips over the side of her face and along her jaw.

She tilts her head slightly and I kiss my way down her neck.

"That," she whispers, her voice breathy and sexy as fuck.

"You mean this?" I suck lightly on her skin, nip it with my teeth, and soothe the sting with my tongue.

Sorcha murmurs something unintelligible and moans. A sound that goes straight to my cock. I grind against her and slip my leg between hers. The voice inside my head reminds me where we are, but an overriding need is much louder. She shudders and one of us must have some sense, because she's whispering in my ear.

"We have to stop." Except her actions are saying something entirely different as she rubs her sweet, hot core against my thigh. "Aidan."

Finally, her words penetrate the haze of lust. We're dry fucking in the middle of the hallway where anyone could walk by. Sorcha would be mortified if she's seen. With every ounce of control I have, I pull myself away. Her face is flushed and the skin along her neck is even redder, either from my facial hair or my mouth. Beneath her shirt, pebbled nipples tempt me. I adjust the throbbing hardness behind my zipper.

How the hell am I going to lie in the same bed with her tonight and not fuck her?

I brush the hair off Sorcha's face and she stares up at me. Slowly, her lips turn up. "You're an evil, evil man tormenting me like that. But you win."

"You'll do whatever it is you want with the money we have, then?"

She nods. "Yes. I'm still not sure what direction I want to go, but you convinced me to at least try."

"I'm happy to *convince* you to my side of any other future debates we have as well." I drop my voice suggestively and Sorcha snorts.

"I bet you will."

614

CHAPTER 22

I FINISH BRUSHING MY TEETH, DRY OFF MY MOUTH, AND walk into the bedroom, turning the bathroom light off on my way out. Aidan is meeting with his Da so I'm alone for the moment. I read Aisling a bedtime story and checked on the boys earlier. It's still hard to believe we're in Dublin and living in this place. It doesn't feel real.

Once I'm under the blankets, I prop myself up against the headboard with some pillows and get out Aidan's laptop again. All the open tabs mock me. There's a lot more to operating an art gallery than the few things I mentioned to him apparently. Considering the terrible job I'd been doing running the pub, I'm not sure I'm cut out to be a businesswoman.

There's a single knock on the door before Aidan steps in.

"Still researching?" he asks as he takes his wallet out and tosses it on the desk.

"It's a bit overwhelming to say the least." And frustrating. "Out of curiosity, I searched for storefronts to let. I know you said not to worry about the money, and I'm trying not to, really, but some of the rent these people are charging is outrageous. Nauseating, in fact."

He reaches up and tugs the neck of his shirt, dragging it over his head—mussing his hair—and exposing every glorious inch of his tattooed chest. The jerk is distracting me whether intentionally or not. Judging by his expression, it's not. *Just ignore it*. Better said than done. I force my eyes back to the computer. "Like this one here. Yes, it's in the center of the city on what I've discovered is a well-traveled street by tourists, but rent is four digits a month. And not four small digits, either."

Aidan comes over and sits on the bed, his knee angled toward me, and his gaze focuses on the information on the screen. The woodsy scent of his cologne hits me and heat radiates off his body. His finger rolls across the touchpad as he scrolls through the listings. "Jaysus. You should just buy a building. That way you'd own it outright and wouldn't need to worry about monthly rent. One of the families in the organization runs a construction company. They did all the renovations on the casino for us and charged us a fair cost."

I glance at him. "You don't think buying an entire building is excessive?"

Aidan's eyes meet mine. "Not at all. Think about it. You'll be the owner. If the space is bigger than you need or want, put up some walls and create a couple extra storefronts. Then *you* become the person who lets it out to people. Plus, any commission you make from the sales is pure profit, aside from the day-to-day operating expenses you have to pay out, which can't be that much. Utilities, cleaners, a couple employees. I also know that, with your talent for picking out brilliant work, you won't lack for buyers."

Barely a second passes and I lean over to kiss him. "Thank you for always knowing the right things to say that make me feel better."

The two dimples on either side of his mouth appear. "You're welcome. I'm being serious about owning your own building, too. I can make a call tomorrow if you want."

"Let me think on it." I don't want to make any rash decisions. Especially when there are so many other things I need to learn. Which gives me an idea. "Do you think your brother would be willing to teach me about managing books and running a business? I had no idea what I was doing with the pub. We survived the past month on pure luck. Although, considering you had to pay off Da's debt, any luck we might have had would have run out soon."

"I can't speak for Finn, but I'll ask him." Aidan palms the back of my neck. "Although, I'm not sure how well I'll be able to deal with you in such close proximity as him if he says yes. I'd hate to have to kill my brother because he flirted too much with you."

I breathe out a laugh. "He's harmless. His charms have no affect on me."

He growls. "You think he's charming?"

I poke him in the center of his chest. "That's not what I meant and you know it."

"Hmm, I'm not sure I do. Maybe you should show me exactly what it is you meant," his tone drops suggestively.

My pulse spikes and heat settles in my belly. An ache grows from my core and spreads through my body. Without looking away from me, Aidan manages to close the lid on the laptop and toss it toward the end of the bed. A dull thud follows.

"You probably broke it," I whisper.

"I'll buy another one." That's the last thing he says before his lips claim mine.

Every kiss brings new sensation with it. Each one swirling around inside me, spreading, until I'm consumed with nothing but need. Desire. Want. Aidan kisses me like it's the last time he'll be able to. It's too much and yet, not enough. The heavy weight of his hand caresses my spine sending shivers dancing down it before he settles it along my shoulder blade and carefully guides me to lying on my back.

He breaks the kiss and his eyes meet mine. He palms the side of my face, his fingers threading through my hair, and rubs his thumb gently along my cheekbone. His touch brings with it more heat and fire that sizzles through my veins.

"You're beautiful. I'm not sure if I've ever told you that," his voice is a gruff whisper that vibrates through me.

I flick my tongue out and further dampen already damp lips. It hadn't been intentionally seductive, by Aidan's gaze drops to them. I reach up and glide my fingertips along the contours of his forehead, nose, and jaw, the hair covering it soft. I dip one into the divot on the left side of his mouth. I meet his eyes again. "I think you're beautiful, too."

He smiles and the crater deepens. "Now you're just trying to make me blush."

I snort. "It takes more than a simple compliment to make a man like you blush."

"What kind of man do you think I am?" He quirks an eyebrow.

My muscles in my cheeks go slack as I grow serious. "A kind and generous one. A man who makes me laugh. One who's smart. Who makes me feel safe. Protected. The kind of man I'm glad I get to spend the rest of my life with. My best friend."

With every word I speak, Aidan's eyes darken, and his gaze sears into me with a burning intensity it's a surprise I don't combust. I mean it all, though. My only hope is that one day we'll find the kind of love my parents have. The kind I've witnessed between Carrick and Nora. A love I never thought I'd have, but discover I desperately want. With Aidan. I'm more than halfway there already and have been for a long time.

His lips crash down on mine and his tongue sweeps in like he's dying to taste me. I meet every thrust with my own and sink into the pleasure that crashes over me in waves. Aidan's body covers mine. My nipples grow harder, and the dull throbbing in my center grows as he settles in the cradle of my thighs. His cock hits right at my clit, and I roll my hips trying to increase the contact where I need it.

He answers by rocking his pelvis against me and swallowing my breathy moan. My fingers clutch at his hair, holding him tightly to me. I don't ever want this kiss to end. His palm covers my breast and gently kneads my flesh. I arch my back and press more fully into his touch, needing more. There's blissful pleasure as his fingers pluck the hardened tip of my nipple through my thin shirt that travels throughout me.

It's as though every nerve in my body is firing. Everything tingles and a low hum dances across every inch of my skin. I've never experienced anything like it before. Aidan's cock hits a spot that makes my toes curl. We both have far too many clothes on. As if sensing my thoughts, he reaches for the hem of my t-shirt and with some maneuvering on my part, he drags it up and over my head. My bra is gone next and I collapse into the mattress.

Aidan rises up on a single elbow and stares down at me. With a fingertip, he traces a line down my sternum and then circles my pebbled nipple. No one has studied me this closely before, and for a second I feel self-conscious enough to want to cover myself. My boobs still sit where they always have, but they're a little small in comparison to the rest of me. Except the desire in Aidan's darkened eyes tells me how much he likes what he sees.

"I've imagined you spread out beneath me more than once over the last five years." His words confirm the thought.

Pleasure flutters in my belly. "Why haven't you ever said anything?"

"Because, like you, I valued our friendship too much to fuck it up by sleeping with you. I didn't want to change anything between us. Or make it weird."

I run my fingers up his bicep, marveling at all the tattoos, and nibble my lip in uncertainty. "Is this going to change it now? More than it already has, I mean?"

Aidan takes my hand and brushes a kiss over my knuckles. "Almost nothing stays the same, but I promise you, no matter what else occurs, you will always be the best thing to ever happen to me."

That doesn't really answer my question.

"Hey," he says and I lift my eyes to meet his. "Are you okay?"

I force a smile to my lips. "Of course. How could I not be with a beautiful, half-naked man in bed with me who, I'm pretty sure, had been about to give me a mind-blowing orgasm?"

Aidan barks out a laugh. "Mind-blowing, huh?"

"Most definitely." I give a succinct nod.

"Nothing like a little pressure to help a man perform."

I pat his cheek. "I'm sure it's nothing you can't handle."

His gaze turns predatory, and any arousal that had dampened during our talk sparks back to life. The faint throbbing ache in my lower pelvis starts up. Aidan bends until his mouth grazes mine and hovers there.

"Challenge accepted," he growls low in his chest.

CHAPTER 23

Aidan

Pushing away any regard for consequences, I claim Sorcha's lips and slip my tongue in between them. Hers tangles with mine, following my lead, and I lap up the mint flavor of her toothpaste. Her kisses are as sweet and sensual as she is. I skim my fingers along her side, running over the ridges of her ribs until I palm the curve of her hip and tug her leg up. She wraps it around me and rolls her pelvis to grind against me. Damp heat soaks through the fabric of her shorts. I let her continue working herself up until I sense she's right on the edge and then draw away.

Sorcha lets out a whimper. "I was so close."

"When you come, I plan on being inside you. But before that, I'm going to have you begging," I promise.

"Is that a challenge? Maybe you'll be the one begging."

I palm her cunt, no doubt dripping with wetness, and she moans. "I beg for no one."

"Challenge accepted," she echoes my words from moments ago.

I rise onto my knees to tower over her. Eyes gone dark with arousal meet mine and I slip my fingers beneath her waistband and slowly lower the fabric that covers what I'm dying to taste. The musky scent of her arousal perfumes the air as I expose her bare cunt to my view. It glistens with wetness and my mouth waters. I toss Sorcha's shorts and underwear over the edge of the bed.

Making room between her legs, I reach down and with my thumbs, spread her wide open. I glide them along her slick flesh until I reach her clit. Her breathing speeds up and a shudder runs over her. A faint moan spills from her lips. I meet her gaze again and rub circles over the sensitive pearl. I study Sorcha's every response. How much pressure, what speed, and in which direction makes her whimper and press herself into my touch.

"Such a pretty sight. Your clit is swollen and begging for me, isn't it?" I repeat the motion that made her cry out and she repeats the sound.

"Yes." She nods shakily. "Please."

I continue playing her body with my thumb and then slide two fingers inside her. She's wet enough there's no resistance. Her cunt clamps down on them. In and out I thrust.

"Please what?" I push ever farther inside her and graze the front inner wall with my fingertips finding the soft spongy spot.

Wetness gushes out of her and Sorcha cries out. "Oh god, please. Fuck me. Please."

Sweat-dampened hair clings to her forehead and her pink nipples have darkened in color to match the flush spreading across her chest. I bend and take one in my mouth, flicking it with my tongue before trapping it agains the roof of my mouth and sucking hard. Her entire body goes rigid and she's almost ready to fly. Quickly I remove my fingers from her and come up on my knees to stare down at her.

Sorcha's entire body shakes, and she whimpers. Taking pity on her, I rip my jeans off, free my cock, and then I'm plunging deep inside her. The second my pelvis brushes against the already over-sensitized flesh of her clit, her climax hits. She fists her fingers and clenches the sheet between them. A scream rips from her throat and I cover her mouth with mine to swallow it down. I pound into her harder and harder.

"You feel so fucking good," I growl against Sorcha's lips.

Her legs clamp around my waist and she digs her heels into my ass. It spurs me on. Another orgasm washes over her. Shudders wrack her body. I don't stop. My thrusts only get faster. Deeper. I reach between us and finger her clit, forcing a third orgasm from her.

"It's too much," she whispers, her voice gravelly and rough. "Aidan, please."

Her pleading triggers my own release, and I erupt inside her with a hoarse yell. When I've finally emptied my cock, giving her everything I have, I collapse half on top of her. Sweat covers both our bodies. Our chests heave with effort to pull in air. I nuzzle my face in the crook of her neck and place soft kisses along her shoulder. A tremor wracks her body and her cunt spasms around me.

I force myself to withdraw from her and roll off the bed for the bathroom. Holding a warm, wet cloth, I come back and clean her. After tossing it in with the rest of our dirty clothes I make my way back to the bed and crawl in next to her. She cuddles into my side and rests her hand on my chest.

"I didn't hurt you, did I?" I can't help but ask.

A satisfied sound comes from her. "Only in a really good way."

I chuckle and kiss the crown of her head. "Did I meet your challenge to your satisfaction? Was that orgasm mind-blowing enough for you?"

"I think my mind exploded with those orgasms. But maybe later we'll have to try again. Just to make sure you can't do better. For research purposes and all. Besides, you still have to meet my challenge. Next time"—she palms my semi-hard cock and it twitches in her grasp—"you'll be the one begging."

She might actually be right.

Before long, Sorcha is softly snoring, and I stare up at the darkened ceiling. I lied to her. Then again, that's what I'm good at.

Because after this, nothing is going to be the same between us. She's not the kind of person who can separate her emotions from sex. It's already evident. I have nobody to blame but myself. I'm the one who told her this marriage was real between us.

God, she'd been perfect though. Every response had made my cock harder than it's ever been. Nothing had prepared me for how good it felt to be deep inside her. Sorcha fit me like a glove. One time and I'm already addicted to her. I want her again and again. She snuggles closer, as though seeking my warmth. I draw the blanket up higher and tuck it beneath her chin. She releases a contented sigh.

I close my eyes, hoping for sleep, but my mind won't quiet. Carefully, I slide out from beneath her and throw my jeans and shirt back on. Glancing over my shoulder to make sure she's still asleep, I walk out into the common room for a drink. I stop short. A lamp is on and the dim light shows Finn's already seated in one of the chairs with a drink in his hand.

"What are you doing home?" I ask quietly as I make my way to the bar.

"The last time I checked, I lived here."

I glance over my shoulder and fill my glass with whiskey. "You know what I mean. Why aren't you at the casino?"

"Needed a break for a night. Brenn is perfectly capable of taking care of things while I'm not there."

With drink in hand, I take a seat in my usual chair. "I never said he wasn't."

We sit in silence for several minutes, each of us sipping our drink.

"I still can't believe you're getting married," Finn breaks it. "You always said you never would. Not after Mother."

If not for Campbell calling my bluff, I wouldn't be. "Sorcha's my best friend. I'm doing what I have to to keep her safe."

He makes a sound I can't decipher and takes another drink. "You seemed a little jealous when you brought her to the casino."

I should have known he'd bring that up. "I wasn't jealous. Merely protective. I know how you are with women."

Finn's eyes narrow. "Not with women who are taken. I've seen what cheating does to a relationship. Do you really think I'd do something like that?"

A pinch of guilt plucks at my chest. "You're right. I'm sorry."

The quiet settles between us for another minute.

"Do you ever hate Da for what he did?" he finally asks.

I turn my head sharply in his direction. "Hate him for what? His affair with Nora?"

"For forcing Mother to marry him knowing she was in love with someone else," Finn says. "If he would have married Nora instead then maybe Mother wouldn't have hated him—hated *us*—so much."

"You forget that it was Grand-da who forced the wedding. He's the one who deserves all our hate. Beside, if Da had married Nora, none of us would have existed *for* Mother to hate. The only person who would even be here is Imogen." I take another sip of whiskey.

No one mourned when Grand-da died a decade ago. He'd been a ruthless prick who actually puts Liam Campbell to shame. At least Campbell loves Imogen enough not to kill any of us unprovoked. Unlike Grand-da who'd had our Uncle Brian murdered.

It's been twenty-three years and I've never told a soul that I was there and witnessed the whole thing. I'll take the secret to my grave. Not to protect the old bastard, but because it would break something in Da if he knew.

Finn tosses back the rest of his drink and stands. "Not that you asked, but you're not fooling anyone other than yourself. We've all seen how you look at Sorcha when you don't think anyone's watching. I know how you feel about Mother and loving someone. But don't let her keep you from what could be the best thing to ever happen to you. She made her own choices and so can you."

Without another word, he walks to the bar and places his empty glass in the sink then turns and heads down the hallway that leads to his room. I finish off my own drink and refill it before grabbing the glass and the bottle from the cabinet and bringing them both back to the chair. Finn's wrong. Whatever he thinks he sees isn't there. Or maybe I am really lying to myself. I've always been a great liar, after all.

CHAPTER 24

I HAD SEX WITH AIDAN.

Panic flutters in my chest.

Oh my god. I had *sex* with Aidan.

And not just any sex but the best I've ever had in my entire life. Taking a deep breath, I roll over. Only to find his side of the bed is empty. I reach over. The pillow beneath my hand is cold. I'm not sure if I'm relieved or disappointed. Maybe a little of both. But mostly relieved because it gives me time alone.

Except being alone only makes my mind spin with too many thoughts all at once. It's overwhelming. I need to focus on something else. Jumping from the bed, I make my way to the bathroom for a shower. There's a twinge of pain between my thighs. Aidan isn't a small man and it's been a while. There aren't a lot of options in Burtonport. And even if there were, I wouldn't have slept with any of them. The village is too small and I never had the desire to be the subject of local gossip. Of course, leaving to marry Aidan no doubt has everyone talking.

I tie my hair up to keep it from getting too wet and step under the spray of warm water letting it beat down on my back soothing some of the aches. Once I've washed up, I throw on a pair of leggings and a comfy shirt. My stomach rumbles, begging for food. Do I dare wander into the kitchen and hope I don't pass Aidan? Based on the dim light filtering into the room, it's still early. In fact, I'm not sure the sun's fully risen yet. My stomach growls again making the decision for me. I'll have to risk it. I'm starving.

The hallway is empty as I make my way through the common room and out of the wing toward the kitchen. My luck holds, because all is quiet. Even it's empty. I don't want to be presumptuous and help myself to anything. *You're marrying Aidan, and for the moment, this is your house, too. No one will care.* Right. With that, I get a few things from the fridge and search for a frying pan.

"Found you." I grab two from the cabinet and raise them up like they're some prize.

I've got potatoes cooking in one pan and eggs in the other when Nora walks in.

"Good morning," I greet her. "I hope you don't mind that I took over the kitchen this morning. I woke up starving and figured I'd help out."

"Thank you, Sorcha. Don't get me wrong, I love cooking, but it's kind of nice to have someone else prepare a meal for a change." She helps herself to something to drink.

"Well, I'm happy to help any time. I've been cooking for the boys and Aisling since my Mum died five years ago, so I understand how good it feels when someone else takes over once in a while." I stir the potatoes and eggs so neither burn.

"Is there something I can do?" Nora asks.

I wave my hand. "You just make yourself comfortable or go take care of anything you have to do."

She hesitates. "Are you sure?"

I twist at the waist to glance back at her and smile. "Positive."

"Thank you." She finishes off her juice, puts the glass in the dishwasher, and disappears. I hum while I continue cooking. Nearly everything is finished by the time the kids stroll in. I glance over at them.

"Good morning. Will one of you set the table, please?"

Aisling comes to stand at my side and I bend to kiss the crown of her head. "Did you sleep better last night?"

She nods. "A little. I still miss my fairy forest though. When will you draw it again?"

"I'll have Aidan take me into town later today and I'll look at what paint I can find. Then, maybe you and I can get started on sketching it out tomorrow, what do you think?" My days are free to be filled with whatever I want to do. A fact I'm still not used to.

"Yippee," Aisling exclaims and dances around.

Laughing, I transfer all the food into serving bowls. "All right boys, breakfast is ready. Take this into the dining room for me, will you?"

Kellen and Carson each grab a bowl and I take the two remaining ones then we head to the next room. The three of them take their seats.

"Shoot, I didn't get any drinks." I turn back to the kitchen and collide with a hard body with an "oof".

Familiar hands steady me as the woodsy smell that's quickly becoming a favorite wafts around me. Right behind it is the strong scent of whiskey. I glance up at Aidan and my lips turn down. Bloodshot eyes scan my face. His hair is rumpled like he's run his fingers through it a thousand times. He's also wearing the same clothes he had on yesterday only they're far more wrinkled.

"Are you okay?"

"Fine. Just didn't get much sleep," he says.

"Why not?" I worry my fingers together. Especially since our epic marathon fucking session last night should have exhausted him. It had me.

"Just thinking about things." With those cryptic words Aidan walks toward the kitchen. Of course, I follow. Not only because it had been my original destination any way.

"Do you want to talk about it?" I ask hesitantly.

He gets a glass from the cabinet and fills it with water from the filtering pitcher in the fridge. I stand there while he drinks the entirety of it, my stomach swirling with nerves and that heavy, uncomfortable sensation burning inside. He refills the glass and leans against the counter. Knots of anxiety tighten. Finally his eyes meet mine. "Not yet."

I swallow. "Okay. You know I'll be here when you're ready."

Aidan smiles, but as someone who knows him almost better than anyone else, it's clearly fake. He unfolds his frame and closes the distance between us until he's close enough to touch. There's a clink of glass hitting the countertop and them he palms my cheeks between both hands and presses the same comforting kiss on my forehead that I've always loved. It feels different this time. Like it's the last one he'll ever give me. Tears sting my eyes for some reason.

He draws back and stares down at me. "You're my best friend, you know that."

I lay my hands over his wrists and try to hold back the panic attack building. "You're mine, too. Always."

"I'm going to be gone for the day. Will you be okay here alone?"

"Of course," I say softly. "Besides, I won't be alone. There are plenty of people here to keep me company."

Aidan releases me and with only a brief glance he walks away. I stand there another minute, slowly breathing in and out, until I take in a long, shuddering breath and go back to what I'd come in here to do in the first place. Moving on automatic pilot, I fill four glasses with juice and, after all the practice carrying drinks at the pub, I manage to pick them all up and take them into the dining room in a single trip. Kellen, Carson, and Aisling are chattering with each other in between bites.

My appetite has vanished, but I force myself to eat a little if for nothing more than sustenance. One by one the kids finish eating.

"Take your plates to the kitchen and rinse them off before putting them in the dishwasher please."

The three of them comply and then I'm left alone. I wallow in self-pity for a short time and then stand. Whatever is going on with Aidan, I need to trust him. Maybe I'm jumping to conclusions and worrying about something that isn't even there. Straightening my shoulders, I clean the rest of the kitchen and then grab Aidan's laptop from the spot on the floor in our bedroom where it had fallen last night. It doesn't appear to have suffered any damage. I take it with me out onto the back patio and click on the first open tab.

I'm going to open that art gallery, and it's going to be incredible. Which means I need to get to work.

CHAPTER 25

AIDAN

I HADN'T SLEPT AT ALL LAST NIGHT. AT LEAST NOT UNTIL I passed out after finishing off the rest of the whiskey left in the bottle I'd pulled from the cabinet. The couple hours I did manage to get weren't near enough and only added to the headache I had from the hangover.

Once I've taken a quick shower and changed my clothes, I walk out the front door and get in my car. Seconds later, I'm on the road toward Dublin. I wind my way through the city streets and across the Liffy until I reach my destination. After finding a place to park I walk down the footpath that leads into the place I haven't visited since right after Sorcha and I met and her mother died.

The atmosphere inside the cemetery is solemn as other pedestrians make their way to their loved one's gravesite. A few stand around an open grave comforting each other. I only give them a passing glance as I continue on my way. Less than ten minutes later I stand in front of where a large marble statue bearing our family's crest towers over the neighboring markers.

I take in the newest ones in the ground at my feet. All of them have been added within the last twenty to thirty years. There's Uncle Brian, an infant daughter of Uncle Conor's, Mhamó, Grand-da, and finally, my mother. Kathleen Róisín Donnelly. The only other inscription besides her birth and death dates is "Beloved Daughter". That's it. Nothing to indicate she'd been a wife or mother or friend.

Did she even have any friends? I'd barely been ten when she died. I hadn't paid attention to that kind of thing. She cried a lot, though.

Was there ever a time when she wasn't crying? Only when she screamed how much she hated us. Hated Da. Hated her life. I'd once walked into her room to ask a question. She'd been sitting on her bed quietly sobbing. In her hands was a picture frame. She stroked it with her fingertips and whispered, "I love you and miss you so much."

The floor must have creaked under my foot, because her head snapped up. Pure hatred spewed from her eyes. She jumped from the bed—yelling at me to get out—and slapped me across the face. I turned and ran out of the room, her screams and curses following me until they only echoed inside my head.

Until that day, I'd hated her as much as she hated us. After, I pitied her for how weak and pathetic she was. How weak love had made her. I swore I would never love anyone if that's what it did to a person.

Except Da's not weak and aside from his children, there isn't anyone he loves more than Nora. Carrick Donnelly rules an entire organization. He's the most powerful man in Dublin.

Maybe I'm the weak one. The one who lets fear rule me.

I stare down at my mother's gravestone. Will mine, one day, read nothing more than "Beloved Son"?

Turning, I walk back to my car. Once I get behind the wheel, I make a couple phone calls.

∼

I DRIVE THROUGH THE IRON GATE OF THE ESTATE AND down the lane toward the manor. The late afternoon sun hides behind the shade of the trees. A few rays of light filter through casting long shadows across the sprawling landscape. I reach the house and park. For a few minutes, I sit there, staring at the front door. The second I cross the threshold, there's no turning back.

Taking a deep breath, I exit, stride forward, and step into the entryway. The faint sound of the boys' voices drift in from the left. I follow it to the common area where the two of them are engaged in a battle on the television screen. They yell out commands to each other and their fingers press wildly on the buttons and knobs of their controllers. Neither of them even glance over at me, too engrossed in their game.

I make my way down the hallway into my bedroom only to find it empty. I'm not sure why I expected otherwise? *Did you really think Sorcha would be sitting here just waiting for you to come back?* I shake my head at the idiocy and go back the way I came. Next, I check Aisling's room. It's just as empty.

The library is quiet as usual. Finally, I walk through the dining room and movement outside catches my eye. I stand at the door and my gaze lands on Sorcha and Aisling. They're sitting at the table, their heads bent close, with paper strewn in front of them. The young girl points at the sheet in front of her older sister and Sorcha's hand moves, the pencil gripped between her fingers moving with it.

I step outside. Sorcha notices me first. Her head jerks up and our eyes meet. Pure happiness radiates from them, but flashes of fear and worry accompany it. I hate that my leaving this morning caused that. She nudges Aisling who whips around. Her smile lights up her face and she rushes over and grabs my hand, nearly dragging me back to the table.

"Aidan, come look what we're drawing. It's a new fairy forest," she squeals in excitement.

I let her pull me over so I can study the art Sorcha's creating. Good Christ, she's talented. It's no wonder Aisling desperately wants her forest back in her room. I study the image in front of me and I can almost imagine I'm there, standing within the trees, smelling the air filled with the scent of flowers and dirt and nature. I can picture the fairies flitting from limb to limb, their iridescent wings sparkling in the black of night.

My eyes meet Sorcha's. "It's stunning. Although that is almost too pale of a word to use."

A flush rises in her cheeks. "Thank you."

I glance at Aisling and back to Sorcha. "Can we talk?"

She swallows. "Of course. Here, take these to your room, please" —she rises and gathers up all the paper in a neat stack and hands it to her sister—"and we'll work on them again later, okay?"

"Bye, Aidan," Aisling says before disappearing into the house.

Sorcha's turns her gaze back to me. Her body is rigid as if she's waiting for a blow.

"Will you take a drive with me into the city?"

She blinks, clearly surprised at the request and nods. "Let me send a quick text to the boys letting them know."

Once she's done that, she passes me on her way to the door. I take her hand and thread my fingers through hers. She startles, but doesn't pull away. Instead, one side of her mouth curls up just slightly in a small half-smile. I'll take it. We get to the car and I'm forced to release her, but the minute we're both seated and driving back into Dublin, her hand is within mine.

I can sense her wanting to ask about this morning, but she doesn't. The only sound is the song coming through the speakers. We ride in silence. Every so often, I squeeze her hand gently. Finally, we come to a stop on a quiet, but frequented-by-locals street in front of a small, two-story building bookended on one side by a bookstore and a popular bakery on the other.

Sorcha sends me a questioning glance when I turn the car off. I just grin and exit the car. Seconds later, her door closes and she rounds the front to stand next to me.

"What is this place?" she finally breaks the silence.

"You'll see." I can't help tease her.

I reach into my pocket, insert the key in the door, and open it. Then I glance over my shoulder. "You coming?"

Sorcha strides forward and follows me inside. I walk over to one wall and flip on the light. The concrete floor is bare and a little dusty. The tall ceiling is fitted with black rafters and exposed black duct-work. White tubed light covers dangle at random intervals, each one bright and shining with brand new bulbs. The cavernous space echoes with Sorcha's footsteps as she gawks from one side of the room to another, slowly pivoting in a circle and taking everything in.

Her chin tips down and she meets my gaze. "This place is lovely. But I'm not sure what we're doing here."

I close the distance between us and reach for her hand, using my thumb to open her palm where I drop the key in it. Sorcha's head jerks up and confusion is written across her face.

"It's yours. If you want it," I tell her.

"Mine?"

"For your gallery."

Her eyes widen and then fill with tears. "Oh, Aidan."

"I'm sorry for leaving and being weird this morning. Especially after last night." I cradle her jaw. "It was nothing to do with you. It was me and my need to let go of the past."

Sorcha lays her hand over mine. "I was worried you regretted it."

"Not at all. I just needed to take care of a few things."

"Did you get them taken care of?" she asks.

I take her hand and kiss her knuckles. "I'm working on it. But while I get my shit together, what do you think? Should we buy the place as a wedding gift to ourselves?"

Sorcha laughs. "To ourselves, huh?"

"Why not? If you can't buy gifts for yourself, who can you buy them for?" I smirk. "Besides isn't there something in the wedding vows about what's mine is yours and what's yours is mine?"

"I don't think that's in the actual vows." She rolls her eyes and walks through the open space taking it all in.

"There's an upstairs that can be used for storage if we need it. Or we can extend the small space in the back that's already there." I gesture in that direction. "You could even make the upstairs into a special events area where you showcase a single artist's work or throw a fancy party."

Sorcha faces me. "You've thought a lot about this, haven't you?"

I close the distance between us and take both her hands in mine. "I know I've asked a lot of you, what with the whole marriage and moving to Dublin, thing. I want you to be happy."

She places her hand on my chest and rises up on tiptoe to kiss me. "I *am* happy. As long as I still have you in my life, I'll be happy."

Her words settle deep in my chest, warming it. I claim her lips with mine, curling my hand around her hip, and tugging her to me. There's no rushing. It's a sweet, perfect kiss. I draw back and press my forehead to Sorcha's. "You make me happy, too."

I reach into my pocket and pull out the small, square velvet box. Sorcha sucks in a breath.

"Do you remember what you asked me to do?" I take out the platinum band with its large round diamond in the center surrounded by emerald accents.

She clears her throat before she can speak. "I asked you not to rule out the possibility of falling in love with me." Still it comes out in a hushed voice.

Taking her trembling hand in mine, I slide the ring down her third finger. "I think it's very possible I already am. Sorcha O'Connell, will you marry me? Not because of any debt or blackmail. But because you're the person I want to spend my life with."

It's not the pretty words every woman wants to hear, but I'm doing my best to open myself up to possibilities. To her. To love. I hold my breath waiting for her to choose me. To choose us.

"Yes."

CHAPTER 26

SORCHA

ONCE AIDAN PROPOSED, WE DECIDED NOT TO WAIT. I mean, when it's the right person, what's the point? Five days after he gave me the best wedding present ever, we're getting married. It's a perfect day for it, too. The gods must be looking down on us and smiling, because the sun is shining brightly in the sky and there's not a single cloud. A rarity in Dublin this time of year.

Caitlín, Nessa, and Lucia had rallied together and with whirlwind speed had a small but adorable venue booked. I would have been happy to have it in the backyard at the manor, but since Liam has refused to step foot on Donnelly property again, it wasn't an option. Nessa told me he'd only done it the one time for Imogen's sake.

The three women had also helped me pick out a dress, flowers, and took care of getting the food for the reception. They even hired a photographer to take some pictures. Although it's only family present, there are still nearly twenty people. That's also counting Aidan and me.

"Aidan is going to want to rip this dress off you the minute you head down the aisle," Caitlín says with an appreciative whistle.

"Let's hope he at least waits until he has her alone." Nessa giggles.

Despite Caitlín still pinning back my hair, I turn in my seat to face the two of them. "Thank you both for being here and standing up with me. I don't really have any girlfriends left and both of you have been so warm and welcoming."

"That's what family is for. Besides, my sister and best friend are halfway across the world. It's nice having sisters here," Caitlín says. "Even if technically we're cousins-in-law."

"I grew up an only child with a shitty Da. Imogen and I are slowly becoming friends, but it's been a challenge. I'm sure because Cian and Liam hate each other. It can't be easy for her to be caught in the middle." Nessa sighs. Does she not realize she's caught there, too?

The wedding ceremony is going to be interesting with everyone, including Liam, in attendance. Aidan had personally invited Imogen and him, although the latter with great reluctance. But he said he knew that if Liam wasn't allowed to come, then his sister wouldn't attend either. I'd been introduced to her when the two of them arrived. They couldn't have been more different. Liam wore a dark, pin-striped suit that showed off his massive build, and his rough and craggy face spoke of someone who'd live a rough life. Imogen, on the other hand, resembled the lead singer of a goth band with her black and white skull dress and the purple and teal streaks throughout her black hair.

"I'm glad they could come. Aidan wouldn't want his sister to miss his wedding. I'm sure everyone can behave themselves for a couple hours," I say.

Nessa and Caitlín exchange disbelieving glances. There's a knock on the door and Aisling skips into the room.

"I brought the flowers." She holds up the basket filled with rose petals nearly spilling some of them in her excitement.

"Look at how pretty you are," I gush.

The white dress with its flared tulle skirt and wide Kelly green ribbon around the waist that ties into a giant bow at the back had been adorable when she'd tried it on. With her hair combed and styled in loose curls, she's the perfect flower girl.

"I'm ready to throw them." Aisling nearly vibrates with giddiness.

"I know you are, but it's not time yet." I face the mirror and meet Caitlín's eyes with a smile and she goes back to putting the finishing touches on my hair.

Nessa calls my sister over and the two of them talk and giggle. Butterflies have been swarming around in my stomach all day. Today I become Aidan's wife. Something I never dreamed possible. The past five days have been surreal. We've both been so busy during the day that we barely saw each other. But the nights? The nights have been incredible.

The first time we'd had sex, it had been fucking. Since he proposed, and although he didn't actually say he loved me, he's made love to me like he does. And while him admitting that he *thinks* he's falling in love with me might not be enough for another woman, it is for me. I've always judged a person on their actions more than their words, and everything Aidan has done over the last few weeks—god, the last five years—tells me he loves me. I can be patient.

"All done," Caitlín announces.

I stare at myself in the mirror. She's pinned the sides back in loose twists and left the rest to cascade down in long waves. My makeup is light and natural with a pale pink lip gloss that shines, but doesn't look wet. Taking a deep breath, I stand and turn to face the three of them. "How do I look?"

"Absolutely stunning," Caitlín breathes out in awe while Nessa and Aisling nod their heads with eyes wide and mouths gaped.

There's a narrow full-length mirror attached to the back of the door and I walk over to it to study myself. My dress is a simple, but beautiful A-line with a sharp V-neckline that shows the perfect amount of cleavage. The asymmetrical skirt is a triple-layered satin that's shorter in the front before lengthening and billowing out around the back. I turn around and twist at the waist to glance over my shoulder. The straps are almost a halter, except they form an X centered right between my shoulder blades exposing my lower back in the triangle-shaped opening. There aren't any other embellishments. The minute I laid eyes on it, my gut told me it was the one.

For the second time, there's a knock on the door. Caitlín goes to answer it. On the other side is Carrick.

"The priest is here and everyone's in their places whenever you ladies are ready," he tells her after a brief kiss on the cheek.

She turns back to me with a huge smile. "You ready to put that ball and chain on my cousin?"

I snort and burst out laughing. "I'm ready."

With Aisling skipping between them, Caitlín and Nessa head to the small suite where the ceremony will take place. Carrick turns toward me with a soft smile that changes his face entirely. He isn't the head of the Irish mafia today. He's the father whose son is getting married and the father-figure who is walking me down the aisle.

He takes both my hands. "You look beautiful. I'm so happy for you and Aidan and I'm proud to call you daughter."

Tears well at his kind words. But they're also a reminder that neither Mum nor Da are here to see me get married. Da had always liked Aidan.

"Thank you, Carrick. Not just for welcoming me as part of your family, but for raising such an amazing son."

"I wish you both a lifetime of happiness." He loops my hand around his elbow and leads me to where everyone—where Aidan —awaits.

The sound of music reaches me through the closed doors of the room and we stop in front of them. Two ushers who work for the venue stand on either side of it. Carrick lays his hand over mine and squeezes it gently. I swallow at the sudden rush of emotion. We stand there for several minutes until finally the song changes and that's our cue. The two men each grab a handle and pull apart the double doors.

Heads turn and then we're slowly moving forward. Both our families are seated in chairs that are placed on two sides of the room forming an aisle in between both sections. At the head of it stands Caitlín, Nessa, and Aisling on the left. To the right are Kellen and Carson who both nearly cried when Aidan asked them to stand up with him. And directly in the center, just in front of the priest, is Aidan. Our gazes lock and neither of us can look away as his Da and I draw closer.

Even from this distance, love shines from his eyes. I feel it deep inside me. No one has ever looked at me like this. I suspect it's the same way I'm looking at him. My heart is full to bursting. It takes far too long, although it's only a minute, but finally, Carrick and I stop next to Aidan. The priest speaks but it's nothing but a buzzing in my ears. All I can focus on is the man in front of me.

There's a soft tug on my arm as Carrick releases my hold on him. He ghosts a kiss across my cheek and then Aidan's strong, calloused hands are wrapped around mine and he brings both sets of knuckles up to his mouth for a soft and gentle kiss.

The priest speaks again, and somehow, I manage to give all the appropriate responses at the right time. Then he faces Aidan.

"Do you have the ring?"

Aidan lets go of my hands and turns to Kellen behind him, who passes him the plain platinum band. Then he's facing me again and taking my left hand.

"You may place the ring on Sorcha's finger and speak your vows now," the priest instructs.

I blink. We were supposed to have our own vows? Mild panic rises, but then it's soothed away by Aidan's voice.

"Sorcha Noreen O'Connell. You've been my best friend. My confidante. My lover. Now, you'll be my wife. The woman I plan on spending the rest of my life honoring, cherishing"—he pauses, a bright light shining from his eyes, and slowly releases a breath as he slides the band in place—"and loving to the best of my ability. Thank you for never giving up on me. I'll do everything in my power to make sure that every day you know how much I care for you. How much I love you. I'm sorry it took so long for me to realize."

I take in a shuddering breath and barely hold back my sob. Tears streak down my cheeks.

"Sorcha would you like to make a vow?" the priest asks, as though he knew ahead of time that I hadn't prepared one.

Except it doesn't matter, because as soon as Caitlín gives me the ring, I speak from my heart. "Aidan Brian Donnelly. Five years ago you saved me. Not just from a bad situation, but from grief. You've been there for me through everything, never wavering in your friendship and support. From that first moment I've loved you and only dreamed that one day you might love me, too. Thank you for making all my dreams come true."

The priest says a final prayer and then, "I now pronounce you man and wife. You may kiss your bride."

Aidan doesn't waste a single second before he palms my cheeks and his lips are on mine. Cheers and clapping echo around us, but the only thing I care about is my husband. Oh my god. Aidan is my husband. Joyous laughter spills from me. He draws away and our eyes meet.

"Wife," he says in a gruff tone.

"Husband."

Aidan threads his fingers through mine and turns us to face our family. Everyone is on their feet whistling and celebrating. The music plays and we step down off the slightly raised dais to walk toward our future. The music is drowned out by a massive boom. The floor shakes.

Confusion is on several faces, but the men's expressions turn fierce and they all share intense glances. Heads swivel like we're all searching for the source of the noise, when there's another explosion and everything around us turns into chaos as the walls collapse with a deafening boom.

CHAPTER 27

Gunfire rings out as debris falls from the ceiling.

"Everybody down," a gruff voice yells out that sounds like Da's.

Sorcha's hand is ripped from mine and she falls to the ground. I scream her name and cover her body as I cough on the dust, and smoke fills my lungs. Children are screaming as more *popping* sounds reverberate around us.

I can still make out shadowy figures. My attention turns to my wife lying still beneath me. I can only pray someone doesn't shoot me in the back.

"Sorcha, baby, look at me." I carefully run my hands over her, searching for a wound.

Blood stains her dress. My hands shake as I shove all the fabric up and out of the way, my heart beating like a drum, and fear like I've never experienced before swells inside me. I can't breathe from it. There's a bullet wound along her upper thigh, although it only appears to have grazed her. She groans and shifts. I search her again and find a large bump on the back of her head.

Roars of pain join the whimpers and cries around us and bodies fall. Fuck. I reach for the ankle holster under my pants and pull out my weapon. Finally the smoke begins to clear giving me a better view of my surroundings. Concrete walls lay crumbled around the perimeter.

The gunfire slows until only a deathly silence fills the air.

"Throw down your weapons or I will kill her," a heavily Arabic accented man breaks it.

I search the room. The women are huddled on the floor protecting the weeping children. Dead bodies—enemies—lie in crumpled heaps. My brothers, Da, Roarke, and Nathan are all standing with their weapons pointed toward where the doors leading into the suite used to be. Several armed Moroccans—none of them Ayman Naji—flank the man in the center, whose arm is wrapped around Imogen's neck and who's holding a gun to her head. Fear lines her face and her eyes are locked on Liam who faces them with his own gun raised. His other arm hangs loosely at his side and blood drips off his fingertips and falls to the floor in a puddle at his feet. I don't have a clean shot and I don't want to move and set off any itchy trigger fingers.

"I said throw down your weapons," the man holding Imogen roars again.

"Not a chance. If you hurt her, you're a dead man. You're all dead," Liam says in a harsh tone.

"My men are closing in as we speak," Da warns, pain etched on his face. "You have nowhere to go."

I study him and spot the blood soaking through his shirt. How bad is it?

The Moroccans exchange glances, as though they're trying to decide whether or not to believe Da. They converse in Arabic until the man holding Imogen slowly backs up, his hold on her not loosening an inch as he brings her with him. The men behind him follow suit, their weapons still trained on all of us.

My family moves as a single unit forward, no one taking their eyes off our retreating enemies. At my feet, Sorcha groans again.

"Aidan," she whimpers.

There's no decision to make. I let Da and the rest take care of things and I drop to my knees next to my wife.

"I'm here, baby. I'm here," I reassure Sorcha, caressing her face and brushing her hair back, taking care to avoid the lump on her head.

Her eyelashes flutter and slowly open. Her pupils are dilated and she blinks rapidly as though she's having trouble focusing. Finally, she's able to lock onto me.

"Wha—what happened?" She tries to sit up and whimpers in pain.

"Careful. A bullet grazed you."

Her head snaps up and she clutches the side of it. "God, my head is killing me. This is worse than any hangover I've ever had."

I carefully lay my hand on top of hers. "You probably have a concussion."

Several shots are fired outside somewhere followed by sharp commands in both English and Arabic. Sorcha jumps. As if remembering where we are, she cries out. "The kids."

Quickly, I scan the room again and find them. Kellen and Carson —whose faces are deathly white—have their arms wrapped around each other. Within their embrace is Aisling, her face equally as pale. Caitlín and Nora guard all three of them with their bodies, both of them staring where their men disappeared.

"They're okay. Caitlín and Nora have them."

On the other side of the room, Nessa and Lucia are protecting her three children. Rubble outside shifts and footsteps approach. Faint sirens blare in the distance. I jump to my feet, gun arm outstretched, ready to defend my wife and our family. Da steps over the pile of rubble—his gaze searching and landing on Nora—slowly followed by Finn, then Nathan and Cian who both head straight for their families, and Roarke who crosses over to Caitlín.

Kellen, Carson, and Aisling run over to us, and I quickly shove the weapon into my waistband at the small of my back under my jacket. A sobbing Aisling throws herself against Sorcha, who hisses in pain, but cradles the little girl in her arms, rocking her with soothing words. The boys cling to me and I bend to pull them tighter against me.

A noise brings my head up. Liam enters with Imogen tucked closely against his side. Rage radiates from him and while she's not crying, there's an eerie stillness to her despite being upright and walking. They come to a stop in the middle of the room.

"Is everyone okay?" Da asks with Nora still in his arms.

Murmurs of assent ripple through the air. I glance down at the boys, who finally release me, but stay close enough to touch.

"Are you two okay?"

They nod their heads shakily, their ashen faces slowly gaining color. I crouch down again and stroke Aisling's hair. "Hey little nightmare. You're not hurt anywhere are you?"

She buries her face in Sorcha's neck and shakes her head. I can tell my wife is in pain, but she won't say anything. Outside, the sirens grow louder.

"Aisling," I say softly, trying to soothe her fear. "Sorcha's leg is hurt. There's going to be some people arriving soon that are going to help, but they'll need to look at her so they can make her feel better. Can I hold you while they do that? I promise it's going to be okay."

Slowly, she loosens her hold on her sister. Her eyes are swollen and her face is flushed as she stares up at me. I smile gently and carefully brush her curls back and tuck her hair behind her ear. The sirens blare loudly directly outside and pounding footsteps approach. Da, Roarke, and my brothers form a protective barrier in front of everyone just to be safe, but when the paramedics and Gardaí step across the rubble, they lose some of their rigidity.

"Come on, let's give them some room to take care of Sorcha,

okay?"

Aisling raises her arms and I pick her up. She wraps all her limbs around me and lays her head on my shoulder. Kellen and Carson stay glued to my side as I take a few steps back and let the men I gesture over do what they need to do. I keep close watch on her though, needing to reassure myself Sorcha's going to be okay. It may be a while before I let her leave my sight.

Da reaches my side. He fusses over the boys, checking to make sure they're not hurt and then glances up at me. Grief shows heavily on his face as his eyes lands on Aisling. Then they meet mine.

"How's Sorcha?" His gaze drifts over to her.

"Her leg was grazed and it's bleeding some, but I'm not sure if it'll need stitches or not. Also some of the falling debris knocked her unconscious. I'm sure she has a concussion, but she'll be okay." I glance at his shoulder. "How bad is it?"

He waves me off. "I'll live. Finn and Cian are unscathed, but Liam took a bullet to the arm."

"And Imogen?"

Da's gaze lands on his daughter whose eyes are no longer dull. She doesn't appear to be in shock anymore. Instead she's fussing over Liam while the paramedics treat him. He may need to go to the hospital, unless he has a private physician that does home visits.

"She's a Donnelly," he says as if that explains everything. And it does. We're all stronger than anyone thinks. Stubborn too.

"What about the Moroccans?"

He darts a glance between the boys and Aisling's back before he turns back to me. "Several of them got away."

I nod. Even if they hadn't, Da wouldn't let this attack on his family go unpunished. If the Moroccans want a war, then they've got one. I glance at Liam again. After this, where does he stand?

The paramedics have bandaged the flesh wound on Sorcha's thigh and after a brief discussion that I can't make out, she waves them off. Da claps me on the shoulder.

"Go take care of your wife."

He walks toward Nora, but is waylaid by the Gardaí. I take Aisling over to Sorcha. The boys are right on my heels. We reach her and she gingerly stands, wincing slightly. She fusses over them, cradling their faces and running her hands over their bodies like they were injured instead of her. They let her, probably knowing she needs it. The three of them probably do, too. Just as much as she does.

"What did they say?" Whatever their instructions, I'll make sure she follows them.

"They cleaned my leg and bandaged it. They said that if I have any headaches or blurred vision to schedule a visit with my GP."

With Aisling still clinging to me, I wrap an arm around Sorcha's waist and pull her against my side. She's a bit slow to move, limping the step closer to me. "I'm going to take you all home. Da will deal with things here."

She nods quietly. I reach for her hand and we carefully weave our way through the mess until we reach outside. The road is blocked by the ambulances, the fire brigade, and more Gardaí. My car is parked a few spaces down and luckily escaped any damage. Everyone climbs inside.

On the drive home, no one speaks. The quiet is louder than any voices. Sorcha is turned away from me and stares out the window. I glance in the rearview mirror and Aisling sits between her brothers with her head resting on Kellen's arm. Carson holds her hand. I've never felt pure unadulterated fear like I did today. If I hadn't been sure I loved Sorcha before, I am after this. I'd be lost if anything ever happened to her.

Needing to reassure myself she's here with me and safe, I reach over for her hand and thread my fingers through hers. Anytime I do this, she always glances over at me with a smile. But she keeps her head turned so only her profile is visible. I rub my thumb up and down hers in a soothing gesture. I'm sure everything's been a shock to her. Once she has time to rest she'll feel better.

I ignore the voice whispering that I'm lying to myself.

CHAPTER 28

I CAN SENSE AIDAN'S ATTENTION ON ME. MY HEAD POUNDS
and the wound on my leg burns. Fear still flows through my veins. So
much so that I am barely managing to keep it together. The pressure
bearing down on my chest makes it hard to breathe. All I want to do
is grab Kellen, Carson, and Aisling and run as far away from Dublin
as I can.

That means running away from Aidan.

An hour ago, I would have scolded myself for such thoughts.
Except they won't stop.

The kids are all quiet and I take a few glances back at them,
making sure they're okay. Jesus, how much therapy are they going to
need after this? How much am *I* going to need? I breathe through
the panic that is starting to take hold, centering myself. *You're okay.
It's okay.*

It takes far too long before we finally drive past the gate and park
in front of the manor. Being careful, I get out and open the back

door for Kellen and Aisling. Carson gets out on Aidan's side. The kids are a mess. The boys' suits are covered in dust as is Aisling's beautiful dress. I glance down at myself and nearly sob. A crimson misshapen stain covers a section of the skirt. *That's never coming clean.* Hysterical laughter threatens to bubble up, but I choke it down because right behind it is a meltdown waiting to be set free.

Aidan reaches for my hand, but I brush past him with Aisling. I just can't. If he touches me, I might shatter. He catches up with us and opens the door. For the second time, I stride past him and head straight upstairs to the boys' rooms.

"Where are you going?" Aidan's voice stops me, and I pause on the second step, forcing myself to glance back at him. There's confusion and worry written across his face, but I harden my heart against it.

"We were all just in the middle of a building exploding around us and a gun battle," my voice rises in pitch and I take a deep breath to calm down. "I'm taking my brothers to their rooms to make sure they're okay and that they're taken care of. They also need to get cleaned up. As does Aisling. Unlike you, we aren't used to being almost killed."

Aidan flinches, but I'm not a single bit guilty. I turn and climb the rest of the steps still holding Aisling's hand. Footsteps follow behind me after only a brief hesitation. All four of us enter Kellen's room and I close the door behind us, effectively shutting Aidan out. Kellen and Carson sit on the edge of the bed with their hands in their laps and I carefully sit in the chair, pulling Aisling on my lap, taking care to avoid my leg wound. She leans against me and rests her head on my shoulder.

I'd love nothing more than to crawl into bed and drag the blankets over my head, but for better or for worse, I'm their parent and their needs come before mine.

"Are you all okay?" I ask for probably the hundredth time.

The twins nod. Aisling does as well.

Kellen fidgets. "Are *you* okay?"

Not even close. "I will be."

"Who were those guys?" Kellen asks. Carson sits still and quiet at his side.

"I don't know."

There's a long pause and then Kellen speaks up again. "Are you mad at Aidan?"

My immediate reaction is to lie, but we've all been lied to enough. "Yes."

"Why?" Carson finally asks.

"Because he put you three in danger. What if any of you had been hurt today? I'd be devastated if I lost one of you." The tears I hadn't managed to shed yet spill down my cheeks. "You're my baby brothers and my baby sister. I love you all so much."

Kellen and Carson rise from the bed and come over to wrap their arms around Aisling and me. The four of us sit together for several minutes holding each other. Finally, the boys let loose of me. I nudge Aisling and she scoots off me and I slowly stand, gritting my teeth at the pain.

"If you're both all right for now, why don't you get cleaned up. Take a shower and put on some clean clothes. Then how about later you come down to the common room and the four of us will watch a movie if you're feeling up to it."

They both say "Okay."

I kiss them both on the tops of their heads, and then run my hand over Aisling's hair. "Come on, little nightmare. Let's go downstairs and get cleaned up as well."

Before I walk out the door, I turn to them. "If you need anything, just holler."

They nod and then Aisling and I walk out of their room. Aidan waits out in the hallway. I move right past him, but he claps my arm to stop me. I go rigid, but he doesn't loosen his light grip.

"Will you please talk to me?"

I shake my head. "I can't right now."

Whatever he sees on my face has him letting me go. Aisling and I move forward and down the stairs, not stopping until we get to her room. Should I be worried that she hasn't spoken since we left the venue? I don't want to push her to talk if she's not feeling up to it.

"Lets get you out of this dress and all cleaned up." Maybe if I keep busy I won't have a breakdown. If only my headache would go away.

Aisling lets me tug it over her head. Her hair is dusty as is the rest of her body that hadn't been covered. I turn on the water and adjust the temperature. When I'm satisfied, I guide her forward with a hand between her shoulder blades.

"In you go."

Together we get her cleaned up including two washes of her hair and then I help her put on her pajamas. I comb out her hair and braid it to help it from tangling when she sleeps. Then I turn her to face me and kneel down in front of her. I brush the wisps of baby hair across her forehead.

"I know today was really scary, and if you want to talk about it, I'm here to listen."

There's a long enough pause that I worry Aisling won't speak to me. But finally she answers. "Why did those bad men try to hurt us?" Her question is spoken in barely above a whisper.

She adores Aidan, and while I may be furious and disappointment in him at the moment, I don't want her to be. She won't understand. Maybe when she gets older. "Some bad people don't need a reason. They just hurt people because they can, and no one knows why."

Aisling's eyes shimmer with tears. "Will the bad men try and hurt us again?"

She asks the one question to which the answer is my greatest fear.

"I'll keep you safe, I promise." Even as I say the words, they resonate through me. I swear I'll keep her, Kellen, and Carson safe even if that means leaving here. No matter how much I love Aidan, the children have to come first. He should understand that.

"Hey, why don't you lay down for a little bit while I get cleaned up too. Then, I'll crawl into bed with you and we'll go back to working on our fairy forest sketch. What do you say?" I give her an encouraging smile, hoping it eases some of her fears.

"Okay," Aisling says quietly.

I take her hand and we walk out of the bathroom and I help her climb into her bed. Once she's settled I kiss her forehead. "Will you be okay while I run to my room to get my own pajamas?"

She nods.

"I'll be right back." I hurry out of the room and pray I don't run into Aidan. I'm not sure I can even look at him yet.

Thankfully both the common area and our bedroom are empty. I grab a clean pair of underwear, a pair of shorts, and shirt and hurry back to Aisling's room. She's still sitting upright in bed, but she jumps when I step into the room. I head for the bathroom and take the quickest shower I've probably ever taken. After I'm done, I hurriedly get dressed so I can get back into the bedroom.

Before I reach the bed, I snag the stack of drawings we've been working on off the desk, along with the charcoal pencils, and her lapdesk, and I settle in beside her.

"What do you think? Do we need more fairies this time?" I glance down at her.

Aisling lays her head against my shoulder. "I like fairies."

"More fairies it is then."

I pick up the pencil and one of the drawings and get to work.

CHAPTER 29

AIDAN

IT'S BEEN HOURS SINCE OUR WEDDING. I'VE CHECKED ON the boys several times. Neither have left Kellen's room and they'd been subdued with each visit. I brought them something to eat earlier since we missed the reception. Same with Sorcha and Aisling, although I left it on a tray outside Aisling's room, knocked on the door, and walked away. As much as it's killing me, I'm giving Sorcha a little space. The expression on her face when she refused to talk to me will haunt me. I'm losing her. I feel it in my soul.

Da, Cian, and Finn should be here any minute They spent this entire time dealing with the Gardaí and news reporters. It's been on television half the day. The door to Da's office opens and he strides in with my brothers trailing behind. They haven't even had a chance to get cleaned up. Right behind them is Nathan and Roarke. It doesn't surprise me that we're having a meeting. What does surprise me is the fact Liam—whose arm is in a sling—brings up the rear. What the fuck is he doing here?

"Everyone take a seat." Behind his desk, Da gestures at the various chairs laid out around the room.

I remain in mine near the bookshelf, while Cian takes his usual near Da's desk, Finn and Roarke sit near the sliding glass door like always, and Nathan sits on the sofa. Campbell remains stiff and standing near the door. From the expression on his face he'd rather be anywhere but here. Da glares at him, but Liam only glares back almost daring Da to say something.

Giving up arguing, Da sits in his own chair and glances at me. "Before we get started, how are the kids? Sorcha?"

I'm not keen on airing my personal business in front of Campbell, but it's clear he's not going anywhere. "The boys have been pretty quiet, but they seem to be handling everything as well as can be expected. I haven't seen Sorcha or Aisling since we returned home. My wife is avoiding me. She's freaked out. Pissed. Terrified. Everything you'd expect from someone who nearly died or whose children could have."

Da grimaces and sympathy lines his face. "I'm sorry. Today's attack took us all by surprise, even though it shouldn't have. I take the blame for it. I knew Naji has been threatening revenge against us. We've been watching him, but apparently not close enough."

"You're not entirely to blame." I turn from him and pierce Liam with a hate-filled glare. "You're the one who's allowed the Moroccans to smuggle weapons in through the port. If you weren't such a cunt, and cut off our own weapon supply, or at least not allowed *our enemies* to import them, then maybe this wouldn't have happened. Even your *Da* didn't deal with the Moroccans."

Campbell's face reddens and his fist clenches at his side. If he had a gun in his hand, he'd shoot me without hesitation. Calling Dónal Sheehan his Da triggers Liam's rage more than anything else. No one in the room contradicts my claim though. Everyone here, Liam included, knows I'm right.

"Regardless of whose fault it is or isn't, Ayman Naji has increased his weapon's stores over the last few months and after today, we know that he will continue seeking his revenge," Cian says. "His men confirmed it before they got away. This has been a declaration of war and we need all the soldiers we can get. Which is why Liam is here."

I stare at my brother. He can't be serious. I glance around the room. No one's surprised by this announcement. My gaze shifts to Da. "You're fucking kidding, right? For the last two months, this bastard has done everything he can to undermine our organization. Before that, he was bent on destroying it. Now we're suddenly supposed to trust him. Maybe he's working with Naji. I wouldn't put it past him. He can cast all the blame on them for killing us all so Imogen won't discover what a piece of shite he is."

"I'll kill you myself," Liam charges me with a roar.

I jump to my feet and surge forward to meet him head-on. Roarke and Cian burst from their seats to hold both of us back. I jab my finger in Campbell's direction over Cian's shoulder, not breaking eye contact with him.

"If you would have just let me pay off Sorcha's loan, she wouldn't have been hurt today. You're to fucking blame for this." Spittle flies from my mouth.

"I did you a favor," Liam growls and then, one-handed, pushes Roarke away. "Get off me."

"A favor?" I lunge again, but Cian's body weight restrains me. "My wife could have died because of you. Imogen, too. Or maybe you don't care about that."

He goes rigid and for a second I'm sure he's about to rush me for a second time. Instead, he remains where he is, his death glare searing into me as he straightens his suit jacket as best he can. He grimaces. "Fuck you."

The raging storm inside me calms by a fraction and I stop trying to barrel past Cian. He slowly loosens his hold on me.

"Look at me," he demands.

I glare at Campbell another second and then move my gaze to my brother. He grabs both sides of my head and gets in my face. "He owes us a life debt."

How?

Cian must see the question in my eyes. "I'm the one who shot the man holding Imogen. He was going to kill her."

A sick sense of glee rises up inside me. My lips twitch. God, it must be killing Campbell to know that he owes Cian—our family—a life debt. Serves the bastard right. It doesn't mean I'll ever forgive him for putting Sorcha and the kids in danger in the first place. But at least Liam's getting what's been coming to him. Cian's grip on my head tightens and he gently shakes it bringing me back to him. I nod and he slowly releases me.

He steps away and we both return to our seats. Roarke's already seated. I don't stop glaring at Liam though. *Prick.*

Da clears his throat. "Now that we've all settled down, we need to get back to business. Liam will be buying up the other two small shipping companies that operate at the docks so we have complete control over every shipment that comes in or goes out. Nathan will be reaching out to our German suppliers and all imports will resume. For the time being, we also plan on taking a financial cut and purchasing our cargo at a slightly higher price than they're selling to the Moroccans."

His gaze travels over us emphasizing his point. "Nathan is also going to reach out to both Emilio and Jack and arrange a...meeting with their contacts in the States to discuss an acquisitions deal with any of them. If the Moroccans want a war, then we will give them one."

"In the meantime," Finn adds, "we're going to borrow Imogen's hacking skills to get all the information we can on Ayman Naji. Bank records. Real estate holdings. We'll find all the Moroccan's hideouts and take them out one by one, drilling away at their defenses until they have none left."

Da rises. "Everyone get some rest. We'll meet at the casino tomorrow night at midnight."

He's barely finished speaking when Liam whips around and marches out of the office. Moments later the front door slams shut.

"Prick," I spit.

Everybody filters out of the room. I'm almost to the door when Da's voice stops me. "You. Stay."

Slowly I pivot.

"Have a seat." He gestures to the chair Cian just vacated.

With a sigh, I settle back in. I'm not in the mood for a goddamn lecture. I just want to find my wife and fix this thing between us. Da sits down as well and leans his forearms on the desk top.

"I know I said this already, but I'm sorry I wasn't vigilant enough in watching Naji and his people. The blame for that lies solely on my shoulders. It's been a lot of years since we've been at war with our enemies. Not since before I was your age. I've forgotten what it's like to always be watching my back. How we can never let our guards down. Not even for a second." Fatigue mars Da's face. He appears to have aged overnight.

"As much as it pains me to admit, it was always going to happen, whether it was Naji or Campbell. At least we have Imogen to thank. By the way, is she okay? My main concern has been Sorcha and the kids."

He nods solemnly. "She's shaken up, of course. But I think she's more worried about Liam than herself. As much as I wish it weren't so, he loves her. If they'd hurt her in any way, Campbell would have razed the entire city to the ground and tried to single-handedly destroy the Moroccans."

Psychopath. *Wouldn't you do the same if it were Sorcha?* Perhaps I shouldn't judge him too harshly when it comes to protecting my sister.

"Being a part of our family—our organization—is dangerous. But we've grown up surrounded by this. We understand how it all works as well as the consequences. I taught you boys from birth. Sorcha has only been part of your real life for less than a month. It's no wonder she's scared and angry." Da sits back and his posture softens. "Go find your wife. I'm sure she needs you."

"Thanks, Da. For everything." I exit his office and head for our wing. She may need me, but I need her more.

CHAPTER 30

THERE'S A FAINT KNOCK ON THE DOOR. WORRIED IT might be either Kellen or Carson needing me, I quickly climb out of the bed, careful not to disturb Aisling. I crack it open only to find Aidan. My heart skips a beat and then races like it always does when I'm in his presence. But then I recall the way it raced in fear earlier.

"Hi," he greets me in a whisper.

"Hi."

"Will you talk to me now?" There's a hint of hope in the question.

"I don't want to leave Aisling, in case she wakes up scared." While true, it's also an excuse.

"Please?"

It's that single word that weakens me. I can probably count on one hand the number of times Aidan has ever said please. I glance over my shoulder. Aisling is sound asleep. We're just a hallway over. If she cries out, I'll come rushing. God, I'm weak. I sigh and open the door wide enough to slide through and then pull it almost closed, but keep it cracked enough that I won't miss any sounds that she might need me.

Side-by-side, Aidan and I walk back to our room. I'm glad he doesn't try and touch me. I'm not sure what I'll do if he does. He gestures for me to enter first. I move past him, trying not to breathe in his fresh woodsy scent, and stand in the center of the room with my arms wrapped protectively around my waist.

He closes the door, but doesn't shut it all the way, and pivots to face me. "How's your head and your leg feeling?"

"They both fucking hurt." Although my head isn't pounding like it had been earlier, but I keep the fact to myself. I have a twinge of guilt for twisting the knife a little deeper, especially when Aidan's face fills with worry.

"I'm sorry. So fucking sorry," he rasps out in another harsh whisper, taking a step forward like he's going to reach for me but stops himself. "I'm sorry for everything. For lying to you all these years. For forcing you into this marriage. For not fully warning you about what this life entails. But most of all, I'm sorry I put not only you, but our children, in danger."

My heart nearly stops beating altogether. The one and only time Aidan has ever said he's sorry was when he confessed his identity. He's said please more times than he's ever apologized. But I can't let go of the fact he called Kellen, Carson, and Aisling our kids. It doesn't matter that I'm their sister. I'm the only mom they have and I love them like they're mine.

"I'm sorry, too."

As much as I want to blame Aidan, I also have to blame myself. It isn't as though him being a member of the mafia had been a secret when we got married. Didn't I watch a news clip of him being arrested for possessing weapons and attempting to break into Liam's house? I'd been not naive, but willfully ignorant. My judgment has been clouded by my feelings for him.

He reaches for me, but I take a step back. His hand drops to his side and pain flashes in his eyes.

"I love you, Aidan. I do. But I need more time to process all of this. I don't know if I can be who you want me to be."

"I don't want you to be anyone else," he says. "I fell in love with this Sorcha, not some imagined version of you."

My arms tighten around my waist. "The Sorcha you think you love wants to take my children and run far, far away. She doesn't want them to have anything to do with gun fights and wars."

Aidan moves before I can guess his intent and pulls me in his arms. "Then we'll go together. The five of us. Start over somewhere as Mr. and Mrs. Broderick. Da will understand."

Tears spill from my eyes as I clutch him tightly and bury my face in his chest. The fact he's willing to leave all this should make me feel better. But it doesn't. I push away from him and at first he doesn't release me, but I push harder until he does. "I can't ask you to do that."

"You're not asking," he points out.

"This is your family. Here is where you belong. With them. You wouldn't be happy living somewhere else. In the end, you'd resent me for taking you away from them."

Aidan straightens and a fierce light enters his eyes. "*You* are my family. You, Kellen, Carson, and Aisling. I belong wherever it is that you are. You're my *wife*, Sorcha. I made a vow to you. One I meant with every breath in my body."

God, this is killing me. I want nothing more than to ignore what my brain says and only listen to my heart. But I can't do that. "I'm not saying we're done. I'm just saying I need time to think before I make any decisions about the future. The future of my kids. Please give it to me."

Several seconds pass before resignation settles in his eyes and his shoulders drop in defeat. He takes a small step forward, presses a kiss to my forehead, and moves back, releasing his hands from mine. "I'll go sleep in another room tonight."

I nod. "Thank you."

Aidan walks out without a goodbye and closes the door behind him. My chest burns and I collapse onto the bed burying my hands in my face. Sobs pour from my throat. I grab a pillow to try and stifle them. This is my wedding night. I'm supposed to be spending it making love with my husband again and again all night long. Instead, I sob for what could be hours. The headache that had only slightly eased is back in full force. It's like someone is taking a jackhammer to my brain. My leg throbs and between the two of them, the pain's enough to make me want to vomit.

Once I've cried all the tears I'm going to, at least for the moment, I wash my face in the bathroom and climb under the blankets. God, they smell like Aidan. I pull his pillow to me and breathe in his scent. My eyes close and far sooner than I expected, I drift off.

MY EYES FLY OPEN AND I JACKKNIFE UP TO SITTING AS MY heart pounds. I glance around and it takes a minute for my harsh breathing to calm. I palm my chest to try and slow it. What woke me? Memories of gunfire and faceless demons haunted my sleep. Aisling screamed more than once in the middle of the night. Each time, Aidan was right there, having rushed in from where he slept. Although, other than the time he reached her first, I'm the one she clung to for comfort.

The pounding is back at the base of my skull and my eyes are gritty like sandpaper. I blink a few times to clear my vision. It's still and quiet. Judging by the light filtering through the shutters, it's later than I normally wake up. I throw back the blankets and climb out of the bed for the bathroom. I wash the sleep off my face and get dressed. The bandage over my wound is clean, so at least it's stopped bleeding. It's still a bit achy, but nothing like yesterday.

My rumbling stomach reminds me it's been since early evening when I last ate. I stop at Aisling's room first, but she's not there. I'm not too concerned, yet. Instead of stopping in the kitchen first, I make my way upstairs to check on Kellen and Carson. They're both sleeping in Kellen's bed. Still no Aisling. That panicked sensation bubbles up in my stomach and I hurry down the stairs toward the kitchen. As I pass through the dining room, I glance outside and stop.

Seated at the table is Aidan's cousin-in-law Lucia. Her gaze is focused out on the sprawling manor landscape. Running around and chasing each other are Aisling and Lucia's eldest son, Enzo. The pair met yesterday, but hit it off talking about art and drawing. On their heels is her middle son, Eoin. I step outside and Lucia turns her head toward me. She waves and smiles. I cross the patio until I reach her.

"Good morning." She tips her head, gesturing toward where the kids are running around. "I thought I'd bring Enzo with me today to maybe provide a much needed distraction. Of course, where Enzo goes, Eoin has to go as well. He idolizes his older brother and follows him everywhere."

"That's kind of you. It will probably do Aisling some good to have something to keep her mind off yesterday." It's a sweet gesture, but also a bit confusing. She's Aidan's relative, and yes, her son is the same age as Aisling, but we all barely know each other.

"Did Aidan tell you I used to live in London working at the British Museum?" Lucia asks, her gaze still trained on the kids.

"No, he didn't. Just that you work for the National Museum here in Dublin."

"I was in London for six years. Hiding."

Hiding?

She finally faces me. "Years ago when I was in my early twenties, I'd been engaged to a young man that was part of our family's...organization. Aidan probably mentioned that my distant cousin Emilio is married to his cousin Brenna."

I shake my head. "No, he didn't mention that. About you and Emilio being related, I mean. He did tell me that Brenna was married to the most powerful man in Brooklyn."

Lucia chuckles. "It's always funny to hear that, because it sounds great, right? Power. Money. Influence. Who wouldn't want to be a part of that, right?"

She's laughing, but I sense a hint of sarcasm behind it. "It does sound tempting."

"It does. And it tempted Michele. He was one of Emilio's soldiers and wanting to work his way up the ranks. We had our lives all planned out. Until he went on a raid and was killed." Lucia pauses and swallows. "I'd been devastated. And furious. I hated everything the mafia represented and wanted nothing to do with it. So, I left."

"To London."

She nods. "To London. I didn't tell a single soul where I was. I came back a few times over the years. Before I left though I attended a family wedding. One in particular. Where I met this far-too-young-for-me eighteen-year old Irishman who swept me off my feet. We danced and flirted and then I ran away back to London. Three years later, we met again. This time a bit more than flirting happened, but I didn't discover the consequences of that *more than flirting* until a few months later."

Lucia's gaze shifts back to the kids. In my head, I do the math. Nathan appears to be around thirty and she around forty. I'm guessing then that Enzo was the result of their more than flirting. Why is she telling me all this? She turns to me again with a sad smile.

"I was terrified. I'd been running from the mafia and all the danger it represented for years. Then, there I was. Pregnant. The father of my child was in the same kind of organization I'd run away from years earlier. I kept Enzo's parentage secret for three years. I didn't even tell my niece, who's my best friend. I thought it was safer that way. There was no way I was going to allow my son to grow up in danger. I'd already lost one person I'd loved to the violence that comes with being a part of a family like ours. I refused to let my son be killed one day."

God, how naive I've been. Not once have I ever considered what it might mean for the boys—or Aisling even—to grow up in Aidan's family's organization. Yet one more thing he and I need to discuss.

"Why are you telling me this?" Another thought occurs to me and anger wells up. "Did Aidan put you up to this?"

Lucia shakes her head and reaches across to clutch my hand. "Not at all, I swear. I'm here on my own because I know you probably weren't aware of the potential dangers that come with being married to someone like Aidan. And I can only guess at how scared you might be. How you might not want anything to do with the organization. How you might want to run from it. I understand exactly how you feel, because I felt it too. You weren't born to this life. Nor were the children. I know how terrifying it can be thinking of what could happen, especially after yesterday."

I sense there's more to her visit. "I hear a but in there."

She squeezes my hand gently. "Not really. I'm the last person to try and wax poetic about how just because things turned out great for me, they will for you, too. Because, while, yes, my life is great, there is always going to be that little voice in the back of my head that whispers about the dangers my sons face. I just wanted you to know you're not alone with your fears."

My eyes burn. "Thank you. That means so much."

"You're welcome. And if you ever need someone to talk to, give me a call, anytime."

We sit out here a while longer while the children play. I'm so glad Aisling is having fun. I'm also really glad Lucia came by. She gave me a lot to mull over.

CHAPTER 31

SITTING OUTSIDE, I BREATHE IN THE FRESH AIR THAT STILL holds a hint of the rain that's been hanging around for nearly every one of the past fourteen days. Everyone is still asleep as the sun crests the horizon. Sunrises are always my favorite time of day. I'm not one for omens, despite being Irish, but I can't help but nurse a small thread of hope that maybe this is a sign of positive things to come.

It's been two weeks since Sorcha and I got married.

And it's been fourteen days of sleeping apart. Fourteen days of stilted conversations. We've kept the children out of school and brought in a home school teacher so they wouldn't fall behind. They've also been talking to a pediatric therapist that specializes in trauma. It's been a slow process, but the light is finally returning to Aisling's eyes. The boys rebounded a lot faster. Despite the distance between Sorcha and I, Kellen, Carson, and I have grown closer.

Behind me, there's the click of the dining room door opening. I glance over my shoulder and my pulse races as Sorcha, wrapped in a blanket and wearing a pair of slippers, steps out. Even sleepy-eyed with her hair a tangled mess around her shoulders, she's still the most beautiful woman ever. She heads straight for me, her pace slow, until she takes a seat in the chair next to me. I can't take my eyes off her. This is the first time we've been alone together since our wedding.

"I'm glad it finally stopped raining," she says quietly, her gaze turned toward the expansive landscape.

"Me too."

We sit in silence for several minutes. I have so many things to say, but where do I start? I'll do anything to save my marriage, but I'm not the only one whose decision it is. Every day, I wake up waiting for her to tell me she and the kids are leaving. Fear has been my constant companion.

"I talked to Lucia a couple weeks ago," Sorcha finally breaks the quiet.

"Nathan told me she'd stopped by." I'd been surprised by the news considering the two had only met once before the wedding, although I'm glad if the women became friends. "Did you have a nice visit?"

"It was informative."

I glance over at her. *What does that mean?* Finally, Sorcha shifts in the chair so she's facing me. Her leg has healed well and her signs of concussion have diminished, although she still suffers from occasional headaches. The doctor said they may never go away or, if they do, it could take years.

"I love you, Aidan."

Fuck. My heart plummets, because my brain hears a but behind it. "I love you, too. More than anything."

Sorcha nods and smiles, although it's a bit sad. "I know you do."

"But?" I have to gently prod, because if she's going to break my heart, she might as well get it over with.

"But I've also never been more scared in my entire life as I was during that attack. I'd been worried for the kids. For you. It was the worst feeling I've ever had. I don't ever want to feel that way again. Ever," she says with a ferocious intensity.

If only I could promise she won't. I ache to reach out for her, but I'm not sure if she'll welcome my touch and I can only afford to be gutted once today. "I wish I could turn back time and make that day disappear like it never even happened."

"I don't," she says, shocking me. "Up until the insanity hit, it was the happiest day of my life. I got to marry my best friend."

"Then I wish I could just make what happened after disappear."

"Wouldn't that be nice?" she chuckles. "It would certainly make people's lives easier if we could just erase all the bad things that happen."

"But we can't."

She shake her head sadly. "No, we can't. I just wasn't prepared for what it meant to be married to you. Not only for me, but for the kids. Will the boys be expected to become a part of your family's organization? What if they don't want to? Do they even have a choice?"

"God, no," I rush to reassure her. "No one would force them to do anything. My grand-da was the ruthless bastard. No one would dare refuse to be initiated into our organization. We were all too afraid of him. But Da isn't like that. He loves his family and only wants them to be happy wherever their path leads."

She nods and some more tension leaves her body.

I take a deep breath. "What do you want me to do to make you happy, Sorcha?"

At last, she reaches across and clutches at my hand. "I want you to keep loving me."

"Always. I'll never stop."

"Five years ago you saved me from Duncan. Then you saved me again when my mum died. Then my Da. And yet again when Liam's men showed up to collect Da's debt. You saved me by marrying me. Everything you've done has been to protect me in some way. From the moment we first met." She breathes in. "I put you up on this pedestal like you were some sort of god to be worshipped. My fierce protector. You had a high standard to maintain. And, I think, when I was hurt and our children could have been hurt, my unrealistic expectations of you made that god-like image I had shatter."

I had no idea she'd seen me like that. "I'm sorry I didn't protect you at our wedding." I'll apologize every day for the rest of our lives if that's what it takes.

"Here's the thing I've thought about over the last two weeks. It's not up to you to protect me for the rest of my life. And it's not fair of me to expect it of you. There's danger everywhere. I could take the kids away from here, back to Burtonport, and we could get into an accident on the way," she says. "We could go back to the pub and any one of us could tumble down the stairs. Anything could happen at any time."

"You know that I will always do everything in my power to keep you safe," I swear to her.

"I know you will. I also know that I can't live my life in fear that *something* could happen. That's no way to live." Sorcha sighs. "And while the thought of being in danger from your enemies is terrifying, I'd rather be happy with you than miserable without you. The children would be miserable without you."

I come to my feet and pull Sorcha with me, dragging her into my arms to hold her close. I've missed the feel of her. The smell of her. "These last two weeks have been killing me. I haven't wanted to put any type of pressure on you or try to influence you one way or another about staying. But know that if you had left, I would have come with you. I would follow you to the ends of the earth and beyond. That's how much I love you."

"I love you, too. I've been miserable as well, but Kellen, Carson, and Aisling had to come before any of my selfish needs." Sorcha lays her head on my chest and squeezes me tightly.

"They're our kids. Of course they're going to come first. I wouldn't expect otherwise." I stroke her hair back and kiss the top of her head. "You're an amazing mother."

She laughs, but there's a hint of self-deprecation. "I have no idea what I'm doing. It's harder than anything I've ever done before."

I lean back and cradle her face between my palms. "Does any new mother know what they're doing? And when it gets hard, you have me. They're my children now, too. We're a team, you and me."

"I love you," Sorcha whispers.

"I love you more."

Our lips meet and it's as though everything has been set right in the world. My wife is here with me and always will be. Our children are safe and I'll make sure they stay that way. The door opens again and I break the kiss to glance back. Kellen, Carson, and Aisling all spill out, still dressed in their pajamas. I pivot and hold my arm out. The three of them race over and collide with Sorcha and me into a giant group hug.

"Did she tell you we're staying?" Kellen asks when we finally let go of each other.

"She did." A wide grin splits my face. "You all made me so happy."

I drop my smile and crouch down so I'm more level with them. My gaze moves from Kellen to Carson to Aisling. "I'll do everything I can to protect you. I love the three of you very much."

"We love you, too," Carson says.

The three of them step into my open arms. Our life isn't going to always be easy, but then again, nothing worth having ever is. As long as the five of us are together, then we can get through anything.

EPILOGUE

Strong arms encircle me, and Aidan presses a soft kiss along the curve of my neck.

"Are you excited for tonight?" he murmurs against my skin that prickles with arousal.

I pivot in his embrace and loop my hands around his neck, threading my fingers together. "I think I'm more nervous than excited. My stomach is in knots."

"It's going to be amazing. And perfect. Just like my wife." Aidan kisses the tip of my nose and then moves to my lips.

I fall into his kisses every time, forgetting everything around me. It's been like that from the beginning. As much as I want to forget what's happening in a few short hours, I have too many things to take care of to get ready for our opening night.

"Okay, stop trying to distract me," I laugh against his mouth and draw away. "I've still got things to do."

"Like what?" He doesn't let me go. "The exhibit is ready and your selections are impeccable. They're going to be sold for a lot of fucking money. The caterers are upstairs now preparing all the hors d'oeuvres. The bar's being set up and stocked and the waitstaff have

679

arrived. Imogen's made sure that your payment system is functioning and your staff is here ready to take people's money. There's nothing else you need to do. You're ready. This place is ready. It's going to be absolutely perfect."

I take in a shuddering breath and sag against him. "I know. You're right. I just keep thinking something is going to go terribly wrong."

Aidan's hands tighten their grip on my hips and he pulls me into the cradle of his thighs. "Nothing will go wrong. And even if it does, nothing so disastrous is going to happen that it'll turn into an utter failure. I'll be here to keep an eye on things and to offer any back up. I do have an expert eye for expensive art."

I snort. "I don't think those specific skills will need to be put to use tonight."

He winks. "You never know. One of these pieces on display tonight might turn into the next Mona Lisa or The Kiss. It could be worth a fortune."

I just shake my head. "I'm not going to encourage your illegal predilections."

"You love my *predilections*," he draws the word out in a suggestive tone.

Rising up on my toes, I press a kiss to his lips. "I love your erections."

Aidan groans. "You're killing me woman. Weren't you the one who just said no distractions? How am I supposed to make it through the night without thinking about you and my erection and how you can take care of it for me?"

I pat his chest. "Poor thing, I'm sure you'll think of something. Now, I need to go check on the caterers."

He lets me go and as I walk past him, I drag my hand across the front of the significant bulge in his pants.

"You're going to pay for that later, wife," Aidan warns making me laugh and waggle my fingers at him in farewell.

I stride through the gallery, my gaze pausing on each pillar or section of wall that displays its piece of focus. Soft lighting illuminates each one, showcasing all the lines, colors, and textures that make up the scene. The evocative images are powerful and resonate with emotions locked deep inside me. Pride swells. Aidan has been making every single one of my dreams come true. If not for him buying this building, I might still be trying to decide what I wanted for my future.

It's only a short climb up the stairs to the second level. We renovated the whole space and had a small kitchen built up here for events like tonight's. I walk through the swinging doors and glance around. Everything appears to be in order.

The owner of the catering company approaches. "Can I help you, Mrs. Donnelly?"

I wave her off. "No, I just popped in to see if you needed anything."

"Thank you, but we've got everything."

"All right, then. It all smells delicious."

She beams. "Thank you."

Since it's clear she has things under control and I'm only here to settle my nerves, I move on.

Aidan was right. We're ready. *I'm* ready.

"Thank you so much for coming. We'll get this boxed up and shipped to you this week." I shake the hand of one of the last remaining patrons. One who just paid over twenty-eight thousand euros on a piece of artwork. On *my* piece of artwork that I hadn't put up for display. Aidan had.

I escort them to the door and once they're gone, I lock it, turn, and collapse against it. My husband comes around the corner and stalks forward with a predatory gleam in his eyes. I rise up and meet him partway. He grips my hips and I lay my palms on his chest.

"You were sneaky adding my piece to the exhibit," I kiss his chin.

"I can't believe you did that. Most of all, I can't believe I missed it. I've memorized every single painting hanging from these walls. Yet somehow, I missed that one."

"I knew you'd never add any of your own work, so I did it for you. It deserved to be displayed front and center."

"Thank you."

Aidan's lips slowly curl in that suggestive way of his. "I believe I should get my reward now."

I chuckle. "Oh, you do, do you? And what kind of reward might that be?"

He walks me backward until my back meets the wall and he flips the lights off until only the faint glow from the upstairs filters down the stairwell. "The kind of reward that ends up with you and me in bed with my cock buried deep inside you."

"That sounds scandalous," I say breathlessly."Oh, it is. Extremely scandalous." Aidan leans into me and nibbles the skin along my jawline, drawing his tongue across the slightly stinging flesh and soothing it.

I tip my head to give him better access and moan as pleasure skates over my body and the ache in my core grows, spreading throughout me.

"Whoever's idea it was to build a small room upstairs deserves a medal," he whispers against my heated flesh, knowing full well it was his.

"I don't have a medal, but I'm sure I can come up with something to make up for it."

"Hmmm. I like the way you think." Taking my hand, Aidan leads me across the gallery floor and up the stairs until we reach the small bedroom just off the kitchen.

Ever so slowly, he takes the pins from my hair and tosses them on the small vanity and then runs his fingers through it, gently teasing out the tangles. I sigh in pleasure. His hands go to my shoulders and he turns me to give him my back.

Far too slowly, he releases the buttons that run from the top of the dress all the way down to the swell of my butt. It's tortuous waiting, as inch by small inch he exposes me. Aidan kisses his way down my spine sending shivers racing over me. Goosebumps prickle at my arms.

He pushes the fabric off my shoulders, kissing along the slope of one, until the dress falls and pools at my feet. I'm left clad in only my bra, panties, and high heels. I've never felt sexier, especially when he groans, dragging me back against his chest, and swipes my hair off my neck to press kisses along the length of it.

"You get more beautiful every day," Aidan whispers into my ear.

He slides his hands around to my front, tickling my ribs in the process. I suck in a breath as he palms a breast while he glides his other hand down my belly and dips under the waistband of my panties.

"You're so wet and perfect." His fingers meet my swollen clit and my knees nearly give out.

Playing my body perfectly, he brings me almost to climax before drawing his hand away.

"You enjoy torturing me, don't you?" I pout.

Aidan, the bastard, chuckles. "Normally, yes, but I've been thinking about this sweet cunt of yours for too long tonight to torment either of us for long."

"Good." I step out of my heels and reach behind me to unclasp my bra.

Turning, I face my husband and drop my gaze to the bulge in his pants. I walk backwards until my legs touch the bed. Slowly, I push my panties down over my hips until they drop to the floor. I sit on the edge of the bed, and with a playful smile, crook my finger, beckoning Aidan to me.

He strides forward, removing his own clothes on his way. I scoot back in the bed, making room for him. He quickly shoves his pants down to his ankles and then with a growl, he pounces. My giggles quickly turn to moans as his lips crash down on mine. Over the past year, he's explored every inch of my body and found all the places on it that drive me wild. Some even I hadn't discovered before.

Never selfish with his pleasure, Aidan takes care of me first. He caresses the one spot between my ribs that should be ticklish, but, instead, has wetness spilling from me and a chill dancing down my spine. Then he moves to the spot along my hip all while deepening the kiss. My fingers clench, gripping his hair and tugging it. Something *I* discovered makes him even harder.

Passion flares higher between us as he rocks his pelvis against mine, rubbing across my already swollen clit and making my body tremble and burn.

"I think it's time for both our rewards, don't you?" I murmur against Aidan's lips.

"You first." He lines up his cock and thrusts deep inside.

I'm already so close, I almost orgasm. Sensing I'm on the edge, he reaches between us and fingers my clit as he rocks his hips and pounds into me. The fuse has been lit and like dynamite, I detonate. The explosive release hits me so hard it takes my breath away. I clutch at Aidan's shoulders, needing a lifeline to keep me from splintering apart.

Another release hits and then warmth spreads through me as he groans out his own release. He collapses on top of me, our bodies sweat-dampened. I love the weight of him and open my legs wider for him to settle deeper. My fingers trace the muscles of his upper back, dancing along the ridges and into the furrows.

"I enjoyed my reward very much." I roll my hips and clench down on his cock to show him how much.

He groans against the crook of my neck and lifts his head. "You're an evil woman Sorcha Donnelly. I've barely caught my breath and already I'm aching to fuck you again."

"What's stopping you?" I lift up and nip his bottom lip.

Despite coming, Aidan's still hard inside me. I guess he really has been thinking about this all night.

"I do deserve another reward, don't I?" he asks as he thrusts shallowly.

"We both do."

"I better give my wife what she asks for, huh?"

I nod and then my eyes snap shut and my breath catches. "Oh yes."

For the rest of the night Aidan and I celebrate the gallery's success and our life together. Never would I have imagined our friendship would turn into our greatest love. We have our children, but most importantly, we have each other.

Thank you for reading **AIDAN**. I hope you enjoyed it. I'd greatly appreciate a review on the platform of your choice. Reviews are so important!

Are you ready for more Dublin Kings?

Be sure to get your copy of FINN!

Doms of Club Eden
Submission
Desire
Redemption
Protect
Betrayal
Mistletoe
Absolution
Merry Eden

To Love and Protect
In Too Deep
Striking Distance
Atonement
Bullet Proof
For Always
Point Blank
Saving Evie

Brooklyn Kings
The Devil I Don't Know
The Enemy in My Bed
The Beast I Can't Tame
Irish Devil
Irish Rogue
Irish Charmer
Irish Rebel

Dublin Kings
Cian
Liam
Aidan
Finn

Other Books
Love Notes: A Dark Romance
SEALs in Love
Say Yes
Black Light: Possession
The Bratva's Enforcer (co-written with Rachel Everly)

FINN

TEAGAN

As far as I'm concerned, men can suck it.

I glare at the back of the rude arsehole I'd had the misfortune of sitting next to during the flight, grab my carry-on bag from the overhead compartment, and disembark. Despite my annoyance, as I make my way up the jet bridge, some of the tension bleeds from my shoulders. The gate area is teeming with people. I dodge several of them blocking me from the exit and the taxi rank, casting furtive glances over my shoulder, reassuring myself I'm not being followed.

You're fine. Safe. He's back in Berlin. He has no idea where you are.

The minute I step outside, I breathe in the fresh Dublin air. God, it's so good to be home. The reason I'm back threatens to overshadow my happiness, but I bury it in the dark recesses of my brain, determined to make the best of my time here. For however long that might be. The driver of the first taxi in the queue opens the door and I slide into the backseat. He circles around the back, gets behind the wheel, and glances at me over his shoulder.

I stumble over an address I'm not used to giving. Aside from the short visit I made to check on Imogen a couple months ago, Berlin and London have been my home.

"You got it." He pulls away and I settle more firmly into the seat.

We're barely two minutes from the airport when the driver glances in his rear view mirror at me. "Are ye visiting?"

"No, I live here." Although that's not entirely true.

"Ah, welcome back, then."

I smile placidly and turn my head to stare out the window, hoping he'll take the hint that I'm not keen on conversation. Thankfully, he does, because the remainder of the trip is spent in blessed silence. He stops in front of my building and while I get out, he grabs my bag from the boot and hands it to me. I pay him the fare, and he nods his head.

"Thank you." I pull the handle up from my luggage and tow it behind me.

The entryway is quiet. Then again, it is the middle of the afternoon and most people are working. I climb the stairs until I finally reach my front door. I open it and take in the clean scent with a hint of floral. The cleaning lady must have been here recently. At least I'm coming home to a clean flat.

Once I toe off my shoes, I head to my bedroom. I'd hired an interior designer when I first moved in to give it a complete makeover. I wanted it to be a calming oasis where, the minute I entered it, I left my stress and worries and anxieties at the door. Up until today, it worked. But not even the pale yellow walls, the cool blues of the accent chair, or the sight of my massive bed with its sky blue tufted velvet headboard is enough to keep my thoughts from spiraling.

Unpacking can wait a bit longer. I flop onto my back on the bed. I stretch my arms up above my head and take in a deep, cleansing breath. I'm going to have to call Imogen soon, but I'm not quite ready.

You know what she's going to say.

Which is why I'm waiting.

I close my eyes and breathe in and out slowly, lengthening my exhales each time until, at last, a nominal amount of peace settles in my chest. Finally, I sit up and make myself put away my belongings. Next, I head for the kitchen where a stack of mail sits. Most of it is probably junk since everything is paperless these days. But as I go through it, I find a few envelopes that contain things I need to take care of.

After I've opened every piece of mail there is, I blow out a huge sigh and walk back into my bedroom to pick up my phone. I've put it off long enough. Lying on the bed, I wait for Imogen to answer.

"Hey, are you in town?" she says, her tone pitched with excitement. I'd never guess she could have been killed two weeks ago at her brother's wedding.

"Hi. Are you feeling better?" I ignore her question.

"I'm doing okay other than getting a little annoyed with a hovering, over-protective maniac," Imogen raises her voice with the last few words like she's speaking pointedly to someone nearby.

"Cut Liam some slack. You were being held at gunpoint right in front of him not that long ago. He may be a bit of a psychopath, but he's a psychopath that loves you."

She sighs. "I know, which is why I'm tolerating the hovering. Nothing's been the same since the Moroccans tried to kill all of us."

I still can't believe that Imogen's Da is the head of the Irish mafia. Or that there are people who want to see the Donnellys dead. And apparently Liam as well because of his connection to them through her. "Are you really doing okay?"

There's a far longer pause after I ask this time.

"Some days are better than others," she finally admits. "I've had more than one nightmare. Who would have thought my life would turn out like this? I'm just a death-metal-loving goth-girl hacker who sits behind a computer all day."

There's a bitter humor in her voice. I try to come up with something else to say, but I've stalled long enough.

"I'm back in Dublin. How about I come over tomorrow? We can

order takeaway, and afterwards we'll eat our weight in cheesecake and drink far too much wine."

Imogen nearly screeches. "Why didn't you tell me you were home before now?"

"I just got to my flat from the airport." I pause. "I wanted to surprise you."

I've only lied to Imogen once before, and it was about something so stupid I barely remember what it was.

"You have no idea how happy this makes me. I've missed you so much. Talking and texting just aren't the same as in person." Her pout is evident all the way through the phone. "You better get over here first thing in the morning. I want to spend the whole day with you catching up on everything. You can tell me all about Ben."

My stomach dips at the name and there's a flutter of panic inside my chest cavity. I can barely form words, but I force them out. "We broke up."

"Oh no, I'm sorry." She makes a sympathetic noise. "I know how much you liked him. I'd really been hoping he was the one."

Every part of me wants to blurt out the truth, but I can't do it. Imogen's dealing with enough shit and doesn't need me to pile my own problems on top of hers. "It's probably for the best. You know how much I travel for my job. Long distance relationships rarely work out anyway."

Especially when a boyfriend turns into a jealous monster who accuses his girlfriend of cheating every time she leaves the house. Or when he threatens to kill her and whoever else she's fucking if she ever leaves him.

"How long are you home for?"

I blink and focus on the present. "I'm not sure, yet."

"Be prepared for me to hang out with you every day you're here then, so I can store up all my Teagan time before you have to leave again," she says matter-of-factly.

"I can't wait. See you tomorrow." I end the call and flop my arm out to the side. The phone tumbles from my fingers onto the bed.

There's a part of me that can't believe I ran. But the greater part can't believe I stayed so long. I cover my face with my arm to block out the sunlight filtering in through bare window. Deep down there had to be a reason why I never let my lease run out and why I continued to pay rent on a flat I didn't even live in ninety-percent of the time. The only person who knows my address is Imogen. I have no family left. It's one of the things she and I had somewhat in common when we first met.

I never knew my pedar and my mādar died a year before I went to Uni. Other than Imogen, I'm alone. It might have bothered me before I met Ben. But after everything he's done, being alone is welcome. It means I'm free. Safe. A shudder runs down my spine and a cold, uncomfortable sensation settles in my belly.

Needing a distraction, I jackknife up and off the bed. A long, hot shower sounds good. I need to wash off the travel odor anyway. If I'm lucky, the water will also wash all my thoughts away. At least for a little while. But even as I grab some clean clothes from the wardrobe, it's pretty clear I'm only fooling myself.

CHAPTER 2

Finn

Soft hands caress my back before slender arms wrap around my waist. The woman presses the entire length of her naked body against mine and kisses the skin between my shoulder blades. The musky scent of sex perfumes the air.

"Why don't you come back to bed?" Aoife murmurs as one of her hands skates down the front of me.

She barely brushes the root of my cock before I step away, forcing her to loosen her hold. I shouldn't have asked her to come up here. Given her false hope. Like a coward, I keep my eyes focused on the lights that cast a faint glow over the city.

"You should probably go." I say it as kindly as I can.

The silence that follows is deafening.

Forcing myself to turn, I face her, doing my best to school my features and keep my gaze trained above her chin. Aoife, on the other hand, isn't keeping her emotions in check. Hurt fills her eyes, along with a sheen of wetness she quickly blinks away. She sniffs, clears her throat, and straightens her spine, forcing her shoulders back and her chest out. It's not a pose meant to seduce, but rather to shield.

"Yes, I suppose I should." Aoife turns and quickly slips into the dress and panties I'd helped her out of a few short hours ago.

I continue standing there as she steps into her heels, picks up the purse she'd dropped just inside the entrance, and turns the handle of the door. She pivots a half-turn and scans my face. Whatever she sees on it causes her to nod so infinitesimally I might have missed it, as though she's confirming something to herself.

"See you around, Finn. Or maybe not." With those softly spoken parting words, Aoife's gone, closing the door behind her with a quiet snick.

Christ. I'd never meant to hurt her. I take the blame for it though, because I broke my own rule about fucking any of the casino's former floor girls. More than once. Or in her case, at least a dozen times over the last six months. *You should have known better.*

I should have made myself more clear regarding the boundaries of our...arrangement. At least then, if—when—Aoife caught feelings, I could have said "I told you it wouldn't be anything more than fucking.". Not that I would have said it that way, because I'm not that much of a bastard, but maybe it would have helped ease some of my guilt.

I turn and stare out the mirrored glass window again, unconcerned that anyone on the outside might be able to see my nakedness. A restless uneasiness has been plaguing me over the past month and I can't pinpoint where it's coming from. When the Moroccans attacked our family during Aidan and Sorcha's wedding a couple weeks ago, my first thought was that this is what my instincts have been warning me about. Except it wasn't.

Tired of wracking my brain and coming up empty to its origin, I walk into the bathroom to wash up. After I've removed Aoife's scent, as well as the sticky remnants of come from myself, I put on a clean suit from the closet. I lock the door of the suite, head to the elevator, and make my way to the casino floor. I don't spend a lot of time down here since I have plenty of employees to act as security, but on occasion, I'll wander around to observe the games in play. Mostly because I need to keep myself acquainted with the members of our exclusive establishment.

I weave in and out of the tables, pausing at a few for inane greetings and pleasantries with some of our richest patrons. The ones who keep our coffers full. We cater to their every need, especially since that prick boyfriend of my sister's will, no doubt, do what he can to lure members away from us when his casino opens.

"Aren't you supposed to be upstairs in between the thighs of some woman?"

Pivoting, I come face-to-face with someone I never expected to become friends with, considering our family history. I smirk at Declan Campbell and shake his outstretched hand. "Sadly, she had to leave early."

"Pity."

"What brings you to our humble establishment tonight?" I ask. "Taking notes to pass off to Liam on how to make his future casino less tacky?"

He barks out a laugh and glances around. "I'd hardly call this place humble. And you know as well as I do that despite slowly repairing our relationship—or at least as much as it can be—my adoring cousin is still a twat. I like you far more than I like him. Which means, your business secrets are safe with me."

"I almost feel sorry for the poor bastard if he can't even get his own family to like him." I pause. "But I don't."

Declan and I continue our trek around the casino conversing casually. We come to a stop at the bar. I turn to him. "Drink?"

"I'll take a Guinness."

I nod at the bartender. "A glass of The Devil's Keep as well, please."

While we wait for our drinks, I lean back against the surface behind me. "How's Aran?"

"Recovering, no thanks to you. He barely limps now." Declan side eyes me, but there's no animosity in his tone.

I throw up my palms in a half-hearted apology. "You know as well as I do that I was only following orders."

When Liam bought out the shipping company we used to illegally import weapons, he blocked all incoming shipments from our German suppliers. In retaliation, several of our organization's soldiers and I paid a visit to Declan and Aran's house. By the time we left, both men needed to go to the hospital. Which is why it's surprising we've managed to become friends since then. "Have you talked to Imogen?" Declan asks. "Is she doing okay after what happened at the wedding?"

"Da and Nora have spoken to her more than me, but I called her a couple days ago. It sounds like she's doing all right physically, but is still a bit shaken up." Rage burns inside my gut that the Moroccans almost harmed her. "She's tough, though. It's just going to take a little more time. I will say one thing about Liam, and that is he definitely loves my sister."

"A fact that shocks me more than it does you."

I don't doubt it. Campbell had only become a threat to his former stepda's organization—and by association, ours—within the last five years. Which means his cousins know him far better than we do. And based on conversations with Declan, Liam hasn't given a shit about anyone in twenty years. He's ruthless, cold, and heartless. Except when it comes to Imogen.

The bartender returns with our drinks and I take a small sip of our family's favorite whiskey, savoring the oaky flavor that burns its way down my throat. Warmth settles in my stomach.

I glance over at Declan. "You never did say what brings you here."

"Aran has a new woman he's trying to impress and he asked me to give him a bit of privacy for the evening. What better place to kill some time on a Thursday night than here? I'm feeling lucky." His gaze follows Shannon as she leaves the bar with a tray full of drinks.

"I've learned a valuable lesson in the years since I've been running this place." I take another drink as Declan pulls his attention from the woman's ass back to me and arches an eyebrow.

"And what is that?"

"Don't fuck anyone in a place you frequent. Things get messy when it turns to shite." I gesture with a finger in Shannon's direction.

He chuckles. "Noted."

"I'm feeling a bit restless myself so maybe I'll join you for a hand or two." I stride to the nearest poker table with two empty chairs.

Aside from raising or calling bets, there's little conversation from the men surrounding us. My brothers and I have gotten used to it whenever we sit in on a game. Cian and I take perverse pleasure from the fact, but we don't abuse our intimidating presence. We want the members to relax and enjoy themselves. We don't want them thinking about the fact we're relieving them of their money most of the time.

Declan wins a few hands, as do I, but by the time we finish, one of the members takes home the final pot.

"Congratulations, Oren." I reach across and shake his hand and nod to the remaining seated men. "I'm calling it. Enjoy your evening gentlemen."

The man on my right rises as well and we head for the bar again.

Declan turns to me once we have our drinks. "What's going on with you tonight? Something feels off."

I glance over at him. It's strange that in the short time we've known each other, Declan has already gauged enough of me to know I'm not myself.

"I don't know what it is." My gaze scans the room. "It's almost as if I'm bored."

His brow wrinkles. "Bored with what?"

"Everything. All of this." I sweep my arm out. "Look around. We belong to the two most powerful families in Dublin. We're rich and people envy us. We can have anything we could ever want or need. Lately, though, it's almost as if there's something missing."

I haven't even mentioned this to Cian and Aidan. Then again, they've been preoccupied. "Maybe you need to take some time off. Aren't you the one who told me you're almost always here? Why not take a break?" Declan suggests.

Because this casino is mine. Without it, I'm not sure who I even am.

CHAPTER 3

With two bottles of wine in hand and a small overnight bag slung cross-body over me, I tap my knuckle to the bell and wait. Barely any time passes before the door is flung open and Imogen throws herself at me. Laughing, I stumble back a step under her attack, but she steadies me.

"Oh my god, I'm so glad you're here. Come in." She takes the bottles from my hand and gestures with her head.

I follow Imogen into the bowels of the massive house. It's exactly how she described. Although she mentioned it, I can barely hold in the gasp at the waterfall spilling down one entire wall of the living area. It doesn't do my imagination justice. Jesus, it's stunning. Same with the massive fireplace built into the opposite one.

"Liam left for the day so it's just you and me," Imogen says over her shoulder.

If she hadn't told me what happened at her brother's wedding, I'd never have guessed she'd been held at gunpoint only a couple weeks ago. She appears to be the same Imogen I've been friends—sisters—with for a decade. Nobody knows her better than me. Not even Liam.

We pass through the dining area and into the kitchen that's clearly designed for a person who knows how to cook. The massive black cast iron stove is intimidating to someone who survives on nothing but takeaway.

"Good god, you weren't lying when you said this place was obscenely over the top." I glance outside and catch a peek of a towering stone plinth with a matching gargoyle perched on top of it.

She places the bottles on the counter, pivots with a laugh, and leans back bracing herself with her elbows. "Aidan and Cian say it's pretentious. They're not entirely wrong. But I've gotten used to the place. My favorite parts are the conservatory and the swimming pool."

I set my bag down on the floor out of the way. "You have an actual conservatory?"

Imogen smirks. "Yes. Although I don't recommend getting down on your knees in there. It's not the most comfortable."

"Ew." I scrunch my face up. "Why'd you have to ruin it for me? Now all I'm going to think about when I walk through it is you and Liam getting freaky in there. I'll never be able to look him in the eye again."

She bursts out laughing. "God, I've missed you."

"I've missed you, too." More than she'll ever know.

Imogen rises up with a huge grin and claps. "All right, let's get this party started."

Instead of opening the wine—it is only ten in the morning, after all—she grabs two bottles of red lemonade from the fridge as well as a platter of scones, cream, and jam.

"Here, let me carry something." I step over, pick up the drinks, and follow her out of the kitchen .

She sets the food on a table, plops down on the sofa, swiveling to bring one leg up onto it, and pats the cushion next to her. I pass her her lemonade and mirror her position.

"I know I asked you this yesterday, but do you know how long you'll be home this time?"

"For now, indefinitely. I'm asking for a transfer from our corporate headquarters to one of the offices here."

The space between Imogen's eyebrows wrinkles. "But I thought you loved all the traveling? Plus, what exactly are you going to do spending all your time in an office? How are you going to monitor systems and all the servers if you're not on site where the main network hubs are? Doing it remotely isn't nearly as secure, you know that."

"It's only temporary. I'm actually looking for a new job entirely. One that will keep me in Dublin for a while. I just haven't told my boss, yet." I've tried to imbue some excitement as well as sheepishness in my voice about moving back for a while.

Imogen scans my face. I sulk a little and huff. "I thought you'd be more excited that I'll be in town for the foreseeable future."

She glares. "Of course I am. I'm ecstatic."

"Then be excited." I give her a pointed stare.

Her expression softens but there's still a flicker of worry in her eyes. "I'm sorry, you're right. Yes, it makes me so happy that we're going to be able to spend more time together. I want you to meet my family, too, while you're here."

Thankful for the opening, I take it. "How *is* the whole new family thing going by the way? Everyone playing nice?"

Imogen pauses and it's clear she doesn't want to let the previous topic go entirely, but finally she chuckles. "Liam is playing as nice as Liam can play. Although he's been extra grumpy because he owes Cian for saving my life and he hates being in Cian's debt. For now, they have a common enemy in the Moroccans, so they're working together. But for fuck's sake, the both of them are trying to prove they're these big bad alpha males. Honestly, it's turned into nothing but a dick swinging contest."

"One big, dysfunctional family. I bet you guys are a lot of fun at reunions." I snort.

Imogen winces. "It's been a challenge, but I'm doing my best to make everything work out between us all."

"What about you and Nora?" I take another sip of my lemonade.

She bobs her head side-to-side. "I'm still not ready to forgive her, but we're spending time together. Getting to know each other. Same with Carrick."

"I can't wait to meet them."

While we eat our scones, we talk about the latest security protocols I'd put in place at the Deutsch Bank in Berlin after a potential hacking scare. It's great to be able to talk code with someone else who actually knows what the hell they're doing. Imogen is the one who keeps me on my toes. I use my cyber security skills to help giant corporations keep not only all the hackers like her out, but their servers and other financials secure. More than once she's managed to bypass all the firewalls I'd put in place. I'm great at my job, but she's even better at hers.

Imogen pops the last bite of scone in her mouth and washes it down with a swig of lemonade. "All right, how about we go swimming for a bit? You brought your suit, right?"

"After you texted me in *all caps* telling me to, of course I did."

She sticks her tongue out and picks up the platter with the few remaining scones. I grab out empty bottles and follow her into the kitchen.

"I'm going to clean up in here, but why don't you go ahead and get changed. Head back through the living room and down the hallway closest to the fireplace you'll find a bedroom on the right you can use." Imogen points in the general direction. "I'll meet you back in here."

I pick up my bag from where I'd dropped it and follow her instructions, which are easy enough not to get lost. I hope. Thankfully, I find the room without any trouble. From my bag, I pull out the yellow string bikini I purchased at an adorable boutique during one of my trips to the Amalfi coast. I'll admit it makes my tits and ass look amazing. I strip down to almost nothing and exchange my ugly, everyday bra and underwear for the barely there scrap of sunshine magic.

There isn't a mirror in here so I can adjust things, but Imogen can help if I need it. I throw my hair up quickly into a messy knot on top of my head, grab the towel I'd also brought, and make my way back to the kitchen.

I come to an abrupt halt in the living room at the sight of the far-too-attractive man standing on the other side of it.

His heated gaze slowly travels down my entire body and back up until his eyes meet mine. The casual curling of his lips bring forth a dimple on the right side of them.

"You're not Imogen," he draws out in a seductive tone.

I chuckle at the obvious. "No, I'm not."

We both keep our eyes on the other until finally he arches an eyebrow. "That usually leads to the other party offering a name."

"I don't like to do the usual thing."

He steps closer until he's only a foot away, but I remain where I'm standing. "I'm Declan, in case you were wondering."

"I wasn't, but it's nice to meet you, Declan." I soften the statement with a smile.

He palms his chest dramatically. "You definitely must be friends with Imogen. Only someone who spends far too much time with her can be this brutal."

"I'll take that as a compliment."

Just then Imogen comes from a different hallway than the one with the bedroom I'd changed in, wearing a black tankini and carrying a towel. Her gaze lands on Declan and widens in surprise and then a toothy grin appears. She rushes over and gives him a huge hug.

"Oh my god, what are you doing here?" She draws back and her gaze bounces between us. "Declan, this is Teagan, my best friend in the whole world."

He over exaggerates a pout. "I thought I was your best friend in the whole world."

"You're my best friend out of all of Liam's cousins." She gives him another cheeky grin.

"Two beautiful women insult me in one day. That might be a record. I'm not sure my ego can handle it."

Imogen snorts. "Your ego will survive and you know it. There are plenty of other women in Dublin that drool over you. You'll be fine if two don't. Besides, how did Teagan insult you? Did you try and schmooze and charm her and she turned you down cold?"

Declan barks out a laugh and glances over at me. "Something like that."

My cheeks heat that I was probably a little rude.

"You still didn't tell me what brings you here. Liam's not home."

"I see that now. It's no big deal. I was just dropping off some paperwork for him about the casino." Declan pulls some folded sheets of paper from his back pocket.

"Why don't I put them on his desk?"

He hands them to her and she disappears down the hallway with an "I'll be right back" over her shoulder. Declan's gaze lands on me again.

"I didn't mean to come off as rude," I apologize.

He grins, this time with actual amusement. "Don't worry about it. Like Imogen said, my ego can take the hit. Although I will say it isn't often that an attractive woman blows me off."

I wince. "If it makes you feel better, it's not you, but me."

Declan chuckles. "Isn't that what women say when they break up with a man and try to let them down easy?"

"I suppose if we hadn't just met, that might be true." I shrug. "But in this case, it really isn't you."

"Well, if you're in town long enough and you change your mind, give me a call." He glances to where Imogen disappeared. "Let her know I said bye and I'll talk to her later."

I nod. "Of course."

Declan turns and walks away. Just as Imogen comes back the sound of the front door closing reaches me.

"Where'd he go?"

"He said he had to leave, but he'd call you later." A memory tickles my brain. "Is he the cousin that helped you get to Carrick's house after Liam kidnapped you?"

She smiles fondly and tugs my arm, pulling me forward with her as she walks. "That would be Declan. Liam's still pissed about that."

I'm sure. Declan seems like a nice enough guy, but Ben was nice at first, too. That didn't turn out so well.

CHAPTER 4

Finn

I step into the quiet house. A rare occurrence over the last few weeks with the addition of two twelve-year old boys and a six-year old girl. Seconds later, Kellen and Carson bound down the stairs.

"Morning, Uncle Finn," they greet me in unison.

I smile at the name. Nora's almost gotten them to call her Mhamó, which she's beyond excited about. Her and Da. "Good morning. Isn't this early even for you guys to be up?"

They exchange glances.

"We've been up for an hour," Kellen says. "Aisling had a nightmare and screamed the house down."

Christ. "How are you two doing? Any nightmares for you? It was pretty scary what happened."

They shake their heads. Carson shifts on his feet and his eyes dart back and forth a couple times. "I've had a little trouble falling asleep, but that's it."

"Sorcha found someone for us to talk to about it with which has helped," Kellen adds.

"That's good. There's nothing wrong with asking for help when you're scared about something." My brothers and I have been surrounded by violence our entire lives. I've almost become immune. Sorcha and her siblings were thrust into this life. Of course they'd be traumatized. "Are you heading to breakfast then?"

They nod their heads. "Make sure you save some for the rest of us." I wink.

The two of them just grin and then hurry off toward the kitchen. Even if Nora's not in there yet, she will be soon. I head for the wing of the house that I've shared with my brothers for the last decade. Since Sorcha and the kids moved in, I share it with her, Aidan, and Aisling.

At first the common room where we sometimes hang out together appears empty, but in the dim light I can make out Aidan lying on the couch. I feel bad for the poor bastard. Married two weeks and he's been sleeping out here for the entirety of his marriage. He stirs and rubs his hands down his face. I close the distance until I'm standing in front of him. He opens his eyes and recoils.

"Jesus. What the hell are you doing hovering over me like a creeper?"

I snort and take a seat in the nearby chair while he sits up. "Pussy."

He gives me the finger in response.

"I heard Aisling had a nightmare?"

Aidan's entire body deflates. "She hadn't had one in a week. I really thought they were gone, but I should have expected it. She's just a little girl who experienced something traumatic. The boys act like they're handling everything okay, but you know how we were at twelve. Acting far tougher than we really were."

"I saw them in the hallway. Carson said he's having a little trouble sleeping, but neither are having any nightmares at least." I lean back in my chair. "How are things with Sorcha? Not great, I imagine, if you're still sleeping out here."

He leans forward and braces his forearms on his knees. His hands hang between them. "I'm giving her the space she asked for while she decides our future. Lucia stopped by right after the attack to talk to her. I keep hoping that whatever she said to Sorcha made some sort of positive impact. We just got married for Christ's sake. We're supposed to be spending the rest of our lives together not on the verge of her leaving me."

"I'm sure processing the fact she or the kids could have died is a lot. None of them—especially Sorcha—were prepared for what happened at your wedding. She loves you though. That has to mean something." I wish I could promise him that things will work out, but I can't.

"If only that was all it took. Maybe sometimes love isn't enough," Aidan says in a rough tone.

As harsh as it might sound—and I would never say this to my brother—maybe Sorcha isn't meant for the kind of life we live. Where danger can occur at any time. We've all gotten lax over the last couple decades with the truce that had settled between Dónal Sheehan and Da. Up until some dumb fuck kidnapped a civilian friend of our top enforcer a few months ago—under the guise of working for the Moroccans— they managed to keep their business to themselves.

After we launched an assault to rescue them, their leader Ayman Naji declared war. I guess they figured Aidan and Sorcha's wedding was the perfect place to take us all out at once. Since then, we've launched several strategic attacks against their businesses and a few of their gathering places. There have been deaths on both sides, but the Moroccans' casualty rate has been far higher.

I stand and clap him on the shoulder. "I really do hope things work out between you."

He barely nods so I leave him alone and head to my room for some sleep. Declan and I went back to my office for a few drinks and discussed the Euronext Dublin well into the night. We've both invested heavily in various stocks, some of the same ones, in fact, and he has a similar head for numbers that I do. No one in the family, not even Da, has an interest in the stock exchange. They all trust me to invest our family's money any way I see fit.

Once I walk into my room and shut the door, I strip off my clothes and take a quick shower before climbing into bed. I stare up at the ceiling, the swarming discontent returning in the quiet. I'd told Declan last night that it was like I'm bored, but that's not really it. Maybe it's the fact that both my brothers have found love and they're moving forward with their lives. While I'm happy for them, it also feels as though I'm being left behind.

Flopping onto my side, I punch the pillow to try and get comfortable. I close my eyes, as if that will help and force my mind to let go of it for the moment. It could be minutes or it could be hours, but I finally drift off.

A BUZZING AWARENESS BRINGS ME OUT OF SLEEP. I TURN onto my back and lie there a minute longer until I throw back the blanket and get up and ready for the day. My stomach growls reminding me it's been since last night that I ate. I head through the common room and find Aisling sitting at the makeshift desk Aidan created for her. She's bent over a sketchpad, and her tongue peeks out of the corner of her mouth in concentration as her hand moves across the page.

"Hey there," I say quietly trying not to scare her. I'd bit back almost calling her little nightmare, the nickname from her siblings considering her name actually means dream. I didn't want to give her any reminders she's been having them.

Aisling raises her head and smiles. "Hi Uncle Finn. You slept really late."

I close the distance.

"What are you drawing?" I squat down next to her.

Aisling sets down her pencil and lifts the pad for me to get a better look. "It's all the twinkle lights we're going to put in my room."

Sure enough, there's a forest full of trees on the paper, but she's decorated each one with small starbursts. For a six-year old, she's pretty good. In a year or two she'll probably be excellent.

"It's beautiful."

Aisling beams up at me, and then her expression stutters. She loses the glow and turns solemn. "Uncle Finn?"

"What?"

"Will the twinkle lights keep the bad men away?"

Ah, fuck. I drop to a knee, gently palm the back of her head, and look her straight in the eye. "The bad men can't get you here. You're safe. Aidan, Grand-da, and I won't let anyone hurt you."

"Do you promise? Da said if you make a promise to someone you have to keep your word."

I place my hand on my heart. "I swear it."

"What do you swear?"

Pivoting on my heel, I find Sorcha walking toward us carrying a tray with two plates on it. Aisling gathers her art supplies and pushes them to the far side of the desk.

"Uncle Finn swore he'll protect us from the bad men."

Sorcha's steps stutter, but she quickly recovers and sets the platter down. She darts a quick glance in my direction. "I'm sure he will, too. Now, it's time for supper."

I stand and let Sorcha set out their plates. "I'll let you two eat."

Aisling's already taken a bite, but her sister nods briefly at me before she takes a seat. I leave them and head for the kitchen, the scent of food growing stronger the closer I get. Nora, Da, and the boys are there with full plates. Da glances up at my arrival and welcomes me with a grin.

"Are you joining us this evening?" he asks.

I hadn't planned on it, but it's hard to pass on one of Nora's home-cooked meals. "For a little bit, but then I need to get to the casino."

Nora sends Kellen and Carson into the dining room and follows them.

"How are things there?"

"Same as always. The Flanagan boys lost more of their uncle's money."

Da shakes his head. "There's going to be trouble if they don't put a halt to their gambling."

"I can always send them over to Liam's casino. They can be his problem then."

Da chuckles. "That might not be a bad idea."

I load up my plate and glance toward the doorway. "The clan leaders are all coming to the casino tonight to strategize our next step."

His mouth tightens. "Good. Make sure Liam's present as well."

"I will."

He and I join Nora and the boys at the table. Kellen and Carson keep up most of the conversation.

Under normal circumstances, Campbell wouldn't be allowed to step foot in *Anamacha Caillte*, but since he owes a life debt to Cian, there's nothing he can do to us. Not unless Cian forgives it. Something I don't ever see happening. He'll lord it over him forever unless Nessa puts a stop to it, which she most likely will. Both she and Imogen want everybody to get along. I suppose it can't be easy for them to be stuck between two people they care about.

Who knows? Maybe after we put the Moroccans back in their place, peace will settle between Campbell and our family. As long as he and Imogen are together, we're all going to have to come to terms with the fact we're stuck with each other.

CHAPTER 5

Today has been one of the best days I've had in a long, long time. We swam earlier, then Imogen took me on a tour of the conservatory and the grounds. When was the last time I'd been able to let my guard down and have fun without watching over my shoulder or worrying I'd do something to set Ben off?

The fact I can't remember scares me.

"Oh my god." Imogen cackles and nearly falls off the couch. "Do you remember that time when I hacked into that shitty professor's computer and uploaded a program that Rick Rolled him every time he tried to open a document?"

I laugh and nearly spew wine everywhere. "I completely forgot about that. He was so pissed, especially since a virus was attached to it for when they tried to remove it."

Unrepentant, Imogen snorts. "He deserved it after what he did to that poor girl. As always, the man is the victim and the girl seduced him. It was her fault he stuck his dick in her. Fuck that guy and fuck the patriarchy."

She raises her arm up above her head nearly spilling the wine from the glass she's holding.

"Men are arseholes," I chime in. "Every single one of them. But especially Ben. I hope that piece of shit gets an itch on his balls that he can never scratch."

Imogen lowers her arm and pierces me with a sharp glare. "Wait a minute. We hate Ben? What happened between you two? I thought you said you broke up because long distance relationships were hard."

Cursing the wine, I drop my gaze and fidget with the stem of my glass.

"Hey." She lays her hand on my leg, sounding surprisingly sober. "What's going on?"

There's no use trying to hide it from her anymore. Imogen is stubborn as hell and with me opening my big mouth, she'll never let it go. I let out a deep sigh and lift my gaze to meet hers.

"He got possessive. Jealous," I finally confess. "Any time I left the house he accused me of cheating on him. I wasn't really going to work, he said. He would grab my arm tight and grill me about where I was really going. Who I was really seeing. If I had to go out of town for a job, he would call my cell non-stop until I was forced to shut it off."

"Oh Teag, I'm sorry." Her eyes harden. "You're right, he is a piece of shit. I'm so glad you broke up with him."

"Actually, I didn't. I mean, I did. He just doesn't know it." I swallow hard and my throat clogs. "Two days ago he went crazy, screaming he'd kill me and whoever I was sleeping with and destroyed my flat. He...he hit me. It was the first time, but it wouldn't be the last. He left soon after, and the minute I knew he was actually gone, I packed a carry-on suitcase and left. Stayed at a hotel that night and got on the first flight back here I could find."

Imogen takes my wine glass from my hand, places mine and hers on the table, and wraps her arms around me. I lay my head on her shoulder.

"Jesus. I wish you would have told me. I would have flown to Berlin and made Liam come with me. He would have kicked Ben's ass. Probably would have shot him, actually."

"That's why I didn't say anything. This was my mess to clean up. I didn't want to involve you in something that could get you or Liam in trouble or hurt. I know you Genny. You don't back down from anything. Besides, it might have stopped Ben for a short time, but as soon as he thought he could get away with it, he would have been back. He would have followed through with his threat to kill me. I just know it."

She squeezes me. "I'm glad you got away from him. Is that the real reason you're requesting a transfer?"

I nod against her. "I can't go back there."

Imogen leans and pushes me to sit upright. Her fierce glare bores into me. "You're damn right you're not going back. I'll kick your ass if you do."

She would, too. "You're a scary woman, Imogen Walsh. You know that?"

"Damn right I am. Now"—she grabs our wine glasses off the table and hands me mine—"we drink to new beginnings without that shitbird, Ben."

I tap the rim of mine to hers with a small German cheer. "Prost."

Imogen scrambles off the couch. "It's time for cheesecake."

Since I could use a refill, I follow her into the kitchen. She brings the dessert out of the fridge, slides it onto a large plate, and grabs two forks from the drawer. Most people would cut it into pieces, but that's not our thing.

"I've been thinking about this all day." She lifts it to her nose, takes a huge whiff, and moans like she's having an orgasm. "God, this smells so good. I haven't eaten cheesecake in so long. It's almost better than sex."

"I'm clearly not doing my job then," a deep grumble comes from the other side of the room.

I turn just as Imogen squeals, smacks the plate on the counter, and launches herself into Liam's arms. He catches her around the hips, his palms gripping her ass, as she wraps her legs around his waist and plants kisses all over his face. I try not to laugh at Liam's startled expression. This can't be the first time Imogen's been tipsy around him, can it? It must be if he has no idea how handsy and affectionate she gets. A pang of pure envy slams into me and I turn away to grab the bottle and top off my glass.

"Why don't I get this response every time I walk through the door?" There's amusement in his tone.

"Because I'm not drinking wine." There's another loud smack and then a light thud.

I finally turn to face them. Imogen's standing, but she's still holding onto Liam whose arm is wrapped around her shoulder.

"Hey." I give a half-hearted wave. "Nice to see you again."

"You as well, Teagan." He raises an eyebrow, which is understandable. The last time I was here I wasn't too friendly to him. Then again, he had just kidnapped my best friend. Even though he and Imogen fell in love, I still don't trust him entirely. Imogen will deny it until her dying breath, but her heart is fragile. I don't want him to break it.

"You and I might be taking a trip to Berlin." Imogen pokes Liam's chest and I cringe.

She's not so great at keeping secrets when she's been drinking either.

"Oh? For what may I ask?" His gaze darts over to me.

I make myself not flinch under his flinty stare.

"Teagan might need an ex-boyfriend—you know—taken care of." Imogen snarls and runs her finger across her throat. "That fucknut hit her and threatened her, too."

Liam goes rigid. Time to defuse things.

"No one needs to do anything. Ben is in Berlin and I'm here. He doesn't know where I'm staying or that I even came here. I just want to forget all about him. Please." My gaze darts between the two of them, my eyes pleading.

Imogen huffs. "Fine. But the offer is always open, isn't it babe?"

"Teagan only needs to say when." If Liam's stare had been intense before, it's nothing compared to how his eyes are laser-focused on me. It's a disconcerting sensation, because there's wrath burning in their depths. *Jesus, he's serious.* He would actually kill Ben if I asked him to.

I swallow. "Thanks."

What do I say to a man who just said he would murder someone for me? Without even blinking an eye. Entirely uncomfortable with the direction the conversation has turned, I grab the plate filled with cheesecake.

"You want to help me eat this or am I going to devour the whole thing myself and be absolutely miserable?" I lift my arms slightly like I'm presenting it to her.

"Sorry babe, cheesecake calls." Imogen pops up on her toes and kisses Liam with a loud smack.

I snag my full glass of wine and hustle out of the kitchen and away from Liam's intensity. I'm definitely going to need more to drink after this. My heart pounds as I set the plate on the sofa cushion between where Imogen and I had been sitting. She plops down on the other side of it and picks up her fork before digging in for the first bite. I take mine a little slower.

"And Liam wonders why I love my favorite bakery so much. This. This right here is why." She moans again in appreciation.

After a couple bites, Imogen finally glances at me. I'm not sure what she sees on my face, but she gets that stubborn tilt to her chin. "I'm not sorry I told him. Someone needs to know what Ben did to you. Especially since Liam can take care of things, if for any reason that fuckwad does find out where you are."

While I appreciate the fact Imogen cares so much about making sure I'm safe, it also makes me itchy that Liam knows my personal business. "I know. Thank you for looking out for me."

Imogen's eyes soften. "We always look out for each other. It's been that way for ten years. You're my best friend and I don't want anything to happen to you."

"It won't."

We go back to eating our cheesecake—Imogen with far more gusto than me—but the whole time I can't ignore the faint warning at the back of my mind that something bad is coming.

CHAPTER 6

FINN

I NOD AS I PASS ENNIS WHO MANS THE DOOR. EVER SINCE he fucked up and let Dónal Sheehan make it into the casino a couple months ago, he's been extra vigilant. That lapse led to Cian and Nessa getting together—and Sheehan getting dead—so it all worked out in the end.

Considering it's still early the tables are surprisingly full. I'm not complaining, but I'm curious as to why. Liam refused to come tonight when I first reached out—something about Imogen having a friend over—but when I mentioned another raid against the Moroccans, he was on board.

Making my way across the floor, I reach the lift, scan my card, and take it up to the restricted top floor, where only family and invited guests are allowed. It's quiet up here. Too quiet. Which leaves me unable to drown out my thoughts. My brain hasn't stopped running for almost a month. It's why I haven't spent much time alone.

I unlock my office door and step inside. The lights turn on automatically and I head for my desk and boot up my computer. Once it's running, I switch on the security feed that Imogen hooked up and study it while I wait for everyone to arrive. The on-screen images change every twenty seconds to a different position on the casino floor as well as the bar. With the new cameras we installed, there's a three-sixty degree view.

Since adding the additional security, I've caught one of the floor girls stealing and another "servicing" some of the members. For a price. Normally, I don't pry into whatever the women do, but I draw the line at taking money for sex. I'm not against prostitution, but I'm not going to jail for it.

My gaze is drawn to the feed of the front door of the casino just as Liam steps through. A grin tugs at my lips at the black-, teal-, and purple-haired woman who appears right behind him. And then there's a thump of some kind in my chest. Imogen's arm is looped around the arm of another woman. Christ, she's stunning.

Dark brown hair is piled on top of her head giving me the perfect view of her slim neck and heart-shaped face with arresting eyes and plush red lips. A few tendrils cascade down to brush the top of her shoulders—one of which is bare, as the collar of the shirt she's wearing dips down exposing it. Her jeans accentuate her hourglass shape and my fingers itch to trace the curve of her hips.

I study her face again. There's something so compelling about her features. She's not Irish, that's for certain. As if a tether is pulling me, I quickly head for the lift and make my way back down to the casino floor. A good host greets his guests personally, after all. The quiet inside of the metal box is broken by the din of conversation the second the doors open.

Trying not to appear overeager, I measure my steps as I scan the room. Towering over nearly everyone, Liam is easy to spot. I make my way forward until his gaze lands on me. The craggy and rough-hewn edges of his face indicate a hard life. Neither he nor Imogen speak of it, but from a few overheard whispers, it's no wonder Liam has hated everything and everyone.

"Donnelly," he greets me with a tone of derision.

"Campbell," I mimic his tone before my gaze skips over him and stops on Imogen.

She grins and loosens her hold on the woman at her side and gives me a brief hug. "It's nice to see you, Finn."

"You, too. You're looking well. Are you still holding up okay?"

Imogen narrows her eyes. "I really wish people would stop asking me that. You all are acting like I'm some delicate flower or something."

I hold up my hands in surrender. "I won't ask again."

"Thank you. Oh," she twists and drags the woman forward. "This is Teagan, my best friend from uni. Teagan, this is Finn."

"A pleasure to meet you." I reach out my hand, and she places hers in my palm.

Her skin is petal soft and the sweet fragrance of blackberries engulfs me as I stare into eyes that remind me of chocolate. Rich and sweet. A hint of pink darkens her cheeks.

"You as well." Far too quickly she pulls her hand from mine.

Already I miss touching her. Jaysus, what's wrong with me? Someone clears their throat, and I blink, breaking eye contact with Teagan who's already looked away. I glance at Imogen who presses her lips together, as though holding back her amusement. Liam, on the other hand, scowls. Even more than he usually does.

"Can I get you ladies a drink?" I'm not ready to walk away yet.

"I thought we were supposed to be having some meeting?" Liam grumbles.

"You're the first one here. Might as well have a cocktail while we wait for the others to arrive." Without waiting for another excuse, I head for the bar and wave over the bartender.

I don't glance over my shoulder, secure in the fact they're following me. Or at least that Imogen and her lovely friend Teagan are. Finally, at the man's approach, I pivot a half turn. Sure enough the three of them are here, although Liam's off to the side.

"We'll both have a glass of shiraz," Imogen says.

I stare at the other man with an arched brow. He grits his teeth. "Whiskey."

After relaying our order, I give them my full attention. Or at least Teagan. "Are you just here for a visit?"

"No. I recently moved back after living in Berlin and London for the last five years." Her husky voice washes over me.

"How did you like Berlin?" There's this sudden urge to know everything about her.

Teagan shifts and glances at Imogen who thins her lips and clenches her jaw. She turns her gaze back to me, but she won't quite meet my eyes. "I enjoyed it for a while, but I missed Dublin."

There's more to that story. "There's no better place than here."

She smiles, but it doesn't ring sincere. The bartender comes back with our drinks. I pass the women their wine and make to pick up Liam's whiskey, but he's already got it in his hand. *Glad I didn't waste any Devil's Keep on him.* I doubt he'd appreciate the flavor as much as our family does.

Movement to the right of him draws my gaze. Cian and Aidan approach. The former glares at Liam's back. There will most likely always be bad blood between the two. As if sensing my brother's stare, Liam turns toward them and goes rigid.

Cian and Aidan finally reach us. They ignore Campbell and focus on Imogen and Teagan. Despite the fact both men are taken, it doesn't stop me from taking a small step closer to Teagan. As though I'm claiming she's mine. Aidan's lips twitch.

"Imogen, I'm so glad to see you." Aidan greets her with a hug. Cian steps up next and repeats the embrace and greeting.

More introductions are made. As much as I don't want to walk away, it's probably time to head up to the office. More of the clan leaders and Da should be arriving any minute. I swivel toward Teagan.

"It was a pleasure meeting you. I hope we meet again soon," I can't help but tack on.

The corners of her mouth lift, but once again I get the impression that it's an automatic reaction of forced politeness. I stuff down the disappointment and walk away, leaving Liam and my brothers to trail behind. No one speaks until we reach the lift.

"Marking your territory already are we?" Aidan quips.

Liam's head jerks in my direction and he narrows his eyes. "Don't even think about it."

I bristle at his tone. "Excuse me?"

Cian and Aidan both stiffen and inch slightly closer to me. I appreciate the united front they're offering, but I don't need them to fight any battles for me. Perceived or not.

"Teagan is under my protection. She doesn't need you panting after her." Liam practically sneers.

If I weren't already interested in her, then his words have only made me more so. I'm a Donnelly. No one, not even Liam Campbell, tells me what I can or can't do.

"The last time I looked—and trust me, I looked—Teagan is a grown woman who I'm sure is quite capable of making her own decisions."

"Not about this," he growls.

"Why don't you worry about Imogen and keep your mouth shut about anyone else," Cian snaps.

Ignoring the fact that the lift door slides open, the two men close the distance between each other with a single step. I hold the button to keep it there while Aidan quickly moves in between them with a hand on their chest. "Why doesn't everyone take a deep breath and relax? There's way too much testosterone in this lift at the moment. Besides, I doubt neither Imogen nor Nessa wants either of you coming home tonight with battle wounds. Save it for the Moroccans."

For a few tense seconds, neither men loosen their rigidity. At last, Cian's the first to back down. Probably with the threat of Nessa getting upset. The man is nothing if not devoted to his woman and wanting to keep her happy.

"If we're done here?" I snark and exit the lift.

Slowly, the three of them follow, with Cian taking up the rear. I move past them and reach my office. Once inside, everyone except Liam takes a seat. With the glares being exchanged, everyone is still on edge. None of us trust Campbell.

I head to the bar, pour three glasses of whiskey, bring them back to Cian and Aidan, and then take a seat behind my desk. The tense silence is loud. Normally, my brothers and I would catch up and discuss business, but not tonight. Not with Liam here. Thankfully, we don't have a long wait before there's a sharp rap and Da enters. Behind him are several clan leaders that are part of our organization.

Everyone files in and Da shuts and locks the door behind him. He glances around the room, his gaze pausing on Liam, before launching into what we're all here for. How to take down the Moroccans.

CHAPTER 7

I'VE HAD DINNERS WITH SOME OF THE RICHEST BUSINESS owners in Berlin and London, and none of them can top the type of money I'm surrounded by in the Donnelly's casino. It's almost indecent.

"So that was interesting," Imogen remarks.

I turn from my perusal to find her staring at me with amusement glinting in her eyes. Damn. I'd kind of been hoping she would leave it, but this is Genny. She doesn't *leave* anything. I take the bait. "What was?"

"Finn was in to you." She scrunches up her face. "I'm not sure how I feel about my brother and my best friend together though."

"First of all, we're not together. Nor are we going to *be* together. He was merely being polite." I try to deflect, but she's not having it.

Imogen snorts. "There was nothing 'polite' about the way Finn was looking at you. He completely forgot any of the rest of us even existed."

My cheeks heat, because I had definitely got that impression as well. I admit to being flattered by the attention. Except after Ben, I have no interest in dating for the foreseeable future. I no longer trust my own judgment. "I've sworn off men, remember?"

"I thought you were just swearing off shitfuckers named Ben?"

Them too.

"All men. Especially dangerous ones. Look what happened to you being with Liam and related to the Donnellys. I'm not like you, Imogen. I'm the straight-laced one, remember. The one who remains on the other side of the law. Where it's safe and I can pretend I'm badass. I'm just boring Teagan who plays around with computers."

She loops her arm around mine and squeezes. "You are anything but boring. You're amazing. Smart. Fun. Fun*ny*. Kind. Beautiful. The best friend a girl could ask for. You're dependable, not straight-laced. There's nothing wrong with that, either."

"Dependable sounds like the tagline for diapers," I deadpan.

Imogen growls. "Come on. You clearly need another glass of wine."

Considering I've barely finished the one I'm currently working on, I definitely don't. "How about I finish this one first and reassess after?"

"Fine." She huffs. "But we're going to go play some Blackjack and spend Liam's money."

I snort and let her lead me to the nearest table. Before long there's a stack of chips in front of us both—one high enough to make me sweat a bit—and as soon as the two cards are in front of me, I place my first bet. I win far more often than I lose and soon I've accumulated another two stacks of chips and drawn a crowd.

Imogen, on the other hand, is down to only a handful of chips. She's shit at cards.

I'm having a lot more fun than I expected to and I can feel my muscles loosen and relax. *I didn't realize how tense I've been.* Encouraged by the increased number of members observing, my bids grow higher and maybe a bit more reckless. I shouldn't be so cavalier about

Liam's money. Then I remember he *did* kidnap my friend and I don't feel as bad.

"Twenty, and we have another winner," the dealer calls out and scoops my cards up.

I draw in my winnings and turn to Imogen, who's lost the last of her chips. "That's it for me, I think. I want to quit while I'm ahead."

Grumbles come from all around, but I ignore them. Imogen swivels in her seat to glare at the people standing behind us. "Piss off."

I bite back my laughter. I suppose that's one way to get rid of them. A different gentleman than the one who dropped off our chips arrives at the table. I let him take everything I've won back to the cage to cash out, and Imogen and I wander around.

"That was fun." I chuckle. "The perfect way to top off the perfect day."

Imogen shoulder bumps me. "I'm glad you've had a great time today."

"The best."

"Impressive play back there." A voice I'm sure I've heard before says.

We turn and Declan Campbell strolls forward.

"What are you doing here?" Imogen asks.

"I should ask you the same thing."

She waves her hand in the general direction the men went earlier. "The boys are having some meeting so I thought it would be fun to come with and show Teagan the casino."

Declan nods. His gaze flicks to me and a lazy grin appears. "Looks like someone got lucky tonight. Nicely done."

"Thank you." A small part of me is soaking up the fact that two brutally gorgeous men have flirted with me tonight. I mean, what girl wouldn't?

"Maybe I'll get lucky as well." There's no mistaking the suggestive tone. Especially since he drags a lazy gaze over me.

"Okay, enough of that. How about getting us a drink? You're

buying though. Liam's already going to side-eye me at the amount of money of his I lost." Imogen grabs his arm and drags him toward the bar.

He barks out a laugh as we stop in front of it. I step up on the other side of her.

"Serves him right," Declan says. "He has far too much of it and I'm glad to see that if anyone is relieving him of it, it's going to be the Donnellys. And you know as well as I do, that he won't say a damn thing about it. Liam lets you get away with far more than he would anyone else."

Imogen smirks. "That's because I'm the one who gives him blow—"

I smother the rest of her sentence with my hand over her mouth. Declan makes a gagging noise.

"No. No. Nope. Keep that shit to yourself." I glare at her and she narrows her eyes right back.

Reluctantly I lower my arm and brace myself for when she finishes the sentence.

"You guys are such babies," Imogen says instead, her gaze bouncing between us.

"No one wants to hear that about their cousin," Declan gripes.

"I'm firmly on his side."

Imogen rolls her eyes. "Traitor. You're supposed to be *my* best friend."

Thankfully we're interrupted by the casino employee. "Miss? Congratulations on your successful evening."

He discreetly hands me an envelope that I quickly shove in my bag. "Thank you."

"Maybe Teagan's buying drinks tonight," Imogen quips.

Declan glances over at us as the bartender arrives next. "What sort of gentleman would I be if I let a beautiful woman pay? I'm buying."

"Two shiraz, please," Imogen orders for both of us without skipping a beat. If she didn't know me so well, I might be annoyed at her presumption. Except she does, so I don't put up a fuss.

"Guinness for me," Declan adds and then turns to lean against the bar. "I don't suppose it's been long enough for you to have changed your mind about meeting me for a drink? And this one doesn't count."

I have to give him credit for at least being persistent. And if he's willing for me to turn him down again, this time in front of Imogen, he really must not be worried about his ego. I do like his confidence, but I'm already shaking my head. "Afraid not."

He grins good-naturedly. "You can't blame a man for trying."

The bartender sets our drinks in front of us and I pick mine up while Declan withdraws his wallet. I probably should offer to pay, but a single glance at him and I resist. Somehow I can tell he was serious about being the type of man who wouldn't let a woman buy his drinks. I don't get a sense that it came from a misogynistic place either.

"They'll let anyone in here, won't they?" Liam pulls Imogen to him and wraps a possessive hand around her waist. He glares at his cousin.

Declan stiffens. "Yes, I guess they will."

"Nope." Imogen shakes her head and pinches Liam's side. He doesn't even flinch. "No dick swinging tonight. Teagan and I are here to have fun. It's been the best day so far. Neither of you are allowed to fuck it up."

Both men continue glaring at each other before Liam tips his head. "Only because you asked so nicely."

I snort, cover it up with a cough, and take a quick sip of my wine. Or at least I mean to. Instead, I stop with the glass pressed to my lips and meet Finn's startling blue eyes. There's a flare of heat in them and then he shifts his gaze to Declan—who's moved to my side—and back to me. It's barely noticeable, but there's a slight thinning of his lips. What is that all about?

Slowly, he approaches and stands so close he's nearly touching me. Despite the narrow distance between us, he still leans in. Almost as though he's sharing a secret. "I heard you made out well at the Blackjack table tonight? Congratulations."

The warm, woodsy scent of teakwood surrounds me. It reminds me of the childhood hikes I used to take with my mādar in the Hyrcanian Forests whenever we visited her homeland. I ignore how good he smells. *Nope, not happening.*

"Thank you." I put on the smile I use in tedious business meetings and hope he takes the hint. I'm not interested. Taking a sip of wine to wet my suddenly dry lips, I glance over at Imogen who's got that irritating smirk on her face again. Declan is studying Finn and Liam is glaring at him. A thick tension comes out of nowhere to settle around us. Suddenly, Imogen yawns. Loudly. She doesn't even bother covering her mouth. I bite back my laugh. It's the same tactic she used in uni when she wanted to ditch someone.

"Sorry, boys," she addresses all of them. "I'm exhausted. And I'm sure Teagan is as well . I think we're going to head home."

She steps away from Liam, plucks the full glass of wine out of my hand, and sets it on the bar. Then she practically drags me away from the three men and doesn't wait to find out if Liam is following. Most likely because she knows he'll be right on our heels. This is why Imogen's my best friend. She's gotten me out of more than one uncomfortably awkward social situation.

"I love you. You know that, right?" She does know, but everyone likes to hear it once in a while.

She barks out a laugh. "Of course I do. What's not to love? Right, babe?"

"I'll refrain from answering until I know what I'm agreeing to," Liam replies since her raised voice—and glance over her shoulder—clearly indicates she's asking him.

Imogen shakes her head and squeezes my arm tight. "I love you, too. Which is why I'm really glad that one day you'll be my sister-in-law. But we're going to have to make Finn work for it."

I sputter and cough. "Never mind, I take it back. I hate you."

"No you don't. But fine, I was just kidding." She bats her lashes at me. "Maybe we'll be cousin-in-laws instead, then."

"You really are the worst." There's no heat in my tone though. "There will be no in-law of any kind happening. I've sworn off men, remember?"

All Imogen does is side-eye me. Maybe if I say it enough times we'll both believe it.

CHAPTER 8

FINN

I DRAW MY GAZE AWAY FROM TEAGAN'S RETREATING figure only to be met with Declan's closed-off expression.

"What?"

He shakes his head. "Nothing. She just doesn't seem like your type is all."

Annoyance sparks. "I wasn't aware I had a type."

Declan shrugs. "Everybody has a type. Even you."

"I suppose next you're going to tell me that Teagan is *yours*." Why is a fire burning in my gut at the thought of the two of them together?

"She and I just met earlier today at Imogen's house. I don't know her well enough yet to determine if she is or not. But what I do know," he emphasizes "is that somebody hurt her. I think recently, too."

I want to track down whoever this unknown person is and beat the hell out of them. "What makes you say that?"

"Because I pay attention. And a woman usually only brushes off a guy she just met by saying 'it's not you, but me' when her heart's been broken and she's trying to get over it," Declan says matter-of-factly.

"So you did ask her out, then?"

He snorts. "Of course I did. She's beautiful, and she's Imogen's best friend. I trust your sister's judgement on what makes a person best friend worthy. Boyfriend-worthy, on the other hand, is where Imogen's clearly not to be trusted for smart choices."

I have to laugh at that, because he's not wrong. "So she turned you down flat, huh?"

"Sooo flat." He widens his eyes for emphasis.

"I guess we'll find out if my luck is any better than yours." It's almost a dare for him to object.

Declan doesn't take it. Instead he claps my shoulder. "Don't come crying to me when she shoots you down."

"I'll keep that in mind. As much as I'd enjoy standing around to talk, I need to get back upstairs. There are some numbers that aren't adding up."

He raises his beer bottle. "Have fun with that."

I nod and head for the lift. Almost immediately the image of Teagan comes to mind. This fascination I have doesn't make sense. What is it about her? I can't explain it, but I want to figure it out. Except I can't at the moment, because business has to come first. Especially when it's possible one of my employees is stealing from us.

Loyalty is the one thing we require of anyone who works for us or who belongs to our family's organization. There is no sin against us worse than betrayal. Caitlín has told us stories about what her Italian brother-in-law over in Brooklyn does to traitors. Every member of their syndicate is tattooed with a crown when they're initiated. If that member betrays them, they burn the crown from their body before ending them. A fitting punishment really.

I get to my desk, pull up all our accounting records, and sift through them. Based on what's in front of me, I suspect it's going to be a long night.

A LOUD BANG HAS ME BOLTING UPRIGHT AND REACHING for the gun in my top drawer only to stop when my sleep-blurred eyes land on a laughing Aidan. My pounding heart slows.

"You have a little drool, right here." He points to a spot on his own face, and I swipe at the opposite place on my own.

"You're an arsehole."

He crosses the room and plops himself in the chair in front of my desk. "I'm having an amazing day and nothing you can say is going to hurt my feelings."

"Why's that? Did you finally grow a pair?"

"Nope, not even bothered. Because early this morning Sorcha told me she, Kellen, Carson, and Aisling aren't going anywhere."

I grin widely. "That's great news. I'm really happy for you. I know how hard the last couple weeks have been on both of you. As well as the kids."

Aidan nods. "I really thought I was going to lose her. I never knew what love was until Sorcha."

That familiar thread of envy wiggles its way through me. Both my brothers have found their person which is only a reminder that I'm alone. An image of Teagan flashes behind my eyes. I blink it away. She interests me, but that's a long way from being in love.

"I'm glad it's worked out for you two. I doubt that's what brought you all the way into town to tell me, though."

"No. Da sent me here because we have a problem." Aidan's tone turns serious.

I sit up in my chair. "What problem?"

"Someone—most likely the Moroccans—set fire to the shipping vessel that arrived overnight carrying our most recently acquired merchandise from our German suppliers. The entire thing sank before they could put the flames out." He pauses. "Everything on board was destroyed. On top of that, we found the body of one of the dock workers under our employ. He'd been shot in the back of the head."

"Fuck." I slam my fist on the desk top. "How did they get past security? Not only that, but how did they know a shipment arrived, let alone which carrier it had come in on?"

Aidan stares at me with a knowing glance. *Someone told them.*

"Money is missing from the casino." I don't believe in coincidences.

"What? How much? Who?"

I gesture to the still open computer in front of me. "The how much is what I've been working on since last night. As far as the 'who'? I don't know. Yet."

Aidan sits quietly for a minute. "Do you think it's one person betraying us or are there more?"

I shake my head. "I don't know. Who has motive? Or opportunity?"

His eyes meet mine. "There's one person I can think of off the top of my head."

"He owes us a life debt."

Aidan leans forward. "That only means he can't physically harm any of us. But he sure as hell can try to put us out of business. And what about that cousin of his? Declan. He's here frequently and the two of you spend a lot of time together. Da, Cian, and I still don't understand how he can be friends with one of the men who put him and his brother in the hospital. Maybe it's a ruse."

My immediate reaction is to deny that Declan would do something like that. Except I stop myself. *Haven't you also questioned how you two could become friends?* Is it possible that I've been blind? I clench my fists. If he's been playing me this whole time, then I don't care if he is Liam's cousin, he's a dead man.

"Let me worry about Declan. If he's betraying us—him *or* Liam —then I'll take care of it."

Aidan nods. "For Imogen's sake, I really hope it's neither of them."

So do I.

He stands and glances down at me. "Keep me or Cian informed if you find something out."

"I will."

Aidan walks out of my office, closing the door behind him. I stare at the numbers on the screen. No matter how long I worked through them last night, I still can't find the source of the discrepancy or a total amount. It's there somewhere. I just have to keep searching. In the meantime, since I should give my mind a break, there's something else I need to do.

I shut down my computer and head out of the casino to where my car is parked on the street in a family designated spot. After a quick stop at Imogen's favorite bakery for a couple things, I make my way toward the north side of the city. *You don't even know if she's still there.* Yet I continue on until I stop in front of an ostentatious home. I grab the bag, both cups of tea, and walk to the front door.

After my knock, several minutes pass. I glance at my watch. Christ. It is a little early. They're all probably still asleep. I knock once more and ring the bell for good measure. Moments later, it's jerked open and a gun is directed at my face.

"For fuck's sake. What is it with you Donnelly's coming to my door at god awful hours? I'll ask you the same thing I asked your brother when he came barging in here a few weeks ago. Give me one reason I shouldn't shoot you?"

"Because then you'll get blood on these scones, and you know how much Imogen loves them." I show my teeth in a cheeky grin and hold up the bag.

Liam whirls away and grumbles something under his breath about pussies hiding behind a woman. I ignore him and step inside, glancing around. Good god. Aidan is right. This place *is* pretentious.

"Finn? What are you doing here?" Imogen moves toward me.

"I brought breakfast." For a second time, I raise the bag.

She rushes forward with a squeal and snatches it out of my hand. "Oh my god, is this from Mannings?"

"Of course. Do you really think I would bring you and your guest second-rate scones and tea? Fortnum's Ginger and Sicilian Lemon, right?"

Imogen quirks her lips and rolls her eyes. "You know, you should be far less obvious."

I palm my chest and bat my eyelashes. She just shakes her head and takes one of the to go cups. "Come on. Teagan is probably still asleep, but I'll wake her."

As much as it pains me to, I stop her. "No, don't disturb her."

"I'm already awake."

My head jerks up and my gaze zeroes in over the top of Imogen's head. The main reason I'm even here approaches.

"I didn't mean to wake you." *Didn't you, though*?

Teagan waves her hand. "It's fine. Did I hear you say you brought breakfast?"

Imogen pivots to face her friend. "He brought Mannings."

Dark eyebrows rise and Teagan cocks her head. "That feels almost like a bribe."

I give her my most innocent look and offer her the second cup. "I hope you like Fortnum's as well."

Her fingers graze mine and a small spark flares from the touch. Teagan takes the drink and quickly pulls her arm back. She clears her throat. "Not as much as Genny, but it'll do."

My gaze flicks to Imogen whose eyes are filled with amusement. "Genny?"

"Only Teagan is allowed to call me that, so don't get any ideas. Now, if you're done flirting with my friend, the scones are getting cold and I'm hungry." She pivots and walks away from us. "You better have brought jam and cream."

A quick glance confirms a pink hue colors Teagan's cheeks.

"Would you mind if I joined the two of you for breakfast?" She opens her mouth and I hold up my hand. "There's no pressure and no expectations of anything more than that."

A short silence settles before she breaks it. "Just breakfast."

I nod in agreement. I'll take it. To start, anyway.

CHAPTER 9

THIS IS A BAD IDEA. A REALLY, REALLY BAD IDEA. I SENSE Finn's eyes on my back as he follows me into the kitchen. Imogen glances up at our arrival and a smile ghosts across her face before she lowers her head and puts a scone on each of the plates she's set on the counter.

"Grab some knives, will you, please?" She gestures to the drawer where they're kept.

I take a step in that direction, but Finn's voice stops me.

"I'll get them. You're a guest."

While he crosses the room, I fidget with the lid on the cup and try to focus anywhere but on him. Both he and Declan are equally attractive with their dark hair—although Finn's is near-black— and razor sharp jawlines dusted with the perfect amount of scruff. While Declan's eyes are a gray that remind me of a windswept storm, it's Finn's blue eyes that seem to pierce me all the way down to my soul. Liam's cousin doesn't affect me in nearly the same way as Imogen's

745

brother does no matter the brief amount of time I've spent with him. There's something about his presence that has my body on high alert.

This is just breakfast.

I'll remind Finn—and myself—that as many times as I need to. I'm not in any kind of headspace to start seeing someone. Ben made sure of that.

A warm heat radiates through me. I glance up to find Finn standing close enough to touch.

"Are you all right?" he asks softly.

"What? Oh, yeah." I wave away his concern. "Just drifted off for a second."

I get the impression he doesn't believe me. Shaking it off, I take a deep, cleansing breath and straighten my shoulders. "What can I do?"

"We're good," Imogen says. "Everything's out and ready to eat."

Sure enough the containers of jam and cream are open and sitting next to the plates. Imogen's already slathering hers. Finn sweeps his arm out.

"After you."

I stride past him and do my damnedest to ignore his woodsy scent and the way my body is completely aware of him. "Thanks."

"My pleasure."

Finn's suggestive tone rolls over me and a small shiver skates down my spine. My belly heats. Flustered, I set my cup on the counter and snatch up a knife. I keep my gaze focused on the task in front of me as though it takes all my concentration. With the heat of those eyes boring into my back, it does. Once I have all the jam and cream I want, I take my plate and tea to the dining room where Imogen is already seated.

"What happened to swearing off men?" she whispers loudly.

I dart a glance toward the kitchen. "It's just breakfast."

"Mmhmm. If you say so."

"I do."

She clamps her mouth closed as Finn walks in. He sits across from me. Damn it. I want to kick him under the table for forcing me to have to meet his eyes every time he talks. Even when he's not talking. I may have only met him last night, but he strikes me as the person who does everything with intention. I should be annoyed since I've already made it clear I'm not interested in anything more than this meal. But somehow I can't find it in me to be.

Thankfully Imogen monopolizes the conversation. I could kiss her. Until Finn turns his gaze from her and locks it on me.

"Cyber security, huh?" he asks. "That sounds complicated."

My gaze bounces to Imogen. Damn. I've missed half the conversation. I set down my scone, take a sip of tea, and clear my throat. "It can be. It's exhausting, because there's always some hacker out there who is trying to make a name for themself."

I give a pointed stare at Imogen. She throws up her hands with a laugh. "I've already made a name for myself in the community. No need for me to impress anyone anymore. They all know what I can do."

She isn't bragging either. Few hackers are as brilliant as her.

"You still working for Paddy, I take it?" Finn asks.

"Going on a decade. It still blows my mind that all this time my own cousin has been one of my clients and I had no idea." Imogen shakes her head.

Liam walks in just then, pauses at the sight of Finn, and glares. "Why are you still here?"

"These lovely ladies invited me to stay for breakfast. Sorry, I forgot to bring you anything."

I almost laugh because we definitely didn't invite him, and the fact he's so flippant amuses me. It's not that I don't like Liam, but it's kind of nice to see him humbled a bit. Or at least as humbled as someone with his amount of self-importance can get.

Imogen heads over to him.

"Be nice," she whispers audibly and rises up to give him a kiss.

I glance at Finn who winks at me and one side of his mouth curls up. A dimple appears. I've always had a weakness for a man with dimples. Which is what got me into trouble in the first place. Ben has them. The sight of that small little furrow is a good reminder that no matter how aware I might be of Finn, I'm nowhere near ready for a flirtation.

"Where did you go just now?"

My head jerks up and I meet his eyes. I glance to where Liam and Imogen stood, but they've disappeared somewhere, leaving me alone with Finn. I'm going to kill her. My gaze darts back to him still waiting for an answer.

"I really appreciate you bringing over breakfast." I'm not answering his question.

He sits back. "But?"

"But whatever this is"—I gesture between us—"it isn't going to happen."

This time, Finn slowly leans forward and rests his forearms on the table. "And what exactly do you think *this* is?"

Flustered by the intensity of his stare, I struggle to answer. "This...this..."

"Attraction?"

I huff in exasperation. "Yes."

A slow grin forms on his lips. "So what you're saying is you're attracted to me?"

"Yes. No." I growl. "You're far too smug. You know that, right?"

"So I've been told." His smile hasn't left.

I take in a deep breath and release it. "Look, I'm going to tell you the same thing I told Declan."

"It's not you, it's me," Finn beats me to it.

I'm not sure how I feel about the two of them discussing me. "Yes."

"That's a cop out."

I sputter. "Excuse me?"

He leans back again, far too relaxed and looking far too good in the suit he's wearing. His black hair, so similar to Imogen's, shines from the light coming in through the windows. Is it as soft as it looks? *Focus.*

"I said, that's a cop out. If you're truly not interested in me, then say so. But if you are, then don't try and hide behind some lame line. What are you so afraid of?"

I'm afraid to open myself up again.

I'm afraid I'll never trust myself again.

I'm afraid of being hurt.

I'm afraid of *Ben.*

But I don't say any of those things. Instead, I get to my feet and walk out of the room. Wood scrapes the floor behind me. I don't get far before Finn latches onto my arm. Unable to control my response, I flinch and throw my hand up to block a blow that doesn't come. Instantly, he releases me and I step away.

"Teagan," he says softly. Gently. "I'm not going to hurt you."

"I'm sorry." The words spill out of me automatically. It's what I've been conditioned to say these past few months. Every time Ben lost his temper.

Finn shakes his head. "No, I'm sorry. I shouldn't have grabbed you. It's my fault."

Stupid tears fill my eyes. Moving so slowly, he closes the distance between us and ever so carefully wraps his arms around me. My fingers clench his shirt as my tears wet the fabric. I breathe in his comforting scent and let the warmth of his body soak into me. We stand at the far side of the dining room, neither of us speaking. Finn just holds me and lets me cry. I never cried, no matter how many times I was screamed at. Berated. I didn't even cry when Ben hit me.

I let the tears wash away all the uncertainty. The pain. The fear. Every emotion I've been holding back over these last few months. I cry until there's nothing left but exhaustion and a sliver of hope that everything is going to be okay. Reluctantly, I loosen my grip and move away. Finn lets me go. I swipe at the remaining wetness dotting my eyelashes and sniffle.

"Thank you for being so nice."

"You don't have to thank me, Teagan."

I let the soft way he says my name wash over me. I'm not sure what happens next. There's a larger part of me that's embarrassed by my breakdown. Especially in front of Imogen's brother. I shift my weight the tiniest bit. As if sensing the overwhelm I'm feeling, Finn gives me a bit more space.

"I enjoyed breakfast, but I'm sure Liam thinks I've worn out my welcome," he says with a small chuckle.

Somehow I manage a small smile. He stares at me a moment longer and I hold my breath, hoping he doesn't say anything else. He grants my wish, because he nods shallowly. "Maybe I'll see you around."

"Yeah, maybe." I'm not sure either of us believe it.

"Take care of yourself."

And then Finn walks away. I stumble back into the wall and slowly slide down until my butt hits the floor. Pulling my knees into my chest, I rest my chin on them and hug myself tight. That's how Imogen finds me. She sits down—her hip pressed to mine—and wraps an arm around me. I lay my head on her shoulder and we sit there quietly together.

CHAPTER 10

FINN

So much for getting work done.

"You've been distracted for days. And it has nothing to do with the missing money from the casino." Aidan pours himself and me a glass of whiskey.

Cian sits in one of the extra chairs in my office already working on his drink. The two of them stopped by for some unknown reason. Based on the glances they keep sharing, this feels like some kind of intervention. Whatever it is, they need to make it quick since we'll be opening in less than an hour and I need to go back to combing through the accounts.

"I'm not distracted."

It isn't often we're all together like this unless we're meeting with Da and the other clan leaders. Even more so since Cian and Nessa moved into her childhood home. Something that surprised Aidan and me considering the house had previously belonged to her Da.

Especially given how much hatred Cian held for the man. Not only because he abused Nessa, but also because he'd almost killed her.

"You're a shite liar, you know that, right?" Cian remarks.

I glance at Aidan who brings my whiskey over. "I feel like we've had this conversation before, but I liked it much better when it was about Aidan's lies."

He drops into the chair next to Cian and raises his glass. "To none of us being shite liars."

We copy the gesture. I take a sip and let the burn travel down my throat to settle warmly in my stomach. Aidan leans forward with his elbow resting on his knees.

"Lies aside. What's got you distracted?"

The two of them are stubborn and once they lock onto something, they don't let it go. I'm annoyed that I've become the object of their focus. There's no point trying to redirect or brush them off. Neither of them will stop pushing until I've told them everything.

"Imogen's friend Teagan." It spills out of me.

Cian and Aidan share a glance that ratchets up my irritation level.

"What's that look for?" I snap.

"Should have known it was woman trouble." Cian nods.

"It's not trouble. I just..."

"Can't get her out of your head?" Aidan cuts in. "Think about her constantly?"

I glare at him. "Yes." She hasn't left my mind since the morning I last saw her almost a week ago.

He laughs and sits back in his seat. "Welcome to the club."

"What club?"

"The club of men who have met the woman that brings them to their knees," Cian explains.

"Teagan hasn't brought me to my knees. I hardly know her." But I want to.

"It doesn't matter," Cian points out. "The minute you start thinking non-stop about a woman is the minute you're done for.

There's no letting go. Trust me. It's the exact same thing that happened with Nessa and me. I knew nothing about her. Not her likes or her dislikes. But every time I looked at her, I saw a spark of something that only continued to grow bigger until it consumed me. I suspect your time is coming."

I stare at my brother. "You're not serious are you?"

"Dead serious."

"If you can't stop thinking about her, then why don't you do something about it? It's not as though you're with anyone. Unless, of course, she is." Aidan adds.

"No, she's not. At least I don't think so." Just remember her reaction to my clasping her arm makes me see red again. "She's...skittish. Somebody has hit her. I'm guessing an ex."

Both Cian and Aidan's expressions turn fierce.

"I hope you have something extremely painful planned for him," Cian grinds out. "And whatever it is, we're in."

As much as we've fought and disagreed over the years, the one thing I can count on is my brothers having my back. I loosen the death grip I have on my whiskey glass so I don't break it. "I have no idea who, or where, he is. Although, if it is her ex, I suspect he's in Berlin since that's where she was living before moving back here."

"Have you asked Imogen?" Aidan inquires.

"No."

Cian raises his eyebrows. "Why not?"

"If Teagan wants people—me—to know, she'll tell them. I don't want to go behind her back and invade her privacy. It doesn't feel right." I pause. "Besides, the last time I saw her she made it pretty clear she's not ready to date anyone."

"Why does it have to be all or nothing?" Aidan asks. "How about trying to be her friend? I mean, look how well it's worked out for me. Sorcha and I fell in love."

Cian snorts. "Is that before or after you spent the first two weeks of your marriage with your wife barely speaking to you and sleeping on the couch?"

Aidan gives him the finger. "Fuck off. Sorcha and I are good. Great, even. Because we started out as friends and had built trust between us."

I stare at my older brother. His suggestion isn't a bad idea actually. I've never been just friends with a woman before. Not really. I glance at Aidan. "It's certainly worth trying."

"Exactly," he says.

"Good luck," Cian adds and gets to his feet. "Now that we have that settled, I'm heading home. Nessa and I leave in a couple weeks for Brooklyn for Caitlín's wedding, and I want to make sure I have everything I need."

This time, Aidan and I share a glance. I grin and turn back to Cian.

"You picked up her ring, I take it?"

He nods. "Earlier today. Now it's just waiting for the perfect moment. I don't want to upstage Caitlín since we're there for her wedding after all. I've heard women get weird about that kind of thing."

I'm really happy for him and Nessa. "I'm sure you'll figure out the right time. Congratulations, Cian."

His gaze moves between Aidan and me. "Can you believe that barely six months ago it was just us three and Da? Look at our family now. We have a sister! I've added Nessa and Aidan's got not only a wife, but three damn kids. I have no doubt that before long, Finn, you're going to bring someone into the family as well."

Aidan laughs. "Now all we need to do is convince Nora to marry Da."

It came as a shock to all of us that Da's long-time mistress Nora was Imogen's biological mother and he her father. It's been an adjustment for all of us since finding out the news.

"I'm sure we will," Cian says and sets his glass on the bar. "We'll talk later."

Once he's gone, Aidan turns to me. "Take it from someone who's been there. If you're going to be Teagan's friend, then you need to be her friend. Don't make anything between you sexual. I'm not saying you two will fall in love like Sorcha and me, but if you're really interested in her, meet her where she's comfortable."

Since I'm sure he's only trying to be helpful, I swallow down my sarcastic comment about not being an idiot. Instead I just nod. "Understood."

He stands. "I'll let you get to work. If you need anyone to talk to, you know I'm always available."

"Thanks. I appreciate it."

Aidan heads out the door as well and I sit back in my chair and nurse my drink. Friends with Teagan. Will she even accept that much from me? Guess I'll find out. But not tonight. Tomorrow, though, I'll call Imogen and get a phone number. Having to be satisfied with that, I boot up my computer and open the accounting software.

Hours later, eyes blurry, I stare at the screen and all the numbers that have run together. I've cross-checked everything. The books say one thing, but the money being reported at the end of each night aren't matching. Not even the security cameras have picked up who might be pocketing it. I've watched hours and hours of footage.

"Fuck." I slam the lid down on the laptop and push away from the desk.

I need another drink and then I need sleep. After a single shot, I head for the suite I sleep in more often than not. Once I'm undressed, I climb into bed and close my eyes. Immediately my brain pulls up an image of Teagan and then I drift off.

Gentle hands roam over my back and down my shoulders. I turn and Teagan smiles up at me. Her top front tooth is slightly crooked. She doesn't say anything. Just lifts up onto the balls of her feet and presses a kiss to my lips. It's sweet, and yet a fire sizzles and burns through my veins. I palm her bare ass and drag her closer. A breathy moan spills from her. She rubs her pelvis against mine. The musky scent of her cunt fills my nose. I breathe it in even deeper.

Teagan's nails score my back. Not hard, but enough to send a shiver straight to my throbbing cock. Fuck. I grit my teeth. The sensation of her skin against mine only makes me harder. I want to bury myself deep inside her until neither of us knows where I end and she begins.

I grip her hips tightly and hoist her up, my lips never leaving hers. Teagan wraps her long, supple legs around my waist, pinning my cock between us. The pressure is both agonizing and yet not enough. Wet heat spreads across my flesh from where our bodies meet. Careful not to trip over anything, I walk forward carrying her towards the bed. I set her down gently and she stares up at me with chocolate eyes gone dark.

A seductive smile appears on a passion-kissed mouth and Teagan crooks her finger, beckoning me closer. Her small pink tongue peeks out to tease me. I'm dying for another taste of her. Dipping my head, I cover her lips and drag a stuttering breath from her. Another moan escapes from her throat.

I kiss my way across her jaw and neck, nibbling lightly here and there. Teagan tilts her head to give me better access. I take full advantage of it. I lick a path downward. Pert brown nipples rise up as though begging for their turn. I lift my gaze until our eyes meet and then latch onto the first one. Her back arches, pushing her breast up. I devour her.

"More," she whimpers.

Teagan moves her hands from my shoulders and her fingers tunnel through my hair. Her fists clench gripping me tight as though she can't bear for me to stop. I have no intention of doing any such thing. Not until she comes apart beneath me with my cock inside her.

"Tell me again what you want." It's a hard demand.

"More," Teagan repeats.

"More what?" I want her begging.

"Kisses. Touches. Everything."

I give her exactly what she asks for, kissing my way down her stomach to breathe in her scent. Beneath the musky scent is a hint of blackberries. My tongue flicks out to tease Teagan's swollen clit. I palm one breast, pinching then rolling the hardened tip between my fingers and slowly insert a finger from my other hand into the hot, wet heat of her cunt.

My mouth and fingers work in tandem to bring her to the pinnacle of pleasure. She squirms and bucks beneath me and I bite down on her clit with a sharp nip to keep her still. Only Teagan does the complete opposite. She screams and digs the sharp point of her nails into my scalp. Her pelvis jerks up so sharply she nearly bucks me off.

Her cunt clenches my finger and a full tremor rushes over her body. Liquid spills from her soaking the sheets. She cries out again, my name echoing through the room in the sweetest symphony. Unable to hold myself back any longer, I move and line my cock up with her entrance and thrust my hips forward, impaling her on my length.

My eyes jerk open and I suck in air. I'm fisting my cock and almost explode, but I squeeze the base of it to hold my seed back. My heart pounds like a drum. I shudder with the need for release. Like a teenage boy who's jerking himself off for the first time, it's coming and there's no stopping. I let go and let it happen. When I have nothing left, I drag myself out of the bed and into the bathroom for a shower.

I stare at myself in the mirror. How am I going to try and be just friends with Teagan after that?

Christ. I'm so fucked.

CHAPTER 11

My designed-to-be zen room has lost its zen. It doesn't matter that everything is where it's always been and everything looks the way it's always looked. Even my bed doesn't feel right. In fact, nothing feels right anymore. Berlin isn't home, but I'm not sure Dublin is either. I've been gone too long. Yes, I've missed Imogen, but maybe I've changed too much. I'm definitely not the same person I was when I left for London five years ago and then Berlin the year after that.

From the hallway my intercom buzzes. I throw back the duvet and hurry out to it. It's probably a good thing since I've been moping in bed for way too long today.

"Yes?"

"I brought takeaway and a friend. Let us up." Imogen's voice crackles with static.

Shit. I'm glad I at least put on regular clothes, even if it is only leggings and a t-shirt. She'd never let it go if she found me still in my pajamas since it's nearly one. I press the button to release the lock on the front door of the building and open my own while I wait. Footsteps plod up the stairs until her tri-colored head appears first and then the rest of her follows. In her hand is a brown paper takeaway bag. Right behind is a pretty woman I've never met. Her hair is down around her shoulders and a pair of sexy librarian-esque glasses is perched on her nose. I'm envious of the stunning yellow and white wrap dress that hugs her curves perfectly.

Imogen pivots and gestures toward her. "Teagan, this is Nessa, Cian's girlfriend."

"It's so nice to finally meet you. Imogen has told us so much about you," Nessa says kindly.

"Please, come in." I step back so the two of them can walk past and close the door behind them.

Imogen leads us to the kitchen and sets the bag on the counter. The scent of my favorite restaurant fills the small space. "Did you get me corned beef and colcannon?"

She glares at me with eyes widened in disbelief as she pulls out small white takeaway containers. "Of course I did."

I blink innocently. "Just checking."

Imogen glances over at Nessa. "Teagan and I started getting food from Davy Byrne's during our...second year at University, wasn't it?"

"That sounds about right."

She continues emptying the bag and then folds it up and sets it on the other counter. "We ordered from there at least once a week, if not more. And every time, no matter what, Teagan ordered the exact same thing."

"Hey." I gasp in offense, circling around to get utensils for us. "You're not supposed to make it sound weird. I just know what I like. Why make it hard on myself trying something new when I always end up getting what I really wanted in the first place? At least with colcannon, I know I'm going to enjoy it."

Nessa laughs softly. "I completely understand. More often than not I tend to do the same thing."

"See?" I gesture. "Nessa gets me."

Imogen snorts, peeks inside the first container, and passes it over to me. "This is yours."

She does the same thing with the second one. "This one's mine. Which means this one is yours." She hands the third container over to Nessa and then grabs three glasses from a cabinet and fills them with filtered water from the pitcher in the fridge.

"I'm sorry I don't have enough chairs at the table for all of us. But we can go into the living area. It's where I usually eat anyway." It's been too long since I've entertained anyone.

"I'm a no fuss kind of person, so I don't mind," Nessa says relieving me of the pinch of guilt for not being a better hostess.

We take our food and drinks into the other room. Imogen drops into the chair while Nessa and I take the sofa.

"How goes the job hunt?" Imogen mumbles around a mouth full of food.

"Not well. Every single manager I talk to says I'm over-qualified for the position." It's really pissing me off too.

"You know, I can always refer a couple of my clients to you. Nothing big or, you know, illegal." She grins.

I'm not that desperate yet. "I'll let you know. Thank you for the offer."

Imogen stares for a minute before I turn toward Nessa. "I love your dress, by the way."

A hint of pink fills her cheeks. "Thank you. Cian's cousin Caitlín picked it out for me on one of our shopping trips. I have no eye for fashion—nor do I care about it. I'm all about comfort and casual. Except she's made it her life's mission to pick out all my clothes. Which, truthfully, I don't mind. She has far better taste than I do anyway."

"Well, she did a great job with that one. It's beautiful."

"Wait until you meet her." Imogen chuckles. "That woman is a force to be reckoned with. I've never known anybody who can be both obnoxious and yet funny and charming like her. If you thought

I didn't have a filter, Caitlín surpasses even me with the whole saying what's on her mind thing."

"She certainly lets you know how she feels about things, that's for sure," Nessa adds with a small laugh.

"I can't wait to meet her." A lack of filter is one of the things I love most about Imogen. A person always knows where they stand with her.

I dealt with too many people growing up who said one thing to my face and something entirely different behind my back. Mostly my mādar's family. If Caitlín is even more blunt, then I'm sure I'll love her.

"When she and Roarke get back from their honeymoon, we'll have to call Sorcha and Lucia and have a ladies night out," Imogen announces and glances at me. "Sorcha is Finn's sister-in-law and Lucia is married to Caitlín's brother."

It's also been far too long since I've gone out with friends. I had a few acquaintances in Berlin, but they were closer to colleagues than friends. It had taken me too long to realize that Ben had kept me isolated from everyone. One more reason to be grateful I'm away from him.

"I can't wait for my first trip to America. Cian and I are going to Caitlín and Roarke's wedding in Brooklyn," Nessa chimes in. "It'll be my first plane ride, too. I'm so nervous."

"It's going to be great," Imogen reassures her. "You and Cian will have a great time. Eat some New York pizza for me, please, and tell me if it's as amazing as I've heard everyone say it is."

"Oh, I will."

Imogen then launches into a story about her latest hacker job while I sit back, enjoy my lunch, and savor being around girlfriends again. I've missed this so much. Just as we finish eating, Imogen holds up a finger.

"Before I forget," she swallows. "Finn texted me earlier wanting your phone number. Are you okay with me giving it to him? I told him I would ask."

My heart stutters for half a beat. It's been five days since he walked out of Imogen's house after my epic breakdown. Five days where I cringe at my reaction to him when he did nothing more than clasp my arm as well as at my inability to control my emotions. I swallow. *Tell her no. Two little letters. N-o.*

"I suppose it's all right," I say instead and mentally smack myself.

Clearly she hears the uncertainty in my tone, because she cocks her head. "Are you sure? If you don't want to talk to him, I'll tell him to bugger off."

"No. No," I hurry to assure her. "It's okay. Really. You can give it to him."

Imogen narrows her eyes slightly, but tips her chin. "I'll text him with it later then."

"Okay." A swirling sensation starts up in my belly. It's a combination of trepidation and excitement.

That's all I'm going to be thinking about the rest of the day. Finn's call. I'd gotten the impression when he left Imogen's house that he had no interest in pursuing the...attraction between us. At first I'd been relieved. But if he asked her for my number, then maybe I'm wrong.

"As much fun as this has been, we should probably get going." Imogen picks up her glass on the floor near her feet and stands. "I need to head into my office soon. I'm expecting a call from Paddy about a job he needs me to do for him."

Nessa and I get up as well and we all walk to the kitchen to toss out the containers and put the glasses and utensils in the dishwasher. I give Imogen and Nessa both a hug.

"Thank you for bringing lunch over. I've been going a little stir-crazy here being alone." I glance over at Nessa. "And it was so nice meeting you."

She smiles wide. "You too. I'm looking forward to our girls' night out when Cian and I get back from Brooklyn. I have years of them to catch up on."

I blink at that. I'll need to ask Imogen about it later. I walk them to the door and close it behind them. Turning I sag against it with a long sigh. From the living area, my phone rings. Maybe it's someone calling me about a job. I rush into the room and answer it.

"Hello?"

"You've been a very bad girl, Teagan."

I nearly drop the phone at the sound of Ben's voice. God, I'm going to be sick. "How did you get this number?"

Before leaving Dublin I blocked him. Changing my number was the first thing I did after arriving back in Dublin.

"What did I tell you would happen if you ever tried to leave me?" he asks, completely ignoring my question. "You only brought this upon yourself."

My hands are shaking and my knees almost buckle. It takes me a moment, but as the silence lengthens, I pull the phone from my ear. The screen displays a picture of Imogen and me on our graduation day. Bile rises in my throat. I run into the bathroom and barely make it to the toilet before I throw up. More vomit comes until there's nothing left in my stomach and I collapse onto the floor. The cold tiles feel good against my fevered skin.

I lay there long enough to get a cramp in my side. Pushing myself up to seated, I lean against the wall while my whole body shakes. Finally, I manage to get to my feet and stagger into the living area like a zombie. I pick my phone up from where I dropped it and pull up my favorites. Seconds later, it's ringing.

"Hey," Imogen answers. "Did you miss me already?"

"I think Ben found me."

There's a split second of silence. "Lock your door. Don't open it for anyone. We'll be there in ten minutes."

"Hurry. Please." I do as she says.

"I'm already out the door." Imogen ends the call.

I go into the kitchen and grab a knife from the drawer. Then I go back into the living area, sit on the couch with the blade clutched tightly in my hands, and wait.

CHAPTER 12

FINN

I STARE AT THE COMPUTER, BUT MY GAZE IS UNFOCUSED. I've been waiting most of the day for Imogen to text me. What if Teagan tells her not to give me her number? I can't remember a time when I was this hung up on a woman. Have I ever been?

Every time I pick up my phone to text Imogen, I slam it back down on my desk. This is ridiculous. Maybe I should call Aoife. Except she's not the person consuming my thoughts and making it difficult to concentrate on anything else. Fuck it. I punch the screen for Imogen's number and wait. She answers after a couple rings.

"I can't talk at the moment."

Her voice doesn't sound right. I straighten in my chair. "What's wrong?"

"Look, Teagan needs me right now. I have to go." She ends the call.

What the hell? Did something happen to Teagan? Without even

pausing to think, I jump out of my chair, throw on my suit jacket, and head for the lift.

"Come on." I drum my fingers against my leg as I wait for it to arrive. Why is it taking so long?

Finally the bell dings and the door slides open. I barely cross the threshold when I push the button for the ground floor. Once again, it takes forever to get there. I ignore the people trying to get my attention. There's still a bit of light left in the sky when I make it outside and into my car.

"Shite." I don't have Teagan's address.

I'll start at Imogen's place. The roads are far too crowded for me and more than once I lay on the horn. Curses spew from my mouth. Impatience nips at my heels until at last I come to an abrupt halt in Liam's driveway. The soles of my shoes pound on the concrete and I ring the bell incessantly. The door is ripped open.

"What the fuck do you want?" Liam snaps.

"Where's Teagan?"

"For Christ's sake." He walks away without closing the door.

For the second time in a week, I step into Campbell's house. The only rooms I've been in are the kitchen and dining room so I make my way in that direction. They're both empty. I head back to the entryway and am about to search every room when Liam comes back. His shoulders are rigid and there's a tick in his right cheek beneath his eye.

"They're this way." He spins and moves in the direction from where he just came.

I follow him through the living area and down a hallway where he stops outside the first room on the right. He gestures with a slight head tilt. Slowly, I step forward until I stand in the doorway. Teagan and Imogen are on the bed. Imogen sits with her back against the headboard and Teagan is on her side with her head in Imogen's lap. Her eyes are closed and my sister is stroking her friend's hair.

Imogen lifts her head and her eyes widen in surprise. Liam walks away.

"What are you doing here?" Imogen whispers.

"I was worried." My voice is just as soft. "What happened?"

She glances down at Teagan who hasn't stirred. Since I haven't been kicked out yet, I come farther into the room and stop when I reach the side of the bed. Tear-stains line Teagan's cheeks. Every protective instinct rears up inside me. I want to pull her in my arms and make sure no one hurts her again.

"Her ex-boyfriend called," she finally says. "Threatened her again."

My body goes rigid. "The same one who hit her?"

Imogen's head pops up. "She told you?"

So it's true. "I took a wild guess."

She lets out a sigh. "Ah. I wondered. She didn't say what happened between the two of you before you left the other day, but I knew something had after I'd found her."

"Does he know where she is?"

Imogen shrugs. "I'm not sure. He knows she's not in Berlin anymore."

"I'll take care of him." Whoever he is, he's going to regret threatening Teagan.

"Why? You don't even know her."

I glance back down at the woman who's consumed my thoughts during every waking hour and even while I'm sleeping. I've never believed in love at first sight. I'm not saying that's what this is. But there's something between us. Or could be. I'm sure of it.

"Because I can." It's the only answer I have for Imogen.

She's quiet another minute as she continues running her hand over Teagan's head. "Are you planning on killing him?"

Yes. "That depends on him, I suppose."

There's a knowing in her eyes that says I'm probably lying, but she doesn't call me out on it.

"I don't want her going back to her flat alone," Imogen says.

"She can stay in the suite at the casino." I'd invite her to the manor, but it's gotten crowded.

"Is anyone going to ask me what I want?" Teagan opens her eyes and slowly pushes herself to seated. Pink tinges her cheeks as she swipes a few stray strands of hair off her face.

Imogen turns toward her. "About anything else but this, yes. You've already told me you don't doubt Ben will follow through with his threat. He's already found your phone number. What happens when he shows up at your door?"

"Dublin is a big city, and you're the only one who knows where I live."

"It doesn't matter, T. You and I both know that if he's that determined to find you, he will." Imogen clutches her friend's hand. "Will you please stay at the casino? At least until that cocktwat has been taken care of. For me?"

I keep my mouth shut and let the two of them work things out. *Say yes, Teagan.* I send the unspoken request out. Her gaze flicks toward me but she quickly focuses back on Imogen. The two stare at each other, neither giving an inch, until finally, Teagan's body deflates.

"Fine." She holds up a finger when Imogen opens her mouth. "But only for a week. If there's no sign of Ben by then, I'm going home."

If her ex is willing to track down her phone number after a week, call and threaten her, then he's not going to give up finding her. Even if it takes another week. Maybe not ever. The guy sounds unhinged. That only means I have to find him first.

Imogen must realize that's the best offer she's going to get because she nods. "Thank you."

"I need to get some of my things." Teagan swings her legs off the bed and stands.

"I'll drive you there and then take you to the casino if you'd like." The sooner I can get her under our tight security the better.

For a second, I'm not sure she'll agree, but finally she meets my gaze. "I appreciate it. Sorry to put you out."

"You're not putting me out. No one lives there permanently. It's a place where anyone in my family can crash if we don't feel like driving out to our estate. I'll make sure they all know that you'll be staying there. No one will bother you. We also have round-the-clock security." I'll need to get a description, or better yet a picture, of this Ben bastard so I can show it to any member of security who mans the door. I want to know if he tries to step foot into the place.

Teagan glances at Imogen who's rounded the bed and wraps her in a hug. My sister whispers something in Teagan's ear, but they're too far away for me to make it out. After a minute or so they separate and Teagan faces me.

"I'm ready when you are, I guess."

I walk out of the room. Footsteps follow. Liam has made himself absent as we head out the front door and toward my SUV.

"Call me when you get settled, please," Imogen calls out from the doorway.

Teagan nods and raises her hand in farewell. I walk her to the passenger side, which makes her blink, and open it.

"Thanks." She climbs in.

I come back to the driver side and glance over at Imogen. "I'll make sure she's safe."

"You better." There's a bright sheen in her eyes. "Oh, and Finn? Hurt him. A lot. Even if it's permanently."

"It will be my pleasure."

She turns and disappears into the house. I climb behind the wheel and after a brief check on Teagan I drive away. I break the silence shortly after we leave.

"Where to?"

Her address is in a quiet, but upper class neighborhood. Given her career, I'm not surprised. As I head that direction, Teagan stares out the window. I hate the way her shoulders curl in on themselves, like she's trying to make herself smaller.

"Do you want to talk about it?" I ask, wanting to hear the sound of her voice.

She barks out a humorless laugh. "Not really, no."

"If you change your mind, I've been told I'm a good listener. Not by my brothers, though. Mostly because I try to tune out everything they say." Maybe some humor will cheer her up.

Teagan swivels her head partly in my direction and a tiny smile appears. I'll take it. It's far better than her being morose.

"As an only child, I wouldn't know anything about that, but I have heard siblings can be both a blessing and a curse," she says.

"Mine are straight up a curse. Full stop." She snorts and it does something to me that I can amuse her under the circumstances. "The things I've had to put up with my whole life being the youngest would make you glad you're an only child. I'm glad Imogen showed up. Now there's someone younger than me for the rest of us to torment."

"I've known Imogen far longer than all of you. Believe me, if anyone is going to get tormented, it's most definitely not going to be her." At last, a full-blown smile creeps out.

I glance over at her and chuckle. "Yeah, you're probably right."

In that moment, I vow to make her laugh more often.

CHAPTER 13

Teagan

If a person could die from embarrassment, then I should be dead. I hate, hate, *hate* that Finn has somehow been placed in the middle of this whole mess. Did Imogen call him to let him know what happened? I don't want to ask why he suddenly showed up at Liam's given the hostility between him and Finn's family. Mostly, because I don't want to be mad at her if she did. But if I'm being completely honest with myself, I'm terrified to go back to my flat.

It's also really hard for me to ask anyone for help. My mādar raised me all by herself. Not once did she ask anyone to help her. She always said to me we were doing fine on our own. Since I never wanted for anything, I believed her. She passed that independent mentality onto me. It was Imogen and her mother Maire who taught me that it's okay to not only ask for help, but also accept it when offered. It doesn't make a person weak or desperate or any of the other reasons my mādar had for doing everything on her own.

I steal glances at Finn and study his profile. It's well past dusk and the street lights have turned on. We pass under them and with each one his features become clear before falling back into the shadows. Every time I've seen him, he's been wearing a perfectly tailored suit. His broad shoulders fill it out well.

"You're staring."

I blink and he comes into focus. A small grin is on his face as he turns his head quickly getting his eyes back on the road.

"Sorry." Another habitual response.

Finn's mouth tightens. "You don't have to apologize to me. Ever. About anything. And stare all you want. I enjoy having a beautiful woman's eyes on me."

His facial muscles have relaxed and amusement filters into his tone. Heat floods my cheeks. Not only at the compliment, but also at the slight reprimand that preceded it. How long will it take me to break free of Ben's hold on me? I glance out the window. The neighborhood is familiar. Finn turns onto my street and comes to a stop at the curb just down from my building.

"Wait here, please." He exits the car and I lean forward to keep my gaze on him.

What is he doing? It only takes me a minute before I figure it out. His eyes slowly pan up and down the street twice before he comes around to my side and helps me out of the vehicle. We walk the short distance and I unlock the gated entrance. Finn follows me inside and up the stairs until we reach my place.

I have the key in the lock and turning the knob when he lays a hand on my arm making me pause. I glance up at him.

"Let me go in first." He pauses. "Just in case."

I nod and take a small step back so he can slide in front of me. He opens the door and sweeps his hand up and down the wall for the light until he finds it. Slowly, we walk inside. I strain my ears for any sound, but everything is quiet. He holds up a hand and I come to a halt while he moves forward. Finally, he straightens a couple inches and his limbs loosen. He turns back to me.

"Go ahead and get your stuff. I'm going to make a couple phone calls."

"Okay." I walk past him and down the hallway to my room.

I turn on the light and let out the breath I'd been holding. Once I drag down the same carry-on suitcase I ran away from Berlin with, I pack it full of several changes of outfits and all the toiletries I need. I glance around my room. What once used to soothe and calm me only makes me anxious and on edge. It's as though shadows lurk in every corner. Will I ever feel safe again?

The conversation between Imogen and Finn comes back to me. There had been a note in his response when she'd asked if he was going to kill Ben. My eyes had been closed so I missed his expression, but despite his almost denial, there'd been a hint of dishonesty in it. *Or maybe you're just imagining things.*

Finn is part of the mafia. Considering what happened at his brother's wedding, violence is nothing new to them. While I don't understand all the workings of their organization, I'm pretty certain they're not strangers to murder. Hell, Liam admitted he'd kill Ben if I asked. The fact should terrify me more.

I take a final glance around to make sure I have everything I need, heft my suitcase off the bed, and roll it down the hallway to the living area. Finn stands in the middle of the room holding a small picture frame. It's one I keep on the table next to the couch.

"That was Imogen's and my first year at University."

He runs a finger over the glass. "God, she was so young. You both were."

A pang of sorrow hits my chest that he and his family missed out on so much time with her. I understand why Nora gave Imogen up at birth for Nora's sister Maire to raise. She'd been protecting her from Carrick's wife who'd threatened to kill both Nora and her unborn baby. Threatened to kill Imogen.

As someone who'd had a mother who would die for her, I can sympathize with the agony Nora must have been going through to have to give up her child and never be able to know her. Although, the person I feel the worst for is Carrick, Imogen's father. Nora knew Imogen was safe. He didn't even know she existed until a few months ago.

"We've both certainly changed in the decade since it was taken. Our lives' paths have taken us into completely different directions." One I never imagined mine would take.

Instantly I regret bringing it up. I don't want Finn asking questions I don't particularly want to answer. He sets the picture frame back in its place and glances up at me.

"Are you ready to go?"

What will he do if I say no? "Yes."

He strides forward and reaches for my suitcase. "I'll take it."

I glare at him. "You know I'm not completely helpless, right?"

Finn stares at me intently. "There's nothing wrong with accepting help sometimes."

It's like he read my inner thoughts earlier. Teagan Shah doesn't ask for help. Never has, so why should she start? Except, I can hear Imogen's voice in my head scolding me for not accepting it when it's offered. Wordlessly, I pass the handle off to him. His fingers brush mine as he grasps it. The same zing of electricity that sparked between our skin the other time we touched happens again. Maybe it wasn't a fluke.

I yank my arm down to my side and rub my fingers together. Finn's gaze drops to it and then back up to meet mine. The world stops turning for a few brief seconds while we stare at each other. Far too soon, he breaks the connection and heads for the door. I take in a long, slow breath to try and slow my galloping heart.

After I lock up, we walk back to the SUV in silence. Like Finn had when we arrived, he scans the street. Taking a cue, I do the same. I focus on the cars lining each side of it and concentrate on any shadows that might indicate someone is sitting inside one watching us. A shiver skates across the back of my neck and down my spine. My pace increases and I lengthen my stride so I can reach the safety of the vehicle faster.

Finn glances over at me as I manage to overtake him. I don't relax until we're enclosed inside and he's heading away from my flat. My gaze drifts to the side mirror and I keep an eye on any moving traffic behind us. Except there isn't any. We're alone on the road. No one is following. Finally I relax and glance over at him. Will he tell me I'm being paranoid?

He doesn't though. In fact, he doesn't say anything. Not one to let silences linger, I force myself to make conversation.

"I really do appreciate you letting me lay low for a bit."

His grip tightens on the steering wheel. "I told you already it's not a problem."

So he did. I just can't help but feel like I'm an inconvenience. The need to not bother him wars with the relief of not being alone. Ben's phone call rattled me more than I like to admit. His voice alone yanked me back into the past several months of constantly being on edge.

"How long has the casino been open? Imogen only said a few years. And what made you all decide to start one?"

Finally, Finn's fingers loosen their hold and his shoulders relax. "We first opened for business about six years ago. It was our cousin Caitlín's idea. Apparently her brother-in-law runs a successful one over in Brooklyn. Given everything she told us about it, we thought it was a sound investment."

Considering its success, they were right.

"Plus, it helps to make our organization appear more legitimate on paper and to the authorities," he adds. "It's the perfect front for some of our less...legal activities."

I whip my head in his direction and widen my eyes. Finn glances over at me and one side of his mouth curls.

"What? You didn't think we were completely on the straight and narrow did you?"

"Um, no. I guess I didn't think you would be so honest and forthright about your organization's...activities, as you say." I really hope this isn't one of those 'if I tell you, I'll have to kill you' type situations.

Finn's smile turns into full on laughter. "Don't look so worried. It's not as though the entirety of Dublin doesn't know the types of things our family and the syndicate are involved in. It's more of an unspoken topic. But considering how close you are to Imogen, it's almost like you're family anyway."

Oh god. Does that mean he sees me as nothing more than like a sister? No. Not with the heated way he stares at me. Not that I care.

"I'll be honest. I'm not sure I'm ready for what it means to be a part of your family."

Finn glances over at me. Only this time, I can't read his expression. Did I say something wrong? I shift in the seat as he faces forward again without comment. I'm not sure why, but it's as though a sudden chasm opened wide between us. I'm not sure how to close it though.

CHAPTER 14

Finn

TEAGAN'S WORDS ECHO IN MY HEAD. HADN'T I JUST MADE a similar assessment that Sorcha might not be ready or cut out for this kind of life? Not that Teagan and I are in the same situation as Aidan and his wife, but the fact that I'm even considering how she might fit into our family is certainly telling.

Unlike my brothers before they met Nessa and Sorcha, I've never been opposed to marriage and everything that entails. In fact, I've always kind of looked forward to it when I found the right woman. Except I somehow always imagined she would be someone who fit seamlessly into our family. Who didn't care about what obstacles might stand in our way. Who was more than ready to become a part of my life.

It's just one more reminder that despite the strong attraction we have, neither of us knows the other. With Teagan being just down the hall from where I spend the majority of my time, this is the perfect opportunity for that to change.

"When we get to the casino I'll show you around and introduce you to our security team. Let them know you'll be occupying the suite for a while so you're free to roam around the casino as you please."

She swivels slightly toward me. "Thank you."

"I know the situation isn't what you'd been hoping for, and I don't want you to think you're a prisoner"—I glance over—"but I'm not sure it's a good idea for you to leave the premises. At least not until we're sure it's safe."

Given Teagan's resistance in staying at the casino in the first place, I expect her to argue.

"It's only for a week. I suppose I can manage to keep put for that long."

She already has it in her head that this Ben fucker is going to just give up locating her. I'll let her live under the illusion—for the moment anyway—that she's right. Which means I have a week to track him down first. I'm already waiting for the lecture from either Da, Cian, or Aidan that my head should be on finding out, not only who our thief is, but also on putting the Moroccans back in their place. In fact, we plan on hitting one of their safe houses tonight.

I turn down the narrow, residential street where the casino sits and pull into one of our family's designated parking spaces.

"Must be nice that you don't have to try and find any open spots blocks away from the casino," Teagan remarks with a hint of amusement.

"The perks of having a lot of money to be able to buy special privileges." I wink and exit the SUV so I can grab her suitcase from the back seat.

Placing my hand on her lower back, I escort her to the front door where Ennis stands. As soon as I can get an ID on the ex, he'll get it.

"Miss..."—I pause and glance at her.

"Shah," Teagan supplies.

"Miss Shah is a personal guest of mine. She'll be staying in the upper floor suite for the time being. Make sure she gets whatever she asks for. Until I have time to introduce her to the others, make sure everyone knows she's here."

Ennis nods. "Yes, Mr. Donnelly."

We stride through the entrance. Tables are full and play is well underway given the late hour. Teagan leans close.

"A please goes a long way, you know." she says.

"Are you scolding me?" It's an amusing concept.

She lifts and lowers one shoulder. "I'm merely making a suggestion."

"Noted."

As we make our way across the casino floor, I draw the attention of several more nearby members of our security staff and introduce Teagan to them as well.

"Whatever she needs, make sure she gets." I cast her a quick glance. "Please."

"Yes, Mr. Donnelly."

We continue forward. She hides her smile. "See? That wasn't so hard was it?"

"Painful to the extreme." I inject enough sarcasm that she can't hold it back any longer and she grins widely.

"You poor thing."

We step into the lift and a second later we're enclosed in the small space together.

"I really am." I'm enjoying the teasing banter with Teagan. I lower my tone to one far more suggestive. "What are you going to do to soothe me?"

The adorable pink color spreads across her cheeks again making her appear far too innocent. "I think you're more than capable of soothing yourself."

Unable to help myself, I move closer. She backs up a few steps, and I follow her until she's pressed against the wall. I stop before my chest touches hers, although I lightly caress the flaming hot side of her face with a fingertip.

"But it's so much more fun when a beautiful woman does the...soothing."

Teagan's eyes darken from chocolate to nearly black and the rate of her breathing picks up speed. It's not from fear either. Not with the way she flicks her tongue out to wet her lips. My gaze holds on the shininess of them and the memory of the vivid dream rears up. God, I want to taste her so bad.

The lift comes to an abrupt halt and bell dings a second before the door slides open. Teagan jumps at the sound and quickly scoots around me. I sigh and grab her suitcase handle. She takes a step back as I exit. Never one to not face things head on I don't move any farther except for the middle of the entryway.

"So are we going to ignore what happened just now?"

She won't meet my eyes. "Nothing happened."

"Is that really the lie you're going to tell yourself?"

Finally Teagan shifts her gaze to meet mine. "Yes."

"Why?" I keep pushing.

"Because it has to be."

I scoff. "Because of that piece of shit ex of yours?"

She crosses her arms and tilts her chin the same way Caitlín does when she's about to dig her heels in based only on pure stubbornness. "Do you always bully women when you don't get your way?"

"Oh, is that what I'm doing?" There's enough sarcasm in my voice to make Teagan glare at me.

"Yes. You told me the other day that if I truly wasn't interested then to tell you. Well," she pauses for a breath. "This is me telling you."

I grit my teeth. *Way to go, dickhead. You should have known better than to push too hard.*

"Understood." Forcing myself not to grab her suitcase and storm off like a toddler having a tantrum, I calmly reach for it and head to the double doors of the suite. I swipe the keycard in the reader and swing one of them open. Teagan walks in right behind me.

"I'll put this in the bedroom."

When I come back, she's standing in the middle of the living space with her arms wrapped around herself. There's such a solemn air to her that I want to do nothing more than pull her against me and try to comfort her. But as soon as she spots me, she drops her arms and straightens, wiping any trace of unease off her face.

"Help yourself to anything in the bar or the fridge. I'm going to assume you either blocked the bastard or turned off your phone. If so, I'll get a burner for you. I will have meals brought here if you'd like since I usually have meals delivered to my office anyway. Unless you'd rather have takeout delivered. Just let me know." I try to make myself sound as impersonal as possible—to hide my irritation—but I'm not sure how well I'm doing. "If you need anything or have any questions, just dial 0 on the phone over there. I'll leave you to get settled."

I stride past her and just reach the door when Teagan calls out. "Finn?"

Pausing with my palm on the handle, I glance over my shoulder and arch a brow.

"I really do appreciate everything you've done," she says quietly.

With a simple nod, I walk out and softly close the door behind me. The first place I head is to my office down the hall and make a phone call.

"Hey. Did you get Teagan settled?" Imogen asks as soon as she answers.

"Yes. I just left her in her suite so I'm sure you'll hear from her soon. But that's not why I called."

"Is everything okay? You sound weird."

Because I'm pissed at myself. I'm pissed at the fuckwit that hurt Teagan. But I'm also disappointed that she closed herself off from me. "I need you to send me either a description of this ex-boyfriend or, even better, a picture."

There's a rustling sound. "I got you. Give me about twenty minutes."

I glance at my watch. There's still time before I have to meet up with Cian and Aidan. "Call me the second you find something."

"Will do."

Setting the phone down, I head for the bar and pour myself half a whiskey. Not enough to impair my reflexes or senses, but enough to ease some of my tension. I'm going to need to be at full capacity when we attack the Moroccans. My gaze drifts to the wall that separates my office from the suite. What is Teagan doing at this moment? Is she lying in the same bed where I just laid last night and this morning? Where I dreamed about her and all the wicked things I want to do to her?

Impatience nips at me and I pace the length of my office floor while I sip my drink. I glance at the clock on the wall, already antsy with the silence and the wait. Imogen is good, but I need to give her the time she needs without interruption.

I go back to my desk and drop into my chair. Back and forth I rock, my gaze landing and sticking on my phone in front of me. I tap my fingers on my desktop while I wait. Far too many times to count, I glance at my watch and check my phone until finally it rings.

"Did you find it?"

"Of course I did." Imogen huffs obviously annoyed I doubted her skills. "Check your email. I just sent you a copy of that little shit-fuck's ID. Oh, hold a minute. Teagan's calling."

While she switches lines, I quickly log into my laptop and open my email. There in front of me is an image of a soon-to-be dead man. I study him. Depending on a woman's standards, he's a nice enough looking guy with light brown curly hair and hazel eyes. Two dimples bookend a toothy smile that reminds me of a shark's. He's clean-shaven without a hint of shadow along his jawline. Nothing about him radiates power. Maybe that's why he has to abuse women.

"Okay I'm here."

"Everything all right?"

"Yeah. I told her I'd call her back.Anyway, while I was getting his ID, I also managed to locate some recent expenses, including a plane ticket purchased two days ago from Berlin to Dublin. The only problem is that was the last charge made that I've been able to find." Imogen's tone is pure aggravation. "I'll keep searching though. If he charges anything to any credit card, I'll know."

"Keep me updated."

"I will. You better make sure he doesn't find her, Finn."

My fist clenches around the phone. "He doesn't stand a chance."

I end the call and dial another number. Imogen isn't the only one with tricks up her sleeve. I'm going to guess that this Ben fucker has no idea the kind of allies Teagan has or that money buys not only power, but information.

"What?" A two-pack a day voice rasps.

"I have a job for you. Meet me tomorrow at one at the usual place."

"You got it, boss."

Wherever the little rat is hiding, my contact will find him.

CHAPTER 15

TEAGAN

I HAVE A RIDICULOUS URGE TO CRY. IT'S MY OWN FAULT though. Sniffing back the pressure building behind my eyes, I acquaint myself with my temporary home. If I'm stuck in hiding from a crazy, abusive ex-boyfriend, there are worse places I could be. Giant wall-to-wall windows cover one entire side of the suite. Judging by how dark they are, I'm going to guess they're tinted.

The furnishings are all clean sharp lines in a contemporary color scheme of black and silver with a few pops of color in the pillows that fill the sofa. An abstract shaped white rug lies within the L placement of the furniture and a glass and silver coffee table is centered on it. The strong teakwood scent that fills the place tells me Finn might spend a lot of time in here.

A quick visit to the kitchenette offers a wide range of alcohol including some top brand whiskey and sparkling water. My next stop is the room I've been avoiding. If the fragrance of Finn's cologne in the living area was overwhelming, it's even more so in the bedroom.

I'd been engulfed in the woodsy scent when he cornered me in the lift and it had taken every ounce of my willpower not to throw myself at him.

I'm so angry at the way I reacted. How I'd so vehemently denied there is anything between us, when all I want is for Finn to wrap his arms around me and tell me everything is going to be all right. That he'll take care of me. My mādar would be so disappointed. Maybe I'm not as strong as she was. Maybe I don't want to be. It's hard, sometimes, not relying on other people for anything.

My bag sits at the edge of the bed. I open it and take all my toiletries into the bathroom. Once I've emptied my clothes and placed them in two of the drawers of the bureau, I head back out to where the bar is and fix myself a drink. I kick off my shoes and, with my phone in hand, curl up against the arm of the couch with my feet tucked beneath me. I'm surprised Imogen hasn't blown up my phone yet making sure I'm okay. Then again, she trusts Finn to make sure I am.

I did promise I'd call when I got settled, so I tap her number on the screen and take a sip of my gin and tonic while it rings.

"Hey. Give me two minutes, please. I'm on the other line with Finn."

A weight settles in my stomach. What are they talking about? Is he telling her he regrets offering to put me up? Or how much of a coward I am? I take a bigger drink this time. And another.

"Okay, I'm back," Imogen announces. "So, give me all the details."

I choke on the liquid and break into a coughing fit.

"Shit, are you all right?"

"I'm fine." It's a raspy and breathy confirmation as I finally clear my throat. "I'm fine, it just went down the wrong pipe. What details exactly are you wanting?"

"What do your new digs look like? I haven't been up to the family level yet. Is it as obnoxiously upper class as the rest of the casino? Or did Finn manage to make it more comfortable and lived in?" Imogen asks.

Ah, so that's what she meant and not the details of the near-kiss that happened in the lift. "Um, it's a little bit of both, I guess. I mean, I'm sitting on the couch and while I'm deathly afraid of spilling anything on it, it's also remarkably soft and squishy. I suspect the matching chairs and love seat are the same."

"I should have expected as much. My family tends to not throw their wealth in people's faces, but shows it in far more subtle ways. Unlike some broody men I know."

That's a pretty accurate way to look at it. I'm surrounded by wealth, but it doesn't make me feel inadequate or uncomfortable in any way. *Kind of like its owner*. God, I really need to stop thinking about Finn.

"Is everything okay? You got really quiet there for a second," Imogen says.

"Sorry. It's just been a day and I'm tired."

She tsks. "Get some rest. Things will be better in the morning."

Her sudden increase in positivity is a bit unnerving. Imogen has always been more of a realist. At least in comparison to me. "Thank you for being my best friend."

For some reason overwhelming emotion is threatening to drown me.

"There's no one I'd rather be best friends with. Now, go to sleep and call me tomorrow, will you?" she instructs.

"I will. Good night. Love you."

"Love you, too," she says softly.

I set my phone on the cushion beside me and stare at a spot in the distance until my gaze grows unfocused. A droplet of condensation falls off the bottom of the glass onto my hand resting in my lap. I wipe it off on my pant leg and blink away the haze. I've always considered myself to be an honest person. Except I lied to Finn and I'm not sure I've ever regretted anything more. There'd been frustration on his face, but worse? His eyes had been filled with disappointment.

Maybe Imogen's right and things will look better in the morning. I get up from the sofa, toss back the rest of my drink, and rinse the glass in the sink. After turning off most of the lights, I walk into the bedroom to get undressed. I slip into a pair of sleep clothes, perform my nightly ritual of brushing my teeth and washing my face, and then crawl under the covers in the massively large bed.

The sheets have been freshly washed, but there's still a hint of Finn on them. I bury my face in the pillow and breathe in deep. I'm not sure I'll ever be able to smell the woodsy, teakwood scent again without thinking of him.

"Ugh." I groan and flop onto my back.

I close my eyes and do the breathing exercises my therapist gave me to help control the spiraling thoughts I get from time to time. Maybe I should turn on my soothing music as well. Anything to calm my nerves and anxiety. Except I'm far too comfortable lying here and the smell is actually helping me. I keep breathing in and out until my body loses all its rigidity in slow increments. Already sleep is creeping in. I'm glad, because I'm so ready for this day to be over.

WHY AM I SO RELAXED? NOT ONCE SINCE I'VE BEEN BACK in Dublin have I been this well-rested. I shift and the soft fabric rubs across my cheek. A familiar earthy scent comes with it as does the memory of yesterday and last night. Slowly, I open my eyes preparing myself for my surroundings. I'm still lying in Finn's bed in his family's suite. Although, based on how strongly it smells of him, I'd guess it's more his than anyone else's. I glance over at the window. Even with the tint, there's not a hint of sunlight. What time is it anyway?

There isn't a clock in here and I left my phone out in the living room. My stomach grumbles. I haven't eaten since yesterday afternoon when Imogen and Nessa came over for lunch, but then I vomited it all out. No wonder I'm hungry. And thirsty. I should have gotten a glass of water before I went to bed.

I push off the blankets and head into the kitchenette area. Water first. I guzzle half of a glass then check the fridge for anything to eat. Except it's empty. I guess Finn forgot to go shopping. The few cupboards bring almost more of the same. There are a few things there, but nothing that constitutes an actual meal.

We passed a small coffee shop less than a block from here when we arrived yesterday. Maybe they're open this early and I can get a pastie. I pause though. Finn did ask that I not leave the casino. But he also said I could have food delivered. I grab my phone and bring up the local food delivery app. A few quick scrolls and I place an order.

While I wait, I take a quick shower and change into clean clothes. It's been twenty minutes which means the delivery person should be here soon. I slip into my shoes and leave the suite to meet them at the door. The lift bell rings and its doors open. I cry out softly and stumble backward with my hand on my chest.

"Teagan, it's just me." A blood-covered Finn carefully steps out. His left arm hangs loosely at his side.

Finally I get my bearings. "Oh my god, what happened to you?"

"Nothing you should worry about. Just family business." He moves and then hisses, clamping onto his arm.

I stiffen my spine and lift my chin. "You need to have that injury looked at. Come inside and let me see what you've done to yourself."

He tries to wave me off. "It's fine. I can take care of it."

"Damn it Finn, get in there, now." I jab my finger in the direction of the suite.

A small grin curls his lips despite his eyes being glazed over with pain. "You know you're even more sexy when you're bossy."

I hold back my snort. After last night I wasn't sure he'd ever talk to me again, let alone flirt. I need to stop being so wishy-washy. Either there's something between us or there isn't. Tabling that for later, I place my hand on his lower back and guide him to the door. Shit. I don't have a key card.

"Left inside pocket of my suit," Finn says. "I'll make sure you get one before lunch."

As gently as I can, I reach in and my fingers clamp onto it. I swipe it through the reader and let us both inside.

"Is there a first aid kit anywhere?"

He heads toward the living area and points toward the bedroom. "Check under the sink in the bathroom. There should be something there."

I hurry to find it. Relief floods me and I rush back to Finn with it in hand. My steps stutter, but I quickly recover. He removed his suit jacket and he already has his shirt half unbuttoned with more smooth flesh being displayed with the release of more buttons. He shrugs his good arm out of the sleeve and drags the shirt completely off exposing his entire upper body.

There's a small patch of hair in the middle of his chest and my vision latches onto the glint of silver in both nipples. I would never have suspected Finn of being a guy with piercings. *Focus Teagan. The man is injured for god's sake.* My gaze darts to his bloodied arm.

"You have a habit of doing that. Not that I'm complaining," Finn remarks.

I jerk my gaze upward to meet his. "Doing what?"

"Staring." His eyes dart to the box in my hand. "I see you found it."

Jerked out of my stupor, I cross the room. "Sit down, please."

He gingerly sits just as my phone rings.

"Oh, shit." I set the first aid kit down and grab the device. "Hello?"

Pause.

"Give me a minute, please."

I end the call and turn to Finn. "My breakfast is here."

"Wait." He holds up a finger and brings out his phone. "There's a delivery at the front door for Miss Shah. Make sure they're paid and bring the food upstairs. Please." Finn tosses the thing on the couch. "Security will get it for you."

"More perks of having a lot of money?" I grin. "And I noticed you said please."

His matches mine. "Maybe your manners are rubbing off on me."

I can only shake my head as I stand next to him and then lower myself to my knees to tend to the nasty looking wound. Swallowing at the blood, I open the first aid kit for something to wipe it off with. Finn lays his hand over mine.

"Thank you for doing this."

"You're welcome." I find what I'm looking for and get to work.

CHAPTER 16

FINN

MY ARM BURNS LIKE A MOTHER FUCKER. SHE RUNS THE alcohol swab over it and I hiss at the sting.

She jerks her gaze up and she winces. "Sorry."

"It's fine," I reassure her. "You know, you're a much better nurse than my cousin Caitlín. She would have laughed and called me a pussy."

As was my intention, Teagan chuckles and goes back to tending the wound. "Considering I'd probably be in tears right now if I had this kind of injury, I have no right to call you anything."

I shake my head. "Nah. You're stronger than you think."

She cocks her shoulder, but keeps her eyes on her task. "I'm not so sure about that."

Almost against my will, I lift her chin with a finger under it until she looks at me. "Don't discount yourself."

Teagan's gaze remains on me for another second and then she gives a shallow nod. I lower my arm and she reaches for the bandages, but she's interrupted by the knock on the door. She jumps to her feet and hurries to answer it. Lee stands there with a brown takeout bag. He passes it over with a polite, "Miss" and glances at me before turning away. She closes the door and comes back to her place in front of me, setting the bag off to the side.

"What happened anyway?" she asks, her hands gentle as she places a large bandage over the injury.

"Bullet grazed me."

Her hands stop moving and I gauge her expression. There's nothing beyond a slight widening of her eyes.

"I see. Is the other person worse off?"

"People, and yes."

Teagan's eyes flick up for only a second and then she's focused back on adding another bandage. I should tell her that the minute I take a shower all her hard work will be for nothing, but I like how she's taking care of me. My mother died when I was young—not that she was any kind of mother—so I've never known the soft, gentle hands of anyone nursing my hurts. Or someone trying to ease my pain by comforting me.

Words like soft, gentle, and tender don't exist in our world.

"I'm sorry. For last night." She finishes bandaging my arms and sits back on her heels. In her lap, her hands are clasped together and she stares down at them.

Calling on every ounce of patience I have, I wait for her to say more. I'm rewarded for it when she raises her head.

"You were right. There is...*something* between us. But I'm terrified of it. Of what it could lead to. I'm not a woman who can do casual. When I'm with someone, I'm all in. And the last person I was all in with abused not only my heart, but me. I'm not saying you would do either of those things, but I just don't know that I can take the chance that my heart might get broken again."

I lean forward and slowly raise my uninjured arm to palm Teagan's cheek. "All I have is my word. I've never physically hurt a woman in my life and would never. Not only because it goes against a moral code I *do* possess, but also because there are too many women in my life who would make me regret it. I don't think you've met Caitlín yet, but she would be the first in line."

She smiles slightly and curls her fingers over my wrist. "Considering everything Imogen has told me about her, that doesn't surprise me in the least. It still leaves me with the possibility of a broken heart though."

"There are no guarantees with anything in life, Teagan. But I can promise you that if you ever do entrust your heart to me, I will do my best to treat it with the utmost care." Having learned my lesson from last night, I drop my arm and give her some breathing and thinking room. I have no idea where this attraction between us will lead.

That's the best part of it though. The not knowing.

"Since there aren't too many places open this early, I'm going to assume you ordered something from Mannings. Why don't you go ahead and eat? If it's not too much trouble, I'd like to borrow the shower so I can wash up a bit."

Teagan quickly rises and swipes her palms down her thighs. "Of course. This is your place. I'm just a guest. I'll get this stuff cleaned up and eat while you're busy. There were some K-cups in the cabinet. I can make us some coffee if you'd like."

"Thanks. I won't be long." Letting her do what she needs to, I head for the bathroom.

On my way, I pass through the bedroom. The bed is unmade and the clothes Teagan wore yesterday lie scattered on the floor. I like getting this slight glimpse into her personality. From a young age our mother made sure our bed was made as soon as we woke up. Otherwise we weren't allowed out of our rooms. To this day, Aidan and Cian refuse to make theirs, as a fuck you to the woman they hated. I never really hated her. I just felt sorry for her.

Crossing the room, I grab a clean shirt and pants from where I keep extras in the closet and go into the bathroom. It smells like blackberries. Just like Teagan. It might have suddenly become my favorite fruit. It's impossible to take a shower without getting the bandages on my arm wet, but I do the best I can.

Once I've finished and gotten dressed, I go back out into the living area. The strong scent of coffee greets me. Teagan stands within the kitchenette area pouring a cup. She glances over her shoulder.

"Perfect timing." She finishes filling it up and then hands it over to me. "I wasn't sure if you took it black or not, so I didn't add any cream or sugar.

"Thank you, black is fine."

She picks up her own cup and takes a drink. I follow suit and lean my hip against the counter. "How was your breakfast?"

"Delicious as always. Imogen turned me onto that place years ago. I missed their scones while I've been in Berlin. No other place I've ever eaten compares."

"I've never had them."

Teagan gapes. "Are you kidding?"

I smile broadly. "Nope."

"That, my friend, is a travesty. You haven't lived until you've had a scone from Mannings. Tomorrow, I'm getting you one," she promises. "I swear you'll never want to eat another one anywhere else."

"Those are big words."

She leans against the counter as well and folds her arms. "I can back it up."

"I look forward to it."

A charged silence settles between us as though neither of us are talking about scones. Teagan clears her throat and quickly straightens. She picks up her mug and cradles it between her palms. "I meant to ask if you'd mind me using the television. Aside from a book I'd been reading, I didn't bring anything to keep me occupied while I'm here."

"Of course. You're free to use anything here."

"Thank you. I'm going to place a small order for a few groceries as well. Just enough to last me the week."

It's clear she's desperate to believe that this is all going to go away in that time, so I let her. If the meeting with one of my informants today leads to my prey, she might be right.

"Let me know when you're ready to order everything you need, and I'll give you my credit card."

Teagan recoils slightly and narrows her gaze. "You don't have to pay for me. Letting me stay here is more than enough."

"What happens if your ex can track your card?"

She opens her mouth, but closes it. Then opens it again. "I'm paying you back."

I've learned to pick my battles over the years and based on her mulish glare, this isn't one I'm going to win, so I acquiesce. "Fine."

"Fine."

Despite the shower, fatigue is hitting me hard. I'd love nothing more than to stay and talk, but I need to get a few hours of sleep before I meet my contact. I rinse out my mug and set it on the counter. "I won't keep you any longer. Thank you again for fixing me up. And for the coffee."

"You're welcome."

I grab my bloodied and soiled shirt and jacket and let myself out. Normally after a night like last night, I'd crash in the suite. But the couch in my office is going to have to do. I toss the clothes in the corner and call the security room.

"Miss Shah needs a key card for the suite. Can you get one to her within the hour?"

"Yes, Mr. Donnelly."

"Thank you."

I toss the phone on my desk and lie down, trying to make myself comfortable. With my attention no longer on Teagan, I'm aware of the pulsing pain in my arm. We lost one of our men last night, and there were a few other injuries, but it could have been worse. The frequency in which we've been fighting is taking its toll on us. We need to come up with a way to end things once and for all. Word has been spreading in the underground network that we're closing in on the Moroccan leader's whereabouts. Let's hope we corner him soon.

A heaviness is beginning to weigh my shoulders down. I still haven't located our thief or narrowed down where the casino is bleeding money. Da hasn't said anything yet, but I expect him to any minute. Hopefully after some much needed sleep and my meeting later, I'll be able to focus on the books again. With that in mind, I close my eyes and try to get some rest.

CHAPTER 17

I'M BORED.

Bored and antsy. Shortly after Finn left, a gentleman knocked on my door with a key card for me. Since then, I've explored nearly every inch of the casino I've been able to access, even using the stairs instead of the lift to get some exercise in. Not once did I encounter Finn.

I passed his office during my self-guided tour. Had he been in there, or did he return to his family's estate to sleep after I'd taken care of his wound? Imogen and I have talked about the violence she's become a victim of with her connection to them. It's scary witnessing it first hand. I also hate the fact I've essentially kicked him out of this place since it's obvious he spends a lot of time here.

Without any people present, the place is a little eerie. Okay, a lot eerie. It's far too quiet in here. There aren't any windows so the only light is provided by a few wall sconces leaving far too many shadowed corners where someone could hide. It had made me hurry back up to the suite. That was a couple hours ago.

Even my book isn't keeping me entertained. I glance at the time on my phone. Again. Groceries were delivered not too long ago and I put everything away, only keeping out what I needed for lunch. Which I've already eaten. I'm making myself not call Imogen. She has work to do and can't be entertaining me all the time since I'm officially on a leave of absence from my job.

Outside the suite, a door closes. I sit up from where I collapsed on the couch earlier. Is that Finn? Is he coming or going? Before I can stop myself, I hurry across the length of the living area and quietly open the suite's door to peek out. He's standing in front of his office with his back to me, but glances over his shoulder as though sensing my presence. God he looks good. Better than he had this morning when he'd appeared tired, run down, and in pain.

He wrinkles his brow and turns to fully face me. "Is everything okay?"

My fingers have a death grip on the edge of the door. "Oh, um, yeah. I was just wondering if you wanted to come in and watch a movie or something?"

I nearly smack my forehead with my palm. *A movie? Really, Teagan? You couldn't come up with something better than that?*

Finn hesitates a beat too long.

"Sorry, never mind, you're probably busy. Maybe another time." Since when do I ramble?

"I'd love to," he says quickly and walks over.

I startle in surprise, but step aside to let him in. "There's a new comedy that just came out I've been wanting to see. Unless you have a preference for something else?"

"No, that sounds good."

A weird awkwardness lingers between us for the first time. I gesture to the couch with a small flailing of my arm. "Please, have a seat. Can I get you something to drink or a snack?"

Finally, a small grin appears on Finn's face. "I'm okay, but thank you."

I'm acting like a teenager having a boy over to her house for the first time while her parents are away. I take a step toward the living area the same time he does. We both stop. My chuckle is far less natural than his.

"Ladies first." Finn sweeps an arm out.

I hurry over to the couch and grab the remote. Anything to give me something to do. The cushion dips with his weight as he settles next to me. I could have sworn the sofa wasn't this small when I sat on it earlier. Expect he's far too close and his body heat warms my side. I take a quick peek at him in my periphery. He leans back and casually crosses an ankle over the opposite knee.

Fumbling with the buttons, I manage to turn the television on. The smart menu pops up and I click on one of the streaming services I'm subscribed to. I've already logged into all the ones I have. Sweat makes my palms clammy.

"Teagan," Finn says gently and places his hand on my arm.

I jump and jerk my head in his direction.

"Relax. We're just watching a movie."

"Right." I take a deep breath and try to calm my racing heart.

Finally, I locate what I'm searching for and click the play button. With each second that passes, I grow more aware of Finn sitting next to me and less on the film. Every time he shifts, I hold my breath. Then I have to relax all the muscles I've tensed up. I'm getting so drunk on his scent, the movie is nothing but a blur. I can't concentrate. More than once I'm tempted to open my mouth and interrupt the movie, but each time I stop myself. What am I even going to say? I've never been this tongue-tied around a man before. I don't like that I am with this one.

Movement to my left has me darting a quick glance out the corner of my eye. Behind my shoulders the cushion moves. Sinks. Without being obvious—I hope—I slowly inch backward in small increments until I brush up against something hard. I can't help it. I turn my head in Finn's direction. His eyes are on the movie I've all but completely missed, but his arm is resting on the cushion behind me.

It's like I'm standing at a crossroads and two choices are staring me in the face. I just have to decide which one to make. Imogen's voice whispers in my ear pushing me in a single direction. Before I second-guess myself, I scoot over until my hip presses against Finn's and I lower my head to his shoulder. He doesn't say anything, but he gently lays his arm around me and tucks me closer against his side.

We remain like that until the credits roll. Finally, I raise my head and Finn turns his toward me until our eyes meet. My gaze drops to his lips and slowly, I lean forward and press mine against them. It barely qualifies as a kiss, but I feel it all the way down to my toes. He lets me lead as I flick my tongue out for a small taste. His mouth parts a sliver in a welcome invitation. I don't deepen the kiss. Not yet.

Instead I acquaint myself with the feel of him. The taste.

I swing my leg over Finn's so I straddle him. He grips my hips and I balance myself with my palms on his muscled chest. Following the movement with my eyes, I run my hands over him, starting with his shoulders and down to his elbows and back up being mindful of his injury.

I glide my fingertips up the sides of his neck until his head is cradled between my hands. Our eyes meet briefly and then I return my gaze to where I hold him. Up and down, my thumbs brush across his cheekbones. With the tip of a finger, I trace a line across his forehead, down his temple, his cheek, and along his jaw. The dark bristles of his facial hair lightly abrade my skin, and a shiver skates down my back causing goose pimples to dot my arms.

Finn's grip on my hips tightens and he pulls me a fraction of an inch closer to him. The hard ridge of his cock slots itself right in the center of my thighs. I'd already been wet, but I grow even wetter. I fight against my body's instinct to rock my pelvis and increase the friction. It might be ready, but my brain hasn't caught up.

I meet his gaze and discover eyes gone nearly black with blown pupils. The intensity of Finn's stare sets my blood on fire. I swallow.

"You won't be upset if we don't go any farther than this, will you? I'm not quite ready yet." The whispered words hang in the air.

"God no." He shakes his head. "I'll accept only what you're willing to give and be glad for it. Take whatever time you need to get ready."

I suck my lower lip. "What if I'm never ready?"

"Then I hope at least we might be able to manage being friends."

Friends.

"I'd like that." I pause and brush my lips across Finn's a final time.

He loosens his hold on me like he knows I need the break and I climb off his lap. My stomach rumbles. I slap my hand over it as though that will stop the sound.

"It's getting close to supper. Could I tempt you to eat with me if I order something or are you sick of my company?" he asks.

I'm feeling vulnerable at the moment after what just happened, and I open my mouth to politely decline, except that's not what comes out. "Yes. To eating together, I mean."

"Excellent. Anything particular you're in the mood for?"

"Not really." I shake my head. "I'm not really picky."

"I have just the place then." Finn grabs his phone.

"I'll have whatever you're having." I need a breather. "If you'll excuse me for a minute?"

He nods and I rush into the bathroom. I stop in front of the mirror. Staring back at me isn't the same reflection from only a few days ago. She'd had tension lines around her eyes and mouth. The brown eyes that normally sparked with amusement and joy had been dull and almost lifeless. This woman in front of me has flushed cheeks and there's a flicker of...possibility residing inside her darkened pupils.

Laying my hand on my chest, there's a racing heart beneath it. One that could easily get broken if I don't guard it. Except the more time I spend with Finn, the more I want to drop my walls and let whatever might happen between us.

CHAPTER 18

Finn

The knock on the door must be our food. Teagan rises, but I hold up a hand.

"Sit. Relax. I'll get it."

She settles back against the couch cushion with her drink in hand, and I cross the length of the floor. Lee stands on the other side and hands me the bag from my favorite restaurant. I take it with a nod of thanks and then bring it over to Teagan.

"Is that from Davy Byrne's?"

I blink. "Yes. How can you tell?"

"Because I would know that takeaway bag from anywhere. It's one of my favorite restaurants."

That makes me raise my eyebrows. "Mine, too."

Excited energy vibrates off Teagan. It's actually pretty sexy. I take my seat next to her and bring out the first container and the plastic utensils that came with it. "I hope you like corned beef and colcannon."

She practically snatches it from my hand and moans in a way that makes my cock stand at attention. It's the kind of moan a woman makes during really good sex. "You talked to Imogen, didn't you?"

My forehead wrinkles. Why would she think that? "Not since last night. Why?"

Teagan holds the container up to her nose and breathes deeply. "Because this is the only thing I ever order from there. It can't be a coincidence that you just happened to order not only from my favorite restaurant, but also my absolute favorite entree."

I palm my chest with a short laugh. "I swear I absolutely have not talked to Imogen since last night."

She narrows her gaze like she doesn't believe me. Finally, Teagan huffs out a laugh.

"This is just too weird."

"We both have good taste, I guess." I know I do anyway.

As we eat, there's a comfortable silence. Possibly our first since we met. It's either been awkward or sexually charged. This, though, it's relaxed. Like we're old friends who don't feel like they have to fill it with inane conversation. It's a novelty, actually. I'm not sure I've ever sat comfortably with a woman I wasn't related to. Definitely not one I have an intense interest in.

"So is Shah your mother or Da's name?"

Teagan covers her mouth and finishes chewing. "My mādar's. I didn't know my pedar."

"I'm sorry."

She shakes her head. "Don't be. I'm not. She and I always had each other and I never felt like I was missing out on anything by not knowing him."

I lean back. "There are times I wish I hadn't known my mother. She wasn't a kind person. Then again, I'm sure you've heard what she tried to do to Nora and Imogen."

For a second, anger flashes across Teagan's face. "Yes, Imogen told me. I don't like to speak unkindly about the dead, but she sounds like a horrible person. Which I shouldn't say, since she was your mother after all."

"It's my turn to say don't be. I have no illusions as to who my mother was." I pause. Did she have any good qualities? It's been so long since she's been gone, I'm not sure if any I might remember are fact or wishful thinking. "I know Cian and Aidan hate her. Da and probably Nora too—though she's never spoken a bad word about her despite what Kathleen tried to do to her."

Teagan cocks her head. "You mentioned your brothers, but not yourself. Did you hate her as well?"

"I was young when she died. The most I remember about her is that she was always sad. More than once I heard her crying. I think she was exceptionally cruel to Aidan. I don't have any proof. Just a gut feeling." My brother's never spoken about it, but I've caught glimpses of sharp pain whenever someone talks about her. "Truthfully, I feel sorry for her. Married to a man who not only didn't love her but also did nothing to hide his extra-marital affair. That has to do something to a woman."

Teagan lays her hand on my arm. "I'm sorry you didn't have a relationship with her. I'm not sure who I would have turned out to be if I hadn't had my mādar. She was my best friend up until the day she died. We did everything together. My favorite memories are of us hiking through the Hyrcanian Forest during my breaks from school when I was a kid."

"I'm not familiar with that place. It's not in Ireland is it?"

"Iran. It's where my mādar was born and raised."

That explains where her dark hair and eyes come from. "What brought you to Dublin, then, if you don't mind me asking?"

Teagan smiles. "We're well past the point of holding secrets, don't you think? I doubt you tell just anyone about your mother."

I chuckle. "You're right, I don't."

"Thought so. As far as why she moved us to Dublin, I don't know." She takes a sip of her drink. "I was barely two years old when we came here. By the time I got old enough to ask questions, it never really mattered. I didn't think of Iran as home, merely a place we would go to on vacation every break. Of course, now that she's gone, I do often wonder what it was about Ireland—about Dublin—that made her choose it."

I reach across and palm Teagan's cheek. "Well, I for one am glad she did."

She covers my hand with hers and leans into my touch. "I am, too."

Someone pounds on the door and we break apart. She darts a nervous glance in its direction. I set my food container on the table and go to answer it. Aidan stands on the other side. His gaze travels over my shoulder, and I sidestep to block his view.

"What do you want?"

He arches an eyebrow. "We've been trying to reach you for hours, but you're not answering your phone. I volunteered to come make sure you weren't dead. Answer your fucking phone next time."

Shit. I turned the ringer off before I laid down after Teagan patched me up and forgot to turn it back on. "Sorry I made you come all this way for nothing."

"I'm not sure it was all for nothing." Aidan jerks his chin up. "Dinner date, huh? Does Imogen know you're making the moves on her best friend?"

I bristle at him talking about Teagan that way. "I'm not 'making the moves' on her."

He makes a non-committal sound. "If you say so. Since I know you're not dead somewhere I'll let you get back to your non-date. But turn your damn phone back on."

"Got it."

Aidan leaves and I go back to the couch where Teagan sits with a concerned expression.

"Everything okay?"

I nod. "Yeah. With what's going on with the organization lately, I should have made sure I turned my ringer back on. Aidan was checking in."

"That's nice that you have such a close family."

"Sometimes I wish we weren't quite as close." I laugh with a bit of self-deprecation. "Being the youngest in our family comes with its challenges."

Teagan sets her empty container on the table, swivels to face me, and folds her leg up on the cushion. She leans her elbow on the back of the couch and props her head on it. "What kind of challenges?"

I mirror her position so we're eye-to-eye. "Cian's the oldest. Since birth he's been groomed to take over the organization after Da's done. He was born into the role. Aidan is, what I guess you'd consider, the spare. Although, it's not a title he has any interest in. He'd rather spend his time on his artistic endeavors. Then there's me."

"What about you?" Teagan asks gently.

"My interests have never really aligned with the rest of my family's. I've never told them this, nor will I ever, but I hate being part of our organization. I don't want to worry about the various dangers that come with it. Not just for myself, but for those I care about, present or future. It's exhausting waiting around for our enemies to decide they want to take everything away from us." I try to gauge what she's thinking but there's no discerning hint to her thoughts. "I got high marks in school. In fact, they were some of the highest. I've always had an aptitude for numbers. The stock exchange fascinates me. No one in my family cares about it. I just feel like other than being related, we don't have anything in common."

Teagan squeezes my knee. "That must be hard for you. Not only feeling like that, but also keeping it secret."

"I know I shouldn't complain. What person would if they belonged to the most powerful family in the country? If they had all this money at their fingertips? If Caitlín hadn't come up with the bright idea of us opening this casino, I'm not sure where I would be right now or what I'd be doing. This place gives me a purpose."

There's a brief silence. "My mādar pushed me into computers. She said that they were the best way for me to get somewhere in life, because I should rely on my brains and not my looks. Like I was some shallow person who would try to do the bare minimum, because I knew people—men—would take up my slack. My entire life, every one I've ever met has remarked on them as though there's nothing more to me than that. As though that's the only thing that defines me. At first, I'd been hurt by her words, but then I realized she'd done me a favor."

"I'm sure she knew how absolutely brilliant you are."

Teagan's smile is small. "I sometimes wonder if she didn't project her life onto me somehow. My mādar was one of the most beautiful women I've ever met. Absolutely gorgeous. She used that to her advantage, too. I witnessed it more than once as I got older. Sometimes it bothered me. A lot."

Her hand is still on my knee and I take it and thread my fingers through hers, rubbing my thumb along hers. "She sounds like a wonderful mother."

"She was. The best."

"That's kind of how I feel about Nora. She's been a better mother figure to us than Kathleen ever was. There are times when I think all three of us boys had wished she was our real mother. Which makes me feel guilty."

Teagan gently squeezes my hand. "It's a terrible burden for us to carry so much guilt about our parents."

It really is. There are a lot of burdens that rest unnecessarily on my shoulders. Maybe I should let some of it go. "Thank you for an enjoyable day. I hate to go, but I should probably head to my office and get some work done."

"Of course." She stands and I follow.

Slowly, I lean close and brush a brief kiss across her lips. "I'll talk to you later?"

Teagan nods. "That would be lovely."

Each step I take is like I have lead in my shoes. I'm reluctant to leave. All I want to do is spend the rest of the night with her talking.

Getting to know one another. But duty, as always, calls. I pause at the door and glance back.

"Have a good night and call if you need anything at all."

She smiles. "Thank you."

I close the door softly behind me and take in a deep breath. Even out here, the scent of blackberries follows me.

CHAPTER 19

TEAGAN

MY FINGERS COVER MY LIPS LONG AFTER FINN WALKS OUT the door. I want to savor that last, sweet kiss. It had been brief and only a whisper of a touch, but it had held the hint of more. I'm terrified to explore this thing between us, but also filled with a giddy excitement. There's that fluttery sensation in my stomach of a first-time crush.

I glance at the clock. It's still early, so I call Imogen. She's made more than one comment about Finn and me. I'm not sure she's one hundred percent serious though. Will it be weird for her if something does happen with Finn and me? Or worse, what if it doesn't?

"You okay?" she asks the second she answers.

"I'm fine. Good, actually." I curl up on the couch in the same place where Finn sat. It's still warm. "Your brother just left."

Might as well get it out in the open.

"Oh," Imogen draws out the word in a sing-song tone. "And?"

"We watched a movie and had dinner together." It wasn't *only* that.

"And?" she repeats, because no one knows me better than her and when I'm hiding something.

I huff. "Fine, and we kissed. Nothing more."

She squeals so loudly in my ear I have to pull the phone away from it. "I *knew* it. You guys are totally into each other."

"It was just a kiss, Genny." It was more than that.

"A kiss is something. Especially since I'm pretty sure you're the one who told me repeatedly that you had sworn off men."

It's really annoying when she's right. "You're not...you know? Weirded out or anything by it?"

There's a lengthening pause that makes my stomach drop. If she is, then whatever is starting with Finn and me will have to stop. Imogen—and our friendship—is more important to me than any guy. Maybe I want her to say it's okay more than I realize.

"I think if I'd grown up with Finn, then maybe it might be weird. But even though we share the same father, I only met all of them a few months ago. Yes, they're my brothers, but they don't *feel* like my brothers. Not really. Not yet, anyway. Maybe never, although I hope that's not the case."

The tension flows out of me as relief hits. "That makes me feel better. Not about them not feeling like your brothers, but that you're okay with it if whatever between Finn and me goes anywhere."

"Just don't tell me when you two bang. I'm not sure I can handle knowing *that much* about my best friend and my brother."

She almost makes me spit. Instead, I cough and sputter. "I absolutely will not tell you if, or when, that ever happens. You know everything there is to know about me, but I'm not sure you need to know that."

"Good." I can almost hear her nod. "I'm really happy for you, T. I was worried that fucknut had broken your spirit. God, I can't wait until Finn finds him."

"I didn't know he was looking for him." Sure, he said if he found

Ben, he'd take care of him, but to actually go searching him out? I had no idea.

"The one thing I've learned since becoming a part of the Donnellys is that they don't tend to wait until things happen. They're proactive and take care of shit before it becomes a bigger problem. That shitty ex of yours is a problem." Imogen's disgust is clear. "My brothers protect the people they care about. Which means Finn is going to do what he can to make sure you not only feel safe, but that you *are* safe."

I never want to see Ben again, but can my conscience take knowing that someone is purposefully looking for him with the intent to hurt him? Maybe even get rid of him?

"He hit you and threatened to kill you, Teagan," Imogen says as though she can read my mind. "What if you haven't been the first woman he's abused? Or the last? If he's treated you like this, who's to say he won't keep doing it? What happens if he *does* find you? I'm not normally the type of person who wishes violence on people, but in this case I'll make an exception."

What if she's right? I don't doubt what Ben will do if he finds me. Why am I feeling bad for that bastard? Do I wish him dead? No. But will I mourn him if, or when, he's gone? Another no.

"I'm sure I'd feel the same if I were in your position."

"You definitely would," Imogen says succinctly. "What are your plans for the rest of the night?"

"I was probably going to crawl into my bed early and read. Why?" It's the only thing *to do* unless I want to watch more TV. This is going to be the longest week ever if I can't leave.

"Because Liam is out and I'm bored. And now that you're back in town I've realized how much I missed you. I want to make up the time we lost since you moved away. The few sporadic visits I got weren't enough."

No, they weren't. "What were you thinking? You know Finn asked me not to leave the casino."

"I'll come to you. We can either spend more of Liam's money

at the tables or we can sit at the bar and judge all the rich old men." Imogen laughs. "If neither of those sound good, then you can give me a tour of the swanky place you're staying in. I'll bring the wine."

After spending all these months apart, I've missed her as well. So much. "I approve of any of those three options."

"Excellent. I'll see you in less than an hour."

"Can't wait."

As soon as the call ends, I head for the shower. If Imogen and I go down to the casino, will Finn be around? Even though he only just left, the thought of seeing him again makes me fluttery. Man, I have it bad.

I take a little longer to get ready than I normally would. Mostly because the selection of clothes I brought with me aren't really up to *Anamacha Caillte* standards. Although it's not like anyone is going to kick me out. But I want to look somewhat nice. I settle on a pair of black leggings and my favorite yellow sweater. The color goes well with my skin tone.

Just as I leave the bathroom, there's a knock on the door of the suite. I hurry across the room to open it.

"Damn, look at you." Imogen strides past me with a bottle while her gaze tracks a path from my head to my toes. She whistles and wags her eyebrows. "Trying to impress a certain someone I see."

My cheeks heat like they always do when someone ever says something the least bit suggestive to me. It's not that I'm embarrassed, but my body decides to act in some stupid way. Taking her teasing in stride, I drop into a curtsey.

"I dress to impress."

Imogen nods. "That you do my beautiful friend. Finn's not going to want to leave your side the whole night if we find ourselves downstairs. And since you're all dressed up, I'm going to assume that's where we're headed?"

I wince. "You don't mind do you? I know you brought the wine."

She recoils slightly. "Of course not. It will still be here when we get back. Or we'll save it for another night."

That's a relief. "I'm not sure I'm up for gambling tonight though. Sitting at the bar sounds like a good plan."

"You're speaking my language." Imogen sets the bottle in the kitchenette and when she returns, she loops her arm around mine. "Let's go have some fun."

We walk to the lift and my eyes lock on Finn's door as though I might be able to see through the wood or willing him to step out. But the bell rings and the doors slide open and then close us inside.

"Let me tell you about this newest job I just got." Imogen breaks the silence during our ride down to the main level. "I got to hack into the American FBI's system."

My eyes goggle. "What? Jesus, Genny are you insane?"

The lift jerks to a halt and we exit.

She poo-poos and waves me off. "Don't worry. I was in and out with no one even knowing I'd been there. It's not as though I added a virus as a good-bye gift. I just needed to get some information about one of their cases and the two agents involved. Let me tell you, they are some shady bastards."

I close my eyes and rub my forehead. "I'm most certainly going to need a drink after that revelation."

Imogen sticks her tongue out at me. "You know, you could be doing all the cool stuff I get to do if you want. We could be like co-workers. It's not as though you don't have the skills. Plus, it would be the perfect cure for your boredom. It has to be mind-numbing sitting in that suite by yourself all day, no matter how pretty the place is."

"You have this really annoying habit of talking me into entirely poor life choices." I glare at her.

She barks out a laugh and several heads turn to stare before returning to what they were doing. "I'm going to take that as a yes."

"It's an I'll think about it." Which is, fine, a yes. But I'm going to draw it out a bit longer, because she can't always get what she wants right away all the time.

Imogen eyeballs me. We both know I'll cave soon. The idea of doing what Imogen does *is* a bit thrilling. I can at least admit that much. We continue walking toward the bar and I let my gaze wander. We pass behind one of the tables and I happen to glance over at the dealer. Then I do a double take. *Did I see what I think I saw?*

"Yoo-hoo." A hand waves in front of my face.

I blink and Imogen comes into focus. "Sorry, did you say something?"

"Yeah. I asked if you saw Finn anywhere. That's who you were looking for wasn't it?" She flashes a cheeky grin.

I take another quick glance over my shoulder at the dealer, but he's got a deck of cards in one hand and he's laying down new cards in front of the players with the other. Maybe I'm mistaken. I lean into her to speak softly in her ear.

"Don't look, but I could have sworn that dealer back there pocketed a chip. Maybe two." I can't be certain of either. "I don't want to accuse anyone of something though."

"We need to tell Finn. If it's an honest mistake, then no harm, no foul. But if he has someone stealing from him..." She pauses. "Loyalty is the one thing they require of the men not only in their organization but in their employ."

I hesitate. "What if I'm wrong, though?"

"It's better to err on the side of caution."

Still, after learning what I have about how Finn's organization deals with things, I'm worried about making things worse for someone. Finally, I nod shallowly. *Please be wrong.*

CHAPTER 20

Finn

I'd almost been hoping Teagan might decide to come down to the casino, but security mentioned that Imogen showed up a short while ago without Liam. I suspect the two of them will remain in the suite. Which is why I'm surprised when they appear in my line of sight and approach me. Neither are smiling when they stop in front of me. My gaze lands on Imogen.

"I didn't expect to see you here."

"Liam wasn't home so I thought I'd come hang out with Teagan for the night. We opted to head to the bar so we can sit and judge everyone."

My lips quirk. "Of course you did. Why don't I escort you?"

"Actually," Imogen glances around. "We wanted to talk to you for a minute. In private."

My brow furrows and look from her to Teagan and back. "Everything okay?"

"We're not sure."

I tilt my head to the side. "Follow me."

The three of us weave around tables until we reach a secluded corner toward the back of the casino floor. I pivot to face them. "What's going on?"

Imogen glances over at Teagan who turns my way. "We were walking around down here and I think I saw one of the dealers pocket a chip. Maybe two. I'm not absolutely certain though. I could be wrong. If I am, I apologize to him and you."

My body goes rigid. "Who? Which table?"

"I can show you. It was near the other side, not far from the entrance leading to the lift." I try to gesture inconspicuously in that direction.

"Show me, please." I let Teagan lead and I place my hand on her lower back. Imogen tags along.

Slowly, we make our way across the floor. Several people follow us with their gaze. I catch the eye of Ronan who heads security and signal him over. He says something to the rest of the team through his mouthpiece and comes abreast of us as Teagan stops just to the right of a table and tips her chin up a fraction toward the dealer in question. I don't take my eyes off her for a second just for confirmation. She doesn't call back her response. Merely stares back.

I take a step away from them until I'm next to Mason, who glances over at me. His eyes widen slightly and he attempts a smile, but he looks away guiltily. When his gaze lands on the guard nearby, he swallows. The people at the nearby tables shift their attention to us.

"Mr. Donnelly," he says in a shaky voice. "Is everything all right?"

Ronan moves to stand just behind and to the side of him while I turn to the men seated at the table and paste on my most conciliatory smile. "Gentlemen. I apologize, but I need to call a halt to your game in play. If you would, please collect your remaining chips. I'll double the amount they're worth as an apology for the inconvenience."

Although they mumble under their breath, they all pick up their winnings and walk away. Most likely to head to another table. Once they're out of earshot, I turn to Mason.

"Come with me."

"What's this about, sir?" His eyes dart around as though he's searching for an escape.

"Don't make me repeat myself."

For the second time, he swallows, albeit harder and finally moves. We pass Imogen and Teagan.

"Stay down here, please," I say to both of them, but I'm looking at Teagan. "I'll come get you in a bit."

She nods and with Ronan taking up the rear, I head for the lift. The silent ride up to my office is only interrupted by the harsh breathing of Mason. I unlock my office door and take a seat behind my desk. Ronan closes it behind him and leans against the nearby wall with his arms folded over his chest. Mason remains standing, twitching.

"Empty your pockets."

He jerks. "Sir?"

Instead of answering, I reach into the top desk drawer and set my gun on the surface, keeping the grip within my palm and my finger along the outside edge of the trigger. With noticeably shaking hands, Mason does as I commanded.

"They threatened to kill my wife and kids," he says, his voice trembling with something between remorse and fear, as he pulls a single chip out of each pocket and sets them on top of my desk. He takes a quick step back, as though wanting to put as much distance between me and him.

"Who did?"

"The Moroccans. They followed me home one night after a shift and forced their way inside. They"—his voice cracks—"they hurt Freya. One of them went upstairs and brought down one of Evie's dolls from the room where she slept. He was within feet of my baby girl."

While a part of me sympathizes with him, he should have come to us with this. We would have protected his family. "These chips are worthless outside of this building. You'd have to cash them in. Except, as a dealer, you can't."

I lean back and wait. Is he going to give up his partner? The fact we have two traitors within our ranks is not only troubling, but it pisses me off. Why Mason did it is understandable—even if unforgivable. But for someone else to betray us? We can't let either stand.

"It's not his fault." He shakes his head. "They threatened us both."

Not good enough. "Give me a name."

The silence lengthens until finally I get what I want.

My gaze shoots over to Ronan. "Have him escorted up here as well."

He nods and uses his comm system to relay the command. Without taking my eyes off Mason, I bring out my phone. Da answers.

"I need you, Aidan, and Cian here at the casino. Now. We have a problem."

He doesn't hesitate. "I'll let them know."

I set the phone on the desk and palm the weapon again. Mason's gaze shifts to it and back up to my face before he straightens and lifts his chin.

"If you're going to kill me sir, will you please make sure that my family is safe? I know I have no right to ask after betraying the organization like this, but I'm asking anyway."

His punishment isn't up for me to decide. As the head of the syndicate, it's Da's. While he takes our council, ultimately it comes down to his decision.

"Sir," Ronan says when he returns. "No one can find Samuel. I had my team check the security feeds and right after we left the floor to come up here, the time stamp shows him exiting the casino out the back."

That's unfortunate. If he hadn't run, we might have—although doubtful—shown some leniency. After this? He's a dead man, I'm sure of it. I shift my attention to Mason.

"Where will we find him?"

I get an address.

"And if he's not there?" Knowing we'll be looking for him, I doubt he'll stay there longer than it takes to pack some shit and make himself scarce.

"He has a mother in Galway, I believe."

Limerick is closer. It might be a job for Uncle Conor. As the silence lengthens, my anger at this entire situation grows. I'd much rather be downstairs where Teagan is than up here dealing with this fuckery.

"What about the fire at the docks? Did you give that information to the Moroccans as well?"

His brows draw together. "What fire? I don't know anything about that, sir."

I study him for several minutes. His surprise appears to be genuine. If he didn't, then was it Samuel? Or are there even more traitors in our ranks? Since there's nothing more to be said until Da gets here, I sit back in my chair and wait with my gun resting on my knee. I don't offer Mason a seat. He doesn't deserve to get comfortable after this.

After an indeterminable wait, there's a sharp rap on the door. Ronan turns and opens it. Da strides in. In this moment, he's not our loving Da. He's Carrick Donnelly, head of the Irish syndicate and the most powerful man in Dublin. The man even the Gardaí don't cross. Yet, here stands someone who did and judging by Da's fierce expression, payment will most likely be made in blood when he discovers what Mason has done.

He meets Da's eyes and flinches. Moments later Cian and Aidan arrive. They take in the room and the heavy tension as well, I suspect. They both have a seat while Ronan closes us inside and remains guarding the exit. Da stays standing.

I launch into why they're all here. "It was brought to my attention that Mason here had pocketed chips this evening. He and Samuel—who is currently missing since being outed—have been working together to exchange them for cash. Cash they've, in turn, handed over to the Moroccans. Apparently, they abused his wife and threatened to kill her and their children if he didn't comply. It's the reason why I haven't been able to find where the missing money is coming from in the books. It's never been in the books."

Cian and Aidan both curse. Da's face turns bright red and he whips his head in Mason's direction. To his credit, he meets Da's gaze head-on.

"I'm sorry, Mr. Donnelly. I needed to protect my family."

Da switches his gaze to me. "What are we doing to find the other traitor?"

"I have an address. If he's not there, we might need to reach out to Uncle Conor. Samuel's mother is in Galway and he's closer."

Da turns to Cian. "Send some men to the traitor's house. If they're unable to locate him, then reach out to Conor with the information. Ask him to put someone at the mother's house and wait to see if he shows up. If, or when, he does, have him detained until we can get there."

"Yes, sir."

Then it's Aidan who Da's attention shifts to. "Gather a couple men and take this one to the warehouse until I decide his punishment. For the moment treat him as we would anyone who betrayed us, but don't kill him. Not yet anyway."

Aidan nods and exits the office with his phone already in hand. In less than five minutes he returns with two of our men from downstairs. They flank Mason and with only a short glance at us, they escort him out with Aidan in the lead and Ronan in the rear. It's for this exact situation that, while rare, we restrict access to the back stairwell. We certainly can't be seen either in the lift or on the main floor removing men from the premises who may soon turn up dead. Although it's been a while since we've had to use it.

It leaves Da, Cian, and me.

"I never would have expected Mason to betray us," Cian notes.

"A man will do a lot of things in order to protect his family," Da says. "Still, loyalty is the backbone of our organization. It's our oath. If an example isn't made of those who betray us, even within our own ranks, it demonstrates weakness. This role doesn't come with easy decisions."

I don't envy Cian his legacy or the responsibilities he'll have to carry.

"He should have come to us." Although it's too late for that.

Da runs a hand down his face with a heavy sigh. "Christ."

"At least we have one problem solved," Cian says. "If the Moroccans are using our own men against us, it's time to end this once and for all."

I couldn't agree more.

CHAPTER 21

Teagan

For the past hour I've cast glances in the direction of the passageway leading to the lift, waiting for any sign of Finn. Imogen had pointed out her Da and two other brothers when they'd headed that way forever ago and none of them have returned either.

"What do you think is going on up there?" I haven't taken my eyes off the other side of the room.

"I don't have a clue," Imogen answers. "Although I doubt anyone is being murdered. Too messy to clean up."

I whip my head in her direction, expecting her sarcastic smile—dark humor has always been her go to in uncomfortable situations—but her lips are downturned at the corners. She actually appears worried. Guilt nearly swallows me whole. Did I do the right thing?

She lays a warm hand over mine and stares at me intently. "Whatever happens, it's not your fault. People make bad decisions and when they're caught they have to realize there are consequences to their actions. Whether or not you said anything, eventually, Finn would have discovered the theft. It was only a matter of time."

I flip my palm up and squeeze her fingers, grateful for her and how well she knows me. "I know you're right, but it doesn't make it any easier."

"No, it doesn't, but it's still not up to you to shoulder the blame." Her gaze drifts to something behind me. "There's Finn. He looks like he might need some company. Why don't you go ahead? I'll call Liam to come get me when he's finished with his business."

I hesitate. "Are you sure? I feel like I've ruined our mini girl's night."

"You didn't ruin anything. Besides, it isn't like we can't have another one tomorrow or the day after."

True. I'm here—not just at the casino, but in Dublin—for the foreseeable future. It's going to take some getting used to. I circle the table and give her a huge hug. "Thank you. For everything."

"That's what best friends are for." Imogen hugs me even tighter. "Now go. And don't forget, I don't want to know when you bang my brother."

I snort and twist my fingers against my lips to seal them. She gives me a little nudge and I take a couple small, slow steps until I lengthen my stride and walk confidently toward Finn. I'm only a short distance away when he spots me. A noticeable change comes over him. It's like having a front row seat to all the tension completely leave his body. His rigid shoulders drop and he loosens the tightness around his mouth and eyes. I come to a stop in front of him.

"Hi." It's whisper soft.

"Hi," Finn replies just as quietly.

"Are you okay?"

His lips curl the tiniest bit, but doesn't reach completion. "I will be."

"Do you want to come up to the suite and I'll make us some tea?"

He glances around. "Where's Imogen? I thought you two were having some girl time."

"She was ready to go. Liam is coming to pick her up." It's not the complete truth. "So, would you like that tea?"

"I'd love some."

A compulsion has me threading my fingers through his and pressing my arm against his as we walk hand-in-hand to the lift. Warmth spreads through my whole right side from the contact. His woodsy scent engulfs me and I breathe it in a little deeper.

We step out of the lift and into the suite.

"If you want to sit, I'll make that tea." I loosen my hold on him and release his hand. Except I want to call it back. It's been a long time since I've done something as simple as hold a guy's hand. Ben always complained I made his palm clammy.

Don't think about him. Tonight it's just you and Finn.

I head to the kitchenette while he sits on the sofa and within minutes, I have the electric kettle full and heating. "Do you have a flavor preference?"

"I'll have whatever you're having."

Easy enough. I grab my favorite flavor and get everything set up. The whistle on the kettle blows and I pour each of us a cup and bring them into the living area. Finn takes his from me and I sit beside him.

"Do you want to talk about it?" Maybe it would assuage some of the guilt I can't stop clasping onto.

"Sorry, I can't discuss organization business outside the family. I appreciate the offer, though."

"I understand." That answers my question anyway. If it was nothing, wouldn't he say so?

"Thank you for accepting it so easily."

"Have women not in the past?"

Finn gives me a half-smile. "Generally speaking, no."

I merely nod and sip my tea. "I'm sorry you're having to deal with this kind of stuff. I know you said you don't care for it."

"This is the life I was born into."

"Have you ever thought about leaving?" Is it even possible? How does the mafia even work?

"No," Finn responds in an instant. "You can't truly leave. Da gives us far more leeway than our Grand-da did. If he was still alive and someone even considered leaving the organization, the only way they'd do so is through death. Colm Donnelly was a brutal and hated man. We all feared him. His temper was legendary and he didn't hesitate to...take care of someone who disobeyed him in any way."

My god. "He sounds terrible."

Finn raises his cup in a salute. "May the bastard rot in hell."

I can't even imagine how horrible he must have been if his own family curses him and is glad he's dead. It makes me thankful Imogen's Da isn't like that. "Is that why you're still single? Because you don't want to bring someone into the potential dangers of your life?"

Some form of madness makes me ask.

Finn reaches over and toys with a lock of my hair. He's not touching my skin yet a tingle spreads through me. He raises his eyes to meet mine. There's a fire burning deep within the depth that makes my breath catch and nearly scorches me alive.

"There's danger everywhere," he points out. "I guess it's more because I hadn't found a woman who is unimpressed with my family name or our money, or more accurately, I hadn't found one who sees *me*."

I blink at the usage of past tense. Is that a slip of the tongue or does that mean he's found her? Am I reading way too much into it? Wealth means nothing. I know plenty of wealthy people. I care about honesty. Integrity. Kindness. Someone who builds me up instead of tearing me down.

Can I imagine Finn being that person?

Yes.

"What do you see when you look at me?" I study his face.

He drops the strands of hair he'd still been rubbing between his fingers and carefully takes my cup from my hand and sets it and his on the coffee table. Then reaches up and caresses my cheek. I lean into his touch.

"I see a woman who possesses more strength and determination than she realizes. A fierce and independent woman, but one with a tender heart. I see a loyal friend. Mostly though, I see someone that I could end up caring about."

My eyes burn with unshed tears. For far too long I've seen myself as a coward. Someone who's always scared. Someone who lets life happen to her instead of living what should be her best life. I cradle Finn's jaw in my palm and run my thumb up and down the shallow divot in the outer corner of his mouth.

"I see a man who carries a heavy weight on his shoulders. But he bears it because of how much he loves his family." I stare more intently, my eyes scanning his face, memorizing each feature and seeing beyond the surface. "I see a man who's surrounded by people, but keeps a part of himself hidden. I also see loneliness behind the laughter. Most of all, I see a protector. A guardian."

I see someone I could fall hopelessly in love with.

Bolstered by the courage I'd been lacking only a few short hours ago, I rise up onto my knees and palm both sides of Finn's head. For another few seconds I stare down at him. He doesn't move an inch. He doesn't even blink. He merely waits for me to take the lead. To set the tone for what I'm ready to give and take.

Slowly I bend and lightly brush my lips across his. My hair falls around us like a curtain closing off the outside world. His earthy scent and my fruity one combine to create the perfect blend. Finn's hands find my hips and his grip around them firms. I love the strength that's evident in the way he holds me.

I keep my kisses light. Soft. But my hands glide down his neck and across his shoulders where they continue along the sloped lines of his thick upper arms. Even through the thickness of his suit jacket, the power in them is evident. Yet, I have no fear that Finn would use that strength and power against me.

With a final kiss, I draw away. Carefully, I put a foot on the floor and stand. He tips his head back and waits for my next move. There's no pressure. No nudge. If I called a halt to this again after only a couple kisses, he'd accept it. Which is the biggest reason why I hold out my hand.

There's no hesitation in Finn when he lays his in mine and rises to tower over me. Instead of being overwhelmed by it, I step closer and lay my head against his chest. His heart beats a steady rhythm in my ear. We stand there for another minute before I step back, tugging him along with me and guide us toward the bedroom. Tonight I'm going to do something for myself. Take back some of the control I'd given up. Embrace that fierceness I used to have.

CHAPTER 22

Finn

Walking into the bedroom with Teagan is the last thing I would have suspected I'd end up doing tonight. Especially after earlier. Has something happened in the last few hours that made her change her mind about us? I won't complain, but I also plan on letting her lead in case she changes her mind. She should never feel like she can't put a halt to things.

It's hard to come to terms with the fact that we have traitors within our organization. Have we gotten too soft? No one would have dared betray Grand-da back when he was alive. Times are different I suppose. Carrick Donnelly is nothing like Colm Donnelly had been. While not cruel like his Da, it doesn't mean Carrick's any less ruthless when he needs to be.

Except this isn't the time to be thinking about business. Instead, all my focus and attention should be on this beautiful woman who has put her trust in me. I don't want to do anything that might cause her to regret doing so.

The fragrant fruit scent of her has permeated the bedroom. There's not a single trace of my cologne left. Not that I mind.

She comes to a stop not far from the bed and turns to me.

"You know, I've only ever seen you in a suit," she remarks, almost off-handedly as she runs her fingers along my shoulders. "Imogen pointed out your Da and brothers when they arrived tonight and none of them wore one. I admit to being curious why you do. Not that I don't think it's hot."

That faint shade of pink colors her cheeks again as her eyes meet mine. One side of my mouth curls. Her flushed face is what's hot.

"I noticed a long time ago that in here"—I twirl my finger in the air—"men respect other men in suits. We have a few younger members who tend to wear a slightly more relaxed attire. Dress slacks and a sweater or a plain shirt and blazer without a tie. Still expensive, but far more casual than the old-school members who wear their perfectly tailored suits. They don't have nearly the commanding presence as their older counterparts. Maybe it's intentional on their part. I've never asked. But it's obvious how much differently they're treated."

"And since you own this place, it's important that you look the part," Teagan notes with accuracy.

"Exactly." I rarely even take my suit jacket off in my office in case someone shows up. Everything is always about appearances.

She stares up at me intently. "You don't have to look or play any part with me. I always want to see the genuine Finn Donnelly. The Finn you don't show to just anyone."

When was the last time I'd been the true me with a woman? Have I ever? Aoife might have been the closest, but even with her, I never gave her everything of myself.

"What about you?" I grip Teagan's hips and slowly guide her into the cradle of my thighs. "Will I get to see the true Teagan? The one I'd take a guess only Imogen sees?"

She lays her palms on my chest and smooths out the non-existent wrinkles. "I think I've lost that part of myself over the last few months. The real me. I'm really trying to find my way back to her. I've missed who I used to be."

"I bet she's only more amazing than this version of you."

Teagan chuckles and lifts her gaze to meet mine. "I'd like to think so."

"While we all question her taste in men, she has impeccable taste in friends."

Pure laughter spills from her perfect, plump lips. "That she does."

Unable to resist any longer, I palm her cheeks and her laughter fades. Either I bend or she rises up on her toes, but in the next second we're kissing. It's not a frenzied move, but rather a long, slow tease. I lap at Teagan's sweetness and savor her flavor. The fabric of my jacket glides over my shoulders and down my arms as she pushes it off me.

She hesitates as though unsure what to do with it until I take it from her and toss it off to the side. I don't need to keep up appearances in here. Not with her. With far too agonizing slowness, she plucks at each button of my shirt, exposing a fraction of my skin at a time. The cool air feels good against the heat being this close to Teagan brings. She tugs the shirttails out from beneath my waistband, and in seconds it joins my jacket on the floor.

Her gaze shifts to the white bandage wrapped around my upper arm and her fingers hover over it. "How is your wound doing?"

It aches like a fucker. "If I tell you it still hurts, will you kiss it and make it feel better?"

She rolls her eyes. "It must not be bothering you too bad if you can joke about it."

"Nothing but a flesh wound." I don't want her worrying.

"Would you actually tell me if it hurt?" Teagan narrows her gaze.

"Not a chance." I shake my head. "A man doesn't want the woman he's trying to woo to think he's a baby whining about something like a cold."

"Wooing me, huh?"

I cock my head. "Is it working?"

"Maybe." A soft touch ghosts over the barbell in my right nipple. "You don't strike me as a man who would get his nipples pierced."

I chuckle. "Call it the mishaps of youth as well as being the unlucky loser of a bet against my brothers."

"Not that you're ancient, but it's been a few years since you've been a youth. Why not just take them out?"

"I don't know, I've sort of gotten used to them." The added sensation of having them played with during sex is also a perk. If the nipples surprise Teagan, then she's in for a bigger shock soon. I can hardly wait.

She lightly tugs on one and sure enough it sends a spike of pleasure straight to my cock. "They're a lot sexier than I expected them to be."

"No piercings for you then, I take it?" I tease.

She shakes her head. "I'm a chicken when it comes to pain. I don't even have my ears pierced."

"You're not a chicken for not wanting to experience pain. Maybe that just makes you smarter than the rest of us."

"Ha. Maybe."

Teagan flicks both barbells again in obvious fascination. She reaches for my belt next, but I lay my hands over hers. "I think fair play is in order here, don't you?"

She lowers her hands and quirks her lips almost like a dare. I reach for the hem of her sweater whose color reminds me of sunshine and tug it upward and over her head. Her hair tumbles into messy waves around her shoulders. I brush back the wild strands that spilled over her forehead. Hard nipples spear the thin fabric of her bra begging for attention, and the shadow of areola is visible. Reaching behind her, I expertly release the hooks and Teagan slips the straps down her shoulders, her eyes never leaving mine. The scrap of fabric drops to the floor. Only then do I drop my gaze. My tongue sticks to the roof of my mouth. I can't wait to taste them.

"It looks like we're even," she says in a husky tone.

"So it does."

When she reaches for my belt again, I let her. There's the sound of metal against metal and the tension gives. It releases farther when Teagan slips the button free of its hole. The zipper is undone next and her gaze drops to where she pushes my pants down freeing my aching cock. I press my lips tightly together as her eyes widen and slowly rise to meet mine.

A slow smile curls her lips. "Another mishap of your youth, I take it? Or maybe you didn't learn your lesson about not betting against your brothers the last time?"

I bark out a laugh and palm my cock, rubbing my thumb over the silver ring in its tip. "I can't blame either of those things for this decision. This was all me."

Teagan's head rocks up and down. "I see."

Her words are bland, but there's certainly curiosity in those deep chocolatey eyes of hers. "Not to be indelicate in our current situation, but I haven't had any complaints."

She snorts and slowly reaches out. "I'm sure you haven't."

Her hand pauses just before she touches the piercing. It's only for a brief second and then she's tracing the entry point, which sends a shudder of pure pleasure coursing through me. Patience has never been my strong suit, but I practice every ounce of it I can while Teagan explores. I recite multiplication tables in my head and run through the stock prices of all my investments just so I don't come.

When I'm not sure I can take it any longer, she drops her arm, giving me a moment of relief. It only lasts long enough for her to get to her knees and take me in her mouth. Fuck. Nothing has ever felt as good as Teagan's tongue flicking out to latch onto the ring and give it a gentle tug. I clench my fists for a measure of control. She takes me deep and adds her palm to increase the sensations.

I let her continue for a few minutes, but then reach down and with hands under her arms, I pull her to her feet. Teagan pouts.

"I wasn't done."

"Later. I need to taste you first." With far less patience than she showed, I remove her pants—taking her panties with—palm her ass and lift.

She wraps her legs around my waist and I lay her on the bed, following her down. I claim her lips with mine and have no plans on stopping until Teagan screams my name.

CHAPTER 23

Holy shit, Finn's cock is pierced.

My pussy clenches at the thought of it rubbing along all the rights spots inside. I run my fingers through his hair as he rains kisses down my body, pausing and paying homage to my breasts first. He laves his tongue around my nipple and gently nips it with his teeth before tugging it just to the point of pain. Then he soothes them with soft and sweet kisses, lapping at them with his tongue.

Beneath my fingertips, his hair is the slightest bit coarse. It's long enough for me to grasp onto and anchor myself. I want to feel every touch. Every kiss. And not forget a single one. Although I'm not sure I'd be able to even if I tried. No one has treated me with this gentleness in a long, long time. I soak it all up and hoard the sensations away as though nothing will feel like it again.

The bristles of the scruff along his jaw abrades the skin under my breasts. A tremor runs through me, hardening my nipples even more. They ache but in a good way. As though sensing how much, Finn takes each one in his mouth for a bit longer before finally moving down. His facial hair tickles my belly. I squirm and giggle, unable to help myself.

He lifts his gaze to meet mine and that sexy smile curls his lips, both dimples prominently displayed. I wait for the unease to hit, but only pleasure fills me. I love those small furrows. They make him appear even more playful. Without breaking eye contact, Finn scoots down until he's directly over my core. He kisses my inner thigh. First the right, then the left. Each time avoiding my throbbing center that is dripping with wetness and waiting for his touch.

"Please," I beg in a needy whimper.

He tongues my flesh, nibbling only along the length of my leg he can reach and ruthlessly taunting me. "Have you been a good poppet?"

I nod frantically, thrusting my pelvis upward, trying to reach closer to his mouth. "Yes."

A calloused fingertip grazes my swollen clit. I cry out, but that simple touch isn't enough. "Don't be cruel. Touch me."

"Poor poppet. Where do you want me to touch you?" Finn glides his thumb along my inner knee, nowhere close to where that bastards knows I'm practically begging him to reach.

A growl rumbles up my throat. He only laughs. Frustrated, I yank his hair and clutch his head tightly, pushing his face to where I am desperate for his touch. As though sensing how on the edge I am, he finally gives me what I want. Lips and tongue and teeth, Finn feasts on me. There isn't a single inch of heated flesh he leaves untouched. From my back hole to my clit, he devours me.

My hold on him tightens as I rise to the pinnacle. His face has to be soaked with as much wetness he's drawing from me. But he doesn't stop. I clench down on the finger that slowly pushes its way inside me.

"Yes. Oh god, I need more." It's a plea.

One he answers as I stretch around two fingers. Or maybe it's three. I'm too delirious with pleasure to know or care. It's still not enough and won't be until Finn fills me with his thick cock. Still, I'm close. Hovering on the brink of release. He doesn't waste any time coaxing it from me. Blunt teeth latch hard onto my clit and pinch the sensitive flesh between them. The bite of pain along with the tightness of his thrusting fingers pushes me over the edge.

My back arches off the bed and I let loose a scream. There's movement over me and the faint sound of foil tearing, but it's hard to focus on anything but the wash of sensations rushing through me. My chest heaves with every breath I take. Slowly, I open my eyes and find Finn above me.

I reach up and caress his cheek. He leans into my touch and then glides his hands up my arms, gently loosening my hold on him, and laces his fingers through mine. Our eyes meet and lock and slowly, he lines his cock up at my entrance and far too gently pushes inside. With careful strokes, he stretches my inner walls to accommodate him. My wetness eases his way. The ring at the tip of his cock scrapes along the sensitive flesh and I gasp at the sensation. It's like nothing I've ever felt before.

Every move is amplified with more pleasure than I might be able to handle. It's too much and yet not enough all at the same time. Needing more, I tilt my pelvis, and Finn slides another inch in. He freezes and nips my skin. My whole body shudders.

"Impatient little poppet," he growls against the side of my throat.

"Unnnh." It's not even a word, only a sound.

There are no thoughts. Only pleasure. Intense, consuming pleasure. I'm burning up with it. Sweat-dampened hair sticks to my forehead and along the back of my neck. I'm trapped with Finn in a bubble of mindless ecstasy. Finally he moves, rolling his hips and rocking his pelvis against mine. His piercing hits a spot inside me that makes my toes curl. I lock my feet behind the small of his back and arch into each of his thrusts urging him on.

I don't want gentle. I want him to take. To lose control. "Fuck me. Hard. Please."

Finn lifts up on his forearms, our fingers still intertwined, and stares into my eyes. There's a feral glow in the deep blue depths of his. His lips form a snarl and he unleashes the beast he'd been holding back. With punishing thrusts, he goes deeper filling me full of his cock. Skin slaps against skin echoing loudly around us. The musky scent of sex surrounds me and I breathe it in. Filling my lungs with it. Beneath it is the earthy woodsy fragrance that I'll forever associate with Finn. With tonight.

He's almost vicious with his need. My fingers leave his hair and I grip his shoulders. I clutch at him and dig my nails into his flesh, anchoring him to me. I don't even want this to end. He rocks into me with a force that pushes me higher up the bed. I don't care. I want this. Need this.

It's a reminder that I can make a man lose himself inside me. That I can be this close to another human. With Finn. It's as though we're one being. Two halves making a whole. As though he's the missing piece of me. The one I've been searching for but haven't been able to find until this exact moment. Tears fill my eyes. Feelings of completeness overwhelm me.

It's almost too much.

I scream out my pleasure as my release hits. Finn throws his head back, and the muscles along his neck grow taut. He comes with a shudder that transfers into my body, a rolling wave of pleasure that runs from my head to my toes. He collapses half on top of me. I run my hands up and down his sweat-slicked back. My fingers play along the ridges of the muscles that flex and writhe while I try to calm my racing heart.

Finn's breathing slows and he rolls to the side bringing me with him. We're still connected intimately and I'm not sure I'll be ready for when we have to separate. I lay my cheek on his chest and draw random designs over his pec. His arms tighten around me keeping me secure and protected. A shiver skates down my back and he throws the blankets over us to keep the warmth in. He's a furnace beneath me and I snuggle deeper into it.

"That was..." my voice trails off, unable to find the words adequate enough to describe what just happened.

Finn chuckles and the vibration rumbles through me. "Yeah, it certainly was."

We lie there basking in the afterglow of the best sex I've had in my life. I pick my head up, cross my arms on top of him, and lay my chin on my folded hands to stare down at him. He brushes my hair off my forehead and tucks the stray strands behind my ear.

"You're stunning. You know that, right?"

We've just been closer than two people can get and yet those few simple words bring a flush to my face. A woman can never hear from the man she's with that he's attracted to her too often.

"It's always nice to hear. And thank you. You're good for my ego."

"It's true and it has nothing to do with your ego. You should be told every day how beautiful you are. Inside and out." Finn palms my jaw and I lean into his touch.

"So where does this leave us?"

"Where do you want it to?" he asks.

I pause. Where *do* I want it to leave us? I hadn't lied when I said that when I'm with someone, I'm all in. Do I want to be all in with Finn? My heart gives a resounding *'yes'*.

CHAPTER 24

Finn

From somewhere in the pile of clothes on the floor, my cellphone rings. I drag my gaze from a sleeping Teagan and carefully roll out of the bed, trying not to disturb her. Quickly rifling through everything, I grab the device and walk out of the bedroom. A quick glance toward the windows tells me it's still the middle of the night.

"Finn Donnelly."

"I have something for you," the rough, gravelly voice on the other end replies.

"What is it?" I pause in the middle of pacing the living area.

"Pretty sure I found our friend, but I need another day to confirm."

Impatience thrums inside me. "Where?"

"A hostel on the north side of the city. Near St. Mary's Chapel of Ease," my informant replies.

Fuck. That's far too close to Teagan's flat.

"I want guaranteed confirmation tomorrow."

The man coughs deep from his lungs. "You'll have it."

I end the call, head over to the bar to set my phone down, and pour myself a drink. My glass is half empty when Teagan steps out of the bedroom with only a sheet wrapped around her. She crosses the distance and leans against the counter.

"Is everything okay?" she asks.

Indecision wars within me, but I don't want to lie or keep secrets from her. I saw what they almost did to Aidan and Sorcha. "My man believes he's found your ex."

A flash of fear appears in Teagan's eyes and she straightens. "Ben? Where?"

I tug on the length of the sheet until I can wrap my arms around her. She trembles in my embrace and I lay my chin on the crown of her head, tightening my hold on her. "I told you I'd take care of it. He's not going to hurt you."

"It just scares the shit out of me that he managed to follow me all the way here. What kind of psychopath does that?"

"The kind who likes to control women through fear. It's the only way he can feel powerful, because in all other ways he's nothing more than a weak bastard."

Teagan sighs heavily. "What happens if it's not him?"

"Then my men will keep looking until he's found."

She lifts her chin to stare up at me. "What if you don't? Find him, I mean? Am I just expected to put my entire life on hold out of fear? I don't want to live that way."

"That's not going to happen." It's a vow.

"How can you be so sure? I know you like to think that you're untouchable, but crazy people do crazy things."

I cradle Teagan's jaw between my palms. "I swear to you I will find him."

She holds my stare until finally she gives a small nod. "I trust you."

I kiss her forehead and wrap my arms around her again. Hers

encircle my waist and we remain that way for several minutes until I draw back.

"How about a drink? Something to help you relax?"

Teagan rises up and brushes a kiss over my lips. "I can think of much better ways you can help me relax."

"You're absolutely right."

I guide her back into the bedroom and by the time I'm finished with her, she's so relaxed she can barely move.

THE SCENT OF BLACKBERRIES WAKES ME. I OPEN MY EYES. My nose is buried in dark brown hair splayed out over the pillow. Faint snores come from the woman in my arms. Our limbs are tangled together and Teagan's soft breath ghosts along my chest. I lost track of how many orgasms she had. But at least she's slept soundly since we came back to bed.

I lift my head and glance toward the windows. Even through the tint, it's noticeably well into the day. The sun is actually shining. Who knows how long it will last though. I'm not ready to separate myself from Teagan. She feels too good—too right—in my arms. In this bed. She's the first woman I've spent an entire night with in it.

She shifts and arches her back in a small stretch. A moan escapes her. Slowly, she tips her chin up and smiles.

"Good morning," she says without a hint of embarrassment. If I expected her to be shy in the light of day, I'd have been mistaken.

"Morning. Or afternoon, rather. How'd you sleep?"

"I'm not sure much sleeping went on last night."

Pride swells at the satisfaction in her tone. "Maybe we can take a nap together after lunch." I waggle my eyebrows and Teagan chuckles.

"Why does that sound like a euphemism for something else and no actual napping will be involved?"

I blink, trying to appear innocent. "I'm not sure what you're trying to say."

She just rolls her eyes and shakes her head. "You fool no one sir."

"Sir, is it? I kind of like the sound of that."

Teagan pokes the center of my chest. "Don't get any ideas."

I drop a quick kiss on her nose. "How about we take a shower and get cleaned up? I'll order us breakfast—or lunch as the case may be—and we can have a nice meal. Get some of your strength back."

"I'm not opposed to either of those suggestions."

"Excellent." I roll out of the bed and she follows, but at a slower pace.

Before long the water is the perfect temperature. "Let me know if it's too hot."

"If it doesn't turn my skin pink then it's not hot enough," she says.

"A woman after my own heart." I step under the spray and wet my hair.

I slick it back and face her. "You're staring again."

"Yes, I am. I like looking at you."

To my shock, it's my cheeks that heat this time. I know I'm relatively attractive, but it's not something I put much stock in. But it does make me want to preen a little that Teagan likes what she sees. "You're good for my ego."

"I doubt you need me to stroke your ego."

I tug her to me, keeping my back to the water so it doesn't hit her face. "Maybe I need you to stroke something else instead?"

"Something like this?" Her hand skates across my thigh until she reaches my cock that's been no less than semi-hard since last night.

Teagan grips my length with the right amount of pressure and I growl low in my throat with how good it feels. She strokes up and down, squeezing at the base, and dragging her hand toward the tip, milking my release from me. I'm tempted to take control, but she curls her hand around the back of my neck and pulls me down for a kiss. Her tongue slicks over mine and mimics the push and pull of what she's doing to my cock.

It doesn't take much before I'm coming like it's my first time. Ropes of viscous white splash onto Teagan's stomach like I'm marking her as mine. I want her to smell like me—like us—to anyone who tries to get close to her. I've never had this feral possessiveness for anyone before her.

With a heaving chest, I press my forehead to hers while I try to catch my breath. "I swear you'll be the death of me."

Her breath huffs across my face. "Yeah, but what a way to go."

"I can certainly think of worse ways." I lift my head. "As much as I would like to continue, we should probably get cleaned up and get both of us fed. I also have a couple things I need to take care of before this evening."

Teagan exaggerates a pout and I nip at the plump bottom lip. Once we're clean and dressed I follow her out to the living room and gesture toward the couch. "Have a seat and I'll make us something to eat."

She widens her eyes. "You can cook?"

I laugh lightly. "I wouldn't go that far, but I can put enough together that I won't poison us and we won't starve."

"You're not instilling a lot of faith in me." Teagans swivels and props her elbow on the back of the sofa and rests her cheek against her fist.

"Didn't you tell me you trust me?" The minute I ask the question I regret it. I hadn't planned on bringing up the reminder of the call last night.

She must be thinking the same thing, because her expression shutters and then she blinks and it clears. "I do trust you."

I smile to try and bring back the light mood. "One poison-free meal coming right up."

The fridge is stocked with enough things that I manage to put together a meal of mashed potatoes and a couple slices of corned beef. Enough to satisfy us until dinner. The whole time I could feel

Teagan's gaze following me. I take two plates into the other room and hand one to her.

"Nora gave me her special recipe for the potatoes. They're one of my favorites."

"I'm sure they're delicious." She picks up a forkful and tastes. I wait impatiently for the verdict. She glances over and nods. "These are really good."

"Glad I exceeded your low expectations of my culinary skills." I dig into my own food.

We eat in silence until Teagan sets her fork down. "Maybe we can watch another movie later. If you have some free time, that is. I don't want to keep you from work. I know you have things to do."

"If I can get away, I'd love to." I have to take care of some things, especially in light of discovering traitors.

Once we finish eating and clean up, I check my phone. I'm surprised neither Cian or Da have called.

"Thank you for lunch." She leans against the counter.

"You're welcome." I move in front of her and kiss her forehead. "I'll call you later."

Teagan looks up at me and nods. "Okay."

I have to drag myself away and out the door. This is the first time I've had to balance work with a relationship. It pisses me off that she has to stay hidden to keep her safe. Although, after today, that shouldn't be an issue. Because I plan on taking care of this ex of hers.

Permanently.

CHAPTER 25

I collapse in a heap on the sofa. Last night had been incredible. Same with this morning. I'd forgotten how it felt to feel sexy. Beautiful. Wanted. I hadn't expected to trust someone again as much as I trust Finn. And while I do trust him to find Ben, I'm also tired of hiding. Of letting my fear rule. Of feeling helpless. That's not the kind of woman Finn deserves. It's not the kind of woman I want to be. Pushing myself upright, I head into the bedroom and find my phone.

Imogen answers. "Everything okay?"

"Do you think Liam can teach me how to use a gun?" I probably should ask Finn, but I hesitate for a couple reasons. Mostly because he has family business he has to take care of. But also because something tells me he might say no. Whether because he thinks it's too dangerous or because he wants to be the one to protect me.

There's a long pause on Imogen's end. "I can ask him. But, Teag, are you sure this is something you want to do?"

"I'm positive." I sit on the edge of the bed. "As much as I appreciate the fact I've had a safe place to stay, and as beautiful as it is, it's also starting to feel like a prison. The walls are slowly closing in. I know it could be dangerous to leave, but I'm not sure how much longer I can remain here."

Not after last night.

Finn would also try to talk me into staying here. As much as I've loved having him nearby, last night made me realize I don't want to be the type of person who lets other people solve her problems for her.

"I'm sorry you're stuck in there. I'd be going stir-crazy as well. Let me talk to Liam and I'll call you right back."

"Thank you."

"Give me a few." Imogen ends the call and I set the phone next to me.

I glance around the room that still smells of sex. Last night had been amazing. One of the best nights of my life. And I want more of them. A lot more. I also want to walk through Stephens Green holding Finn's hand. I want to go to our favorite restaurant and eat our favorite meal. I want to go to a football match and cheer on the Bohemian F.C. from the stands.

Most of all, I don't want to be scared anymore.

Finn said a man like Ben lords control over women. I'm done with letting Ben control me. My phone rings and I snatch it up. Imogen's number is displayed.

"And?" My impatience is evident.

"We can be there in thirty minutes."

"I'll be waiting." I end the call and sit there for a minute.

Straightening my shoulders, I grab my runners from the wardrobe and put them on. Then I head back into the living area and instead of sitting, I make my way to the bar in the kitchenette and pour myself a small drink. I finish it in one swallow.

Am I really doing this? I have to.

Not wanting to take the risk of running into Finn and explain where I'm going, I pace the length of the suite to give myself some-thing to do. I have no idea how many laps I do before my phone rings again.

"We're downstairs," Imogen says.

"I'm on my way." I grab my phone and key card and make it to the lift without incident.

Seconds later I'm out on the casino floor and can make out Imogen, Liam, and one of Finn's security team. They all turn at my approach.

"Miss Shah," the security guard—Lee, I believe—says. "Mr. Donnelly asked that you not venture outside."

"She's not a prisoner," Imogen grinds out, but I hold up my hand. I can handle it.

"I understand what Mr. Donnelly has probably explained to you, and I appreciate you following his directive, but I'm leaving for a little while. I'll be back in a few hours. And unless you have plans to physically restrain me, I'll ask you to please step aside."

He hesitates for so long I brace myself for a fight. I highly doubt Liam will allow anyone to put their hands on me. Lee's gaze bounces between Imogen, Liam, and me until finally, he moves out of the way. "I'm going to have to notify Mr. Donnelly."

I expect nothing less. His loyalty is to Finn after all. "I understand."

"Are we leaving or not?" Liam grumbles.

Imogen elbows him in the side and he doesn't even grunt.

"Yes, we're leaving." Before I lose my nerve.

Liam pivots and leads the way. Imogen snags my arm and we leave together. The sun has disappeared and the gray sky appears more dismal than usual. But the air smells fresh and clean and also a bit like rain. I cast several glances around, but there are far fewer cars parked at the curbs then there had been when Finn and I arrived a few days ago. Nothing jumps out at me as suspicious. It's just a regular day in Dublin.

We come to a stop next to a black town car and driver who opens the back door. To my surprise, Liam steps to the side and holds a hand out for Imogen. She takes it and he helps her in. It's my turn next and while he doesn't offer his hand, he waits until I'm sitting on the other side of Imogen before he gets in and the driver closes the door. I'm not sure why I'm shocked by his gentlemanly behavior. I guess because of how hard he always is. Maybe there is more to Liam than he presents to everyone. Everyone other than Imogen, I suspect.

The driver makes his way down the city streets and away from the casino. Imogen turns to me.

"Did something happen to bring on this sudden change?"

Since she's already said she doesn't want to know about Finn and me being together, I come up with another reason. "I just couldn't take staying inside another day."

She eyeballs me and finally nods, because she knows what I'm saying is true. I'd told them a week. Granted, I'm only on day four, but enough is enough.

I redirect the conversation. "Where are we going anyway?"

"Liam has a place we can go for you to practice where no one can hear. Some warehouse at the shipping yard."

Considering he owns over half the shipping companies in Dublin, that makes sense. It isn't long before we arrive at the docks. We stop at a security booth and then the gate opens for us to drive through. The town car stops in front of a large building. He exits the vehicle and lets us out. We trail Liam who leads us to the entrance and stands there with his face angled upward toward where a camera in the corner above the door points down.

The sound of locks is loud and the metal door swings open on well-oiled and noiseless hinges. A scarred mountain of a man wearing a suit stands just inside. Judging by the size of him, I'm surprised the seams at the shoulders don't split. He's massive.

The three of us step past him and we're enclosed in darkness for a second before a light flares to life brightening the entryway we're standing in. The large man nods at Liam and then walks down a hall-way. We follow him until we reach another door. I can't help but glance around. It's deathly quiet in here. A few wall sconces give off light, but it's an eerie yellow instead of the bright sunshine yellow that's my favorite color.

From my pocket, my phone rings. I startle at the noise and reach for it. Everyone's staring at me. I wince.

"Sorry."

Still, I answer it. "Hello?"

"Why did I have to hear from Lee that you left the casino?" Finn's question is filled with disappointment.

I flinch at it and turn away from three pairs of eyes to try and give myself the illusion of privacy. "I'm sorry. It was a spur-of-the-moment decision."

"You still could have let me know. There was no need to call Liam. If you needed to leave that badly, I would have taken you where ever you wanted to go. I may not have liked it, but I would have taken you." More hurt colors his tone.

Guilt floods me and I sigh. "You're right. I should have told you."

"Where are you?"

"Um," I hesitate, not wanting him to know.

He blows out a harsh breath. "Call me when you're about to leave so I know you're on your way back. You *are* coming back, aren't you?"

Was I? The whole point of me learning to shoot was so I felt somewhat safe returning home. At least it was a pretty illusion that I might be able to protect myself if I need to. But I'm also not sure I'm ready to be that far away from Finn.

"Teagan?"

"At least for tonight."

The lengthening silence indicates he's not happy. "Call me when you're finished doing whatever it is you're doing with Liam and Imogen. Please?"

"I will." I glance back. "I'm sorry, but I have to go."

I'm not sure who ends the call first, him or me, but either way,

Finn's gone. I turn back to face everyone and pocket my phone. "I'm ready."

The large scarred man pushes open the interior door and steps back. Liam strides past him, then Imogen. I skate by his intimidating presence and the door shuts behind me. I jump at the dull sound. In front of me, spread across a waist-high table, are guns of different sizes as well as rectangular shaped bars, each one holding a stack of bullets. I swallow and wipe my sweaty palms on my thighs.

Liam picks up a gun and slams one of the bars into the bottom of the grip. Imogen moves to the side and behind me as he hands me the weapon with it pointed away from both of us.

"Let's see what you can do."

I stare at it. What the hell am I doing?

CHAPTER 26

Finn

I TRY TO SOOTHE AWAY THE HURT AND DISAPPOINTMENT that Teagan left the casino. Not just with Liam, of all people, but especially after last night. For someone who said they trusted me, she sure isn't showing it. I'll have to deal with my feelings regarding that later. In the meantime, I have a grubby bastard to take care of.

Before he finds her.

The interior of the pub is dimly lit, and the stench of beer is mixed with the sour scent of vomit. Ratty booths line the wall and tables sit tightly packed together with barely any room to move around. A few raggedy-looking blokes sit with a pint in front of them, and the single television mounted on the wall displays a staticky picture of replays from the most recent football match at Daly-mount Park.

In the back corner sits the man I'm here to meet. I weave my way to the shadowy alcove and take a seat across from him. A pock-marked face is half hidden beneath a tattered gray tweed flat cap. His eyes are barely visible. The fingers threaded together on the table top are tar-stained and the stale scent of cigarettes emanates from him.

"Did you get confirmation?" I'm on edge to take this guy out.

Billy shifts around and he clenches his hands tighter. "He didn't come back after he left early this morning. I've had a guy sitting outside all day, but nothing."

Goddamn it. "Where did he go when he left?"

"I don't know. He got on a bus and I followed him, but I never saw him get off. It was packed with people heading to work so it was hard to keep track of where he stood. All I know is by the time the crowd had thinned enough that I could see everyone, he was gone."

"Which bus?"

Billy pauses. "The number nine, I believe."

"Do you think he knew you were following him?"

"Maybe." He shrugs. "Could be how he ditched me."

Which means he could be anywhere in the city. "You promised you'd have confirmation."

"I know, boss, and I'm sorry."

"Keep your guy there and let me know the second he gets back," I bite out. "In the meantime, make sure your network is still looking for him."

He nods. "Yes, sir."

I get up from the table and walk out the door without a backward glance. Fuck. We're back to square one.

Maybe Imogen can help. From some of the things we've all heard she's done for our cousin Paddy, she can hack into almost anything. I reach my SUV and glance up. There's a flash of black, and then chaos. A barrage of bullets fly, hitting all around me. Tires squeal. A searing pain shoots across my face as I dive behind the vehicle.

Screams fill the air and people run for cover. I yank out the gun from a holster beneath my jacket and peek around the front end of my SUV. I sweep my gaze back and forth, but there's nothing there. Rapid footsteps and raised voices that echo around me. Warm liquid runs down the side of my neck. I swipe it away with my hand and hiss at the sting that follows.

Carefully, I stand but stay hunched over and protected behind my vehicle. I jerk upright for a quick glance, but the street is devoid of any cars. Rising fully, I glance up and down the length of the street, but other than the cars parked along the curb, there's nothing. No movement other than a few people who rouse from their hiding spots. I put my gun away, get in the SUV, and call Da. Shards of glass cover the passenger seat in the front and the back. I'm sure a few bullets are stuck in the exterior paneling as well. I drive away from the curb just as he answers.

"Someone just tried to take me out."

"Where?"

"Outside of Grogan's Pub. I was meeting one of my informants about something and was about to leave when a vehicle drove by and opened fire." I grab the rearview mirror and yank it downward. A long trail of blood runs from just above my ear to down my neck. My shirt collar is soaked in dark red. "Bullet grazed me. I'm heading out to the estate. Not sure if I'll need stitches or it's just a bleeder."

"I'll call Dr. McGowan and have him meet you out here." Da pauses. "Be careful."

"Yes, sir."

I toss the phone in the console between the seats and make my way through the city and onto the road leading toward the manor. As carefully as possible, I shrug out of my jacket and rip the buttons off my shirt to remove that as well. I bunch it up and press it to the side of my head to try and stop the blood that keeps flowing. A little over twenty minutes later, I come to a stop at the large iron gate blocking the drive. It opens in seconds and I make my way down the narrow lane, my head swimming.

It takes forever to get there—or at least feels like it—but I finally come to a stop in front of the house. The doctor's vehicle is parked behind Aidan's. I make it up to the front door which opens before my hand curls around the knob. Da's arm comes around me and he helps me inside.

"Nora, bring Dr. McGowan to my office. Now."

Everything fades in and out. Sounds reach my ear and my head pounds with throbbing pain. I open my eyes and a man in a jacket bends over me.

"Almost finished, Mr. Donnelly."

I close my eyes again. Finished with what?

THERE'S A POUNDING INSIDE MY SKULL. I OPEN MY EYES which takes more effort than it should. Where the hell am I? I turn my head slowly and wince. Da's office comes into focus and with it the memories. The drive-by shooting outside Grogan's. The sting of pain. The blood. Although the ride out here is a little foggy.

"You're awake."

I turn toward Da's voice. He's sitting in a chair he's dragged near the couch I'm lying on. Gingerly, I sit myself up and groan with the effort.

"How long have I been out?"

"An hour, maybe."

I glance down. "Sorry for all the blood."

He huffs. "It'll clean. How're you feeling?"

I'd chuckle, but it hurts too much. "Like I got shot." Christ, even the bullet grazing my arm didn't hurt as much as this.

"You're lucky you didn't pass out before you got here. Doc said you lost a lot of blood."

"I'm glad I didn't." Try explaining that to the Gardaí.

Da stands and gently palms the uninjured side of my head. "Why don't you go get some rest? Nora is making you some soup for later."

"I can't stay." Carefully I get to my feet. "I have to get back to the casino."

I'm not leaving Teagan there alone.

"Finn, the casino will survive without you for a night."

"It's not that." I hadn't planned on mentioning her yet. Not until there was something more between us. "Imogen's friend Teagan is staying in the suite. I don't want her by herself."

Da's nod is knowing. "Is this the woman that's been keeping you distracted?"

There's no denying my focus hasn't been where it should, ever since Teagan came into the picture. "Yes."

He studies me. "I take it things are serious with you two?"

Are they? Before she left with Liam and Imogen I might have said yes. Now I'm not sure. "I want them to be."

"If that's the case, then maybe you should bring her out here and introduce us. I'm sure the rest of the family would like to get to know her." He raises an eyebrow in expectation.

"Fine. I'll call her with an invitation."

"I'll let Nora know to expect one more for dinner." Dropping that proclamation he leaves me standing in his office while he goes off to talk to her.

Great. There are times when I love how close we are as a family, but I'm not sure this is one of them. I take a seat back on the couch and reach for my phone.

"Hello?" Teagan answers, her tone pitched with a frantic note.

"Hey, it's me."

"Are you okay? Imogen got a call from one of your brothers."

Christ. "Yeah, I'm fine. Just a little banged up."

"What happened?"

No lies, remember? Except I'm not sure the truth is better. "Someone shot at me."

"Oh my god. Where are you?" She mumbles something indecipherable that's not directed at me.

"I'm out at the estate."

"Imogen and Liam are going to drive me there."

Relief flows through me, so I don't argue. I want her here. Not just because Da wants an introduction, but because I need to reassure myself that she's fine. That we're both fine. "I'll be here."

"We'll be there soon." Teagan ends the call.

I lean back and blow out a breath. At least Da will be happy. Me too. I'll just rest my eyes until she arrives.

CHAPTER 27

Teagan

Imogen's hand is warm in mine. She squeezes gently.

"He's going to be fine."

I nod, because she's expecting it, but inside I'm petrified. What if he isn't fine, though? The last words between us were tense and, while not angry, certainly filled with disappointment. My stomach is in knots recalling this latest phone call. Finn had sounded so tired. Far more fatigued than I've heard him be. Even after his other bullet wound. Is this really what his life is like? Getting shot at all the time?

Thankfully Liam keeps his thoughts and opinions to himself, although I sense some irritation. Probably at being inconvenienced with having to take me to Finn. I'm not sure how I'd react if he were to be his usual cranky self. The drive out to the Donnelly estate takes far too long. At least compared to the one and only other time I drove out here with Imogen when she confronted Nora about her parentage.

Finally the driver pulls up to the iron gate leading into the property. He rolls down his window, and after a brief conversation, it opens and he drives forward. I can't help but take in the beauty of the trees the lane cuts through. They tower over us providing a canopy of green. The narrow driving path curves slightly one way and then the other until around the next bend, the sprawling manor house appears.

Sunlight glints off all the windows across the front. More greenery weaves its way up the sides of the house, climbing toward the roof and threaded through the spaces between each window. Multiple cars line the circle drive. Finn's SUV brings up the rear. Liam's driver parks behind it and I'm already out of the town car before he can open the back door.

I rap at the door several times. There's only a brief wait and then a crack appears between the double doors that quickly widens. An older version of Finn stands in the bright entryway. They have the same dark hair, although his pedar's is threaded with silver, and vibrant blue eyes. Age lines radiate from around Finn's Da's and across his forehead, but Carrick Donnelly is still an attractive man with broad shoulders and tapered waist. His gaze shifts over my shoulder and then his eyes meet mine again.

"You must be Imogen's friend, and the woman who has my son distracted." Even his voice is similar to Finn's with its whiskey gruffness.

I flush at his statement, but don't deny it. "Teagan Shah, sir."

Imogen and Liam reach us. Finn's Da makes a noise and reaches out to shake my hand. "None of that sir stuff. Call me Carrick."

"Yes, si—Carrick." I place my palm in his.

He releases me and his face lights up. In two steps he's got him arms wrapped around Imogen. "It's always so good to see you."

She hugs him back. "Nice to see you too Carrick."

"Liam." Her Da's greeting is far less welcome this time.

"Donnelly."

The tension between the two of them is thick enough to choke a person. God, how does Imogen deal with the obvious animosity between them? I don't envy her. Thankfully, Finn's Da doesn't let it fester for long before he turns his gaze back to me.

"Please, come in. I'll get Finn for you."

He backs inside and I move to follow, but pause and glance over at Imogen. "You don't have to stay if it's uncomfortable for you. I'll be okay."

She latches onto Liam. "We'll stay for a few minutes."

His jaw tightens, but he doesn't argue. I nod my thanks and follow Carrick inside. The three of us stand in the entryway while Finn's Da goes down a hallway. He isn't gone more than a few seconds when an older woman walks in from another room. Her eyes spark and she smiles broadly. This must be Imogen's biological mother. Despite being an obvious Donnelly, there are still noticeably similar features between the two women.

She rushes over for a hug. "Imogen, dear, I didn't realize you were coming."

"Neither did we." Imogen releases her and half-pivots in my direction. "Nora, this is my best friend, Teagan. Teagan, this is Nora."

Before I can even say hello, warm arms are wrapped around me and she squeezes me tightly. "It's so lovely to meet you. Imogen can't say enough good things about you."

"Thank you, Nora. It's nice to meet you as well."

She loosens her hold on me and gives Liam a soft and surprisingly genuine-appearing smile. "Hello, Liam."

"Nora." His voice is maybe a bit kinder and he nods with slightly less hostility than he gave Carrick.

I guess it's just Imogen's Da and brothers he doesn't like. Footsteps approach from the direction Finn's Da went and then Finn's there. His face is pale and a bandage covers the side of his head that matched the one on his bare arm that's evident since he's shirtless. The second his gaze lands on me, I rush forward and into his waiting arms.

Tears fill my eyes as he whispers indistinguishable words in my ear and strokes my hair. He's not as warm as he usually is, but at least he's standing on his own two feet. I draw back and scan his entire upper body, carefully brushing my fingertips along his hairline where dried blood still clings.

"I was so worried," I whisper.

Finn palms the back of my neck and rests his forehead gently against mine. "It's just a scratch."

That makes me chuckle. "The same kind of scratch that's on your arm that you refuse to admit probably hurts like a bitch?"

"If I say yes, will you kiss it and make it better?" he echoes the same question he asked me the last time.

"If you say yes, it means I won't smack you for putting yourself in danger again."

Finn smiles. "The next time you scold me, will you wear a short, sexy skirt and white shirt with librarian glasses and a bun, so I can live out my primary school boy fantasy?"

Behind me, Imogen clears her throat. Red-hot heat burns my cheeks and I turn to face her and Liam. I'd completely forgotten them. Finn tugs me closer to his side.

"You're clearly feeling better," Imogen quips with a sly smirk.

"I have this beautiful woman in my arms. Of course I feel better."

She rolls her eyes.

"Now that the reunion is over, we can leave," Liam states.

Imogen elbows him in the side with a hiss and a glare, but he just stares down at her with an arched brow.

"Actually," Finn interrupts. "Da invited Teagan to stay for dinner. I'm sure Nora wouldn't mind if the two of you joined."

I could reach up and kiss him, because it's more than obvious how hard that had been for him to say. But at least it's a small olive branch extended in Liam's direction. The question is, will he take it? For Imogen's sake, I really wish there weren't so many bad feelings between everyone.

Liam doesn't answer at first, but the silently pleading look from

Imogen has him sighing. "Fine. But don't expect us to hang around after."

My guess is the warning is more for Imogen's sake than anyone else's, since she dips her chin in agreement. It's a small step, I guess.

"Great. If you two don't mind, I need to go get cleaned up and dressed." He glances down at me. "Come with?"

"Of course."

Imogen laces her fingers with Liam's. "We'll go find Carrick and Nora and most likely head out to the back portico. Take your time."

Finn takes my hand and leads me away from the entryway and down a hallway that opens up into a large living space. "This is the wing where Aidan, Cian, and I live. Although, it's Aidan and Sorcha's more than anyone's now. And Aisling."

"Aisling?"

"Sorcha's baby sister. They've made Cian's old room into hers." He points toward a second hallway that branches off the large room. "Aidan and Sorcha live in Aidan's room down there. And this is my section of the wing."

Finn leads me down a third hallway and into a massive bedroom. It's bigger than my sitting room in my flat. I gape at everything. It's almost as expensive-looking as the suite back at the casino. Lush blues and earthy greens cover the whole room. It's like being surrounded by the ocean. The only thing missing is the sand and sun. It's absolutely beautiful.

"Have a seat if you want." He points to a large velvet tufted chair in a rich hue of peacock blue.

I drop into and stare as Finn kicks his shoes off to the side and strips out of his pants. His toned ass is the perfect peach shape and makes me want to take a bite out of it. He glances over his shoulder and all I do is set my elbow on the armrest, prop my jaw on my fist, and take in the gorgeous view. I even waggle my eyebrows. He bursts into laughter and then groans.

"Don't make me laugh." Yet he still chuckles lightly.

Instantly I'm contrite. "I'm so sorry."

Finn walks over to me and I keep my gaze above his waist as he stops in front of me. He thumbs my chin, bends, and kisses me softly. "I'll take any pain if it makes you smile and look at me like that."

I soften at how weirdly sweet the sentiment is. Having him naked and this close is doing something to me. "You should probably get dressed."

He straightens and winks at me. "Only because if we make Liam wait too long there might be bloodshed."

My gaze follows him as he walks to the other side of the room and turns the light on in a connecting door that illuminates the bathroom. The water from the sink runs and then shuts off. Finn steps back out with a wet washcloth and stands in front of a mirror wiping away the dried blood.

I stand and close the distance between us. His gaze meets mine in the reflection and I take the cloth from him and gently take over. As I wipe away all the evidence of violence, I can feel his eyes on me. I dart a quick glance and meet his gaze head on and then go back to my task so I can't see his expression.

"Liam and Imogen took me some place for me to shoot a gun."

Finn goes rigid. "Why?"

I swallow and shrug. "At the time, I thought it was a good idea. I was feeling on edge and also tired of letting Ben win. It felt like something that gave me a sense of control."

There's a lengthy pause. "And now?"

My eyes meet his again briefly. "I hated it. The gun felt awkward in my hands and they shook the whole time. With my luck I'd end up shooting myself."

"I wish you would have just told me."

"Would you have agreed to take me somewhere so I could try?" I raise my eyebrows.

"Probably not."

I go back to cleaning Finn's blood. "That's why I didn't tell you."

He cradles my jaw until I lift my head. "How about this? Next time, please talk to me and I promise that I'll listen if you explain why you feel like you need to do something I might not agree with."

"All right." I nod shallowly.

Once I finish wiping away all the remnants, Finn grabs clothes from his closet—surprisingly not a suit—and gets dressed. He reaches for my hand. "Ready to go join everyone for the most tense and uncomfortable family dinner ever?"

I snort. "I can't wait."

CHAPTER 28

FINN

Despite the still pounding headache, I feel remarkably better with Teagan here. We walk out of my room and toward the common space I've shared with my brothers since we built this wing a decade ago. No sooner do we step into it than Aisling comes skipping in from the direction of her room. She see us and comes rushing over.

"Hi, I'm Aisling. Who are you?" She stares up at the woman at my side.

Teagan squats down loosening her hold on me and sets her hands on her knees. "Well, hello. I'm Teagan. It's very nice to meet you."

"Are you Uncle Finn's girlfriend?"

Teagan glances up at me with lips pressed tightly together like she's trying not to laugh. She turns back to Aisling. "Yes, I suppose I am."

"Cool." With that, the little girl takes off, heading wherever she'd been intending to go before stopping.

Teagan stands with a short burst of laughter. "She seems like fun."

I take her hand again and thread my fingers through hers. "You have no idea. It's been an adjustment for all of us having a six-year old and twin almost-thirteen-year old boys in the house. Da and Nora love it, though. Aidan and I do too, of course, but in a different way."

"The boys are Aisling's brothers?" Teagan asks.

I nod. "Kellen and Carson. They're also Sorcha's younger brothers. When Aidan married her, the four of them came as a package deal."

"A ready-made family."

"They're great kids. The boys are big gamers so the three of us hang out on occasion when I'm here." We walk through the family room, but it's empty. I suspect with the nice weather, everyone is outside.

"I'm not sure why the fact you're a gamer doesn't surprise me." Teagan shoulder bumps me.

"Why? Do I have nerd written all over me?"

She pinches my arm, but it's hardly anything. "No. It just seems like something you'd enjoy considering how much you said you enjoyed the Exchange. I picture you as extremely strategic and focused, which I imagine are two skill sets you employ with your video games."

"I suppose that's better than my girlfriend thinking I'm a giant nerd."

Teagan smirks. "You caught that, huh?"

I pretend to think about it. "I like it. A lot."

"Me, too."

I guide her into the dining room and through the windows a group of people congregated outside are visible. "Guess we found everyone."

We head out the door and several heads turn in our direction. Da, Nora, Aidan, Sorcha, and Imogen are all seated around the table with glasses of various drinks in front of them. Liam remains standing but he's directly behind Imogen who's holding onto his hand just below her shoulder and leaning against him. Kellen, Carson, and Aisling run around the backyard. Or rather, she's chasing them and they're running away.

Da stands and walks toward us. "Glad you're able to join us."

He sweeps his arms out and I pull out the chair next to Imogen for Teagan. Once she's seated, I move next to her. Da returns to his place beside Nora. I glance at Aidan. He and Teagan haven't been officially introduced yet.

"Aidan, Sorcha, this is Teagan." I place my arm along the back of her chair.

"It's lovely to meet you," she tells the both of them.

"You as well." Sorcha's smile is welcoming.

From what Aidan has said, she's felt a bit out of place with the women of the family as its newest member. I'll be sure to arrange for Teagan and her to get to know each other better.

"I have dinner in the oven and it should be ready in about forty minutes," Nora says. "I hope you all enjoy beef pasties."

Aidan groans in obvious delight and leans back slightly to rub his stomach. "You know they're my favorite."

She quirks her lips. "I didn't make them just for you."

He over-exaggerates a wink. "It's okay. I won't tell anyone you love me the most."

Nora shakes her head and Da snorts. I observe Teagan, curious what her thoughts are about our weirdly dysfunctional family. Liam is the only one not relaxed. Then again, he always looks like he's got a stick up his arse.

"How's the fairy forest coming along, Sorcha?" Imogen asks.

My sister-in-law's face lights up. Her artwork is the thing she loves to talk about the most. Aidan brags on her more than anything, too. Rightfully so. I've never met anyone with as much artistic talent as Sorcha has. Aidan's a close second. Aisling also, considering she's only six.

"It's going really well. Aidan is helping me, and, of course Aisling is making her contribution."

"Fairy forest?" Teagan inquires.

Aidan slings his arm around Sorcha. "My wife is an artistic genius. She's creating a mural for Aisling's room that will cover the entire wall and ceiling with trees, fairies, and twinkle lights. It's pretty magical."

Sorcha's cheeks turn bright red and she playfully smacks at him. "I'm not a *genius*."

"I beg to differ," my brother tells her.

"I'd love to see it when you've finished," Teagan adds. "I don't have artistic talent, but I can certainly appreciate someone else's."

The fact that she thinks she'll still be around by the time Sorcha completes the work gives me a huge sense of satisfaction.

"Cian's going to be disappointed we didn't invite him to this little impromptu family get together," Aidan snarks, his gaze on Liam who bristles and glares.

Da sighs heavily and Nora flinches. It's Imogen that gives him the evil eye, though. "We only stayed because Finn asked nicely. But we're more than willing to walk out the door if you're going to intentionally push buttons that don't need to be pushed."

An awkward silence fills the space. The animosity between Cian and Liam is a touchy subject. Aidan—who should have known better—shrinks a bit and appears properly chastised.

"I apologize, Imogen."

She shakes her head. "I'm not the one you owe the apology."

My brother winces, but he brought it on himself. He clears his throat. "Apologies, Liam."

Christ, I bet that hurt.

Liam's glare doesn't lessen, and his nod is succinct and shallow. Not actually forgiveness, but it's the best Aidan's going to get. A high-pitched squeal breaks the tension as Aisling comes barreling up the incline with her brothers hot on her heels.

"Uncle Liam, save me," she cries out and collides with his legs, shaking her arms above her head and wiggling her fingers frantically.

A flash of terror crosses his face. He shoots a panicked glance at Imogen but hauls Aisling up into his arms since she's nearly climbing up him already anyway. She curls her legs around his waist and clutches his shoulders. The boys come to an abrupt halt a couple feet away and stare up at the hardened man holding their sister. The little shit glances down at her brothers from Liam's considerable height and sticks out her tongue.

The stand-off is almost comical.

"Cheater," Kellen scolds her.

"I'm not a cheater," she snaps back. "You were being mean, and Uncle Liam is gonna yell at you if you don't stop."

"Okay, everyone. How about we all get along?" Da says and considering it's all the adults he's glancing at, the sentiment pertains to us more than the kids.

"Come on, let's go," Kellen grabs Carson's arm and the two of them take off running back down the slight hill and around the small copse of trees to the left of the lawn.

Aisling—still in Liam's grasp—busses his cheek with a kiss. "Thanks, Uncle Liam."

She wiggles, and he sets her down quickly. He even takes a half-step away from her like she's diseased and contagious. Sorcha tugs her hand and pulls her over to whisper something in her ear. Aisling's shoulders drop, and she climbs into her sister's lap and sits there.

Nora stands. "I better go check on the food."

"I'll help," Da says and with a hand on her lower back, he guides her into the house.

"When are Caitlín and Roarke leaving for New York, again?" That should be a neutral enough topic.

"Early next week, I think. He's busy dealing with that *thing* at the moment," Aidan says pointedly. "They wanted to get there far enough before the wedding to have time to visit family and take care of any last minute wedding details."

As our head enforcer, he's no doubt currently occupied with the traitor from last night. But considering we're also still at war with the Moroccans, it's not the ideal time for Roarke to be leaving. Aunt Moira has been working hard on Caitlín's wedding for months though. It would break both their hearts if they had to cancel.

"How are things coming with the art gallery?" Imogen directs the question to Sorcha.

"Slowly, but I don't want to rush anything. We've got some contractors lined up to get quotes on a few renovations and upgrades we want to make. It's going to be beautiful when it's all said and done."

"You're opening an art gallery?" Teagan asks.

Sorcha nods and glances at Aidan with a soft smile. "One of these days. It's been a dream of mine since uni, so Aidan bought this cute little building just on the edge of the city center in the perfect spot. It's tucked in between a bookstore and the second-best bakery in Dublin, after Mannings."

"I've trained you well," Imogen grins.

"Please let me know when you open the doors. I have a few former colleagues who are huge art collectors. I'll happily send them your way," Teagan offers.

"Oh goodness, thank you so much," Sorcha exclaims. "It may be a while, but I'll ring you when it's complete."

The dining room door opens and Nora sticks her head out. "All right everyone, supper is ready."

Aisling jumps off Sorcha's lap and races inside while we all get to our feet.

"I'll go find the boys," Aidan tells her and kisses his wife on the cheek.

Everyone heads into the house with Imogen and Liam trailing behind. I clasp Teagan's hand and lean in close. "Are we at all like you expected?"

She laughs. "Not even remotely like it. I'm not sure what I

expected, but it definitely wasn't this. I love how close you all are. Or at least seem to be. The kids are adorable, by the way."

"They're a handful. I don't envy Sorcha and Aidan at all."

"Do you not want children, then?"

I glance over at her, trying to gauge her tone, but like her expression, it's bland. I can't get a read on where she stands on children. "I don't *not* want them."

She nudges me with her elbow, but she smiles. "That's not really an answer."

We walk through the dining room, but before we get any closer to the kitchen, I tug Teagan to the side and let Imogen and Liam pass so it's just the two of us.

"I guess it's one of those things where if it happens, I'll be happy, but if it doesn't happen, I'll also be okay with that. Finding the perfect woman for me is really what I've always wanted. Anything beyond that is a bonus." I pause. "What about you?"

She twists her lips side-to-side. "I'm not sure. I love the idea of having a big family since I'm an only child. But I also love the independence and freedom that comes with not having the kind of responsibility required to be a parent."

"There is something to be said about freedom."

The door swings open and Aidan walks through. He pauses for a second when his gaze lands on us, but then he keeps coming. Kellen and Carson trail him.

"Didn't mean to interrupt," my brother says.

"You didn't. We were just about to head in." I place my hand on Teagan's lower back.

The five of us make our way to the kitchen where everyone is getting their food. We get in the back of the line, and the only thing I can do while we stand here is picture a sweet little girl with her mom's chocolate brown eyes and dark hair.

CHAPTER 29

Teagan

Finn's Da and Nora walk us to the door. The sun's gone down and the moon is cresting the sky. It shines an eerie white light down between the branches, which sway in the light breeze, sending shadows scurrying across the front lawn. Imogen and Liam left a while ago and Aidan and Sorcha sent the boys upstairs to their room and then disappeared into their wing of the house with Aisling.

"Thank you for a lovely dinner, Nora." Once I'd gotten over being nervous around Finn's family, I'd had an incredible time. I'm envious of Imogen having all these people caring about her.

She hugs me tight. "You're welcome. It was wonderful getting to know one of Imogen's dearest friends. Please come back anytime."

"I will." I turn to Finn's Da, who is far more down to earth than I imagined the head of the Irish mafia to be. "It was a pleasure meeting you both."

"The pleasure was all ours." With a smile, Carrick puts his arm around Nora and brings her close to his side. His gaze shoots to Finn and his expression shifts to one more serious. "I need you to come to my office tomorrow."

Finn nods. "Yes, sir."

He places his hand on my lower back and guides me out to his SUV. He opens the door and helps me in. Then he gets behind the wheel and slowly heads down the drive and onto the lane leading out of the estate. I glance over at him.

"I hope I didn't do anything to offend your Da."

Finn's gaze darts to me and a wrinkle appears between his eyes. "Why would you think that? Because of him wanting to see me tomorrow? I can promise it had nothing to do with the two of us."

"You're sure?" I'm annoyed that I sound so needy, but I really want his parents to like me.

"Absolutely."

The complete certainty in his tone makes me feel better.

"So aside from that single worry, you made it through an entire evening with most of my family intact," he jokes with a cheeky grin.

I laugh. "It was touch and go at first. I'm not surprised that Imogen and Liam don't spend time together out here. The whole night, there was an underlying bit of tension." I hate that for her.

Finn sighs. "She and Nessa have it the worst. They're both caught between family and the person they love. I admit to not being very good at forgetting about the past and trying to cultivate a less hostile relationship with Liam. At least for Imogen's sake. It's not fair that she and Nessa are stuck in the middle."

No, it isn't. She's told me more than once how guilty she feels if she spends time with her family without Liam. They weren't terrible to him today—at least not after that first snarky comment by Finn's brother—but they certainly weren't welcoming. Other than Nora anyway. Of course, considering how closed off he is and the fact he tried to take down their entire organization not that long ago, he isn't making it easy on them.

"I've also been less friendly than I could be. Holding grudges is not one of my better qualities. If Imogen can forgive him for kidnap-ping her, then I should be able to as well." She's always been a more forgiving person than I am. "And inviting them to stay for dinner was nice of you."

"I suppose if someone is going to reluctantly extend an olive branch, it's going to have to be me." Finn huffs. "Cian definitely won't do it. Not unless Nessa forces the issue. And Aidan's too focused on his new family to put any effort into it."

I reach across and lay my hand over his. "It's not easy being the bigger person, but somebody has to be. It's hard on Imogen, so for you to make the effort tonight...it goes a long way. I'm sure she appreciated it."

Finn turns his palm up and laces his fingers through mine. "You're a good friend to her. I'm glad Imogen has you in her life."

"I'm the lucky one. She bulldozed her way into my life and hasn't let me go. I've always had a hard time keeping friends." I shrug a little self-deprecatingly. "I have hundreds of acquaintances. People I know through various work organizations. But true friends are few and far between. Imogen is the only one who's stuck around through all the good and bad."

He brings our connected hands up to his mouth and brushes a kiss over my knuckles. "I don't have any plans on going anywhere any time soon."

My heart does a little flip-flop. I was doomed from the moment I met Finn. He's everything I always hoped for in a part-ner. The thought is absolutely terrifying. But I'm done with letting fear rule me. Wherever this thing between us goes, I'll let it happen.

"Me either."

We turn down the street for the casino and park in a family spot. Before I can step out of the vehicle, Finn is already there with an outstretched hand. I take it in mine and let him help me out. Neither of us attempt to release the other. Tonight is going to be the last night I stay here, though. I'll ask about hiring a bodyguard or something, but as beautiful as the suite is, it doesn't feel like home. I prepare myself for a debate.

The guard manning the front door opens it for us and we step inside. It's filled with people. Finn and I make it to the lift and up to the top floor.

"Would you like to come in for a drink, or do you have work to get done?" Other than the bookkeeping, I'm not sure what else his job entails.

"Let me check on a couple things, and then I'll be over. Give me about thirty minutes." We pause outside the suite door and he kisses me, then heads for his office.

I let myself in and drop my purse on the side table. After the day I've had, a drink is calling me. At the bar, I pour myself a gin and tonic and collapse onto the couch with a huge sigh. I toe off my shoes and curl my feet beneath me while I sip my drink.

The silence should be a blessing. Between how loud firing a gun was and so many voices talking at the same time for the last few hours, I should appreciate the silence. It never bothered me before. I often enjoyed the quiet. The stillness. Not so much anymore. Now it's stifling. Claustrophobic. Suffocating. Maybe because it was always so quiet before Ben erupted. Before the shit storm hit.

"Grrrr." I slam my hand down on the cushion. "Fuck him."

The fear I've been holding onto for months is slowly bleeding out of me. In its place is a slow burning rage that's soon going to become a wildfire of pure hate. It's nearly reached its fever pitch. I can feel it sizzling through my veins gaining strength.

I toss back the rest of the drink and glance at the clock. Maybe a quick shower will help release some of the tension. I should have time before Finn gets back. I make my way to the bathroom, stripping my clothes off on the way, and chucking them on the floor to pick up later. Imogen always got on me about my messy habits when we roomed together. It ended up becoming a running joke with us.

Once I've got my hair tied up in a messy bun, I step under the steaming hot spray and close my eyes. I stand there, letting the water wash over me and lightly massage my neck and back. I'm thankful for the strong water pressure, because it's not like this at my flat. After I'm reasonably less tense than I'd been when I got in here, I shut off the water, wrap a towel around me, and head back into the bedroom to get dressed.

Twenty minutes after Finn left, I'm on the sofa with another drink in hand. I've got music playing from my phone and I'm far more relaxed than I was not so long ago. There's a beep from the door and the lock disengages. In walks Finn. I drink in the sight of him. The top three buttons of his shirt are undone giving me only a tease of his muscled chest.

"I hope you don't mind that I let myself in." He crosses the room, stands over me so I have to bend my neck, and kisses me.

"Of course not. You're welcome to come and go anytime you want."

Finn circles around and sits next to me. He reaches for my hand and tugs me onto his lap. "You were too far away."

I laugh and lay my arm around his shoulders. "Is that what it was?"

He winks. "You taste like gin."

"And you taste like sin."

"I do, huh? And what exactly does sin taste like?" Finn nuzzles the side of my neck.

"Like hot toffee pudding."

He lifts his head and chuckles. "I taste like hot toffee pudding?"

"No," I draw out the word. "You taste like sin and *sin* tastes like hot toffee pudding. Two different things."

Finn snorts. "That makes no sense. How much have you had to drink while I was gone?"

"Just this one." I raise my glass up in front of his face. "And another one."

"Uh huh."

"I take it you got all your work done?"

He covers my hand with his and brings my glass up to his lips.

They touch the same spot where the faint imprint of my lipgloss shows, and our eyes meet while he drinks from the same place I did. Why is that so damn hot?

"I did," Finn finally answers.

"What exactly is it you *do* anyway? I mean besides the accounting? What does owning and running a casino actually involve?" I've been curious about it from the first night I stayed here and we had dinner together.

His stare intensifies. "Do you know that you might be the first person who's actually asked me that. After Caitlín broached the idea with Da, he basically handed everything over to me and let me run it how I wanted. Aside from a few questions, he's never been a part of the business. Same with Cian and Aidan."

"It sounds like he really trusts you. I'll guess the casino brings in *a lot* of money for your organization."

Finn blinks and recoils slightly. "I've never actually thought of it like that. I always got the impression that he gave me the position of overseeing it because it kept me occupied while he and Cian did all the hard stuff."

He sits there, almost stunned. As though he's seeing things for the first time. I soothe my hand over his chest. "So, are you going to show me what it takes to be in charge of such an important part of your family's organization?"

Both dimples appear. "It's not that exciting, but I'm happy to do so."

Finn taps my thigh and I hop off his lap so he can stand. Together we leave the suite and head across the hall to his office. He opens the door and sweeps his hand forward. "After you."

CHAPTER 30

Finn

I'M PRETTY SURE I'M DONE FOR.

No one has seen me like Teagan has. Or made me see myself the way she does. All this time, and I never even would have thought that Da actually trusted me. But this casino is a huge bulk of our income. Between membership fees, the constant flow of alcohol, and the money lost in high-stakes games, *Anamacha Caillte* makes up nearly fifty percent of our entire wealth. And it's only been in business for six years. All under my reign.

Teagan's blackberry scent sweeps over me as she steps into my office. She glances around and I study her. What does she see? For once, I'm proud of all I've done with this place. I move behind my desk and fire up the computer.

"This is pretty much where I control everything." I key in my password and open a few windows.

She circles around to stand next to me, her gaze intent on the screen.

"We have a high-tech security system that Imogen worked with us on. I can keep an eye on the entire casino floor from here. We have a central security station on the floor below us along with a team who monitors things. But I like to be aware of what goes on as well." I point to one of the feeds displayed. "See that guy there? He gets VIP treatment. I make sure that he never has to ask for anything. We anticipate his need, because he is one of our highest 'sponsors' if you will. Whenever he's here I always make sure I go and personally speak with him. Schmooze a little. Stroke his ego."

"You're an ambassador." Teagan chuckles.

"I suppose I am." I point at another feed. "These two are brothers. Habitual gamblers and habitual bad losers. More than once I've had security escort them out. They've always gone more or less without incident so I let them come back. As soon as Liam opens his casino, I'm going to figure out how to entice them to join, so they can be his problem instead of mine."

Teagan nudges me with her elbow. "Sneaky. I like it."

"I thought you might." My gaze drifts back to the computer. I lean in, stare, and jerk upright. "Fuck."

I slam my hand under my desk sounding the silent alarm, run over to the bookcase, press a hidden button, and it springs open.

"What's going on?" Teagan asks.

From inside, I grab a rifle as well as several magazines and shove them in my pockets. I spin and rush over to her. I palm the back of her neck and press my forehead to hers. "Lock the door. Don't let anyone in but me. No one, Teagan. There's a gun in the top drawer. Use it if you have to."

I kiss her quickly and race out to the staircase, praying she does what I say. My feet pound with each step and the sound echoes through the cavernous space. My harsh breathing joins it. I reach the bottom of the stairs and shove the door open. It's fucking chaos. Gunfire spits. People yell. Smoke is everywhere. I shade my eyes and cough as I make my way toward the casino floor.

An armed man appears in front of me and I fire my weapon. He collapses to the ground. Another appears as the smoke slowly dissipates. I fire a few more rounds and he joins the first man.

"Finn, down," a harsh voice commands.

I drop as a gun goes off and I snap my head sideways to find a third man lying close by. Blood slowly pools around his head. I whip around and stand. Declan jogs over, a weapon in his hand.

"You okay? What the fuck is going on?" he barks.

"It's the goddamn Moroccans."

Yelps of pain fill the air along with the continuous *rat-tat-tat-tat* of weapons firing. Not having time for conversation or to wonder why Declan is here, we scurry forward. My head swivels side-to-side as I scan the place. Bodies lie scattered around. Some unmoving, while others moan in pain. A bullet flies by my head, narrowly missing me, and splinters the wall behind. I fire back and then Declan and I flip one of the tables to give me some type of protection. We duck behind it and when more bullets hit it and splinter the wood, I flinch.

"You are all alone, Mr. Donnelly," a harshly accented voice calls from the other side of the casino floor. "And when your men come, we will take each of you out one by one. There are more of us than there are of you. I will take great pleasure in killing you. All of you will pay in blood for our brothers you took."

"Good luck with that." I shouldn't antagonize them, but fuck if I'm dying tonight. Teagan needs me. It's killing me that she's upstairs without protection. I swore I'd keep her safe.

Declan glances over at me and nods. He springs up and opens fire while I lean around the side of the table and do the same. Until the smoke clears more, we're shooting blindly at only voices. My gaze darts to the hallway and there's a flash of a weapon before Lee steps into view. Behind him is the fully armed security team.

I jerk my chin and he repeats the gesture. He and his men spill out from their spot like a swarm of ants scattering around the outer walls firing back at the shadows that are slowly becoming visible through the wisps of smoke. Rounds of gunfire come from the enemies. There's no way to tell if anyone is hit. Lee and one of his men station themselves behind the table next to ours.

"More back up should be coming." We had a silent alarm installed a few years ago that sends a signal out to our soldiers as well as a flashing indicator of where the signal is coming from.

"Did you see how many men they had?" Declan asks.

"No." I shake my head. "The smoke's too thick. You?"

"A few. I'd been in the middle of a game when they rushed the casino floor and started shooting. It was madness. People stampeding toward the exit, knocking others over. I made my way toward the lift to try and find you."

"I saw it on the security feeds. Christ." I slam my elbow into the bottom of the table. "Teagan's upstairs."

Declan's eyes widen. "What?"

"She's been staying in the suite." I open my mouth to say more, but the ceiling sprinklers open up and rain sprays down everywhere. "What the fuck?"

I glance around the side of the table again as the water clears out the smoke completely. More bodies lie scattered around. I swipe my hair out of my eyes and water spills off my nose. Everything is soaked. My phone dings. I grab it quickly. It's a text from Da. I stab out a reply and then shove it back in my pocket.

Tired of this standoff, I glance over at Lee and gesture with two fingers. He acknowledges and whispers to the man at his side who relays the message through his mouthpiece. I turn to Declan while I remove my magazine and replace it with a full one.

"We're moving forward at the count of three. We need to push the Moroccans toward the entrance and box them in. Our men should be arriving shortly."

He swings his head and bangs it on the table behind. "If I get shot again, I'm going to be pissed."

"Hey, at least this time I won't be the one shooting you."

Declan huffs. "Alright, let's do this."

I lift my arm to shoulder height and raise a finger. Then the second one. With only a brief pause, the third goes up. All of us jump to our feet and open fire. I don't focus on what anyone else is doing. My eyes stay trained ahead and ready to lock onto any moving target. Someone hollers out in Farsi and then they return fire. I dodge behind a table, wait for a second, and then I'm on the move again.

Figures retreat and then fall. In my periphery, there's movement on both sides. I quickly glance in each direction. All of our men are tightening formation and flanking the enemies, pushing them back. My ears are ringing. I squeeze the trigger again, but I'm empty.

I remove the magazine, grab another from my pocket, and ram it in place.

"Put down your weapons!"

Fuck, is that Gardaí?

Bright lights blind me and I'm knocked to the ground. My gun slides across the floor. Rough hands jerk my arms behind my back and restrain them. I turn my head to the side. Declan is also being restrained by two Gardaí. They yank me to my feet.

Half my men are held at gunpoint by the authorities, while the other half's arms—along with the few remaining Moroccans—are tied behind their back. Da pushes through the melee, Cian and Aidan right behind him.

"Find Teagan." She's the only thing I care about. "She's in my office. Make sure she's okay."

Da gestures for my brothers to head toward the lift. "We'll take care of her. I'll put a call into our solicitor."

I nod and then I'm dragged outside and placed in the back of a car. Even as it drives away, I don't take my eyes off the casino, willing Teagan to appear so I know she's all right.

CHAPTER 31

Teagan

THE SECOND FINN RUSHES OUT OF THE ROOM, I RUN OVER and lock the door. I collapse against it with a rough sigh and hurry back to the desk. What had he seen on the security feed that I hadn't?

Oh god.

I slap my hands over my mouth to hold back the scream. Armed men are shooting. People scatter like cockroaches under a bright light.

All I can do is stare in silence. More men collapse. There's no sign of Finn anywhere. Didn't he say there was a way to see more than one angle? To be able to see the entire casino floor? I grab the chair and then my fingers fly across the keyboard. Imogen was always the best at this kind of thing, and my hacker muscles haven't been flexed in over five years. I've been on the other end trying to keep hackers out.

Finally, I get four quadrants to pop up and give me a better look at what's going on. Holy shit. There's Declan. What do I do? What do I do? Praying Finn doesn't hate me, I switch windows away from the feed and key in more code. God, I wish I had a second computer, but mine's in the suite and I'm not leaving this office. It takes a few minutes—or maybe it's hours, but finally, I'm in the Gardaí's system. I send a widespread message across their email servers that there's an armed attack on the casino. The second I hit return, I go back to the security footage.

Where's Finn? I scan all the quadrants until I spot him and Declan behind a table lying on its side. They're firing through the smoke that still fills the air. It's got to be hard for them to see. What if they hit one of their own men?

I have to do something to help besides just sit here and wait while Finn could be killed.

I locate the schematics of the the building and my finger runs across the screen searching for...anything. Maybe I can create some sort of distraction or disruption. Suddenly, there's someone pounding at the door and I yelp.

"I know you're in there, Teagan," a raised, but muffled, voice comes from the other side.

My stomach lurches and nausea churns.

"Open this door before I break it down and maybe I'll go easy on you."

How did Ben find me here? Only able to focus on one thing at a time, I ignore his threats and the creepy knocking he's doing and go back to what I'd been trying to do. Find something to help Finn. My hands shake over the keys and sweat slicks my palms. I open and close my fists with several deep breaths to ease the cramping.

Finally, I find it. How much good it will do, I have no idea, but at least I tried.

"Open the door now, Teagan." Ben's voice is no longer muffled, but instead loud and raging. He pounds even harder.

Pay attention to what you're doing. Don't look at the door. Concentrate. I get into the casino's sprinkler system and hit it. I glance at the security feeds and in less than a second, the sprinklers open and spray everywhere. Relief hits.

There's a massive thud at the door. And another. Like Ben's throwing himself against it or kicking it. I jump up from the chair and my entire body trembles. There's a sharp crack, and the wood splinters. Another crash and it flies open and bangs against the wall.

My breathing gets rapid and I'm on the verge of hyperventilating. He strolls in like he doesn't have a care in the world.

"You've made me very unhappy, Teagan."

I'm more scared of the casual tone than the words themselves. Casual always equalled pain. Suffering. Terror.

"What are you doing here? How did you find me?" My voice trembles and I curse the fact Ben can probably hear the fear in it.

His grin is pure evil. The dimples I loved at first only remind me of the pits of hell and the face of a demon. "Funny thing. Did you know I have distant relatives that live here? I'm sure I told you that when we first got together. It was one of the things you and I had in common, remember? Having family emigrate to Dublin. While you spent summers with your mother in Iran, I spent a few of them here. Until my parents refused to allow me to come anymore. Something about staying away from that side of the family."

I shake my head. Maybe he told me that once, but it was so long ago I can't remember. He comes a little closer,. As though he's confident he has me right where he wants me. And he does. He's a predator toying with its prey. The one thing standing between me and the door. If I want to escape, I have to make it past him first.

A memory sparks. Can I actually do it, though?

"I had no idea what they were talking about until I got older," he continues. "It would seem that my father broke off all contact with an uncle on his mother's side. Said they were dangerous, and he wanted nothing to do with them. Me, on the other hand, I found it fascinating. I love the thought of being feared by people. It turns me on."

Decision made, I yank open the top drawer of Finn's desk, grab the gun, and point it at him. "Don't come any closer."

My hand shakes and the weapon wobbles in my grip. I grab it

with my other hand to steady it. Still, my arms bob with the weight. Ben pauses his advance. His grin only grows more terrifying.

"Well, would you look at that." He cocks his head. "Do you really think you can shoot me?"

I step back, farther away from his encroachment. "I will if I have to."

He just laughs. "Your little boyfriend down there is dead. Or soon will be. My great-uncle's men will make sure of it."

What?

"I see you haven't quite figured it out yet, have you?" Ben takes another step closer.

"I said stop." I back up a pace and scurry to the left as he rounds the desk. It puts me nearer to the door.

"When you ran off, I knew the one place you'd come was back here." Step. "So I rang up my great-uncle for a favor. He has connections, you see. It didn't take them long to find you. Especially considering the company you're keeping. Tsk, tsk, Teagan. Fraternizing with criminals. Don't worry. My great-uncle's men down there will take care of the bastard you're fucking for me."

None of this makes sense. "Your family is Moroccan?"

Ben takes two quick steps forward like a dance and I jump backwards. He laughs. God, my arms ache, but I can't lower my guard.

"They're half-family, technically."

I glance over my shoulder, gauging the distance between me and the door. It's a mistake, because he leaps the narrowed distance between us and grabs my hands. He jerks my arms up and away and the gun goes off. Plaster from the ceiling rains down, but I refuse to let go.

"I'm going to kill you, you little bitch." Spittle hits my face.

We wrestle for control. It has to be adrenaline giving me strength, because I manage to keep hold. Ben throws me to the ground. I cry out in pain when I hit, and I barely have time to catch my breath before he's rolling me onto my back and straddling me. The punch comes before I can block it. Pain radiates through my face, and blood fills my mouth.

Not again. White-hot rage blinds me and I slam the gun I've still managed to keep hold of against the side of Ben's head. He tumbles off me and I try to scramble to my feet. He recovers quickly and slams me back to the ground, trapping the gun between us. I kick and scream trying to get away. The weapon goes off and my whole body jerks. We both freeze as I wait for the pain.

But it doesn't come. I stare up at Ben. His eyes are wide and his mouth opens and closes, but he doesn't actually speak. A warm wetness spreads across my skin. Frantic, I push him off me with every ounce of strength I have. He falls to the side and onto his back. A dark red stain mars the front of his shirt. His hands cover where it spreads.

Vomit rises in my throat. I fling the gun off to the side, unable to stand touching it any longer, and scramble backwards away from him. Pounding footsteps approach, but I can't take my eyes off Ben and the pool of blood forming beneath him. Someone says my name, but I don't move. Then he's no longer in front of me. Instead, I stare into the face of Aidan.

"It's okay. You're okay." He reaches out carefully and places his hand on my shoulder.

Pain clutches at my chest. I'm having a hard time breathing. My face throbs and the taste of blood is still strong in my mouth and down my throat.

"Teagan. Look at me."

My panicked gaze meets Aidan's and he takes a slow, deep breath in.

"Breathe with me. In and out. Easy." His chest rises and falls and mine follows suit. "Good. Again. In and out."

Finally, I get it under control and return to my normal breathing. I grab his arms. "Finn."

"He's fine. I swear." Aidan wraps his arms around me.

"Da and I are going to take you to the estate, all right?" he asks. "Cian will take care of...things here."

All I can do is nod. He helps me to my feet and keeps between me and the body on the floor. Finn's Da meets us just outside the door. Aidan transfers me into Carrick's hands and with eyes blinded by tears, he escorts me down the back stairs and into the waiting vehicle behind the casino. He sits with me in the backseat while I tremble. Time passes slowly, but at last, Aidan gets behind the wheel and we leave madness and death behind.

CHAPTER 32

Finn

THIS ISN'T THE FIRST TIME I'VE BEEN ARRESTED. DA HAS enough men in his pockets that I'm not too concerned. My biggest worry is Teagan. I'd been allowed to make a call and Cian assured me Aidan and Da were taking care of her and were driving her out to the estate to stay.

"Get out there as soon as you're released. She's going to need you after what happened up in your office."

That's all he would tell me so I've been sitting in this cell for hours waiting to be released and trying not to freak out over why she would need me. What the fuck happened up there?

"Donnelly." One of the Gardaí approaches the cell with a set of keys and unlocks it. The same one who tried to start shit with me.

I walk through it, wink as I pass him, and head for the desk to pick up my things. Aidan's waiting for me outside. It's not even dusk yet. The moon isn't visible, but it gives off a faint light from behind the clouds. A cool breeze skates across the back of my neck and through the thin layer of my shirt. As soon as we're in the car and on the road, I fire off my questions.

"What the fuck happened with Teagan? Is she okay? Cian sounded worried."

He glances over at me before turning his attention back to the road. "Physically, she's fine. Imogen, Sorcha, and Nessa are with her at the moment. Mentally? I'm not sure. She kind of just keeps getting this blank stare."

"If you don't tell me exactly what happened, I swear to god as soon as we get out of this car, I'll beat the shit out of you." My fists clench as I try to rein in my anger.

"The door to your office had been kicked in and there was a dead, or nearly dead, guy on the floor when we got there. You'll have to ask Cian, since he's the one who handled it. I was busy keeping Teagan from having a panic attack. Considering your gun was near her, I'm going to assume she's the one who shot him."

"Who was it?" I snap.

Aidan raises and lowers his shoulder. "No idea. Dark brown hair. Clean shaven. Posh clothes. I'd guess maybe somewhere in his early thirties."

Christ. "That sounds like her abusive ex. How the fuck did he happen to show up at the same time the Moroccans did? And at the casino?"

"I don't know. You're going to have to get any more information from her. We did find our missing thievery accomplice though."

"Where?"

"On the footpath outside the casino. Shot in the back of the head. Along with Ennis." Aidan glances over.

"Fuck," I bite out. "So he's how the Moroccans made it through the front doors?"

He nods. "Most likely. I'm going to have Lee check the security footage from the outside cameras. Maybe Imogen, too. They had to have blocked the signal somehow. Or disrupted it in some way, because the security team said they never saw anything on their feed."

I slam back into the seat and punch the dashboard. Whatever happened, Teagan needed me and I wasn't there. It takes far too long, but finally we pass through the gated entrance and stop in front of the manor. Aidan hasn't even put the car in park when I'm jumping out and running inside. Our wing is the first place I go.

Teagan sits on the sofa with Imogen on one side of her and Nessa on the other. They're both holding her hand and she's resting her head on Imogen's shoulder with her eyes closed, and one side of her face battered, bruised, and swollen. The rest of it is a pale stark contrast. Sorcha sits on the floor at her feet, as though they're cocooning her within their small safety net.

Imogen turns in my direction first. Relief flashes across her face and she murmurs something to Teagan who jerks her head up and opens her eyes. Tears fill them and she harshly whimpers my name. We both move at the same time and then she's in my arms. I hold her tight and let her cry. She clutches my shirt, and it's soon soaked with her tears. Imogen helps Sorcha off the floor. My sister and Nessa leave the room with a sad smile and Sorcha heads down the hallway that leads to her and Aidan's bedroom.

I do nothing but stand there, whispering words of comfort until finally Teagan's cries slow. She draws back first and swipes the wetness away from her eyes and face. I palm her cheeks—being careful of her injury—and bend down until we're face to face. A stray droplet hangs on her lower lashes and I wipe it away with my thumb.

"I'm sorry I wasn't there." I'm not sure I'll ever forgive myself.

She sobs a little, but shakes her head. "You needed to be downstairs to stop those men."

I lay my forehead against hers. "I should have protected you."

Teagan cradles my head. "You did what you had to do."

I breathe her in for another minute and then tuck her under my arm. I may never let her go. "Come on."

Together, we walk to my room. I help her undress—someone else got her into pajamas at some point—and lay her down on the bed. A few strands of hair have escaped the long plait and I brush them off her forehead.

"Will you be okay for five minutes while I wash?"

Teagan nods. Not wanting to waste any time, I hurry into the bathroom—stripping my shirt off on the way—and wet a cloth. Once I'm as clean as I'm going to get without a shower, I yank off my pants and then climb in beside her. She scoots close and rests her head on my chest.

"Do you want to talk about what happened?" I ask quietly. Gently.

Teagan stiffens a little and shakes her head. "Not yet. Please."

"Okay." My arms tighten around her and I rest my chin on her crown. "I'm here whenever you're ready."

She snuggles closer until finally the tension leaves her body and soft snores ghost hot air across my flesh. I close my eyes intent on getting some sleep, if I can. I must have fallen asleep, because jerky movements wake me. A bit groggy, I slowly open my eyes, and Teagan bolts upright, gasping for air. Sunlight spills across the bed.

I jackknife up and cradle the back of her head. There's pure fear in her expression. "It's okay, Poppet. It's just a nightmare. You're safe. Breathe."

She tucks her chin and slowly breathes in and out until it returns to normal. One long exhale later and she lies back down and rolls to her side to face me. I do the same and patiently wait for whatever she does next. Whether it's to talk or attempt to go back to sleep. Teagan brushes her fingers up and down the middle of my chest. Her gaze follows each movement.

"I shot him," her voice cracks. "Killed him. I didn't mean to."

"Of course you didn't." I lay my hand over hers and press her palm hard against my chest. "You were defending yourself against someone who hurt you."

Teagan swallows hard and sniffs. In the shadows, her bruise is even more discolored. I smother the rage that he was able to even touch her.

"He was going to kill me. I had to protect myself." She's almost pleading for me to believe her.

"Look at me, poppet," I firm my tone.

She lifts her eyes to meet mine.

"You don't have to justify yourself to me or anyone else. No one is judging you. Least of all me." I sweep Teagan's hair over her shoulder and run my hand down her arm. "Certainly no one in the family. Besides, he was a dead man either way. It was just a matter of when."

"You were going to kill him regardless, weren't you? After you found him, I mean?" Her voice drops to a whisper.

"Yes." I don't even hesitate.

Teagan nods shallowly and drops her gaze back to my chest. "I thought as much."

I let the silence settle a moment longer. "Do you know how he found out where you were?"

She laughs bitterly. "Apparently, he's some distant relative to those men. Or one of the men anyway. Used to come to Dublin to visit when he was just a kid. He said he knew I'd run back here, so he called them and asked for help locating me."

Christ. No wonder he found her far too easily. Considering they almost took me out the other day, it's obvious the Moroccans have been following us. Monitoring our movements. They had to have seen Teagan and I arriving. Or maybe her leaving with Imogen and Liam. By bringing her here, I put her in danger. I'm such an idiot.

"You probably would have been safer at your flat. I'm so sorry, poppet."

She jerks her gaze up to mine. "No, it's not your fault. If Ben had these connections, he would have found me anyway. All he had to do was follow Imogen. She'd already been to my place once. If I'd stayed there, she would have come to visit another time. They just as easily could have tracked her there."

I gently run my finger along the bruises marring her skin. "I'd never been so scared in my life when Aidan told me what happened. I thought I'd lost you."

"And I thought I'd lost you, too. All I could think about was how could I help you."

A smile curls my lips. "Were you the one who contacted the Gardaí? While I was being held, they told me someone sent them an anonymous email."

Teagan sucks in her bottom lip. "Yes. I hacked into their system and sent it through there. I didn't know what else to do."

Another thought occurs to me. "Were you responsible for the sprinklers as well?"

Her cheeks turn pink. "It was such a dumb idea, but it was the only thing I could think to do to cause a distraction. Plus, I thought it would help alleviate the smoke."

I tip up her chin and kiss her. "It was bloody fucking brilliant is what that was. If you hadn't cleared the smoke out, we wouldn't have been able to see well enough to fight like we did. You, little poppet, are a genius."

Teagan's face turns an even brighter hue. "Honestly, it was nothing but pure damn luck. I'd forgotten half of the things Imogen had taught me when we were in uni about hacking. I had no idea what I was doing."

"I promise I won't tell anyone." I grin. "We'll just let everyone think you saved the day with your amazing skills. Because you did."

Finally, a small smile graces her lips. "Maybe there is something to be said about bending the law a little. If I hadn't been so terrified, I might have gotten a small rush from being able to tap into the Gardaí's system."

I laugh and kiss her again. "I think you'll fit right in with our family."

She slowly turns serious. Intent. "Yeah. Maybe I will."

EPILOGUE

Teagan

Children from the age of four to thirteen run past us screaming and laughing. They chase each other down the hill behind the manor and disappear into the trees. Autumn has arrived, and today's the first day we've had in two weeks where it hasn't rained. I sit back in the chair and tug my sweater a little tighter around me while my gaze wanders and takes in all of Finn's family. Everyone is here. It's been three months since that night at the casino. Three months of occasional nightmares and a lot of damn therapy. More than anything, though, it's been filled with family. Laughter. Love.

Nessa and Cian are a short distance from where I sit talking to his cousin Nathan and his wife Lucia. She's carrying an adorable redheaded toddler on her hip and admiring Nessa's engagement ring. Imogen and Liam were on their way over when they stopped for a second to say hi to Aidan and Sorcha as well as Caitlín and Roarke who just got back from an extended honeymoon.

"I brought you dessert." Finn bends and gives me a kiss.

"Mmmm. *Now* you taste like sticky toffee pudding."

He sits next to me with two small bowls and places one of them in front of me."You were right, too. It does taste like sin."

"Told you." I dip my spoon in the gooey cake and toffee sauce and take a huge bite. My eyes meet Finn's heated ones as I slowly draw the utensil out from between my lips. His gaze drops and I lick the corners of my mouth to make sure I didn't leave any behind.

"I think you and I are going to have to use that mouth of yours in another way later." The pitch of his voice drops an octave.

"Gross." Imogen collapses in the chair on the other side of me with a cheeky grin. "I thought I told you I didn't want to hear about any of your sex-capades with each other."

My whole face bursts into flames. Especially as Liam takes a seat next to her. Oh god, how much did he hear? Judging by the tiny curl of his lips, I'd guess more than enough. It's incredible what a difference the last few months have made in him.

"So I shouldn't tell you about the time with this swing—"

I screech and slam my hand over his mouth. Imogen cackles like a mad woman. Even Liam cracks an actual smile. Behind my hand, Finn laughs as well and then licks my palm.

"Ewww." I jerk my arm away and grab the napkin, but I'm chuckling. "If you're not careful, mister, there won't be any more sex-capades for you to gloat over."

"Oh, shit," Imogen says. "You better watch yourself, Finn. This woman can hold a grudge like no one's business. If you're not careful, she may never have sex with you again."

He jerks his head in my direction and widens his eyes. I stare him down, trying to keep my amusement at his appalled expression at bay, but I can't do it. I burst out laughing.

"Can I have everyone's attention, please?" Carrick clacks a spoon against his glass and then sets the utensil on the nearest table to him.

Conversation dies down. Nora comes to stand next to him and

he wraps a hand around her waist pulling her close. She lays her head on his shoulder for a second. Then they both look at us all again.

"I never thought a man could be as lucky as I am. I've been blessed with four amazing children who couldn't make me more proud. Each one of you has brought so much joy to my life. More than I could have ever imagined. You've brought grandchildren, as well as incredible partners into our family. People you love and who love you in return. Nessa, Sorcha, Teagan." Carrick raises his glass to each of us and then smirks when his gaze shifts slightly to my right. He raises his glass a fourth time. "Even you Liam. But don't get too cocky about it."

We all laugh and Imogen shoulder bumps Liam who gives her a genuine half smile. I'm not sure I'll ever get used to that, but he's become a bit less hard and cold. I'm happy for him and Imogen.

"But beyond all that," Carrick continues. "I have this beautiful woman at my side. A woman I've loved for half my life. And who, finally, after all these years and countless proposals, has finally agreed to marry me and make me the happiest man alive."

A chorus of "holy shit", "oh my god," and "it's about damn time" follow the announcement. Finn stands and pulls me to my feet and we join the entire Donnelly clan and extended family who circle around Carrick and Nora offering their congratulations.

Imogen hugs Nora. "Congratulations...mam."

Tears spill down Nora's cheeks. Emotion hits me hard. I'm pretty sure this is the first time Imogen has called her anything close to mother. She's always been Nora.

"Thank you...daughter."

Imogen reaches for Carrick next, whose eyes glisten with tears as well. "You too, Da."

A lump forms in my throat. I hug them both and offer my congratulations before stepping aside for Finn. He hugs his Da hard and claps him on the back.

"I'm so happy for you guys."

Carrick palms the back of Finn's neck and kisses his son's forehead. "I love you, Finn."

"I love you too, Da."

Finn pulls Nora in for a hug and whispers something in her ear. More tears fill her eyes and she palms his cheek. He gives her a soft smile and moves away so the rest of the family can offer their well wishes. Soon, all the children join us and the excitement starts anew when they hear the news. Aidan disappears inside and comes back with five bottles of champagne.

Glasses get filled and passed around. We spend the next hour celebrating until the sun reaches the horizon and the temperatures drop. Everyone cleans up so Nora doesn't have to and then all the guests slowly depart. Finn walks me out to his SUV and we head back to the city and my flat where he spends almost all of his nights anymore. The casino needed to be completely remodeled after all the destruction, but it should be back open and operational within the month.

In the meantime, Finn's been investing more of their money in the Exchange to increase their earnings while the casino's closed. He finds a place to park on the street and we head inside. I set my keys and bag on the table and kick off my shoes. I glance over my shoulder on the way to the kitchen. "Do you want something to drink?"

Finn doesn't let me get far. He snags my hand and tugs me back to him. I tumble against his chest and brace my palms against it.

"I want you," he says staring down at me with an expression that makes my pulse race.

"You have me." He does, too. All of me. My heart and my soul.

He sweeps my hair over my shoulder and caresses my cheek with his thumb sending tingles rushing through me. Finn's eyes dart side to side as he scans my face. "Da was right, you know."

"About what?"

"About having partners we love."

My breath catches. Finn cradles my jaw between his two palms and his eyes lock with mine.

"You're the best thing to ever happen to me, Teagan Shah. You make me be a better man. And I love you."

Happy tears threaten to fall. "I love you, too. So much."

He lowers his head and kisses me hard. Shockwaves run through me, like they do every time his lips touch mine. But what started out as just a kiss becomes more. Clothes quickly come off and are tossed to the floor as Finn walks me backward down the hallway toward my bedroom. Ever since he's been staying over, the zen has come back into it. It's become my sanctuary again. Finn's too, if the way he worships my body every night is any indication.

Our kisses grow more heated. More frantic. More intense. But along with all of that they're filled with love that shines so bright it's almost blinding. His tongue lashes against mine. A hard surface meets my back and the air is pushed from my lungs, but Finn fills them again.

"I need you." My fingers clutch desperately at his back and my nails dig into his flesh.

He grips my hip and slides his hand down toward my knee to pull my leg up. He hooks it over his arm so I'm splayed wide open for him. He rocks his cock against me and it notches along the track of my pussy. The ring at the end rubs me in all the right places, and wetness spills from me, coating his entire length.

Not once has he stopped kissing me. I rub my breasts against his chest. The bars in his nipples abrade my skin and a shiver races down my spine. Finally, Finn breaks the kiss.

"What do you need, poppet?" he murmurs against my lips.

"I need you to fuck me. Please."

He rolls his pelvis and slides back and forth along my slickness. With each push and pull, the ball of his piercing butts up against my clit. I press myself harder into him, needing more friction.

"Say it again," Finn commands.

"Fuck me."

"Again. Louder."

"Fuck me." The scream is ripped from my throat.

"I'll always give you what you want," he says as he lines his cock up at my entrance and thrusts deep and hard.

I throw my head back and cry out with so much pleasure. Oh my god, why does it feel different? So fucking better? When Finn thrusts again and his ring scrapes my inner walls, it hits me. He's completely bare. For a second I panic that we forgot protection, but then he penetrates me deeper and grinds against my clit. Every other thought flies out of my head as all I can do is feel the overwhelming pleasure.

He keeps up the brutal pace that soon becomes too much. Every nerve in my body fires and sends their signal straight to the center of me where it builds and builds until it has nothing to do but explode. Bright lights flash behind my eyes and my whole body shudders. My knee weakens and I nearly collapse, but Finn holds me tight. He thrusts a second time. Then again. On the fourth one he goes completely rigid and erupts inside and fills me up.

His head drops to my shoulder and his harsh breath is loud in my ear. He slowly releases my leg and I let it fall to the floor so I'm standing on two feet. His cock remains inside me, pulsing. Throbbing.

"I love you," Finn whispers.

"I love you, too."

He slips out of me and his come leaks down my inner thighs, coating them. "Fuck, I'm sorry, Teagan. I should have asked."

I palm his cheek. "It's okay. I just got my shot not long ago. And I trust you."

Finn kisses me. "Why don't we go get cleaned up?"

We take a quick shower together. Or at least we try. But one thing led to another and we got dirty again. Finally, we manage to wash up and then climb into bed.

"Thank you for loving me," I whisper against his chest once we've settled in together.

He tips my chin up so I meet his gaze. "You don't ever have to thank me for that. Just keep loving me back."

I smile up at him. "I promise."

When I escaped to Dublin only a few months ago, I never would have imagined I'd end up here. With Imogen's brother. In love. But as I close my eyes and smile, my heart knows there's no place else I'd rather be than here with Finn.

Thank you for reading **FINN**. I hope you enjoyed it. Be sure to sign up for my newsletter to stay up-to-date on what's coming next!

Can you believe Nora finally said "YES!"?
They have a winter wedding and you can get their short story Meant to Be as a Patreon exclusive! As a patron, you'll also get:

✓ A new short "slice of life" featurette every month
✓ A Monthly "Ask Me Anything" Zoom call
✓ Early access to future books before everyone else
✓ Exclusive sneak peeks at covers
✓ Exclusive sneak peeks at WIP
✓ Other Patreon only content
✓ Voting priority for future "featurette" stories

Have you started the Brooklyn Kings featuring the Brooklyn Donnellys?
Get THE DEVIL I DON'TKNOW today